STEPHEN JONES is the winner of two World Fantasy Awards and two Horror Writers of America Bram Stoker Awards, as well as being a nine-time recipient of the British Fantasy Award and a Hugo Award nominee. A full-time columnist, television producer/director and genre film publicist and consultant (all three *Hellraiser* movies, *Night Life*, *Nightbreed*, *Split Second* etc.), he is the co-editor of *Horror: 100 Best Books*, *The Best Horror from Fantasy Tales*, *Gaslight & Ghosts*, *Now We Are Sick*, *The Giant Book of Best New Horror* and the *Best New Horror*, *Dark Voices* and *Fantasy Tales* series. He has also compiled *The Mammoth Book of Terror*, *The Mammoth Book of Vampires*, *The Mammoth Book of Zombies*, *Clive Barker's Shadows in Eden*, *James Herbert: By Horror Haunted*, *Clive Barker's The Nightbreed Chronicles*, *The Hellraiser Chronicles*, *The Illustrated Vampire Movie Guide* and *The Illustrated Dinosaur Movie Guide*.

RAMSEY CAMPBELL is the most respected living British horror writer. He has received the Bram Stoker Award, the World Fantasy Award three times and the British Fantasy Award seven times—more awards for horror fiction than any other writer. After working in the civil service and public libraries, he became a full-time writer in 1973. He has written hundreds of short stories (most recently collected in *Alone With the Horrors* and *Strange Things and Stranger Places*) and the novels *The Doll Who Ate His Mother*, *The Face That Must Die*, *The Parasite*, *The Nameless*, *The Claw*, *Incarnate*, *Obesession*, *The Hungry Moon*, *The Influence*, *Ancient Images*, *Midnight Sun*, *The Count of Eleven* and *The Long Lost*. He has also edited a number of anthologies, reviews films for BBC Radio Merseyside, and is President of the British Fantasy Society. He is much in demand as a reader of his stories to audiences.

BEST NEW

# HORROR 4

# BEST NEW
# HORROR 4

Edited by
STEPHEN JONES
and
RAMSEY CAMPBELL

Carroll & Graf Publishers, Inc.
New York

First published in Great Britain in 1993 by Robinson Publishing.

First Carroll & Graf edition 1993

Carroll & Graf Publishers, Inc.
260 Fifth Avenue
New York, NY 10001

ISBN: 0-7867-0004-1

Manufactured in the United States of America

# CONTENTS

# ACKNOWLEDGEMENTS

We would like to thank Kim Newman, Jo Fletcher, Gordon Van Gelder, David Pringle, Stefan Dziemianowicz, Sue Irmo and Randy Broecker for their help and support. Thanks are also due to the magazines *Locus* (Editor & Publisher Charles N. Brown, Locus Publications, P.O. Box 13305, Oakland, CA 94661, USA) and *Science Fiction Chronicle* (Editor & Publisher Andrew I. Porter, P.O. Box 2730, Brooklyn, NY 11202–0056, USA) which were used as reference sources in the Introduction and Necrology.

INTRODUCTION: HORROR IN 1992 Copyright © 1993 by Stephen Jones and Ramsey Campbell.

THE SUICIDE ARTIST Copyright © 1992 by Scott Edelman and Necronomicon Press. Originally published in *Suicide Art*. Reprinted by permission of the author.

DANCING ON A BLADE OF DREAMS Copyright © 1992 by Roberta Lannes. Originally published in *Pulphouse: A Fiction Magazine*, Volume 2, No. 1, November 1992. Reprinted by permission of the author.

THE DEPARTED Copyright © 1992 by Clive Barker. Originally published as "Hermione and the Moon" in *New York Times*, October 30th, 1992. Reprinted by permission of the author.

HOW TO GET AHEAD IN NEW YORK Copyright © 1992 by Poppy Z. Brite. Originally published in *Gauntlet 4*. Reprinted by permission of the author.

THEY TAKE Copyright © 1992 by Brunner Fact & Fiction Ltd. Originally published in *Dark Voices 4: The Pan Book of Horror*. Reprinted by permission of the author.

REPLACEMENTS Copyright © 1992 by Lisa Tuttle. Originally published in *MetaHorror*. Reprinted by permission of the author.

*For*
*ROBERT BLOCH*
*Who still has that heart*
*of a small boy . . .*

# INTRODUCTION: HORROR IN 1992

WITH AN OVERALL DECREASE in the amount of genre books appearing on both sides of the Atlantic last year, the number of horror titles published in 1992 once again significantly trailed the totals for the fantasy and science fiction markets.

Although the output of horror published in America remained fairly constant, the number of titles appearing in the UK dropped slightly for the first time in two years. However, despite this decrease, the long-touted collapse of the horror market still failed to materialise.

In fact, almost all the Big Names in the genre had new novels published in 1992:

As always, Stephen King led the field with two new non-supernatural thrillers, *Gerald's Game* and *Dolores Claiborne*. Dean R. Koontz once again top-and-tailed the year with a pair of guaranteed bestsellers, *Hideaway*, involving near-death experiences, and *Dragon Tears*, about a cop marked for demonic vengeance.

James Herbert returned to his fictional roots with the ecological disasters of *Portent*, while Clive Barker successfully crossed over into the Young Adult market with *The Thief of Always*, a dark fantasy effectively illustrated by the author.

Anne Rice continued to chronicle the exploits of her popular vampire hero Lestat in *The Tale of the Body Thief*. *Midnight Whispers* was the fourth volume in the gothic horror thriller series about the Cutler Family, bylined V. C. Andrews™ in America and The New Virginia Andrews™ in Britain. Despite an apologia from the Andrews family, admitting the books weren't written by her, real author Andrew Neiderman still remained uncredited.

Following *The Wild* last year, Whitley Strieber remained in the horror field with *Unholy Fire*, a novel about occult possession. John Saul's *Shadows* contained his usual demonic children, Michael Stewart resurrected a 300-year-old murderess in *Belladonna*, and *Nightworld* was the sixth volume in F. Paul Wilson's loose series which began with *The Keep*.

Basil Copper's long-awaited occult novel *The Black Death* finally appeared from Minneapolis publisher Fedogan & Bremer, who look set to become a second Arkham House perhaps. *Absolute Power* by Ray Russell was produced as a limited edition by Maclay and Associates, Curt Siodmak's medical chiller *Gabriel's Body* marked the return of the veteran author/screenwriter, and Ronald Chetwynd-Hayes updated his terrors to an urban milieu in *Kepple*.

Richard Laymon's killer played with nubile young girls in *Blood Games*, inexplicable accidents plagued the protagonist of Peter James' *Prophecy*, Marvin Kaye added a note of musical menace to *Fantastique*, and Tanith Lee transformed a family of shapechangers in *Heart-Beast*. The ubiquitous Graham Masterton pushed out *The Pariah*, conjured up Native Indian curses for *Burial* and revived H. P. Lovecraft's Brown Jenkin in the Cthulhu Mythos novel *Prey*.

There were also welcome new novels from K. W. Jeter (*Wolf Flow*), Stephen Gallagher (*Nightmare, With Angel*), Lisa Tuttle (the Arthur C. Clarke Award-nominated *Lost Futures*), Michael Cadnum (*Ghostwright*), Ray Garton (*Dark Channel*), Stephen Laws (*Darkfall*), Christopher Fowler (*Red Bride*) and Thomas Monteleone (*Blood of the Lamb*).

When he wasn't being V. C. Andrews, Andrew Neiderman found time to write *The Need* and *Sister, Sister* under his own byline. T. M. Wright also published two new titles last year, *Little Boy Lost* and *Goodlow's Ghosts*. Michael Slade (a pseudonym for several Canadian lawyers) tried for a slice of the psychokiller market with *Cutthroat*, and Shaun Hutson attempted to tone himself down in *Heathen*.

There is no doubt that 1992 will be remembered as the Year of the Vampire, in no small way influenced by Francis Ford Coppola's much-hyped movie *Bram Stoker's Dracula*. In fact, vampire fiction accounted for almost 20 per cent of all the horror titles published last year.

Not counting the large number of reprint volumes spruced up by avaricious publishers to look like new books, the aforementioned Anne Rice bestseller, and various reprintings of Bram Stoker's out-of-copyright original, there were still plenty of new titles for fans of the undead to sink their teeth into.

*Blood Brothers* by Brian Lumley was the first volume in his new

Vampire World trilogy and a follow-up to the hugely popular Necroscope series. In *Children of the Night* Dan Simmons placed his vampires in a post-Ceausescu Romania and combined them with AIDS. S. P. Somtow's *Valentine* was the long-awaited sequel to his 1984 novel *Vampire Junction*, again featuring vampiric rock star Timmy Valentine; and Kim Newman continued to play literary mind-games by setting *Anno Dracula* in a Victorian Britain ruled by the Count himself.

*Morningstar*, the first novel by *Hellraiser* sequel-writer Peter Atkins, deftly combined the two icons of modern horror, the serial killer and the undead. Fred Warrington took a more traditional route with her vampires in *A Taste of Blood Wine*, Storm Constantine's *Burying the Shadow* featured a race of angelic vampires, while Tanith Lee's *Dark Dance* was about a family of not-quite-vampires.

*Blood on the Water* was the sixth in P. N. Elrod's series about vampire reporter/private investigator Jack Fleming, set in Depression-era Chicago. Another PI, Christopher Blaze, searched Miami for a drug smuggling vampire kingpin in Vincent Courtney's *Harvest of Blood*, the sequel to his earlier *Vampire Beat*.

*Blood Trail* and *Blood Lines*, the second and third books respectively in Tanya Huff's Blood Prince series, featured vampiric romance writer Henry Fitzroy and private investigator Vicky Nelson hunting for a serial killer of werewolves and a murderous living mummy.

Scott Ciencin kicked off his series about a half-vampire, half-human girl with *The Vampire Odyssey* and quickly followed it up with *The Wildlings* and *Parliament of Blood*. Gary Raisor's *Less Than Human* featured an unlikely pair of pool-playing vampires, Kathryn Meyer Griffith gave an apocalyptic twist to *The Last Vampire*, and we were also treated to *The Vampire's Apprentice* by Richard Lee Byers, *Kiss of the Vampire* by Lee Weathersby, *Thirst of the Vampire* by T. Lucian Wright, *Sweet Blood* by Pat Graversen and *Liquid Diet* by William Telford.

At least *Child of an Ancient City* by Tad Williams and Nina Kiriki Hoffman attempted something different by combining Arabian Nights storytelling with the undead in a short novel illustrated by Greg Hildebrandt in America and Bruce Pennington in the UK. Charles L. Grant rightly decided to lampoon the entire subgenre under his "Lionel Fenn" byline in *The Mark of the Moderately Vicious Vampire*, and followed it with another spoof, *668: The Neighbor of the Beast*, both featuring his comedic hero Kent Montana.

Because the revival of interest in vampires was mostly sparked by the influence of Hollywood, it was perhaps inevitable that we would get the novelisation of *Buffy the Vampire Slayer* by Richie Tankersley Cusick. Somewhat more surprising was *Bram*

*Stoker's Dracula* by Fred Saberhagen and screenwriter James V. Hart—presumably because they didn't think the original was close enough to the film version.

The other dominant trend in 1992 was the explosion of the Young Adult market for horror fiction. It quickly established itself as a major marketing force within the field, and horror titles comprised around one-third of the entire YA market.

This was mainly due to new teenage horror lines being created by several major publishers and the runaway success of such bestselling authors as Christopher Pike (*Chain Letter 2: The Ancient Evil* and *Monster*) and R. L. Stine (*Goosebumps: Welcome to Dead*, *Goosebumps: Stay Out of the Basement*, and a vampire entry in the rival series, *Fear Street: Goodnight Kiss*).

The undead proved to be just as popular amongst teen readers as their adult counterparts, with L. J. Smith continuing the exploits of two vampire brothers and the girl they both love in *Vampire Diaries Volume IV: Dark Reunion*, Caroline B. Cooney promising *The Return of the Vampire*, and Nancy Garden discovering *My Sister, the Vampire*.

Teenage hauntings manifested themselves in *A Christmas Ghost* by Robert Westall, *Shapeshifter* by Laurence Staig, three further volumes in Barbara and Scott Siegal's *Ghostworld*: series (*Dark Fire*, *Cold Dread*, and *Fatal Fear*), *Mirror, Mirror* by D. E. Athkins, and two volumes in the *Phantom Valley*: series, *Stranger in the Mirror* and *The Spell*, both by Lynn Beach.

The Young Adult market proved so lucrative that even a couple of well-respected horror writers added their own contributions under *nom de plumes*: Ray Garton catalogued a series of supernatural murders as "Joseph Locke" in *Kiss of Death*, while as "Simon Lake" the ever-prolific Charles L. Grant introduced us to *Midnight Place*: (a YA variation on his Oxrun Station setting) in *Daughter of Darkness* and *Something's Watching*.

As always, the emerging stars of horror fiction were busy establishing themselves, and Kathe Koja (*Bad Brains*), Melanie Tem (*Blood Moon* and *The Wilding*), Mark Morris (*The Immaculate*), Graham Joyce (*Dark Sister*), Joe Donnelly (*The Shee*) and Daniel Easterman (*The Name of the Beast*) all continued to build upon their growing reputations. There were also impressive novel-length debuts by Poppy Z. Brite (*Lost Souls*, about decadent Southern vampires), Elizabeth Massie (*Sineater*), Susan Palwick (*Flying in Place*), Jessica Amanda Salmonson (*Anthony Shriek*) and Wayne Allen Sallee (*The Holy Terror*).

Horror also proved itself the mainstay of the midlists with such titles as *Chiller* by Randall Boyll, *Dark Fortune* and *Dead Time* by Richard Lee Byers, *Boneman* by Lisa Cantrell, *Darkborn* by Matthew J. Costello, *The Hoodoo Man* by Steve Harris, *Dark Silence* by Rick Hautala, *Deathgrip* by Brian Hodge, *Succubi* by Edward Lee, *Chaingang* by Rex Miller, *Dark Time* by Maxine O'Callaghan, *Kiss of Death* by Daniel Rhodes, *Hell-O-Ween* by David Robbins, *Skeletons* by Al Sarrantino, *The Dead Man's Kiss* by Robert Weinberg and *The Monastery* by J. N. Williamson.

Content to hide their lights under bushels were fantasy author Charles De Lint (*From a Whisper to a Scream* by "Samuel M. Key"), science fiction novelist John Brosnan (*Bedlam* by 'Harry Adam Knight') and crime writer Ed Gorman (*The Long Midnight* by "Daniel Ransom").

Of course, there were always those books which were kept a healthy distance from the horror shelf, despite their content: Robert R. McCammon continued his drift into the mainstream with *Gone South*, a Southern Gothic thriller. Christopher Moore's *Practical Demonkeeping: A Comedy of Horrors* was somewhat predictably compared to Clive Barker's work, while Emma Tennant's *Faustine* was a contemporary retelling of the Faust legend and *Augustus Rex* by Clive Sinclair had Beelzebub as its narrator. The refined haunting of Jonathan Aycliffe's *Whispers in the Dark* was amongst the best the field had to offer last year, and Susan Hill continued the theme in *The Mist in the Mirror*. At least Jonathan Carroll's latest novel, *After Silence*, was as genuinely unclassifiable as usual.

Although masquerading as a novel for marketing reasons, Thomas Ligotti's *Grimscribe: His Lives and Works* was actually a series of interconnected narratives. Fifteen superior science fiction and horror stories lived up to the subtitle of Lisa Tuttle's *Memories of the Body: Tales of Desire and Transformation*, while Christopher Fowler chronicled fourteen tales of urban horror in the aptly-titled *Sharper Knives*. *Element of Doubt* by A. L. Barker included thirteen ghost stories, several of which were broadcast by BBC Radio 4 over Hallowe'en, and Elizabeth Engstrom explored the darker side of human nature in the twenty stories collected in *Nightmare Flower*.

*Fearful Lovers and Other Stories* by Robert Westall and *The Burning Baby and Other Ghosts* by John Gordon each contained five tales ostensibly aimed at younger audiences, but still powerful enough to resonate with an adult readership.

More regional terrors were showcased in *Aisling and Other Irish Tales of Terror* by Peter Tremayne (Peter Beresford Ellis) and *Whistling Past the Churchyard: Strange Tales from a Superstitious*

*Welshman* by Jon Manchip White. For those who preferred the classics, there were always *Charles Dickens' Christmas Ghost Stories* edited by Peter Haining, and Richard Dalby's not-quite-definitive *The Collected Ghost Stories of E. F. Benson*, which included fifty-four tales compiled from four earlier volumes.

Given the popularity of vampires in 1992, it was not surprising that a number of editors were quick to jump upon the undead bandwagon. Chief among these was the always-prolific Martin H. Greenberg who, besides editing the all-new *Dracula: Prince of Darkness*, also teamed up with Robert Weinberg and Stefan R. Dziemianowicz to produce *Weird Vampire Tales*, a collection of thirty stories from the pulp magazines, and with Dziemianowicz alone for the somewhat similar *A Taste of Blood*. Reprints and original stories were combined for both *The Mammoth Book of Vampires* edited by Stephen Jones, and Richard Dalby's *Vampire Stories*, the latter at least boasting an introduction by Peter Cushing.

Probably the best original anthology of the year was Dennis Etchison's *MetaHorror*, the long-awaited follow-up to his 1986 volume *Cutting Edge*. *In Dreams*, edited by Paul J. McAuley and Kim Newman, contained an eclectic mix of science fiction and horror stories celebrating the 7-inch single. It was certainly more ambitious than the year's other music anthology, Jeff Gelb's *Shock Rock*, despite the latter's inclusion of a new novella by Stephen King and an introduction from Alice Cooper.

Editors John Skipp and Craig Spector returned to the world of George Romero's zombies for *Still Dead: Book of the Dead 2*, and F. Paul Wilson did a creditable job integrating the nineteen stories comprising the second Horror Writers of America anthology, *Freak Show*. The Midnight Rose collective of Neil Gaiman, Mary Gentle and Roz Kaveney mostly ingnored the horror potential of another shared-world anthology, *The Weerde: Book 1*, in which a race of shapechangers co-exist with humans.

Peter Crowther's *Narrow Houses* included all the requisite Big Names, while *Dark at Heart* edited by Joe and Karen Lansdale featured twenty crime and suspense stories by many writers better known for their horror work. *The Pan Book of Horror* reached its thiry-third year of publication with *Dark Voices 4*, edited by David Sutton and Stephen Jones.

David G. Hartwell's *Foundations of Fear* was a hefty 660-page follow-up to his other excellent reprint anthology, *The Dark Descent*. Fedogan & Bremer continued their bid to take on the Arkham House mantle with *Tales of the Lovecraft Mythos* edited by Robert M. Price, which featured twenty classic Cthulhu Mythos tales. Ramsey

Campbell's *Uncanny Banquet* included a new story by the editor and Adrian Ross' rare 1914 novel *The Hole of the Pit*.

Only book club members were given the opportunity to see Marvin Kaye's *Lovers and Other Monsters*, while other seasoned anthologists fared somewhat better with *Terror by Gaslight: An Anthology of Rare Tales of Terror*, the second book with that title edited by Hugh Lamb, *Great Irish Stories of the Supernatural*, edited by Peter Haining, and Richard Dalby's *Horror for Christmas*.

*The Oxford Book of Gothic Tales* edited by Chris Baldick contained thirty-seven stories dating from the eighteenth century to the present, and Brian Stableford unearthed some equally obscure finds for *The Second Dedalus Book of Decadence: The Black Feast* and *The Dedalus Book of Femmes Fatales*, which mixed in new material as well. *Midnight Graffiti*, edited by Jessica Horsting and James Van Hise, contained reprints from the glossy small press magazine along with original stories, while David B. Silva's *The Definitive Best of The Horror Show* was exactly what the title suggested. *Reel Terror: The Stories that Inspired the Great Horror Movies* was an uninspired selection by Sebastian Wolfe, but the same editor showed more originality with *The Little Book of Horrors: Tiny Tales of Terror*, which managed to squeeze in seventy short-short stories, poems and cartoons.

As always, Ellen Datlow and Terri Windling's *The Year's Best Fantasy and Horror: Fifth Annual Collection* was the most substantial of the year's prime volumes, containing forty-four stories and six poems. Karl Edward Wagner's *The Year's Best Horror Stories* celebrated its twentieth anniversary with volume XX, Robert Morrish and Peter Enfantino's *Quick Chills II* collected twenty-five stories which appeared in the small presses during 1989–91 and, as usual, our own *Best New Horror 3* was the only annual showcase to appear on both sides of the Atlantic.

The inevitable collapse of the Pulphouse publishing pyramid, supported by multifarious magazines and overpriced "collector's editions", proved that you still can't fool all of the people all of the time.

Otherwise, in America horror fiction continued to flourish in the small press magazines with John L. Herron's *Aberrations: Adult Horror, Science Fiction and Dark Fantasy*, four issues of the World Fantasy Award-winning *Cemetery Dance*, edited by Richard T. Chizmar (including a new Stephen King story), two issues each of Mark Rainey's *Deathrealm*, Crispin Burnham's *Eldritch Tales* and Gretta M. Anderson's *2AM*. There was just one new issue each of Peggy Nadramia's WFA-winning *Grue* and Jon B. Cooke's *Tekeli-li!*, although the latter weighed in at an impressive 128 pages.

Jeff VanderMeer's *Jabberwocky* grandly billed itself as 'The Magazine of Speculative Writing', and the first issue of Rachel Drummond's *Sequitar* suffered from the same pretentious tone. *The Scream Factory* devoted an issue to listing the worst horror fiction, including short stories which one editor thought insulted his intelligence, clearly an achievement.

After an absence, *Midnight Graffiti* published a new issue featuring fiction by Rex Miller, Ray Garton and David J. Schow, while W. Paul Ganley's long-running *Weirdbook* (another WFA-winner) also managed a single issue with stories by Brian Lumley and Scott Edelman, and poetry by the late Joseph Payne Brennan.

Darrell Schweitzer's revived *Weird Tales* produced a pulp-sized issue showcasing John Brunner's fiction, but the somewhat delayed F. Paul Wilson special marked an unattractive change of format. The anti-censorship periodical *Gauntlet: Exploring the Limits of Free Expression* published two volumes which included fiction and articles by Ramsey Campbell, Robert Bloch, Steve Rasnic Tem, Richard Christian Matheson, Poppy Z. Brite, Harlan Ellison and a comic strip adaptation of a F. Paul Wilson story.

*Shivers* was a new British horror film magazine launched by the publishers of *Starburst*. A bit on the thin side, it at least had the distinction of being edited by one of the field's premier critics, Alan Jones. Also worth a look was David J. Schow's "Raving & Drooling" column in the American horror movie magazine *Fangoria*, in which the creator of the "Splatterpunk" appellation vented his spleen in an often forthright and funny manner.

Possibly one of the most prolific publishers of horror material, much of it devoted to the so-called "Lovecraft Circle", was Necronomicon Press. As well as producing a multitude of chapbooks devoted to HPL and his colleagues, they also published three issues of Robert M. Price's *Crypt of Cthulhu*, two issues of S. T. Joshi's *Lovecraft Studies* and a single issue of *Studies in Weird Fiction*, also edited by Joshi. Three issues of *Necrofile*, the premier critical review of horror fiction, edited by Stefan Dziemianowicz, S. T. Joshi and Michael A. Morrison, also appeared.

The third issue of Leigh Blackmore's *Terror Australis* was a "Jack the Ripper Special". In Britain, David Pringle's *Interzone* continued to publish some of the most interesting short fiction around, and the second paperback volume of David Garnett's revived *New Worlds* also included some offbeat material.

*Interzone*'s companion title, *Million, the Magazine About Popular Fiction*, included features on Robert Bloch, Stephen Gallagher, James Herbert and Robert Aickman, and *The New York Review of Science*

*Fiction* also published the occasional piece of interest to horror fans. For straight news and reviews, American readers could pick from either *Locus* or *Science Fiction Chronicle*, while in UK the choice was *Critical Wave* and *The British Fantasy Newsletter*.

In fact, the British Fantasy Society's irregular *Newsletter* finally found a new editor and a new identity, and was supplemented by the sixth issue of Peter Coleborn's *Chills*, *Dark Horizons* No. 33, edited by Phil Williams, the fourth *Mystique* from Mike Chinn and Mark Morris' short story chapbook *Birthday*. Rosemary Pardoe produced another welcome volume of *Ghosts & Scholars*, and *Peeping Tom* put out four issues edited by Stuart Hughes. The 80th issue of Gordon Linzner and Jani Anderson's long-running *Space & Time* was going to be the last, but it might continue under a new publisher.

Despite the proliferation of professional anthologies and collections and small press magazines, one of the expanding outlets for short horror fiction in 1992 was signed, numbered or illustrated limited edition chapbooks and paperbacks.

Colorado's Little Bookshop of Horrors put out a number of titles under the Roadkill Press imprint, including *For You, The Living* by Wayne Allen Sallee, *Beautiful Strangers* by Melanie and Steve Rasnic Tem, *Cannibal Dwight's Special Purpose* by Nancy Holder, *Steppin' Out, Summer '68* by Joe R. Lansdale, the fiction double *Kill Shot/Cuttings* by Roger Zasuly and Pamela J. Jessen, and the collections *Mr. Fox and Other Feral Tales* by Norman Partridge and *Darker Passions* by Edward Bryant.

The Wildside Press reprinted F. Paul Wilson's story *The Barrens* as a chapbook, then moved into collections with *Courting Disasters and Other Strange Affinities* by Nina Kiriki Hoffman, *Rosemary's Brain and Other Tales of Weird Wonder* by Martha Soukup, and a trio of cat stories by Fritz Leiber entitled *Kreativity for Kats and Other Feline Fantasies*. From TAL Publications came Lucy Taylor's impressive collection *Unnatural Acts*, *Edward Lee's Quest for Sex, Truth and Reality* by Edward Lee, and Elizabeth Massie's Bram Stoker Award-winning short story *Stephen*. Joe R. Lansdale's *God of the Razor* was reprinted by Crossroads Press, who followed it with *Cold Turkey* by Nancy A. Collins, a new novella featuring her vampire Sonja Blue from the novels *Sunglasses After Dark* and *In the Blood*.

In Britain, author/illustrator A. F. Kidd published a chapbook collection of six ghost stories under the title *Bells Rung Backwards*. Crimson Altar Press produced David G. Rowlands' *The Living & the Dead*, a collection of seven ghost stories featuring E. G. Swain's protagonist the Rev. Roland Batchel, while from The Ghost Story

Society came *No. 472 Cheyne Walk: Carnacki: The Untold Stories* by A. F. Kidd & Rick Kennett, featuring four new stories about William Hope Hodgson's famed ghost-finder. Two tales featuring John Whitbourn's psychic detective Admiral Slovo appeared in the Haunted Library publication *Popes & Phantoms*, and *Haunted Pavilions* included nine ghost stories about cricket, edited by Mark Valentine.

Also in the UK, editor Nicholas Royle followed his British Fantasy Award-winning anthology with twenty-three new stories in *Darklands 2*, Jack Hunter edited *Red Stains* for Creation Press, and Chris Kenworthy included seven science fiction and horror stories with a political slant in Barrington Books' *The Sun Rises Red*. On the other side of the Atlantic, George Hatch's Horror's Head Press offered thirteen "adult" stories in *Souls in Pawn*, Stanislaus Tal's *Bizarre Bazaar '92* was subtitled "A Magazine Anthology", and Michael Brown's *Demons and Deviants* was a slim volume published by Phantom Press/Fantaco Enterprises which included new fiction by Clive Barker, Peter Atkins, Dan Chichester and Steve Niles. In Australia, Bill Congreve's anthology *Intimate Armageddons* appeared from Five Islands Press.

With so much vampire fiction around, it was no surprise that *Vampire: The Complete Guide to the World of the Undead* by Manuela Dunn Mascetti failed to live up to the promise of its title. John L. Flynn's *Cinematic Vampires* was also a disappointment, despite coming from the usually reliable McFarland & Company.

Tony Magistrale managed to wring a few more facts out of his subject in both *The Dark Descent: Essays Defining Stephen King's Horrorscope* and *Stephen King, The Second Decade: Danse Macabre to The Dark Half* (the latter including an interview with King). These might even have helped with the answers in *The Second Stephen King Quiz Book* by Stephen Spignesi.

Britain's own bestselling horror writer was profiled in the multi-faceted *James Herbert: By Horror Haunted*, edited by Stephen Jones, which collected together articles, interviews and Herbert's short fiction. From the University Press of Mississippi came Mary R. Reichardt's *A Web of Relationship: Women in the Short Fiction of Mary Wilkins Freeman* and the companion volume, *The Uncollected Stories of Mary Wilkins Freeman*. *Wandering Ghosts: The Odyssey of Lafcadio Hearn*, by Jonathan Cott, and *Lafcadio Hearn and the Vision of Japan*, by Carl Dawson were both biographies of the American writer who retold the myths and legends of his adopted homeland. After Kenneth Silverman's ground-breaking 1991 biography *Edgar Allan Poe: Mournful and Never-Ending Remembrance*,

Jeffrey Meyers attempted the same feat with *Edgar Allan Poe: His Life and Legacy*.

New English Library published an updated and revised edition of the Bram Stoker Award-winning *Horror: 100 Best Books* edited by Stephen Jones and Kim Newman, Darrell Schweitzer's *Discovering Classic Horror* contained eleven essays on the subject, and Cosette Kies' *Supernatural Fiction for Teens* appeared in an updated second edition recommending 1300 annotated titles. In Starmont House's *Fear to the World*, Kevin Proulx interviewed eleven horror writers, including Clive Barker, Ramsey Campbell, John Farris, F. Paul Wilson and Richard Christian Matheson, while more dedicated scholars may have wanted to track down the comprehensive *Reference Guide to Science Fiction, Fantasy and Horror* by Michael Burgess (Robert Reginald).

Gordon Sander's *Serling: The Rise and Twilight of Television's Last Angry Man* was a biography of Rod Serling, creator of TV's *The Twilight Zone*. Editor Peter Goodrich's *Cut! Horror Writers on Horror Film* included interviews with Clive Barker and Anne Rice, and *The Video Watchdog Book* reprinted Tim Lucas' invaluable articles in a single volume with a new foreward by director Joe Dante.

Certainly the most attractive art book of 1992 was *Graven Images: The Best of Horror, Fantasy, and Science Fiction Film Art from the collection of Ronald V. Borst*, which reprinted more than 500 vintage posters and lobby cards in full colour, boasted an introduction by Stephen King, and included essays by Forrest J Ackerman, Clive Barker, Robert Bloch, Ray Bradbury, Harlan Ellison and Peter Straub.

Probably the bestselling illustrated book of last year was James Gurney's *Dinotopia*, set in a lost world populated by sentient dinosaurs, while Underwood-Miller's *Virgil Finlay's Women of the Ages* beautifully showcased the delicate stipple work of the late pulp illustrator.

For fans of the Cenobites, *The Hellraiser Chronicles* edited by Stephen Jones contained full colour photographic portraits from all three movies, supplemented with text by screenwriters Clive Barker and Peter Atkins. Along the same lines, *Bram Stoker's Dracula: The Film and the Legend* by Francis Ford Coppola and James V. Hart included the script for the most expensive vampire movie ever made, profusely illustrated with colour stills from the film. Capitalising on the Count's renewed popularity, *Dracula: A Symphony in Moonlight and Nightmares* was a collection of watercolours by Jon J. Muth based on Bram Stoker's novel.

* * *

Vampires also meant big business in comics, as the phenomenal sales of Malibu's adaptation of Brian Lumley's *Necroscope* series proved, with each issue featuring a distinctive cover painting by Bob Eggleton. Inevitably, Coppola's *Bram Stoker's Dracula* also received the graphic novel treatment, scripted by veteran comics writer Roy Thomas.

*Revelations* was the latest in Eclipse's series of Clive Barker adaptations, scripted by Steve Niles from Barker's short story, with art by Lionel Talaro. Bantam Spectra published three volumes of *The Ray Bradbury Chronicles* which collected new and reprint graphic adaptations of Bradbury's stories with new introductions and notes by the author.

Tim Burton's darker and much improved *Batman Returns* topped the American box office at the end of 1992 with receipts of more than $162 million, although it was soon overtaken by Walt Disney's animated *Aladdin* (well past the $200 million mark by now) and the dire *Home Alone 2: Lost in New York* ($173 million). In Britain, the Batman sequel could only manage fourth place behind *Basic Instinct*, *Hook* and *Lethal Weapon 3*.

In fact, 1992 was the third best year on record for movie admissions, with genre films making up almost a quarter of the year's total. One of the surprise hits of the year was *The Hand That Rocks the Cradle*, a slick psychothriller that cost $12 million to make and grossed $88 million. Far less successful was Francis Ford Coppola's visually striking but incoherent version of *Bram Stoker's Dracula* which, although it grossed around $82 million, had a reputed negative cost of nearly $70 million.

Despite ILM's incredible special effects, the decidedly unfunny horror comedy *Death Becomes Her* grossed nearly $60 million and still managed to finish ahead of the underrated *Alien*$^3$. Two dumb Stephen King adaptations, *The Lawnmower Man* and *Sleepwalkers*, both came in around the $30 million mark, and the disappointing adaptation of Clive Barker's *Candyman* was not far behind.

Wes Craven returned to form with *The People Under the Stairs*, but the Stephen King sequel *Pet Semetary Two* proved a disappointment. The failure of either *Buffy the Vampire Slayer* or John Landis' *Innocent Blood* to set the box office alight killed off the predicted vampire boom before it even got started.

*Hellraiser III: Hell on Earth* was the most successful entry yet in Clive Barker's Cenobite series, and it managed to make more money than *Dr. Giggles*, *Twin Peaks: Fire Walk With Me* and Brian DePalma's demented *Raising Cain*.

*The Resurrected*, Dan O'Bannon's version of H. P. Lovecraft's

*The Case of Charles Dexter Ward*, and Peter Jackson's tasteless zombie gorefest *Braindead* (aka *Dead Alive*) deserved wider exposure, however it was probably just as well that *Amityville 1992: It's About Time*, *Children of the Night*, *Critters 4*, *Cthulhu Mansion*, *The Devil's Daughter* (aka *The Sect*), *Evil Toons*, *House IV*, *Killer Tomatoes Strike Back*, *Maniac Cop III: Badge of Silence*, *Prom Night IV: Deliver Us from Evil*, *Puppet Master III: Toulon's Revenge*, *Scanners III: The Takeover*, *Seedpeople*, *Xtro II* and others of their ilk were relegated to the video wastelands.

Genre films did surprisingly well at the 1992 Academy Awards with *The Silence of The Lambs* (Best Film, Director, Adaptation, Actor and Actress!), *Beauty and the Beast* and *Terminator 2: Judgment Day* each earning multiple Oscars. George Lucas was presented with the Irving G. Thalberg Memorial Award and the Gordon E. Sawyer Award went to Ray Harryhausen.

Television had little of interest to offer in 1992. Wes Craven's *Nightmare Cafe* quickly disappeared and *The Young Indiana Jones Chronicles* failed to recapture the excitement of the original films. The small screen's high points were all animated shows—*The Simpsons*, *The Ren and Stimpy Show* (despite the firing of creator John Kricfalusi) and the impressive animated *Batman* series.

At the second World Horror Convention, which returned over March 5–8 to Nashville, Tennessee, Stephen King won the 1992 Grand Master Award. Predictably, he was not on hand to receive it.

The Horror Writers of America's Bram Stoker Awards were presented on 19 June in New York. Robert R. McCammon's *Boy's Life* won in the Novel category, while the result for First Novel was a tie between *The Cipher* by Kathe Koja and *Prodigal* by Melanie Tem. "The Beautiful Uncut Hair of Graves" by David Morrell beat out the other nominations for Novella/Novelette and "Lady Madonna" by Nancy Holder did the same in the Short Story category. *Prayers to Broken Stones* by Dan Simmons won for Collection, and *Clive Barker's Shadows in Eden* edited by Stephen Jones picked up the Non-Fiction award. The Lifetime Achievement award was accepted by cartoonist/writer Gahan Wilson.

The British Fantasy Awards were presented at Fantasycon XVII in Birmingham, England, on 4 October. The August Derleth Award for Best Novel went to *Outside the Dog Museum* by Jonathan Carroll. Michael Marshall Smith won the Best Short Fiction award for the second consecutive year, for "The Dark Land", and the anthology it came from, *Darklands*, edited by Nicholas Royle, won in the Best Collection/Anthology category. The Best Small Press award went to *Peeping Tom*, edited by Stuart Hughes, and Jim Pitts was voted Best Artist. Melanie Tem was announced as the winner of The Icarus Award for Best Newcomer, and the Special Committee Award went to Andrew I. Porter, editor and publisher of *Science Fiction Chronicle*.

The World Fantasy Awards were presented on 1 November at Pine Mountain, Georgia. *Boy's Life* by Robert R. McCammon picked up another award for Best Novel. The Best Novella award went to "The Ragthorn" by Robert Holdstock and Garry Kilworth, and "The Somewhere Doors" by Fred Chappell won Best Short Story. Lucius Shepard's *The Ends of the Earth* was voted Best Collection and Tim Hildebrandt named Best Artist. The Best Anthology award went to *The Year's Best Fantasy and Horror: Fourth Annual Collection*, edited by Ellen Datlow and Terri Windling, and George Scithers and Darrell Schweitzer won the Special Award Professional for *Weird Tales*. The Special Award Non-Professional went to W. Paul Ganley for *Weirdbook*/Weirdbook Press, and artist Edd Cartier won the Life Achievement Award.

Californian book dealer Barry Levin announced Stephen King was the Most Collectable Author of the Year. Charnel House's lettered state of *Last Call* by Tim Powers was Most Collectable Book of the Year, and Robert Reginald received the special Lifetime Collectors' Award for His Invaluable Contribution to Science Fiction, Fantasy and Horror Bibliography.

In an editorial provocatively entitled "Daring to Care" in the spring 1992 issue of the British small press SF magazine *Nexus*, Paul Brazier claimed that "the abbatoir aspect of horror fiction has come to dominate the genre, until it seems we can expect blood to drip from every page . . . Certainly, writers of [Mark] Morris' calibre mar their books with the blood-letting which seems to be *de rigueur* nowadays, and it would be nice to see more real psychological value creeping back into horror fiction."

It would appear from Mr Brazier's comments that he hasn't read very much *good* horror fiction lately. Otherwise, he might not have dismissed the entire genre in quite so cavalier a manner. Over the past couple of decades a tolerance between the genres has been established, with many authors, editors and publishers now content to blur the demarcation lines between the categories.

Then, in the grand tradition of fanzine writing, along comes Mr Brazier giving the impression that the horror field hasn't developed since the *bad* old days of *The Pan Book of Horror Stories*. Even a brief perusal of any of the three Year's Best horror anthologies currently available would reveal the breadth and scope of horror fiction being published today.

Of course, the very nature of *some* horror fiction dictates "blood to drip from every page" (in the same way that *some* science fiction still uses the trappings of spaceships and ray-guns), however that alone does not necessarily mean that it is *bad* fiction.

We would be the first to admit that there is a great deal of bad horror fiction being published (we are exposed to much of it every year when compiling this anthology!), but that argument also applies to every other publishing category.

The undeniable strength of horror fiction is the very *diversity* the field has to offer. One of the most enjoyable aspects of editing *Best New Horror* is discovering how horror (or terror, or suspense, or dark fantasy, whatever you want to call it) can be incorporated into almost any other type of fiction, be it war stories, westerns, crime or, yes, even science fiction.

If, as Mr Brazier claims, all he is asking horror writers to do is "to care about their characters," perhaps he should read more fiction by those authors currently working in the field before he dismisses the entire genre out of hand. He might even be pleasantly surprised . . .

The Editors
May, 1993

BEST NEW

# HORROR 4

# SCOTT EDELMAN

## The Suicide Artist

SCOTT EDELMAN's short fiction and poetry have been published in *The Twilight Zone Magazine, Fantasy Book, Amazing Stories, Isaac Asimov's Science Fiction, Eldritch Tales, Weirdbook* and the Necronomicon Press chapbook, *Suicide Art*.

He has also written comic books for both Marvel and DC (*House of Mystery, Weird War Tales, Welcome Back Kotter* etc.) and various television scripts ranging from Saturday morning cartoons for Hanna-Barbera to *Tales from the Darkside*. His novel *The Gift*, published by Space & Time in 1990, was a finalist for a Lambda Literary Award in the category Best Gay SF/Fantasy Novel, and he is currently the founding editor of the magazine *Science Fiction Age*, launched in 1992.

As always, we lead off *Best New Horror* with one of the most powerful stories in the volume. As the author explains: "'The Suicide Artist' comes out of my desire to wrestle with the question not only of 'What is a horror story?' but also the equally important questions '*Why* is a horror story?' and 'What is a horror story *for*?'

"I have always felt that a story must do more than merely pass the time. It must defend its very existence as well. It must justify itself, and the demands it makes on your time.

"When I read 'The Suicide Artist' aloud at conventions, the audience response is unlike that I receive for anything else I've ever written. Other stories of mine insist on getting mixed emotions out of a group. But no such dichotomies occur with this story. 'The Suicide Artist' receives a singularity of response such as I've never seen before. I dive into the performance, and within a few paragraphs

I realise that the room has grown hushed, as if people had become too fearful to breathe. I have considered the audience reaction, and I think I have finally figured out why that happens. It is because they know that the voice of 'The Suicide Artist' is more than a narrator just speaking to some faceless listener. They know that the narrator is speaking to them.

"And to you."

I LONG AGO DECIDED THAT NOTHING, *nothing* should suit a person's life so much as the leaving of it, and the universe has supported me in this notion.

The use of the word "decided" is perhaps inaccurate here. I am very concerned with accuracy, for it is important to me that you understand my story, perceive the reason I am telling it to you, and absorb it with all its exacting nuances. So let me retract the word "decided" right now, and strive henceforth to be more precise in my prose. For can it ever be said that we "decide" to learn the lessons that life, in its hammerlock on our attention, endeavors to teach us?

I was not as old as you might think I would have needed to be to have first learned that central precept. I was at an age when life was still vague, and death itself seemed apocryphal.

Will you listen while I tell you of it? Of course you will. Forgive my disingenuousness in asking, when of your attention I have no doubts.

I was never a social animal. Whether I took that path by personal choice or molded by cosmic design I do not know, and at this point in my life it is far too late to invest much concern in the issue. So entering kindergarten was in itself something of a shock to me. I had never even been inside a nursery school, as mother intended to keep me as far from churches and synagogues for as long as possible, and it seemed as if the only nursery schools she could find were affiliated in some way with a religious institution of one kind or another. Kindergarten, therefore, was my first exposure to peer humanity en masse.

I did not like it. Did you honestly expect that I would?

The short, stout woman who squinted at me through thick glasses was not the only teacher I encountered there. My brother and sister five and six year olds, who were better teachers of knowledge than she, taught me everything I need to know about cruelty and intolerance, about prejudice and insult, about hatred and pride. The lessons were not ones I wished to absorb, but obviously, at that age, I had little control over my attendance. So I went, and I learned.

I did not like the other children very much. I do not understand those who, as children, *did* like other children. To me, they were the ones who with angelic demeanor would deliberately bump into me when I was eating my milk and cookies, who pinched me and punched me, who would share with me only under warning of some undisclosed parental threat, who would not let an accidental sin of mine, such as spilling fingerpaint or coming back from the bathroom with my fly open, go unobserved and unreported if passing it on to the teacher would create a greater entertainment, who turned faces of menace to me and faces of innocence to adults. So when some of the children began to disappear and the parents when gathered together started speaking only in muffled whispers, I did not mind. At the time, I did not understand what was happening. I only knew that to me, a world with one less bully in it was a relief.

During this period, parents were not as lackadaisical as they had once been about being there in the playground waiting for us when school let out. Their faces as they stood by the open gate, puffing on their cigarettes, were no longer calm and happy ones; even I could read the tension. Momma was always early, but then, Momma was early for everything. My childhood had been populated with mad dashes, as if out of fear that if we ever took it slow, life would get away from us. One day, Momma was not there. I watched as all the other kids vanished with their parents. I was eventually left alone in a darkening schoolyard.

You might have thought that there would have been at least one parent who, in his or her concern for the safety of his or her own child, might have spared one iota of that concern for me. I know, years afterward, that is what *I* thought. I have resigned myself to the fact that it was just another one of my life lessons.

I stood there solitary for about fifteen minutes, holding in my hands a lion mask we had made that day out of a paper plate. While I was staring into the lion's eyes, a man approached and told me that my Momma had asked him to drive me home.

Yes, I know. And it seemed strange even at the time, but then, grownups were grownups, and to be obeyed. I followed him a long way from the school to where he had parked, and then we drove through winding streets I had never seen. During our entire ride, he spoke only once, and then in a soft, breathy voice.

"Your shirt," he said. "It's so . . . so white."

When we parked, it was in front of a house unfamiliar to me. He must have noticed a puzzled expression, for he quickly told me that my Momma would not be getting home until later, that she wished me to wait there with him. He took my hand with cold and sweaty fingers, and led me inside. When the door clicked shut behind me, I did not like the sound of it.

You can guess what happened now, can you not? You have heard stories that have begun like this before, are familiar with the overtones, can intuit the direction in which this little incident is heading. Can I not simply leave you to *imagine* the rest, if details are what you require? Do I need to go on? I would rather not, but I know you, so I guess I must, I guess I must.

When, in the center of the room, I turned around at the sound of the locking door, when I saw the man's face in its home base light, stripped of what must have been its previous strained pretense of innocence, I realized that what I had up until then been interpreting in his eyes as levity was really insanity, that what I had been mistaking as nervousness was really desire.

He moved towards me, and I began to fight. I had never been a fighter, though I had been given many opportunities to learn. In the schoolyard, in response to the boys who took great delight in tormenting me, I normally rolled into a ball and waited for them to tire. At that instance, in that house, I intuitively knew that would not suffice. I kicked and punched wildly, only occasionally connecting with flesh as he pulled at my clothing. Buttons popped and cloth tore as I protested, and he had me naked almost before I knew it. He let me go and backed away, the clothing bunched tightly in his hands. Gasping, my nose bloodied, I crawled slowly away from him into a far corner of the room.

"You shouldn't have done that," he said, staring down at a bloodstain on my shirt. "You shouldn't have put up such a fight. Why do they always put up such a fight? Look at it. You've . . . *soiled* it."

"I didn't mean to," I whimpered, able from the tone in which he'd spoken to tell the seriousness of my supposed crime. I looked around the room for a way out, and could see none. I was amazed that I had not earlier noticed the room's bizarre decor. Fear had been clouding my perception, I imagine. The room's only piece of furniture was a small cot, its rumpled sheets stained and yellowed. The door through which we had come was not visible, for it and all four walls of that room were hung with a crazy quilt of shirts and pants and shorts and socks, all small and childlike and delicate. Some were ripped to shreds, some clean but used, some covered with blood, some neat and fresh with creases still showing as if hardly worn at all. At the time I did not understand enough of the world to know what this odd collection might mean. Now I know, but I try not to think about it.

The man, who I fear I must keep referring to as simply that, "the man," because his name I was never to learn, kept glancing from my clothing to me to my clothing again. His eyes would widen when they sought out the fabric, and I tried to imagine what it was he saw there in its folds. I could not even come close then to describing that look, but these days, I often wonder if it is the same gleam that others find in my eyes. He finally turned from me, muttering, as if I was not there. He sat down on the edge of his bed, and began to ramble in a slurred speech. I shivered and strained to hear each word he said.

"There is so much . . . evil in the world. So much. Only innocence can ward it off, protect me. I can feel it, yes, oh yes, I can feel it.

The innocence has been . . . absorbed. This one is a good one. He will help me mend my shield. I can be safe again. I can be. I can be safe."

Repeating himself, he slumped back, and then began to snore. I listened to the ticking of a clock, and made myself count along with it until I had measured out sixty ten times, wanting to be sure that he was really asleep. Once I felt confident about his lack of consciousness, I searched for the door beneath the makeshift curtain, and having found it gently turned the knob. It of course would not open. Did you expect that my travail would end so easily? You know better, don't you? You would not have bothered coming along with me on my journey if that is what you'd calculated, would you? You desire, you need, you must have . . . *more*, mustn't you?

I tiptoed quietly through the house of this man who thought he knew the secret of how to hide from evil. (If he could ask me now, I would tell him what I have learned: that evil cannot hide from evil, or from good.) For all my youth, the inventory I took on my wide-eyed tour was not difficult to interpret. It was as if a gruesome Grimm's fairy tale had suddenly become real before me.

Pots and pans of a slowly simmering stew bubbling on the kitchen burners.

The walls a badly patched tent, sewn together of children's clothes.

In the basement, which I descended into most trepidatiously, deep trenches filled with bones. I prayed they were those of neighborhood cats and dogs, but knew they were not.

I returned upstairs and surveyed the sleeping man. Unconscious as he was, he did present an appearance of innocence, did seem as innocent as he hoped was the cloth which his obsession told him would protect him from whatever unknown evil was his demon. The flesh of his face hung calmly, peacefully, unmolded by his mania, and I could almost believe the man belied his environment. But then I looked down to see my clothing within his slack fingers.

I grasped hold of my collar, and started slowly to pull my shirt from those fingers. If the man's digits jerked or tightened, I would stop my efforts, but as soon as he relaxed again, I would begin once more to pull. I stared at his trembling eyelids while I worked, wondering what dreams raced through his mind. After a span of time that to me seemed longer than my life had been up until then, at last it was in my hands.

I calmly watched him breath (oh how amazed I was at my own calmness), and at that very special moment when, chest concave and mouth wide, he reached for his next breath, I as quickly as I could shoved the fabric into his open mouth and pinched his nostrils closed.

His eyes immediately bulged wide, and as he looked at me, I knew he was looking *into* me. I knew what he saw there, and I was afraid of it. I jumped atop him and wrapped my spindly legs about his chest, and amazed myself by holding on tightly as he bucked and tried to knock me from his chest, me, a six year old. Where did my strength come from to be able to steal the life from a grown man, and a lunatic at that? I do not know.

I never know.

Once I was sure that he was dead, I pulled my shirt from his mouth, and the rest of my clothing from his hands. I took them to the bathroom sink, the grout of which was red from the man's madness. There, I carefully washed my clothes. In the kitchen, I found an old iron with which to dry them as I had sometime seen my Momma do.

Momma. As I dressed I thought of Momma, and wondered how it was that she had failed to meet me at our appointed time. She had never failed me before. I hurriedly rummaged through the man's pockets, and found a key, with which I made my escape. I did not take the time to lock the door behind me. I had to get home quickly, to tell Momma . . . I was not sure what.

It took many long hours of wandering before I found a street that was familiar to me. I then walked slowly home in a dark that I had never before seen alone. Even after what I had endured, maybe *because* of what I had endured, I took my time, almost blinded by the beauty of the night sky. As I turned the corner onto my street, I saw a police car parked in front of my house, its light flashing soundlessly. I well recall thinking that the lights flashed for me, for my absence. I was wrong.

I have perfect recall for so much else, yet I cannot remember how I reacted when they told me that Momma was dead. I can remember the moment before I learned of that death, and the moment after, but of the moment itself . . .

She died, as I understand it, as she lived, always racing. She had been rushing towards me as if by a pull of gravity, probably after having grown impatient behind a slow moving driver, or perhaps after having been frustrated even earlier behind a long line at the supermarket, and so zoomed forward at the sight of an amber light. She had not deviated from her usual style, only this time she was hit by another car jumping at the first trace of green. One of my great losses is that I do not know what I would have told Momma had we been reunited that night, had I returned home from my detour to discover her sitting pale and worried in our living room. I never had the chance. My father and the other relatives were too lost in their grief to notice anything other than my reappearance itself. They did not act as if anything unusual could have occurred during the absence that prefaced it. They never questioned me about anything that might have happened; perhaps they lacked the imagination.

Momma would have questioned me.

And so it is that up until this day I have told no one about what that dying man saw in my eyes—that (are you ready?) I *enjoyed* his death. Even then, even before my newfound discovery turned to well worn habit, it seemed . . . *apt*. I knew that he deserved his end and his end came in a way which made artistic sense of his life, such as it was, transforming chaos into poetry. And to discover that my mother had been taken from this world with that same sense of correctness, of artistry, of flair, well . . . that taught me a lesson.

I learned how death should be.

And that was a good thing, too, because there seemed to be so much of it.

I haven't yet told you about the rest of my family, and I'm sure you're probably wondering about them. (No? How sad. Yet how typical of you, to be so self-centered. I should have expected it.) I'll have you know that Momma's death affected not just me. It affected the entire family. Dad, oh how Dad did change. And Kate. It affected Kate.

Kate was my older sister by four years, which meant that she was almost ten when Momma died. Once we were down to a familial trinity, the whole chemistry of our house changed. At first, Kate tried to be Momma for both of us, but it didn't work for long. She would cook for us, and play with me, and when Dad would come home from work and sit wet-eyed before the flickering television set, silent to both of us, she would bring him a drink, and massage his temples. She so wanted to make his pain go away. She never seemed to act with as much tenderness to me, but I guess she figured I was too young to have any true pain.

The more she became like Momma to my father, the less she could be a Momma to me.

There came a time when I was awakened by Kate crying late at night. The wall between our rooms was not sufficient to contain her sobbing. My first thought was one of surprise, for Kate had always been a stoic, never one to give in to outward displays of emotion. She hadn't even cried at Momma's funeral. My next thought was fear. For if *Kate* was crying, something was terribly wrong. (Notice that I had not yet learned of the healthy, curative power of tears. I now know that I should have rejoiced at my sister's tears; they were the first sign of true recovery in our home in months.) I slipped from my room into hers quietly.

I had learned to move quietly through the house. I'd *had* to learn that; my survival depended on it. If I became an actual presence in the home, my father would sense me and look up and remember his pain, and I did not want to be the cause of that pain, both because of the way it would make him feel, and the way causing it would make *me* feel. (Guilt is another one of the lessons life teaches us young. It is one I have spent a lifetime, however, trying to forget.) I entered the room without my sister noticing.

She was curled up on one side, facing away from me. Her sheet was wrapped around her, and the moonlight made her bare shoulders gleam with perspiration. Her crying, as I stopped and watched her, grew very quiet. Now and then her body would tremble. Her pajamas were in a pile with her blankets in a far corner of the room. The sheet which enfolded her had been gathered and stuffed between her legs, and the panda bears were stained red. She moaned, and I crept over and lightly placed a hand on her arm to comfort her.

She screamed and spun, flinging me from her. Her eyes were full of hate and fear. As I was babbling apologies, the light clicked on. I covered my eyes with my hands, and squinted through the cracks between my fingers. Dad stood beside me, a towel wrapped around his waist, the dark hair on his chest damp, as if fresh from a shower. I looked from Dad to Kate and back again.

"Go to your room," Dad whispered. I turned to Kate. She nodded.

I went back to my room.

Do I have to make it any plainer? You are an adult, I was a child, do I have to decode it for you? Well, I will not. I refuse.

I grow tired of the explicitness you demand. Can't I just tell you that not long thereafter my father died, and leave it at that? I am a doer, a man of action, not one of your foul storytellers. Can't I just slip ahead past all of this . . . *horror*, and make my point?

No, you will not let me. And I guess . . . I guess that if I am to make you see whereof I speak, that part deserves to be told.

Having gone back to my room, I did not simply go to sleep that night. I snuck past my sister's closed door and went back to the house where death had first shown me its bulging face. Though weeks had passed, the door was unlocked, as I had left it. That no one had been there since me I could tell before I entered the room, for the rotting body announced its presence to me before I ever saw it. The man still lay on the bed, his flesh puffy and foul-smelling.

It took me hours, but I ripped down the clothing that lined the living room walls. Neatness scored no points for my purpose. I carried the fabric to the basement and used the swatches to make bundles of the bones. The stew, which had long since congealed in its pots, I took to the bathroom and poured down the drain. In an upstairs bedroom, I found a display cabinet filled with a variety of trinkets: bracelets, some jacks and balls, baseball cards, barrettes, some rolled comic books, a necklace locket with a picture of a dog, a pair of broken glasses. I added these things to my packages. Throughout the night I walked back and forth to our house, secreting what I'd brought with me in our basement.

My task completed, I peered in once more upon my sister. She slept, but from the noises that she made, I could tell her sleep was not a peaceful one.

I punched three buttons on the phone, and whispered briefly to the man who answered.

I tucked into my bed, content.

Later, as the sun was beginning to rise, I was awakened by a loud knock on the door. Out the window I could see a police car parked out front. One policeman was already at our front door while a second moved around towards the back. I stayed in my room, listening to what transpired, acting as an uninvolved audience as my father's voice grew very loud and then quiet again, before seeing him walk off between the two policemen.

I was not to be left alone with him again before his death.

I met with him once in a small room with a large guard, and he seemed very confused, unsure why it was what had happened to him had happened. The guard kept his eyes fixed on my Dad's hands during the entire visit. Dad felt that for him to be there in prison meant there was no justice in the world. I left him with comforting words, but little else. I wonder whether Dad had that look of confusion on him still when he was stabbed to death in the showers by an embezzler bereft with grief who had lost a child to cancer just before coming into custody.

My sister and I were split up between family members, and never spoke about any of the things that had happened. I guess I can understand why she would feel that way. I don't like having to speak of any of it to you.

But you insist, don't you?

You'd have me tell you about all the deaths that followed, about the boy in grade school who would beat me up daily and take my lunch money, about the cigarette executive who pimped for the coffin nails that killed an uncle, about . . .

Never mind. You'd have me tell you about all of them, and the ends they met, each and every one, in extreme and nauseating detail.

But no.

I'd rather talk about you. You, who sit there reading these words, you who *delight* in the reading of these words, when you know as well as I, if you'd only admit the truth about yourself, that there is something oh so wrong with your liking of them.

I know you as well as I know myself.

You are reading these words in a magazine. On its cover is some putrid illustration of a man being tortured, or eaten by monsters, or having rotting flesh fall off his face. Maybe a woman is being raped. Maybe a child is being threatened. Perhaps the picture is crudely drawn. Perhaps it is not.

Maybe you are not holding a flimsy magazine, maybe it is a sturdy book, a handsomely bound volume with gold lettering embossed across its spine.

It does not matter. You have been reading my words, and you have actually, may God forgive you, been *enjoying* them. You have read the other stories before mine, both at this time and for years before, and you have smiled at the most horrible of things.

I have lived these things. This is not a story to me. I must continue living with them forever. If I could trade my life for another's, I would pay any price. And yet you find in yourself the ability to think it is fun to visit with me. You actually consider this a way of having a good time.

You go to movies of this type, with people in pain and buckets of blood. You read novels with rats gnawing still pulsing flesh. You read comic books, rife with mass-produced nightmares.

You discuss these books, these movies, with your friends, as casually as discussing a lunch order. You are the deadly market which creates these horrible demons. Just as illegal narcotics would not be grown if there were no addicts to purchase them, so it is that no miseries would be nurtured in the lonely dark if you were not there to be an audience for them.

And what an enthralled audience you are.

So enthralled, in fact, that as you read these words, you will not hear me creeping up behind you, coming to direct you to your most poetic of ends. Of all the fiends I have known, and I have had the misfortune to know many, there has been none who has so enjoyed the agony of others as have you. For you I have a special plan. I will not tell you of it. It must be a surprise.

Do you think you feel my breath hot on your neck even now, even though I am not yet there? Good. That is how I want it to be, until I come for you. You shall have no peace ever again as you read your morbid fantasies, for you will constantly be thinking, "Is that him yet? Is it time?" The sensation of my breath on your neck will be a constant companion. And when the anticipatory tingle you presently feel is replaced by warm reality, and you start to turn, but do not turn quickly enough, you will realize that yes, everything

I have told you is true, your death is right, it is just, this is your correct and proper end.

You disagree? You think your final thoughts when I shortly come for you will be different ones? I don't see how you will possibly be able to deny the aptness of it all. Do you know why?

For you have had the stomach to travel with me so that we find ourselves still together at the end of this tale.

I look forward to meeting you in the flesh.

Soon.

# ROBERTA LANNES

## Dancing on a Blade of Dreams

ROBERTA LANNES lives in Southern California where she works as a fulltime teacher, graphic designer and photographer, writing whenever she can find the time.

Since the publication of her story, "Goodbye Dark Love", in Dennis Etchison's 1986 anthology *Cutting Edge*, her dark and distinctive short fiction has appeared in the anthologies *Lord John Ten*, *Alien Sex*, *Fantasy Tales 5*, *Splatterpunks: Extreme Horror*, *The Bradbury Chronicles: Stories in Honor of Ray Bradbury*, *Still Dead: Book of the Dead 2*, *Dark Voices 5: The Pan Book of Horror*, and such magazines as *Iniquities* and *Pulphouse*. She is currently working on a novel titled *The Hallowed Bed*.

The author should have made her debut in this series with "Apostate in Denim" in *Best New Horror 2*. However, at the very last moment, the publisher decided the story was too extreme for the sensibilities of British book retailers and cut it from that volume. Most of Lannes' stories *are* deeply disturbing but then, after all, isn't that what all the best horror fiction should be? "Dancing on a Blade of Dreams" is no exception, and we extend to her a belated welcome to these pages . . .

THE COUPLE UPSTAIRS WAS SCREWING. Loudly. Patty picked up the book from her nightstand and tossed it to the ceiling. It made a barking noise and fell into her lap, along with some flakes of plaster. She dusted the book off and sent it up again. This time a little harder. For a moment, they were quiet. Then, with dramatic flourish, they resumed their debauchery.

"Assholes! It's two-thirty in the morning. People do sleep at this hour!" she yelled.

She threw off the blanket and stormed into the living room. She paced, lit a cigarette, trailing smoke like a locomotive.

It was the trial. Normally, she would be asleep by ten o'clock, but jury duty was fouling up her routine. The case was stirring—a kidnapping-rape-murder—they hadn't gotten into anything juicy yet. But, Patty found it difficult to sit still all day, felt that she had to be moving, doing *something*. She found herself wound up at night, unable to fall easily to sleep.

The trial had taken over her thoughts. She wanted them to get to the point and be done with it. All she knew from the testimony and legal drivel was that the accused, David Allen Garrick, believed that the death of Marianne Murphy was not by his hand, but a frame by an ex-army buddy of his. Alibis had been devised and told, the chronology of the case delineated, and witnesses brought in to corroborate the same old stuff. The case was four weeks old and due to go on for another two.

Patty stared out her window to the silent street below. She could still hear them upstairs. Her stomach churned. It had been a long time since she'd last been in someone's arms.

The defendant, Garrick, was something of an anomaly. She had expected someone deranged, loutish, over the edge. Garrick was a startlingly handsome man in his early forties; over six feet tall, fair-skinned with a slight blush to his cheeks, dark haired, with intense, intelligent looking, brilliant-blue eyes rimmed with dark lashes. Then there was his white, even smile. He hadn't shown it much in the four weeks. His pose was that of a victim. He often peered into the jury box from under his eyebrows, shyly reverent, hopeful.

Patty also took notice of his build. Under the frayed and baggy prison uniform, she could see evidence of lean hard muscle, broad shoulders and narrow hips, and she wasn't alone. Though the jury was admonished not to talk about the trial, the women took to terse accolades of Garrick's appearance when on restroom breaks.

She stubbed out her cigarette and lit another. She watched the clock. Three-fifteen. She fumed.

At first, she had found staring at Garrick mildly distracting. She noticed how each member of the jury reacted to Garrick's returning glance. Some of the men sat up straighter, the women squirmed, fussed with their hair, and sighed heavily. But Patty wasn't about to be taken in by a pretty face. She'd just divorced Michael, who blamed his own fatal attractiveness for his numerous, flagrant, and painful indiscretions. She swore she would never allow a man's sensuality, his appearance, the *effect*, to sway her again.

Yet that afternoon, when the jury was filing out of the box, she let Garrick catch her eye. Just for a second, she felt the heat of his stare penetrate to the back of her head and down to her toes, making her swoon. Only when Garrick was turned away by the sheriff did she feel a release, the return of her composure. The incident bothered her still.

She heard the thump of footsteps on the floor above, the flush of the toilet, the murmuring that followed, and the clack of a light switch. It would be quiet now, but she wouldn't be able to sleep feeling so worked up. She pulled a half-filled fifth of Jack Daniels from the bar, and downed it. That, she thought, would speed the coming of dreams.

Patty greeted the other jurors already seated around the long table in the poorly lit, cramped, windowless room. Ralph, a huge black man, a postal worker, eyed her up and down, then laughed with a jocular familiarity borne of the weeks they had all spent together.

"That musta been some night you had last night, girl. You look like somethin' the cat drug in." He leaned back in his chair and pressed the "all here" button on the wall behind him.

Melanie, a meek, dowdy housewife from Culver City, added, "You're never late. You all right?"

"Well, yes and no. I couldn't sleep and tried this old remedy my grandfather used, only it didn't do the trick for me."

The one person Patty hadn't quite warmed up to, a care-worn lesbian bus driver named Dawn, crossed her heavy legs and snorted. "I know that remedy and a sleepless night and a hangover are not good company. What you needed was. . . ."

The bailiff peeked in and announced the judge was ready for them. They filed out solemnly, took steno pads off their seats, and sat down.

Patty flipped to her last entry. She found the doodles and sighed. The meaningless shapes of yesterday had a definite phallic quality to them today. Perhaps Dawn had been about to tell her she needed a lover to help her sleep. Sex. That was it. Maybe Dawn would have been right.

Garrick sat stone-still at the defense table as the judge swept in, greeting those present, admonishing the jury, getting things up to date. So far, Garrick's defense was airtight. His partner, Ken Stolte, had verified Garrick's whereabouts during the twenty days Murphy was missing, his girlfriend Anita had testified he was with her the evening Marianne disappeared, and all of his character witnesses painted a pristine picture of a good man; honest, virtuous, hard-working, easy-going. It seemed a matter of Garrick's and his friends' words against some circumstantial evidence.

Patty wanted to believe what she heard, but sensed there was a prevailing lack of sincerity in the testimonies.

The bailiff escorted an attractive, athletic, college-aged blonde to the stand. The prosecution introduced Cindy Howard to the court and asked her to describe her relationship with the girl Garrick was accused of murdering. Howard was stiff, anxious with the eyes of the court on her. She avoided looking at Garrick, and fidgeted with a shredded tissue. She told them she had been Marianne's roommate and that they'd worked together at the Big Deal, a burger joint near the college they both attended. They'd had separate friends and different interests and majors, yet they had been real close friends.

Then the prosecutor asked if she was acquainted with the defendant.

"I hardly knew him. He came into the restaurant where Marianne and I worked with his big friend, Ken, the guy he's partners with. They usually sat in Marianne's station."

The prosecutor stopped her, then routed her to the evening she last saw Marianne Murphy.

"Yeah, right." She sneered at Garrick for a moment then turned toward the jury. "Marianne had finally relented after months. Dave had been bothering her for a date a long time, but she thought he was too old for her. She chickened out that day when he came in for lunch and he began grabbing her and stuff, like he'd already slept with her, real familiar-like. She said she wanted to get out of there, so I lent her my car and told the manager Marianne was sick." Howard hung her head. "That was the last time I saw her. I tried to get the police to look into it but they won't do anything for forty-eight hours."

The prosecutor then asked her if she called her father.

"Yes. My father is an insurance fraud investigator with lots of connections. He knew a private investigator who could help. That was on Friday. Sunday the guy was calling me down to the morgue to identify a body that might be Marianne's. It wasn't hers, but seeing a dead girl my age like that really scared me. I kept bothering the police department after that."

Patty was still holding onto her healthy skepticism. This roommate was an angry girl, but composed, sure, and *honest*. That's what had been missing so far, truth. Patty looked at Cindy Howard and wondered how this girl could find the strength and audacity it took to take the stand like that and sneer in Garrick's face.

Cindy was asked what happened on the seventeenth of August.

"My father called. Told me the police had who they thought was Marianne. I offered to identify her. That's when they told me they were contacting her parents, and sending off to Arkansas for dental charts." Cindy let one tear roll slowly down her cheek; so went her bullet-proof poise. "But they *had* found her."

Patty knew what Cindy *wasn't* saying. She finally felt she could believe what she heard. Garrick had somehow intercepted Marianne that afternoon and made off with her. In the next ten days, he'd repeatedly raped her and eventually horribly murdered her. The probability gave Patty gooseflesh, yet it inexplicably jibed with her intuition. Patty wrote down the words.

GARRICK KILLED MARIANNE MURPHY

Then she glanced at him. He was staring at Cindy, his face a dark mask of simmering rage. Abruptly he turned and looked at Patty. It was as if he knew she was condemning him at that very moment. He frowned a little and held her stare for what seemed a very long while. Patty lost her sense of time, heard little else than the rustling of steno pages being turned beside her. She felt something like the rush of adrenaline one has when having just missed colliding with another car. That feeling mingled with a revulsion for what she thought him to be—and a surprising slow burn of desire.

The judge's gavel startled her. Garrick turned away. She let out her breath, feeling violated, unclean, as though he'd actually touched her. She would have to be more careful, though she knew what had occurred was just a silly manifestation of her boredom. Her resistance was faltering and this vulnerability disturbed her.

Patty pushed the feelings aside as she walked from the courthouse to the garage. She chatted animatedly with her juror friends before climbing into her car. Once alone, she felt uncomfortably restless. She hurried home, stopping only to get a fast food meal before turning onto her street. As she sat in her car, she ate half her dinner, fooled with the radio and lit cigarettes that she left smoldering in the ashtray. When the claustrophobic quality of the car got to her, she ran upstairs. She went from room to room, switching on the radio, the television, her CD player. She finished her meal as she stood staring out at the Technicolor sunset over the distant coastline, the collection of sounds soothing her.

"God, what's happening to me?" She looked down at her trembling hands. She reached for the phone and called the one friend she'd managed to salvage from the divorce. Michael, the bastard, had charmed away the bulk of the others.

"Liz, it's me, Patty. I'm going crazy with this jury thing. I figured I'd take ten days, do my duty, you know, get a vacation from work at the same time, then go back refreshed, with a new perspective. Hell, I can't wait to get back to that dungeon at Valencia Studios. I'm yearning for the tedium, the overtime, the stress!"

"So quit. They have alternates, don't they? Just say you're sick."

Patty looked up at her ceiling and watched a tiny spider wend its way down to her torchère lamp. "Well, I guess I am sick, aren't I? Sick of the grind. Oh, God, I can't. I want to, but I can't."

"You are a true schizoid, Patty. Half wants to stay, half wants to go. It's like you, though, isn't it? The ambivalence. Trust the part that wants to go. If I can't sit still all day, I can't imagine how you, the super human-*doing*, stands it."

"I can't. If I don't have something to do, a cigarette to smoke, coffee to sip, a nail to bite, I feel hysterical. But, I also feel compelled to sit this out. Besides, I *am* an alternate. The last three have already filled in for other jurors. If I go, and one other juror, they'll have to retry Garrick, and I know the guy is guilty . . . oops. I'm not supposed to talk about the case. You think my phone's tapped?"

"God, now you're paranoid too? Shit."

Patty lit a cigarette, dropping the match into the residue of sauce left in the styrofoam plate from her dinner. It hissed and sizzled. "Look, it makes me feel responsible, important. Since I divorced Michael, I haven't felt like I matter anywhere. Even my family deserted me. It was as if *I* was the big loser because I dumped Mr Perfect."

"What Mr Perfect? The bastard prince? If you would tell your folks what an awful son-of-a-bitch he truly was, maybe they wouldn't treat you like you're nuts. Why keep the truth to yourself? Hell, I had to pry it out of you. What did you get out of keeping your misery to yourself, Saint Patty? Explain this to me."

"Hey, we're getting off the point. I feel like I could make a difference on this jury." Patty sighed heavily.

"I feel for you, Patty. Look, as soon as you meet a new guy, you'll forget this jury problem. It's all the emptiness in your life. Wanna go to McGinty's tonight? There are some truly great specimens there. . . ."

"I'm not ready for anything."

"I'm not talking affair here, not a major relationship, just a night of fun. Hey, I'm single, but I'm never lonely. My nights aren't empty." A wink of an eye was implied by her tone.

"I would rather be lonely." Patty couldn't explain it. The anxiety about not stopping for even a moment, for fear she might feel the loneliness, the pain. If there was another man, there would also be more pain. She was merely being self-protective.

She made an excuse to cut the call short and hung up. She showered, got into bed, took out her book. The couple upstairs was arguing at the other end of the apartment. She fell quickly to sleep.

She dreamed of the trip she'd taken with Michael to Palm Springs when the air conditioner in the van broke. She sat in the rear, the heat stifling, her hair matted to her head, stinking from not having bathed in two days. Her neck hurt where he'd tried to strangle her. Her wrists and ankles were raw under their rope bonds. Her breasts ached from his twisting them, poking them with sharp, hot things. Every bump the van hit, her private parts burned from the repeated violations, but she was happy to be alive.

He spoke to her as the van took them further into the desert. He told her how she would love him even more when she saw the house with a pool they would be staying at. How could he think she could love him more? He had given her such pleasure once, in the beginning. She loathed what he was doing to her now. Why couldn't he just be done with her? Let her go home. She wouldn't tell anyone. She'd be too ashamed.

The house was everything he had said it would be. He carried her in from the back yard, into the bedroom, and laid her down on the bed. The room was beautiful. The bedspread, curtains, and wallpaper were all the same fabric. She'd seen homes like this in magazines.

From where he left her on the bed, she could see a sunken marble bathtub. She wriggled off the bed after he had gone, and hopped to the sink. With her teeth, she turned the faucet and slurped thirstily at the water, letting it run over her face.

She heard his footsteps in the hallway. She tried to get back to the bed in a dream-slowness, but he caught her and tossed her into the tub. She cracked her head, biting her tongue. The coppery sweet taste of blood filled her mouth.

He ran the water into the tub. Standing over her, he took off his shirt and jeans. When he was naked, he stroked himself, watching in the mirror. The water felt so good to her. She stared at it as it flowed over her.

"Look at me!" he shouted.

She obeyed him. He was so pretty. So perfectly built. And those blue eyes . . .

He stepped into the tub with her, then pulled off her torn soiled clothes and bloody ropes. He caringly soaped her, washed her. He shampooed her hair and rinsed it. He held her for a moment, like their first night together, caressing her.

That night had been romantic, exciting, scary. He'd gone to her apartment and lured her away to a motel near the ocean. She'd never been with a man before. Not like that. She apologized so many times for asking all those questions, but it didn't seem to matter. He was so angry. She just wanted to know why the skin on his penis was so funny-looking. How did the strange skin disappear when he was hard? Were other men's penises like his? So innocent. Besides it had felt fine. Really.

He'd said she would pay for the questions, and she had. Now couldn't he just let her go?

He bent to kiss her. She felt the heat of his tongue on hers, the blood mingling with saliva. Then he struck her across the face. Again and again. Her lips swelled; blood ran down into the soapy water. She tried to hold up her arm to stop him.

Patty jerked awake. Her hair was wet, her nightslip soaked with sweat, her heart racing. It was four-thirty in the morning. Trembling, she turned on the light. Her thoughts were jumbled; she felt drugged. She remembered the trip, the torture, Michael. . . . Wait. She'd never been to Palm Springs before. It hadn't been Michael. It had been Garrick. She'd dreamed she'd been one of his victims!

Patty lit a cigarette. She couldn't stop shaking. She changed her bedclothes, showered, and stood shivering in the bathroom. Her breasts felt tender, ached as they had in the dream. Her vulva burned, too. A phantom pain. Like remembering having once broken a leg; a tiny echo of the pain. And she remembered the love-hate feelings.

She was fine by the time she sat in the jury box later that morning. She stared at Garrick, willing him to look back, but he kept his eyes on the witness stand. It was as if he'd had his way with her and now. . . Patty dismissed the thought as crazy and turned her concentration to the trial.

The witness was a maid for the Neidorff family of Palm Springs. The hair on Patty's back and neck bristled. She straightened in her chair.

The maid had come the day before the Neidorffs were to return from a month's travel. She found the house had been lived in for some time, though no one was there when she arrived. It was a mess. The worst of it was the blood. In the Misses' closet, behind her gowns, were the words scrawled in blood, "DG has me. Help me." It looked as though Marianne had tried to write her name, but the letters M-A-R were all she could get down. Then the police photographs of the house were passed around. Patty tried not to look, to pass them on, but she couldn't help noticing the matching fabric of the wallpaper, the bedspread, and the curtains.

Too anxious to eat during her lunch break, Patty sat feeling lightheaded and nauseous. The sounds around her were loud and sharp. When the testimony resumed, Patty listened to it with a fierce tenacity. She wanted to hear something that would make all that she'd dreamed the night before just a nightmare. But word after word confirmed her dream, moment to moment.

The maid looked at Garrick as she was dismissed from the stand. Garrick made a strange face at her. She became visibly upset, moaned, and ran from the courtroom. Garrick's eyes followed her until they caught Patty's. She felt the conflicting feelings from the night before.

That was when he parted his lips and soundlessly mouthed the words. They were unmistakable.

"Sweet dreams." He turned away, leaving her shaken.

Patty wanted to scream, run in panic out into the corridor. But she couldn't betray herself to the others. Explanations would have to be simpered out over embarrassed silences, then they would simply laugh at her, unbelieving. She looked around at the stoic faces of the jury. Even she didn't know whether to believe what was happening. It was possible he had mouthed the words to someone else or they weren't what she imagined them to be. Or all of this was nothing but a coincidence.

The judge allowed a half hour recess while he handled other business. Patty gladly sprinted from her seat to the sanctuary of the garden outside the courthouse. She sat still, waiting for the beat of her heart to slow to a comforting rhythm. The sun warmed her as she began to relax.

Lighting a cigarette, she stared at Dawn who was heading over to a young woman with a small boy beside her. The two spoke quietly for a few minutes, then broke into a loud argument. She couldn't make out the subject, but when Dawn stomped away past where Patty sat, she had tears on her cheeks. Dawn's emotion seemed so out of character to Patty. Dawn was so *hard*.

Masks confounded Patty. She had hers; the perfectionist, the always cool, always composed, usually right, and sometimes impervious, as well as others. But they were so automatic, so natural, they felt like they *were* her. Yet in her gut, she knew they were about hiding the desperate loneliness, the emptiness, and the anxious feeling of knowing she was so horribly imperfect, ordinary and inept. Dawn had her brick wall toughness and barroom raunchiness. What tender, marshmallow heart might that mask be covering up?

She thought of Michael; his steel-plated heart masked by a face of sweet passion, ardor. She hadn't been able to see it until the marriage seemed over. Well, she'd sensed it in the beginning, but there had been so many wonderful things about him to distract her. She bit her lip and began pacing. There was still so much she resisted thinking about Michael. Denial, Liz called it. By the time they were finally called into the courtroom, she was actually excited to return. Her feelings confused her.

She sat down and watched as Richard Dahlquist walked to the stand. Garrick slouched in his seat and looked away petulantly. His attorney whispered to him, shaking his head. Patty took up her notepad and turned to the top of a new page. This witness was important. She knew it the moment she saw Garrick grow uncomfortable.

Dahlquist had been a Vietnam buddy of Garrick's, twenty years back. They had been stationed together at Pleiku. Dahlquist was a newlywed then and Garrick a lonely bachelor. After lengthy questioning, under cross and re-cross examination, Richard Dahlquist told a story of deceit and betrayal. Garrick had been invited to live with Dahlquist upon his discharge from the army, and did stay for almost a year. Garrick then disappeared with Dahlquist's wife and the eight thousand dollars the couple had saved to buy a house. Seven months later, Dahlquist's wife was found incoherent and near death from malnutrition, chained to a motel bed. She managed to commit suicide less than three weeks later in a psychiatric hospital without having spoken a word. Until he was called for trial, Dahlquist had not seen or heard from Garrick. He'd put the past behind him. Dahlquist told the jury that for Garrick to think Dahlquist would want to dredge it up by framing him twenty years later for a murder was ridiculous.

Patty wanted to tell Dahlquist she was sorry, that she would make sure Garrick was found guilty, but she knew she couldn't. It had to be enough to know it herself. She smiled at him as he passed by, hoping her feelings were conveyed.

All the way home, Patty thought about what a relief it was going to be to have the weekend ahead of her to get away from the trial. There was just one more day. One more night . . .

She drank an entire pot of coffee. As the caffeine began its tap dance on her nerves, she got the jitters. She wouldn't be sleeping this night. No way. No more dreams. She turned on the radio, the television, flicked on all the lights, squinting in their brightness, and put out a carton of cigarettes. She read the juicy, backstabbing, Hollywood gossip novel she'd been saving for an occasion such as this. Shortly after Johnny Carson, she fell asleep in her chair.

She dreamed she was sick. Very sick. She was sitting in a bathtub in a motel, a few inches of water and her own wastes beneath her. Her arms were covered with sores, festering, her legs a map of infected gouges and burns. Her throat hurt and she was dizzy with fever. Her chest felt tight and ached when she coughed. She was naked and cold, shivering under a bare light bulb. She gagged as she coughed and threw up bits of cracker and bile.

He kicked open the bathroom door. He wore new red cowboy boots and a pair of pre-faded blue jeans. Tight ones. He still looked good to her, though it was painful to feel any desire.

He asked her what she wanted. She told him water, some clothes, a blanket. A doctor, couldn't he see she was sick? He knew she was sick, he told her as he poured her a glass of water. When it was full he turned and tossed it on her. That would clean her up some. He laughed at her. She was disgusting to look at. She should see herself.

When she began to cry, he knelt down beside the tub. She could smell the alcohol on his breath as he breathed through his mouth. He held his nostrils pinched. She stunk, she knew it. She hoped he would soften as he had so many times now when she cried. Sometimes he made love to her. When was that? Days ago, weeks? Before she got sick. If only he would hold her, make her warm.

He told her he knew she wanted it, that he knew she was addicted to his lovemaking, but now, she would have to watch. He unzipped his jeans and began to jerk off. She watched the strangely scarred foreskin shrink off his glans until she could only see the blur of his fist moving. He grabbed a towel and held it over his mouth and nose, grunting. His eyes burned into her, as if to say "suffer as I have." She tried to raise her hand to touch him, but the chains were heavy and she was so weak. He howled as he ejaculated over the rim of the tub. Then he rose, unsteady, and told her he didn't need her anymore.

She lay still after he left, feeling more lonely and tortured inside than hurt by any of the physical abuse. There was no one in her life but him. He couldn't see she loved him, that he was her life, that she was willing to do the penance if she could be released to make him truly happy. Now, he didn't need her. She had nothing. Was nothing. She pulled her filthy hands up, put her fingertips to her forehead, the chains softly clinking in her lap, and prayed she would soon die.

Her chapped lips opened to say the words. "Please, God, take me."

Patty heard her own voice saying the words and wakened with a start. "Damn!"

The lights blinded her, the sound of the radio and television overwhelmed her, the bang of the newspaper being slammed against her front door pulled her from the chair. She ran into the bedroom and stood before her mirror. Shaking, she slowly peeled her robe off, afraid the sores would be there. She swallowed to see if her throat was raw. She felt her head for fever. She remembered the man was Garrick. Again.

"You can't let this thing get to you!" Patty laughed nervously. She wrapped the robe tightly around her and reminded herself it had just been a dream. She took a cigarette and lit it. The smoke of her cigarette smelled like feces and urine and rotting flesh. She felt her gorge rising and made it to the toilet in time to vomit.

She drove to the courthouse with the car windows down. By the time she arrived, the smell was gone. She stood outside the building, shaken. An emotional boxing match was going on inside of her. She was compelled to go in, to continue subjecting herself to the influences of a man who was stealing into her sleep, who somehow might be able to reach inside her and know what she thought, what she felt. If she believed that, then he could own her as he had the victim she dreamed she had been just hours ago. She wanted to run.

"You going to stand out here all day or come on in?" Ralph came up beside her and touched her shoulder. She winced and jerked away.

"Ah! Uh . . . yes, of course. Sorry. I'm a bit jumpy this morning. Too much coffee, not enough sleep."

"Right. Well, come on then. We don't want that judge to come down on us for being late, now do we?"

Patty shook her head. She looked at Ralph as they crossed the street then walked the polished granite halls of the courthouse to Department 83. Was he being affected by the trial? Were his dreams being colored by Garrick?

The first witness was a detective, Louis Molina. He was the chief investigating officer. He was present when they found Marianne Murphy's body in the alley behind a Quick Stop Market. He testified to the body's condition. Then came the photographs. The jury was warned the photos were disturbing, and everyone tried to glance at them quickly and pass them on, yet it was impossible to look at them with detachment, without morbid curiosity. Patty was the third juror to see them. She found herself staring after them as they were passed on. It astounded her that no one fainted or ran to throw up or moaned in distaste, yet she, too, felt stunned into silence.

Next up was a Sergeant Les Duncan from the Bakersfield sheriff's department. A couple meeting the description of Murphy and Garrick had stayed in the Del Rey Motel, which led to an investigation there. A male had paid for the room with a stolen credit card.

The prosecution then called in the motel owner who was working the day the man meeting Garrick's description showed up. When he was asked to look around the courtroom and tell the jury if he saw the man who had registered as a Max Lerner, the owner of the stolen credit card, the motel owner pointed to Garrick. He told the jury he hadn't checked the credit card because Garrick had looked so honest.

Patty tried to listen, but the image of Marianne Murphy's remains was burned into her brain. She hoped she would not be dreaming the events that led to Marianne's disfigurement, the missing parts of her.

Then the attorneys proceeded to play with two psychiatrists called in as experts in the field of sensational murders and sex crimes. The line of questioning proved to be argumentative, long, loud, and moot. Patty shut it out when her stomach grew tight and she began to feel faint. More psychobabble.

The drive home was excruciatingly tedious. Smog wafted in with the air conditioned cool, and a head-ache turned into a full-blown migraine. At six-thirty, Patty was on her way to the emergency ward with Liz. By seven she was throwing up, her vision was blurred; a vise had a death grip on her head making her skin too painful to touch. She begged to be put to sleep. She hadn't had a migraine since college. Or was it the divorce? She finally slept a deep, drugged sleep, dreaming of nothing.

Saturday, Liz picked Patty up and took her home. Patty was still suffering a drug-muffled pain. She curled up in her bed as Liz sat beside her, frowning.

"It's the damned trial, isn't it?"

"Please. Don't use any words with consonants in them. They hurt my ears. I just need my drugs and silence."

"The doctor said no stress for twenty-four hours. Not that you should move into a monastery."

"No stress means a weekend in the Bahamas. Christ, I have a migraine from the smog, the heat, the traffic, not getting enough sleep, not just the trial. I know I shouldn't be saying this, but I know the fucker is guilty and I'm going to be sure we all come to the same verdict. Now, leave me alone with some ice cream, my cigarettes, and I'll be just fine."

"I want to stay with you. I'm worried about you."

Patty was not in the habit of asking for anything from anyone. She found it difficult to say she needed someone, much less allow herself to feel it. But now, maybe now.

"Okay. I really don't want to be alone. Just promise me one thing."

Liz brightened. "Sure, anything."

"Don't let me fall asleep."

"I don't get it." Her face fell.

"I can't explain it. Just don't let me sleep, all right?"

Liz nodded, suspicious. They played games that forgave Patty's drugged limitations, laughed about their long history together, ate too much, and watched rented movies. Liz finally collapsed, exhausted, into sleep. Patty watched Liz's even breathing, beatific face, and felt envious of her dreams. With Liz there as a comfort, Patty believed that with the aid of a sleeping pill, she might get another dreamless night's sleep. She took a yellow capsule, lay down, and stared at Liz's jittering eyelids until her own began to droop.

It was dark and incredibly hot. She was being jostled about. She was fading in and out of consciousness. She smelled car exhaust and hot asphalt, blood and a wool blanket. She could hear the faint sound of a radio, cars and trucks passing, the hum of their tires on the road beneath her. She was in the trunk of the car. She was on fire, her wounds were dull constant aches. Everything went blank a moment, then it was dark, but cold, very cold. She smelled oil and metal and sawdust. She was lying on something hard, a bench, a coffin? She heard the distant sound of a buzz saw, the crunching of bone, the brittle screams of someone tired and scared and wracked by the pain. She felt a warm wetness splashing at her face, then the feathery slap of flesh freed from its bonds. She wanted to reach to her eyes, pull away the gauze that covered them so she could see, but when she willed her arm to rise, there was nothing to raise. She tried to blink, then realized she had no eyes beneath the useless flaps of skin that wriggled wormlike over empty orbs. She wanted to scream "why?" one more time. Perhaps he would answer now. But, the effort was too much and with her last breath, she could only think it.

*Why?*

Patty gasped for air, grabbed for something, anything, to feel her arms, her legs. She struggled her eyes open, closed them, touched them, blinked. Liz lay sleeping below her on the cot, snoring softly. Reality. She held herself and cried softly.

When they sat down to breakfast, the truth was trapped, captive in her throat. Patty knew that telling Liz about the last week was admitting she was crazy. Liz was already worried about Patty. This would simply confirm her worst fears.

Patty would get through this on her own. She'd done it with the divorce and she could do it with the trial. She had always done things this way. It was all she knew.

The next night, her sleep was full of dreams of light and color and peace. She woke surprised yet relieved. It was finally over.

As the trial went on, Garrick increased his intimidating stares and the jury grew more nervous as he did. Except for Patty. He was done with her. Perhaps he was working on another juror. She didn't know, and didn't care. She listened with detached ease, relaxed, took notes, and felt her old self again. She chatted with the others on breaks, even taking time to talk with Dawn; who seemed more troubled every day, yet revealed nothing. Garrick wasn't bothering Patty, but then she wasn't going to let him catch her eye, either. It felt good to cheat him, deprive him of his power over her.

One night, she and Liz met for dinner. She watched Liz scan the room for men like a great white shark at the beach on Labor Day. Soon, Patty's obsessing was forgotten as Liz managed to lure two urologists from the bar to sit with them. The talk went from dull chit-chat to genitalia and circumcision. The more wine they drank, the more graphic the detail. Liz had that effect on men.

Patty found herself mesmerized by the medical jargon, the immense amount of information about things she had believed she knew most all there was to know. She asked them about the foreskin she had seen in her dream, saying she'd seen a photograph once. One of the doctors told her her description reminded him of an odd case he'd seen in his residency of a boy of seventeen who had been sexually abused by his Satan-worshipping parents. They had inserted rings through his foreskin and hung him from an inverted cross. The man had come in for help when the scar tissue was so severe, the foreskin would not retract and he couldn't urinate properly.

Liz balked. She had her limits and after all, she just wanted to move onto the next part of the ritual. "God, this is revolting party conversation. Let's go into the bar and dance. I can hear the band. They sound great."

Patty wasn't in a mood to dance after learning about what she'd seen in her dreams. She excused herself and went home.

Once in bed, she had the sensation of yearning to fall asleep, craving it. As if something wonderful was waiting there. She could feel the wine had dulled her senses, quelled her fears. She fell slowly, deeply asleep.

He was faceless. He came to her from a brilliant light that kept him in silhouette. His voice was deep and calm, so like Michael's. He was naked. He stood at the foot of her bed and held his arms out to her. She kneeled before him, tentative, yet desirous.

"I am who you have longed for all your life, Patricia. I am love and light and security. I am giving and caring and constant. I am a reflection of your desires. Let me hold you. Allow me to be all you deserve and more. Share with me the pleasures I can assure you of for as long as you live. You have but to open your heart."

With a willingness she never knew she possessed, she leaned into him. The sensation of warm flesh, firm muscle, and gentle caresses seemed so real though she knew she was in a dream. Even as she kissed him, his face remained vague, insubstantial. His tongue met hers with the cool heat of passion and she was lost.

He moved with liquid ease over her, until she was lying spread open beneath him. His tongue traveled over her body with the knowing progress of her ancient fantasies' longings. She climaxed a second and third time before the dream man rose up, turned halfway away from her, revealing a huge erection, then walked back into the light. She awoke with the after-glow radiating through her body.

How sweet sleep was now.

The dream was the same each night. During that week, the trial began winding down. Witnesses were called mainly to corroborate previous testimony. Others were recalled. Patty was growing bored. She began taunting Garrick with surreptitious glances every few minutes. It was as if the new dreams were making her stronger, giving her a sense of fullness, invulnerability. *She* was choosing the dream now, not Garrick. With the security of that knowledge, she let her eyes fall on him and easily pulled away when he caught her eye. Each time she tried it, she felt better. She kept it up for two days.

She began to feel irritated by her dream lover's turning away. Soon after the irritation grew into angry frustration, the dreams began to change. He stopped opening his arms to her, and instead stood at the foot of the bed and stroked himself. She leaned toward him, eager to touch his penis, pull him into her, then the dream would fold into darkness. The dream continued for a few more nights, resisting Patty's strong desire to conform it to her will. She could almost make out his face, handsome and smiling as he disappeared. Was it Michael now? No. Please, no.

The last few witnesses shocked the courtroom back into active interest. A maid from the motel in Bakersfield testified she saw Marianne Murphy in the motel bathroom, chained to the faucets in the bathtub. She had been afraid to come forward, even to tell her boss, because the girl told her to go away, to be afraid of the man, he could hurt her too. Fearfully, she pointed Garrick out.

Then there was a gardener for the Neidorffs who said he noticed a van parked outside the house, but that he'd seen many vans delivering things before. After seeing it there for three days, he remembered what it said on the side. He told the jury, "Stolte Moving Company."

Lastly, the police's latest discovery. The police found blood and hair samples in tools and on the work bench in Dahlquist's mountain cabin and attached workshop. He hadn't used it in the over two years he'd been renting it out. From whom had the samples come? Marianne Murphy. The name on the rental agreement? Ken Stolte's.

Patty's head swam with testimony, the dreams, thoughts she fought to banish. She stared off, her eye lighting on Garrick. He turned, stared at her. She could feel unwanted desire from her dreams inflame her; the feeling swelled and eclipsed her awareness until they were alone in the courtroom, just the two of them, the razor sharp blade of her dreams edging them closer. She was being consumed, her breath sucked from her. He *wasn't* through with her.

She gasped. He smiled, triumphant. This was some kind of game to him. She forced herself to frown, to shake her head. No. She wasn't going to play. He put his head back and let loose a silent laugh. She looked at her hands shaking in her lap, her pencil broken on the pages of her notepad.

She drove home numbly, unsure of what to do. The imagined strength of her new dream had faded into real despair. If Garrick were simply someone her unconscious had chosen to teach her something in her dreams, then she couldn't be hurt by him. Not in reality, in her waking life. This all had to be about Michael, about the unexamined feelings she still harbored about the relationship. The desire she still felt for him, for the perfection he promised but couldn't make good on. Perhaps what she was about to learn would garner her the strength she'd only imagined. She could hope so.

With that aspiration, she went to bed. She let the dream come as she knew it would. When she reached for his cock this time, he didn't leave. She felt it, real and warm to the touch. She heard a low throaty chuckling as his body moved closer toward her. His cock stood erect, darkened rose, and pointed up at her. She pulled closer to see. The foreskin was mottled with holes and the flesh was pulled into strange configurations, some winged out in petals of scar tissue. He asked her to draw him into her mouth. His voice was not the deep masculine one she'd heard before. It was soft, deliberately breathy. She wasn't going to be afraid. This man was harmless. A teacher. She laughed at her passing anxiety, then she realized she was looking right at his penis as she did. His mutilated foreskin.

She heard herself scream as his hands came out of the darkness to strangle her. She saw his face, Garrick's face, angry, full of vengeance, and she woke up. Why had she laughed? She felt the pressure of his fingers, still on her neck.

When she arrived at the jury room the next morning, she discovered Dawn had gone out sick. She asked around—did anyone else notice Dawn hadn't been feeling well? Had she been the only one to see Dawn's darkening mood?

It was up to Patty now as the last alternate to fill in. The responsibility she'd longed for was hers. She felt cold and shivery all day.

Garrick took the stand. His attorney told the jury the defendant didn't have to testify, but he wanted to tell how Dahlquist had framed him. David Allen Garrick rose from his seat wearing an orange uniform with large stenciled letters across the front. L.A. COUNTY JAIL. He swaggered to the witness stand and sat down. The prosecutor asked him what his relationship with Marianne Murphy was.

"We were friends. I met her where she worked. I liked her. She was young and naive and sweet. I knew she had a crush on me and I guess I'm guilty of enjoying it. I called her, she called me. We talked. I asked her to meet me sometimes for coffee or Coke, whatever, but she always said no. It was okay with me. I had a girl, sort of. Anita, you know, she testified before. . . . Anyhow, I never wanted to sleep with Marianne. She was a virgin and wanted to stay that way. I respected that."

The dream voice, soft and breathy. Patty recognized it, only now it was close, clear, and deeper. She squinted at him and thought, "bull-shit." "She believed she loved you, asshole. She wanted to love you so much it cost her her life. I know that voice, that body, those hands, that cock." But there was no response. Garrick never glanced at the jury.

When he was asked about Dahlquist's wife, he told a complex fabrication of how the wife left because she was being abused, beaten, by a suspicious and jealous Dahlquist, that they had lived together for a while, then she left Garrick. He'd last seen her five months before she was found in the hotel bed.

The questions went on all day and Garrick answered them with precision. Nothing he said put a dent in Patty's certainty of his guilt. She was uneasy in her condemnation, knowing he was aware of it, and could, if she let him further into her dreams, give her cause to fear for her reality. She thought of Dawn. Dawn's dreams.

Liz called her at seven. Patty let her answering machine pick it up. She wanted to be left alone. It could all be over the next day when they went into deliberations. She just had to get through the night. She drank a few wine coolers just to take the edge off her angst, then fell asleep on her couch.

The haze of her dream vision cleared as the man's hands went to her throat. He knelt into the light. Garrick. She could smell him. Sweat and aftershave. He put his mouth close to her ear.

"You loved the way I made you come, didn't you?"

His hands tightened around her neck. She nodded.

*Wake up. Wake the hell up*!

"You want me as much as I want you, don't you?"

She nodded. She hated the truth that drifted heavy through her denial.

*Please wake up. Damn it.*

"But you laughed at me because I'm not like your pretty husband, all smooth. He was perfect; had a prick like a porn star, didn't he?"

Again she nodded. Except for his foreskin, Garrick's was just as . . . good. So very good. If only the reality were possible. *No.*

"You know what I'm going to do, because I like you? I'm going to make you a deal. If you see to it the jury comes to a verdict of 'not guilty,' or hang it with your refusal to go with them, I'll come see you, make love to you, just like I have been. But if you don't, I'll come back and kill you. Slowly. And you know how that is. So, how about it?" He let go of her neck and pulled her face to his and kissed her deeply.

*Wake up you stupid girl. This isn't real. He is just in your imagination. He can't hurt you.*

She agreed. Yes, please. Be my perfect lover. She ached for him.

"Good girl. Now Dave will just leave you to your dreams. See you in court."

The haze returned. A beach, water lapping at a sandy shore, the sun was on her body. Trees swayed around her. She turned over to let the sun touch her back. She opened her eyes.

She could hear her alarm down the hall in her bedroom. She moved her tongue over coated teeth. Another hangover. She avoided looking at herself as she dressed. She kept telling herself the same thing over and over. By agreeing to Garrick's bargain, she had taken the easy way out, but just to buy herself some time.

That morning Garrick went back on the stand to clarify loose ends, then both sides made closing arguments. Garrick stood as the jury filed out for their deliberations. He looked a little sad, a little hopeful, and very weary. Patty was nearly the last out the box. He looked at her as if she were the final card he was turning up in a game of blackjack. She smiled weakly, holding onto the façade.

The door had barely settled into its jamb when they began shouting to hang the bastard. Ralph tried to get them into some semblance of order to pick a foreman. In three minutes, by secret ballots, they voted him foreman. He asked for a show of hands. Who thought Garrick was guilty? All went up but Patty's.

"What the hell is wrong with you?" The housewife from Culver City frowned at her. "Weren't you in that courtroom with the rest of us, or were you too busy ogling that killer's ass to hear the truth?"

Patty's face went red with shame. Just how much had she bought into the dreams? What was she stalling for?

"I think we need to review the judge's instructions and follow the rules the bailiff gave us. We're totally disregarding the system." She shrugged toward Ralph.

"Bullshit." Ralph shook his head.

Her voice quivered. "Ralph, how is it going to look if after only ten minutes we walk out with a verdict? It should appear we took some time and considered the testimony."

Ralph mulled the thought over, then nodded. "Patty has a point. Well, let's just read the law." He shuffled the bound sheets the bailiff had given them to read.

Patty was begging for more time, but she knew she was acting futilely. Garrick was guilty. She just didn't want to die. Even if he wanted to kill her, which was beginning to seem a viable alternative to living in the hell of wanting to experience the perfection of his lovemaking under the threat of becoming nothing more than a Marianne Murphy-throwaway, she wanted more time.

She really did want to feel she had done something important, and if she joined the others in the jury, she would get what she wanted. And very shortly after that, she could die. The small angry voice of desire in her was muffled into silence.

Garrick would have to find some way out of prison to get at her and kill her. After all, she couldn't die in reality when she died in a dream. She'd lived through Marianne's death as Marianne. All he'd done so far was convince her she was being seduced. He could scare her, make her believe he was capable, but he couldn't really hurt her. She smiled. She would vote against Garrick. And even if he owned her sleep for the rest of her life, he'd be behind bars.

Then desire raised its lecherous head. Why couldn't he just be happy to have her in his dreams where perfection was easy and no one ever had to be let down? Perhaps, she could try to convince him, as she had once with Michael.

Patty gripped her notepad. "All right. I'm being overly cautious. The verdict is obvious. I'm with you."

When Ralph read the verdict, Garrick slumped in his chair. He hadn't expected it. Patty knew that. His attorney tried to touch him. Garrick flinched. The sheriff had to support him as they hauled him from the courtroom, limp, beaten.

Patty felt miserable, yet strangely free. She joined the jury members for a drink and to talk openly about the case. She didn't dare ask about anyone's dreams, and no one volunteered anything. They got drunk, laughed themselves silly, and spoke of reuniting for the sentencing hearing. She thought a lot about Dawn, flirted with a lawyer she met and ended up making out with the guy in her car. What the hell, she figured.

Finally home, she slipped into bed and languished in the memory of feeling a man's arms around her. The sheets felt cool and inviting, and she had no reason to get up early. The fear and nightmares were merely lapping at the corners of her mind. She read a few chapters in her novel, now bent into a mass resembling a spastic's attempt at origami, and smoked a cigarette. She fell asleep with the light on, the book in her lap.

She was at her wedding. Michael was dancing with her mother, she was dancing with Michael's father. They reached out for each other, spinning and whirling, Michael released Patty's mother and pulled Patty to him. They fell laughing into a chair. Michael's arms went around her. Everyone looked at the happy couple and applauded.

"They think we make a great couple, Patty." It wasn't Michael's voice. She turned to see Garrick smiling sadly.

"YOU!" Patty struggled to get up. She was no longer in her wedding dress, but wore her nightslip and nothing else. Everyone stared.

"Yes, I made you a bargain. You changed your mind. I'm just keeping my end. Now you're going to die."

"Please. We can continue the lovemaking. It will make the time in jail go easier. For both of us. Easier." She whimpered.

She kept struggling, feeling a warmth emanate from beneath her. "You can't kill me in my dreams. I know. All the times I was Marianne, I wasn't hurt. I didn't die when she did."

Garrick waved his hand and a circle of flames rose up around them. "Maybe I didn't want you to die yet, so you didn't. I just wanted you to know what I could do, so that when I made my deal, you would do as I asked."

Patty was feeling hot, unbearably hot. And she was feeling pain. Far worse than when she was Marianne in the trunk of the car. "Like Dawn? You make her the deal too?"

The flames grew higher. Garrick now stood outside the fire and shouted to her through the smoke, over the crackling and spitting sounds of Patty's burning flesh. She felt weak, paralyzed. The pain was so real, so terribly real.

"Yes, and you know what that bitch did, don't you? I came to her as the woman of her dreams. The dyke wasn't interested, no. But she paid for it." He spat.

"Getting hot enough yet?" He laughed at her.

"You know you did me a favor. I would have hated to have sex with you every night. It was really a chore, just like Michael said. He was right about you—so repressed, so emotionally withholding. All those conditions you put out there. Shit. He wanted to see you come alive, learn to accept all of his and your imperfections, didn't he? He thought it was such a pity a beautiful woman like you was wasted on all that pretense and bullshit about how it *should* be. He tried for three years. I sure wouldn't have. You aren't worth it. He wouldn't have needed other women if you just hadn't held on so fucking hard to your uptight values. . . ."

She couldn't breathe. *Wake up. Now. Wake up*! Her mind was growing muzzy. She could smell the stench of her flesh burning. It seemed so real.

"You want to wake up, don't you? Well, wake up, Patty. You sure made this easy, choosing your own way to go. Thanks for the help. Good death to you."

Garrick disappeared and the dreaminess was gone. Patty coughed in the thick black smoke and felt the flames lick at what was left of her face and arms, her lower body already charred to the bone. Her thoughts raced from her with her breath and she remembered the cigarette she'd been smoking when she fell asleep. She could hear the sound of knocking at her door, shouting outside. She thought of Dahlquist's wife and Marianne Murphy, and all the jurors who had fallen ill during the trial, the dreams. Fatal synchronicity? Then thought of Garrick's voice telling her what she'd known all along, been too afraid to admit because she knew she couldn't live with the truth. And she felt the bite of tears welling in her eyes, too late to put out the flames.

# CLIVE BARKER

## The Departed

SINCE THE PUBLICATION of his ground-breaking sextet of *Books of Blood* collections (1984–5), Clive Barker has produced very little short fiction, prefering to concentrate on such novels as *The Damnation Game*, *Weaveworld*, *The Hellbound Heart*, *Cabal*, *The Great and Secret Show*, *Imajica*, *The Thief of Always* and *Everville*.

However, he did find time to contribute "Lost Souls" to *Time Out*, "Coming to Grief" to *Good Housekeeping*, and "On Amen's Shore" to *Demons and Deviants*. The atmospheric ghost story published here originally appeared under the title "Hermione and the Moon" in the *New York Times* the day before Hallowe'en 1992, and it was reprinted the following day under its present title in Britain's *The Guardian Weekend* magazine.

More recently, Barker was executive producer on the movies *Hellraiser III: Hell on Earth* (1992), *Candyman* (1992, based on his story "The Forbidden"), and a feature-length animated adaptation of his bestselling Young Adult novel *The Thief of Always*.

Eclipse is continuing the series of handsome graphic novels based on his stories, he has created the concepts for a "Barkerverse" of new titles from Marvel Comics (*Hyperkind*, *Hokum and Hex*, *Ecktokid* and *Saint Sinner*), and New York's Bess Cutler Gallery mounted an extensive exhibition of his paintings and drawings in 1993. There have also been a number of recent stage productions based on his fiction.

With all the above and more happening, perhaps it is not so surprising that Barker rarely gets the time nowadays to write short stories. But he hasn't turned his back on them, or on the macabre, as the following proves . . .

IT WAS NOT ONLY PAINTERS WHO were connoisseurs of light, Hermione had come to learn in the three days since her death; so too were those obliged to shun it. She was a member of that fretful clan now—a phantom in the world of flesh—and if she hoped to linger here for long she would have to avoid the sun's gift as scrupulously as a celibate avoided sin, and for much the same reason. It tainted, corrupted, and finally drove the soul into the embrace of extinction.

She wasn't so unhappy to be dead; life had been no bowl of cherries. She had failed at love, failed at marriage, failed at friendship, failed at motherhood. That last stung the sharpest. If she could have plunged back into life to change one thing she would have left the broken romances in pieces and gone to her six-year-old son Finn to say: trust your dreams, and take the world lightly, for it means nothing, even in the losing. She had shared these ruminations with one person only. His name was Rice; an ethereal nomad like herself who had died wasted and crazed from the plague but was now in death returned to corpulence and wit. Together they had spent that third day behind the blinds of his shunned apartment, listening to the babble of the street and exchanging tit-bits. Towards evening, conversation turned to the subject of light.

"I don't see why the sun hurts us and the moon doesn't," Hermione reasoned. "The moon's reflected sunlight, isn't it?"

"Don't be so logical," Rice replied, "or so damn serious."

"And the stars are little suns. Why doesn't starlight hurt us?"

"I never liked looking at the stars," Rice replied. "They always made me feel lonely. Especially towards the end. I'd look up and see all that empty immensity and . . ." He caught himself in mid-sentence. "Damn you, woman, listen to me! We're going to have to get out of here and party."

She drifted to the window.

"Down there?" she said.

"Down there."

"Will they see us?"

"Not if we go naked."

She glanced round at him. He was starting to unbutton his shirt.

"I can see you perfectly well," she told him.

"But you're dead, darling. The living have a lot more trouble." He tugged off his shirt and joined her at the window. "Shall we dare the dusk?" he asked her, and without waiting for a reply, raised the blind. There was just enough power in the light to give them both a pleasant buzz.

"I could get addicted to this," Hermione said, taking off her dress and letting the remnants of the day graze her breasts and belly.

"Now you're talking," said Rice. "Shall we take the air?"

All Hallows' Eve was a day away, a night away, and every shop along Main Street carried some sign of the season. A flight of paper witches here; a cardboard skeleton there.

"Contemptible," Rice remarked as they passed a nest of rubber bats. "We should protest."

"It's just a little fun," Hermione said.

"It's our holiday, darling. The Feast of the Dead. I feel like . . . like Jesus at a Sunday sermon. How dare they simplify me this way?" He slammed his phantom fists against the glass. It shook, and the remote din of his blow reached the ears of a passing family, all of whom looked towards the rattling window, saw nothing, and—trusting their eyes—moved on down the street.

Hermione gazed after them.

"I want to go and see Finn," she said.

"Not wise," Rice replied.

"Screw wise," she said. "I want to see him."

Rice already knew better than to attempt persuasion, so up the hill they went, towards her sister Elaine's house, where she assumed the boy had lodged since her passing.

"There's something you should know," Rice said as they climbed. "About being dead."

"Go on."

"It's difficult to explain. But it's no accident we feel safe under the moon. We're like the moon. Reflecting the light of something living; something that loves us. Does that make any sense?"

"Not much."

"Then it's probably the truth."

She stopped her ascent and turned to him. "Is this meant as a warning of some kind?" she asked.

"Would it matter if it were?"

"Not much."

He grinned. "I was the same. A warning was always an invitation."

"End of discussion."

There were lamps burning in every room of Elaine's house, as if to keep the night and all it concealed at bay.

How sad, Hermione thought, to live in fear of shadows. But then didn't the day now hold as many terrors for her as night did for Elaine? Finally, it seemed, after 31 years of troubled sisterhood, the mirrors they had always held up to each other—fogged until this moment—were clear. Regret touched her, that she had not better known this lonely woman whom she had so resented for her lack of empathy.

"Stay here," she told Rice. "I want to see them on my own."

Rice shook his head. "I'm not missing this," he replied, and followed her up the path, then across the lawn towards the dining room window.

From inside came not two voices but three: a woman, a boy, and a man whose timbre was so recognisable it stopped Hermione in her invisible tracks.

"Thomas," she said.

"Your ex?" Rice murmured.

She nodded. "I hadn't expected . . ."

"You'd have preferred him not to come and mourn you?"

"That doesn't sound like mourning to me," she replied.

Nor did it. The closer to the window they trod, the more merriment they heard. Thomas was cracking jokes, and Finn and Elaine were lapping up his performance.

"He's such a clown!" Hermione said. "Just listen to him."

They had reached the sill now, and peered in. It was worse than she'd expected. Thom had Finn on his knee, his arms wrapped around the child. He was whispering something in the boy's ear, and as he did so a grin appeared on Finn's face.

Hermione could not remember ever being seized by such contrary feelings.She was as glad not to find her sweet Finn weeping—tears did not belong on that guileless face. But did he have to be quite so content; quite so forgetful of her passing? And as to Thom the clown, how could he so quickly have found his way back into his son's affections, having been an absentee father for five years? What bribes had he used to win back Finn's favour, master of empty promises that he was?

"Can we go trick-or-treating tomorrow night?" the boy was asking.

"Sure we can, partner," Thomas replied. "We'll get you a mask and a cape and . . ."

"You too," Finn replied. "You have to come too."

"Anything you want . . ."

"Son of a bitch," Hermione said.

". . . from now on . . ."

"He never even wrote to the boy while I was alive."

". . . anything you want."

"Maybe he's feeling guilty," Rice suggested.

"Guilty?" she hissed, clawing at the glass, longing to have her fingers at Thomas's lying throat. "He doesn't know the meaning of the word."

Her voice had risen in pitch and volume, and Elaine—who had always been so insensitive to nuance—seemed to hear its echo. She rose from the table, turning her troubled gaze towards the window.

"Come away," Rice said, taking hold of Hermione's arm. "Or this is going to end badly."

"I don't care," she said.

Her sister was crossing to the window now, and Thomas was sliding Finn off his knee, rising as he did so, a question on his lips.

"There's somebody . . . watching us," Elaine murmured. There was fear in her voice.

Thomas came to her side; slipped his arm around her waist.

Hermione expelled what she thought was a shuddering sigh, but at the sound of it the window shattered, a hail of glass driving man, woman and child back from the sill.

"Away!" Rice demanded, and this time she conceded; went with him, across the lawn, out into the street, through the benighted town and finally home to the cold apartment where she could weep out the rage and frustration she felt.

Her tears had not dried by dawn; nor even by noon. She wept for too many reasons, and for nothing at all. For Finn, for Thomas, for the fear in her sister's eyes; and for the terrible absence of sense in everything. At last, however, her unhappiness found a salve.

"I want to touch him one last time," she told Rice.

"Finn?"

"Of course Finn."

"You'll scare the bejeezus out of him."

"He'll never know it's me."

She had a plan. If she was invisible when naked, then she would clothe every part of herself, and put on a mask, and find him in the streets, playing trick-or-treat. She would smooth his fine hair with her palm, or lay her fingers on his lips, then be gone, forever, out of the twin states of living death and Idaho.

"I'm warning you," she told Rice, "you shouldn't come."

"Thanks for the invitation," he replied a little ruefully. "I accept."

His clothes had been boxed and awaited removal. They untaped the boxes, and dressed in motley. The cardboard they tore up and shaped into crude masks—horns for her, elfin ears for him. By the time they were ready for the streets All Hallows' Eve had settled on the town.

It was Hermione who led the way back towards Elaine's house, but she set a leisurely pace. Inevitable meetings did not have to be hurried to; and she was quite certain she would encounter Finn if she simply let instinct lead her.

There were children at every corner, dressed for the business of the night. Ghouls, zombies and fiends every one; freed to be cruel by mask and darkness, as she was freed to be loving, one last time, and then away.

"Here he comes," she heard Rice say, but she'd already recognised Finn's jaunty step.

"You distract Thom," she told Rice.

"My pleasure," came the reply, and the revenant was away from her side in an instant. Thom saw him coming, and sensed something awry. He reached to snatch hold of Finn, but Rice pitched himself against the solid body, his ether forceful enough to throw Thom to the ground.

He let out a ripe curse, and rising the next instant, snatched hold of his assailant. He might have landed a blow but that he caught sight of Hermione as she closed on Finn, and instead turned and snatched at her mask.

It came away in his hands, and the sight of her face drew from him a shout of horror. He retreated a step; then another.

"Jesus . . . Jesus . . ." he said.

She advanced upon him, Rice's warning ringing in her head.

"What do you see?" she demanded.

By way of reply he heaved up his dinner in the gutter.

"He sees decay," Rice said. "He sees rot."

"*Mom?*"

She heard Finn's voice behind her; felt his little hand tug at her sleeve. "Mom, is that you?"

Now it was she who let out a cry of distress; she who trembled.

"Mom?" he said again.

She wanted so much to turn; to touch his hair, his cheek; to kiss him goodbye. But Thom had seen rot in her. Perhaps the child would see the same, or worse.

"Turn round," he begged.

"I . . . can't . . . Finn."

"*Please.*"

And before she could stop herself, she was turning, her hands dropping from her face.

The boy squinted. Then he smiled.

"You're so *bright*," he said.

"I am?"

She seemed to see her radiance in his eyes; touching his cheeks, his lips, his brow as lovingly as any hand. So this was what it felt like to be a moon, she thought; to reflect a living light. It was a fine condition.

"Finn . . .?"

Thom was summoning the boy to his side.

"He's frightened of you," Finn explained.

"I know. I'd better go."

The boy nodded gravely.

"Will you explain to him?" she asked Finn. "Tell him what you saw?"

Again, the boy nodded. "I won't forget," he said.

That was all she needed; more than all. She left him with his father, and Rice led her away, through darkened alleyways and empty parking lots to the edge of town. They discarded their costumes as they went. By the time they reached the freeway, they were once more naked and invisible.

"Maybe we'll wander awhile," Rice suggested. "Go down south."

"Sure," she replied. "Why not?"

"Key West for Christmas. New Orleans for Mardi Gras. And maybe next year we'll come back here. See how things are going."

She shook her head. "Finn belongs to Thom now," she said. "He belongs to life."

"And who do we belong to?" Rice asked, a little sadly.

She looked up. "You know damn well," she said, and pointed to the moon.

# POPPY Z. BRITE

## How to Get Ahead in New York

POPPY Z. BRITE first appeared in these pages back in 1991 with her story "His Mouth Will Taste of Wormwood". Since then she has become one of the new rising stars of horror fiction, with the publication of two novels, *Lost Souls* and *Drawing Blood*, and the collection *Swamp Foetus*.

She has lived all over the American South and recently returned to her birthplace of New Orleans to live. When she was a child, her father used to take her around the voodoo shops in the French Quarter, and she wrote her first horror story, "The Attack of the Mud Monster," while still in second grade. Brite started submitting her stories to magazines at the age of 12, and sold her first story to *The Horror Show* when she was 18. She has worked as a candy maker, gourmet cook, mouse caretaker, artist's model and stripper, and she appeared nude in a 1992 short film *John 5*, directed by Athens GA artist Jim Herbert, who also directs the REM videos. She is currently looking forward to seeing an autopsy.

"How to Get Ahead in New York" is part of the further adventures of her characters Steve and Ghost, who also appear in the story "Angels" (1987) and her debut novel *Lost Souls*. "'How to Get Ahead' takes place the spring after *Lost Souls*," explains the author, "as the guys are preparing to take off on an extended cross-country road trip and band tour (which should provide lots of other tales).

"I've only been in the Port Authority Bus Terminal once and never intend to go back, but I did get a story out of it. I wasn't attacked by homeless people, but the lady with cocoons in her hair was real."

She adds, "The thing with the heads didn't happen to me (hell, I would've bought one), but it did happen to someone I know, right there on St Mark's Place. Actually, I love New York. I hope that's evident in the story."

We'll leave it up to the reader to decide . . .

## *HOW TO GET AHEAD IN NEW YORK*

CONSIDER THIS SCENE:

Four a.m. in the Port Authority bus terminal, New York City. The Port Authority is a bad place at the best of times, a place where Lovecraft's wrong geometry might well hold sway. The master of purple prose maintained that the human mind could be driven mad by contemplation of angles subtly skewed, of other planes where the three corners of a triangle might add up to less than a hundred and eighty degrees, or to more.

Such is the Port Authority: even in the bustle of midday, corners do not appear to meet up quite right; corridors seem to slope from one end to the other. Even in full daylight, the Port Authority terminal is a bad place. At five a.m. it is wholly soulless.

Consider two young men just off a Greyhound from North Carolina. They were not brothers, but they might be thought brothers, although they looked nothing alike: it was suggested in the way the taller one, crow-black hair shoved messily behind his ears, kept close to his fairhaired companion as if protecting him. It was implied in the way they looked around the empty terminal and then glanced at each other, exchanging bad impressions without saying a word. They were not brothers, but they had known each other since childhood, and neither had ever been to New York before.

The corridor was flooded with dead fluorescent light. They had seen an EXIT sign pointing this way, but the corridor ended in a steel door marked NO ADMITTANCE. Should anyone find this message ambiguous, a heavy chain had been looped through the door handle and snapped shut with a padlock as large as a good-sized fist.

The fair boy turned around in a complete circle, lifted his head and flared his nostrils. His pale blue eyes slipped halfway shut, the lids fluttering. His friend watched him warily. After a minute he came out of it, shook himself a little, still nervous. "I don't like it here, Steve. I can't find my way anywhere."

Steve didn't like it either, wished they could have avoided the terminal altogether. They'd planned to drive up, but Steve's old T-bird had developed an alarming engine knock which threatened to become a death rattle if not dealt with kindly. The trip was all planned; they were booked to play at a club in the East Village—but they also meant to embark on a cross-country road trip next month. Steve left the car with his mechanic, telling him to fix it or scrap the motherfucker, Steve didn't care which. Ghost stood by half-smiling, listening to this exchange. Then, while Steve was still bitching, he had walked up the street to the Farmers' Hardware store that doubled as Missing Mile's bus station and charged two round-trip tickets to his credit card. He hated using that card, hated the feel of the thing in his pocket, but this surely counted as an emergency. That same night they were New York bound.

"It's just the damn *bus station*," Steve said. "You ever know a town that could be judged by its bus station?" But as usual, there was no use arguing with Ghost's intuition. The place set Steve's teeth on edge too.

Ghost hitched his backpack up on his shoulder. They turned away from the padlocked door and tried to retrace their steps, but every corridor seemed to lead further into the bowels of the place. The soft sound of Ghost's sneakers and the sharp clatter of Steve's bootheels echoed back at them: *shush-clop, shush-clop*. Through Ghost's thin T-shirt Steve saw the sharp winglike jut of his shoulderblades, the shadowed knobs of his spine. The strap of the backpack pulled Ghost's shirt askew; his pale hair straggled silkily over his bare, sweaty neck. Steve carried only a guitar case, the instrument inside padded with a spare shirt and a few extra pairs of socks.

They came to another dead end, then to the motionless hulk of an escalator with a chain strung across its railings. A KEEP OUT sign hung from the chain, swinging lazily as if someone had given it a push and then ducked out of sight just before Steve and Ghost came around the corner. Steve began to feel like a stupid hick, to feel like the place was playing tricks on them. *Came to the Big City and couldn't even find our way out of the bus station. We ought to sit down right here and wait for the next bus headed south, and when it comes, we ought to hop on it and go right back home. Fuck New York, fuck the big club date. I don't like it here either.*

But that was stupid. The city was out there somewhere, and it had to get better than this.

Port Authority, Ghost decided, was about the worst place he had ever been in. Everything about it looked wrong, smelled wrong, leaned wrong. There were patterns on the floor made by the grime of a thousand soles; there was a bloody handprint on the tile wall. Looking at it, Ghost tried to close off his mind: he didn't want to know how it had gotten there. He managed to block out all but a faint impression of dirty knuckles plowing into a soft toothless mouth.

All at once the corridors shook and shuddered. The floor vibrated beneath his feet, throwing Ghost off balance. He had no way of knowing that this loss of equilibrium was caused by the subways constantly passing through; it made him feel as if the place were trying to digest him.

*How did you ever get here?* he thought. *How did you get from the green mountains, from the kudzu traintracks and the lazy hot summers, all the way to this city that could chew you up and spit you out like a wad of gum that's lost its flavor? How did you get to this place where you can never belong?*

Immersed in his thoughts, he had let Steve get a little ahead of him. He looked up an instant before the apparition of death reeled around the corner; he heard Steve's curse, the sharp "*Fuck!*" that was nearly a gag, as the apparition lurched into Steve.

Steve's arms shot out reflexively, found the man's shoulders and shoved him away. The bum fell back against the wall, leaving a long wet smear on the tiles. His ragged suit jacket and the wattles of his throat were webbed with pale stringy vomit that dripped off his chin and made small foul splatters on the floor. His skin was grey, flaccid. It made Ghost think of a pumpkin that had sat too long in his grandmother's cellar once, waiting for Halloween; when he'd poked it, his finger had punched through the rind and sunk into the soft rotten meat. This man's skin looked as if it would rupture just as easily. One of his eyes was filmed over with a creamy yellowish cataract. The other eye listed toward the ceiling, watered and seemed about to spill over, then managed to track. When the eye met his, Ghost felt ice tingle along his spine. There was no one home behind that eye.

A wasted claw of a hand came up clutching a Styrofoam cup in which a few coins rattled. Veins stood out on the back of the hand. In the dead light they were as stark and clear as a map of the man's ruined soul. "Spare change for my li'l girl," he muttered. His voice caught in his throat, then dragged itself out slow as a bad recording. "My li'l girl's sick. Gotta catch the mornin' bus to Jersey."

Ghost looked at Steve. The understanding passed clearly between them: *bullshit*. There was no little girl in Jersey, there was nothing waiting for this man except the love at the bottom of a bottle. But the reality of him staggering through the desolate corridors in his vomit-caked coat, with his lone empty eye—that was worse than any sob story. Steve pulled out his wallet; Ghost dug through the pockets of his army jacket. They came up with a dollar each and stuffed the bills into the broken Styrofoam cup.

The bum threw his head back and a weird hooting sound came from his cracked lips. It was not quite a word, not quite a whistle. It reverberated off the tiles and ceilings.

And then the walls and the corridors of the Port Authority seemed to split wide open, and the legions of the hopeless spilled forth.

The bums were everywhere at once, coming from every direction, their eyes fixed on Steve's wallet and Ghost's open hands and the crisp bills poking out of the cup. Most of them had their own jingling cups; they shoved them at Steve, at Ghost, and their eyes implored. Their voices rose in a hundred meaningless pleas: *cuppa coffee . . . sick baby . . . hungry, mister, I'm hungry.* In the end the voices only meant one thing. *Give me. You who have, when I have none—give me.*

They kept coming. There seemed to be no end to them. Their hands reached for the money and grasped it. A persistent young brother grabbed a handful of Steve's hair and wouldn't let go until Steve reared back and punched him full in the face. He got a fistful of snot and ropy saliva for his trouble. As the boy fell away, Steve saw angry red holes in the pale flesh of his outstretched palms: needle marks. *He was my age*, Steve thought wildly; something in the eyes made him think the kid might have been even younger than twenty-four. *But he was already worn out enough to shoot up in the palms of his hands.*

Steve found himself flashing on *Dawn of the Dead*, a movie that had terrified him when he was a kid. He'd seen it again a couple of years ago and been surprised by how funny it really was: Romero's allegory of zombies roaming a modern mega-mall had escaped him at twelve. But now the original kid-terror flooded back. This was how it would be when the zombies ate you. They weren't very smart or quick, but there were a *lot* of them, and they would just keep coming and coming until you couldn't fight them any more.

Filth-caked nails scraped his flesh. The wallet was torn out of his grasp and dumped on the floor. Steve saw dirty hands shuffling through the trivia of his life. His driver's license. Ticket stubs from concerts he'd seen. A tattered review of Lost Souls?, his and Ghost's band, that had been written up in a Raleigh newspaper. Rage exploded like a crimson rocket in his brain. He had *worked* to get that money; he had *worked* to have a life, not see it trickle away from him like vomit on a dirty bus-station floor.

He hefted the guitar case—none of them seemed interested in that—and swung it in a wild arc. It connected with flesh, filthy hair, bone. Steve winced as he heard the jangling protest of the strings. He'd hit the first bum in his vomit-caked jacket, the only one they had willingly given money. *Try that for a handout, motherfucker.* The bum fell to his knees, clutching the back of his skull. Even the blood welling up between his fingers had an unhealthy look, like the watery blood at the bottom of a meat tray. It spattered the dirty floor in large uneven drops.

Ghost was grappling for his backpack. An old woman with skin like spoiled hamburger pulled at one shoulderstrap. The buttons of her flannel shirt had popped open and her shrivelled breasts tumbled out. The nipples were long and leathery as the stems of mushrooms. Her hair was a uniform grayish-yellow mat overlaid with a layer of white gauze which seemed to thicken, to form dense little balls, in several spots. Networks of delicate threads led away from these; dark shapes moved sluggishly within them. *Cocoons*, he realized sickly. *She has cocoons in her hair*.

He grabbed the woman by the shoulders and shoved her away. Ghost's notebooks were in that backpack—the lyrics to every song they had written. Ghost's eyes met Steve's, pale blue gone darker with panic.

Then, for no discernible reason, the creeps began to lift their heads and scent the air. A silent alarm seemed to pass among them. One by one they shrank away, sidled along the walls and disappeared like wraiths into the maze of corridors. The money in their Styrofoam cups rustled and jingled. Steve thought of cockroaches scuttling for cover when the kitchen light snaps on. In less than a minute they were all gone.

Steve and Ghost stared at each other, sweating, catching their breaths. Ghost held up a shaky hand. The cocoon lady's nails had left a long, shallow scratch along the back of it, from his knuckles to the bony knob of his wrist. A moment later they heard heavy, measured footsteps approaching. They edged closer together but did not otherwise react; this was surely the soul of the city itself coming to claim them.

The cop came around the corner all hard-edged and polished and gleaming, stopped at the sight of them, saw Steve's wallet and its contents scattered on the floor, frowned. His face was broad, Italian-looking, freshly shaved but the beard beneath the skin already showing faintly blue-black. "Help you with something?" he asked, his voice sharp with suspicion.

Steve drew in a long trembling breath and Ghost spoke quickly, before Steve could. Cussing cops was never a good idea, no matter where you were. "I think we got a little lost," he said. "Could you tell us how to get out of here?"

He was relieved when the cop pointed them in the right direction and Steve bent and scooped up his wallet, then stalked off without a word. Ghost's brain still ached from the long bus ride and the attack of the homeless people—or the people who lived, perhaps, in Port Authority. Worse than their grasping hands had been the touch of their minds upon his, as many-legged and hungry as mosquitoes. Their raw pain, the stink of their dead dreams. On top of that he hadn't needed Steve to get himself arrested. But Ghost was used to being the occasional peacemaker between Steve and almost everyone they knew. Steve bristled and Ghost calmed; that was just the way things were.

The sky was already brightening when they came out of the bus terminal. The city soared around them, bathed in a clear lavender light. The first building Ghost saw was an old stone church; the second was a four-storey sex emporium, its neon shimmering pale pink in the dawn. Steve leaned back against the glass doors and began to laugh.

"Good morning, Hell's Kitchen," he said.

Washington Square Park was in full regalia, though it was still early afternoon.

There were street musicians of every stripe, rappers clicking fast fingers and rattling heavy gold chains, old hippies with battered guitars and homemade pan pipes and permanent stoned smirks, young hippies singing solemn folk lyrics *a capella*, even a Dixieland brass band near the great stone arch. There was the savory mustard-chili tang of hot dogs, the harsh smoulder of city exhaust, the woodsy smell of ganja burning. There were homeboys and Rasta men and hairy-chested drag queens, slumming yuppies and street freaks. There were the folks for whom every day was Hallowe'en, faces painted pale, lips slashed crimson or black, ears and wrists decorated with silver crucifixes, skulls, charms of death and hoodoo. They huddled into their dark clothes, plucked at their dyed, teased, tortured hair, cut their black-rimmed eyes at passersby. There were punks in leather; there were drug dealers chanting the charms of their wares (*clean crystal . . . sweetest smoke in the city . . . goooood ice, gooooood blow*). There were cops on the beat, cops looking the other way.

And, of course, there were two white boys from North Carolina whose feet had just this morning touched New York City asphalt for the first time.

They had drunk vile coffee from a stand in Times Square, then walked around for a while. They kept losing track of the Empire State Building, which was the only landmark they recognized. The tranquil light of early morning soon gave way to the hustle and shove of the day. The air came alive with shouts, blaring horns, the constant low thrum of the city-machine.

Eventually—as soon as they could stand to go below street level again—they descended into the subway at Penn Station and didn't get out again until the Washington Square stop. At that point Ghost swore he would never enter a transit station or board any subway in New York City or anywhere else, ever again. It wasn't the crowds; since Port Authority the only panhandlers they'd seen had been shaking discreet cups or quietly noodling on saxophones. No one else had bothered them. It was the merciless white light in the stations and the bleak garbage-strewn deadliness of the tracks and the great clattering ratcheting roar of the trains. It was hurtling through sections of tunnel where the tracks split in two at the last heartstopping second before you smashed into solid stone. It was the abandoned tunnels that split off like dead universes. The very idea of the trains worming along beneath the city, in their honeycombed burrows, seemed horribly organic.

But topside, he was fine. Ghost found himself liking the stew of sounds and smells that comprised the city, and the colorful variety of the minds that brushed his, and the carnival of Washington Square. Steve stopped to watch the Dixieland band, and Ghost listened to the dipping, soaring brass for several minutes too.

But in his peripheral vision a man was rooting in a garbage can. He tried not to look, but couldn't help himself as the man pulled out a whole dripping chilidog, brushed flies away, and bit into it.

The man was old and white, with long gray dreadlocks and mummified hands and the universal costume of the drifter, army jacket, baggy pants, Salvation Army shirt that just missed being a rag: an ensemble ready to fade into the background at a moment's notice. The chilidog was a carnage of ketchup and pickle relish and flaccid meat, the bun limp, sponge-soggy. The man's face registered more pleasure than distaste. The dog might taste awful, but there was still warm sun on his shoulders and a half-full bottle in his pocket and a goddamn huge party going on right here, right now. His eyes were curiously clear, almost childlike.

*But it was* garbage, *he was eating* garbage. The wire trashcan was crammed with ripening refuse. A redolent juice seeped out at the bottom, a distillation of every disgusting fluid in the can, moonshine for bluebottle flies. Ghost felt his mind stretching, trying to accommodate something he had never had to think closely about before. There were poor people in Missing Mile, sure. Most of the old men who played checkers outside the Farmers Hardware store were on some kind of government or military pension. Lots of people got food stamps. But were there people eating out of garbage cans? Were there people so desperate that they would band together and attack you for the change in your pocket?

*You bet there are. They're everywhere. Your life has been just sheltered enough, just sanitized enough, that you didn't see them. But you can't get away from it here . . . this city chews up its young and spits them back in your face.*

Ghost looked up, startled. He wasn't sure what had just happened; it felt as if the world, for an instant, had split and then reconverged. As if someone had had the exact same thought as him, at the exact same time.

He saw a young black man leaning on the low concrete wall nearby, also watching the old drifter. The young man was handsome, trendily barbered, dressed in casual but expensive-looking sport clothes. He wore gold-rimmed glasses with little round lenses, carried a radio Walkman in his breast pocket and a copy of *Spy* tucked under his arm. In his face as he watched the old man chewing was an ineffable sadness, not quite sympathy, not quite pity.

*The hearts that would swell with rage back home—if you could call them hearts—to see a black man looking upon a white man with anything resembling pity . . .*

*(Get outta that garbage, boy)*

The man shifted on the wall and looked straight at Ghost, warm mocha eyes meeting startled pale blue. And suddenly Ghost knew many things about this man. He was from a tiny town in south Georgia—Ghost didn't get the name—and his family had been crushingly poor. Not trash-eating poor . . . but there had been a man in the town who *was*. Ancient and alone, black as midnight, brains pickled by half a century of rotgut wine. He was no town hobo of the sort people laughed at but looked out for; he had no colorful nickname, no family, no history. He was a smelly old wino who pissed his pants, and most of the whites in town, if they were aware of him at all, called him Hey Boy. As in *Hey, Boy, get outta that garbage*. As in *Hey, Boy, I'm talkin' to you*. As in *Hey, Boy, get off my property before I blow your nigger guts to Hell*.

And this young man, as a hungry scrawny child in this stagnant backwater of a town, had seen that happen.

Ghost saw the blood exploding through the air, smelled flame and cordite, redneck sweat and the raw sewage odor of Hey Boy's ruptured, blasted guts. He felt the giddy terror of a child hiding—where?—he couldn't get it—viewing death up close for the first time, afraid its twin black barrels would swing his way next. He could not move, could not look away from the young man's calm brown eyes, until Steve touched his shoulder. "Somebody just gave me directions to the club. It's real near here. You want to go check it out?"

Ghost glanced back over his shoulder as they left the park. The young man was no longer looking at him, and Ghost felt no urge to speak. They had already had the most intimate contact possible; of what use were words?

They crossed a wide traffic-filled avenue and turned east. Ghost wasn't sure just where the Village began, but the streets seemed to be getting narrower, the window displays more fabulous, the crowds decidedly funkier. People wore silver studs in their noses, delicate hoops through their lips and eyebrows. A boy in a black fishnet shirt had both nipples pierced, with a filigree chain connecting the rings. There were shaved and painted scalps, long snaky braids, leather jackets jangling with zippers and buckles, flowing hippie dresses of gossamer and gauze. The streets of the East Village by day seemed a shrine to mutant fashion.

Steve pulled a joint from his sock, lit up, took a deep drag and passed it to Ghost. Ghost grabbed the burning cigarette and cupped it gingerly between his palms, trying to hide it, expecting a big cop hand to fall on his shoulder at any second. "Are you *crazy*?"

Steve shook his head, then blew out a giant plume of smoke. "It's cool. Terry said you could smoke right on the street up here, as long as you're discreet. He gave me this as a going-away present."

Terry owned the record store where Steve worked, and was the best-travelled and most worldly of their crowd; also the biggest stoner, so he ought to know. But Ghost could not stretch his definition of *discreet* to include walking down one of the busiest streets in New York City with a cloud of pot smoke trailing behind. Still . . . He looked thoughtfully at the joint in his hand, then brought it up to his lips and took a cautious toke. The spicy green flavor filled his throat, swirled through his lungs and his brain. New York probably imported every exotic strain of reefer from every country in the world, but Southern homegrown had to beat them all.

A few blocks later the crowds thinned out. The streets here felt older, greyer, somehow more soothing. More like a place where you could actually live. There were little groceries on every block with wooden stands of flowers and produce in front. Ghost smelled ginger and ripe tomatoes, the subtle cool scent of ice, the tang of fresh greens and herbs. Sage, basil, onions, thyme, sweet rosemary and soapy-smelling coriander. As long as he could smell herbs he was happy.

New York, Steve decided, was a city bent upon providing its citizens with plenty of food and information. In other parts of the city there had been hot dog carts everywhere, pizza parlors and cappuccino shops, restaurants serving food from Thailand, Mongolia, Latino-China, and everywhere else in the world; newsstands on every corner carried hundreds of papers, magazines, and often a wide selection of hardcore porn. There were radios and TVs blaring, headlines shrieking. In the first part of the Village Steve had seen more restaurants, comics shops, and several intriguing bookstores he planned to check out later. Here you had the little groceries, though not quite so many restaurants. For information, there were the street vendors.

Steve had started noticing them a while back, though he'd been too busy noticing everything else to pay much attention at first. But here they were more frequent and less obscured by the flow of the crowd. They set up tables or spread out army blankets, then arranged the stuff they wanted to sell and sat down to wait until somebody bought it. There were tables of ratty paperbacks, boxes of old magazines, tie-dyed T-shirts and ugly nylon buttpacks, cheap watches and household appliances laid out on the sidewalk like the leftovers from somebody's yard sale.

But as they walked farther, the wares started to get a little strange. At first it was just stuff that no one could possibly want, like a box of broken crayon-ends or a shampoo bottle filled with sand. Then they passed a man selling what looked like medical equipment: bedpans in a dusty row, unidentifiable tubes and pouches, some jar-shaped humps covered with a tattered army blanket. In the center of his display was a single artificial leg that had once been painted a fleshy pink. Now the paint was chipped, the limb's surface webbed with a thousand tiny, grimy cracks. The toeless foot was flat and squared-off, little more than a block of wood. At the top was a nightmarish jumble of straps and braces meant, Steve supposed, to hold the leg onto a body. He could not imagine walking around on such a thing every day.

"Where is this club?" Ghost asked nervously.

"Well . . . I know we're near it." Steve stopped at the corner, shoved sweaty hair out of his face, and looked around hoping the place would appear. "The guy who gave me directions said it would be hard to find in the daytime. We're supposed to look for an unlit neon sign that says *Beware*."

"Great."

"WHAT PLACE YEZ LOOKIN' FOR?" boomed a voice behind them. It took Steve several seconds to realize that the vendor had spoken and was now motioning them over.

"Yez look like gentlemen in search of the unusual," the vendor told them before they could say anything about clubs or directions. He was a white man of indeterminate age, dishwater-brown hair thin on top but straggling halfway down his back in an untidy braid. His eyes were hidden behind black wraparound shades, his grin as sharp and sudden as a razor. Steve noticed a strange ring on the second finger of the guy's right hand: a bird skull cast in silver, some species with huge hollow eyesockets and a long, tapering, lethal-looking beak that jutted out over the knuckle. It was lovely, but it also looked like a good tool for putting an eye out or ventilating a throat.

"Well, right now we're looking for this club – "

"Something UNUSUAL," the vendor overrode. "A collector's item maybe." His hand hovered over his wares, straightened tubes and straps, caressed the artificial leg. "Something yez don't see every day." His face went immobile, then split back into that sharp crazy grin. "Or rather—something yez DO see every day, but most of the time yez can't take the fuckers HOME WITH YA!"

His hand twitched back the army blanket covering the jar-shaped humps. A small cloud of dust rose into the air. Sunlight winked on polished glass. Steve cussed, took two steps back, then came forward again and bent to look.

Ghost, who had never in his life felt so far from home, burst into tears.

The man had six big glass jars arranged in two neat rows, sealed at the tops and filled with what could only be formaldehyde. Inside each jar, suspended in the murky liquid, was a large, pale, bloated shape: an undeniably real human head.

The necks appeared to have been surgically severed. Ghost could see layers of tissue within the stumps as precisely delineated as the circles of wood inside a tree trunk. One head was tilted far enough to the side to show a neat peg of bone poking from the meat of the neck. Several had shaved scalps; one had dark hair that floated and trailed like seaweed. Parts of faces were pressed flat against the glass: an ear, a swollen nostril, a rubbery lip pulled askew. Blood-suffused eyeballs protruded from their sockets like pickled hard-boiled eggs.

"How much do you want for them?" Steve asked. Ghost sobbed harder.

The grin seemed to throw off light, it was so wide and dazzling. "Two apiece. Ten for all six of 'em."

"Ten *dollars*?"

"Hey, I'm in a hurry, I gotta unload these puppies today, yez think this is *legal* or somethin'?"

As if on cue, sirens rose out of the general distant cacophony, approaching fast. A pair of police cars rounded the corner and came shrieking up the block. Revolving blue light flickered across the lenses of the black wraparound shades. The grin disappeared. Without even a *good day to yez* the vendor scooped up the artificial leg and took off down the street. One car roared after him. The other slammed to a halt at the curb where Steve and Ghost still stood staring stupidly at the heads.

"You weren't really going to buy one, were you?" Ghost whispered.

"Course not." Steve snorted. "I don't have any money anyway, remember? The bums got it all. I'm lucky to have an I.D. to show this cop." He dug out his wallet and flipped it open. "We're just a couple of hicks from North Carolina, Officer. We lay no claim to these jars or their contents."

*Minds like butterflies preserved in brine, trapped under thick glass . . .*

It seemed that their friendly vendor, a gentleman whose given name was Robyn Moorhead but who was known variously as Robyn Hood, Moorhead Robbins, and (aptly enough) "More Head," had robbed a medical transport truck en route from Beth Israel Hospital to the Mutter Medical Museum in Philadelphia while it was stopped at a gas station. The truck's door had not latched properly, and More Head and an unidentified girlfriend had simply climbed in and cleaned it out. He had already sold several items before Steve and Ghost came along. The artificial leg, though, was his own. He used it for display purposes only, to call attention to whatever shady wares he sold; it was a valuable antique and not for sale; he carried it everywhere.

*No*, Ghost told himself. *You did* not *feel their minds beating against the jars like dying insects. You did not feel the raw burn of formaldehyde against your eyeballs, the dead taste of it in your mouth; you did not feel the subtle breakdown of the molecular dream that was your brain. They were not alive. You could not feel them.*

"I gotta know," said the cop as he finished writing up their statement. "How much did he want for 'em?" Steve told him, and the cop shrugged, then sighed. He was a decent sort and the affair seemed to have put him in a philosophical mood. "Man, even'f I was a crook, even'f I was tryna sell yuman heads, I'd't least be askin' more'n ten bucks. Kinda devalues the sanctity a'yuman life, y'know?"

*Jewelled wings, beating themselves to powder against thick glass . . .*

They had overshot the club by five blocks. The cops pointed them in the right direction and ten minutes later they were descending below street level again, past the unlit neon sign that said not *Beware* but *Be Aware*, though Ghost guessed it amounted to the same thing, and into the club. The poster they had sent was plastered everywhere: TONIGHT—LOST SOULS? They were too tired to consider doing a soundcheck yet, but it was just the two of them, Steve's guitar and Ghost's voice, and they didn't really need one. At any rate they wouldn't be going on till midnight. Right now they needed sleep. One of the bartenders was out of town and had left them the keys to her apartment, which was just upstairs.

Too tired for the stairs, they rode the ancient, terrifying elevator up seven stories. Steve had bummed two beers at the bar. He guzzled most of one as they rode up. "New York is pretty interesting," he said.

"No shit."

Steve snorted into his beer. And then at once they were both laughing, losing it in a rickety box suspended from an antique cable in a building that was taller than any building in Missing Mile but small by the standards of this magical, morbid, million-storied city. They fell against each other and howled and slapped high-five. They were young and the one had a voice like gravelly gold and the other could play guitar with a diamond-hard edge born of sex and voodoo and despair, and it was all part of the Great Adventure.

They staggered out at the top still giggling, fumbled with three unfamiliar locks, and let themselves into the apartment. The place was decorated all in black: black walls, black lace dripping from the ceiling, black paint over the windows, black silk sheets on a huge futon that covered the floor. The effect was soothing, like being cradled in the womb of night. Their laughter wound down.

Steve stood his guitar case in a corner, gulped the second beer after Ghost refused it, and stretched his tired bones out on the futon. Ghost toed his sneakers off and lay down beside him. It was absolutely dark and, for the first time since Port Authority, nearly quiet. How strange to think that the whole teeming city was still out there, just beyond the walls of the building. Suddenly Ghost felt disoriented in the little pocket of blackness, as if the compass he always carried in his head had deserted him.

He shifted on the mattress so that his shoulder touched Steve's arm, so that he could feel Steve's familiar warmth all along the left side of his body. Steve heaved a great deep sigh like a sleeping hound. Ghost thought of all the highways, all the back roads, all the train tracks and green paths that led back home, and he did not feel so far away.

And there was music, there was always music to carry him wherever he wanted to go. Soon the distant thrum of the city and the tales it wanted to tell him faded completely, and the gouge of Steve's bony elbow in his side lulled him to sleep.

# JOHN BRUNNER

## They Take

JOHN BRUNNER is one of Britain's most prolific and respected science fiction authors. Since the late 1950s, he has won two British Science Fiction Awards, The British Fantasy Award, the French Prix Apollo, Italy's Cometa d'Argento twice and the Europa Award. He also received the Hugo, science fiction's top honour, in 1969 for his novel, *Stand on Zanzibar*.

His many other books include *The Sheep Look Up*, *The Jagged Orbit*, *The Compleat Traveller in Black*, *Shockwave Rider* and the recent *Muddle Earth*.

Besides science fiction, Brunner has written mysteries, thrillers and fantasy, and he has turned his hand to horror in recent years, with great success, in *Weird Tales* and the *Dark Voices* series.

"They Take" is proof (if any was needed) that the author is as proficient in this genre as he is in all the others . . .

"ARE YOU SURE WE'RE GOING THE RIGHT WAY?" demanded Ann Bertelli. Strictly she was Annunziata, but in the trendy circles of Milan and Turin the shorter English name was far more fashionable, like her sleekly coiffed fair hair, her wraparound sunglasses, her brief clinging frock and massy gold bracelets.

At the wheel of their Alfa Twin Spark, whose shiny red paintwork was dull with dust, her husband Carlo snapped, "It's the way you told me to take! You've got the map Anzani sent us!"

"Who in his right mind trusts a lawyer?" Ann retorted. "In his letter he described Aunt Silvana's estate as 'fertile and productive,' but I can't imagine that being true of any land in this area!"

Late summer sun beat down on the countryside. Either side of the rough road crops bent their weary heads: beans, maize, tobacco. In the distance they now and then saw peasants at work, helped or hindered by balky donkeys and scrawny oxen. More than once Ann had said this trip was like travelling back in time—yet it wasn't as though they were in the deep Mezzogiorno. Indeed, they were still well north of Rome!

Ahead lay a T-junction. Braking, wiping sweat from his forehead with the sleeve of his slub-silk jacket, Carlo demanded, "Which way now? Right or left?"

And when she delayed an answer, trying to orientate the photocopied sketch-map that was their only guide, he went on savagely, "When I think that but for your damned aunt we could have spent the rest of our fortnight in Nice – "

"Getting off with that German girl you had your eye on?" murmured Ann.

"Oh my God!" Carlo shifted out of gear and applied the handbrake. "We're not going to have another fit of jealousy, are we?"

Ann raised her head and glanced around. "Not right now," she replied composedly, pointing through the dusty windscreen. "Later if you like . . . But what about that?"

Fallen from its post, a white on blue sign lay among dry yellow grass, spattered with rust-marks as if it had been used for target practice. But the name Bolsevieto was just legible, and its arrow-shaped end pointed right.

Annoyed at having overlooked it, Carlo spun the car's wheels in dust as he made the turn. From the corner of his mouth he said, "What's the time?"

"Two hours later than it ought to be."

"How the hell was I to know there'd be such a jam on the *autostrada*? A crash like that happens only – "

"It would have helped if we'd got away on time! We're only going to look my aunt's place over and you insisted on packing enough for a month in – "

"Oh, shut up! At least we're practically there."

"There"—Bolsevieto—was a village of a hundred or so houses, plus outlying farms, encircled by a ring of low hills. The central square, where they were to meet Signor Anzani, was easy to find, for it was the only place the road led to. There was a church, of course; there were a few trees, a few shops, and a *bar ristorante* outside which stood iron chairs strung with red and yellow plastic.

And sitting on one of the chairs, looking distinctly bad-tempered, was a glum middle-aged man sweating in a black suit, with an empty glass and a briefcase on the table at his side. Parking the car, jumping out without waiting for Ann, Carlo strode over hand outstretched.

"Signor Anzani? I'm sorry we're late! There was a big crash on the *autostrada*—did you hear?"

The lawyer hoisted himself to his feet, forcing a polite expression that didn't really qualify as a smile.

"Ah, what is another couple of hours when you had to miss the funeral of your wife's aunt more than a week ago? You are Signora Bertelli?"—to Ann as she joined them. "Charming, charming!" He bent to kiss her hand. But Carlo detected a transient frown of disapproval at her too-short dress.

There were few other people in sight: the waiter at the door of the bar; a blank-faced man of about thirty with a slack mouth and dirty clothes, possibly a village idiot—such creatures did still exist in remote areas like this—two elderly women in black who seemed to be complaining about the price of tomatoes, although their accent was so thick he couldn't tell whether it was the cost in a shop or what they were offered for their garden produce; and, glimpsed at opening shutters, people rising from siesta.

Those apart, there were no living creatures in view save birds, flies and a couple of large, loose-limbed black dogs that now and then yawned to display their red maws, but showed scant interest in the arrival of strangers.

Yet he felt a sense of being under scrutiny, like an itch. As he and Ann accepted Anzani's offer of a drink he cast his eye around the square in search of its cause. The fronts of the houses—some of them once fine, now losing plaques of stucco, the ornamentation of their porches eroded by wind and weather—offered no clue. The façade of the church, on the other hand . . .

Yes, the church struck him as unusual, more French perhaps than Italian. It bore many carved faces, most of a style he would term demonic, up to its eaves and beyond. He turned to ask Ann's opinion. He himself was an ordinary commercial sort of person and earned his living selling whatever might turn a profit: formerly, food and furniture, at present life insurance. Ann, though, had graduated in the history of art and currently worked for one of the most prestigious galleries in Milan. Occasionally he felt a trifle envious of her broader knowledge.

But she was already riffling papers that the lawyer had produced from his briefcase, saying, "Carlo darling, you ought to be looking at these. You're much more business-like than I am."

Sighing, Carlo complied.

Yet there seemed to be no real need to consult him, for shorn of legal jargon her aunt's will said what had been summarized in Anzani's letter: she had become the owner of a run-down house, its contents, and a parcel of land. They had promptly reached an agreement to dispose of the lot, in spite of their frequent quarrelling—and why not? As the proverb put it, *L'amore non e bello se non e litigiello*. An occasional row lent spice to life. But it didn't have to affect genuinely important decisions.

He cut short the pointless conversation by suggesting that they ought to head for the house at once if they were not unduly to delay Signor Anzani. His office was not here in tiny, time-forgotten Bolsevieto, but the nearest town of any size, Matignano, eleven kilometres away.

Glancing gloomily at his watch, the lawyer nodded agreement, drained his glass, and rose.

So, to the second, did one of the dogs. He had been stretched out on the church steps. Now he jumped up, tail wagging, as the door swung open and a priest emerged in a black cassock and a broad-brimmed hat: a thick-set man, heavy boned, heavy jowled, clean shaven but with what Ann and Carlo had learned to call by the English name "five o'clock shadow" in preference to that absurd American term "designer stubble".

By now, Carlo noticed, people had begun to appear on the street again. The opening of shutters at the end of the siesta had harbingered their emergence. Unlike the incurious dogs they stared at the outsiders, making him feel like a specimen under a microscope with a score of observers.

Yes: definitely it would be best to sell Ann's inheritance for whatever they could obtain. Small towns—town? Bolsevieto was at best a village!—got on his nerves.

Hers too, he imagined.

Elderly people, slow moving, crossed themselves on noticing the priest, who responded with a wave as, the dog at his heels, he headed towards Anzani. The two were clearly well known to one another. Each uttered a few phrases in a dialect too broad to follow. Then Anzani addressed the Bertellis in a formal tone.

"As possible future residents of our community, you should be introduced to Father Maru."

Ann and Carlo exchanged glances on hearing the peculiar name, but forbore to comment. Presumably it was a local pronunciation of Mario, conceivably still influenced by the Latin Marius after all these centuries.

Its bearer, with an expression appropriate for meeting people who had so recently lost a relative, shook their hands, regretted that they had been unable to attend their aunt's funeral, and said he would expect them at Mass next Sunday (*Fat chance*! freethinker Carlo married to a freethinker growled to himself). Then he tried to present his dog, who turned out to be called Ercle. But the animal's only response was another yawn.

To Carlo's surprise, and somewhat to his annoyance also, for he was anxious to avoid more delay, Ann reacted on hearing the dog's name. "That's unusual!" she exclaimed. "Isn't it the Etruscan for Hercules?"

"Why, indeed it is!" the priest beamed. "But I assure you it's not unusual hereabouts. We are, after all, on the terrain of Etruria, are we not? You'll find many survivals of that sort. The very name of our *paese*"—he used the word that means both village and country—"is half Etruscan: the same root that one finds in Volsci, plus the Latin for old. There are many ancient patronymics here, as well. Have you visited your aunt's grave? No? Well, I have half an hour to spare. If you like I can take you to it now and show you what I mean on the way."

"I'm sure that would be very interesting," Carlo said hastily. "But we shouldn't detain Signor Anzani too long."

"No, of course not," Father Maru granted. "Well, doubtless there will be another chance."

With visible relief the lawyer stumped towards his car, a sober dark blue Fiat, instructing them to follow.

As Carlo was starting up Ann said thoughtfully, "I think that priest has an Etruscan name, too."

"What?"—swinging into the wake of the Fiat.

"Maru. You assumed it was a variant of Marius at first, didn't you? So did I. Now I suspect it's much older."

"Since when do you know so much about Etruscan?"

"Since last year when we held an exhibition of Etruscan art," she retorted. "I wrote the notes for the catalogue, remember?"

Embarrassed at having forgotten, Carlo said, "So what does Maru mean?"

"I'm not sure—I don't think anybody is—but either priest or magistrate, maybe both. Back in those days there wasn't much distinction between religious and civil office."

Carlo said nothing further for the time being. Now they were out of the village Anzani, more familiar with the area and perhaps less concerned about damage to his car, was setting a fast pace along a rough and stony track, and he was having trouble keeping up without being blinded by the clouds of dust.

Aunt Silvana's former home was a typical farmhouse of the region, its roof of tiles unaltered in design since Roman times, its walls of hollow bricks covered with flaking stucco and partly masked by a sprawling vine. Chickens were scratching around a disused well in what passed for its front garden; near by a donkey brayed; there was a noticeable odour of goat; sweet peppers and tomatoes were laid out to dry in the sun. An elderly woman clad in black, her face lined, her hands gnarled, several of her teeth missing, awaited them at its door with the timeless patience of one to whom clocks were still a novelty. Emerging from his car, Anzani gave her a curt greeting, and would have gone on to introduce Ann and Carlo but that she interrupted.

"Ah, so you are Signora Silvana's niece. I don't need to be told. There is something about your eyes. One can tell your ancestors hailed from our *paese*." Her voice, though wheezy, was clear and easy to understand despite a trace of the regional accent they had heard in Bolsevieto. "And you, *signore*, must be her husband. Welcome! Please call me Giuseppina. I am used to it. Sometimes I almost forget I have another name. Come, let me show you to the room I have prepared."

Ann and Carlo exchanged glances. They had been planning to return to Bolsevieto, or even Matignano, for the night. Ann turned to the lawyer intending to say as much, but he forestalled her.

"You'll lodge better here than at the *albergo* in Bolsevieto," he grunted. "And in a cleaner bed, most like. Besides, the property is an extensive one. You'll need to take your time inspecting it . . . Oh! Before I forget!"

He strode back to his car, leaned in, and reached for something on the back seat. Returning, he held out to Carlo a bottle of Asti Spumante.

"A token to mark your arrival," he said. "Well, now I must leave you. There's no phone here, I'm afraid, but you have my number and if you need any more information you can ring me from the bar where we met. *Signora—signore*—Giuseppina—*arrivederci*."

The abruptness of his departure left them astonished. Not until his car was a hundred metres down the lane did Ann murmur to her husband, "He could at least have made it champagne."

Not only was there no phone; there was no electricity, water came from a spring on the hillside—here they were just below the high ground that encircled Bolsevieto—and the outside privy was so noisome Ann declared her intention of hiding behind a bush rather than make use of it. But the huge brass-framed bed was indeed clean, and looked rather comfortable, and despite being cooked over a wood fire the mess of spaghetti, eggs and wild mushrooms that Giuseppina prepared for their supper was tasty as well as filling. Moreover the *grana* cheese she served with it was *stravecchio*—extra mature, of the highest quality. Also there was a salad of tomatoes from the garden dressed with fresh basil and local olive oil. And even though there was no refrigerator, half an hour in the running water from the spring chilled Anzani's wine to acceptable coolness—made it, indeed, quite palatable.

They had expected Giuseppina to eat with them in the *salone*, but she retreated to the kitchen. When they asked why, she shrugged and indicated her sunken lips, implying that it was embarrassing for her to eat in company lacking so many teeth. They nodded understanding but insisted she take a glass of wine along. When she came to clear the table and deliver grapes and figs by way of dessert, she left them with a warm good night.

"Bedtime?" Carlo said as the door closed behind her.

"Well, we're out in the wilds," Ann sighed. "No TV, no radio even—unless you want to sit in the car until the battery runs flat. We might as well take the hint. If we get up early we can look over the estate before lunch and be on our way by afternoon." She glanced around the room, fitfully lit by a paraffin lamp that Giuseppina had set on a handsome but neglected nineteenth-century side-board. "We ought to be able to raise a fair price, don't you think? There's a good deal of land."

Carlo nodded firmly. "Enough to pay off the mortgage on our apartment, at the least."

"You're not tempted to sell up and return to nature?" Ann enquired with such mock gravity that for a second he took her seriously and almost choked on his last swig of wine. When he recovered he started to laugh.

"Come on, let's turn in," he managed at length.

"OK. I just hope that donkey doesn't start braying in the night. And there's bound to be a cockerel, too." She reached for her handbag, checking abruptly.

"Damn. I meant to save a mouthful of wine to swallow my Pill. I hope that water's safe. Pass me the jug."

Luckily the night proved tolerably quiet. The only noise that did disturb them was the barking—rather, the baying—of a large dog, perhaps one of those they had seen in the village. But it didn't last for long, and by the time Giuseppina's movements disturbed them at six they had had plenty of rest. Besides, it was a fine morning.

After breakfast Ann kept her promised rendezvous with a bush, as did Carlo, and having arranged with Giuseppina to return for lunch at noon they set off on their tour of exploration armed with the sketch-map Anzani had supplied.

The land had been neglected, but the lawyer had told the truth after all. Thanks to the spring welling from the hillside it was indeed exceptionally fertile compared with the area they had driven through yesterday. It was also less flat than the surrounding terrain, forming a series of gently undulating hills, some adorned with trees and bushes planted by past owners: chestnuts, olives, mulberries, lemons. For a wild moment Carlo felt tempted by the idea Ann had mooted as a joke, then dismissed it sternly. Certainly it would be possible to survive off a farm like this—one might even live quite well—but he had no wish to be transported back in time, as Ann had put it.

Then, abruptly, everything changed.

In shorts today, Ann had run up the next hill ahead with a laughing accusation about smoking too much—it wasn't true, he'd given up at her request when they got married—and come to a dead stop. Not until he had caught up did she recover from her shock.

"Carlo, I don't believe it!" she whispered. "*Look*!"

Ahead, in a sort of bowl, there stood a tumulus in the form of a wide low cone. The irrelevant thought crossed Carlo's mind that it was exactly the shape of one of Ann's breasts. Though it was covered in scrub, a single glance sufficed to show that it was artificial, for it was ringed by a stone wall, about shoulder height, and it had a door, or rather a doorway: a low stone porch was crudely blocked by wooden planks nailed to a wooden frame and lashed in position with ropes that served for both hinges and latch. All around were signs that this was or had recently been someone's home: a pile of rubbish, another of ashes, a bucket, an axe, a stack of firewood.

"Something like the *nuraghi* we saw on Sardinia the other year?" Carlo hazarded, shading his eyes against the sun.

"Idiot!" She strode down the slope, leaving him to keep up as best he might. "We're slam in the middle of an Etruscan necropolis! I bet the sides of these hills have as many burrows as a rabbit-warren! And look at this!" Halting beside the mound, she pointed at a long box-like object, half full of water. Its reddish-brown sides, patched with lichen, bore traces of elaborate moulding.

"What is it?"

"An Etruscan coffin! Lord, it must be worth millions and it's being used as a drinking-trough!"

Darting towards the porch, she attacked the rope that fastened its door.

"Ann, do you think you ought to?"

Over her shoulder she snapped, "According to the map we're on my land, aren't we? I suppose I have some rights as the new owner!"

The rope fell away. She dragged the door aside and peered in. Reluctant, Carlo followed her example.

Cut into the side of the tumulus there was a large, low-ceilinged room, its roof upheld by square pillars. There were more signs of occupation: a bed, a table, tools, kitchen utensils. In a niche beside the entrance stood four primitive statuettes, presumably very old, garlanded with withered flowers, and these stopped Ann in her tracks with an exclamation under her breath: "*Lares and penates!* And still receiving offerings! In this day and age!"

But what really seized and held her attention were the walls—rather, the paintings on them. Grimy and faded, they were none the less astonishing.

"My God," she whispered. "Look! This scene of two men in hoodwinks, that one with a club and this one with a dog roped to his arm! Only one other like it is known to have survived. It's supposed to represent some sort of trial by ordeal, maybe a precursor of the Roman Games. Presumably the man with the club had to flail about hoping to cripple the dog before it could sink its teeth into him. Carlo, you realize what this means, don't you? I've inherited a fortune! There must be other tombs all around us, so provided they haven't been ransacked – "

"Listen," Carlo broke in.

A moment, and it came again: a deep baying sound, the cry of a dog such as Father Maru owned.

"I think the occupier may be coming home," he whispered. "Let's get out of here."

They returned to daylight, and his guess proved right. Staring down at them from the crest of the same hill over which they had passed stood a thick-set man with a heavy black beard, cradling on his left arm a broken shotgun, at his right a dog that might have been litter-brother to the priest's. At their appearance he shook the gun closed with a swift and practised motion, and made to raise and point it.

He shouted something they failed to understand, to which the dog added a growl, its hackles bristling.

"We're the—the new owners!" Ann called back. "I'm Ann Bertelli and this is my husband Carlo!"

Eying them suspiciously under bushy brows, the man advanced. It could now be seen that he had a pouch slung at his side, from under the flap of which protruded the ears of a fresh-killed rabbit. He halted five or six paces away, studying them from head to toe. Especially Ann. He scrutinized her, the way, she imagined, he would inspect a horse or ox he planned to buy.

He had extraordinary eyes, not just dark, but actually black—as black as though she were looking through them into nowhere.

Eventually he said, his accent thick but his meaning clear enough, "All right. Just don't come poking around again, hear? This is mine! So unless you want Cerbero to help himself to dinner off your backside . . . In your case"—with a nod at Ann—"that would be a shame. Now be on your way!"

"Now look here!" Ann began hotly, setting her hands on her hips. Carlo checked her with a touch on her arm.

"Gun," he said succinctly.

Not to mention dog. She conceded the wisdom of beating a strategic retreat. But she fumed all the way back to the house, describing what she was going to say to Anzani for not having warned them they had a squatter in residence.

Carlo uttered occasional murmurs of agreement.

"Odd!" she said at last as they approached their goal. "I couldn't help feeling that that fellow looked familiar. As though I've seen him somewhere before."

Her husband shrugged. "Probably a local type," he suggested. "I imagine there's a lot of inbreeding in communities like Bolsevieto. Everybody's probably everyone else's cousin."

"Yes, perhaps . . . Now where's Giuseppina? I have a few questions to put to her, as well!"

They found her at her wood-fired hearth stirring a *bollito misto* of kid meat, sausage, and assorted vegetables. "So you met Tarchuno Vipegno," she said when she heard Ann out. "Yes, he has the right to live there."

"But those are Etruscan tombs! They must be full of priceless archeological relics! If they haven't been plundered, of course."

"None the less," Giuseppina said composedly. She turned away from the pot, wiping her hands on her apron. "There were Vipegnos living here long before my day, let alone yours. They do say: since a hundred generations."

"Oh, that's ridiculous!" Ann stamped her foot. "Does he have a wife, does he have a family?"

Giuseppina let her apron fall.

"The Vipegnos don't marry," she said. "They take."

After an ill-tempered meal nothing would satisfy Ann but that they drive to the bar in Bolsevieto and ring Anzani. Carlo's reminders about the siesta fell on deaf ears, and at last he reluctantly gave in.

It was, however, as he had predicted: there was no reply from the lawyer's office, and the bored waiter assured them it was useless to try again before half-past three. Too restless to sit for so long, Ann cast around for distraction. Carlo suggested they might visit her aunt's grave, and she listlessly agreed. They found it without trouble—there were few recent tombstones in the little cemetery—stared at it inanely for a while, and turned back the way they had come. As the priest had mentioned, many of the names above the other graves were unusual and archaic, and the sight of them set Ann complaining again.

"What I don't understand," she muttered, "is why the site isn't famous. It doesn't look as though it's ever been properly excavated. Certainly this—this Tarchuno has no business treating it as . . ."

The words tailed off. Carlo glanced a question at her.

"I just realized," she said after a pause, "that his name is literally Etruscan."

"How do you mean?" They were strolling side by side towards the village square and the church again.

"Tarchuno—Tarquinus, as it was in Latin. And Vipegno—that's too like Vibenna for coincidence. There were two brothers called Aulus and Caelius Vibenna who lived during the last years of kingly rule in Rome, supposed to have been friends and allies of Servius Tullius . . . Did you know the Etruscans were the first people to use the modern European style of naming, a given name plus a family name?"

Without waiting for an answer, she plunged on.

"Soon as we get back to Milan, I must get in touch with the people I met while I was writing up those exhibition notes. Heavens, this place ought to be one of the biggest tourist attractions in the area! And couldn't it do with a shot in the arm?" They were in sight of the square now, where the only signs of life consisted of a few buzzing flies and the usual drowsy dogs; the human inhabitants were still in hiding from the heat.

Carlo hesitated. After a pause he said, "Does this mean you've changed your mind about selling?"

"Not at all! But now we know what comes with the property we'd be fools not to milk it for every lira. And if there are a decent number of saleable relics in the necropolis we might well consider doing up the house and keeping it on for weekends, hm? It's not all that far from Milan, and it wouldn't half impress people." Ann checked her watch. "Damn, still another quarter-hour to go. Suppose we take a look at the church."

And, as though her eyes had been newly opened, she found much to comment on there, too. The sinister carvings Carlo had noticed yesterday—most of them had semicircular recesses, much ornamented, around the faces, not at all like the haloes usually accorded to Christian saints—she referred to as *antefissi* and said they must have developed from the protective icons the Etruscans used to mount on the corners of roofs. The very structure of the church, which to Carlo seemed dull and ordinary, excited her, too. Apparently it was built to an Etruscan pattern with three distinct chambers, or one chamber and two cells, instead of the conventional Christian layout.

"I wish there were a guidebook!" she exclaimed.

"Even if there were," Carlo sighed, "we couldn't buy one. There aren't any shops open, and if yesterday is anything to go by there won't be until four o'clock. But it's half-past three and we can try raising Anzani again. I suppose they take a shorter siesta in the big city."

At the idea of Matignano as a big city she managed to crack a smile, and they headed for the bar arm in arm.

Anzani sounded as though he had not yet fully woken up, but at the sound of Ann's angry voice he briskened.

"Yes, I'm sorry not to have explained about Vipegno," he cut in. "It was one of the things I planned to discuss with you. But do remember you were over two hours late, so I scarcely had time to go into detail."

"I wouldn't have thought an Etruscan necropolis was a mere detail!" she snapped. "Especially one that's being ruined by a squatter!"

"Ruined? Not in the least." Anzani had regained his normal professional tone. "One thing the Vipegnos have always been noted for is the way they guard the site. You sound knowledgeable on this subject. Can you name anywhere else like it that's actually in occupation?"

"Of course not, but . . ." Ann drew a deep breath. "You said Vipegnos, plural. Giuseppina said something about them having been there for a hundred generations. I never heard anything so ridiculous!

Why, that would take us right back to Etruscan times—twenty-five centuries!"

"All I can say," Anzani answered after a pause, "is that he holds rights in perpetuity. How far back they date I can't say, but the generally accepted term is 'from time immemorial'."

"Oh, this is getting more and more absurd!" Glancing at Carlo, who nodded vigorous agreement; she was holding the phone a little away from her ear so he could eavesdrop. "What about—what's the term?—eminent domain, isn't that right? Nobody has any business monopolizing part of our national heritage! Especially not on someone else's land!"

"I'm afraid his claims have been challenged over and over," Anzani sighed. "And they've always had to be upheld—even against the *Soprintendenza dell' Etruria*, even the *Direzione Generale delle Antichità e Belle Arti*. The reason your late aunt lived in such straitened circumstances was because her father attempted to dispossess Tarchuno Vipegno's predecessor, and it virtually bankrupted him. Of course, if you have a taste for expensive lawsuits – "

Taking the phone, Carlo broke in. "How would Vipegno meet his legal bills, then?"

"Ah, Signor Bertelli. I can guess what you're thinking—it might be worth trying to exhaust his presumably limited resources, is that right? Drive him to surrender? I can only say I wouldn't advise you to try. Certainly it didn't work in the case of his father, though of course that was before my time."

"This is getting us nowhere," Ann sighed. She reclaimed the phone and promised—or rather threatened—to call again.

They had bought some wine in the village, marginally more interesting than Asti Spumante, and sat gloomily after their evening meal—the broth from the lunchtime *bollito* plus mixed broken pasta of the kind that children call *tuono e lampo*, thunder and lightning—sipping a second bottle and debating what to do. Clearly the opinion of another lawyer would be called for; Ann's contacts among Etruscan scholars offered a further line of approach; and in any case it was impossible to imagine a government department being defied by a dirty-nailed peasant.

In the end, this time having remembered to save enough wine to wash down her Pill, Ann announced her intention of turning in. Carlo, though, felt too much on edge, and preferred to sit up a while longer. Shrugging, she headed for the back door, saying that if they were going to keep this as a weekend retreat the first thing they'd have to do something about was that revolting privy.

"Want the lamp?" he called back.

On the threshold, she glanced at the sky. "No, the moon's up. It's a bit cloudy, but I can see my way."

"OK. With you in a little while."

And he delivered himself to the tantalizing contemplation of a billion-lire windfall.

Finally it dawned on him that he hadn't heard Ann come back. Puzzled, he consulted his watch. Fifteen minutes had gone by. Muzzy from the wine, he debated whether to go looking for her. She could scarcely have missed her way, but the ground behind the house was rough and she might have twisted her ankle, or caught her foot in a treeroot. Sighing, he rose, reaching for the oil-lamp and was struck by a better idea. There was a flashlight in the car. Where were the keys . . .? Ah, here in his pocket.

Duly equipped, he set out in search, calling her name softly for fear of waking Giuseppina. Swinging the beam from side to side, he caught sight of marks in the dust among the bushes Ann would have made for.

Footprints. Not his—they were too big—and certainly not hers. Besides, they were paralleled by the paw prints of a dog.

Vipegno? Surely not! But—who else?

Advancing in bafflement, he abruptly noticed something else. There was a wet patch with scuff-marks near by. The footprints leading towards it, approaching the house, were shallow. Those leading away were much deeper.

Made by someone carrying a heavy load.

Carrying Ann –?

Without thinking Carlo began to run.

He lost the prints as soon as dry grass covered the ground, but that didn't matter. He knew where he must go. Shortly, panting, he breasted the final rise overlooking Vipegno's ancient home, and only then wondered what use he could be, without so much as a stick to wield against the kidnapper's shotgun—not to mention his dog. Oh, there was no doubt he had come to the right place; light could be dimly seen in the porchway, and a moving shadow.

An armed man, a dog . . . and not even a stick. This was ridiculous! Feeling all the agony of a city dweller confronted with primitive rural violence, he cast around for something, anything, to serve as a weapon. Aided by the half-moon, veiled by scudding clouds but shedding useful light, he spotted the woodpile he had earlier noticed by the door. Perhaps there . . .

Switching off the flashlight, he stole towards it, hoping against hope he would not alert the dog. Sweat ran down his dusty face;

he felt streaks of the mixture on his skin, foul as mud. There was a branch that looked as if it might be suitable –

The ramshackle door slammed wide. With a gasp Carlo found Vipegno confronting him, Cerbero beside him with lowered head and sharp, bared teeth.

But he had no gun. Instead, he carried objects in both hands: in his right, a cudgel and a rope; in his left, two bags made of cloth.

At a gesture the dog circled around behind Carlo to cut off his retreat.

Nodding approval, his master spoke.

"You've taken a woman of our *gens*. I shall reclaim her if I can so she may bear a *zili's* heir. That was the custom of my ancestors. It has endured a hundred generations. But by ancient law you – "

Carlo finally found his tongue.

"What have you done with her?"

"Look inside," Vipegno invited, stepping back so he could approach the doorway. A guttering lamp revealed Ann slumped against one of the square pillars, her eyes closed, her shirt torn from shoulder to waist in testimony to the resistance she had put up.

How could he not have heard her screams? Thoughts of chloroform crossed his mind. He caught sight of pale cloth on the beaten-dirt floor; had that been what Vipegno used?

Then he focused on it: Ann's shorts and panties. They would have been down around her knees so she was unable to flee, then ripped from her legs on arrival . . .

He began to curse under his breath.

"Take this," Vipegno said, holding out one of the black bags. "And your chance of rescuing her with it!"

"What?"

"I said take it!"—throwing it at Carlo, who caught it by pure reflex. "Don't don it yet. First tie this rope to my wrist. I'll have to put it on Cerbero because he won't let anyone else touch him."

"I –" Carlo's mouth had already been dry. Now as it dawned on him what he was condemned to, it became like a desert.

That picture. The one Ann had explained . . .

"Move! If you don't, I'll let Cerbero attack!"

Cerbero—Cerberus. Of course. The guard-dog at the gate of hell!

Whimpering, Carlo accepted the rope and did his clumsy best to knot it tight. Then Vipegno looped it around his dog's neck.

"Take the club," he commanded, straightening. "And put on the hood."

So saying, he did the same himself, and waited, muttering what might have been a prayer, or an incantation. It was not in any language Carlo recognized.

Wild hope seized him. If the hoodwinks were indeed opaque Vipegno could no longer see him, and he would take a while to release himself from the rope. To run, reach the car, bring help—it would be too late to save Ann from what the devil had in mind for her, but . . .

"Put it on!" Vipegno rasped. "I may not be able to see you but there are plenty who can!"

*Who?*

Slowly Carlo turned around. On the slope of the hill behind him were ranged half-seen figures; he could not tell how many were men, how many women. But they numbered at least a score.

Bring help? Oh God! There wasn't going to be any help!

Of a sudden his brain was ice cold. Fixing his and the other man's relative positions as exactly as he could, he picked up the cudgel; Vipegno had let it fall while fastening the rope around Cerbero's neck. It felt reassuringly massive. Perhaps he might smash the dog's snout. Grasping it in his right hand, with his left he drew the bag over his head. At once there was an unmistakable sigh from the onlookers.

Belatedly he began to swing the club, aiming for where he recalled the dog had been—and it met air. Losing his footing and almost his balance, he cried out and tried again. This time he connected with something, but it was not the dog: Vipegno's arm, perhaps, for the blow elicited a grunt of pain. For a fatal instant he dared to remember what hope used to be like.

And the cudgel was gone, snatched from his hand.

Screaming in terror, he ripped off his hood. The dog had seized the stick in his enormous jaws. Now he dropped it and lunged, his blunt muzzle slamming into Carlo's midriff, driving the wind out of him. An instant later he was sprawling on his back with Cerbero standing over him. Drops of slaver fell on his throat, like acid.

"Hah!" Vipegno said with contempt. "When my father took Giuseppina her brother put up a better show than that! Broke the dog's foreleg before it bit his ankle to the bone. Walked with a limp until his dying day!"

He added something harsh in dialect, and Cerbero responded with a growl.

Hood discarded, he untied the rope and cast both aside. Carlo tried to follow what he was doing, but if he so much as rolled his head the dog snarled again, so he dared move only his eyes. He thought he made out that Vipegno was bringing—leading, dragging, carrying?—Ann into the open and laying her down. Some kind of mantle was spread over them, though he couldn't see by whom. There followed moans.

Vaguely he grew aware that the witnesses had descended from the hillside and were watching intently from close by. Ann had said something about the Etruscan trial by ordeal being a precursor of the Roman Games. Here was the nearest to their vicious audience he had ever dreamed might still exist in modern times . . .

And there was another dog! Beside it stood its owner—and oh God, it was the priest's, here was the priest, and no wonder Ann had thought she recognized him, for were you to shave Tarchuno's beard you'd find Father Maru's double underneath!

He moved too far, and Cerbero administered a warning nip, not even hard enough to break the skin, but fearful. He lay rock-still again, ears tortured by the loathsome sounds of glutted lust.

"You can get up now," the priest said eventually. Carlo felt as though he might never move again, but managed to, cramp-stiff in every limb.

"Has the world gone mad?" he mumbled as he forced himself upright. "The bastard's kidnapped my wife, and raped her, and you—*you*—and all these people *watched*!" Words failed him. Fists clenched, he rocked back and forth on his heels, staring towards Ann. She lay with eyes closed, her torso at least obscured by the mantle Carlo had seen being delivered to Vipegno, but her long lovely legs bare to the thighs and bruised and smeared with grime.

"It was done beneath the mantle, as is proper," said the priest. "There has been no offence."

The mere effort of standing had drained Carlo of the ability to wonder what that meant. He could think only of the pathetic broken figure on the ground.

"Help her, damn you!" he moaned.

"Mother, see to the girl," Maru commanded after a pause. Mother? Carlo jerked his head around.

Of course. Giuseppina. Who else? But she was making no move to comply. She was showing something, a bag—Ann's handbag. She was showing something from it to her son the priest. It was flat, and shiny on one side, and . . . and it was the dispenser pack holding Ann's monthly supply of the Pill.

For one wild second Carlo wanted to laugh. If the purpose of this loathsome ritual was to ensure there would be another generation of Vipegnos, this time it had misfired. Then he was snatched back to the horrors of reality.

Face darkening, Maru flung down the foil pack and ground it under his heel. "An abomination!" he rasped. "Now it will all have to be done again!"

Tarchuno was standing by the door of his home, fastening his belt, his expression indecipherable thanks to his dense beard. His brother stormed over to him and muttered in his ear. At once he tensed with rage. He strode towards Ann, cuffing aside Giuseppina and other women approaching to attend her, snatched away the mantle, and spat upon her naked belly with a curse. The sight drove Carlo over the brink. No matter what it cost, that must be avenged!

But he couldn't move. He was held tightly by his arms, and far too weak to break away.

Furious, he turned to see who gripped him, and said after a terrible pause, "You too?" He almost uttered the words in Latin. Sad-faced, slump-shouldered, this traitor, this Brutus, was Anzani.

"It's no use fighting what you're up against," he said after a pause. "They've had too much practice. The Romans couldn't stamp out this tradition, nor the Church, nor the Fascists . . . Sometimes I think the Bolsevietans aren't people any more, not as we think of people. Not individuals, I mean. More like a collective organism. At any rate they behave like one."

He seemed to be talking for the sake of talking, to distract himself.

"You wondered whether you might exhaust Tarchuno's funds by taking him to law. I told you the father of your wife's late aunt tried that and failed. I didn't tell you why. It was because they act together. He wasn't only suing one man. He was suing the whole community, and it would take a billionaire to match their resources. They've been here a long time, Signor Bertelli. When they speak of a hundred generations they're not exaggerating. Two thousand five hundred years . . . and in all that while they've never lacked a protector, a *zili*. At present they are especially strong, for as you must have realized Giuseppina bore twin boys, so they have a *maru* too."

"What"—Carlo barely recognized his own voice—"what if the child is a girl?"

"At least they no longer kill it out of hand. Now they try again with someone else. I'm afraid this won't apply to your wife. They regard her as having evaded her obligation. When her contraceptive has worn off – "

"No! No!" Wrenching himself free, Carlo seized the older man by his lapels. "It's impossible! The whole idea is crazy! They can't just imprison us here! We have jobs, friends who'll come looking for us, we have – "

"As much chance of resisting as of stopping Etna from eruption," declared the lawyer. "To my cost, I know."

Carlo dropped his hands, searching Anzani's face.

"You . . .?"

A nod. "My late wife was one of these people. I made the mistake of coming here last year with our daughter."

"But –" Carlo hesitated. What he wanted to ask seemed so terrible, he could not frame the words.

"Why has he taken your wife too, so soon after?"

"Uh . . . Yes!"

"Serafina's baby is a girl."

"They did the same to her? And you—you come here, you do their work, you . . . Oh, God. The world *has* gone mad."

"It's a very old kind of madness. So old, it may in fact be more like sanity." Anzani's face was grey in the moonlight.

"Nonsense! Rubbish!" Carlo cried. The lawyer ignored him.

"You see, they will give you a dog."

"What do you mean?"

"A dog that will make sure you don't go away."

"This grows madder by the moment!" Carlo set his fists to his temples. "I'm going to take Ann back to our car, and I'm going to drive her home, and I'm going to rout out a notary to take her sworn deposition that she was raped, and a doctor to verify there's semen in her vagina, and get it typed so it can be proved that it's not mine, and . . . Why do you keep shaking your head? They'd have to kill me to stop us!"

"Your car isn't there," Anzani said. "You don't own a car any more."

"*What*? Goddamn it! I still have the keys in my pocket! See?" He fumbled for, produced and dangled them.

"Do you think that matters to these people? No, you sold it this morning and the new owner collected it soon after you reclaimed your flashlight. By morning it will be in Yugoslavia, or on a ferry to Greece. The proceeds have been deposited in the bank account you've opened in Matignano. Your apartment in Milan is up for sale. You see, when you arrived here you fell in love with Bolsevieto and decided it was the only possible place to live. Letters confirming the fact have already been delivered to your respective employers. They may be surprised at receiving them so promptly, considering the state of the post these days, but at least they will appreciate being notified, though no doubt annoyed at losing your services with so little warning. Still, your holiday has a week to run."

"No! It's impossible!"

"I assure you it isn't. How often do I have to tell you? These people have had two and a half thousand years of practice! And the letters and other documents, including the authority to sell your apartment, will withstand the closest scrutiny. I can assure you of that, too."

"You? *You* faked them? Why, you bastard!" (An echo of Ann: "Who in his right mind trusts a lawyer?")

"Your wife seems to be recovering," Anzani said, ignoring the fist that Carlo raised before his face. "You'd better go to her."

"Not until you tell me what drove you to throw in your lot with these monsters, this spawn of hell!"

"Haven't you guessed?" the lawyer whispered. "I love my daughter. Poisoning your aunt, forging her will—the land was never hers, of course, but the Vipegnos' as it's always been—that was the only way they'd let me have her back, and my grandchild. You see what I mean about them being sane? They are dreadfully, terribly, horrifyingly sane. They obey the most pitiless kind of logic. They belong to an old world that had no room for generosity or kindness. They are what all of us might have remained had there not arisen teachers to reveal a better way . . . Go to your wife. If you can prove you love her in spite of what they've done, even their iron hearts may some day soften. I pray to that end, every morning, every night."

His voice broke as he turned away, stifling sobs.

"They did it to me as well," Giuseppina said as she sponged dirt from Ann's bruised legs. "I'm still here. And I do have two fine sons."

The reality of the trap had closed on Carlo. The Alfa had indeed disappeared. Photostats of the letters forged by Anzani had been waiting here for him to read.

"Mind you," the old woman went on—she was not truly old, he realized, just aged—"no other man would look at me after I'd born children out of wedlock. Men don't understand. The women were kinder. She's lucky: your wife, I mean. You're a modern husband. Things are different nowadays, aren't they? You hear about it, read it in newspapers and magazines. Even married women can take lovers and their husbands think it only fair. Well, so it is. They've always been used to having mistresses. They say that's how it was in the old days. The Romans insulted Etruscan women because they dined with the menfolk and drank wine in company. So they told me when I was a little girl. But they still wouldn't help me find a husband . . . It's the cruelty of the Church, you know."

Someone—perhaps her son the priest—had provided a bottle of grappa. Carlo had drunk three glasses, not before persuading Ann to sip a little, and that had helped. He thought of the contrast between Giuseppina's view of the Church and Anzani's reference to teachers and kindness. The lawyer had been wrong, totally wrong, to say these people had remained unchanged. They were obviously trying to, yet their mental armour had been breached.

Only not enough. How long would it take? Another two millennia?

Ann stirred as Giuseppina completed her work and bore away the bowl of water and the washcloth. She had shed all the tears she could; her swollen eyes were dry.

"Carlo . . .?" she whispered.

He darted to kneel at her bedside.

"Carlo, I cheated him, didn't I? I figured out what he had in mind. I remembered what Giuseppina said: Vipegnos don't marry, they take. But he didn't reckon with my being on the Pill, did he? When I realized that, I stopped fighting him off. Wouldn't you rather have me more or less in one piece? He could have beaten me unconscious, scarred me for life! He gave me some kind of drug—he had something in his palm when he put his hand over my mouth to stop me screaming, and even though I didn't swallow when he forced it in I suddenly felt weak and dreamy . . . Carlo?"

"Here!" he whispered, sliding his arm under her head.

"We'll go home in the morning, won't we? And we'll call in the police, and somebody will put a stop to all this, and the Etruscan relics will be put in a museum where they belong." She was trying to keep her eyes open, but failing, and her voice was growing fainter.

What was he to do? Tell the truth? Say, "They stole our car, Anzani is in league with them, it's no use prosecuting or suing because they've been around since before money was invented and they know more nasty tricks than the Mafia and the Camorra and Freemasons added together—and anyhow that lot were probably taught by them in the first place!"?

But Ann was asleep.

There had been a tap at the back door, and half-heard speech. Now Giuseppina reappeared. On a leash she held one of the tall lean dogs. Rising to his feet, Carlo stared in sick despair, remembering Anzani's words.

"This is Aplu," she announced. "Apollo, you would say. Great-great-grandson of Tin that watched over me and my sons. He will guard you until the child is born and nursed and old enough to live with his father and learn the knowledge he must learn. If he dies beforehand they will send another. He will sleep outside your door. Don't try and pass him. I've put a chamber pot beneath the bed. Now get what rest you can. It's been a busy night."

Carlo was too stunned to speak. As the door closed, Ann stirred a little and seemed to smile, as though hope had occurred to her in a dream. Convinced that hope was an illusion for them now,

Carlo poured more grappa and sat drinking until the oil in the lamp ran out. Dying, the flame smoked its chimney as black as the future.

And the past.

# LISA TUTTLE

## Replacements

LISA TUTTLE was born in Texas and currently lives in Scotland. Her most recent novel, *Lost Futures*, despite being marketed as horror, was short-listed for the 1993 Arthur C. Clarke Award. Her other full-length works have included *Familiar Spirit*, *Gabriel* and the award-winning collaboration with George R. R. Martin, *Windhaven*.

She also edited the acclaimed horror anthology by women, *Skin of the Soul*, and her science fiction tales have been collected in *A Spaceship Built of Stone*. However, Tuttle is best known for her disturbing stories of physical and psychological transformation and twisted desire. Some of her best horror and fantasy tales have been collected in *A Nest of Nightmares* and *Memories of the Body*. "Replacements" is a jolt of the pure stuff.

# *REPLACEMENTS*

WALKING THROUGH GREY NORTH LONDON to the tube station, feeling guilty that he hadn't let Jenny drive him to work and yet relieved to have escaped another pointless argument, Stuart Holder glanced down at a pavement covered in a leaf-fall of fast-food cartons and white paper bags and saw, amid the dog turds, beer cans and dead cigarettes, something horrible.

It was about the size of a cat, naked looking, with leathery, hairless skin and thin, spiky limbs that seemed too frail to support the bulbous, ill-proportioned body. The face, with tiny bright eyes and a wet slit of a mouth, was like an evil monkey's. It saw him and moved in a crippled, spasmodic way. Reaching up, it made a clotted, strangled noise. The sound touched a nerve, like metal between the teeth, and the sight of it, mewling and choking and scrabbling, scaly claws flexing and wriggling, made him feel sick and terrified. He had no phobias, he found insects fascinating, not frightening, and regularly removed, unharmed, the spiders, wasps and mayflies which made Jenny squeal or shudder helplessly.

But this was different. This wasn't some rare species of wingless bat escaped from a zoo, it wasn't something he would find pictured in any reference book. It was something that should not exist, a mistake, something alien. It did not belong in his world.

A little snarl escaped him and he took a step forward and brought his foot down hard.

The small, shrill scream lanced through him as he crushed it beneath his shoe and ground it into the road.

Afterwards, as he scraped the sole of his shoe against the curb to clean it, nausea overwhelmed him. He leaned over and vomited helplessly into a red-and-white-striped box of chicken bones and crumpled paper.

He straightened up, shaking, and wiped his mouth again and again with his pocket handkerchief. He wondered if anyone had seen, and had a furtive look around. Cars passed at a steady crawl. Across the road a cluster of schoolgirls dawdled near a man smoking in front of a newsagent's, but on this side of the road the fried chicken franchise and bathroom suppliers had yet to open for the day and the nearest pedestrians were more than a hundred yards away.

Until that moment, Stuart had never killed anything in his life. Mosquitoes and flies of course, other insects probably, a nest of hornets once, that was all. He had never liked the idea of hunting, never lived in the country. He remembered his father putting out poisoned bait for rats, and he remembered shying bricks at those same vermin on a bit of waste ground where he had played as a boy. But rats weren't like other animals; they elicited no sympathy. Some things had to be killed if they would not be driven away.

He made himself look to make sure the thing was not still alive. Nothing should be left to suffer. But his heel had crushed the thing's face out of recognition, and it was unmistakably dead. He felt a cool tide of relief and satisfaction, followed at once, as he walked away, by a lagging uncertainty, the imminence of guilt. Was he right to have killed it, to have acted on violent, irrational impulse? He didn't even know what it was. It might have been somebody's pet.

He went hot and cold with shame and self-disgust. At the corner he stopped with five or six others waiting to cross the road and because he didn't want to look at them he looked down.

And there it was, alive again.

He stifled a scream. No, of course it was not the same one, but another. His leg twitched; he felt frantic with the desire to kill it, and the terror of his desire. The thin wet mouth was moving as if it wanted to speak.

As the crossing-signal began its nagging blare he tore his eyes away from the creature squirming at his feet. Everyone else had started to cross the street, their eyes, like their thoughts, directed ahead. All except one. A woman in a smart business suit was standing still on the pavement, looking down, a sick fascination on her face.

As he looked at her looking at it, the idea crossed his mind that he should kill it for her, as a chivalric, protective act. But she wouldn't see it that way. She would be repulsed by his violence. He didn't want her to think he was a monster. He didn't want to be the monster who had exulted in the crunch of fragile bones, the flesh and viscera merging pulpily beneath his shoe.

He forced himself to look away, to cross the road, to spare the alien life. But he wondered, as he did so, if he had been right to spare it.

Stuart Holder worked as an editor for a publishing company with offices an easy walk from St Paul's. Jenny had worked there, too, as a secretary, when they met five years ago. Now, though, she had quite a senior position with another publishing house, south of the river, and recently they had given her a car. He had been supportive of her ambitions, supportive of her learning to drive, and proud of her on all fronts when she succeeded, yet he was aware, although he never spoke of it, that something about her success made him uneasy. One small, niggling, insecure part of himself was afraid that one day she would realize she didn't need him anymore. That was why he picked at her, and second-guessed her decisions when she was behind the wheel and he was in the passenger seat. He recognized this as he walked briskly through more crowded streets towards his office, and he told himself he would do better. He would have to. If anything drove them apart it was more likely to be his behavior than her career. He wished he had accepted her offer of a ride today. Better any amount of petty irritation between husband and wife than to be haunted by the memory of that tiny face, distorted in the death he had inflicted. Entering the building, he surreptitiously scraped the sole of his shoe against the carpet.

Upstairs two editors and one of the publicity girls were in a huddle around his secretary's desk; they turned on him the guilty-defensive faces of women who have been discussing secrets men aren't supposed to know.

He felt his own defensiveness rising to meet theirs as he smiled. "Can I get any of you chaps a cup of coffee?"

"I'm sorry, Stuart, did you want . . .?" As the others faded away, his secretary removed a stiff white paper bag with the NEXT logo printed on it from her desktop.

"Joke, Frankie, joke." He always got his own coffee because he liked the excuse to wander, and he was always having to reassure her that she was not failing in her secretarial duties. He wondered if Next sold sexy underwear, decided it would be unkind to tease her further.

He felt a strong urge to call Jenny and tell her what had happened, although he knew he wouldn't be able to explain, especially not over the phone. Just hearing her voice, the sound of sanity, would be a comfort, but he restrained himself until just after noon, when he made the call he made every day.

Her secretary told him she was in a meeting. "Tell her Stuart rang," he said, knowing she would call him back as always.

But that day she didn't. Finally, at five minutes to five, Stuart rang his wife's office and was told she had left for the day.

It was unthinkable for Jenny to leave work early, as unthinkable as for her not to return his call. He wondered if she was ill. Although he usually stayed in the office until well after six, now he shoved a manuscript in his briefcase and went out to brave the rush hour.

He wondered if she was mad at him. But Jenny didn't sulk. If she was angry she said so. They didn't lie or play those sorts of games with each other, pretending not to be in, "forgetting" to return calls.

As he emerged from his local underground station Stuart felt apprehensive. His eyes scanned the pavement and the gutters, and once or twice the flutter of paper made him jump, but of the creatures he had seen that morning there were no signs. The body of the one he had killed was gone, perhaps eaten by a passing dog, perhaps returned to whatever strange dimension had spawned it. He noticed, before he turned off the high street, that other pedestrians were also taking a keener than usual interest in the pavement and the edge of the road, and that made him feel vindicated somehow.

London traffic being what it was, he was home before Jenny. While he waited for the sound of her key in the lock he made himself a cup of tea, cursed, poured it down the sink, and had a stiff whisky instead. He had just finished it and was feeling much better when he heard the street door open.

"Oh!" The look on her face reminded him unpleasantly of those women in the office this morning, making him feel like an intruder in his own place. Now Jenny smiled, but it was too late. "I didn't expect you to be here so early."

"Nor me. I tried to call you, but they said you'd left already. I wondered if you were feeling all right."

"I'm fine!"

"You look fine." The familiar sight of her melted away his irritation. He loved the way she looked: her slender, boyish figure, her close-cropped, curly hair, her pale complexion and bright blue eyes.

Her cheeks now had a slight hectic flush. She caught her bottom lip between her teeth and gave him an assessing look before coming straight out with it. "How would you feel about keeping a pet?"

Stuart felt a horrible conviction that she was not talking about a dog or a cat. He wondered if it was the whisky on an empty stomach which made him feel dizzy.

"It was under my car. If I hadn't happened to notice something moving down there I could have run over it." She lifted her shoulders in a delicate shudder.

"Oh, God, Jenny, you haven't brought it home!"

She looked indignant. "Well, of course I did! I couldn't just leave it in the street—somebody else might have run it over."

Or stepped on it, he thought, realizing now that he could never tell Jenny what he had done. That made him feel even worse, but maybe he was wrong. Maybe it was just a cat she'd rescued. "What is it?"

She gave a strange, excited laugh. "I don't know. Something very rare, I think. Here, look." She slipped the large, woven bag off her shoulder, opening it, holding it out to him. "Look. Isn't it the sweetest thing?"

How could two people who were so close, so alike in so many ways, see something so differently? He only wanted to kill it, even now, while she had obviously fallen in love. He kept his face carefully neutral although he couldn't help flinching from her description. "*Sweet?*"

It gave him a pang to see how she pulled back, holding the bag protectively close as she said, "Well, I know it's not pretty, but so what? I thought it was horrible, too, at first sight. . . ." Her face clouded, as if she found her first impression difficult to remember, or to credit, and her voice faltered a little. "But then, then I realized how *helpless* it was. It needed me. It can't help how it looks. Anyway, doesn't it kind of remind you of the Psammead?"

"The what?"

"Psammead. You know, *The Five Children and It*?"

He recognized the title but her passion for old-fashioned children's books was something he didn't share. He shook his head impatiently. "That thing didn't come out of a book, Jen. You found it in the street and you don't know what it is or where it came from. It could be dangerous, it could be diseased."

"Dangerous," she said in a withering tone.

"You don't know."

"I've been with him all day and he hasn't hurt me, or anybody else at the office, he's perfectly happy being held, and he likes being scratched behind the ears."

He did not miss the pronoun shift. "It might have rabies."

"Don't be silly."

"Don't *you* be silly; it's not exactly native, is it? It might be carrying all sorts of foul parasites from South America or Africa or wherever."

"Now you're being racist. I'm not going to listen to you. *And* you've been drinking." She flounced out of the room.

If he'd been holding his glass still he might have thrown it. He closed his eyes and concentrated on breathing in and out slowly. This was worse than any argument they'd ever had, the only crucial disagreement of their marriage. Jenny had stronger views about many things than he did, so her wishes usually prevailed. He didn't mind that. But this was different. He wasn't having that creature in his home. He had to make her agree.

Necessity cooled his blood. He had his temper under control when his wife returned. "I'm sorry," he said, although she was the one who should have apologized. Still looking prickly, she shrugged and would not meet his eyes. "Want to go out to dinner tonight?"

She shook her head. "I'd rather not. I've got some work to do."

"Can I get you something to drink? I'm only one whisky ahead of you, honest."

Her shoulders relaxed. "I'm sorry. Low blow. Yeah, pour me one. And one for yourself." She sat down on the couch, her bag by her feet. Leaning over, reaching inside, she cooed, "Who's my little sweetheart, then?"

Normally he would have taken a seat beside her. Now, though, he eyed the pale, misshapen bundle on her lap and, after handing her a glass, retreated across the room. "Don't get mad, but isn't having a pet one of those things we discuss and agree on beforehand?"

He saw the tension come back into her shoulders, but she went on stroking the thing, keeping herself calm. "Normally, yes. But this is special. I didn't plan it. It happened, and now I've got a responsibility to him. Or her." She giggled. "We don't even know what sex you are, do we, my precious?"

He said carefully, "I can see that you had to do something when you found it, but keeping it might not be the best thing."

"I'm not going to put it out in the street."

"No, no, but . . . don't you think it would make sense to let a professional have a look at it? Take it to a vet, get it checked out . . . maybe it needs shots or something."

She gave him a withering look and for a moment he faltered, but then he rallied. "Come on, Jenny, be reasonable! You can't just drag some strange animal in off the street and keep it, just like that. You don't even know what it eats."

"I gave it some fruit at lunch. It ate that. Well, it sucked out the juice. I don't think it can chew."

"But you don't know, do you? Maybe the fruit juice was just an aperitif, maybe it needs half its weight in live insects every day, or a couple of small, live mammals. Do you really think you could cope with feeding it mice or rabbits fresh from the pet shop every week?"

"Oh, Stuart."

"Well? Will you just take it to a vet? Make sure it's healthy? Will you do that much?"

"And then I can keep it? If the vet says there's nothing wrong with it, and it doesn't need to eat anything too impossible?"

"Then we can talk about it. Hey, don't pout at me; I'm not your father, I'm not telling you what to do. We're partners, and partners don't make unilateral decisions about things that affect them both; partners discuss things and reach compromises and . . ."

"There can't be any compromise about this."

He felt as if she'd doused him with ice water. "What?"

"Either I win and I keep him or you win and I give him up. Where's the compromise?"

This was why wars were fought, thought Stuart, but he didn't say it. He was the picture of sweet reason, explaining as if he meant it, "The compromise is that we each try to see the other person's point. You get the animal checked out, make sure it's healthy and I, I'll keep an open mind about having a pet, and see if I might start liking . . . him. Does he have a name yet?"

Her eyes flickered. "No . . . we can choose one later, together. If we keep him."

He still felt cold and, although he could think of no reason for it, he was certain she was lying to him.

In bed that night as he groped for sleep Stuart kept seeing the tiny, hideous face of the thing screaming as his foot came down on it. That moment of blind, killing rage was not like him. He couldn't deny he had done it, or how he had felt, but now, as Jenny slept innocently beside him, as the creature she had rescued, a twin to his victim, crouched alive in the bathroom, he tried to remember it differently.

In fantasy, he stopped his foot, he controlled his rage and, staring at the memory of the alien animal, he struggled to see past his anger and his fear, to see through those fiercer masculine emotions and find his way to Jenny's feminine pity. Maybe his intuition had been wrong and hers was right. Maybe, if he had waited a little longer, instead of lashing out, he would have seen how unnecessary his fear was.

Poor little thing, poor little thing. It's helpless, it needs me, it's harmless so I won't harm it.

Slowly, in imagination, he worked towards that feeling, *her* feeling, and then, suddenly, he was there, through the anger, through the fear, through the hate to . . . not love, he couldn't say that, but compassion. Glowing and warm, compassion filled his heart and flooded his veins, melting the ice there and washing him out into the sea of sleep, and dreams where Jenny smiled and loved him and there was no space between them for misunderstanding.

He woke in the middle of the night with a desperate urge to pee. He was out of bed in the dark hallway when he remembered what was waiting in the bathroom. He couldn't go back to bed with the need unsatisfied, but he stood outside the bathroom door, hand hovering over the light switch on this side, afraid to turn it on, open the door, go in.

It wasn't, he realized, that he was afraid of a creature no bigger than a football and less likely to hurt him; rather, he was afraid that he might hurt it. It was a stronger variant of that reckless vertigo he had felt sometimes in high places, the fear, not of falling, but of throwing oneself off, of losing control and giving in to self-destructive urges. He didn't *want* to kill the thing—had his own feelings not undergone a sea change, Jenny's love for it would have been enough to stop him—but something, some dark urge stronger than himself, might make him.

Finally he went down to the end of the hall and outside to the weedy, muddy little area which passed for the communal front garden and in which the rubbish bins, of necessity, were kept, and, shivering in his thin cotton pajamas in the damp, chilly air, he watered the sickly forsythia, or whatever it was, that Jenny had planted so optimistically last winter.

When he went back inside, more uncomfortable than when he had gone out, he saw the light was on in the bathroom, and as he approached the half-open door, he heard Jenny's voice, low and soothing. "There, there. Nobody's going to hurt you, I promise. You're safe here. Go to sleep now. Go to sleep."

He went past without pausing, knowing he would be viewed as an intruder, and got back into bed. He fell asleep, lulled by the meaningless murmur of her voice, still waiting for her to join him.

Stuart was not used to doubting Jenny, but when she told him she had visited a veterinarian who had given her new pet a clean bill of health, he did not believe her.

In a neutral tone he asked, "Did he say what kind of animal it was?"

"He didn't know."

"He didn't know what it was, but he was sure it was perfectly healthy."

"God, Stuart, what do you want? It's obvious to everybody but you that my little friend is healthy and happy. What do you want, a birth certificate?"

He looked at her "friend," held close against her side, looking squashed and miserable. "What do you mean, 'everybody'?"

She shrugged. "Everybody at work. They're all jealous as anything." She planted a kiss on the thing's pointy head. Then she looked at him, and he realized that she had not kissed him, as she usually did, when he came in. She'd been clutching that thing the whole time. "I'm going to keep him," she said quietly. "If you don't like it, then . . ." Her pause seemed to pile up in solid, transparent blocks between them. "Then, I'm sorry, but that's how it is."

So much for an equal relationship, he thought. So much for sharing. Mortally wounded, he decided to pretend it hadn't happened.

"Want to go out for Indian tonight?"

She shook her head, turning away. "I want to stay in. There's something on telly. You go on. You could bring me something back, if you wouldn't mind. A spinach bahjee and a couple of nans would do me."

"And what about . . . something for your little friend?"

She smiled a private smile. "He's all right. I've fed him already." Then she raised her eyes to his and acknowledged his effort. "Thanks."

He went out and got take-away for them both, and stopped at the off-license for the Mexican beer Jenny favored. A radio in the off-license was playing a sentimental song about love that Stuart remembered from his earliest childhood: his mother used to sing it. He was shocked to realize he had tears in his eyes.

That night Jenny made up the sofa bed in the spare room, explaining, "He can't stay in the bathroom; it's just not satisfactory, you know it's not."

"He needs the bed?"

"I do. He's confused, everything is new and different, I'm the one thing he can count on. I have to stay with him. He needs me."

"He needs you? What about me?"

"Oh, Stuart," she said impatiently. "You're a grown man. You can sleep by yourself for a night or two."

"And that thing can't?"

"Don't call him a thing."

"What am I supposed to call it? Look, you're not its mother—it doesn't need you as much as you'd like to think. It was perfectly all right in the bathroom last night—it'll be fine in here on its own."

"Oh? And what do you know about it? You'd like to kill him, wouldn't you? Admit it."

"No," he said, terrified that she had guessed the truth. If she knew how he had killed one of those things she would never forgive him. "It's not true, I don't—I couldn't hurt it any more than I could hurt you."

Her face softened. She believed him. It didn't matter how he felt about the creature. Hurting it, knowing how she felt, would be like committing an act of violence against her, and they both knew he wouldn't do that. "Just for a few nights, Stuart. Just until he settles in."

He had to accept that. All he could do was hang on, hope that she still loved him and that this wouldn't be forever.

The days passed. Jenny no longer offered to drive him to work. When he asked her, she said it was out of her way and with traffic so bad a detour would make her late. She said it was silly to take him the short distance to the station, especially as there was nowhere she could safely stop to let him out, and anyway the walk would do him good. They were all good reasons, which he had used in the old days himself, but her excuses struck him painfully when he remembered how eager she had once been for his company, how ready to make any detour for his sake. Her new pet accompanied her everywhere, even to work, snug in the little nest she had made for it in a woven carrier bag.

"Of course things are different now. But I haven't stopped loving you," she said when he tried to talk to her about the breakdown of their marriage. "It's not like I've found another man. This is something completely different. It doesn't threaten you; you're still my husband."

But it was obvious to him that a husband was no longer something she particularly valued. He began to have fantasies about killing it. Not, this time, in a blind rage, but as part of a carefully thought-out plan. He might poison it, or spirit it away somehow and pretend it had run away. Once it was gone he hoped Jenny would forget it and be his again.

But he never had a chance. Jenny was quite obsessive about the thing, as if it were too valuable to be left unguarded for a single minute. Even when she took a bath, or went to the toilet, the creature was with her, behind the locked door of the bathroom. When he offered to look after it for her for a few minutes she just smiled, as if the idea was manifestly ridiculous, and he didn't dare insist.

So he went to work, and went out for drinks with colleagues, and spent what time he could with Jenny, although they were never alone. He didn't argue with her, although he wasn't above trying to move her to pity if he could. He made seemingly casual comments designed to convince her of his change of heart so that eventually, weeks or months from now, she would trust him and leave the creature with him—and then, later, perhaps, they could put their marriage back together.

One afternoon, after an extended lunch break, Stuart returned to the office to find one of the senior editors crouched on the floor beside his secretary's empty desk, whispering and chuckling to herself.

He cleared his throat nervously. "Linda?"

She lurched back on her heels and got up awkwardly. She blushed and ducked her head as she turned, looking very unlike her usual high-powered self. "Oh, uh, Stuart, I was just – "

Frankie came in with a pile of photocopying. "Uhhuh," she said loudly.

Linda's face got even redder. "Just going," she mumbled, and fled.

Before he could ask, Stuart saw the creature, another crippled bat-without-wings, on the floor beside the open bottom drawer of Frankie's desk. It looked up at him, opened its slit of a mouth and gave a sad little hiss. Around one matchstick-thin leg it wore a fine golden chain which was fastened at the other end to the drawer.

"Some people would steal anything that's not chained down," said Frankie darkly. "People you wouldn't suspect."

He stared at her, letting her see his disapproval, his annoyance, disgust, even. "Animals in the office aren't part of the contract, Frankie."

"It's not an animal."

"What is it, then?"

"I don't know. You tell me."

"It doesn't matter what it is, you can't have it here."

"I can't leave it at home."

"Why not?"

She turned away from him, busying herself with her stacks of paper. "I can't leave it alone. It might get hurt. It might escape."

"Chance would be a fine thing."

She shot him a look, and he was certain she knew he wasn't talking about *her* pet. He said, "What does your boyfriend think about it?"

"I don't have a boyfriend." She sounded angry but then, abruptly, the anger dissipated, and she smirked. "I don't have to have one, do I?"

"You can't have that animal here. Whatever it is. You'll have to take it home."

She raised her fuzzy eyebrows. "Right now?"

He was tempted to say yes, but thought of the manuscripts that wouldn't be sent out, the letters that wouldn't be typed, the delays and confusions, and he sighed. "Just don't bring it back again. All right?"

"Yowza."

He felt very tired. He could tell her what to do but she would no more obey than would his wife. She would bring it back the next day and keep bringing it back, maybe keeping it hidden, maybe not, until he either gave in or was forced into firing her. He went into his office closed the door, and put his head down on his desk.

That evening he walked in on his wife feeding the creature with her blood.

It was immediately obvious that it was that way round. The creature might be a vampire—it obviously was—but his wife was no helpless victim. She was wide awake and in control, holding the creature firmly, letting it feed from a vein in her arm.

She flinched as if anticipating a shout, but he couldn't speak. He watched what was happening without attempting to interfere and gradually she relaxed again, as if he wasn't there.

When the creature, sated, fell off, she kept it cradled on her lap and reached with her other hand for the surgical spirit and cotton wool on the table, moistened a piece of cotton wool and tamped it to the tiny wound. Then, finally, she met her husband's eyes.

"He has to eat," she said reasonably. "He can't chew. He needs blood. Not very much, but . . ."

"And he needs it from you? You can't . . .?"

"I can't hold down some poor scared rabbit or dog for him, no." She made a shuddering face. "Well, really, think about it. You know how squeamish I am. This is so much easier. It doesn't hurt."

It hurts me, he thought, but couldn't say it. "Jenny . . ."

"Oh, don't start," she said crossly. "I'm not going to get any disease from it, and he doesn't take enough to make any difference. Actually, I like it. We both do."

"Jenny, please don't. Please. For me. Give it up."

"No." She held the scraggy, ugly thing close and gazed at Stuart like a dispassionate executioner. "I'm sorry, Stuart, I really am, but this is nonnegotiable. If you can't accept that you'd better leave."

This was the showdown he had been avoiding, the end of it all. He tried to rally his arguments and then he realized he had none. She had said it. She had made her choice, and it was nonnegotiable. And he realized, looking at her now, that although she reminded him of the woman he loved, he didn't want to live with what she had become.

He could have refused to leave. After all, he had done nothing wrong. Why should he give up his home, this flat which was half his? But he could not force Jenny out onto the streets with nowhere to go; he still felt responsible for her.

"I'll pack a bag, and make a few phone calls," he said quietly. He knew someone from work who was looking for a lodger, and if all else failed, his brother had a spare room. Already, in his thoughts, he had left.

He ended up, once they'd sorted out their finances and formally separated, in a flat just off the Holloway Road, near Archway. It was not too far to walk if Jenny cared to visit, which she never did. Sometimes he called on her, but it was painful to feel himself an unwelcome visitor in the home they once had shared.

He never had to fire Frankie; she handed in her notice a week later, telling him she'd been offered an editorial job at The Women's Press. He wondered if pets in the office were part of the contract over there.

He never learned if the creatures had names. He never knew where they had come from, or how many there were. Had they fallen only in Islington? (Frankie had a flat somewhere off Upper Street.) He never saw anything on the news about them, or read any official confirmation of their existence, but he was aware of occasional oblique references to them in other contexts, occasional glimpses.

One evening, coming home on the tube, he found himself looking at the woman sitting opposite. She was about his own age, probably in her early thirties, with strawberry blond hair, greenish eyes, and an almost translucent complexion. She was strikingly dressed in high, soft-leather boots, a long black woolen skirt, and an enveloping cashmere cloak of cranberry red. High on the cloak, below and to the right of the fastening at the neck, was a simple, gold circle brooch. Attached to it he noticed a very fine golden chain which vanished inside the cloak, like the end of a watch fob.

He looked at it idly, certain he had seen something like it before, on other women, knowing it reminded him of something. The train arrived at Archway, and as he rose to leave the train, so did the attractive woman. Her stride matched his. They might well leave the station together. He tried to think of something to say to her, some pretext for striking up a conversation. He was after all a single man again now, and she might be a single woman. He had forgotten how single people in London contrived to meet.

He looked at her again, sidelong, hoping she would turn her head and look at him. With one slender hand she toyed with her gold chain. Her cloak fell open slightly as she walked, and he caught a glimpse of the creature she carried beneath it, close to her body, attached by a slender golden chain.

He stopped walking and let her get away from him. He had to rest for a little while before he felt able to climb the stairs to the street.

By then he was wondering if he had really seen what he thought he had seen. The glimpse had been so brief. But he had been deeply shaken by what he saw or imagined, and he turned the wrong way outside the station. When he finally realized, he was at the corner of Jenny's road, which had once also been his. Rather than retrace his steps, he decided to take the turning and walk past her house.

Lights were on in the front room, the curtains drawn against the early winter dark. His footsteps slowed as he drew nearer. He felt such a longing to be inside, back home, belonging. He wondered if she would be pleased at all to see him. He wondered if she ever felt lonely, as he did.

Then he saw the tiny, dark figure between the curtains and the window. It was spread-eagled against the glass, scrabbling uselessly; inside, longing to be out.

As he stared, feeling its pain as his own, the curtains swayed and opened slightly as a human figure moved between them. He saw the woman reach out and pull the creature away from the glass, back into the warm, lighted room with her, and the curtains fell again, shutting him out.

# GRAHAM JOYCE

## Under the Pylon

GRAHAM JOYCE was born in 1954. After attending teacher training college in Derby, he won the George Fraser Poetry Award while taking an MA at Leicester University. He had a variety of jobs—fitter's mate, kitchen porter, bingo-caller, holiday camp attendant, fruit picker, supply teacher—before becoming a development officer for the National Association of Youth Clubs.

He quit in 1988 and went to live on the Greek island of Lesbos to concentrate on his writing. His first novel, *Dreamside*, was published to critical acclaim by Pan Books in 1991. Since then, two more books have appeared from Headline, *Dark Sister* and *House of Lost Dreams*.

Although his stories have been published in *Dark Voices 5: The Pan Book of Horror, In Dreams, Darklands 2* and *Interzone*, he has hardly been prolific in this area. It's quality not quantity that we may expect from him, as "Under the Pylon" shows.

AFTER SCHOOL OR DURING THE LONG summer holidays we used to meet down by the electricity pylon. Though we never went there when the weather was wet because obviously there was no cover. Apart from that the wet power lines would vibrate and hum and throb and it would be . . . well, I'm not saying I was scared but it would give you a bad feeling.

Wet or dry, we'd all been told not to play under the pylon. Our folks had lectured us time and again to keep away; and an Electricity Board disc fixed about nine feet up on the thing spelled out DANGER in red and white lettering. Two lightning shocks either side of the word set it in zigzag speech marks.

"Danger!"

I imagined the voice of the pylon would sound like a robot's speech-box from a science-fiction film, because that's what the pylon looked like, a colossal robot. Four skeletal steel legs straddled the ground, tapering up to a pointed head nudging the clouds. The struts bearing the massive power cables reached over like arms, adding a note of severity and anthropomorphism to the thing. Like someone standing with their hands on their hips. The power cables themselves drooped slightly until picked up by the next giant robot in the field beyond, and then to the next. Marching into the infinite distance, an army of obstinate robots.

But the pylon was situated on a large patch of waste ground between the houses, and when it came down to it, there was nowhere else for us kids to go. It was a green and overgrown little escape-hatch from suburbia. It smelled of wild grass and giant stalks of cow parsley, and of nettles and foxgloves and dumped housebricks. You could bash down a section to make a lair hidden from everything but the butterflies. Anyway, it wasn't the danger of electricity giving rise to any nervousness under the pylon. It was something else. Old Mrs Nantwich called it a shadow.

Joy Astley was eleven, and already wearing lipstick and make-up you could have peeled off like a mask. Her parents had big mouths and were always bawling. "The Nantwiches," she said airily, "could only afford to buy this house because it's under the pylon. No one wants a house under the pylon."

"Why not?" said Clive Mann. It was all he ever said. Clive had a metal brace across his teeth, and even though he was odd and stared at things a lot, people mostly bothered to answer him. "Why?"

"Because you don't," said Joy, "that's why."

Tania Brown was in my class at school (she used to pronounce her name Tarnia because of the sunshine jokes) and agreed with Joy. Kev Duffy burped and said, "Crap!" It was Kev's word for the month. He would use it repeatedly up until the end of August.

Joy just looked at Kev and wiggled her head from side to side, as if that somehow answered his remark.

The Nantwiches Joy was being so snobbish about were retired barge people. Why anyone would want to rub two pennies together I've never understood, but they were always described as looking as though they couldn't accomplish this dubious feat; and then in the same breath people would always add "yet they're the people who have got it". I doubted it somehow. They'd lived a hard life transporting coal on the barges, and it showed. Their faces had more channels and ruts and canals than the waterways of the Grand Union.

"They're illiterate," Joy always pointed out whenever they were mentioned. And then she'd add, "Can't read or write."

The Nantwiches' house did indeed stand under the shadow of the giant pylon. Mr Nantwich was one of those old guys with a red face and white hair, forever forking over the earth in his backyard. Their garden backed up to the pylon. A creosoted wooden fence closed off one side of the square defined by the structure's four legs. One day when I was there alone old Mrs Nantwich had scared me by popping her head over the fence and saying, "You don't wanna play there."

Her face looked as old as a church gate. Fine white bristles sprouted from her chin. Her hair was always drawn back under a headscarf, and she wore spectacles with plastic frames and lenses like magnifying glasses. They made her eyes huge.

"Why?" I'd croaked.

She threw her head back slowly and pointed her chin towards the top of the pylon. Then she looked at me and did it again. "There's a *shadow* orf of it."

I felt embarrassed as she stared, waiting for me to say something. "What do you mean?"

Before she answered, another head popped alongside her own. It was her daughter Olive. Olive looked as old as her mother. She had wild, iron-grey hair. Her teeth were terribly blackened and crooked. The thing about Olive was she never uttered a word. She hadn't spoken, according to my mother, since a man had "jumped out at her from behind a bush". I didn't see how that could make someone dumb for the rest of their life, but then I didn't understand what my mother meant by that deceptively careful phrase either.

"Wasn't me," said Mrs Nantwich a little fiercely, "as decided to come 'ere." And then her head disappeared back behind the fence, leaving Olive to stare beadily at me as if I'd done something wrong. Then her head too popped out of sight.

I looked up at the wires and they seemed to hum with spiteful merriment.

Another day I came across Clive Mann, crouched under the pylon, and listening. At that time, the three sides of the pylon had been closed off. We'd found some rusty corrugated sheeting to lean against one end, and a few lengths of torn curtain to screen off another. The third side, running up to the Nantwiches' creosoted fence, was shielded by an impenetrable jungle of five-foot-high stinging nettles.

It had been raining, and the curtains sagged badly. I ducked through the gap between them to find Clive crouched and staring directly up into the tower of the pylon. He said nothing.

"What are you doing?"

"You can hear," he said. "You can hear what they're saying."

I looked up and listened. The lines always made an eerie hissing after rain, but there was no other sound.

"Hear what?"

"No! The people. On the telephones. Mrs Astley is talking to the landlord of the Dog and Trumpet. He's knocking her off."

I looked up again and listened. I knew he wasn't joking because Clive had no sense of humour. He just stared at things. I was about to protest that the cables were power lines, not telephone wires, when the curtains parted and Joy Astley came in.

"What are you two doing?"

We didn't answer.

"My Dad says these curtains and things have got to come down," said Joy.

"Why?"

"He says he doesn't like the idea."

"What's it got to do with him?"

"He thinks," Joy said, closing her eyes, "things go on here."

"You mean he's worried about what his angelic daughter gets up to," I said.

Joy turned around, flicked up her skirt and wiggled her bottom at us. It was a gesture too familiar to be of any interest. At least that day she was wearing panties.

I had to pass by the Dog and Trumpet as I walked home later that afternoon. I noticed Mrs Astley going in by the back door, which was odd because the pub was closed in the afternoon. But I thought little of it at the time.

Just as we were accustomed to Joy flashing her bottom at us, so were we well inured to the vague parental unease about us playing under the pylon. None of our parents ever defined the exact nature of their anxieties. They would mention things about *electricity* and *generators*, but these didn't add up to much more than old Mrs Nantwich's dark mutterings about a *shadow*. I got my physics and my science all mixed up as usual, and managed to infect the rest of the group with my store of misapprehensions.

"Radiation," I announced. "The reason they're scared is because if there was an accidental power surge feedback . . ." (I was improvising like mad) ". . . then we'd all get *radiated*."

Radiated. It was a great word. Radiated. It got everyone going.

"There was a woman in the newspaper," said Joy. "Her microwave oven went wrong and she was *radiated*. Her bones all turned to jelly."

Tania could cap that. "There was one on television. A woman. She gave birth to a cow with two heads. After being *radiated*." The girls were always better at horror stories.

Kev Duffy said, "Crap!" Then he looked up into the pyramid of the tower and said, "What's the chances of it happening?"

"Eighteen hundred to one," I said. With that talent for tossing out utterly bogus statistics I should have gone on to become a politician.

Then they were all looking up, and in the silence you could hear the abacus beads whizzing and clacking in their brains.

Joy's parents needn't have worried. Not much went on behind the pylon screens of which they could disapprove. Well, that's not entirely true, since one or two efforts were made seriously to misbehave, but they never amounted to much. Communal cigarettes were sucked down to their filters, bottles of cider were shared round. Clive and I once tried sniffing Airfix but it made us sick as dogs and we were never attracted to the idea again. We once persuaded Joy to take off her clothes for a dare, which she did; but then she immediately put them back on again, so it all seemed a bit pointless and no more erotic than the episode of solvent abuse.

It was the last summer holiday before we were due to be dispatched to what we all called the Big Schools. It all depended on which side of the waste ground you lived. Joy and Kev were to go to President Kennedy, where you didn't have to wear a school uniform; Clive and I were off to Cardinal Wiseman, where you did. It all seemed so unfair. Tania was being sent to some snooty private school where they wore straw hats in the summer. She hated the idea, but her father was what my old man called one of the nobs.

Once, Tania and I were on our own under the pylon. Tania had long blond hair, and was pretty in a willowy sort of way. Her green eyes always seemed wide open with amazement at the things we'd talk about or at what we'd get up to. She spoke quietly in her rather posh accent, and for some reason she always seemed desperately grateful that we didn't exclude her from our activities.

Out of the blue she asked me if I'd ever kissed a girl.

"Loads," I lied. "Why?"

"I've never kissed anyone. And now I'm going to a girls' school I'll probably never get the chance."

We sat on an old door elevated from the grass by a few housebricks. I looked away. The seconds thrummed by. I imagined I heard the wires overhead going *chock chock chock*.

"Would you like to?" she said softly.

"Like to what?"

"To kiss me?"

I shrugged. "If you want." My muscles went as stiff as the board on which we perched.

She moved closer, put her head at an angle and closed her eyes. I looked at her thin lips, leaned over and rested my mouth against hers. We stayed like that for some time, stock-still. The power lines overhead vibrated with noisy impatience. Eventually she opened her eyes and pulled back, blinking at me and licking her lips. I realised my hands were clenched to the side of the board as if it had been a magic carpet hurtling across the sky.

So Tania and I were "going out". Our kissing improved slightly, and we got a lot of ribbing from the others, but beyond that, nothing had changed. Because I was going out with Tania, Kev Duffy was considered to be "going out" with Joy, at least nominally; though to be fair to him, he was elected to this position only because Clive was beyond the pale. Kev resented this status as something of an imposition, though he did go along with the occasional bout of simulated kissing. But when Joy appeared one day sporting livid, gash-crimson lipstick and calling him "darling" at every turn, he got mad and smudged the stuff all round her face with the ball of his hand. The others pretended not to notice, but I could see she was hurt by it.

Another time I'd been reading something about hypnotism, and Joy decided she wanted to be hypnotised. I'd decided I had a talent for this, so I sat her on the grass inside the pylon while the other three watched. I did all that "you're feeling very relaxed" stuff and she went under easily; too easily. Then I didn't know what to ask her to do. There was no point asking her to take her clothes off, since she hardly needed prompting to do that.

"Get 'er to run around like a 'eadless chicken," was Kev's inspirational idea.

"Tell 'er to describe life on Jupiter," Clive said obscurely.

"Ask her to go back to a past life," said Tania.

That seemed the most intelligent suggestion, so I offered a few cliched phrases and took her back, back into the mists of time. I was about to ask her what she could see when I felt a thrum of energy. It distracted me for a moment, and I looked up into the apex of the pylon. There was nothing to see, but I remembered I'd felt it before. Once, when I'd first kissed Tania.

When I looked back, there were tears streaming down Joy's face. She was trembling and sobbing in silence.

"Bring her out of it," said Tania.

"Why?" Clive protested.

"Yer," said Kev. "Better stop it now."

I couldn't. I did all that finger clicking rubbish and barked various commands. But she just sat there shaking and sobbing. I was terrified. Tania took hold of her hands and, thankfully, after a while Joy just seemed to come out of it on her own. She was none the worse for the experience, and laughed it off; but she wouldn't tell us what she saw.

They all had a go. Kev wouldn't take it seriously, however, and insisted on staggering around like a stage drunk. Clive claimed to have gone under but we all agreed we couldn't tell the difference.

Finally it was Tania's turn. She was afraid, but Joy dared her. Tania made me promise not to make her experience a past life. I'd read enough about hypnotism to know you can't make people do anything they don't already want to do, but convincing folk of that is another thing. Tania had been frightened by what happened to Joy, so I had to swear on my grandmother's soul and hope to be struck by lightning and so on before she'd let me do it.

Tania went under with equal ease, a feat I've never been able to accomplish since.

"What are you going to get her to do?" Joy wanted to know.

"Pretend to ride a bike?" I suggested lamely.

"Crap," said Kev. "Tell her she's the sexiest woman in the world and she wants to make mad passionate love to you."

Naturally Joy thought this was a good idea, so I put it to Tania. She opened her eyes in a way that made me think she'd just been stringing us along. She smiled at me serenely and shook her head. Then there was a thrum of electrical activity from the wires overhead. I looked up and before I knew what was happening, Tania had jumped on me and locked her legs behind my back. I staggered and fell backwards on to the grass. Tania had her tongue halfway down my throat. I'd heard of French kissing, but it had never appealed. Joy and Kev were laughing and cheering her on.

Tania came up for air, and she was making a weird growling from the back of her throat. Then she power-kissed me again.

"This is great!" whooped Kev.

"Hey!" went Clive. "Hey!"

"Tiger tiger!" shouted Joy.

I was still pinned under Tania's knees when she sat up and stripped off her white T-shirt in one deft move.

"Bloody hell!" Kev couldn't believe it any more than I could. "This is brilliant!"

"Gerrem off!" screamed Joy.

Tania stood up quickly and hooked her thumbs inside the waist of her denims and her panties, slipping them off. Before I'd had time to blink she was naked. She was breathing hard. Then she was fumbling at my jeans.

"Bloody fucking hell!" Joy shouted. "Bloody fucking hell!"

The lines overhead thrummed again. Tania had twice my strength. I had this crazy idea she was drawing it from the pylon. She had my pants halfway down my legs.

Then everything was interrupted by a high-pitched screaming.

At first I thought it was Tania, but it was coming from behind her. The screaming brought Tania to her senses. It was Olive, the Nantwiches' deranged daughter. Her head had appeared over the fence and she was screaming and pointing at something. What she pointed at was my semi-erect penis; half-erect from Tania's brutal stimulation; half-flaccid from terror at her ferocious strength.

Olive continued to point and shriek. Then she was joined at the fence by Mrs Nantwich. "Filthy buggers," said the old woman. "Get on with yer! Filthy buggers!"

A third head appeared. Red-faced Mr Nantwich. He was just laughing. "Look at that!" he shouted. "Look at that!"

Tania wasn't laughing. She looked at me with disgust. "Bastard," she spat, climbing quickly back into her clothes. "Bastard!"

I ran after her. "You can't make anyone do what they don't want to," I tried. She shrugged me off tearfully. I let her go.

"Filthy buggers!" Mrs Nantwich muttered.

"You can't make anyone!" I screamed at her.

"Look at that!" laughed Joe Nantwich.

Olive was still shrieking. The power lines were still throbbing. Clive was trying to tell me something, but I wasn't listening. "It wasn't you," he was saying. He was pointing up at the pylon. "It were *that*."

I never spoke another word to Tania, and she never came near the pylon again. I was terrified the story would get back to my folks. I didn't see why exactly, but I had the feeling I'd reap all the blame.

But a few days later something happened which overshadowed the entire incident.

And it happened to Clive.

One afternoon he and I had been sharing a bottle of Woodpecker. He'd been *listening* again.

"Old man Astley's found out."

"Eh? How do you know?"

He looked up at the overhead wires. "She's been on the phone to the Dog and Trumpet."

He was always reporting what he'd "heard" on the wires. We all knew he was completely cracked, but it was best to ignore him. I changed the subject. I started regaling him with some nonsense I'd heard about a burglar's fingers bitten clean off by an Alsatian, when Clive took it into his head to start climbing the pylon. I didn't think it was a sensible thing to do but it was pointless saying anything.

"Not a good idea, that."

"Why?"

Climbing the pylon wasn't easy. The inspection ladder didn't start until a height of nine feet—obviously with schoolboys in mind—but that didn't stop Clive. He lifted the door we used as a bench and leaned it against the struts of one of the pylon's legs. Climbing on the struts, he pulled himself to the top of the door, and standing on its top edge he was able to haul himself up to the inspection ladder. He ascended a few rungs and seemed happy to hang there for a while. I got bored watching him.

It was late afternoon and the sky had gone a dark, cobalt shade of blue. I finished off the cider, unzipped my trousers and stuck my dick outside the curtains to empty my bladder. A kind of spasm shot through me before I'd finished, stronger even than those I'd felt before. I ignored it. "So the burglar," I was telling Clive, "knew the key was on a string inside the letter box. So when the owners came home they got into the hallway and found," I finished pissing, zipped up and turned to complete the story. But my words tailed off, "two fingers still holding the string . . ."

I looked up the inspection ladder to the top of the pylon. I looked at the grey metal struts. I looked everywhere. Clive had vanished.

"Clive?"

I checked all around. Then I went outside. I thought he might have jumped down, or fallen. He wasn't there. I went back inside. Then I went outside again.

Spots of rain started to appear. I looked up at the wires and they seemed to hum contentedly. I waited for a while until the rain came more heavily, and went home.

That night while I was lying in bed, I heard the telephone ring. I knew what time it was because I could hear the television signature blaring from the lounge. It was the end of the late night news. Then my mother came upstairs. Had I seen Clive? His mother had phoned. She was worried.

The next day I was interviewed by a policewoman. I explained we were playing under the pylon, I turned my back and he'd disappeared. She made a note and left.

A few days later the police were out like blackberries in September. Half the neighbourhood joined in the fine-toothcomb search of the waste ground and the nearby fields. They found nothing. Not a hair from his head.

While the searches went on, I started to have a recurring nightmare. I'd be back under the pylon, pissing and happily talking away to Clive. Only it wasn't urine coming out, it was painful fat blue and white sparks of electricity. I'd turn to Clive in surprise, who would be descending the inspection ladder wearing fluorescent blue overalls, his face out of view. And his entire body would be rippling with eels of electricity, gold sparks arcing wildly. Then slowly his head would begin to rotate towards me and I'd start screaming; but before I ever got to see his awful face I'd wake up.

We stopped playing under the pylon after that. No one had to say anything, we just stopped going there. I did go back once, to satisfy my own curiosity. The screens had been ripped away in the failed search, but the nettles bashed down by the police were already springing up again.

I looked up into the tower of the pylon, and although there was nothing to see, I felt a terrible sense of dread. Then a face appeared over the Nantwiches' fence. It was Olive. She'd seen me looking.

"Gone," she said. It was the only word I ever heard her say. "Gone."

Summer came to an end and we went off to our respective schools. I saw Tania once or twice in her straw boater, but she passed me with her nose in the air. Eventually she married a Tory MP. I often wonder if she's happy.

Inevitably Kev and I stopped hanging around together, but not before there was a murder in the district. The landlord of the Dog and Trumpet was stabbed to death. They never found who did it. Joy moved out of the area when her parents split up. She went to live with her mother.

Joy went on to become a rock and roll singer. A star. Well, not a star exactly, but I did once see her on *Top of the Pops*. She had a kind of trade mark, turning her back on the cameras to wiggle her bottom. I felt pleased for her that she'd managed to put the habit to good use.

Just occasionally I bump into Kev in this pub or that but we never really know what to say to each other. After a while Kev always says, "Do you remember the time you hypnotised Tania Brown and . . ." and I always say "Yes" before he gets to the end of the story. Then we look at the floor for a while until one of us says, "Anyway, good to see you, all the best." It's that *anyway* that gets me.

Clive Mann is never mentioned.

Occasionally I make myself walk past the old place. A new group of kids has started playing there, including Kev Duffy's oldest girl. Yesterday as I passed by that way there were no children around because an Electricity Board operative was servicing the pylon. He was halfway up the inspection ladder, and he wore blue overalls exactly like Clive in my dream. It stopped me with a jolt. I had to stare, even though I could sense the man's irritation at being watched.

Then came that singular, familiar thrum of energy. The maintenance man let his arm drop and turned to face me, challenging me to go away. But I was transfixed. Because it was Clive's face I saw in that man's body. He smiled at me, but tiny white sparks of electricity were leaking from his eyes like tears. Then he made to speak, but all I heard or saw was a fizz of electricity arcing across the metal brace on his teeth. Then he was the maintenance man again, meeting my desolate gaze with an expression of contempt.

I left hurriedly, and I resolved, after all, not to pass by the pylon again.

# THOMAS LIGOTTI

## The Glamour

*NOCTUARY*, THOMAS LIGOTTI's third collection of supernatural fiction (following the acclaimed *Songs of a Dead Dreamer* and *Grimscribe: His Lives and Works*), was published in 1993 and contains several previously unpublished stories and a novella written especially for the book.

*The Washington Post* described him as "the most startling and unexpected discovery since Clive Barker," and his atmospheric ghost stories can be found in such anthologies as *The Best Horror from Fantasy Tales*, *Prime Evil*, *Fine Frights*, *A Whisper of Blood*, *The Dedalus Book of Femmes Fatales*, *The Year's Best Fantasy and Horror* and all three previous volumes of *Best New Horror*. The fourth issue of the small press magazine *Tekeli-li! Journal of Terror* (Winter/Spring 1992) included a special Ligotti section, with stories, an interview and bibliography.

"Horror fiction serves as a reflecting surface in which we may glimpse a blurry image of this infinite and eternal medusa in whose arms are held our whole lives and from whom, one hopes, we are finally released at death," explains the author. "At certain angles and from the proper distance, the medusa seems to be quite a looker. Weird tales provide these angles and this distance, and they do so without flinching toward the hell of happy endings."

With "The Glamour", we are delighted to welcome back to these pages one of the most original writers in modern horror fiction with another unnerving tale seen from his unique perspective.

## THE GLAMOUR

IT HAD LONG BEEN MY PRACTICE to wander late at night and often to attend movie theatres at this time. But something else was involved on the night I went to that theatre in a part of town I had never visited before. A new tendency, a mood or penchant formerly unknown to me, seemed to lead the way. It is difficult to say anything precise about this mood that overcame me, because it seemed to belong to my surroundings as much as to myself. As I advanced further into the part of town I had never visited before, my attention was drawn to a certain aspect of things—a fine aura of fantasy radiating from the most common sights, places and objects that were both blurred and brightened as they projected themselves into my vision.

Despite the lateness of the hour, there was an active glow cast through so many of the shop windows in that part of town. Along one particular avenue, the starless evening was glazed by these lights, these diamonds of plate glass set within old buildings of dark brick. I paused before the display window of a toy store and was entranced by a chaotic tableau of preposterous excitation. My eyes followed several things at once: the fated antics of mechanized monkeys that clapped tiny cymbals or somersaulted uncontrollably; the destined pirouettes of a music box ballerina; the grotesque wobbling of a newly sprung jack-in-the-box. The inside of the store was a Christmas-tree clutter of merchandise receding into a background that looked shadowed and empty. An old man with a smooth pate and angular eyebrows stepped forward to the front window and began rewinding some of the toys to keep them in ceaseless gyration. While performing this task he suddenly looked up at me, his face expressionless.

I moved down the street, where other windows framed little worlds so strangely picturesque and so dreamily illuminated in the shabby darkness of that part of town. One of them was a bakery whose window display was a gallery of sculptured frosting, a winter landscape of swirling, drifting whiteness, of snowy rosettes and layers of icy glitter. At the centre of the glacial kingdom was a pair of miniature people frozen atop a many-tiered wedding cake, but beyond the brilliant arctic scene I saw only the deep blackness of an establishment that kept short hours. Standing outside another window nearby, I was uncertain if the place was open for business or not. A few figures were positioned here and there within faded lighting reminiscent of an old photograph, though it seemed they were beings of the same kind as the window dummies of this store, which apparently trafficked in dated styles of clothing. Even the faces of the mannikins, as a glossy light fell upon them, wore the placidly enigmatic expressions of a different time.

Actually, there were several places doing business at that hour of the night and in that part of town, however scarce potential customers appeared to be on this particular street. I saw no one enter or exit the many doors along the sidewalk; a canvas awning that some proprietor had neglected to roll up for the night was flapping in the wind. Nevertheless, I did sense a certain vitality around me and felt the kind of acute anticipation that a child might experience at a carnival, where each lurid attraction incites fantastic speculations, while unexpected desires arise for something which has no specific qualities in the imagination yet seems to be only a few steps away. My mood had not abandoned me but only grew stronger, a possessing impulse without object.

Then I saw the marquee for a movie theatre. It was something I might easily have passed by, for the letters spelling out the name of the theatre were broken and unreadable. The title on the marquee was similarly damaged, as though stones had been thrown at it and a series of attempts made to efface the words that I finally deciphered.

The feature being advertised that night was called "The Glamour."

When I reached the front of the theatre I found that the row of doors forming the entrance had been barricaded by crosswise planks with notices posted upon them warning that the building had been condemned. This action had apparently been taken some time ago, judging by the weathered condition of the boards that blocked my way and the dated appearance of the notices stuck upon them. In any case, the marquee was still illuminated, albeit rather poorly, so I was not surprised to see a double-faced sign propped up on the sidewalk, an inconspicuous little board that read: ENTRANCE TO THE THEATRE. Beneath these words was an arrow pointing into an alleyway which separated the theatre from the remaining buildings on the block. Peeking into the otherwise solid facade of that particular street, I saw only a long, narrow corridor with a single light set far into its depths. The light shone with a strange shade of purple, like that of a freshly exposed heart, and appeared to be positioned over a doorway leading into the theatre.

It had long been my practice to attend movie theatres late at night, and I reminded myself of this. Whatever reservations I felt at the time were easily overcome by a new surge of the mood I was experiencing that night in a part of town I had never visited before.

The purple lamp did indeed mark a way into the theatre, casting a kind of arterial light upon a door that reiterated the word "entrance." Stepping inside, I entered a tight hallway where the walls glowed a deep pink, very similar in shade to that little beacon in the alley but reminding me more of a richly blooded brain than a beating heart. At the end of the hallway I could see my reflection in a ticket window, and on approaching it I noticed that those walls so close to me were veiled from floor to ceiling with what appeared to be cobwebs. Similar cobwebs were strewn upon the carpet leading to the ticket window: wispy shrouds that did not scatter as I walked over them. It was as if they had securely bound themselves to the carpet's worn and shallow fibre, or were growing out of it like postmortem hairs on a corpse.

There was no one behind the ticket window, no one I could see in that small space of darkness beyond the blur of purple-tinted glass in which my reflection was held. Nevertheless, a ticket was protruding from a slot beneath the semi-circular cutaway at the bottom of the window, sticking out like a paper tongue. A few hairs lay beside it.

"Admission is free," said a man who was now standing in the doorway beside the ticket booth. His suit was well-fitted and neat, but his face appeared somehow in a mess, bristled over all its contours. His tone was polite, even passive, when he said, "The theatre is under new ownership."

"Are you the manager?" I asked.

"I was just on my way to the rest room."

Without further comment he drifted off into the darkness of the theatre. For a moment something floated in the empty space he left in the doorway—a swarm of filaments like dust that scattered or settled before I stepped through. And in those first few seconds inside, the only thing I could see were the words "rest room" glowing above a door as it slowly closed.

I manoeuvred with caution until my sight became sufficient to the dark and allowed me to find a door leading to the auditorium of the movie theatre. But once inside, as I stood at the summit of a sloping aisle, all previous orientation to my surroundings underwent a setback. The room was illuminated by an elaborate chandelier centered high above the floor, as well as a series of light fixtures along either of the side walls. I was not surprised by the dimness of the lighting, nor by its hue, which made shadows appear faintly bloodshot—a sickly, liverish shade that might be witnessed in an operating room where a torso lies open on the table, its entrails a palette of pinks and reds and purples . . . diseased viscera imitating all the shades of sunset.

However, my perception of the theatre auditorium remained problematic—not because of any oddities of illumination but for another reason. I experienced no difficulty in mentally registering the elements around me—the separate aisles and rows of seats, the curtain-flanked movie screen, the well-noted chandelier and wall lights—but it seemed impossible to gain a sense of these objects, and the larger scene they comprised, in simple accord with their appearances. I saw nothing that I have not described, yet . . . the round-backed seats were at the same time rows of headstones in a graveyard; the aisles were endless filthy alleys, long desolate corridors in an old asylum, or the dripping passages of a sewer receding into the distance; the pale movie screen was a dust-blinded window in a dark unvisited cellar, a mirror gone rheumy with age in an abandoned house; the chandelier and smaller fixtures were the facets of murky crystals embedded in the sticky walls of an unknown cavern. In other words, this movie theatre was merely a virtual image, a veil upon a complex collage of other places, all of which shared certain qualities that were projected into my vision, as though the things I saw were possessed by something I could not see.

But as I lingered in the theatre auditorium, settling in a seat toward the back wall, I realised that even on the level of plain appearances there was a peculiar phenomenon I had not formerly observed, or at least had yet to perceive to its fullest extent. I am speaking of the cobwebs.

When I first entered the theatre I saw them clinging to the walls and carpeting. Now I saw how much they were a part of the theatre and how I had mistaken the nature of these long pale threads. Even in the hazy purple light, I could discern that they had penetrated into the fabric of the seats in the theatre, altering the weave in its depths and giving it a slight quality of movement, the slow curling of thin smoke. It seemed the same with the movie screen, which might have been a great rectangular web, tightly woven and faintly in motion, vibrating at the touch of some unseen force. I thought: "Perhaps this subtle and pervasive *wriggling* within the theatre may clarify the tendency of its elements to suggest other things and other places utterly unlike a simple theatre auditorium—a process parallel to the ever-mutating images of dense clouds." All textures in the theatre appeared similarly affected, without control over their own nature, but I could not clearly see as high as the chandelier. Even some of the others in the audience, which was small and widely scattered about the auditorium, were practically invisible to my eyes.

Furthermore, there may have been something in my mood that night, given my sojourn in a part of town I had never been, that influenced what I was able to see. And this mood had become steadily enhanced since I first stepped into the theatre, and indeed from the moment I first looked upon the marquee advertising a feature entitled "The Glamour." Having at last found a place among the quietly expectant audience, I began to suffer an exacerbation of this mood. Specifically, I sensed a greater proximity to the point of focus for my mood that night, a tingling closeness to something quite literally *behind the scene*. Increasingly I became unconcerned with anything except the consummation or terminus of this abject and enchanting adventure. Consequences were evermore difficult to regard from my tainted perspective.

For these reasons, I was not hesitant when this focal point for my mood suddenly felt near at hand, as close as the seat directly behind my own. I was quite sure this seat had been empty when I selected mine, that all the seats for several rows around me were unoccupied, and I would have been aware if someone had arrived to fill this seat directly behind me. Nevertheless, like a sudden chill announcing bad weather, there was now a definite presence I could feel at my back, a force of sorts that pressed itself upon me and inspired a surge of dark elation. But when I looked around, not quickly yet fully determined, I saw no occupant in the seat behind me, nor in any seat between me and the back wall of the theatre.

I continued to stare at the empty seat, because my sensation of a vibrant presence there was unrelieved. And while staring, I perceived that the fabric of the seat, the inner webbing of swirling fibres, had composed a pattern in the image of a face: an old woman's face with an expression of avid malignance, floating amidst wild shocks of twisting hair. The face itself was a portrait of atrocity, a grinning image of lust for sites and ceremonies of disfigurement. It was formed of those hairs stitching themselves together.

All the stringy, writhing cobwebs of that theatre, as I now discovered, were the reaching tendrils of a vast netting of hairs. By virtue of this discovery, my mood of the evening—which had delivered me to a part of the town I had never been and to that very theatre—became yet more expansive and defined, taking in scenes of graveyards and alleyways, reeking sewers and wretched corridors of insanity, as well as the immediate vision of an old theatre that now, as I had been told, was under new ownership. But my mood abruptly faded, along with the face in the fabric of the theatre seat, when a voice spoke to me.

"You must have seen her, by the looks of you."

A man sat down one seat away from mine. It was not the same person I had met earlier; this one's face was nearly unblemished, although his suit was littered with hair that was not his own.

"So did you see her?"

"I'm not sure what I saw."

He seemed almost to burst out giggling, his voice trembling on the edge of a joyous hysteria. "You would be sure enough if there had been a private encounter, I can tell you."

"Something was happening, then you sat down."

"Sorry," he said. "Did you know that the theatre has just come under new ownership?"

"I didn't notice what the showtimes are."

"Showtimes?"

"For the feature."

"Oh, there isn't any feature. Not as such."

"But there must be . . . something," I insisted.

"Yes, there's something," he replied excitedly, his fingers stroking his cheek.

"What, exactly? And these cobwebs . . ."

But the lights were going down into darkness. "Quiet now," he whispered. "It's about to begin."

The screen before us was glowing a pale purple in the blackness, although I heard no sounds from the machinery of a movie projector. Neither were there any sounds connected with the images which were beginning to take form on the screen, as if a lens were being focused on a microscopic world. In some mysterious way, the movie screen might have been a great glass slide which magnified to gigantic proportions a realm of organisms normally hidden from our sight—but as these visions coalesced and clarified, I recognised them as something I had already seen, or more accurately *sensed*, in that theatre. The images were appearing on the screen as if a pair of disembodied eyes were moving within venues of profound morbidity and degeneration. Here were the reflections of those places I had felt were superimposing themselves on the genuinely tangible aspects of the theatre: those graveyards, alleys, decayed corridors, and subterranean passages whose spirit had intruded on another locale and altered it. Yet the places now revealed on the movie screen were without an identity I could name: they were the fundament of these sinister and seamy regions which cast their spectral ambience on the reality of the theatre but which were themselves merely the shadows, the superficial counterparts of deeper, more obscure regions. Farther and farther into it we were being taken.

The all-pervasive purple colouration could now be seen to be emanating from the labyrinth of a living anatomy: a compound of the reddish, bluish, palest pink structures, all of them morbidly inflamed and lesioned to release a purple light. We were being guided through a catacomb of putrid chambers and cloisters, the most secreted ways and waysides of an infernal land. Whatever the condition of these spaces may once have been, they were now habitations for ceremonies of a private sabbath. The hollows in their fleshy, gelatinous integuments streamed with something like moss, or a fungus extended in thin strands that were threading themselves into translucent tissue and quivering beneath it like veins. It was the sabbath ground, secret and unconsecrated, but it was also the theatre of an insane surgery. The hairlike sutures stitched among the yielding entrails, unseen hands designing unnatural shapes and systems, weaving a nest in which the possession would take place, a web wherein the bits and pieces of the anatomy could be consumed at leisure. There seemed to be no one in sight, yet everything was viewed from an intimate perspective, the viewpoint of that invisible surgeon, the weaver and webmaker, the old puppetmaster who was setting the helpless creature with new strings and placing him under the control of a new owner. And through her eyes, entranced, we witnessed the work being done.

Then those eyes began to withdraw, and the purple world of the organism receded into purple shadows. When the eyes finally emerged from where they had been, the movie screen was filled with the face and naked chest of a man. His posture was rigid, betraying a state of paralysis, and his eyes were fixed, yet strikingly alive.

"She's showing us," whispered the man who was sitting nearby me. "She has taken him. He cannot feel who he is any longer, only her presence within him."

This, at first sight of the possessed, seemed to be an accurate statement of the case. Certainly, such a view of the situation provided a terrific stimulus to my own mood of the evening, urging it toward culmination in a type of degraded rapture, a seizure of panic oblivion. Nonetheless, as I stared at the face of the man on the screen, he became known to me as the one I encountered in the vestibule of the theatre. Recognition was difficult because his flesh was now even more obscured by the webs of hair woven through it, thick as a full beard in spots. His eyes were also quite changed, and glared out at the audience with a ferocity which suggested that he did indeed serve as the host of great evil. All the same, there was something in those eyes that belied the fact of a complete transformation—an awareness of the bewitchment and an appeal for deliverance.

Within the next few moments, this observation assumed a degree of substance, for the man on the movie screen regained himself, although briefly and in limited measure. His effort of will was evident in the subtle contortions of his face, and his ultimate accomplishment was modest enough: he managed to open his mouth in order to scream. No sound was projected from the movie screen, of course; it only played a music of images for eyes that would see what should not be seen. Thus, a disorienting effect was created: a sensory dissonance which resulted in my being roused from the mood of the evening. The spell that it had cast over me echoed to nothingness.

The scream that resonated in the auditorium originated in another part of the theatre: a place beyond the auditorium's towering black wall.

Consulting the man who was sitting near me, I found him oblivious to my comments about the scream within the theatre. He seemed neither to hear nor see what was happening around him and what was happening to the members of the audience. Long wiry hairs were sprouting from the fabric of the seats, snaking low along their arms and along every part of them. The hairs had also penetrated into the cloth of the man's suit, but I could not make him aware of what was happening.

Finally, I rose to leave, because I could feel the hairs tugging to keep me in position. As I stood up they ripped away from me like stray threads pulled from a sleeve or pocket.

No one else in the auditorium turned away from the man on the movie screen, who had now lost the ability to scream and had relapsed into a paralytic silence.

While proceeding up the aisle I glanced up towards a rectangular opening high in the back wall of the theatre: the window-like slot from which images are projected on to the movie screen. Framed within this aperture was the silhouette of what looked like an old woman with long and wildly tangled hair. I could see her eyes gazing fiercely and malignantly at the purple glow of the movie screen, and these eyes sent forth two shafts of the purest purple light, which shot through the darkness of the auditorium.

While exiting the theatre the way I had come in, it was impossible to ignore the sign that said "rest room," so brightly was it now shining. But the lamp over the side door in the alley was dead; the sign reading ENTRANCE TO THE THEATRE was gone. Even the letters spelling out the name of that evening's feature had been taken down.

So this had been the last performance; henceforth the theatre would be closed to the public.

Also closed, if only for the night, were all the other businesses along that particular street in the part of town I had never before visited. The hour was late, the shop windows were dark—but how sure I was that in every one of those dark windows I passed there was the even darker silhouette of an old woman with glowing eyes and a great head of monstrous hair.

# JOHN GORDON

## Under the Ice

JOHN GORDON lives with his wife in Norwich. Born in Jarrow-on-Tyne, he grew up in the Fens and during World War Two joined the Navy from school and served on minesweepers and destroyers. After the war he became a journalist and worked on papers in East Anglia and Plymouth.

His acclaimed books for Young Adults include the wonderful *Catch Your Death and Other Ghost Stories*, *The Ghost on the Hill*, *The Grasshopper*, *The House on the Brink*, *The Spitfire Grave and Other Stories*, *The Waterfall Box* and *The Burning Baby and Other Ghosts*. He has also written his autobiography, entitled *Ordinary Seaman*.

Gordon's journalistic background created the impetus for the atmospheric ghost story which follows, as the author explains: "Working as a reporter in the Fens I found myself having to write about everything from the Crown Jewels of England, which King John is supposed to have lost in the marshes near Wisbech, to court cases, inquests, water diviners, and men who knew what it was like to skate for the prize of a leg of mutton to keep their families from hunger.

"There's a lot of water in the Fens, and I heard of one farmworker who, coming out of the pub on a Saturday night, would regularly fall into the dyke and flounder about calling out, 'I'm a swimmer! I'm a swimmer!' He did it one night in winter, nobody heard him, and they didn't find him until the thaw.

"'Under the Ice' started there . . ."

VERY FEW PEOPLE HAVE ACTUALLY SEEN a ghost. I have. But I wish I hadn't.

Rupert saw it long before I did, and I was the only person he ever told about it. I just wish he'd kept quiet, and then things might have turned out differently—at least I wouldn't have been there on that terrible day and I would never have seen what I did see. And I would never have known how unfair it was. There was no justice in it. None.

I have often thought I could have done something to stop it—but now I know that was impossible; I couldn't have done a thing. I'm only telling you this because I can't keep it to myself any longer.

I suppose you'd expect anybody who'd seen a ghost to tell everyone about it. Rupert was different. He kept things to himself. Quite a lot of people are like that, out in the flat fens. He had nobody much to talk to, so he got out of the habit, even with me, and I was always reckoned to be his best friend. He was a thin, gangly sort of boy, a bit taller than me, and he was tough in all sorts of ways you'd never guess just by looking at him.

I knew something was bothering him, but I didn't know what, although it had to be pretty important because one day, out of the blue, he asked me if I'd go home with him after school. It was a half holiday, in the middle of a bitter winter, and I didn't fancy cycling such a long way.

"It'll be dark before long," I said, trying to make an excuse.

"That doesn't matter," he said in a rush. "My father will take us, and we can go skating. There's no danger, the ice is rock hard . . . So that'll be all right, will it?"

"Hold your hosses," I said. This wasn't like Rupert at all, the quiet boy from far out of town. "What am I going to do with my bike?" I wasn't going to leave that in the cycle shed all night, not with some of the characters I knew hanging about. "And what about my tea—my mum'll be expecting me."

"I'll give you some tea," he said, just as if he owned the whole house, the bread and butter and everything. "Give your mum a ring—and you can put your bike in the boot." His father had a Volvo like a battle tank, so that was OK.

"Skates," I said. "I haven't got any." My lovely brother in the sixth form nicked everything that belonged to me. "William's screwed my skates on to his boots," I told Rupert, "so what's the use?"

"How big are your feet?" he said suddenly.

"Not as big as his."

"Same size as me." He plonked his foot down next to mine. "You can have my old fen runners."

"Gee," I said. "Thanks a million."

He went red. "Or you can have my Norwegians. I don't mind."

"Don't worry about it, Rupe." I was beginning to feel sorry for him; he seemed so eager for me to go with him that it would have been just like disappointing a little kid if I'd said no. So I said yes. You never do know what you're letting yourself in for.

He was in a fidget waiting for his father after school and he didn't calm down until we'd stowed the bike and were sitting side by side in the back seat. You could have told it was a farmer's car by the old fertilizer sacks in the boot, but even the back of his father's neck would have let you into the secret because it was brown and creased, and the trilby hat he wore was a mud colour through always being out in the sun and rain. I used to get on with his father quite well, chatting about this and that, but I hadn't seen him for some time, and now he was like Rupert—so quiet that after a while I began to feel as if he was some sort of servant in the front seat, just doing his job by driving us home. This made me so awkward that I kept silent, too.

Rupert practically ignored me. He sat back in his corner and gazed out of the window with his mind on something else while the heater blew warm air at us and I began to wish I was at home by the fire. If I'd had any sense I would have stopped feeling sorry for myself and would have remembered what it was that kept them so subdued. Everybody knew what had happened last summer, but that afternoon it just didn't come into my mind.

It had been freezing for a week so I was used to a nip in the air when I was cycling home, but when we got to where Rupert lived and stepped out of the car the cold was something else. In town it lay in chunks like massive ice cubes between the houses and you felt you could dodge some of it, but out here, where there were no streets and no street lights, the cold was a solid black mass that seemed to press even the birds to the ground.

"Don't know what there is to eat," said Rupert's father. "Bread and pull-it, I reckon." I couldn't tell if he smiled because he turned his head away, but I guessed he didn't bother. "The wife wasn't expecting anyone."

Nice welcome, I thought, but I was polite. "I don't mind, Mr Granger," I said. "I'm not very hungry."

"That's all right, then," and he left us, striding away over the crackling gravel to the farm out-buildings.

"I don't think I should've come," I said, but Rupert was already taking me past the frozen bushes to the back door.

He went ahead of me, and the instant the door opened his mother gave a little cry and called out "Who's there?" as if we were burglars. Even when Rupert told her it was just the two of us she kept peering over his shoulder to make sure exactly who was following him out of the shadows.

"It's only me," I said.

"Oh," she said, and some of the alarm went out of her eyes, but the worry remained. "David Maxey. What are you doing here?"

This time even Rupert could tell I wasn't being given a very warm welcome, and he was embarrassed. "He's hungry," he said.

"But you never said you were bringing anyone." She was quite bitchy with him. "You never told me."

I butted in. "I'm sorry, Mrs Granger," I said, and wished more strongly than ever to be somewhere else. "It's Rupert's fault. He wants me to go skating."

"Skating?" The idea seemed to confuse her.

"Mother." Rupert went close to her. "You know you don't like me to go skating on my own—so that's why I brought him. Two together are quite safe."

She was looking from one to the other of us, and I said, "If she cracks she bears, if she bends she breaks." It was something they said about the ice in the fens, where everybody was a skater and knew about such things. "It's very thick now, Mrs Granger, and it'll never bend an inch."

She didn't answer. Instead, she turned to the dresser and took down plates to set a new place for me. "I'm afraid there's not much," she said.

I'd always liked Rupert's mother. She'd never seemed as if she belonged out here, miles from anywhere, with no neighbours. It was partly the way she dressed I suppose, as if she was ready to leave the farm behind at that instant and take us both up to town for a good time. But now there wasn't a trace of make-up on her face, and the shadows around her eyes were genuine.

"I'll get the skates," said Rupert. "They're in the garage."

I didn't want him to leave me, but I made the best of it by trying to help his mother. There wasn't as much on the table as I was used to when I went there, and she apologized. "I haven't been able to get out to the shops in this weather," she said. It wasn't true; there hadn't been enough snow to make the roads dangerous, and I knew she had her own car.

"This is fine, Mrs Granger," I said. "I can hardly eat a thing."

At any other time she would have seen through the lie and laughed; now she just turned towards me, her face full of anxiety, and said, "Are you sure? Are you really sure?"

I'd always thought that, as mothers go, she was rather pretty, and I was so shocked at how pale and lined her face had become that I found I had no words, and I was very relieved when Rupert returned with the fen runners for me. The little skates, which were like the blades of table knives set in blocks of wood, were those he'd started with when he was younger. The boots were tight, but I managed to squeeze my feet into them.

Dusk was beginning to fall by the time we'd eaten and left the house. Mrs Granger stood at the door with her hands clenched in front of her as if she had to struggle not to reach out and hold us back.

"The ice is rock hard, Mrs Granger," I said, making a new attempt to stop her worrying. "We couldn't go through it even if we tried."

"Don't," she said, "please don't say things like that." She looked around the yard. "Rupert, why don't you get your father to go with you?"

But Rupert was already walking away and his father, who had not joined us at tea, was nowhere to be seen.

I'd always known that the farmhouse was lonely, but I'd never realized just how isolated it really was until I caught up with Rupert on the road outside. In summer, green trees and bushes and tall grass crowded around the house and disguised its loneliness, but now the curtains of leaves had been stripped away, and the flat fields, the black furrows ridged with white, stretched away like the bare boards of an empty house.

"Cold," I said, and the blades of the skates that swung in our hands rattled like chattering teeth.

The proper road petered out just beyond the farmhouse and became a track that only tractors could use. There were no hedges out here, only ditches with thin crusts of ice where the water had seeped away beneath. I would have stopped to throw stones through the ice sheets except that Rupert was hurrying ahead, intent on getting somewhere—even though there seemed to be no place better than any other out here.

"It's getting dark early," he said. "It's all this cloud. You won't be able to see it soon."

"See what?" I asked, but he had run on as if he didn't want to answer.

We came to a gate across the track and beyond it a low bank stretched away to left and right like the rampart of an ancient fort. On the other side lay the waterway, except that now it was an iceway, reaching in a dead straight line to the black horizon.

"When there's a moon," said Rupert, "you can skate out of sight."

Our voices were so small in the vast space that I doubt if they reached the far bank of the wide channel, not that there was anybody in the whole of creation to hear us. An ice age had made the world a waste land, and we were alone in it.

"Where are you taking me?" I asked, because I'd guessed by now that he had something more than skating on his mind.

"Hurry up and get those runners on," he said, and he had laced up his Norwegians and was crabbing down the bank almost before I'd started. I heard his long blades strike the ice as I still struggled with my laces. "Wait for me," I called, because he was already gliding out from the bank.

"Hurry up. It's getting dark."

He was out in the middle of the channel when I reached the edge, caught the tip of one skate in a tussock of frozen grass and stumbled forward. I was sure I was going to get a wet foot in the seepage that is always at the margin, but my blades ran through the grass on solid ice. It was as hard as a marble floor from bank to bank. There was no risk of falling through; none at all—but Rupert was leading me on to a danger that was much worse.

We skated, sawing the air with our arms and feeling it bite back at our cheeks and noses, but he, riding high on blades twice the length of mine, easily outpaced me, and I was so far behind that there must have been a hundred metres of ice between us when I saw him circling, waiting for me to catch up.

I was a breathless plodder following a racehorse, and I had lost patience with him so I deliberately dawdled, bending low from time to time, merely letting myself slide slowly along. It must have been infuriating for him, but he gave no sign of it, and continued to cut his slow circles as I drifted closer.

"We don't need a moon," I called. "You can still see for miles." The scatter of snow had made the banks white enough to catch all the thin light that came from the sky and we stood out like dark birds gliding low over frozen fields. But what food would birds find out here? What could they peck at? I was soon to find out.

"I'm flying!" I cried, and I leant forward and spread my arms wide. He had stopped and was waiting for me, and I wondered if I could reach him without pushing again, so I allowed myself to glide.

I was looking down, watching the little blades of the fen runners barely rocking as they skimmed forward, and I realized how smooth the ice was. It was a glassy pavement, polished, without cracks or blemishes, and it came as a shock to see that it was so clear I was actually looking through it. Even in this light I could see into the dark water below, where I knew the long weeds trailed in summer, and I gazed down into a giddy blackness.

My glide had been so successful that I was laughing as my skates came to rest almost at Rupert's feet, and I was just about to raise my head when I caught a glimpse of something beneath the ice. At first I thought it was a twist of weed, and I stooped to look closer. The shape became clear, and in that instant it reached inside me with a sick coldness that held me fixed to the spot. And then, horrified, not wanting to touch the ice anywhere near what I had seen, I eased myself backwards, still crouching, and stood up.

It was only then that I raised my eyes to Rupert.

There was a bridge behind him, in the distance. It was a single span where the track from the farm crossed the channel, and I remember it because it made a black shadow on a level with his shoulders and he seemed for an instant to have enormous arms that stretched from bank to bank. At that awful moment even he terrified me, and I was beginning to draw further back, when he spoke.

"So you can see it, too." The words were like frost on his lips.

I nodded. I saw it clearly. There was a drowned man under the ice.

I could see the folds of his trousers and a shoe twisted at an awkward angle. The sleeves of his jacket were rigid, but his fingers seemed to lie at ease in the ice, resting, as plump and white as the flesh of a plucked chicken. His head was turned away from us, so all we saw was hair and one ear.

I said something, but I can't remember what. All I knew was that we had to go for help even if it was too late—we had to let someone know. That object locked beneath us had to be freed. Words came from me, but Rupert did nothing. He stood quite still.

"Look again," he said.

I turned my eyes to the ice between us but I must have drifted too far back because now I could see nothing. I edged forward. The ice was black, and empty. I cast around, stooping to peer closer, but nothing showed itself.

"Where is it?" I said. The hideous thought came to my mind that a current still flowed under the ice and that the man was rolling slowly beneath our feet. "Where is it now?" I was beginning to panic, taking timid steps on my skates away from the spot as if the ice were about to open and take me down to join the corpse in its frozen coffin. "Where?" I said. "Where?"

"It's still there." His voice was so flat and calm it made me jerk my head up. "It's my uncle," he said.

He skated slowly forward. The extra height of his Norwegians made him tower over me, and once again I was afraid of him. His uncle! He had seen his uncle dead under the ice, and now he was gliding towards me without a sign of grief or even surprise on his face. I was backing clumsily away when he came level with me, and a thin smile appeared on his lips.

"You're not thinking of skating backwards all the way home, are you?" he said.

The fact that he could say something so ordinary, and smile as he spoke, jolted me out of my panic. I even managed to shrug. "How can it be your uncle?" I began . . . and then I remembered. It all came flooding back to me, and at the same instant I knew why his mother was so haggard and his father so silent. The tragedy that had slipped from my mind was still strong within them.

"Oh," I said feebly, "your uncle."

And then my stomach turned over yet again, for his uncle had been dead many months, drowned out here in the fens.

"That was where it happened," Rupert said. "Last summer."

I was ashamed of myself for having forgotten, and for a moment this blotted everything else from my mind. "I'm sorry," I said. "I should have remembered."

"I was there when he was found." He began to move away. "That's how I know who it is in the ice."

So there really was a body there . . . but he was talking nonsense to say it was his uncle. "It can't be," I said. "It's just some old clothes."

"With fingers?"

"Well, it's another body." I didn't want to admit it. "Someone else. We've got to tell somebody. We've got to."

He said nothing. He moved away and I went with him. Our skates were silent and we drifted like ghosts through the bitter dusk. I twisted my head to look behind.

"There's nothing to see," he said. "Even if you go back you won't find it. It's gone."

"How do you know?"

He turned a gaunt face towards me, and once again he smiled. "Do you think I haven't tried?"

"But I saw it. If I can see it, so can somebody else. Have you tried to show anybody?"

Suddenly, as though we were racing, he lowered his head and stretched his legs in long, sweeping strokes that left me behind. I did not catch up with him until we reached the place where we had left our shoes. He was already crouching on the bank unlacing his boots. "Too late to go any further," he said. "Too dark."

We had just seen something impossible to explain, and that was all he had to say.

"It was a ghost," I said, "wasn't it?" And when that had no effect on him, I added, "Or a shadow or something. Some sort of cracks and bubbles in the ice. The light might just catch them at times." He remained silent, but I wasn't going to leave it there. "You ought to tell somebody about it," I said. "Why not your mother?"

"She's got too much on her mind." He concentrated on his laces for a while, and then, speaking so low I could hardly hear him, he said, "She liked my uncle. She liked him a lot."

"Well, you've got to speak to your father—you've got to tell him."

"I can't." He shook his head without looking up. "I can't." His fingers ceased fumbling with his laces but his head remained bowed, and after a while I saw his shoulders tremble and I realized he was crying.

We were side by side in the frozen grass and Rupert had bent his head to his knees and was sobbing like a little child. I had never seen him in tears; and now that it had happened, I did not know what to do. I began unfastening my own skates, waiting until his sobbing subsided, trying to think of something to say, and failing. His grief was too deep for me to reach. Then, suddenly, he raised his head and was once again speaking clearly.

"He hated him," he said. "My father hated him. They used to be friends and then he hated him."

"But they were brothers."

"What difference does that make?" His voice was harsh. "He liked my mother! My uncle liked my mother, didn't he? A lot. Too much. I heard him say so, didn't I?"

He spat the words at me so fiercely I had to face up to him. "I don't know what you heard," I said.

"I heard everything!" He sucked in his cheeks and glared at me as though I was the most detestable creature on earth. "My father said he'd kill him if he didn't go away. Kill him!" He stooped forward suddenly and hauled off his skates. "Now you can go home," he said. "Get lost!"

Neither of us said another word. I climbed the bank alone and got to his house ahead of him. I could see his mother and father through the kitchen window, but I didn't go in. I was in a hurry to get away from that place, so I found my bike and left.

The freeze got worse. Rupert and I saw each other at school and were still friends, but we never once mentioned what had happened. His outburst seemed to have shut the door on it, and there was a kind of haughtiness in him that made me see that he was so deeply ashamed of what he had told me he could never speak of it. I told myself that what I had seen in the ice was made by weeds frozen near the surface, and that it was Rupert's imagination because of the terrible time he'd been through that had somehow forced us both to see what he'd seen last summer when they found his uncle.

Then one day the sun shone. The clouds, that for weeks had ground their way towards the horizon as slowly as a glacier, showed gaps of blue, and the sun began to put its fingers through the thin crust of snow on gardens and gutters. Even Rupert smiled and said, "We shan't get much more skating this year, I reckon."

"Too bad," I replied, thinking that he wanted to shrug the whole business away for ever.

"So why don't you come over tomorrow before it's too late?" he asked.

He had taken me by surprise and I looked so sharply at him that he reddened and mumbled something, saying that there were bound to be other people around as it was a Saturday, so there was nothing to worry about. It was the nearest he'd come to mentioning what was on our minds, and I was a bit nettled that he thought I may have been afraid to go skating alone out there, so of course I said yes.

I even managed to get my skates from my brother, so I was properly equipped when I cycled out to see him. The sun was bright, but I had to push against a biting wind which kept the temperature so low that I knew the ice would still be in good condition. And Rupert was right about other people being there. You could never say the ice was crowded because there was so much of it, but there were skaters wherever you looked, and their tiny black figures were dotted away into the distance. An occasional speed man came slicing by, one arm behind his back and the other swinging, and we decided we would join these long-distance skimmers.

Without either of us saying a word we set out towards the distant bridge and this meant we had to go over the spot where the shadows had frightened us so badly. We did not ignore it, but neither did we linger. We circled once, gazing down, and I was certain of the exact spot because the ice there was clear even though its surface was now criss-crossed by blade strokes. The sunlight would have shown any dead man beneath the ice, but there was nothing. There was only darkness below, and when I looked up and caught Rupert's eye he grinned sheepishly and skated off at speed as if to put it behind him once and for all.

We could hear the squeals of girls and the shouts of boys long before we reached the little groups that were strung out over the ice, but we skimmed by until we were far out in the fens. The sun, although now a blazing red, had shed the last of its heat for the day and was beginning to bury itself in the horizon before we thought of turning back. We stretched out on the frozen grass for a few minutes to rest our ankles.

"It's good out here," said Rupert. He was panting and there was even some colour in his cheeks. "I'm glad you could come today."

We weren't in the habit of paying each other compliments, so I just mumbled that I, too, was enjoying myself. I expected the matter to end there, but Rupert had something on his mind; unfinished business.

"Sorry I was such an idiot last time," he said.

"That's OK." I didn't look at him.

"It's just that everything was getting on top of me—Mum and Dad not being very happy and all that. Things had just been getting worse and worse, ever since . . ."

He seemed to want me to say it for him.

"I know what you mean," I said, but that wasn't good enough for him; he wanted it out in the open.

"Since my uncle drowned himself." He spoke very clearly, forcing me to look at him. "Drowned himself," he repeated. "I told you something stupid about my dad last time. It wasn't true."

"I know it wasn't." I had to agree with him. His father could never have done such a terrible thing as murder his brother, no matter what he might have said. "You were feeling pretty bad," I told Rupert. "And we'd just seen that thing in the ice."

"*Thought* we'd seen. It's not there now."

"And it wasn't there then," I insisted, backing him up. "It was just imagination. By both of us."

"Both of us." He nodded. He was glad he had a friend, and to know that between us we'd scattered all the shadows from his mind. "Right," he said, "I'll race you back."

It was no race. He had done much more skating than me and his ankles were stronger, so from time to time he had to wait for me to catch up. We had gone further out into the fen than I had realized and, with my slow progress, the sun had dipped below the horizon and had left only an afterglow before the bridge came in sight.

We were alone, the other skaters having long since climbed the banks and gone home, so when we came up to the bridge it was our voices alone that echoed beneath it.

"One at a time," said Rupert. "The thaw has made it wet under there."

He went first. There was no suggestion of a crack as he went forward cautiously, but when I followed I could see that his weight had made a pulse of water spill from the edge, so I kept to the centre as he waited for me to come through.

I was concentrating so intensely on the ice beneath my skates that I almost ran into him and had to make a wide swerve to keep my balance. That was why I saw his father before he did. Mr Granger was at the top of the bank, looking down.

"Where have you been?" he called to Rupert. "Your mother was worried."

Rupert did not answer. He was leaning forward like a runner trying to get his breath, and I went up alongside him to taunt him. He did not even turn his head my way and I was stooping to look into his face when I saw that, although his mouth was open, he was not gasping for breath. He was in the grip of terror.

I did not wish to follow his gaze, but I was forced to turn my head and look down.

It was there. I saw the frozen shoe and trouser leg, the stiff folds of the jacket and the fingers cased in ice. Even the hair on the back of the twisted head was visible.

Neither Rupert nor I moved. We were locked to that dreadful place.

"What are you doing down there?" It was his father's voice from the bank. "It's time to go home."

I had my hand on Rupert's arm. I was beginning to pull him back, gently tugging at him, and my skates were making a faint rasping sound on the ice when it happened. The head began to turn. It was as though I had been scratching at the other side of a window pane and had aroused it. The head within the ice came round to face us. Yellow cheeks and an open mouth. And then the eyes, tight shut.

"What's happening?" Mr Granger's voice died and, as it did so, leaving the air empty of all sound, the eyelids lifted. A handspan of ice lay over them, but the eyelids slipped back like a flicker of moonlight, and a pair of dead eyes, grey and as pale as milk, stared up at us.

The cold air brushed the back of my neck as I jerked backwards, but Rupert did not stir. He remained where he was as the fingers came through the ice, and with them, the bulge of the head. It came up like a sleeper pushing back a sheet.

I heard Rupert's name shouted from the top of the bank, and his father came thudding and slithering towards him and snatched him away.

I had slid backwards and was beneath the bridge when the dead figure stood upright and came to collect them. Water ran from its sleeves and dripped from its pale, plump fingers, and its sodden shoes swished on the ice as it advanced.

Without realizing it, I had backed even further away, out of the shelter of the bridge, so I was clear of what happened. I was a spectator . . . as Rupert should have been. But he was with his father.

I saw them enter the shadow of the dark arch together, and I saw Rupert slip and fall full length. His father stooped for him, but never got a chance to lift his son upright. The dripping figure came moving towards them and, in the black shadow under the bridge, embraced them both.

The impact of Rupert's fall had been too much for the ice. There was a soft, rending crack and a sheet the size of a table up-ended itself and in an instant, without a sound, the huddle of figures had gone. I flung myself forward, but the ice had slid back into place. I kicked it, but it was wedged. I put my full weight on its edge, and still it did not budge. I knelt and hammered on it, but Rupert was with his father on the other side of that door, and I never saw him again.

# JOEL LANE

## And Some Are Missing

JOEL LANE was born in 1963 and lives in Birmingham. His short stories have appeared in various magazines and anthologies, including *Fantasy Tales*, *Winter Chills*, *Ambit*, *Critical Quarterly*, *Panurge*, *Skeleton Crew*, *Exuberance* (issue four was a Joel Lane special, featuring two stories, an interview and bibliography), *Darklands* and *Darklands 2*, *The Sun Rises Red*, *Sugar Sleep* and three volumes of Karl Edward Wagner's *The Year's Best Horror Stories*. His criticism has appeared in *Foundation* and *Studies In Weird Fiction*. A selection of his poems appeared in *Private Cities*, a three-poet anthology from Stride Publications.

Like his story "Power Cut", which we reprinted in *Best New Horror 3*, "And Some Are Missing" ("The title comes from a line in a Pet Shop Boys song" reveals Lane) depicts a bleak vision of Britain in the early 1990s.

THE FIRST TIME, IT WAS SOMEONE I didn't know. Inevitably. I'd gone out to use the phone box, around eleven on a Tuesday night. This was a month after I'd moved into the flat in Moseley. I phoned Alan, but I don't remember what I said; I was very drunk. Coming back, I saw two men on the edge of the car park in front of the tower block I lived in. It looked like a drunk was being mugged. There was one man on the ground: grey-haired, shabby, unconscious. And another man crouching over him: pale, red-mouthed, very tense. As I came closer, he seemed to be scratching at the drunk's face. His hand was like a freeze-dried spider. I could see the knuckles were red from effort. With his other hand, he was tugging at the man's jacket.

Too far gone to be scared, I walked towards them and shouted "What are you doing?" The attacker looked up at me. His eyes were empty, like an official behind a glass screen. I clenched my fist. "Fucking get off him. Go on . . ." He smiled, as if he knew something I didn't. Then he got up and calmly stalked away into the darkness behind the garages. The man on the ground looked about fifty; from his clothes and stubble, he could have been a vagrant. There were deep cuts on his face, slowly filling up with mirrors of blood. He was sweating heavily.

I ran back to the phone and called an ambulance. Then I went back to the injured man and dabbed uselessly at his face with my sleeve. Now the shock was wearing off, I needed to go to sleep. I looked at my wristwatch; it was past midnight. There was no blood on my sleeve. I looked again at the drunk's face. It was pale with sweat and blurred by a greyish stubble. But there were no wounds. *Jesus*, I thought, *I've started to hallucinate. It's strictly Diet Coke from now on.* Leaving him for the ambulance, I struggled into the building. Living on the top floor meant I didn't have to keep count. The next thing I knew, my alarm clock was ringing. I didn't remember setting it, let alone going to bed.

The flat's okay, though it costs more to rent than a poorly furnished studio flat should. At least it's pretty secure. You'd need wings or a sledgehammer to break in. Before I paid the deposit, I asked if there was a phone point; the landlord showed me where it was. It was only when I'd moved in that I discovered the phone point hadn't been used in decades and was no longer viable. When I tried to contact the landlord, a snotty assistant told me it was hard luck, but they weren't responsible for telephones. I said that having been told there was a phone line, I had a right to assume it was viable. She said they hadn't told me it was. I thanked her for explaining, then hung up. My hands were shaking. Unless I was prepared to make the landlord a free gift of an installation costing a month's rent, I'd have no telephone until I moved.

A few nights after the incident in the car park, I woke up in the middle of the night. I'd been dreaming about Hereford, Alan's home town. We'd spent the last Christmas there with his family. I remembered the cathedral, the old houses, the hills out towards Fownhope that were so heavily wooded you seemed to be indoors. Suddenly I was crying. Then I felt something touch my face. Fingers. They seemed to be following the tears. One of them scratched my right eye. I lay very still, sweating with fear. The touching was gentle, but there was no kindness in it. A cold palm slid over my mouth. I pulled away, then lashed out in the darkness, cursing. Something moved at the side of the bed. I switched the light on, but the room was empty. There was nobody else in the flat.

I was more scared than I'd been when I thought there was someone in the room with me. I'm a real coward when it comes to dentists and hospitals, but with people my temper takes over. A few years ago, I was walking home late at night when I was stopped by this massive bloke. He asked for directions to somewhere or other, then pushed me against the wall and tried to take my wallet. I pushed him hard, shouted "Fuck off" and ran; he didn't follow me. I sat on my bed, remembering this, staring at the walls of the flat. There was a picture of a town covered with snow at night, done in pastel blue and white on black paper; Alan had drawn that for me. There were Picasso and van Gogh prints, stills from James Dean films, and a sketch of mine that showed an abandoned card table on a bridge over a canyon. I'd filled the flat with images that made me feel at home. But it didn't work.

Some evenings, my head was full of a violence I could only control by drinking myself unconscious. The new flat had been rented in a hurry, while I was staying with friends after the split. Alan was in love with another man: a bearded American, younger than me and more intelligent. Two years of living together, and now suddenly it was all gone. Hard to believe; but every day I had to rediscover it by waking up. Alan and I were still close: we met regularly for coffee or lunch in the city centre, to exchange news or just spend time together.

He wanted to go to America with Paul, and live there. Until that happened, I needed to hold onto whatever feelings for me still lived in him. Perhaps by refusing to let go of him completely, I was damaging both of us—as though the relationship were a kind of wound that we both carried, and which the contact between us kept reopening.

It was at one of those awkward meetings that he told me Sean was dead. I hadn't known him well—a familiar face in one or two pubs, always chatty, but genuinely friendly underneath the banter. He invented nicknames for people that were invariably perfect, and never malicious. One Sunday afternoon we met by chance at the Triangle cinema, and he gave me a lift home. He struck me then as rather subdued and thoughtful. We talked about people we both knew; Sean said he'd grown out of the scene, and wanted a more settled life.

And now—what, eighteen months later?—he'd killed himself. From what Alan said, he'd been suffering from mental illness and couldn't see himself recovering. I cried suddenly, briefly. Sean was only twenty-three. I wish I understood why so many people don't value themselves. Why someone with vitality and humour and warmth should deliberately end his life. Perhaps it's people like that who get hurt the most, and can't hide from it. Somehow they come to believe that they don't matter. And there's nobody to tell them they're wrong.

Everyone seemed to be in trouble that week. It was late summer; the days were hot and sticky, you had people wearing sunglasses and carrying umbrellas. That kind of weather makes everyone restless and uneasy. A couple that Alan and I had known for years split up unexpectedly, and had to sell their house in order to live apart. I started losing track of who was seeing whom, and which affairs were open and which were secret.

Jason, a good friend of mine, lost his job as the result of a pointless row. He was working for the council, answering phone calls from the public. A few of the senior management people had started complaining about the way he dressed. His clothes were colourful and stylish enough to have some of the grey people muttering about "flamboyance". Perhaps Jason was too stubborn for his own good. Or perhaps he felt that, after four years of successful work, he deserved more acceptance from his colleagues. Either way, he tried to shame the management into an apology by offering his resignation. They accepted it.

I didn't have problems like that at work, but sometimes the general level of unhappiness in the company was frightening. Our salaries had been frozen indefinitely, while mishandling of computer files had cost the company a fortune. The directors blamed the recession; but the recession didn't force them to be arrogant, inept and cynical. Nor, indeed, to be absent most of the time.

At the end of that week, I went out to the Nightingale. They'd redecorated it in black wood-chip wallpaper, with black leather seating. The effect was deadpan and oppressive. I brought someone back to the flat. He was a quiet, sensitive guy in his mid-thirties, with a strong Black Country accent. It was more for company than anything else. We were both quite drunk. He used amyl nitrate in bed, which only seemed to distance him. I tried it, but it just made me sweat. Probably I was too tired. When he climaxed his body was immobile, like a statue melting in the rain.

He was asleep when I woke up and saw a figure at the foot of the bed. It seemed hardly more than an outline, and it was somehow too jagged, stretched-looking, like some kind of satirical cartoon. It was just watching. Perhaps waiting for something to happen. That was when I first thought: *the antipeople*. I shifted closer to the sleeping man, touching his arm, his shoulder, his hair. But the cold feeling remained. In the morning we both felt a bit awkward, and didn't arrange to meet again.

A few days later, Alan drove round with some things I needed from the house. Because my new flat was so small, I'd left a lot of possessions behind. I'd have to collect them soon, before Alan moved out. He hoped to be with Paul in New York by the end of the year. We circled around each other nervously, able to hug but not kiss. He'd already said that I could sleep with him again if I wanted to. Paul wouldn't mind—after all, he'd been seeing Paul for three months while I was still in the house. Moving out had reduced the stress, enabled me to get some kind of grip on things. But underneath, I still felt the same way.

It didn't happen until Alan was on the point of leaving. I kissed him fiercely and started to unbutton his shirt. "Lie down. Please." It took less than fifteen minutes, but it was as good as any sex I can remember. Afterwards, we lay there and rested, no longer touching—as always when we slept together. Then I saw the creature sitting over him. It was probing his face with its narrow fingers; the nails were broken. Then it bent further down and pressed its teeth against his arm, just above the wrist. The creature looked a bit like me, but not very much. I hope.

For a few seconds I wondered if I should just let it happen. It wasn't that I wanted to hurt Alan. But . . . why should I protect him, after what he'd put me through? Then I reached out, grabbed the pale thing's shoulder and pulled hard. My fingers sank into the stale flesh and hooked on the bone. The creature pawed at my arm, scratched it with one ragged finger. The skin turned white and hard. Then I was alone with Alan. He opened his eyes and reached for me.

After he'd gone, I put a record on the stereo. Leonard Cohen sang: *Now I greet you from the other side of sorrow and despair / With a love so vast and shattered it will reach you everywhere*. I poured myself a glass of gin and tried to think. Was human love enough to motivate life, to give everything a meaning? Or was it so debased that the only source of meaning was something above humanity? I didn't know.

In fact, I didn't trust people who claimed that they knew. The scar on my arm was numb; it seemed to be frozen. About a week later, the strip of dead skin fell away.

From the window in my flat, I can see out beyond the garages, to where a semicircle of trees forms a natural skyline. There's a cedar, a few birches and a pine tree of some kind. It makes me think of forests, green places full of shadow and drifts of leaves; places where there are no people.

The last few weeks of that summer were close and humid. The newspapers were full of road accidents, murders, rapes. I can remember walking through the city centre and seeing the crowd of people suddenly blur and sway, as though they had all started to dance. Alan and I kept in touch; he was under increasing stress, not knowing whether Paul really wanted to be with him in the future. He was holding onto a job and a home while hoping that he'd be asked to leave them behind. He said he still missed me. We were uneasy with each other, not really knowing what to say or to hope for. For me, it wouldn't have been hard to forgive him. The most difficult thing would have been to trust him.

In spite of this uncertainty, the glare of madness was fading in my head. I was drinking less heavily, though that had never been the core of the trouble. Many people helped me, friends and strangers; and while nobody's help was crucial in itself, the total effect got me through. There's more humanity around than I've tended to think. It's not human nature that gives power to the vultures and maggots; it's only human culture. Dead things like money and authority.

The last time I saw one of the antipeople was in August. It was outside the Nightingale, between two and three a.m. on a Saturday night. I was drunk and on my own, wishing I had someone to share the taxi fare with; or even pay it myself, but not have to go home alone. Opposite the Hippodrome, I saw a body crumpled against a wire fence. Somebody was kneeling over it. As I crossed the road, the figure reared up and gave me an unmistakeable look that meant *Go away. This one's mine*. When I saw the face of the man on the ground, my skin turned cold. It was Jason, and he was bleeding from a deep cut above one eye. The creature's long fingers were pressed against the wound. I saw them turn red and stiffen like tiny pricks. They were hollow.

For a moment, I hesitated. It seemed impossible to change what was happening. Then I lurched towards them, almost falling, and grabbed at the thing's hair. It felt like a mesh of dry plastic threads. I was afraid the hair would pull out and leave me with no grip. But he tilted backwards and twisted around to face me, his arm stretching before the fingers came loose from Jason's face with a kind of tearing sound. The creature's own face was flat and expressionless, with eyes like holes in the ground. He fell against me, knocking me over; when I picked myself up, he'd gone.

Jason was lying very still, but he was breathing. One arm was pinned under his body. His face was like a copper mask, melting at the nose and forehead. I shook him gently; his eyes opened. "David," he said. "My God. What time is it? I must . . . I got beaten up. Did you see them?"

I shook my head. "You'll be all right. Take it easy." He stood up, then wavered and nearly fell. I caught hold of him, and we hugged each other for a few moments. He was wearing a crimson silk shirt which was dark with sweat. The cut in his forehead was like a jewel, and suddenly I thought of Douglas Fairbanks as Sinbad in a film I'd seen as a child. Still holding onto him, I steered Jason across the road and down the sidestreet to the club entrance. They were about to close up, but I told them what had happened and one of their staff went to get some tissues and ice. They knew Jason. He sat down on the doorstep, quite calmly. There was hardly anyone about. The night was blue and warm.

When the wound was cleaned up, I could see a bruise forming around it. His nose and right cheek were puffy too, though the skin was even paler than usual. The ice seemed to lessen the pain. After a few minutes, we walked down to the taxi-hire firm. I told him we'd have to go to the hospital. "Can't I just go home?" he said.

"If you don't get that cut stitched up, it won't heal properly." He nodded slowly. We waited in silence, Jason holding a ball of clotted tissues like a rose stiff with colour. I bit my lip to stay awake. Eventually a taxi came.

The casualty department at the General Hospital was brightly lit and reassuringly blank. Several rows of plastic chairs marked out the waiting area. In front of Jason was a rather gaunt-looking man of thirty or so, who was explaining loudly to the nurse that he'd swallowed a penny and was now unable to shit. It had been three days, he said. "I don't know why I swallowed it. It was just something I had to do." The nurse, with well-concealed impatience, suggested he try a curry. "Nothing works," he said. The look of hopelessness in his face betrayed him. I could pencil in his background easily enough: he lived alone, was unemployed, an incipient schizophrenic or perhaps an outpatient at Highcroft. But no amount of psychiatric help could change the fact that he had no friends and no way of gaining affection from another human being. When the nurse dismissed him, he took a seat behind us and waited to be seen again.

After Jason had talked to the nurse, we went and sat in another waiting area, with red upholstered seats and a number of silent people, all with minor injuries. I thought about the antipeople. They seemed to be everywhere in this hospital, waiting just out of sight. Perhaps they hung around the little curtained rooms where patients were left alone. One thought kept recurring to me, something Alan had said once. *The opposite of love is indifference*.

Eventually, Jason's name was called and he followed a nurse out through the swing doors. I waited, still drunk but sober in whatever part of me reacted to what was happening. Half an hour later he came back, with fourteen stitches in his forehead. It was past four o'clock. Jason lived in Kidderminster with his parents; he'd had to move back there after losing his job. I took him back to my flat, where he slept like a child. In the morning, I woke up and lay there for a while, looking at him. If anything visited him in the night, I didn't see. He woke up around midday and left soon afterwards, thanking me repeatedly for my help. But somehow, I still felt responsible. Fourteen stitches are not enough.

# LES DANIELS

## The Little Green Ones

LES DANIELS was recently honoured as co-Writer Guest of Honour with Peter Straub at the 1993 World Horror Convention, held in Stamford, Connecticut.

His short fiction has been published in *Cutting Edge*, *Borderlands*, *Dark Voices 4* and *5*, *After the Darkness*, *The Mammoth Book of Vampires* and *The Mammoth Book of Zombies*, but he is perhaps best known for his series of novels about the vampire anti-hero Don Sebastian de Villanueva. They include *The Black Castle*, *The Silver Skull*, *Citizen Vampire*, *Yellow Fog*, *No Blood Spilled*, and the still forthcoming *White Demon*.

A long-time devotee of comic books, Daniels has contributed a chapter on vampire comics to *The Compleat Vampire's Companion*, is the author of the recent bestseller *Marvel: Five Fabulous Decades of the World's Greatest Comics*, and he is currently working on a similar volume about the history of DC Comics.

The initial inspiration for the "The Little Green Ones" occurred when the author attended the 1988 World Fantasy Convention, held in West London. The child-like statues in the story can be found in the cemetery adjacent to the convention hotel, and we can attest to the fact that they are definitely as creepy as Daniels' chilling description . . .

He never knew who it was that he followed into the cemetery, much less why. His mind was on something else entirely as he wandered down the leafy London street, and evidently he had fallen into step behind some stranger, for when he looked up he was just inside the gate. He felt as if he were teetering on the edge of a dream. Behind him was a modern street, and he knew that if he turned his head he would see a photocopy shop with a bright orange sign, but in front of him was a shady expanse of ancient trees and weathered stone.

"The Public Are Permitted to Walk in the Cemetery Daily," proclaimed a sign, as if it were the most natural thing in the world for people to stroll through rows of corpses for their pleasure, and in fact he saw figures in the distance, moving slowly through the autumn haze. He couldn't see their faces. He wondered what his friends in Phoenix would say if they saw him go inside himself; it certainly wasn't like him to be morbid, but somehow this spot aroused his curiosity. He felt that this was the real London, that the cars and television sets outside were only a façade hiding something much less modern. Even the cemetery, apparently Victorian, was only a few layers deeper into the layers of disguise that covered something almost sinister in the city, something unutterably old.

He didn't like that, and he wanted to go home.

He had come on business, but there wasn't much business: he wouldn't have been walking around if someone hadn't cancelled an appointment. He didn't even have a room at the convention hotel: some mix-up had shunted him off to a dingy, dark place where the elevator creaked and his room was a box just barely big enough to hold a bed. He was beginning to think he didn't even care if franchises for Cowboy Bob's Bar-B-Q sprang up all over London or not. All that glass and plastic and concrete would be just another trick to fool the eye; the real London stretched out before him.

He stepped through the stone arch in the wall and went into the cemetery. It was quiet, and so big he couldn't see the end of it. Dead leaves littered the pathway, crunching unpleasantly under his feet, but there was still green in the trees overheard. He noticed a squirrel fleeing frantically from his intrusion, and scrambling up the side of a small mausoleum. The motion drew his eyes to the words "Devoted and Gentle Son", and to the pale stone face of a youth beside them. He looked to be about twenty, but his countenance was blackened in spots by time, especially around the eyes. The sculpture was giving way to some sort of rot, like the decay that long ago had turned the face inside the tomb to putrid fruit.

He felt the first hint of a shudder, looked away, and saw the children. There were two of them, standing on the other side of the path, and they were green.

He realized almost at once that they were statues, but somehow he was not reassured. Both of them, the girl and the boy, were staring at him with that disconcerting directness which only small children can summon; they appeared to be about seven, and they had been made lifesize. Except for their colour, which really was quite odd, they looked like figures from an antiquated textbook, a typical pair of typical children from several generations ago. The girl wore a dress that hung straight down from her shoulders to her knees; her shoes had little straps and there was a big bow in her short hair. The boy wore a sailor suit, complete with cap and kerchief; he had short pants and long stockings. They had their heads thrust forward, as if to increase the intensity of their gaze, and they had their arms behind their backs. They stood straight, almost at attention, yet time had tilted each one slightly away from the other, as if they might at any moment fall rigid to the ground. Their faces were earnestly expressionless.

He was only a few paces from the gate, yet in the presence of these little ones he felt terribly alone; he decided on the spot that he would not venture any further into the realm they seemed to guard. After all, he had no business in a graveyard anyway. Still, he stepped across the path to take a closer look at them. He couldn't quite resist the pull of these odd little figures, which seemed so commonplace and yet so horrible. Evidently someone's kids had died, and been commemorated in a fashion that was perhaps not in the best of taste, especially since the statues had turned green. He never would have contemplated such a thing if anything had happened to his two boys, who of course were safe at home, and certain to outlive him in any case. There was no connection with his family anyway; these really quite atrocious little figures were from another time and place.

The girl and boy stood watch over a slab of granite, conventionally grey and shaped somewhat like a coffin. There was an inscription on either side of it, and he discovered to his astonishment that the people buried here were a married couple who had died in middle age. She had given up the ghost in 1927, and he had followed her less than a year later. These were not the graves of children after all.

Then what was the significance of these little green ones who gazed at him so balefully, their loathsome, almost iridescent colour a match for the few leaves clinging to a tumorous old tree behind them? Why were they looking at him, and why was he looking back?

What weird sentiment had inspired these nasty little statues? Who had commissioned them? Was it some whimsical relative, or perhaps the grieving husband, who realized that his time was near and chose to commemorate their early days as childhood sweethearts? Had he killed himself to join her? Had he been hanged for killing her? And why were they so damned green?

It was a sickly, milky green, like lichen or moss, although it might have been oxidation if the things were made of metal. He could have found out easily enough, but he was damned if he was going to touch them. It was too easy to imagine them crumbling beneath his touch, held together by nothing but the strange stuff that encrusted them. Worse yet, his hand might sink into a mass of fungus. People thought green was the colour of life, but this was a festering life that fed on death.

He hurried away from there, hardly taking time to notice another sign beside the gate: "Persons in Charge of Children Are Required to Control Them."

His nerves were shot, no doubt. The trip wasn't going well, and he hadn't been sleeping much: jet-lag. But it was this city, too, and the whole country, really. It was on the wrong side of the world. The gravity was wrong here, and so was the light. He longed to be back in God's country, where things stood new and clean against a desert sky, where nothing was old and nothing was green.

On his way back to the hotel, he had to wait for a hateful and ridiculous traffic signal. Instead of an honest and direct "WALK" or "DON'T WALK", the electric sign displayed a slumped red figure to keep pedestrians immobile, and a strutting, glowing green figure when it was time to march. He stared at something green taking its first step and felt his eyelids twitch.

He was bone weary, no doubt about that, and he would be expected to perform like a happy salesman at the reception that was only a few hours away. He stumbled into his hotel, made his way to his room, locked the door behind him and fell into his little bed. He told himself he was taking a nap. After all, your health is more important. The room grew dark around him while he lay like a man who had been poleaxed.

Half asleep in his overpriced coffin, he heard a quiet voice, something between a groan and a sigh. It was right there in the cramped confines of his room. He jerked upright like an old-fashioned mechanical toy and peered into the twilight. Was someone there? Or had he made that noise himself?

He got up, more drained than ever, and turned on the light. There was nothing to be seen, but the bathroom door was closed and he decided to leave it that way. He went out to the convention without bothering to shave or shower or change his clothes.

The party was noisier and stupider than he would have thought possible. He drank heavily and tried not to talk to anyone. A man got up on a table and took his pants down. The future of Cowboy Bob's Bar-B-Q was in his hands. Amazingly, nobody seemed to object. Even the English seemed crude and crass, oblivious to the verdant mysteries that slept beneath their soil. Christ, even Robin Hood had dressed in green. Was everybody blind?

He took a cab back to his hotel and wondered whether his wife was going to leave him. He was in London, but there wasn't even any goddam fog. He could see every landmark they passed, even Brompton Cemetery. The gates, thank God, were locked, and the little green ones safe inside—unless they'd been out for hours. Do you know where your children are tonight?

The cab dropped him off, and every building he could see around him was the work of men long dead. The sky was gigantic. Everyone was going to die, no matter what they did, and something small was going to come around the corner unless he got inside. Why was this happening to him? He hadn't done anything—he'd only looked.

He stood outside his room, so sure the little green ones were inside that he couldn't even bring himself to open the door. He thought about them for a long time, then said the hell with it and went inside, which was a reasonable plan since they didn't visit him until after he was asleep. It wasn't sleep, really, just the fitful snooze of the ageing and the afraid, but it was good enough until he saw the kids again, their arms locked behind their backs as if they were tied. They didn't reach out for him, and they didn't come toward him; instead they went into the bathroom and stood in the shower. They made no sound, but all at once the silence seemed shrill, as if someone had turned up the volume on an unplugged radio. The boy and the girl waited under the running water, their little faces bland and boring and reproachful, and the green that covered them dribbled away, filling the tub and overflowing on to the floor. It slopped toward him, while the children, washed free of it, gave forth a blistering white light that streamed into his eyes and woke him up.

It was sunlight, of course, and it was his last day in London. All he had to do was survive this, and he would be safe.

A phoney banquet at the big hotel. International food franchise folks, eat this. It couldn't have been worse. Everything was green.

He had walked past the cemetery on his way, and had peered in for long enough to see the kiddies still standing there, but he sensed that they were not through with him, and every course he ate confirmed it. Watercress soup. Avocado salad. Lamb with mint sauce, the green flecks swimming up through the innocuous oil. Green beans, potatoes sprinkled with parsley. Lime mousse for dessert, and mints wrapped in green foil. It was all fucking green, and he didn't eat much. Green Perrier bottles were all around him, but he was slugging back cheap Scotch.

He ran for the plane.

Whatever it was that there was dropped behind him as he soared into the sky, but not before he looked out of the window and saw the whole accursed island spread out below him. It was green, green from stem to stern, green for hundreds of miles in every direction, as far as the eye could see. An alien empire, drifting into insignificance. Christopher Robin's dead.

It was hard to shake them, of course. Their grave little features were engraved on each one of the peas in his plastic plate, and when the plane hit an air pocket he would see their small, sad faces.

They were gone, however, by the time he got to Phoenix, and Death was something that grew in the old world.

He told himself that, even when his wife showed up in a green rented car and asked him for a divorce. She had spent his money on green contact lenses, which transformed her eyes into something glassy, cold, and enigmatic. Maybe she was right, but how could fake and hate bring happiness? It was all nonsense, right up to the last moment, the land around him brown and clean and honest and American. The dead kids were a thousand, thousand miles away. There was nothing to remind him of them.

Dead was dead, and green was green, and that was the end of it.

Yet when his own children ran out to greet him at the door, he saw to his dismay that they were not alone.

# STEVE RASNIC TEM

## Mirror Man

As usual, it's been a prolific year for Steve Rasnic Tem, with short stories published in *MetaHorror*, *In Dreams*, *Narrow Houses*, *The Mammoth Book of Vampires*, *The Dedalus Book of Femmes Fatales*, *Gauntlet 3*, *Dark at Heart*, *Best New Horror 3*, and elsewhere.

He collaborated with his wife Melanie on the chapbook *Beautiful Strangers*, and contributed three new stories to the solo booklet, *Decoded Mirrors: 3 Tales After Lovecraft*.

"Mirror Man" comes from the latter and, as the publisher's blurb reveals: "The sources of horror in Steve Rasnic Tem's fiction are not monsters, but moments of revelation and self-discovery, when characters find their deepest doubts and fears reflected in the world around them ... Through its powerful evocation of personal alienation, this triptych of 'tales after Lovecraft' reminds us that Lovecraft, in teaching us new ways to view our world, also taught us new ways in which to view ourselves."

By way of a coda to that insightful evaluation, the author explains that, "'Mirror Man' was the reason I did the *Decoded Mirrors* chapbook—I actually wrote it several years ago, liked it, but couldn't sell it anywhere (most everybody didn't like the Lovecraft angle in it). So when Necronomicon Press started up their chapbook line, a Lovecraftian trilogy seemed to be in order."

We are delighted to present Tem's disturbing story to a wider audience . . .

JEFF LIKED TO THINK OF THE white hairs in his ears as signs of maturity, although he suspected they were really the first outcroppings of old age. He hadn't even noticed them until they were a half-inch or more long; that bothered him. They were pale and looked slightly rubbery, like the hairs on some mutant onion. Once he knew they were there he spent hours examining himself for any new phenomena. Sometimes he would use Liz's magnified makeup mirror. He was convinced that his face was changing every day, but other than the somewhat dramatic ear-hairs he had found nothing to confirm this.

In the mirror, silvered fog turned to beads, then rivulets that bent his flesh and attempted to drag his face into the sink. He wondered if Susan would still love him if he were deformed. Adults *were* mutants—he could think of no better way to define the accretion of distortions as children grew into adults.

He remembered his embarrassment over his own father—the man's appearance, his views about race and nationality. During his teen years he had sought a theory to explain his father's condition—the brain parasite, the secret society, his father's hidden lizard face.

Some day Susan would find him hideously embarrassing. That was why he had to take her on this trip with him. The time when she was uncompromisingly proud of him was fast approaching an end.

Liz had stopped loving him years ago. There must have been a final day when she'd passed beyond her love for him into whatever indifference or resentment she felt now, but he'd been unable to pinpoint it. There was a kind of unspoken pact between them that they not speak of it, perhaps the ultimate in the series of unspoken pacts which had characterized their marriage. But it had been so obvious, so stupid and banal. He'd continued to love her even after that, in that youthful love-sick and inarticulate way he always had, until that too was gone one day, maybe the same lost day he'd first become the adult mutant, when he'd started growing hair in his ears.

An area of cleared mirror containing a section of his left jaw and earlobe fogged over again beneath his breath. His face had fractured in the mirror, broken out into a collage. Some of the layers of his face were as young as his first memories (his lost tricycle half-buried in a pile of coal behind the house, his mother's breath smelling like warm bread), and others were far older than he was. In fact some of the layers of the mirrored face, he was convinced, didn't even belong to him.

"Are we ever going, Daddy?" He saw Susan in one corner of the mirror, dolled up in her party dress, ready for the trip out. Liz had done up her hair in a mass of tight curls—it must have taken hours. "Well, are we?"

"Just give me a few more minutes, honey. I want to look good for the reunion, haven't seen some of these people in a very long time." He couldn't make himself turn around. The mirror was much safer. If he looked at his daughter directly he would want to hold her all the time, until that day she stopped breathing.

Sometimes she made him want to cry—out of some strange sadness because he was growing older every day or because he loved her so much or because he'd recently realized she was the only person in the world he really did love, and even there he wasn't sure he was very effective at it. As he'd grown older he seemed so frightened and suspicious, so inept at loving. So he contented himself with staring at her reflection, admiring the light she cast. "We'll be leaving real soon, honey. I promise."

Liz was waiting in the bedroom when he walked in. "She'll be bored to tears, Jeff. I really don't understand this."

Her shadow rippled across the wall as she paced the room. That flicker of grey reminded him of a small bird that had been trapped in the house one night. They couldn't quite see it, they were just aware of its grey wings beating and beating against the light's reflection on the glossy wallpaper. In the morning they had found torn feathers, spots of blood on the bed. He spoke to Liz's shadow as it moved across the wall. "None of my old classmates or teachers have ever met my daughter. I want to show her off. I have a right—I'm proud of her."

"Providence is a long way to drag an eleven-year-old. Just to stroke your vanity." Her shadow danced a graceful ballet across the wall. It was a terrible irony that adult mutants cast the delicate shadows of children.

He'd always believed that saying things more than once was pointless. And during the course of an unusually verbal marriage he'd said about everything possible. It was like looking in the mirror every day: if things did change it was too gradual to notice. But if he didn't say something, she'd embrace him with silence until he'd left the house. "I'm sorry," he said. "I don't think that's what I'm doing." The words cracked in his mouth from all the years of repetition. One day they'd degenerate into another, far more primitive language. Some sort of eldritch, decadent phrasing. If he didn't do something. If he was still capable.

There was the expected pause while she decided whether there was going to be an argument this morning. Jeff found himself holding his breath in anticipation of her decision, and that made him resentful. Some mornings that would be enough to make him say the little more which would guarantee an argument, but not today. Today he was going to take his beautiful daughter down to Rhode Island for that ten-year reunion. Everyone from the graduate school was going to know that he'd had it in him to have a family, a normal family like other people. With a beautiful daughter, a daughter who depended on him and who called him Daddy.

He heard the agitated beating of grey wings in his head, but he tried to ignore it, moving about the bedroom getting dressed as quickly as he could, waiting for Liz to say whatever she was going to say. He wanted to ask her what ties he should take, if his grey corduroy jacket with the elbow patches would take one more important wearing, but first he had to know if there was going to be an argument or not. If there was going to be an argument he thought he might never be able to ask such questions of her again.

He caught her reflection in the dresser mirror as she sat on the bed, staring at his half-full suitcase on the other end. She looked so unhappy he wanted to go over and sit beside her, take her in his arms, but then she would tell him all that he had done to make her feel the way she did, and that would start the argument he could not have this morning.

In the mirror he saw the silvering in her long black hair. He'd never noticed it before, looking at her every day, watching her eat breakfast before she left for the university. Again the mirror provided him with secret, arcane knowledge. But then she always wore her hair up for work, and she was usually in good humor—she actually enjoyed the work she was forced to do. Sadness brought out the silver in her hair. Not for the first time, Jeff realized how difficult he must be for her to live with.

"You used to be so impressive," she began softly. "You were the only person I'd ever met who early on decided what kind of person he was going to be, and then became that person. You used to make me feel so good about myself."

Her reflection stared at him, talked to him. Liz had learned where to look if she wanted to look into his eyes. Her image in the mirror was so clear, so direct, that Jeff thought he might be loving her again, if he had ever in fact stopped loving her. The room's reflection around her image looked vaguely warped, shimmering with distortion. The contrast between the room's distortion and Liz's clear image brought a tremor of anxiety into his hands struggling with the tie, and he wondered vaguely at the physics involved. There appeared to be dark pockets where the vertical lines of the room's image warped or broke. There appeared to be distant movement behind Liz where the reflected colors of the room bled. Liz's face was singular and unwavering, her eyes fixed on him, even as the rest of the world appeared chaotic with layers, the room about to dissolve around her, peel away revealing . . . what? He could see in the mirror that she was silently crying now. But if he didn't turn to look at her directly she was not crying at all. If she was sad only in his mirror, he had not made her sad at all. In the mirror her eyes begged him for the first time in years. Jeff looked away, embarrassed, and fumbled again with his tie, trying to imagine it tied.

"I'll . . . talk to you about it just as soon as we get back tomorrow. I promise."

"Okay, Jeff. Whatever. Whatever you say." When Jeff looked back up at the mirror she had left it. The lines of the room moved jaggedly, the furniture blending with increasing speed, as if the world of the mirror was being heated.

Susan was good in the car. It made him proud when Susan was good. "Am I going to meet your friends?" she asked.

"Old friends," he said.

"But are they still your friends?"

He didn't know what to say. He pretended to busy himself with the rearview mirror, adjusting it in order to view as much of the landscape behind him as possible. Early in their marriage Liz would kid him about his habit of fiddling with the mirror, as if something was following him. He had never laughed, and eventually she dropped the joke. "I don't know, honey," he said now. "Adults don't always know who their friends are, I guess. It's simpler at your age. Friendships get complicated when you're an adult. You get set in your ways, and then you forget how to make friends."

Liz nodded solemnly in his rear-view mirror. Jeff stared at the mirror until his wife's face vanished and Susan's reappeared. He adjusted the mirror both to expose the maximum amount of receding landscape and to see as much of Susan as he could, while limiting her view of his own mutating expressions. He had to keep an eye on her, he had to keep her safe—that was his responsibility as a father—and yet he didn't want her to feel that he was spying on her.

"Why won't you look at me, Daddy?" Obviously he had the mirror adjusted correctly. She hadn't asked the question in a long time.

He licked his lips. But he couldn't see himself in the mirror now, so he had to wonder if he was in fact licking his lips. "I'm driving, honey. I can't look at you and drive at the same time."

She nodded again. "That's why I can't sit in the front seat with you. That's the rule."

Every few months she seemed compelled to check out his expectations. He hated it when she called them rules. He preferred to think of them as guidelines which held reality in place. Mutants needed as many of these mini-strictures as they could generate, just to get through the day. Jeff didn't bother to tell Susan about all of them, thinking that if she knew them all it would hasten her evolution into mutancy. So he had always told her strictly on a need-to-know basis. "When you sit in the front seat, it distracts me, honey. And when that happens things aren't so safe any more. I guess you distract me because you're so pretty." He laughed but Susan did not laugh with him. "Driving is serious business," he continued. "Daddy has to concentrate."

"Someday I still want to sit in the front seat, Daddy."

"I know." And someday soon, he knew, she would no longer accept his interpretations of what was safe.

They passed through Attleboro on Highway 123 before connecting with 1–95 which would take them south out of Massachusetts and down into the heart of Providence. Jeff had taken the long way out of New Hampshire, avoiding Concord, Portsmouth, the entire Boston area. He hadn't exactly planned it that way. He drove as he always drove, allowing himself plenty of time, constantly referring to the map so he would have some vague idea where the roads led. Vague because maps lied—he'd discovered this a long time ago—taking you into all manner of locales not even hinted at by the pale colors and wandering veins etched into the paper.

He never chose the shortest route. You couldn't tell anyway because traffic and road conditions were never indicated, and the nature of the driving experience itself was beyond the scope of any map. He avoided the interstates as much as possible—he was scared of not seeing those hidden taints in the bypassed towns.

He preferred to feel his way through the landscape, watching not only the road but also the ambient architecture and the local residents, constantly checking his mirrors for the backward look that often revealed all—the secret faces, the unconscious expressions.

Then he would find the next road on the map, and, if the drive had been pleasant, he would choose routes which he sensed would somehow maintain the experience. But if the look of the buildings or the people or even the particular rake or curvature of the road disturbed him, he would search the map for the quickest, most likely release.

But the indigenous inhabitants were most important. They were the ones who built and maintained the buildings, who landscaped the environment. Even the most neutral of settings would reveal some sort of signature.

They stopped for gas in a small New England town which had somehow escaped the urban sprawl. Perhaps no one had ever noticed it was there. It was tucked away beneath one edge of the highway, a faded green sign hanging askew on rusted bolts pointing to a narrow exit lane. Jeff took the lane past a row of dilapidated houses to a one-pump station.

The boy appeared suddenly at the driver's side window. His dark skin was mottled by patches of pink and grey peeling away beneath his eyes, like poorly-applied makeup. His eyes were narrow and dark. The phrase *melting pot* came to mind. Jeff's father used to talk a great deal about a "melting pot" when Jeff was a child. The phrase had filled him with unease.

"Gas you?" The dark spaces of the boy's eyes betrayed no life. Jeff found himself grunting an affirmative. The boy nodded, replying with a series of expressions, gestures, even simple looks Jeff could not fully understand. It made him uncomfortable. So perhaps he wasn't so different from his father at all, only marginally better-educated. Educated enough to feel the guilt.

In Jeff's mirror, Susan was layered in shadow and light, her deepset eyes unreadable. But he suspected she felt it, too. He'd always wanted to blame his own father for teaching him such profound unease. But he suspected it wasn't upbringing. Unease was bred in the womb.

He tipped the boy much too generously and hurried back to the main highway. He passed through several similar villages. He changed routes several times, and still the worn out houses and patchwork faces continued, the accumulation of them sloughing off his mirror into memory.

In Jeff's rearview mirror shadowed faces appeared in backwards perspective, layer after layer of them in grey doorways and open windows and behind polarized windshields. But what disturbed him more than the faces themselves were the eyes they held—as a bare setting might hold its jewel—too small to see and yet which themselves might see so much. Thousands of eyes glittering with dark color, moving slowly, scanning, telescoping, perhaps jittering a wild, drug-induced dance within the ravaged face within a ravaged hovel. The eyes his rearview mirror could not catch in the act.

He knew such things weren't safe to talk about. Early in his graduate history studies he had been interested in the writings of such American nativists as Madison Grant, Lothrop Stoddard, and H. P. Lovecraft. He'd wanted to know if they had had certain perceptions, and if perhaps they'd so misunderstood these perceptions that their rather bizarre racial theories had come about. He'd wanted to know what they saw when they looked into the mirror.

Regularly he checked on Susan in the mirror. She slept off and on, slumped against the right-hand door. Now and then she would wake up and gaze into the mirror with bewildered eyes, as if this were something she had never seen before, as if she had seen her adult self, her mutancy, her lone animal self. Then she would nod off again. Children were blessed with an expansive capacity for sleep, because the world was too complicated a place for them to take in all at once. Now and then she would wake again and look, and as it grew darker outside the car there came a time when Jeff could not see her eyes in the mirror, although he sensed their heat.

It was night by the time they'd reached the outskirts of Providence. But not the complete dark he would have experienced at home, surrounded by open fields and with the nearest streetlight miles away. This was the brown dark that surrounded large cities, diluted by chemical smoke and exotic lighting.

He'd always found driving at night to be disorienting. Each vehicle was a bubble of dim light, a marginally sufficient and self-contained ecosystem. You wandered up and down grey ribbons of highway you could barely see, seeking clues as to your route. It was a wonder any one of you reached your destination. Night driving seemed a matter of blind and ancient instinct, aided by appeals to the gods of luck.

He remembered being lost one time and driving with the window down, seeking some sort of guidance from the local smells: wet salt, cedar smoke, or a thick, treacly plasma that seemed to cling to his clothing. He'd read somewhere that smells often had a powerful impact on people's moods, especially the moods of children. He wondered how many sociopaths had grown up with stale, evil fragrances.

Now he rolled the window up tight, cursing himself for exposing Susan to the air of the highway. He searched for her in his rearview mirror, eventually finding her curled up against the right-hand door, the top half of her face eaten by shadow. "Susan?" She didn't move. He spoke it again, louder, and still no response. He felt her panicky, screamed name rising swiftly up his throat, but held it back. He should have been watching her all the time. Then she stirred in her sleep. He was relieved, and then suddenly a little irritated with her. He needed to have her alert and charming for his reunion. He pulled off the road and into a small convenience store on the northeast edge of the city.

The man behind the counter seemed too old for the long silver chain dangling from his left ear. His eyes were greasy. He gazed past Jeff out the front window. "Your little girl sick?" he asked, with minimal movement of his lips.

For some reason the very idea that the clerk had noticed his daughter in the car, had used the words "your little girl," alarmed Jeff. He found himself searching the man's face for a lascivious wink or tongue across the lips. In the high chrome polish of the cash register, shelves, and counter trim, Jeff could feel a thousand fragments of the clerk's slick eyes, watching him, sliding closer.

Jeff turned and found himself looking at his daughter directly, without the protection of reflection. She sat like an elderly doll slumped with a heavy weight of medication, her forehead pressing the car window, staring at him. The red and yellow neon of the store's sign washed her face, made it seem thinner, the shadows darker. She was his beautiful doll, his Auschwitz doll. He turned and almost desperately his gaze latched on to the clerk's greasy eyes. "It's just the reflection from your sign. That damned garish neon. That's what makes her look so ill." He said it inviting argument, but there was none. The clerk cast his subhuman eyes down and waited for Jeff's order.

When he got into the car he handed the sack of food back to her without looking. He held his breath a beat, anticipating some sort of terrible breakage—the car windows, the store beyond, perhaps even the tight sheen of skin stretched over his skull, but after a moment a hand took the bag from him. "I couldn't remember what you liked." He forced a laugh and it sounded oddly falsetto. "So I bought enough for six . . . six daughters, six little girls."

He was embarrassing himself. She said nothing in reply; he thought she must be terribly angry with him now. He was glad Liz wasn't there to point out how badly he was handling things. It was obviously much too trying a trip for a little girl. He had given her coffee and donuts, cupcakes and a nut bar and two colas in the bag, brands he had never heard of, Rhode Island brands he supposed. He thought she was too young for coffee but he couldn't remember. He couldn't remember any of the things she liked to eat. Suddenly he didn't know her at all. She had grown up much too fast and soon she would be dead. They all would be dead. Everyone had told him that all his life but he hadn't believed it until now.

She didn't say anything. But he thought he could hear her eating now. Not loudly, but slowly consuming everything he had given her. Good.

He didn't recognize any of the streets around Brown. They were all torn up, decades of asphalt pulled up like geologic strata, detours leading him around the gaping excavations floored with oily liquid to oddly-shaped parking spaces overlooked by black ruins. He thought he recognized the Rockefeller Library but he couldn't be sure. He finally pulled the car into what may or may not have been a parking space, opened Susan's door, and reached into the shadows there. Her hand caught his timidly. "We're late," he barked nervously, turning his head as he dragged her from the car and started racing up the steps. Her tread grew lighter the harder he pulled. He had a vision of his beautiful daughter entering the reception hand-in-hand with proud papa. He whispered back into the cool wind blowing off the damp pavement, "You're beautiful." He knew her shyness would not permit her to reply to that, and she didn't.

The night air in Providence seemed a far more substantial thing than he remembered, but it had been a very long time since he had done more than drive through the city during daylight hours. He supposed there was much more pollution these days, more dust from all the reconstruction. Shadows underwent a congealing process; black spaces solidified. At times it was like walking through veils. The air had a feeling of age, as in a room long kept shut. Try as he might, he couldn't imagine how as a student here he had ever tolerated such Lovecraftian gloom.

The printed sign on the door said that the City Works department had ruled this particular classroom building "unsafe." Another hastily-scrawled red note on blue paper—Professor Lawrence's old stationery?—explained that the reunion had been moved to the Biltmore hotel.

Rather than trying to maneuver those torn and reshuffled streets again, Jeff decided they would walk. He wouldn't worry about getting lost; everyone knew where the Biltmore was.

After several blocks he had to remove his coat. He could not believe the heat. His shirt stuck to his skin like layers of molt—he suspected it was ruined. Liz would be unhappy—she had given it to him last birthday, although it was the only present he could remember receiving. Perhaps an ugly tie from Susan with her child's taste. He vaguely remembered looking into the mirror and seeing a line of distortion hanging from his neck, squeezing it so tightly he couldn't breathe. Susan kept slipping from his grasp; he regripped her hand so tightly he was surprised when she didn't cry out. In the dark puddles spotting the pavement his reflection looked bodiless, his head screaming as it flew through the night air.

Store windows strangely refused to give up all of his reflection. In passing he would see a cheek and an eye, downward slash of a mouth, an outthrust leg, one hand trailing back, desperately clutching at a daughter who seemed to have lost her bright image in their flight across town. He tried to attribute the gaps in his own image and his daughter's complete absence to dust and grease on the glass.

Now and then he lost track of the Biltmore's direction in the tangle of disrupted streets and gutted buildings. He stopped and gave a dark passerby his best "lost" look—the man's shambling made it impossible to ask him directly. He wasn't surprised that the man ignored him. He tried this tack again and again, finally working up the courage to at least touch the shoulder of one or two. Some of those citizens obviously didn't take kindly to his touching them so—some looked as if they might have killed him had there been no witnesses. All his life, he had met people who seemed somehow too cold, too cruel to be human; they behaved in ways Jeff believed no human should behave.

A man turned suddenly and gestured awkwardly toward a narrow side street. Jeff was struck by the mouth, which seemed too wide, as if he had undergone one of those mouth surgeries movie stars had had, but in this case the incision had gone much too far. Jeff stared, but the man's eyes refused to blink, collecting more and more water which caught the dim light and magnified it, making them look heavy with ground glass. Jeff finally turned away.

The gathering at the Biltmore was sedate, and no one seemed to recognize him. The hotel itself was under reconstruction, tall scaffolding leaning precariously against the walls where workers in white coveralls labored overtime at replastering the cracked and stained surfaces. Or perhaps they themselves were applying the cracks and stains. Jeff drank until the workers and scaffolding disappeared, and then he had a vision of the hotel's more elegant future firmly in mind.

"Bill, is that you?" Someone clutched his shoulder, as if desperately seeking directions.

"No," Jeff replied to the staggering fat man in front of him. "Tonight I'm not me at all."

Now and then a stranger would smile and slap Jeff on the back, chant a few endearments and then leave again. Jeff thought that in another time and world they might have been his friends. Everyone had always liked him, but he had no talent for friendship.

Some time near midnight Jeff discovered Professor Lawrence chatting with some men and women Jeff's own age whom he vaguely remembered as having been in his classes in graduate school. He watched the elderly man for some time before he could muster enough courage to speak to him. He wore glasses still, but a different, squarer shape. His speech, his entire presentation seemed a bit more hesitant, his former students interrupting frequently to take command of the conversation and discuss their own researches.

"Professor Lawrence?" he said, pushing himself right up to the old man's glasses. "Jeff Reynolds. It's great to see you again!"

The old man nodded absently, then raised an eyebrow slightly. "Oh, I remember," he said, sounding tired. "You did some work on the nativists, as I recall. Most peculiar. Those old bigots. Most peculiar," he said again, as if describing Jeff himself, and Jeff watched as his reflected face in his imagined father's glasses turned dark, broad, lizard-like.

"Here," Jeff said suddenly, rocking forward and spilling his drink on Lawrence, who blanched and stepped back. "I have a *family* now! Me! A wife and a beautiful . . . beautiful daughter. Susan!" He called, looking around, and suddenly realizing in a panic he had no idea where she was. "Susan!" He tried to grab Lawrence's hands in both of his but Lawrence stumbled and jerked away from him. As if Jeff's touch might contaminate the old fraud. "Susan!" He stared at Lawrence in horror. "You have to believe me!" he cried. "You were important to me. I *do* have a daughter!" But the hotel shimmered so loudly Jeff had no idea if Professor Lawrence heard him at all.

After a few hours Jeff stopped calling out the name of his beautiful daughter, wondering—helpless not to—whether that was truly her name. If she was alive, if she even existed anymore, he felt she would find him. If only he could cover enough ground in time. The sky had lightened somewhat—dawn would be there soon—but as yet there were only night people out on the Providence streets.

He did not know what he could tell Elizabeth, if there was ever an Elizabeth to tell. He didn't think he would ever be able to tell her anything if he could not find Susan.

The pale light falling between the buildings into the narrow streets had its own kind of solidity, as if there were a clear line between this light and what lay beyond and the ordinary morning this side of it. Like a curtain, or a sheet of glass. He stepped through.

In the expanding light Providence tried to reveal its secrets to him. Where store fronts had been torn open metal armature was revealed, a multitude of electrical cable and the complex network of plumbing added to and subtracted from so often over the years that he doubted anyone could trace it all. Posters had been rubbed away unevenly from the exterior walls of shops so that the portions of words remaining spelled out bizarre phrases which nonetheless seemed vaguely familiar to him. Ornate architectural decoration had been weathered so that even more ornate subsurfaces showed through. Disparate building styles had been jammed together to create new styles. The city appeared unfinished, and yet already renewing itself.

Two of the men with too-broad mouths rode huge street cleaning machines, running over the same spots again and again.

From broken window panes fragments of many eyes reflected down. At the bronzed edges of buildings mishappen limbs attempted to stir from the reflective surfaces. In the finish of a shiny red car he saw his body beginning to warp and catch fire. In the polished tile of a pedestrian plaza he caught a glimpse of his true eyes. In the curve of a broken bottle he watched himself striking again and again at the child he loved so much, whom he could not find in all these mirrors.

"This is the way it begins," he thought, as world rubbed against world, and his own skin grew veined and layered. "This is the way it ends," he thought, as stink and dark erupted from every crack in the pavement, every opening in the walls, and the raw edges of his reality. "This is simply one of those moments," he thought, when suddenly and just for the moment you forget that you are a human being in the company of human beings, and you find that you are capable of doing something truly terrible. Just for that moment there seems no reason not to do the worst thing you can think of. There seems to be no one to judge you, and for that moment you are incapable of guilt. A life is defined by the choices made during moments like these.

He found Susan's body somewhere between the world he had always dreamed he lived in and the dark impulses beyond. Her body had been taken apart beyond all hope of reassembly. In the dull mirror of her eye he could see the lizard he had become, and the goat, a lone member of that dark mysterious race that would forever corrupt the lives of the human animal.

# SARAH ASH

## Mothmusic

Sarah Ash trained as a musician and studied composition at Cambridge. Since then she has taught music and collaborated on several theatre pieces for young performers, the most recent being *Spaced Out!*, a 1960s space opera based on the legend of Psyche.

"Mothmusic" marked her debut in *Interzone* and was only the second of her short stories to be published (the first appeared in *Far Point* 4 in 1992). It is a baroque tale of creeping metamorphosis reminiscent of the best work of Clark Ashton Smith.

Her first novel, *Moths to a Flame* (which she reveals "develops some of the themes first started in 'Mothmusic'") will be published in Britain by Orion's Millennium imprint in 1994.

OBSERVATIONS OF ASTAR TAZIEL (personal physician to the House of Memizhon) on the symtoms of boskh-addiction.

*Boskh*: The Aelahim Moonmoth was indigenous to the remote Island of Ael Lahi until this year when a spice merchant brought back live specimens, claiming that the dust from their wings is used extensively by the islanders both as a hallucinogen and a medicinal remedy. This merchant made extensive claims as to its healing properties which the Arkhan commanded me to investigate. The results of my findings are recorded below.

*Medicinal Uses*: When administered in minuscule quantities, boskh has proved to be most efficacious in curing mortal fevers and aiding the healing of infected, gangrenous wounds. A miraculous substance without any like in all Ar-Khendy. One to five grains is usually enough and in the case of a large area of suppurating tissue, a light dusting—no more.

*Addiction—warning signs*: Repeated use of boskh creates dependency. Visual disturbances are the first signs—sore, watering eyes, intolerance of light, etc. When I tried boskh for myself, the sense-enhancement was—magical; quite beyond my wildest imaginings. But as the drug wore off I experienced nausea, agonizing stomach cramps, aching eyes—and the oddest intuition that if I were to take more boskh, the symptoms would be instantly relieved. However, I held firm to my resolve and recovered within a day's span.

**Journal of the Plague Year**

Called at dawn to the house of Torella Sarillë, favoured mistress of X –. There found all the house-hold in darkness and disorder, Sarillë herself, her hair down, half-dressed, wandering the upper corridors like one distracted. When I had calmed her with an infusion of powdered horn-poppy, I examined her. I have never seen anything like this before. Her eyes appear to be swelling within their sockets; the pupil has grown so large has grown so large that there is little iris still visible. The pain caused by the swelling—and by any light—is so excruciating that the patient screams aloud.

When asked, Sarillë admitted to ingesting boskh in large quantities. Now I learn that at Myn-Dhiel all the courtiers have been taking boskh—by mouth and by incising the veins and sprinkling the powder into the bloodstream. Apparently it leads to a greatly enhanced sexual prowess and stamina. They call this "Yskhysse," a word in the Old Tongue that defies accurate translation. She described several erotic practices to me which made even this old physician blush; I will not record them here but mention only that the boskh appears to facilitate some kind of hallucinatory mind-merging and that these exquisites at Myn-Dhiel have devised some bizarre concepts of using the various bodily orifices in ways that the All-Seeing certainly did not intend!

Called again to Sarillë. All shutters closed, no lights. Sarillë supine upon her bed, the brocade curtains drawn. Blind. Crazed. Crying out for more boskh. And everywhere, in the moonlit garden, in the streets, the shrill fluting of these creatures and the sweet stench from their iridescent wings. When I left the house, the night air was filled with moths, swirling like snow. Girls played weirdflutes to them, sang, to entice them into their chambers.

Sarillë. I have never seen the like before. This . . . corruption of the skin. Puncture marks on her arms and legs; I thought at first they were scars from gross intravenous boskh-abuse but they look more like the bite of some insect or leech.

More cases to attend to. Three courtesans of the House of Red Khassia, a house of ill-repute much frequented by young bloods from the Palace. And the boy Khal, the paramour of the Tarrakhan, a Tarkmyn of some seventeen years, famed for his great personal beauty, a uniquely exquisite blending of white-fair hair with soft black eyes, deep enough to drown a man—But I digress. Those famed dark eyes have lost their lustre and become filmed and dull. Khal is going blind—yet he screams with pain if anyone approaches with a lantern or candle. The Tarrakhan is beside himself with grief. He has offered me gold by the bushel if I can but find a cure for the lad.

When I arrived at the Tarkhas House at dusk, the air was filled with the beat of the moths' soft wings, their lirruping songs. The very air—*glittered*. I tied a scarf over my mouth and nostrils so that I should not inhale the noxious substance. In Khal's room, the windows were wide open and a flock of the creatures fluttered about the room. The boy lay motionless on the bed—they were crawling all over him, a heaving coverlet of white down. I went to drive them off but the Tarrakhan stopped me. "Look," he said, "their presence has calmed him—surely this proves the healing properties of this boskhdust!"

Outside in the courtyard dead moths fluttered to the cobbles like dead leaves. Soon a carpet of pale husks covered the ground.

"They are dying!" cried the Tarrakhan, grabbing my arm. "They are dropping by the thousand—there will be no boskh left to cure Khal. Can't you do something?"

"But we have seen this before . . . in the common selkh moth on which our livelihood depends. The moths mate, lay their eggs—and die."

"But—where do they lay their eggs, Taziel?"

I turned back to Khal. The creatures were slowly crawling off him, their wings ragged, all glitter dulled. I brushed some away and they dropped sluggishly to the floor, unable to fly. My fingers were smeared with dust from their decaying, disintegrating wings. Khal groaned, muttered incoherently. I bent over him in the dwindling dusk, trying to examine him; it was too dark to see clearly.

"Bring light!"

"He cannot bear the light – "

"I must have light!" There was something in the urgency of my voice that made him obey. As he held the lantern over the boy's slim body, he saw what I had glimpsed in the gloom. Puncture marks. Bruised puncture marks, freshly darkstained with blood, marring Khal's perfect skin, on chest, smooth belly and groin—as if he had been stung by a swarm of envenomed bees.

"Dear God. Dear God." The light flickered as the lantern rattled in the Tarrakhan's shaking hand. He sank to his knees, laying his head on the boy's breast. "He still breathes—have they drained his blood, are they leechmoths, are they –?"

"No."

"Then—what?"

"I do not know. I have never seen anything like this before."

"Taziel! I'm paying you to cure him!" Tears streamed down his cheeks. "Don't let him die!"

I have watched by Khal's bedside for three days and nights now. There are so many similar cases in Perysse that I cannot number them. If I had not seen the moths crawling on the boy's body I would have said from the marks that we were in the grip of some terrible Pestilence. But Khal's torment lies within—and is struggling to *get out*.

Sarillë is dead. She took poison; the Sleep of White Crystal that kills swiftly. I examined her body. Dear God. She was dead but *they* still lived. To see *them* wriggling beneath the skin, to see the undulation within dead tissue, maggots already gone to work in a corpse not yet cold –

The Tarrakhan is losing his sight; his damaged eyes weep scalding tears. He will not leave Khal's side though the boy's mind wanders on far dark shores and he recognizes no-one, not even his lover.

They burned Sarillë's body today, although I entreated the authorities to let me cut the corpse open—if only to prove my theory that –

Today I am certain I saw *them* again. The wriggling tracks beneath the skin. One beneath the left breast, another across the midriff, a third above the groin, a fourth in the thigh. Khal is being eaten away—from within. I pray the Tarrakhan loses his sight before he sees this living corruption in the ruins of his lover's body.

The nights are silent but for the wailing and screaming of those wretches who are infected. The moths have died by the thousand, their dry, dessicated corpses litter the streets and gardens. Yet still the craving for boskh drives the addicts to extraordinary practices: court ladies on their knees in their fine selkhs, scrabbling through the piles of street dirt, searching for a newly-dead moth with a taste of dust left on its wings; respected scholars gathering handfuls of the frail fragments to burn just to inhale a whiff of the dust; shrunken-faced addicts actually licking the brittle shells, crunching the furred bodies, avidly swallowing them down like sweetmeats –

*They* hatched today.

They burrowed their way to the surface and as dusk fell, they slowly oozed their way out of the yellowed pustules of corruption that have erupted all over Khal's body. His screams –

It is as I feared. It is just as I feared. They are parasites, these moth grubs, parasites that feed on live human tissue. Now I have proof. Sletheris, the grubs of these moths, emerge at about a thumb's length, yellowish-pale and glutinous, like an oozing jelly; fattened on their host's flesh and body fluids, they then weave a cocoon about themselves which they attach by a thin silk thread to their host . . .

I have been to the Arkhan. With my proof positive. He has sent his Tarkhasters throughout all the Seven Cantons to destroy the moths. But it is too late. All Perysse is infected. And there seems no way to kill the grubs—without killing the Host.

May Saint Mithiel protect us. We are doomed.

When I returned from the Arkhan to Khal's room, he –

Even now, I can hardly write it. Khal dead. The Tarrakhan dying. He had slain the boy and then, in the manner of Iskhandar, thrust the razhir-blade into his own entrails, twisting it . . . an unspeakably painful death, the room reeked of spilt blood.

He had dragged himself to the bed where the boy's body lay and was trying to reach up to touch his hand. As I entered, he called to me.

"Taziel . . . I could not bear to watch him suffer so—it was the—only way. See—that we—are consumed on the same pyre – "

When will this end? We have not enough wood or pyre-oil to burn all the bodies. Most, on learning what crawls within them, take their own lives. The looms are silent, the bazaars and quais are empty. Every household burns fumigating herbs; the city is choked with the bitter fug and the billowing smoke of funeral pyres hangs in a pall above Perysse both day and night.

Weary. I am so very weary now. There seems to be no way that I, who call myself a physician, can do anything to alleviate the suffering. I truly believed this substance—*boskh*—to be a miracle, a cure for all the diseases we thought incurable.

Now all I can do is stand helplessly by as my patients die, one by one.

My esteemed colleague, Merindyn (who was apprentices with me to crabbed old Maistre Dyrnion) has sent for me. He has discovered a new case in the stews of the Seventh Circle, a girl prostitute known as "Mynah" (I am told she was gifted with a shrill whistle and a good ear for vulgarly popular melodies). This poor creature, abandoned by her pimp, must have lain some two weeks in her garret whilst the sletheris went about their work inside her.

"Have you ever seen anything like this before, Taziel?"

In truth, I had become so used to horrors in the last weeks that I thought I could not be shocked by anything new. This is the most advanced case I have seen. The girl's body lay encased within a web of soft, sticky selkh . . . most like a selkh cocoon and yet she still breathed within. From what I could make out beneath the glutinous threads, her eyes seemed open and unusually prominent and dark . . . she was Changing.

"Tell no-one," whispered Merindyn, "for they will destroy her if they discover her."

He related then that the good citizens of Perysse had burned three such . . . *mutations* in the courtyard of the Tarkhas Zhudiciar, calling them abominations of Ar-Zhoth. And I cautioned him to look to his own safety . . . the mood of the people is such that they will burn him as well as his patient if they find him at her bedside.

Drawn back at night against my will to Mynah's bedside. Scientific curiosity—or morbid fascination? I cannot stop thinking about that pale, emaciated body still breathing within its protective cocoon. What exactly are we witnessing here? When she wakes—*if* she wakes—what will emerge from this soft-spun chrysalis?

She lies there naked but for the woven shroud of gossamer threads, oblivious of my presence, oblivious of this rheumy-eyed, weary old man with his wavering lanthorn and his laboriously scratching pencil. I have ensured the shutters are closed, no chink of light must give me—and her—away. (Strange. I cannot glimpse any trace of sletheri tracks on the white skin. I had thought—but now I wonder if I am wrong.)

No voluptuous whore, this Mynah, just a scrap of a girl, scarce past puberty. Tender breasts, pink-tipped, wildrose buds that bloom amidst tangled briars on waste grounds –

But I digress. It must be understood that my descriptions of the patient's physical condition are merely set down for medical reasons.

Fine drifts of long hair, so fair it seems white beneath the threads. I thought Merindyn had said she was dark, glossy-haired like the mynah bird's plumage . . . But then these whoregirls will dye their hair rainbow colours, tattoo their bodies, anything to attract the customers (so I am told.) If only her eyes were not open. I feel she is watching me. And yet—how could that be? Her pulse, her breathing, everything has slowed—she sleeps the deep sleep of the narcoleptic, of the comatose.

I wonder if she dreams . . .?

*Moon glimmerlights the dust-drifted boards, the bare pallet . . . Moonmotes float, glittering, in the darkness. Glitter of sound, each radiant point of light a line of high, pure crystalline sound, spinning, weaving –*

*Each gossamer threadline of sound encasing her vibrates, lulling her with a shifting texture of thin high starglitter; starmusic, spheremusic –*

*Mothmusic –*

Dreaming. I must have nodded off a moment there. Not one night's uninterrupted sleep since this cursed plague began but I used to be able to weather such hardships; I must be getting old. Yet still an echo of that reverberant threadhum in my ears, high, unearthly –

Wax. Undoubtedly a build-up of earwax. I must remove it or I may go deaf; some gently-warmed olive oil should do the trick.

I had not intended to return. But, called to a child with the quinsy in nearby Naseberry Lane, I could not resist the lure and crept up the cobwebbed stair in the dark to her garret to see if she still lived.

She had shifted a little within the protective threads. Moonlight glistened on her palesilk hair, her soft white body. Even as I leant over her, I caught the breath of a sigh, so faint it was but the beat of a moth's wing.

I am certain sure now that she is not Hosting sletheris, that the smooth skin is unmarked because there is no infestation beneath. What I have been observing is some unique process of change—of metamorphosis—of translation into Something Else. I can only conclude that the ingestion of boskh stimulates—or triggers—this state of irreparable Change in certain susceptible individuals.

If only she would wake. There is so much to be learned from her, so much she could tell. And yet I dare not disturb her; they say that wakening a sleep-walker only results in madness, dementia.

Away just before dawn with a heavy heart. How long now until she is discovered? How long?

I cannot stop thinking about her. Mynah. As I go about the silent streets from household to household to administer what little treatment I can offer to my dying patients, I see her pale face, I hear again that strange, high music, I cannot wait for night to fall so that I can slip back to her garret.

So tired today. Two dead in Spindle Lane; three new cases of blindness confirmed; one whole household found dead in Shuttle Alley, it seems the master had gone mad and killed them all, even his little babe in the cradle. Is there no end to it? If only there were some way to –

"*Ta—zi—el . . .*"

*She is calling to me, her translucent body naked except for the drifting skeins of her whitesoft hair. She leans from the casement, calling to me and as she calls the moonlit night glitters with the fall of petals from the black sky. And the aching sweetness of her voice makes me want to weep with its promise of release.*

"*Let go . . . drift away . . .*"

I woke to find I had fallen asleep, my head on my open journal, the quill pen leaving a dark smeared blot over my last entry . . . The ink was wet, blurred with water.

Saltwater.

"Once you find yourself weeping," Maistre Dyrnion used to say, "then you know it is time to retire. Cultivate the art of detachment, Taziel. Detachment is an essential skill for a physician."

I should have retired last year, left the city, gone to end my days in the quiet of the countryside. Now there is no escape. Even if I can offer no hope of cure, someone has to comfort the dying, someone has to close the sightless eyes, to pull the sheet over the still, set faces of the dead . . .

Moonlight powders the dusty threads of her transparent shroud. Soft curves of her white-fleshed body beneath, breasts whose delicate nipples are round and pink as little shells. So long since I touched a woman—in that way. O, a physician may touch a hundred women in the course of his work, from tender maids to raddled crones—but all for information's sake, not for his own pleasure –

She stirs.

Can she hear my thoughts, can she sense the heat of my desires? She is so weirdly beautiful, lying there swathed in the white filaments of her hair. From the diseased body of this drab little prostitute, a new creature is emerging, white, virginal—inviolate.

Should I waken her? Slit the dusty webs, take her in my arms, feel that soft, naked skin, that whitepeach bloom against my cheek?

Stay a moment, Astar Taziel. The boskh has infected your brain, stimulating obscene desires, unnatural lusts with its insidious musksweet fragrance. It had to happen . . . I have been inhaling the stuff for weeks now. But to have so nearly transgressed the ethics of my profession, to have so nearly –

I must never come here again. This must be my last visit.

"Farewell, Mynah," I whisper, my hand straying out to touch the sticky threads, pulling back at the last moment. Is it just my heated imagination—or does she murmur softly as the shadow of my hand falls across her face?

A straggle of hooded Hierophants was approaching, mumbling chants and burning bitter herbs in their clanking thuribles. In their wake followed the Believers. The fanatics. The zealots.

The greylight was bright with their spluttering torches, the air harsh with their monotonous chanting.

"The fires! The fires! Come to the fires!"

"Well if it isn't Doctor Taziel," a sharp voice said, a splinter piercing my ear.

Farindel. Clerke to the Haute Zhudiciar. Skilled in the ways of inquisition.

"You're out late, Taziel."

"So many patients to attend to." I waved my hands a little too animatedly, hoping my journal with its sketches and notes was safe concealed within my robes. The heat from his torch was making me sweat; must he hold it so close to my face?

"I am told there's one of them sequestered here-abouts," he said, "and the Arkhan's word is that they must be destroyed. Fire." He smiled at me, showing teeth stained from chewing anise root. "They cannot resist it. Moths are drawn to the flames – "

A hoarse shout from down the lane. I closed my eyes, praying. Not Mynah.

The Hierophants had made a circle with their torches. I turned to go but Farindel grabbed me by the arm; remarkable strength in his grip for one who makes his living pushing a feather quill over parchment.

"Watch." Again that slow smile.

And in the confusion of jostling figures, the waving torches, the jeering shouts and cries, I saw a pale figure at an upper window, a whitewraith, a phantasm, more moth than human.

For a moment, the creature seemed to hang, to float in the very air above the flames. I could not avert my eyes. Illusion. It must be illusion –

The fires caught light. That gossamer whiteness crackled, burned, the creature came thudding to the ground and the Hierophants closed in, hacking, stamping, crushing –

The stench of charred flesh was overpowering. I tried to pull away but Farindel had my arm clutched tight within his grip, his eyes glittered fanatically in the pyrelight.

"As physician it is your duty to bring such cases to my notice, is that understood? It would be counted a heinous crime to harbour one of these daemonspawn, Taziel. They must be eradicated. For their own good as well as for the safety of the people."

You are in danger, my beloved. They want to destroy you.

They do not understand.

How can I protect you from the firemobs that roam the streets by night, seeking to draw you and your kind to their flames? Farindel suspects me, I am sure of that. He may have set a watch on my house. As I go about my visits, I think I am shadowed: a glimpse of a watcher slipping out of sight as I turn to look behind me; a flash of movement caught on the edge of the eye's seeing . . .

And I can think of nothing but you, Mynah. Even your name stirs an echo of that crystalline music. Let me hear it one more time, let me hear your voice again, more potent than boskh, more achingly sweet, with its promise of healing.

Of release.

The pull was too strong. I could not help myself. I had to go back. I had to see her. Somehow I knew it would be tonight.

The music was no more than an echo in my memory at first. Then it became more insistent, an iridescent melody that would not leave me be, wreathing round and around my brain.

And as I drew near the shoddy alleyway, as I crept over the refuse-strewn gutters, the music grew stronger, more piercing—more alluring. I stopped in the dark beneath her tenement house and listened. A single moonshaft lit the ragged tiles of the roof, the high open casement with its cracked panes.

From that open casement the music issued, a single, unbroken thread of silverspun sound, liquid as moonlight.

It ravished the soul to hear it.

Now I knew. She had awakened. She was singing.

In the far shadows of the moonlit garret a frail figure, tall and slender, stood watching me, its dark eyes huge and sad. Clothed only in its long drifts of floating hair, white as spun sugar, it lifted one hand to me, whether in welcome or denial, I could not be sure. The long fingers were webbed, the tracery of veins in the transparent skin as delicate as a skeletal leaf, hoar-dusted by winter frosts.

"Mynah?" I said. My voice was unsteady, hoarse with a vivid, unexpected emotion. "I mean you no harm. I—I am a friend. A physician. I have watched over you whilst you slept. I—I – " My words trickled away to nothing. I just stared.

And the thing that had been Mynah stared mutely back at me.

"You cannot stay here," I said all in a rush. "If they find you they will burn you. You must come with me. Look. I can conceal you in my cloak."

For a moment I thought my Mynah had lost all powers of understanding. But then—O miracle—she slowly nodded her head. And I ventured closer, untying my old worsted cloak and hesitantly offering to wrap it about her frail shoulders. She allowed me to do this—and as I did so, my hand brushed against her bare skin. Such a texture—softer than velvet but with the pile, the bloom of a moth's wing. And with that touch, a faint echo of that lost vision, that still, starlit darkness, that promise of . . .

Down the creaking stairs, I led her, flinching at each squeak of the rotten boards.

"Wait." I peered out into the dark-lit street; it was empty. A fitful wind was blowing; a rusty shutter banged. If I could hurry her to my home unobserved, there I could conceal her, care for her, observe her, learn all the secrets of her metamorphosis –

"It's clear."

She hung back, shaking her pale head.

"I can see no-one there. Trust me."

But she was so weak, her limbs so wasted that she could hardly put one foot in front of the other; she sank against me, a featherweight, her fragile frame weighed down by my cloak.

And as I struggled—vainly—to support her, I felt her tense in my arms. Looking up, I saw the splash of fire against the buildings.

Torches.

They stood at the end of the street, barring our escape. As I frantically spun around, I saw them closing in on us from behind. We were trapped.

"Why, Doctor Taziel, I see you have served me well."

Farindel. Coming straight towards us, a pitch torch in his hands, weeping gouts of flame onto the wet cobblestones.

"Served you!" I cried although my voice shook. "What makes you think – "

Mynah whimpered, cowering in my arms, trying to hide her face from the brightness of the flames.

"Don't listen to him," I whispered to her urgently. "This is none of my doing. They must have followed me – "

"And what have we here?" He stood over us. The others formed a ring. I could hear the muttered chants, could smell the acrid smoke of burning incense herbs.

"A patient of mine," I said defiantly "Will you let us pass? She is very weak and must lie down."

"Don't play games with me, Astar," he said, his voice hard-honed as my surgeon's scalpel. "We know what she is. And you know what the penalty is for harbouring one such as she."

He made a sudden slash towards her with his torch; Mynah let out a shrill, keening cry, the cry of an animal meshed in a snare. The cry pierced me like a knife. And the muttered chants began to grow louder, more insistent.

"To the flames, to the flames, to the flames with her – "

Farindel stooped and pulled at Mynah's hood; her white head was exposed to the torchglare, her huge insectile eyes which I had tried to shield from the firelight.

"Stop!" I cried as she flinched away. "Don't torment her!"

"A perfect specimen," he said, smiling. I knew what it meant, that slow smile. I had seen it before. All the while the chanting was rising louder, dinning into my ears with its merciless, mindless monotony. And now Mynah was struggling against me, struggling as the flames burned brighter and her dark eyes reflected their eerie glare.

"You can't hold her back, Astar," Farindel said softly. "She can't resist the flames. She is drawn to them."

"Don't look, Mynah," I implored her. "Hide your eyes."

"Mynah," Farindel echoed, still so softly, so seductively, "come to the fire, Mynah."

And then she broke free. I went sprawling onto the cobbles—as they closed in on her, trampling me, pushing me down into the mud as I tried to stop them, frantically tearing at their cloaks, their coats –

I heard their triumphant shout as the flames caught.

And her cry. I heard her cry. Ecstatic as the bright ring of flames engulfed her—then wordless, mindless agony as her silkspun hair became a tracery of fire, as the fire shot heavenwards in an explosion of star-sparks and the frail creature that had been made of moonshine burned like a moth in a candleflame—until something charred, blackened, dropped lifeless to the damp cobbles.

I think I went crazy then. I charged in amongst them, hitting, kicking, screaming all the curses I could call down upon their heads.

They took me away. And locked me in this cell. Soon they will return to question me. I must set this record down—for even if I do not leave this cell alive, someone else may read this, my journal, and understand.

*My Lord Arkhan,*

*You must stop this massacre of innocents.*

*We have misunderstood the nature of these mutations. Driven by fear, we have mercilessly crushed them at their most vulnerable when, just emerged from their cocoons, they are limp and weak. We have looked on their Otherness and seen it as a token of divine displeasure. Now I know we are wrong. Horribly wrong.*

*Boskh heals—when taken in tiny doses. And those who are Changed by boskh are Healers. They heal by touch—by the touch of sound upon the mind and body, this extraordinary shimmering, piercing web of sound that they weave. If you could but hear it, my lord . . .*

That irresistible sound. It haunts me. Why do I have this feeling—that if I could only hear it again, all would be well?

(They are coming. I can hear their footsteps echoing in the passageway.)

*If you could but hear it, you would understand. And so I beg you to end the slaughter. Else those unearthly voices will be stilled. And we shall remain locked in our brutish ignorance, not knowing that we have –*

Here end the writings of Doctor Astar Taziel. As you can see, my lord Arkhan, Maistre Taziel never completed his Journals. Hints of the physician's rapid mental disintegration are to be found as the work progresses. The balance of his mind became so disturbed that he ended by defending the very mutations he had earlier sought to destroy. His paranoia became so severe that he believed us, the enforcers of justice and mercy, to be his enemies! It was disturbing to have to witness the rapid disintegration of a once-distinguished intellect. Astar Taziel is at present deeply sedated in the Asylum where I give you every assurance, my lord, he will end his days under constant surveillance.

Farindel, Clerke

# KARL EDWARD WAGNER

## Did They Get You to Trade?

KARL EDWARD WAGNER is a regular contributor to *Best New Horror*. DAW Books recently published the 21st volume of his own annual anthology series, *The Year's Best Horror Stories*; his latest collection is entitled *Exorcisms and Ecstasies*; he is completing a medical horror novel, *The Fourth Seal*; and Penguin/ROC in Britain are reprinting his classic Kane series of heroic fantasy novels. However, he disowns the recent DC Comics graphic novel, *Tell Me, Dark*, after the publisher tampered with his storyline.

Like that graphic work, "Did They Get You to Trade?" is also set in a London milieu which Wagner knows well and is fast making his own. More knowledgeable horror fans might recognise a brief cameo appearance by the remains of a well-known Irish Lovecraftian illustrator, but perhaps what makes the following tale even more disturbing is that the author claims he based it on a true story . . .

# *DID THEY GET YOU TO TRADE?*

Ryan Chase was walking along Southampton Row at lunchtime, fancying a pint of bitter. Fortunately there was no dearth of pubs here, and he turned into Cosmo Place, a narrow passage behind the Bloomsbury Park Hotel and the Church of St. George the Martyr, leading into Queen Square. The September day was unseasonably sunny, so he passed by Peter's Bar, downstairs at the corner—looking for an outdoor table at The Swan or The Queen's Larder. The Swan was filling up, so he walked a few doors farther to The Queen's Larder, at the corner of Queen Square. There he found his pint of bitter, and he moved back outside to take a seat at one of the wooden tables on the pavement.

Ryan Chase was American by birth, citizen of the world by choice. More to the point, he spent probably half of each year knocking about the more or less civilized parts of the globe—he liked hotels and saw no romance in roughing it—and a month or two of this time he spent in London, where he had various friends and the use of a studio. The remainder of his year was devoted to long hours of work in his Connecticut studio, where he painted strange and compelling portraits, often derived from his travels and created from memory. These fetched rather large and compelling prices from fashionable galleries—enough to support his travels and eccentricities, even without the trust allowance from a father who had wanted him to go into corporate law.

Chase was pleased with most of his work, although in all of it he saw a flawed compromise between the best he could create at the time and the final realization of his vision, which he hoped someday to achieve. He saw himself as a true decadent, trapped in the *fin de siècle* of a century far drearier than the last. But then, to be decadent is to be romantic.

Chase also had a pragmatic streak. Today a pint of bitter in Bloomsbury would have to make do for a glass of absinthe in Paris of *La Belle Epoch*. The bitter was very good, the day was excellent, and Chase dug out a few postcards from his jacket pocket. By the end of his second pint, he had scribbled notes and addresses on them all and was thinking about a third pint and perhaps a ploughman's lunch.

He smelled the sweet stench of methylated spirit as it approached him, and then the sour smell of unwashed poverty. Already Chase was reaching for a coin.

"Please, guv. I don't wish to interrupt you in your writing, but please could you see your way towards sparing a few coins for a poor man who needs a meal?"

Ryan Chase didn't look like a tourist, but neither did he look British. He was forty-something, somewhere around six feet, saddened that he was starting to spread at the middle, and proud that there was no grey in his short black beard and no thinning in his pulled-back hair and short ponytail. His black leather jacket with countless studs and zips was from Kensington Market, his baggy slacks from Bloomingdale's, his T-shirt from Rodeo Drive, and his tennis shoes from a Stamford garage sale. Mild blue eyes watched from behind surplus aviator's sunglasses of the same shade of blue.

All of this in addition to his fondness for writing postcards and scrawling sketches at tables outside pubs made Chase a natural target for London's growing array of panhandlers and blowlamps. Against this Chase kept a pocket well filled with coins, for his heart was rather kind and his eye quite keen to memorize the faces that peered back from the fringes of Hell.

But this face had seen well beyond the fringes of Hell, and as Chase glanced up, he left the pound coin in his pocket. His panhandler was a meth-man, well in the grip of the terminal oblivion of cheap methylated spirit. His shoes and clothing were refuse from dustbins, and from the look of his filthy mackintosh, he had obviously been sleeping rough for some while. Chalky ashes seemed to dribble from him like cream from a cone in a child's fist. Beneath all this, his body was tall and almost fleshless; the long-fingered hand, held out in hope, showed dirtcaked nails resembling broken talons. Straggling hair and unkempt beard might have been black or brown, streaked with grey and matted with ash and grime. His face—Chase recalled Sax Rohmer's description of Fu Manchu: A brow like Shakespeare and eyes like Satan.

Only, Satan the fallen angel. These were green eyes with a tint of amber, and they shone with a sort of majestic despair and a proud intelligence that not even the meth had wholly obliterated. Beneath their imploring hopelessness, the eyes suggested a still smoldering sense of rage.

Ryan Chase was a scholar of human faces, as well as impulsive, and he knew any coins the man might beg here would go straight into another bottle of methylated spirit. He got up from his seat. "Hang on a bit. I'll treat you to a round."

When Chase emerged from The Queen's Larder he was carrying a pint of bitter and a pint of cider. His meth-man was skulking about the Church of St. George the Martyr across the way, seemingly studying the informational plaque affixed to the stucco wall. Chase handed him the cider. "Here. This is better for you than the meth."

The other man had the shakes rather badly, but he steadied the pint with both hands and dipped his face into it, sucking ravenously until the level was low enough for him to lift the pint to his face. He'd sunk his pint before Chase had quite started on his own. Wiping his beard, he leaned back against the church and shuddered, but the shaking had left his hands as the alcohol quickly spread from his empty stomach.

"Thanks, guv. Now I'd best be off before they take notice of me. They don't fancy my sort hanging about."

His accent was good, though too blurred by alcohol for Chase to pin down. Chase sensed tragedy, as he studied the other's face while he drained his own pint. He wasn't used to drinking in a rush, and perhaps this contributed to his natural impulsiveness.

"They'll take my money well enough. Take a seat at the table round the corner, and I'll buy another round."

Chase bought a couple packets of crisps to accompany their pints and returned to find the other man cautiously seated. He had managed to beg a cigarette. He eagerly accepted the cider, but declined the crisps. By the time he had finished his cider, he was looking somewhat less the corpse.

"Cheers, mate," he said. "You've been a friend. It wasn't always like this, you know."

"Eat some crisps, and I'll buy you one more pint." No need to sing for your supper, Chase started to say, but there were certain remnants of pride amidst the wreckage. He left his barely tasted pint and stepped back inside for more cider. At least there was some food value to cider in addition to the high alcohol content, or so he imagined. It might get the poor bastard through another day.

His guest drank this pint more slowly. The cider had cured his shakes for the moment, and he was losing his whipped cur attitude. He said with a certain foggy dignity: "That's right, mate. One time I had it all. And then I lost it every bit. Now it's come down to this."

Chase was an artist, not a writer, and so had been interested in the man's face, not his life story. The story was an obvious ploy to gain a few more pints, but as the face began to return to life, Chase found himself searching through his memory.

Chase opened a second bag of crisps and offered them. "So, then?"

"I'm Nemo Skagg. Or used to be. Ever heard of me?"

Chase started to respond: "Yes, and I'm Elvis." But his artist's eye began filling in the eroded features, and instead he whispered: "Jesus Christ!"

Nemo Skagg. Founder and major force behind Needle—probably *the* cutting edge of the punk rock movement in its early years. Needle, long without Nemo Skagg and with just enough of its early lineup to maintain the group's name, was still around, but only as a ghost of the original. *Rolling Stone* and the lot used to publish scandalous notices of Nemo Skagg's meteoric crash, but that was years ago, and few readers today would have recognized the name. The name of a living-dead legend.

"Last I read of you, you were living the life of a recluse at someplace in Kensington," Chase said.

"You don't believe me?" There was a flicker of defiant pride in those wounded eyes.

"Actually, I do," Chase said, feeling as though he should apologize. "I recognize your face." He wiped his hands on his trousers, fumbling for something to say. "As it happens, I still have Needle's early albums, as well as the solo album you did."

"But do you still listen to them?"

Chase felt increasingly awkward, yet he was too fascinated to walk away. "Well. I think this calls for one more round."

The barman from The Queen's Larder was starting to favor them with a distasteful frown as he collected glasses from outside. Nemo Skagg nodded toward Great Ormond Street across the way. "They do a fair scrumpy at The Sun," he suggested.

It was a short walk to the corner of Great Ormond and Lamb's Conduit Street, giving Chase a little time to marshal his thoughts. Nemo Skagg. Nova on the punk rock scene. The most outrageous. The most daring. The savior of the world from disco and lame hangers-on from the 60s scene. Totally full-dress punk star: the parties, the fights on stage, the drugs, the scandals, the arrests, the hospital confinements. Toward the last, there were only the latter two, then even these were no longer newsworthy. A decade later, the world had forgotten Nemo Skagg. Chase had assumed he was dead, but now could recall no notice of his death. It might have escaped notice.

The Sun was crowded with students as usual, but Chase made his way past them to the horseshoe bar and sloshed back outside with two pints of scrumpy. Nemo had cleared a space against the wall and had begged another fag. They leaned against the wall of the pub, considering the bright September day, the passing show, and their pints. Chase seldom drank scrumpy, and the potent cider would have been enough to stun his brain even without the previous bitter.

"Actually," Nemo said, "there were *three* solo albums."

"I had forgotten."

"They were all bollocks."

"I'm not at all certain I ever heard the other two," Chase compromised.

"I'm bollocks. We're all of us bollocks."

"The whole world is bollocks." Chase jumped in ahead of him.

"To bollocks!" Nemo raised his glass. They crashed their pints in an unsteady toast. Nemo drained his.

"You're a sport, mate. You still haven't asked what you're waiting to ask: How did it all happen?"

"Well. I don't suppose it really matters, does it?"

Nemo was not to demur. "Lend us a fiver, mate, and I'll pay for this round. Then Nemo Skagg shall tell all."

Once, at the White Hart in Drury Lane, Chase had bought eight pints of Guinness for a cockney pensioner who had regaled him with an impenetrable cockney accent concerning his adventures during the Dunkirk evacuation. Chase hadn't understood a word in ten, but he memorized the man's face, and that portrait was considered one of his very finest. Chase found a fiver.

The bar staff at The Sun were loose enough to serve Nemo, and he was out again shortly with two more pints of scrumpy and a packet of fags. That was more than the fiver, so he hadn't been totally skint. He brightened when Chase told him he didn't smoke. Nemo lit up. Chase placed his empty pint on the window ledge and braced himself against the wall. The wall felt good.

"So, then, mate. Ask away. It's you who's paid the piper."

Chase firmly resolved that this pint would be his last. "All right, then. What did happen to Nemo Skagg? Last I heard, you still had some of your millions and a house in Kensington, whence sounds of debauchery issued throughout the night."

"You got it right all along, mate. It was sex, drugs and alcohol that brought about me ruin. We'll say bloody nothing about scheming managers and crooked recording studios. Now, then. You've got the whole soddin' story."

"Not very original." Chase wondered whether he should finish his scrumpy.

"Life is never original," Nemo observed. The rush of alcohol and nicotine had vastly improved his demeanor. Take away the dirt and shabby clothes, and he might well look like any other dissipated man in his sixties, although that must be about twice his actual age. He was alert enough not to be gauging Chase for prospects of further largess.

"Of course, that's not *truly* the reason."

"Was it a woman?" asked Chase. The scrumpy was making him maudlin.

"Which woman would it have been? Here, drink up, mate. Give us tube fare to Ken High Street, and I'll show you how it happened."

At this point Ryan Chase should have put down his unfinished pint, excused himself, and made his way back to his hotel. Instead he drank up, stumbled along to the Holborn tube station, and found himself being bounced about the train beside a decidedly deranged Nemo Skagg. Caught up in the adventure of the moment, Chase told himself that he was on a sort of quest—a quest for truth, for the truth that lies behind the masks of faces.

The carriage shook and swayed as it plummeted through subterranean darkness, yanking to a halt at each jostling platform. Chase dropped onto a seat as the passengers rushed out and swarmed in. Lurid posters faced him from the platform walls. Bodies mashed close about him, crushing closer than the sooty tunnel walls, briefly glimpsed in flashes of passing trains and bright bursts of sparks. Faces, looking nowhere, talking in tight bundles, crowded in. Sensory overload.

Nemo's face leered down. He was clutching a railing. "You all right, mate?"

"Gotta take a piss."

"Could go for a slash myself. This stop will do."

So they got off at Notting Hill Gate instead of changing for High Street Kensington; and this was good, because they could walk down Kensington Church Street, which was for a miracle all downhill, toward Kensington High Street. The walk and the fresh air revived Chase from his claustrophobic experience. Bladder relieved, he found himself pausing before the windows of the numerous antique shops that they passed. Hideous Victorian atrocities and baroque horrors from the continent lurked imprisoned behind shop windows. A few paintings beckoned from the farther darkness. Chase was tempted to enter.

But each time Nemo caught at his arm. "You don't want to look at any of that shit, mate. It's all just a lot of dead shit. Let's sink us a pint first."

By now Chase had resigned himself to having bank-rolled a pub crawl. They stopped at The Catherine Wheel, and Chase fetched pints of lager while Nemo Skagg commandeered a bench around the corner on Holland Street. From this relative eddy, they watched the crowd stroll past on Kensington Church Street. Chase smelled the curry and chili from within the pub, wondering how to break this off. He really should eat something.

"I don't believe you told me your name." Nemo Skagg was growing measurably more alert, and that seemed to make his condition all the more tragic.

"I'm Ryan Chase." Chase, who was growing increasingly pissed, no longer regarded the fallen rock star as an object of pity: he now revered him as a crippled hero of the wars in the fast lane.

"Pleased to meet you, Ryan." Nemo Skagg extended a taloned hand. "Where in the States are you from?"

"Well, I live in Connecticut. I have a studio there."

"I'd reckoned you for an artist. And clearly not a starving garret sort. What do you do?"

"Portraits, mostly. Gallery work. I get by." Chase could not fail to notice the other's empty pint. Sighing, he arose to attend to the matter.

When he returned, Chase said, with some effort at firmness: "Now then. Here we are in Kensington. What is all this leading to?"

"You really are a fan, then?"

The lager inclined Chase toward an effusive and reckless mood. "Needle was *the* cutting edge of punk rock. Your first album, *Excessive Bodily Fluids*, set the standard for a generation. Your second album, *The Coppery Taste of Blood*, remains one of the ten best rock albums ever recorded. When I die, these go into the vault with me."

"You serious?"

"Well, we do have a family vault. I've always fancied stocking it with a few favorite items. Like the ancient Egyptians. I mean, being dead has to get boring."

"Then, do you believe in an afterlife?"

"Doesn't really matter whether I do or I don't, does it? Still, it can't hurt to allow for eventualities."

"Yeah. Well, it's all bollocks anyway." Nemo Skagg's eyes had cleared, and Chase found their gaze penetrating and disturbing. He was glad when Nemo stared past him to watch the passersby.

Chase belched and glanced at his watch. "Yes. Well. Here we are in Kensington." He had begun the afternoon's adventure hoping that Nemo Skagg intended to point out to him his former house near here, perhaps entertain him with anecdotes of past extravagances committed on the grounds, maybe even introduce him to some of his whilom friends and colleagues. Nothing more than a bad hangover now seemed the probable outcome.

"Right." Nemo stood up, rather steadier now than Chase. "Let's make our move. I said I'd show you."

Chase finished his lager and followed Nemo down Kensington Church Street, past the church on the corner, and into Ken High Street, where, with some difficulty, they crossed over. The pavement was extremely crowded now, as they lurched along. Tattooed girls in black leather miniskirts flashed suspender belts and stiletto heels. Plaid-clad tourists swayed under burdens of cameras and cellulite. Lads with pierced faces and fenestrated jeans modeled motorcycle jackets laden with chrome. Bored shopworkers trudged unseeingly through it all.

Nemo Skagg turned into the main doorway of Kensington Market. He turned to Chase. "Here's your fucking afterlife."

Chase was rather more interested in finding the loo, but he followed his Virgil. Ken Market was some three floors of cramped shops and tiny stalls—records and jewelry, T-shirts and tattoos, punk fashions from skinhead kicker boots to latex minidresses. You could get your nipples pierced, try on a new pair of handcuffs, or buy a heavy-metal biker jacket that would deflect a tank shell. Chase, who remembered Swinging London of the Beatles era, fondly thought of Ken Market as Carnaby Street Goes to Hell.

"Tell me again," he called after Nemo Skagg. "Why are we here?"

"Because you wanted to know." Nemo pushed forward through the claustrophobic passageways, half dragging Chase and pointing at the merchandise on display. "Observe, my dear Watson."

Ken Market was a labyrinth of well over a hundred vendors, tucked away into tiny cells like funnel spiders waiting in webs. A henna-haired girl in black PVC stared at them incuriously from behind a counter of studded leather accessories. A Pakistani shuffled stacks of T-shirts, mounted on cardboard and sealed in cellophane. An emaciated speedfreak in leather harness guarded her stock of records—empty albums on display, their vinyl souls hidden away. An aging Teddy boy arranged his display of postcards—some of which would never clear the postal inspectors. Two skinheads glared out of the twilight of a tattoo parlor: OF COURSE IT HURTS read the signboard above the opening. Bikers in leather studied massive belts and buckles memorializing Vincent, BSA, Triumph, Norton, Ariel, AJS—no Jap rice mills served here.

"What do you see?" Nemo whispered conspiratorially.

"Lots of weird people buying and selling weird things?" Chase had always wanted to own a Vincent.

"They're all dead things. Even the motorcycles."

"I see."

"No, you don't see. Follow and learn."

Nemo Skagg paused before a display of posters. He pointed. "James Dean. Jim Morrison. Jimi Hendrix. All dead."

He turned to a rack of postcards. "Elvis Presley. Judy Garland. John Lennon. Marilyn Monroe. All dead."

And to a wall of T-shirts. "Sid Vicious. Keith Moon. Janis Joplin. Brian Jones. All dead."

Nemo Skagg whirled to point at a teenager wearing a Roy Orbison T-shirt. Her friend had James Dean badges all across her jacket.

They were looking at a poster of Nick Drake. Nemo shouted at them "They're all *dead*! Your heroes are ghosts!"

It took some doing to attract attention in Ken Market, but Nemo Skagg was managing to do so. Chase took his arm. "Come on, mate. We've seen enough, and I fancy a pint."

But Nemo broke away as Chase steered him past a stall selling vintage rock recordings. Album jackets of Sid and Elvis and Jim and Jimi hung in state from the back of the stall. The bored girl in a black latex bra looked at Nemo distastefully from behind her counter. Either her face had been badly beaten the night before, or she had been reckless with her eyeshadow.

"Anything by Needle?" Nemo asked.

"Nah. You might try Dez and Sheila upstairs. I think they had a copy of *Vampire Serial Killer* some weeks back. Probably still have it."

"Why don't you stock Needle?"

"Who wants Needle? They're naff."

"I mean, the early albums. With Nemo Skagg."

"Who's he?"

"Someone who isn't dead yet."

"That's his problem then, isn't it."

"Do you know who I am?"

"Yes. You're a piss artist. Now bugger off."

Chase caught Nemo Skagg's arm and tugged hard. "Come on, mate. There's nothing here."

And they slunk out, past life-size posters of James Dean, mesmerizing walls of John Lennon T-shirts, kaleidoscopic racks of Marilyn Monroe postcards. Elvis lipsynched to them from the backs of leather jackets. Betty Page stared wide-eyed and ball-gagged from Xotique's window of fetish chic. Jim Morrison was being born again in tattoo across the ample breast of a spike-haired blonde. A punker couple with matching Sid and Nancy T-shirts displayed matching forearms of needle tracks. Someone was loudly playing Buddy Holly from the stall that offered painless ear piercing. A blazing skull grinned at them from the back of the biker who lounged at the exit, peddling his skinny ass in stained leather jeans.

Outside it was still a pleasant September late afternoon, and even the exhaust-clogged air of Ken High Street felt fresh and clear to Chase's lungs. Nemo Skagg was muttering under his breath, and the shakes seemed to have returned. Chase steered him across traffic and back toward the relative quiet of Ken Church Street.

"Off-license. Just ahead." Nemo was acting now on reflex. He drew Chase into the off-license shop and silently dug out two four-packs of Tennant's Super. Chase added some sandwiches of unknown composition to the counter, paid for the lot, and they left.

"Just here," said Nemo, turning into an iron gate at the back of the church at the corner of Ken Church and Ken High Street. There was an enclosed churchyard within—a quiet garden with late roses, a leafy bower of some vine, walkways and benches. A few sarcophagi of eroded stone made grey shapes above the trimmed grass. Occasional tombstones leaned as barely decipherable monuments here and there; others were incorporated into the brick of the church walls. Soot-colored robins explored wormy crab apples, and hopeful sparrows and pigeons converged upon the two men as they sat down. The traffic of Kensington seemed hushed and distant, although only a glance away. Chase was familiar with this area of Kensington, but he had never known that this churchyard was here. He remembered that Nemo Skagg had once owned a house somewhere in the borough. Possibly he had sat here often, seeking silence.

Nemo listlessly popped a can of Tennant's, sucked on it, ignored the proffered sandwich. Chase munched on cress and cucumber, anxious to get any sort of food into his stomach. Savoring the respite, he sipped on his can of lager and waited.

Nemo Skagg was on his second can before he spoke. "So then, mate. Now you know."

Chase had already decided to find a cab once the evening rush hour let up. He was certain he could not manage the tube after the afternoon's booze-up. "I'm sorry?" he said.

"You've got to be dead. All their heroes are ghosts. They only worship the dead. The music, the posters, the T-shirts. All of it. They only want to love dead things. So easy to be loyal to dead things. The dead never change. Never grow old. Never fade away. Better to drop dead than to fade away."

"Hey, come on." Chase thought he had it sussed. "Sure the place has its obligatory showcase of dead superstars. That's nostalgia, mate. Consider that there were ten or twenty times as many new faces, new groups, new stars."

"Oi. You come back in a year's time, and I promise you that ninety per cent of your new faces will be missing and well forgotten, replaced by another bloody lot of bloody new sods. But you'll still find your bloody James Dean posters and your bloody Elvis jackets and your bloody Doors CD's and your bloody John Lennon T-shirts, bullet holes three quid extra.

"Listen, mate. They only want the dead. The dead never change. They're always there, at your service, never a skip. You want to wank off on James Dean? There he is, pretty as the day he snuffed it. Want head from Marilyn Monroe? Just pump up your inflatable doll.

"*But*. And this is it, Ryan. Had James Dean learned to drive his Porsche, he'd by now be a corpulent old geezer with a hairpiece and three chins like Paul Newman or Marlon Brando. Marilyn Monroe would be a stupid old cow slapping your Beverly Hills cops around—when she wasn't doing telly adverts for adult nappies and denture fixatives. Jim Morrison would be flogging a chain of vegetarian restaurants. Jimi Hendrix would be doing a golden oldies tour with Otis Redding. Elvis would be playing to fat old cunts in Las Vegas casinos. Buddy Holly would be selling used cars in Chattanooga. How many pictures of fat and fading fifty-year-old farts did you see in there, Ryan? Want to buy the latest Paul McCartney album?"

Chase decided that he would leave Nemo Skagg with the rest of the Tennant's, which should keep him well through the night. "So, then. What you're saying is that it's best to die young, before your fans find someone new. So long, fame; I've had you. Not much future in it for you, is there, being a dead star?"

"Sometimes there's no future in being a live one, after you've lost it."

Chase, who had begun to grow impatient with Nemo Skagg, again changed his assessment of the man. There was more in this wreckage than a drunken has-been bitterly railing against the enduring fame of better musicians. Chase decided to pop another Tennant's and listen.

"You said you're an artist, right? Paint portraits?"

"Well, I rather like to think of them as something more than that . . ."

"And you reckon you're quite good at it?"

"Some critics think so."

"Right, then. What happens the day comes and they say you aren't all that good: that your best work is behind you; that whatever it was you had once, you've lost it now? What happens when you come to realize they've got it right? When you know you've lost the spark forever, and all that's left is to go through the motions? Reckon you'll be well pleased with yourself, painting portraits of pompous old geezers to hang in their executive board rooms?"

"I hardly think it will come to that." Chase was somewhat testy.

"No more than I did. No one ever does. You reckon that once you get to the top, you'll stay on top. Maybe that happens for a few, but not for most of us. Sometimes the fans start to notice first; sometimes you do. You tell yourself that the fans are fickle, but after a while you know inside that it's you what's past it. Then you start to crumble. Then you start to envy the ones what went out on top: they're your moths in amber, held in time and in memory forever unchanging."

The churchyard was filling with shadows, and Chase expected the sexton would soon be locking the gates. Dead leaves of late summer were softly rustling down upon the headstones. The scent of roses managed to pervade the still air.

"Look." Chase was not the sort who liked touching, but he gave a quick pat to the other man's shoulder. "We all go through low periods; we all have our slumps. That's why they invented comebacks. You can still get it back together."

"Nothing to put back together, mate. Don't you get it? At one time I had it. Now I don't."

"But you can get help . . ."

"That's the worst part, mate. It would be so good just to blame it all on the drugs and the booze. Tell yourself you can get back on your feet; few months in some trendy clinic, then you're back on tour promoting that smash new album. Only that's not the way it is. The drugs and the booze comes after you somehow know you've lost it. To kill the pain."

Nemo Skagg sucked his Tennant's dry and tossed the can at the nearest dustbin. He missed, and the can rattled hollowly along the walkway.

"Each one of us has only so much—so much of his best—that he can give. Some of us have more than the rest of us. Doesn't matter. Once the best of you is gone, there's no more you can give. You're like a punch-drunk boxer hoping for the bell before you land hard on your arse. It's over for you. No matter how much you want it. No matter how hard you try.

"There's only so much inside you that's positively the best. When that's gone, you might as well be dead. And knowing that you've lost it—that's the cruelest death of all."

Ryan Chase sighed uncomfortably and noticed that they had somehow consumed all the cans of lager, that he was drunker than he liked to be, and that it was growing dark. Compounding his mistakes, he asked: "Is there someplace I can drop you off? I'm going for a cab. Must get back."

Nemo Skagg shook his head, groping around for another can. "It's all right, mate. My digs aren't far from here. Fancy stopping in for a drink? Afraid I must again impose upon you for that."

In for a penny, in for a pound. All judgment fled, Chase decided he really would like to see where Nemo Skagg lived. He bought a bottle of Bell's, at Nemo's suggestion, and they struggled off into the gathering night. Chase blindly followed Nemo Skagg through the various and numerous unexpected turnings of the Royal Borough of Kensington and Chelsea. Even if sober and by daylight, he'd not have had a clue as to where he was being led. It was Chase's vague notion that he was soon to be one of the chosen few to visit with a fallen angel in his particular corner of Hell. In this much he was correct.

Chase had been expecting something a little more grandiose. He wasn't sure just what. Perhaps a decaying mansion. Nemo Skagg, however, was far past that romantic luxury. Instead, Nemo pushed aside a broken hoarding and slid past, waving for Chase to follow. Chase fumbled after him, weeds slapping his face. The way pitched downward on a path paved with refuse and broken masonry. Somewhere ahead Nemo scratched a match and lit a candle in the near-darkness.

It was the basement level of a construction site, or a demolition site to be accurate. A block of buildings had been torn down, much of their remains carted away, and nothing had yet risen in their place save for weeds. Weathered posters on the hoarding above spared passersby a vision of the pit. The envisioned office building had never materialized. Scruffy rats and feral cats prowled through the weeds and debris, avoiding the few squatters who lurked about.

Nemo Skagg had managed a sort of lean-to of scrap boards and slabs of hoarding—the lot stuck together against one foundation wall, where a doorway in the brick gave entrance to a vaulted cellar beneath the street above. Once it had served as some sort of storage area, Chase supposed, although whether for coal or fine wines was a secret known only to the encrusted bricks. Past the lean-to, Nemo's candle revealed an uncertain interior of scraps of broken furniture, an infested mattress with rags of bedding, and a dead fire of charcoal and ashes with a litter of empty cans and dirty crockery. The rest of the grotto was crowded with a stack of decaying cardboard cartons and florist's pots. Nemo Skagg had no fear of theft, for there plainly was nothing here to steal.

"Here. Find a seat." Nemo lit a second candle and fumbled about for a pair of pilfered pub glasses. He poured from the bottle of Bell's and handed one clouded glass to Chase. Chase sat down on a wooden crate, past caring about cleanliness. The whisky did not mask the odor of methylated spirits that clung to the glass with the dirt.

"To your very good health, Ryan," Nemo Skagg toasted. "And to our friendship."

Chase was trying to remember whether he'd mentioned the name of his hotel to Nemo. He decided he hadn't, and that the day's adventure would soon be behind him. He drank. His host refilled their glasses.

"So, this is it," Chase said, somewhat recklessly. "The end of fame and fortune. Good-bye house in Kensington. Hello squat in future carpark."

"It was Chelsea," Nemo replied, not taking offense. "The house was in Chelsea."

"Now he gets his kicks in Chelsea, not in Kensington anymore," sang Chase, past caring that he was past caring.

"Still," Nemo went on, content with the Bell's. "I did manage to carry away with me everything that really mattered."

He scrambled back behind the stack of cardboard cartons, nearly spilling them over. After a bit of rummaging, he climbed out with the wreckage of an electric guitar. He presented it to Chase with a flourish, and refilled their glasses.

It was a custom-built guitar, of the sort that Nemo Skagg habitually smashed to bits on stage before hordes of screaming fans. Chase knew positively nothing about custom-built guitars, but it was plain that this one was a probable casualty of one such violent episode. The bowed neck still held most of the strings, and only a few knobs and bits dangled on wires from the abused body. Chase handed it back carefully. "Very nice."

Nemo Skagg scraped the strings with his broken fingernails. As Chase's eyes grew accustomed to the candlelight, he could see a few monoliths of gutted speakers and burned-out amplifiers shoved in with the pots and boxes. Nothing worth stealing. Nothing worth saving. Ghosts. Broken, dead ghosts. Like Nemo Skagg.

"I think I have a can of beans somewhere." Nemo applied a candle to some greasy chips papers and scraps of wood. The yellow flame flared in the dark cave, its smoke carried outward past the lean-to.

"That's all right," said Chase. "I really must be going."

"Oi. We haven't finished the bottle." Nemo poured. "Drink up. Of course, I used to throw better parties than this for my fans."

"Cheers," said Chase, drinking. He knew he would be very ill tomorrow.

"So, Ryan," said Nemo, stretching out on a legless and spring-stabbed comfy chair. "You find yourself wanting to ask where all the money went."

"I believe you've already told me."

"What I told you was what people want to hear, although it's partly true. Quite amazing how much money you can stuff up your nose and shove up your arm, and how fast that draws that certain group of sharks who circle about you and take bites till there's nothing left to feed on. But the simple and unsuspected truth of the matter is that I spent the last of my fortune on my fans."

Chase was wondering whether he might have to crash here for the night if he didn't move now. He finished Nemo's sad story for him: "And then your fans all proved fickle."

"No, mate. Not these fans. Just look at them."

Nemo Skagg shuffled back into his cave, picked out a floral vase, brought it out into the light, cradling it lovingly in his hands for Chase to see. Chase saw that it was actually a funeral urn.

"This is Saliva Gash. She said she was eighteen when she hung out backstage. After she OD'd one night after a gig, her family in Pimlico wouldn't own her. Not even her ashes. I paid for the cremation. I kept her remains. She was too dear a creature to be scattered."

Ryan Chase was touched. He struggled for words to say, until Nemo reached back for another urn.

"And this one is Slice. I never knew his real name. He was always in the front row, screaming us on, until he sliced his wrists after one show. No one claimed the remains. I paid for it.

"And this one is Dave from Belfast. Pissed out of his skull, and he stuck his arm out to flag down a tube train. Jacket caught, and I doubt they picked up all of him to go into the oven. His urn feels light."

"That's all right," said Chase, as Nemo offered him the urn to examine. "I'm no judge."

"You ever notice how London is crammed with bloody cemeteries, but no one gets buried there unless they've snuffed it before the fucking Boer War? No room for any common souls in London. They burn the lot of us now, and then you get a fucking box of ashes to carry home. That's *if* you got any grieving sod who cares a fuck to hold onto them past the first dustbin."

Nemo dragged out one of the cardboard boxes. The rotted carton split open, disgorging a plastic bag of chalky ashes. The bag burst on the bricks, scattering ashes over Nemo's shoes and trouser cuffs. "Shit. I can't read this one. Can you?"

He handed the mildewed cardboard to Chase, then poured out more Bell's. Chase dully accepted both. His brain hurt.

"Bought proper funeral urns for them all at first," Nemo explained. "Then, as the money went, I had to economize. Still, I was loyal to my fans. I kept them with me after I lost the house. After I'd lost everything else."

The fire licked at the moldy cardboard in Chase's hand, cutting through his numbness. He dropped the box onto the fire. The fire flared. By its light Chase could make out hundreds of similar boxes and urns stacked high within the vault.

"It's a whole generation no one wanted," Nemo went on, drinking now straight from the bottle. "Only *I* spoke for them. I spoke to them. They wanted me. I wanted them. The fans today want to worship dead stars. Sod 'em all. I'm still alive, and I have my audience of dead fans to love me."

Chase drank his whisky despite his earlier resolve. Nemo Skagg sat enthroned in squalor, surrounded by chalky ashes and the flickering light of a trash fire—a Wagnerian hero gone wrong.

"They came to London from all over; they're not just East End. They told the world to sod off, and the world repaid them in kind. Dead, they were no more wanted than when they lived. Drugs, suicides, traffic accidents, maybe a broken bottle in an alley or a rape and a knife in some squat. I started out with just the fans I recognized, then with the poor sods my mates told me about. After a while I had people watching the hospital morgues for them. The kids no one gave a shit for. Sure, often they had families, and let me tell you they was always pleased to have *me* pay for the final rites for the dearly departed, and good riddance. They were all better off dead, even the ones who didn't think so at first, and I had to help.

"Well, after a time the money ran out. I don't regret spending it on them. Fuck the fame. At least I still have my fans."

Nemo Skagg took a deep swig from the bottle, found it empty, pitched it, then picked up his ruined guitar. He scraped talons across the loose strings.

"And you, Ryan, old son. You said that you're still a loyal fan."

"Yes, Nemo. Yes, I did indeed say that." Chase set down his empty glass and bunched the muscles of his legs.

"Well, it's been great talking with you here backstage. We'll hang out some more later on. Hope you enjoy the gig."

"I'll just go take a piss, while you warm up." Chase arose carefully, backing toward the doorway of the lean-to.

"Don't be long." Nemo was plugging wires into the broken speakers, adjusting dials on the charred amps. He peered into the vaulted darkness. "Looks like I got a crucial audience out there tonight."

It was black as the pit, as Chase blundered out of the lean-to. Nettles and thistles ripped at him. Twice he fell over unseen mounds of debris, but he dragged himself painfully to his feet each time. Panic steadied his legs, and he could see the halo of streetlights beyond the hoarding. Gasping, grunting, cursing—he bulled headlong through the darkened tangle of the demolition site. Fear gave him strength, and sadistic fortune at last smiled upon him. He found the rubble-strewn incline, clawed his way up to pavement level, and shouldered past the flimsy hoarding.

As he fell sobbing onto the street, he could hear the roar of the audience below, feel the pounding energy of Nemo Skagg's guitar. Clawing to his feet, he was pushed forward by the screaming madness of Needle's unrecorded hits.

Nemo Skagg had lost nothing.

# NICHOLAS ROYLE

## Night Shift Sister

1993 HAS BEEN a busy year for Nicholas Royle. Barrington Books published his first novel, *Counterparts*, as a limited edition paperback and New English Library released the first mass-market edition of his British Fantasy Award-winning anthology *Darklands*, with a second and possibly further volumes to follow.

Recent new stories have appeared in *The Mammoth Book of Zombies*, *Dark Voices 5: The Pan Book of Horror*, *In Dreams*, *The Sun Rises Red*, *Sugar Sleep* and *Sunk Island Review*.

Bump in the Night Books recently issued a chapbook of short stories by Royle and Michael Marshall Smith, and his fiction has been selected for five consecutive volumes of *The Year's Best Horror Stories*, all four volumes of *Best New Horror*, and his contribution to *Narrow Houses* was one of only two to be chosen from that anthology for *The Year's Best Fantasy and Horror: Sixth Annual Collection*.

No wonder *Fear* called him "Britain's most successful young writer of short horror fiction."

As the author explains, "'Night Shift Sister' was partly inspired by the video for the Siouxsie and the Banshee's single 'Kiss Them for Me'." It also brings together some of his other favourite things, such as maps, hidden realms/parallel worlds, and gasholders, and became the starting point for a new novel entitled *In the City*.

First Carl found the map. It was a photocopy of a page taken from a book of street maps. He found it on the pavement outside the record shop one night when he'd worked later than usual sorting secondhand singles into categories. He knew that his customers would soon refile so many of them that his system would be ruined. That was partly why he liked doing it: to give the kids something to knock down. These days he rebelled only vicariously.

But there were patterns everywhere. Even in his own filing systems he discerned some arcane force at work. Something which came from above him and directed his hands as they lifted and turned and slotted. When the customers changed the system they did so according to some secret order not even they were aware of.

He left the shop late and became conscious while he was locking up of a fresh wind that carried a faint unpleasant odour reminiscent of domestic gas. For a moment he worried that there might be a leak in the shop but then it dispersed and he saw the map at his feet.

Studying the map as he walked to his old Escort parked a couple of streets away, Carl became confused. It looked like a detail of a city, presumably his own because of where he found it, but the streets were unnamed. They were obviously streets, and railway lines, too, and parks, ponds, canals and open spaces and closed spaces, but none of them were named so he couldn't say what locality it represented.

He unlocked the car door and got in. Dropping the map on the passenger seat he started the engine and pulled away from the kerb. At a red light he looked at himself in the rearview mirror and ran a hand through his long black hair which was perhaps in need of another bottle of dye and certainly a thorough wash. He also needed a shave. His dirty white leather jacket creaked comfortably and he reached down to take the packet of Camels out of his left boot and light one using the car lighter. The light went green, he turned right and the Escort bounced over the uneven road surface in the gathering darkness. Carl liked this time of day. Once he'd shut up shop his time was his own. He liked company but only of his own selection. Crowds weren't his scene. There was a radio in the car but he generally didn't switch it on. He welcomed quiet after spinning singles all day to keep the kids from getting bored.

He called in at the Cantonese takeaway and studied the map while he waited for his food. There were long straight drives and grids of narrow streets, and an area of streets which curved round and round like a game of solitaire where you have to get the ball to the middle. There was even a little circle at the centre.

When he reached the flat he took the map and his A to Z from the glove compartment, and his sweet and sour, and went upstairs. The flat was sparsely furnished but all the walls were shelved to house his enormous record collection. In the living room there was also a battered old sofa, a low sturdy table with an overflowing ashtray, and a pretty good TV and VCR. The white-painted ceiling was nicotine-stained.

He spent most of what remained of the evening going through the A to Z looking for a street layout that mirrored the one on his photocopied fragment, but without success.

It had occurred to him that the map could be of a different city, but then why was the original owner using it here? Carl decided whatever the map depicted was to be found here or nowhere.

The map's patterns attracted him but when frustration set in he lit a cigarette and slid a cassette into the VCR. A big fan of Siouxsie and the Banshees, Carl just couldn't get enough of the latest single. He played it several times a day at the shop and at home he watched the video over and over again. It helped him relax. And just looking at the way she moved made him feel less lonely, which was often a problem since Christine had fucked off to Paris without even leaving him a phone number. Or saying goodbye for that matter. All she'd said was something about him being a worthless drifter with less sense than her little sister. It had seemed harsh to him.

Sometimes he got so miserable he felt like crying. Nearly thirty, he had nothing apart from a scummy record shop, a decrepit Ford Escort, four or five thousand records and a few videos. His only company was Siouxsie Sioux. On video. Christine had left a hole in his life and, rather than try to fill it with someone else, he preferred to slip out through it and find something new.

Most of his old friends were married and couldn't come out because "it's such short notice and we couldn't get anyone to sit". The only one of his old friends who was still single was Baz and all he ever offered Carl was a fix. Things weren't that bad, he always thought to himself. Seeing Baz sometimes had the effect of cheering him up because he realised there was still a lot further to fall. He was determined to hang on. Maybe when the car dropped dead and he could no longer afford the spiralling rent on the shop. Maybe then he'd turn to Baz.

Carl took another cigarette from the pack on the table and reached for his matches because like a dickhead he'd left his lighter at the shop. But the box was very light. He shook it. Empty.

"Shit."

Kitchen.

Carl switched on one of the electric rings on the hob and waited for it to heat up. When it was bright orange he swept his hair away from his face and bent down to light the cigarette. He didn't turn the ring off but watched it becoming brighter and hotter as he smoked.

He flinched as he remembered pressing the flat of his hand down on one of his mother's electric rings when it was on. He'd been trying to climb on to a work surface and was using the cooker to lever his body up. As soon as he had felt the pain he had tried to withdraw his hand, but all his weight was on it, so he had screamed loud enough to pierce his mother's eardrums and she had looked round as he began to fall. He remembered her picking him up off the floor, trying to uncurl his hand. The rings had left dark brown marks on his skin and the smell made him sick.

He pulled on his cigarette. The scars had healed quite quickly but he had been left with a fear of the cooker. When he had bought his flat he had wanted gas but there wasn't any, so he intended to get a cooker with a modern ceramic hob, but Christine bought him a moving-in present: a nice old-fashioned electric cooker with rings just like his mother's.

He stared hard at the orange spiral, mesmerised by it. It wasn't just a bad memory. The shape meant something to him. It both attracted and repelled him without him knowing why.

Carl took the photocopied map to bed with him and fell asleep clutching it.

Carl became obsessed with the map and discovering the place it was based on. He thought about it constantly while serving customers and sorting through boxes of old singles people brought in to sell. He was bored with their mewling complaints and saw the map as an escape route.

An original '76 punk with bad teeth said he wanted £25 for The Skids' "Into the Valley" on white vinyl and £30 for the "Wide Open" EP, twelve-inch on red. Carl suggested wearily he'd do better to advertise in the music papers. He'd already got two copies of one and three of the other in the shop and no one seemed to want to buy them.

"What about Roxy Music 'Viva!' on Island? Forty quid."

"I've got three in stock."

"Not on Island," the punk argued. "It's rare."

"It's rare but I've got three of them."

Two French students asked if he'd got anything by Michel Petrucciani. Carl directed them to the jazz shop a couple of blocks away, then began to wonder if the map was of Paris and he was supposed to use it to find Christine. He discounted this quickly, feeling certain that he was the last person Christine wanted to see. To lift his spirits he stuck "Kiss Them for Me" on the turntable. He took the map out of the back pocket of his jeans and lit a cigarette. Out of the corner of his eye he noticed two young girls playing peek-a-boo with him from behind the soundtracks section. Did they know anything about it? Was it a deliberate plant?

He stepped forward to the till to serve a boy buying a clutch of house singles and when he looked up again the girls had gone. When he gave it some thought, he realised a great many people passed through his shop, trailing their lives and their secrets. Did some of what they carried get left behind? When he shut the shop at night the atmosphere always seemed a little bit richer. The secondhand records contained so many memories, different memories for different people, but each record would reek of the particular recollections of its previous owners. Had he bought the Skids' singles off the punk, he would have taken part of the punk into his shop to stay after the doors were locked. Perhaps that was why he had said no.

He lit another cigarette and held the map up to the light to see if that revealed any clues. It didn't. So he slipped his cigarettes down his boot, locked up and drove home.

The flat was quiet. When the downstairs tenant was in, Carl's life felt like a film with a soundtrack. A heavy metal soundtrack. Which meant you knew it was a crap film. He slung his leather jacket on a chair in the kitchen and took a bottle of Peroni beer from the fridge. He was running low. There were only six boxes left. Lighting a Camel he wandered into the moonlit living room and trailed his finger along rows of singles. He filed them alphabetically by artist. Hundreds had been bought new, but most were second-hand. He thought about what had occurred to him in the shop and wondered if he would be able to sense someone else's memories by playing their single.

He turned his attention to the shelf that held twelve-inch singles and took down "IV Songs" by In Camera. He switched everything on and played the first track. Spidery guitar, deliberately flat vocals, a spiny bass line and chattering cymbals. But no atmosphere. It was a depressing record but only because of the music. He took it off and looked at the words scratched into the runout groove. "Thanks Ilona." Inscribed on to the original acetate by the cutting engineer at his lathe, these messages fascinated Carl because they were like clues to a whole world of secrets and relationships behind the record. He put back the In Camera single and crossed the room to the C section of his LPs and proudly took out Elvis Costello's "This Year's Model". Inscribed on the runout groove was "Special Pressing No. 003. Ring Moira on 434 3232 For Your Special Prize." He had bought the record the day it came out and, noticing the inscription, found a phone box and dialled the number, winning free tickets to a Costello concert. The message had been intended to appear on the first 500 copies, but it overran by about 20,000 and a lot of people got very pissed off. But it was a good gig and now the record felt like a trophy.

He slid the LP back in its sleeve and went and lit another Camel from the electric ring because he'd forgotten his lighter again. The orange spiral burned into his brain and he reflected on how pathetic it was to be going through his record collection trawling for memories, his own and other people's.

He dragged on the cigarette and blew smoke rings. He watched them uncoil and re-form, a series of loops and twists. From his back pocket he took out the map and traced its streets with his eye. He shut his eyes and ran his fingers over the paper to see if that would yield anything. But all he felt were the slight ridges of toner from the photocopier.

He pressed play on the Siouxsie video and lit another cigarette from the stub of the old one. When it finished he rewound and played it again. While he was aware of how they could ensnare and reduce life to a series of repeats, Carl found some comfort at times of stress in following routines and resorting to icons. He fancied Siouxsie like mad and loved the song but he was still restless. Prowling down the shelves into the hallway he came across his huge collection of white labels. At the shop he bought a lot of white label promos in blank sleeves from collectors and if there were any he wanted to keep he just took them home. It was all the same money, whether it was at the shop or at home. Many of the promo copies in his collection had the artist's name scrawled across the white label in felt tip, but some were blank and these he liked best because if there were no distinguishing marks he could forget who the record was by and playing it was always a surprise.

He fell asleep on the sofa and woke with a start when his cigarette burned right down and stung his finger. He sucked it as he drew his legs off the table and stood up. In the bathroom he ran his finger under the cold tap and examined it under the light over the mirror. There was a tiny patch where the whorls of his fingerprint had been smoothed over. He stared fascinated at the pattern of parallel lines. On the third finger of his right hand the lines seemed to fan out in a spiral from a central point, like hair growing from the crown. But Carl realised that when you'd got down to examining your own fingerprints it was time to say goodnight.

He played a random selection of singles at the shop and listened with one ear to the lyrics. He looked carefully at the records he had bought during the morning in case their titles revealed anything. But there was nothing. He knew he could make something up out of all the material at his fingertips, but he would know he'd invented it.

If a genuine message were to stand out from the dross he'd know it because he'd feel it.

By the end of the day he felt saturated by voices and longed for silence. The roads were refreshingly empty. His tyres hissed on wet tarmac and he cruised with the radio off. The red lights in the distance became a cascade of reflections in the puddles as he knocked the gear lever into neutral and coasted down to meet them. He rolled into position behind a girl in a Mini who like him was waiting for the lights to change. She had shoulder-length black hair like Siouxsie Sioux and was bobbing up and down on her seat and moving from side to side, tapping her fingers on the steering wheel and banging the dash.

*What was she listening to?*

Carl suddenly felt his stomach twist as he realised that whatever music the girl was listening to was a clue. If only he could hear it he would share a secret with her and perhaps he'd know the way to drive to the streets on the map. Maybe she'd let him follow her. He wound his window down but her window was up and he couldn't hear anything. She bounced on her seat and the little car moved like a cocoon when she did. He couldn't pull alongside because there was only one lane.

The lights changed and she was off. He jerked into first and followed, reaching across to switch on the radio to see if she was listening to a station he could tune into. The gap between the two cars lengthened as he slewed across the dial, stopping to catch fragments of music. But there was nothing that spoke to him as clearly as the girl's movements. It must have been a tape. She was a long way ahead now. He jumped a red light to keep her in sight but she turned into a side street and although he followed suit she had vanished into a warren of crescents he barely knew.

He was smoking and reading a thriller in bed when the front door rattled in its frame. With a clear view of the door from his bed, Carl looked up and put his book down beside him. When the door opened he wasn't altogether surprised to see the girl from the car. Her black hair framed a face that was Siouxsie's, except that it wasn't. Because it was Christine's. She was like a composite of both of them. The only two women in his life, both now very much on the fringes of it, synthesised into this one girl.

She walked in and turned past his doorway to enter the living room. He noticed as he got out of bed to follow her that she was carrying a long knife in the back pocket of her jeans, the same pocket he kept his map in. He felt in his own pocket and was relieved to find it still there. The girl went over to Carl's stereo equipment and slipped a single from inside her denim jacket on to the turntable. She stood back and Carl came forward to see what she'd brought him. A white label disc spun at 45 and the needle cut into it. He looked up but the girl had gone. He whirled round and ran to the door but it was shut and there was no sound in the stairwell. He bent over the record player again and saw that as the needle travelled round the groove towards the centre it left a fine spiral of blood in its wake.

Carl jumped and woke up. His cigarette had burnt a hole in the duvet cover. He smothered it quickly with a pillow, but there was no need: the cigarette was cold. He shivered and felt sick. Brushing the curtain behind his head to one side he looked down into the street for a Mini, but there was only his Escort and one or two other familiar cars.

He stomped out of his bedroom and checked the front door—undisturbed—and the stereo. There was no record on the turntable and no blood but the power was on. He never left the power on. Groaning, he flicked the switch and went to make as much and as many different uses of the bathroom as his body would let him.

In bed once more he tossed and turned but sleep eluded him. *Got to get up, got to get up*, he thought over and over. He pulled on a pair of boxer shorts and went through to the living room. A cigarette and the Siouxsie video. They had a placebo effect but he was neither completely relaxed nor did he feel sleepy. Yet his body was exhausted. At dawn he was thinking of taking the car for a run down to the crescent where he'd lost the girl in her Mini when he finally fell asleep in front of the TV.

Driving to the shop a couple of hours later he felt like a jigsaw that had been put together wrongly. Someone had tried to force pieces into each other and they held but only just. He had a craving for pure orange juice but made do with a cigarette instead. He pushed in the dashboard lighter and waited for it to pop out. He withdrew it and brought it up to his mouth. While driving he looked down to align the end of the cigarette with the lighter and was shocked by the sight of the burning orange element. He lost his grip on the steering wheel and went the wrong way round a set of bollards. Feeling sick, he righted the car and coasted in to the kerb. He got out, threw the cigarette in the gutter and leaned against the bonnet for a few minutes. The shop would have to open late for once.

He kept seeing the image from his dream of the needle cutting into the record and drawing blood. He got back in the car and set off for the shop again. Every Mini turned his head. He'd never noticed them before but now it seemed like the city streets were full of them. He couldn't remember what colour the hybrid Siouxsie/Christine girl had been driving. It had, after all, been dark when he'd seen it.

During the hours of daylight he imagined it was parked up in one of the nameless streets on his map. Only by night, when there wasn't any, did she venture into the light of the real world.

Carl struggled to concentrate on the business of running the shop. The jigsaw feeling had faded but he still wasn't on top form. He chainsmoked and played randomly selected singles back to back all morning. Customers brought him boxes of records and he bought them all with the briefest examinations and without haggling over the amount he would pay for them. The shop seemed infested with Siouxsie clones but they were all years out of date, painted birds and scarecrows, their faces plastered with the Hallowe'en makeup Siouxsie herself now did without. Over the years, as the masks had been slowly stripped away she had become more and more beautiful to the point where her beauty was now a dangerous, provocative thing, like the music had always been.

Carl slipped 'Superstition' into the CD player and pressed repeat. The album played for the rest of the day.

In a stream of people offering him their old picture discs and limited edition gatefold sleeves a girl's hand pushed a white label single on to the counter. Carl gave a small cry and immediately looked up but the floor was crowded with customers. Out of the corner of his eye he saw the door close but it could have been anybody. Nevertheless, he squeezed under the counter and pushed through the crowd to the door. He craned his neck and looked in all directions but she had disappeared. There was no sign of a Mini parked nearby. His heart pounding, he re-entered the shop and returned to his place behind the counter.

Word must have got round that he was throwing money away today: it seemed as if the whole teenage population of the city had descended on his shop. "Whose is this?" he asked, holding up the white label. No one claimed it. "Is it yours?" he asked the next girl in the queue. She nodded. Someone behind her cackled like a hyena and he felt foolish, but for all he knew it could really have been hers and she'd been too shy to stick her hand up. The colour of the label could have prompted him to imagine someone who hadn't been there at all. He took the other stuff the girl clearly hadn't been expecting to sell, then lit a cigarette and put the white label underneath a stack of CDs to look at later.

It was with enormous relief that he locked the door and flipped the open/closed sign. He didn't need all this unrest. He stood and watched the rain through the glass as he lit a cigarette and put the lighter away in his jacket pocket. Cars squealed softly as they braked for the red light. Carl smoked nervously, unhappy about acknowledging his fear of the unknown girl and the white label she'd brought him. In the brightness of the afternoon it had been easier to rationalise. But in the shadowtime of dusk it seemed indisputable that his obsession was based on fact. He watched car headlamps dazzle and melt into wet reflections like silver waterfalls. Taking a deep drag that caused his head to spin he turned away from the window and went back to the counter. He felt like a bug in a killing jar. They could be watching him through the windows from across the street. They would want to see how he reacted when he listened to the white label. Well let them!

He picked it up and slipped it out of its blank sleeve, holding it by the edges and angling it so that the light fell across it. There was nothing written on the label, but on the runout groove he made out the inscription "It's a gas." It meant nothing to him. It just seemed like the kind of throwaway remark that cutting engineers sometimes went in for.

He placed the record on the turntable with great care and positioned the needle before pressing release. It landed with that satisfying clunk he had heard a million times. It didn't matter how new a vinyl record was, you always heard something apart from the music, even if it was only the hiss of dust. He wondered what he would hear as the needle wound its way towards the music.

But none came. He checked the amp controls. Everything was on and the volume was turned up. He looked at the needle. It was a third of the way into the record and still there was no sound.

He turned the volume higher and listened harder. He heard the usual rumble of ticks and bumps you got at the beginning and end of records. When it finished he repositioned the needle and played it again. With the volume full up he fancied he could hear the needle itself scoring the groove a fraction deeper. He found himself becoming quite drawn to the sound. Without the distraction of music it was somehow purer, more elemental. He played the flip side and it was the same. The more he played it and the harder he listened, the more it sank into him. He noticed also that his forehead had begun to hurt where the skin stretched tightly across it. A sharp irritating pain like a paper cut.

Pain or no pain he was in thrall to the record. He loved its silence just as he soon came to need the sounds that *were* there to be heard if you listened hard enough. He played it again and again until he entered a state approaching rhapsody.

Towards midnight he locked up and walked to the car. The white label was in a padded envelope under his arm. He laid it carefully on the passenger seat and started the engine. He drove like an automaton, unblinking eyes sweeping the road ahead in search of the hybrid's car. He knew what she'd been dancing to and now he'd been there himself. In the shop. Listening to the record over and over again. The walls and ceiling had receded and he had felt himself at the centre of a huge spiral which descended upon him from the sky.

Waiting at a red light, rain lightly stippling the windscreen, Carl pressed in the cigarette lighter and reached into his boot. He stuck a cigarette between his lips. The lighter popped out and he withdrew it. He stared fixedly at the burning spiral for a few moments before sticking the third finger of his left hand inside the lighter and pressing the tip against the element. He didn't blink. Rain fell more heavily on the car, beating a tinny tattoo on the roof. The light went green but he didn't move. The smell of burning flesh infused the air in the car.

Deep inside Carl, in a small part of him, a tiny scream caught like a flame in a tinderbox, then flickered and died.

He only pulled his finger away when he felt his nail grating unpleasantly against the metal coil.

His finger was black and cauterised. His face was blank. The light was red again. He replaced the cigarette lighter and waited for the light to change. When it did he shifted into first gear, wincing and moaning slightly as his burnt finger brushed against the passenger seat.

How long would it be before she appeared? He cruised slowly to give her enough time, but there was no sign of her and soon he was pulling up outside the flat. Maybe she'd be waiting for him inside. He looked at his finger with a curious, childlike expression as he climbed the stairs. It still wasn't bleeding. He stuffed his hand in his back pocket to check on the map. It was still there. His mind dulled in response to the friction against his jeans.

The flat was empty but it didn't feel like his own any more. When he put the record on and turned the volume right up he felt a druggy mixture of euphoria and emptiness. His forehead itched. He wondered dully if Baz was involved. The inscription on the runout groove. "It's a gas." It was the kind of thing Baz would say. The girl couldn't have recorded, cut and pressed a record all on her own; she needed accomplices. Someone had to inhabit the streets on his map.

He looked at the thousands of records lining his walls. He'd wasted so much time searching for all that noise when all along the real music had been waiting for him just a few streets away.

In the kitchen he switched the ring on full and watched it get hot. He could still hear the music swirling around him, making of him its heart. But his forehead was hurting, like scratched sunburn. Maybe he could burn up the pain by lowering his forehead on to the ring. He bent over the cooker and was about to do it when he heard a car pull up outside.

It was her.

He left the kitchen without switching off the cooker and looked out of the living-room window. There was a black Mini parked in front of his Escort. He crossed to the door and as he looked back for a moment before closing the door he felt a tug. He realised this was his last chance. If he didn't turn back now he might never be able to. He looked at the photograph of Christine he still kept by the bed and felt a stab of regret. But as he sharpened his focus on the picture he saw that now she looked more like Siouxsie. And more like the candyman waiting outside in the car.

He left the door open and walked down the staircase. As he stepped into the street he felt a warm breeze and detected the faint odour of gas. The map was in his back pocket. He reached for the door handle on the Mini but the girl gunned the engine into life and moved forward several feet to dissuade him. He walked towards his own car and glanced in through the Mini's windows.

On the back seat lay a long knife.

He followed her in the Escort. She turned off his familiar route into the warren of semi-circular streets where he'd lost her for the first time. Despite his injured finger he kept pace with her. The road curved round to the right, then they turned right and curved some more. They seemed to be drawing in towards some hidden centre. He noticed a clocktower among a group of school buildings, but the clockface was devoid of hands. He accelerated and felt the road, once he'd passed the playground, twist round to the right. The streets were lined with bay-window semis. What suburban relapse could have occurred at the heart of this model landscape?

Carl fumbled the map from his back pocket and unfolded it. As he had vaguely remembered, there was a pocket of circular streets, effectively a spiral.

*Take me back, take me back,* he silently entreated the girl in the car ahead. But she took him on.

They turned right again and eventually the houses disappeared, giving way to waste ground, a procession of electricity pylons and an enormous gasholder.

The girl parked and started walking. Carl had to run to catch her up. They walked over ground dotted with sorrel and belladonna. He looked at the map. They were heading for the circle which lay at the centre of the curled maze of streets. The gasholder.

It reared up before them, a wonderful monster of overlapping curved metal plates. A telescopic spiral ready to expand or contract. It glowed in the moonlight and appeared to hover just above the ground like a ghostly carousel.

Carl followed the girl to the base of the gasholder. The long knife stuck out of the back pocket of her jeans. When she reached an opening she turned and looked back. The moon fell on her face which Carl now saw for the first time outside of his dream. She was, as he had dreamt, the perfect synthesis of Siouxsie and Christine. She had the most beautiful face he had ever seen. His stomach went into a slow dive. But it was love in a void and he felt his heart turn to stone. He would have wept but for the detail on her forehead which, though he caught only the briefest of glimpses, chilled him to the bone.

She turned and vanished inside the gasholder.

Carl followed because, no longer in control of his actions, there was nothing else he could do.

Inside the gargantuan chamber it was dark and Carl was forced to rely on other senses. He raised his arms to protect his face as he stepped forward. The overwhelming impression was of noise: of hundreds or thousands of slowly shuffling feet and in the highest reaches of the metal skin there resounded the magnified hiss and clicks and cannon booms of the white label. It threw its hooks into Carl immediately and he felt himself being drawn into a mass of swaying bodies. He visualised a charnel house of carcasses and raw heads and bloody bones.

There was something else he sensed but couldn't put a name to.

Carl succumbed to the silent music but the darkness awakened his fear and he felt pulled to bits. He pictured the girl's forehead and imagined all the flitting spellbound shapes around him to be similarly disfigured.

They pressed nearer and he was horrified to realise he felt close to them in mind as well as body. He imagined he could feel Christine's breath on his face and for a moment the gasholder almost became a place of paradise. But there was still the niggling feeling that something else was wrong but he didn't know what. Something around him that he should be aware of.

A cold object sliced his forehead and he felt a warm liquid run down into his eyes. Then the girl pressed harder with the knife but it was always a light, intimate touch, intended to brand rather than hurt.

Carl panicked. These weren't his people. It wasn't his celebration. He had never wanted oblivion, just a change. Something secret and new. Now he wanted his life back.

As far as he could tell, they were scared of the light.

He slipped his hand into the pocket of his leather jacket and closed his fingers round his cigarette lighter. He lifted it up to eye level and in the very same moment that he spun the wheel and created a dazzling, vivid snapshot of hundreds of raised foreheads marked by needle-fine spiral scars, he realised what the other thing was. A silly thing really.

The smell of gas.

# SIMON INGS & M. JOHN HARRISON

# The Dead

"THE DEAD" is the first of two contributions M. John Harrison makes to *Best New Horror 4*, so you can find his bibliographical notes with his story "Anima", later in this volume.

Simon Ings works nights as a legal proof reader, days at his third novel or being rude to his elders. He has recently signed to write a short film script for the British Film Institute, based loosely on material from his first novel, *HotHead*, and its sequel, *HotWired*. His short fiction has been published in *Other Edens III*, *Zenith 2*, *New Worlds* and *Omni*, and a literary fantasy novel, *City of the Iron Fish*, is due in 1994. Like rust, he rarely sleeps.

The story which follows was originally published in Chris Kenworthy's small press anthology *The Sun Rises Red* and quickly reprinted in *Interzone*. It marks the first—but, we hope, not last—collaboration between two of Britain's most exciting and original writers.

ONE YEAR, IN THE PARK, there were strange grey birds scavenging the shoreline of the ornamental lake.

"Don't be afraid," Elizabeth's mother said.

She said:

"Feed them. They're hungry."

The birds, which were perhaps geese, looked at Elizabeth with big round greedy eyes. They walked very slowly—very smoothly—back and forth over the snow-speckled gravel. Elizabeth's mother stroked Elizabeth's neck: woollen gloves scratched Elizabeth's skin just above her red scarf.

"Feed them," she repeated.

Her grip was fierce.

Elizabeth's Uncle Tony laughed. It was just his way of trying to cheer her up. He would laugh in exactly the same way at his brother's funeral—which was, of course, her father's too. Uncle Tony was gauche. He found it difficult to speak. Now he laughed at the geese and said to Elizabeth:

"Look. They're almost human."

And indeed they had formed a little line, to wait for the bread.

"Almost human!" said Uncle Tony.

"Shut up," said Elizabeth's mother.

"Nearly human."

Why have a stale bread roll in the pocket of your tailored red coat, if not to feed the birds? Elizabeth, always a punctilious child, took the roll out of its paper bag, broke it up, and scattered the pieces. The geese bobbed up and down in front of her in a slow way, necks curved, beaks open. Elizabeth's mother stared at them with an angry but helpless expression, as if her feelings ran in contrary directions. Her eyes, Elizabeth saw, were more gold than green; there were wrinkles under her jaw.

In those days the winters were colder than the rest of the year. Every month they would visit Uncle Tony, who was a painter in the city. They often set out in darkness, arriving so early that mist still obscured the ends of the cobbled streets. After feeding the birds, they would eat breakfast in the house: fresh rolls, strong coffee for the mother, hot chocolate for Elizabeth.

"Will I have a cake?"

Uncle Tony was delighted.

"No one has cake for breakfast."

"Will I have some cheese?"

He threw up his hands. What a game!

"Cheese is for lunch, Elizabeth."

"Will I have a goose, then?"

Silence.

"Can I have a goose?"
"Shut up Elizabeth," said her mother.
Elizabeth was four years old.

She found Uncle Tony's house hard to sleep in. Pocked bulky wooden beams emerged from the plaster work in one room, to disappear into another. By day the bare, varnished boards were black with trapped reflections. At night they creaked; while the uncle gave great shouts and snores, like communiques from his dream-life. He would speak a full sentence just before dawn, his voice reasonable and calm:

"I wanted blue."

Or:

"Let's get the pegs first."

There were other noises, perhaps less random. One night on a visit not long after her eighth birthday, Elizabeth was woken by a woman sobbing. One moment, this sound was low and contemplative, brooding over events gone by; the next it rose angrily to meet some immediate pain. It came and went in the night, full of the pure pity of the self—present anguish, passing sorrow—but also something raw as a broken tooth.

Elizabeth got out of bed and knocked on her mother's door. The only answer was an inhuman screech. Elizabeth opened the door and looked in. There her mother knelt, quite alone, on all fours on the bare floor in the dark. Moonlight came through the window, picking out the wooden bed-head, the white china jerry. It glistened in the sweat on the mother's forehead, pooled between the muscles in the narrow small of her back, which she first hollowed then rounded in some rhythm of frustration.

"Mother?"

"Go away."

"Mother?"

There was a strong smell in the room. The mother's breasts hung down. She stared emptily ahead.

"Go away and wait your turn," she said.

After that, things went from bad to worse. It rained all winter; and all the following summer, and all the winters and summers which followed that. December was too warm. July was too cold. At home Elizabeth's mother spent her nights on a trestle bed in the conservatory, while Elizabeth's father sat on the stairs practising the violin until his wife was quiet.

When she was fourteen, Elizabeth's father taught her a song.

*Oubliez les anges*, it advised:

*Oubliez les bosseus*
*Et partout*
*Oubliez les professeurs*!

He took her to the cafe by the bus station, where, from a table by the window, a very fat woman called Hetty Calver played clock patience and watched the buses go in and out all day. The air was full of the smell of cigarettes and hot fat. As soon as you entered, Hetty would drag herself to her feet and fetch from behind the formica-topped counter a bottle of marjolaine, a dusty jar of honey. Anywhere else they would warm the honey over a little hotplate before it was added to the marjolaine. That was the modern way. But Hetty Calver still dipped her finger in the jar, licked the honey off, and rolled it round her mouth to liquefy it.

"There you are, dear."

"I'm not drinking that," said Elizabeth.

"It tastes of roses," said her father. He smacked his lips mournfully.

"It's been in her mouth."

"We all loved Hetty when she was young."

He took Elizabeth to the park. It was a miserable day for summer, as if someone had collected all the damp and forgettable moments of the year and strung them together regardless of season. The fair was cancelled. Elizabeth's coloured paper parasol, so necessary in former summers, crumpled in the drizzle and fell to pulp. If the summer was no longer hot, the winter was no longer cold. Elizabeth fidgeted.

"Why is Mummy like she is?"

Her father made no answer.

"Listen," he said.

The town's famous silver band had begun its afternoon practise.

"Listen," he began.

He said "There are a great many dead – "

Elizabeth's father was quite different from his brother. Everything had to be proper for him: a suit, a marriage, a phrase in music. He smelled of lavender water. If he over-wound his watch that morning he would walk round worriedly all day, murmuring: "The spring will be strained. The spring has strained. Perhaps the spring is broken." Uncle Tony had no watch. His paint brushes stuck up surprisingly out of a jam jar, like men with mad and sticky hair. These brushes were responsible for the biggest, most garish pictures Elizabeth had ever seen. Hot yellow fishes hung in a green sky, a sky the colour of her mother's eyes. "Green sky!" Elizabeth ticked him off. "Rubbish! And those fishes are a baby's fishes." Her father was easily defeated by life, but Uncle Tony would never give up. It would be hard to imagine two more different people, but Elizabeth loved them both.

"There are a great many dead," her father repeated.

"They far outnumber the living," he explained. "We must pay our debt to them."

He thought for a moment.

"We must accommodate them somehow."

At his own funeral, some months later, the rain never stopped. The cortege wound its way across town, up a hill, between factories, behind rusty gasometers and over the canal by the derelict lock-gates, corner by corner, junction by junction, as if it had lost its way. It was late afternoon. The pall bearers tried to walk in the centre of the street, where the wet cobbles, gleaming in the light of the boarding-house windows, were less overgrow. Bird droppings mottled the flagstones in the churchyard, piled up in the corners beneath the broken guttering. Elizabeth's father changed hands three times on the journey. His friends from the silver band, somewhat drunk, found him heavy; they played him along on their sodden instruments, with Oubliez les Anges. Hetty Calver followed a little way behind the mourning party. Great fat woman, great fat arms. She had brought her son with her, an idiot with dirt under his nose and breeches several sizes too big, who prowled about the edges of the cortege picking up half-bricks and bits of corroded pipe and calling out, "No more. No more." Over the grave he was the only one to produce tears. "Hush," said Hetty Calver, stroking his hair: "Hush." The cemetery, Elizabeth saw, was full of headstones so worn you could read on them only the word "Father".

Afterwards, as they ate the funeral baked meats in a room above the grocer's shop, a grey bird came tapping against the window. Elizabeth stared at it and burst into tears. She cried until she was sick. The women stood round her, uncertain what to do. The air was absolutely still. The rain fell straight down, and Elizabeth's father was dead, and everything smelled the way it had smelled for weeks. "There, there," said the women. The grey bird ruffled its feathers as if settling into a coat, and looked in at Elizabeth from the window sill.

"Get it away!" she screamed.

What happened to Elizabeth's mother?

She died, too, but not before she explained everything.

"You will remember?" she said anxiously. "Your father would want you to remember."

She sighed and took Elizabeth's hand.

"There really is nothing we can do, is there? About the world? Little one?"

"I hate you," said Elizabeth. "I hate him too."

The mother laughed softly.

"How shocked I was when you came into that room and found me there! All those years ago, when we still had summers and winters."

"I hate you."

Elizabeth inherited her father's house and her mother's advice. "Pick a clear, starless night. Wear a cotton dress. Get up onto the mausoleum. It helps to lick your finger and wet yourself between the legs. If anyone is with you, have them turn away." And then:

"Do you remember our summers by the lake? You used to love them so. Feed the birds my darling. Goodbye."

One other thing she inherited was her mother's chair, an ugly wooden object with a high back and a curious, scooped-out seat. "We must carry it to your room," her mother said. How heavy and awkward it was, for an old woman and a young girl. At first it would not go through the door. But between them they got it in, and set it down in the corner by the window. "There!" the mother said. She tried to smile, but exhaustion made her face immobile. She and Elizabeth, at this astonishing juncture of their lives, could only make together a comedy of domestic affections—each starting to speak, each hanging back for the other, over and over again. In the end, the mother said:

"Well. Sit down."

Then she turned and went tiredly out.

It was a "birthing" chair, designed less for comfort than the correct posture.

"I hate it," whispered Elizabeth, when the door was closed at last.

"Will you come to the funeral?" she wrote to her Uncle Tony. She was seventeen years old, not so much angry as puzzled. "The world is just such a hateful place." In the end, though, he was less support to her than she had hoped. He arrived late, left before the meats were served. She watched him walk away down the rain-silvered cobbles of the high street. He was preoccupied, and his shoes were new. Later, it turned out that he had remarried, to a middle aged woman with a few black curly hairs along the line of her jaw, whose thirteen year old son, gassed by a faulty boiler, had drowned in the bath the year before. She wore a little silver bird on a thin silver chain round her neck, and all she ever talked about was how to cook vegetables. Elizabeth met her only the once.

"How is my uncle?"

"He eats well."

"How are his odd skies and yellow fishes?"

Uncle Tony's wife wiped her upper lip. Uncle Tony was eating his greens: but no one was buying his pictures. They had been called too colourful for the middle-class taste. Uncle Tony, on the other hand, believed they weren't colourful enough. It was his theory that there was something wrong with the paint.

"It isn't lively. The colour is washed right out of it as it arrives on the canvas," he complained to Elizabeth in a letter.

"The world seems washed out too," he admitted.

He and his wife had moved into a smaller house, on a road that was always being dug up.

"I miss the children most," he wrote: "Their bright clothes and ribbons. Do you remember when we fed the birds together? You looked like a little wooden doll in your red coat. So proper, yet you asked: 'Can I have cheese for breakfast?' I miss the language of children, which we forget so easily. Perhaps my eyes are tired, and I have grown out of sympathy with my public; but my ears are perfectly good. The world has grown out of sympathy with us all. Of all the things the dead have stolen from us I miss the children. Of all the children I miss you, Elizabeth, the most."

Elizabeth was obscurely disappointed by this.

She imagined Uncle Tony in an upstairs kitchen, arguing desultorily with his wife. Outside, workmen were shouting, and a mechanical digger went to and fro, shaking the fabric of the house, making it hard to hear what anyone said. Uncle Tony's wife stood by the window, lifting one corner of the faded net curtain. The room smelled of cooked macaroni. As she looked down at the new hole in the road, which was full of muddy water, some thought made her face tighten briefly then relax again.

"You never go to church," she accused.

"Pardon?"

If she wants me to hear, Uncle Tony thought, she'll have to shout.

"You'll have to shout," he said.

His wife looked down at the mechanical digger, rocking backwards and forwards in one place with a mouthful of paving slabs.

"Nothing," she said.

Elizabeth had hoped Uncle Tony would help her, but he came to nothing. Uncle Tony was someone who needed help himself. She wrote to him:

"I remember the breakfasts we had."

She wrote:

"How happy we were, long ago."

"They'll never put the gas back on," he told his wife. "I know that."

* * *

Dawn breaks over the town. Its factories and recreation grounds and terraces of dark bricks are silent in the pale horizontal wash of light. The old chimneys make faint long shadows across the grass. The railway bridges and advertising hoardings are silent. An old bicycle is parked against a wall in the rain. Every wall—every factory or warehouse, every nice house on the outskirts—is carved with the names of the dead. There are dried flowers in the niches. The air chokes on the muddy perfume: lavender and birdlime. Lavender and birdlime, and the smell of yeast from a run-down brewery on Thomas Street.

Elizabeth gets up too early and walks through town. Time has passed. Uncle Tony is dead now too. At nineteen years old—tallish, and with what would have been called a good body—she is already greying at the left temple. Her eyes are rather large, the irises unnaturally wide. She has a thin, anxious smile.

"I'll wear a green and gold dress," she promised herself last night.

By now the town is waking up.

Bicycles go past, wheels hissing in the rain. Workmen will be gathering in the bus station. At the cafe, Hetty Calver is already playing patience at the table by the window. She says to herself aloud:

"Hearts on hearts, my love."

Her cards are soft and sticky with wear. "Hearts on hearts." Then: "Be with you in a minute, love." Her chair scrapes back. Breathing heavily through her mouth, she squeezes behind the counter. "Nasty day." Out comes the marjolaine and honey. "There you are, dear."

Elizabeth smiles and empties the glass.

"Thank you."

"They all loved me when I was young."

In the centre of the town, where the canal flows through the municipal park, there is an iron bridge. At all times of day but especially in the quiet morning, before the town wakes properly up, this bridge is grey with birds. You think they are pigeons: they cover the pavement like a rustling, cooing rug. You think they are starlings: they perch heads cocked on the railings, the mossy rusted beams above and beneath. You think they are great soft grey geese: they fill the sky with creaking wings which obscure the sluggish green water of the canal below. They wheel about you. The air flutters and susurrates with their feathers. They are like a musty grey growth on everything. Elizabeth comes to the mid-point of this bridge, where the oldest birds perch. When you pass they launch themselves from the rails and swoop close to you, brushing your hair for luck.

"Not too close," says Elizabeth.

"I love you, but not too close."

On the other side of the canal she takes the brick-paved lane to gardens, wrought iron benches, and the ornamental lake where her mother and her uncle used to sit talking while she fed the birds. Now she can sit on the same bench and reflect: "How proper of the dead to leave us their ashes, which silt down quietly in the lake." A breeze springs up, full of dust, bringing from the waking cafes the smells of instant coffee and soap. Elizabeth feels it through her mother's dress, against her skin. She grips the bench with her hands and brings her hips forwards so the small of her back rests against the cold iron slats. She bends her knees to take the weight of her body, and parts her legs so the wind can penetrate. Dust on her skin. Dust on her breast. Dust in shapes rotten and terrible and heartbreaking: but the years have passed, all exactly alike, and she has grown so used to them.

She remembers her mother's advice.

"If someone is there, have them look away."

No one else was ever there.

Back in her room, Elizabeth pulls her mother's dress up round her waist, and tells herself:

"It's always cold in here."

Shut the windows, draw the thin curtains.

What light they admit is as grey as a feather.

Elizabeth sits in the birthing chair. Her pains begin.

"What? Are you so beautiful?"

She groans: "Oh, oh, nnnnh, oh no."

The first of them is stillborn, a draggle of wet feathers. The next two unwrap in an instant, flutter to the window and beat their wings against the glass. Elizabeth is dizzy. Pushing the last one out, she has wet herself. Birds, little birds, flutter round the room, all colours first, then fading to grey. They throw themselves so helplessly against the glass. "If only I could get them to the light!" As soon as she can Elizabeth goes to the windows to release them. Out they go, one after the other, glisten for an instant in the light as if they might regain their colour; then they're gone, round the corner of the building, off towards the bridge. Exhausted, Elizabeth washes the blood-streaked mucus from her thighs—cleans the window, looking out—rubs half heartedly at the stain on the carpet. Mid afternoon: she lies upon her bed and goes to sleep. The boundaries between states have all crumbled: no more snow, no more sunshine. The dead leave no room for us: if anyone is there when you do it, make them look away. Oubliez les professeurs. Why do you have a stale bread roll in the pocket of your red coat, if not to feed the birds?

So that they will feed you.

It would be an odd world, Elizabeth thought, if we could really forget our teachers.

She wakes hungry, looks out. The birds have left a heap of things under the window while she slept—some peanuts from the floor of a bus shelter, breadcrusts, a square of chocolate with the blue silver paper still on it. Elizabeth squats down on the bricks outside her room to go through this stuff, the air still and warm on her skin. Everything sorts quite easily into a meal. While she is eating, a single starling flies in and settles on the bricks beside her. Its feathers have a mad, sticky, iridescent look. One of its eyes is green, the other gold. In its beak is a cigarette butt, which it drops in front of her.

Elizabeth looks at it and smiles.

"Thank you," she says.

She says: "I don't think I'll eat that though."

# CHRISTOPHER FOWLER

## Norman Wisdom and the Angel of Death

FOR HALF OF EACH DAY, Christopher Fowler works with the writers, producers and artists at The Creative Partnership, the Soho film promotion company he runs, creating poster and trailer images, writing publicity scripts, producing behind-the-scenes films and designing title sequences.

For the other half of the day he writes short stories and such novels as *Roofworld, Rune, Red Bride* and *Darkest Day*, which loosely make up a "London Quartet" set in an alternative city. His stories have been collected in *City Jitters, City Jitters Two, The Bureau of Lost Souls* and *Sharper Knives*, while recent anthology appearances include *The Mammoth Book of Zombies, I Shudder At Your Touch, Dark Voices 4: The Pan Book of Horror, Narrow Houses, In Dreams, The Time Out Book of Short Stories* and *London Noir*.

On the movie front, both *Roofworld* and *Rune* are in development (the latter from *Total Recall* director Paul Verhoeven); his story *The Master Builder* was recently filmed as a CBS-TV movie starring Tippi Hedren; *Left Hand Drive* has been produced as a feature short, and he has written an original screenplay, *High Tension*, for State Screen Films.

The author reveals that he "watched every single Norman Wisdom film" to write the following story and that the idea came from "reading about Asperger's Syndrome, the insidious disease that exists by degree in people who become obsessed with everything from train-spotting to *Star Trek*. If you've ever seen the home video footage of mass-murderer Dennis Nilson with his victims, you'll know that far from being a *Red Dragon* type, he was a deeply boring man."

Possibly even more disturbing is that Fowler admits he actually wrote the story because "I happen to find Norman Wisdom really funny. Not many people are prepared to admit *that* in print, eh?"

Too right, they're not.

**Diary Entry # 1 Dated 2 July**

THE PAST IS SAFE.

The future is unknown.

The present is a bit of a bastard.

Let me explain. I always think of the past as a haven of pleasant recollections. Long ago I perfected the method of siphoning off bad memories to leave only those images I still feel comfortable with. What survives in my mind is a seamless mosaic of faces and places that fill me with warmth when I choose to consider them. Of course, it's as inaccurate as those retouched Stalinist photographs in which comrades who have become an embarrassment have been imperfectly erased so that the corner of a picture still shows a boot or a hand. But it allows me to recall times spent with dear friends in the happy England that existed in the fifties; the last era of innocence and dignity, when women offered no opinion on sexual matters and men still knew the value of a decent winter overcoat. It was a time which ended with the arrival of the Beatles, when youth replaced experience as a desirable national quality.

I am no fantasist. Quite the reverse; this process has a practical value. Remembering the things that once made me happy helps to keep me sane.

I mean that in *every* sense.

The future, however, is another kettle of fish. What can possibly be in store for us but something worse than the present? An acceleration of the ugly, tasteless, arrogant times in which we live. The Americans have already developed a lifestyle and a moral philosophy entirely modelled on the concept of shopping. What is left but to manufacture more things we don't need, more detritus to be thrown away, more vicarious thrills to be selfishly experienced? For a brief moment the national conscience flickered awake when it seemed that green politics was the only way to stop the planet from becoming a huge concrete turd. And what happened? Conservation was hijacked by the advertising industry and turned into a highly suspect sales concept.

No, it's the past that heals, not the future.

So what about the present? I mean right now.

At this moment, I'm standing in front of a full-length mirror reducing the knot of my tie and contemplating my frail, rather tired appearance. My name is Stanley Morrison, born March 1950, in East Finchley, North London. I'm a senior sales clerk for a large shoe firm, as they say on the quiz programmes. I live alone and have always done so, having never met the right girl. I have a fat cat called Hattie, named after Hattie Jacques, for whom I have a particular fondness in the role of Griselda Pugh in Series Five, Programmes One to Seven of

*Hancock's Half Hour*, and a spacious but somewhat cluttered flat situated approximately one hundred and fifty yards from the house in which I was born. My hobbies include collecting old radio shows and British films, of which I have an extensive collection, as well as a nigh-inexhaustible supply of amusing, detailed anecdotes about the forgotten British stars of the past. There's nothing I enjoy more than to recount these lengthy tales to one of my ailing, lonely patients and slowly destroy his will to live.

I call them my patients, but of course they aren't. I merely bring these poor unfortunates good cheer in my capacity as an official council HVF, that's a Hospital Visiting Friend. I am fully sanctioned by Haringey Council, an organisation filled with people of such astounding narrow-minded stupidity that they cannot see beyond their lesbian support groups to keeping the streets free of dogshit.

But back to the present.

I am rather tired at the moment because I was up half the night removing the remaining precious moments of life from a seventeen-year-old boy named David Banbury who had been in a severe motorcycle accident. Apparently he jumped the lights at the top of Shepherd's Hill and vanished under a truck conveying half-price personal stereos to the Asian shops in Tottenham Court Road. His legs were completely crushed, so much so that the doctor told me they couldn't separate his cycle leathers from his bones, and his spine was broken, but facial damage had been minimal, and the helmet he was wearing at the time of the collision had protected his skull from injury.

He hasn't had much of a life, by all accounts, having spent the last eight years in care, and has no family to visit him.

Nurse Clarke informed me that he might well recover to lead a partially normal life, but would only be able to perform those activities involving a minimal amount of agonisingly slow movement, which would at least qualify him for a job in the Post Office.

Right now he could not talk, of course, but he could see and hear and feel, and I am reliably informed that he could understand every word I said, which was of great advantage as I was able to describe to him in enormous detail the entire plot of Norman Wisdom's 1965 masterpiece *The Early Bird*, his first colour film for the Rank Organisation, and I must say one of the finest examples of post-war British slapstick to be found on the face of this spinning planet we fondly call home.

On my second visit to the boy, my richly delineated account of the backstage problems involved in the production of an early Wisdom vehicle, *Trouble In Store*, in which the Little Comedian Who Won The Hearts Of The Nation co-starred for the first time with his erstwhile partner and straight-man Jerry Desmonde, was rudely interrupted by a staff nurse who chose a crucial moment in my narration to empty a urine bag that seemed to be filling with blood. Luckily I was able to exact my revenge by punctuating my description of the film's highlights featuring Moira Lister and Margaret Rutherford with little twists of the boy's drip-feed to make sure that he was paying the fullest attention.

At half past seven yesterday evening I received a visit from the mentally disoriented liaison officer in charge of appointing visitors. Miss Chisholm is the kind of woman who has pencils in her hair and "Nuclear War—No Thanks' stickers on her briefcase. She approaches her council tasks with the dispiriting grimness of a sailor attempting to plug leaks in a fast-sinking ship.

"Mr Morrison," she said, trying to peer around the door of my flat, presumably in the vain hope that she might be invited in for a cup of tea, "you are one of our most experienced Hospital Helpers"—this part she had to check in her brimming folder to verify—"so I wonder if we could call upon you for an extracurricular visit at rather short notice?" She searched through her notes with the folder wedged under her chin and her case balanced on a raised knee. I did not offer any assistance. "The motorcycle boy . . ." She attempted to locate his name and failed.

"David Banbury," I said, helpfully supplying the information for her.

"He's apparently been telling the doctor that he no longer wishes to live. It's a common problem, but they think his case is particularly serious. He has no relatives." Miss Chisholm—if she has a Christian name I am certainly not privy to it—shifted her weight from one foot to the other as several loose sheets slid from her folder to the floor.

"I understand exactly what is needed," I said, watching as she struggled to reclaim her notes. "An immediate visit is in order."

As I made my way over to the hospital to comfort the poor lad, I thought of the ways in which I could free the boy from his morbid thoughts. First, I would recount all of the plot minutiae, technicalities and trivia I could muster surrounding the big-screen career and off-screen heartache of that Little Man Who Won All Our Hearts, Charlie Drake, climaxing with a detailed description of his 1966 magnum opus *The Cracksman*, in which he starred opposite a superbly erudite George Sanders, a man who had the good sense to kill himself when he grew bored with the world, and then I would encourage the boy to give up the fight, do the decent thing and die in his sleep.

As it happens, the evening turned out quite nicely.

By eleven-thirty I had concluded my description of the film, and detected a distinct lack of concentration on behalf of the boy, whose only response to my description of the frankly hysterical sewer-pipe scene was to blow bubbles of saliva from the corner of his mouth. In my frustration to command his attention, I applied rather more pressure to the sutures on his legs than I intended, causing the crimson blossom of a haemorrhage to appear through the blankets covering his pitifully mangled limbs.

I embarked upon a general plot outline of the classic 1962 Norman Wisdom vehicle *On The Beat*, never shifting my attention from the boy's eyes, which were now swivelling frantically in his waxen grey face, until the ruptured vessels of his leg could no longer be reasonably ignored. Then I summoned the night nurse. David Banbury died a few moments after she arrived at the bedside.

That makes eleven in four years.

Some didn't require any tampering with on my part, but simply gave up the ghost, losing the will to go on. I went home and made myself a cup of Horlicks, quietly rejoicing that another young man had gone to meet his maker with a full working knowledge of the later films of Norman Wisdom (not counting *What's Good For The Goose*, a prurient "adult" comedy directed by Menahem Golem which I regard as an offensive, embarrassing travesty unworthy of such a superb family performer).

Now, standing before the mirror attempting to comb the last straggling wisps of hair across my prematurely balding pate, I prepare to leave the house and catch the bus to work, and I do something I imagine most people have done from time to time when faced with their own reflection. I calm myself for the day ahead by remembering the Royal Variety Performance stars of 1952. The familiar faces of Naughton & Gold, Vic Oliver, Jewel & Warriss, Ted Ray, Winifred Atwell, Reg Dixon and the Tiller Girls crowd my mind as I steel myself to confront the self-centred young scum with whom I am forced to work.

It is no secret that I have been passed over for promotion in my job on a number of occasions, but the most terrible slap-in-the-face yet performed by our new (foreign) management was administered last week, when a boy of just twenty-four was appointed as my superior! He likes people to call him Mick, walks around smiling like an idiot, travels to work wearing a Walkman, on which he plays percussive rubbish consisting of black men shouting at each other, and wears tight black jeans which seem specifically designed to reveal the contours of his genitalia. He shows precious little flair for the job, and has virtually no knowledge whatsoever of the pre-1960 British radio comedy scene. Amazingly, everyone seems to like him.

Of course, he will have to go.

**Diary Entry # 2 Dated 23 August**

Mick is a threat no more.

I simply waited until the appropriate opportunity arose, as I knew it eventually should. While I watched and listened, patiently enduring the oh-so-clever remarks he made to the office girls about me (most of whom resemble prostitutes from Michael Powell's excessively vulgar and unnecessary 1960 film *Peeping Tom*) I comforted myself with memories of a happy, sunlit childhood, recalling a row of terraced houses patrolled by smiling policemen, uniformed milkmen and lollipop-ladies, a place in the past where Isobel Barnet was still guessing contestants' professions on *What's My Line*, Alma Cogan was singing "Fly Me To The Moon" on the radio, cornflakes had red plastic guardsmen in their packets and everyone knew his place and damned well stayed in it. Even now when I hear the merry tickle of "Greensleeves" heralding the arrival of an ice-cream van beset by clamouring tots I get a painful, thrilling erection.

But I digress.

Last Tuesday, while shifting a wire-meshed crate in the basement workroom, Mick dislocated his little finger, cutting it rather nastily, so naturally I offered to accompany him to the casualty ward. As my flat is conveniently situated on the route to the hospital I was able to stop by for a moment, trotting out some absurd excuse for the detour.

After waiting for over an hour to be seen, my nemesis was finally examined by Dr MacGregor, an elderly physician of passing acquaintance whose name I only remember because it is also that of John Le Mesurier's character in *The Radio Ham*. My experience as an HVF had familiarised me with basic casualty procedures, and I knew that the doctor would most likely inject an antibiotic into the boy's hand to prevent infection.

The needles for the syringes come in paper packets, and are sealed inside little plastic tubes that must only be broken by the attending physician. This is to prevent blood-carried infections from being transmitted.

It was hard to find a way around this, and indeed had taken dozens of attempts over the preceding months. The packets themselves were easy enough to open and reseal, but the tubes were a problem. After a great deal of practice, I found that I was able to melt the end of a tube closed without leaving any trace of tampering. To be on the safe side I had prepared three such needles in this fashion. (You must remember that, as well as having access to basic medical supplies—those items not actually locked away—I also possess an unlimited amount of patience, being willing to wait years if necessary to achieve my goals.)

While we waited for Dr MacGregor to put in an appearance, the boy prattled on to me about work, saying how much he "truly valued my input". While he was thus distracted, it was a simple matter for me to replace the loose needles lying on the doctor's tray with my specially prepared ones.

A little while ago I throttled the life out of a very sick young man whose habit of nightly injecting drugs in the toilet of my local tube station had caused him to become ravaged with terminal disease. I would like to say that he died in order to make the world a safer, cleaner place, but the truth is that we went for a drink together and I killed him in a sudden fit of rage because he had not heard of Joyce Grenfell. How the Woman Who Won The Hearts Of The Nation in her thrice-reprised role as Ruby Gates in the celebrated *St Trinians* films could have passed by him unnoticed is still a mystery to me.

Anyway, I strangled the disgusting urchin with his own scarf and removed about a cupful of blood from his arm, into which I dropped a number of needles, filling their capillaries with the poisoned fluid. I then carefully wiped each one clean and inserted it into a tube, neatly resealing the plastic.

Dr MacGregor was talking nineteen to the dozen as he inserted what he thought was a fresh needle into a vein on the back of Mick's hand. He barely even looked down to see what he was doing. Overwork and force of habit had won the day. Thank God for our decaying National Health Service, because I'd never have managed it if the boy had possessed private medical insurance. My unsuspecting adversary maintained an attitude of perky bravery as his finger was stitched up, and I laughed all the way home.

Mick has been feeling unwell for several weeks now. A few days ago he failed to turn up for work. Apparently he has developed a complex and highly dangerous form of Hepatitis B.

As they say, age and treachery will always overcome youth and enthusiasm.

**Diary Entry # 3 Dated 17 October**

The hopeless liaison officer has returned with a new request.

Yesterday evening I opened the door of my flat to find her hovering on the landing uncertainly, as if she could not even decide where she felt comfortable standing.

"Can I help you?" I asked suddenly, knowing that my voice would make her jump. She had not caught me in a good mood. A month ago, Mick had been forced to resign through ill-health, but my promotion had still not been announced for consideration.

"Oh, Mr Morrison, I didn't know if you were in," she said, her free hand rising to her flat chest.

"The best way to find out is by ringing the doorbell, Miss Chisholm." I opened the door wider. "Won't you come in?"

"Thank you." She edged gingerly past me with briefcase and folders, taking in the surroundings. Hattie took one look at her and shot off to her basket. "Oh, what an unusual room," she said, studying the walnut sideboard and armchairs, the matching butter-yellow standard lamps either side of the settee. "Do you collect Art Deco?"

"No," I said tersely. "This is my furniture. I suppose you'd like a cup of tea." I went to put the kettle on, leaving her hovering uncomfortably in the lounge. When I returned she was still standing, her head tilted on one side as she examined the spines of my post-war *Radio Times* collection.

"Please sit down, Miss Chisholm," I insisted. "I won't bite." And I really don't because teethmarks can be easily traced.

At this instigation she perched herself on the edge of the armchair and nibbled at a bourbon. She had obviously rehearsed the speech which followed.

"Mr Morrison, I'm sure you've read in the papers that the health cuts are leaving hospitals in this area with an acute shortage of beds."

"I fear I haven't read a newspaper since they stopped printing The Flutters on the comic page of the *Daily Mirror*," I admitted, "but I have heard something of the sort."

"Well, it means that some people who are required to attend hospital for tests cannot be admitted as overnight patients any more. As you have been so very helpful in the past, we wondered if you could take in one of these patients."

"For how long?" I asked. "And what sort of patient?"

"It would be for two weeks at the most, and the patient I have in mind for you – " she churned up the contents of her disgusting briefcase trying to locate her poor victim's folder—"is a very nice young lady. She's a severe diabetic, and she's in a wheelchair. Apart from that, she's the same as you or I." She gave me a warm smile, then quickly looked away, sensing perhaps that I was not like other people. She handed me a dog-eared photograph of the patient, attached to a medical history that had more pages than an average weekly script of *The Clitheroe Kid*, a popular BBC radio show which for some reason has never been reissued on audio cassette.

"Her name is Saskia," said Miss Chisholm. "She has no family to speak of, and lives a long way from London. Ours is one of the few hospitals with the necessary equipment to handle complex drug and therapy trials for people like her. She desperately needs a place to stay. We can arrange to have her collected each day. We'd be terribly grateful if you could help. She really has nowhere else to go."

I studied the photograph carefully. The girl was pitifully small-boned, with sallow, almost translucent skin. But she had attractive blonde hair, and well defined features reminiscent of a young Suzy Kendall in Robert Hartford-Davies' patchy 1966 comedy portmanteau *The Sandwich Man*, in which Our Norman, playing an Irish priest, was not seen to his best advantage. What's more, she fitted in perfectly with my plans. A woman. That would certainly be different.

I returned the photograph with a smile. "I think we can work something out," I said.

**Diary Entry # 4 Dated 23 October**

Saskia is here, and I must say that for someone so ill she is quite a tonic. The night she arrived, I watched as she struggled to negotiate her wheelchair around the flat without damaging the paintwork on the skirting boards, and despite many setbacks she managed it without a single protestation. Indeed, she has been here for two days now, and never seems to complain about anything or anyone. Apparently all of her life she has been prone to one kind of disease or another, and few doctors expected her to survive her childhood, so she is simply happy to be alive.

I have installed her in the spare room, which she insisted on filling with flowers purchased from the stall outside the hospital. Even Hattie, never the most amenable of cats, seems to have taken to her.

As my flat is on the second floor of a large Victorian house, she is a virtual prisoner within these walls during the hours outside her hospital visits. At those times the ambulance men carry her and the folded wheelchair up and down the stairs.

On her very first night here I entered the lounge to find her going through my catalogued boxes of BBC comedy archive tapes. I was just beginning to grow annoyed when she turned to me and asked if she could play some of them. No one had ever shown the least interest in my collection before. To test her, I asked which shows she would most enjoy hearing.

"I like Leslie Phillips in *The Navy Lark*, and the Frazer Hayes Four playing on *Round The Horne*," she said, running a slim finger across the spines of the tape boxes. "And of course, *Hancock's Half Hour*, although I prefer the shows after Andre Melee had been replaced by Hattie Jacques."

Suddenly I was suspicious.

This tiny girl could not be more than twenty-two years of age. How could she possibly be so familiar with radio programmes that had scarcely been heard in thirty years?

"My father was a great collector," she explained, as if she had just read my thoughts. "He used to play the old shows nearly every evening after dinner. It's one of the few lasting memories I have of my parents."

Well naturally, my heart went out to the poor girl. "I know exactly how you feel," I said. "I only have to hear Kenneth Williams say '*Good Evening*' and I'm reminded of home and hearth. They were such happy times for me."

For the next hour or so I sounded her out on other favourite film and radio memories of the past, but although there seemed no other common ground between us, she remained willing to listen to my happy tales and learn. At eleven o'clock she yawned and said that she would like to go to bed, and so I let her leave the lounge.

Last night Saskia was kept late at the hospital, and I was in bed by the time the heavy tread of the ambulance man was heard upon the stair. This morning she asked me if I would like her to cook an evening meal. After some initial concern with the hygiene problems involved in allowing one's meal to be cooked by someone else, I agreed. (In restaurants I assiduously question the waitresses about their sanitary arrangements.) Furthermore, I offered to buy produce for the projected feast, but she insisted on stopping by the shops on her way home from the hospital. Although she is frail, she demands independence. I will buy a bottle of wine. After being alone with my memories for so long, it is unnerving to have someone else in the apartment.

And yet it is rather wonderful.

**Diary Entry # 5 Dated 24 October**

What an enthralling evening!

I feel as if I am truly alive for the first time in my life. Saskia returned early tonight—looking drawn and pale, but still vulnerably beautiful, with her blonde hair tied in a smart plait—and headed straight into the kitchen, where she stayed for several hours. I had arranged a ramp of planks by the cooker so that she could reach the hobs without having to rise from her chair.

Hattie, sensing that something tasty was being prepared, hung close to the base of the door, sniffing and licking her chops. To amuse Saskia while she cooked I played dialogue soundtracks which I had recorded in my local cinema as a child during performances of

*Passport To Pimlico* and *The Lavender Hill Mob*, but the poor quality of the tapes (from a small reel-to-reel recorder I had smuggled into the auditorium) was such that I imagine the subtleties of these screenplays were rather lost to her, especially as she had the kitchen door shut and was banging saucepans about.

The meal was a complete delight. We had a delicious tomato and basil soup to start with, and a truly spectacular salmon en croute as the main course, followed by cheese and biscuits.

Saskia told me about herself, explaining that her parents had been killed in a car crash when she was young. This tragedy had forced her to live with a succession of distant and ancient relatives. When the one she was staying with died, she was shunted into a foster home. No one was willing to take her, though, as the complications arising from her diabetes would have made enormous demands on any foster-parent.

As she talked she ate very little, really only toying with her food. The diabetes prevents her from enjoying much of anything, but hopefully the tests she is undergoing will reveal new ways of coping with her restricted lifestyle.

The dining table is too low to comfortably incorporate Saskia's wheelchair, so I have promised to raise it for tomorrow's dinner, which I have insisted on cooking. I was rather nervous at the prospect, but then I thought: if a cripple can do it, so can I.

Saskia is so kind and attentive, such a good listener. Perhaps it is time for me to introduce my pet topic into the dinner conversation.

**Diary Entry # 6 Dated 25 October**

Disaster has struck!

Right from the start everything went wrong—and just as we were getting along so well. Let me set it out from the beginning.

The meal. I cooked a meal tonight that was not as elaborate as the one she had prepared, and nothing like as good. This was partly because I was forced to work late (still no news of my promotion), so most of the shops were shut, and partly because I have never cooked for a woman before. The result was a microwaved dinner that was still freezing cold in the centre of the dish, but if Saskia didn't like it she certainly didn't complain. Instead she gave a charming broad smile (one which she is using ever more frequently with me) and slowly chewed as she listened to my detailed description of the indignities daily heaped upon me at the office.

I had bought another bottle of wine, and perhaps had drunk a little too much of it by myself (Saskia being unable to drink for the rest of the week), because I found myself introducing the subject of him, Our Norman, The Little Man Who Won All Our Hearts, before we had even finished the main course. Wishing to present the topic in the correct context I chose to start with a basic chronology of Norman's film appearances, beginning with his thirteen-and-a-half-second appearance in *A Date With A Dream* in 1948. I had made an early decision to omit all but the most essential stage and television appearances of The Little Man for fear of tiring her, and in my description of the films stuck mainly to the classic set pieces, notably the marvellous "Learning To Walk" routine from *On The Beat* and the ten-minute "Teamaking" sequence from the opening of *The Early Bird*.

I was about to mention Norman's 1956 appearance with Ruby Murray at the Palladium in *Painting The Town* when I became distinctly aware of her interest waning. She was fidgeting about in her chair as if anxious to leave the table.

"Anyone would think you didn't like Norman Wisdom," I said, by way of a joke.

"Actually, I'm not much of a fan, no," she said suddenly, then added, "Forgive me, Stanley, but I've suddenly developed a headache." And with that she went to her room, without even offering to do the washing up. Before I went to bed I stood outside her door listening, but could hear nothing.

I have a bad feeling about this.

**Diary Entry # 7 Dated 27 October**

She is avoiding me.

It sounds hard to believe, I know, but there can be no other explanation. Last night she returned to the flat and headed directly to her room. When I put my head around the door to see if she wanted a late night cup of cocoa (I admit this was at three o'clock in the morning but I could not sleep for worrying about her) it seemed that she could barely bring herself to be polite. As I stepped into the room, her eyes widened and she pulled the blankets around her in a defensive gesture which seemed to suggest a fear of my presence. I must confess I am at a loss to understand her.

Could she have led me on, only pretending to share my interests for some secret purpose of her own?

**Diary Entry # 8 Dated 1 November**

At work today we were informed that Mick had died. Complications from the hepatitis, annoyingly unspecified, but I gained the distinct impression that they were unpleasant. When one of the secretaries started crying I made a passing flippant remark that was, I fear, misconstrued, and the girl gave me a look of utter horror. She's a scruffy little tart who was sweet on Mick, and much given to conspiring with him about me. I felt like giving her something to be horrified about, and briefly wondered how she would look tied up with baling wire, hanging in a storm drain. The things we think about to get us through the day.

At home the situation has worsened. Saskia arrived tonight with a male friend, a doctor whom she had invited back for tea. While she was in the kitchen the two of us were left alone in the lounge, and I noticed that he seemed to be studying me from the corner of his eye. It was probably just an occupational habit, but it prompted me to wonder if Saskia had somehow voiced her suspicions to him (assuming she has any, which I consider unlikely).

After he had gone, I explained that it was not at all permissible for her to bring men into the house no matter how well she knew them, and she had the nerve to turn in her chair and accuse me of being old-fashioned!

"What on earth do you mean?" I asked her.

"It's not healthy, Stanley, surrounding yourself with all this," she explained, indicating the alphabetised film and tape cassettes which filled the shelves on the wall behind us. "Most of these people have been dead for years."

"Shakespeare has been dead for years," I replied, "and people still appreciate him."

"But he wrote plays and sonnets of lasting beauty," she persisted. "These people you listen to were just working comics. It's lovely to collect things, Stanley, but this stuff was never meant to be taken so seriously. You can't base your life around it." There was an irritating timbre in her voice that I had not noticed before. She sat smugly back in her wheelchair, and for a moment I wanted to smother her. I could feel my face growing steadily redder with the thought.

"Why shouldn't these people still be admired?" I cried, running to the shelves and pulling out several of my finest tapes. "Most of them had dreary lives filled with hardship and pain, but they made people laugh, right through the war and the years of austerity which followed. They carried on through poverty and ill-health and misery. Everyone turned on the radio to hear them. Everyone went to the pictures to see them. It was something to look forward to. They kept people alive. They gave the country happy memories. Why shouldn't someone remember them for what they did?"

"All right, Stanley. I'm sorry—I didn't mean to upset you," she said, reaching out her hand, but I pushed it away. It was then that I realised my cheeks were wet, and I turned aside in shame.

To think that I had been brought to this state, forced to defend myself in my own home, by a woman, and a wheelchair-bound one at that.

"This is probably a bad time to mention it," said Saskia, "but I'm going to be leaving London earlier than I first anticipated. In fact, I'll be going home tomorrow. The tests haven't taken as long as the doctors thought."

"But what about the results?" I asked.

"They've already made arrangements to send them to my local GP. He'll decide whether further treatment is necessary."

I hastily pulled myself together and made appropriate polite sounds of disappointment at the idea of her departure, but inside a part of me was rejoicing. You see, I had been watching her hands as they rested on the arms of her wheelchair. They were trembling.

And she was lying.

**Diary Entry # 9 Dated 2 November**

I have much to relate.

After our altercation last night, both of us knew that a new level in our relationship had been reached. The game had begun. Saskia refused my conciliatory offer of tea and went straight to her bedroom, quietly locking the door behind her. I know because I tried to open it at two o'clock this morning, and I heard her breath catch in the darkness as I twisted the knob from side to side.

I returned to my room and forced myself to stay there. The night passed slowly, with both of us remaining uncomfortably awake on our respective beds. In the morning, I left the house early so that I would not be forced to trade insincere pleasantries with her over breakfast. I knew she would be gone by the time I returned, and that, I think, suited both of us. I was under no illusions—she was a dangerous woman, too independent, too free-minded to ever become my friend. We could only be adversaries. And I was dangerous to her. I had enjoyed her company, but now she would only be safe far away from me. Luckily, I would never see her again. Or so I thought. For, fast as the future, everything changed between us.

Oh, how it changed.

This morning, I arrived at work to find a terse note summoning me to my supervisor's office. Naturally I assumed that I was finally being notified of my promotion. You may imagine my shock when, in the five-minute interview which followed, it emerged that far from receiving advancement within the company, I was being fired! I did not "fit in" with the new personnel, and as the department was being "streamlined" they were "letting me go". Depending on my attitude to this news, they were prepared to make me a generous cash settlement if I left at once, so that they could immediately begin "implementing procedural changes".

I did not complain. This sort of thing has happened many times before. I do not fit in. I say this not to gain sympathy, but as a simple statement of fact. Intellect always impedes popularity. I accepted the cash offer. Disheartened, but also glad to be rid of my vile "colleagues", I returned home.

It was raining hard when I arrived at the front gate. I looked up through the dank sycamores and was surprised to find a light burning in the front room. Then I realised that Saskia was reliant on the council for arranging her transport, and as they were never able to specify an exact collection time, she was still in the house. I knew I would have to use every ounce of my control to continue behaving in a correct and civilised manner.

As I turned the key in the lock I heard a sudden scuffle of movement inside the flat. Throwing the door wide, I entered the lounge and found it empty. The sound was coming from my bedroom. A terrible deadness flooded through my chest as I tiptoed along the corridor, carefully avoiding the boards that squeaked.

Slowly, I moved into the doorway. She was on the other side of the room with her back to me. The panels of the wardrobe were folded open, and she had managed to pull one of the heavy-duty bin-liners out of the floor. Somehow she sensed that I was behind her, and the wheelchair spun around. The look on her face was one of profound disturbance.

"What have you done with the rest of them?" she said softly, her voice wavering. She had dislodged a number of air fresheners from the sacks, and the room stank of lavender.

"You're not supposed to be in here," I explained as reasonably as possible. "This is my private room."

I stepped inside and closed the door behind me. She looked up at the pinned pictures surrounding her. The bleak monochrome of a thousand celebrity photographs seemed to absorb the light within the room.

"Saskia. You're an intelligent girl. You're modern. But you have no respect for the past."

"The past?" Her lank hair was falling in her eyes, as she flicked it aside I could see she was close to tears. "What has the past to do with this?" She kicked out uselessly at the plastic sack and it fell to one side, spilling its rotting human contents onto the carpet.

"Everything," I replied, moving forward. I was not advancing on her, I just needed to get to the bedside cabinet. "The past is where everything has its rightful place."

"I know about your past, Stanley," she cried, pushing at the wheels of her chair, backing herself up against the wardrobe, turning her face from the stinking mess. "Nurse Clarke told me all about you."

"What did she say?" I asked, coming to a halt. I was genuinely curious. Nurse Clarke had hardly ever said more than two words to me.

"I know what happened to you. That's why I came here." She started to cry now, and wiped her nose with the back of her hand. Something plopped obscenely onto the floor as the sack settled. "She says you had the worst childhood a boy could ever have. Sexual abuse, violence. You lived in terror every day. Your father nearly killed you before the authorities took charge. Don't you see? That's why you're so obsessed with this stuff, this trivia, it's like a disease. You're just trying to make things all right again."

"That's a damned lie!" I shouted at her. "My childhood was perfect. You're making it up!"

"No," she said, shaking her head, snot flying from her nose. "I saw the marks when you were in the kitchen that first night. Cigarette burns on your arms. Cuts too deep to ever heal. I thought I knew how you must have felt. Like me, always shoved around, always towered over, always scared. I didn't expect anything like this. What were you thinking of?"

"Are you sure you don't know?" I asked, advancing toward the cabinet. "I'm the kind of person nobody notices. I'm invisible until I'm pointed out. I'm in a private world. I'm not even ordinary. I'm somewhere below that."

I had reached the cabinet, and now slowly pulled open the drawer, groping inside as she tried to conceal her panic, tried to find somewhere to wheel the chair.

"But I'm not alone," I explained. "There are many like me. I see them begging on the streets, soliciting in pubs, injecting themselves in alleyways. For them childhood is a scar that never heals, but still they try to stumble on. I end their stumbling, Saskia. Miss Chisholm says I'm an angel."

My fingers closed around the handle of the carving knife, but the point was stuck in the rear wall of the drawer. I gave it my attention and pulled it free, lowering the blade until it was flat against my leg. A sound from behind made me turn. With a dexterity that amazed me, the infuriating girl had opened the door and slipped through.

I ran into the lounge to find her wheelchair poised before the tape archives and Saskia half out of the seat, one hand pincering a stack of irreplaceable 78s featuring the vocal talents of Flanagan and Allen.

"Leave those alone!" I cried. "You don't understand."

She turned to me with what I felt was a look of deliberate malice on her face and raised the records high above her head. If I attacked her now, she would surely drop them.

"Why did you kill those people?" she asked simply. For a moment I was quite at a loss. She deserved an explanation. I ran my left thumb along the blade of the knife, drawing in my breath as the flesh slowly parted and the pain showed itself:

"I wanted to put their pasts right," I explained. "To give them the things that comfort. Tony Hancock. Sunday roast. Family Favourites. Smiling policemen. Norman Wisdom. To give them the freedom to remember."

I must have allowed the knife to come into view, because her grip on the records faltered and they slid from her hands to the floor. I don't think any smashed, but the wheels of her chair cracked several as she rolled forward.

"I can't give you back the past, Saskia," I said, walking towards her, smearing the knife blade with the blood from my stinging thumb. "I'm sorry, because I would have liked to."

She cried out in alarm, pulling stacks of records and tapes down upon herself, scattering them across the threadbare carpet. Then she grabbed the metal frame of the entire cabinet, as if trying to shake it loose from the wall. I stood and watched, fascinated by her fear.

When I heard the familiar heavy boots quickening on the stairs, I turned the knife over and pushed the blade hard into my chest. It was a reflex action, as if I had been planning to do this all along. Just as I had suspected, there was no pain. To those like us who suffered so long, there is no more pain.

**Diary Entry # 10 Dated 16 November**

And now I am sitting here on a bench with a clean elastic bandage patching up my stomach, facing the bristling cameras and microphones, twenty enquiring faces before me, and the real probing questions have begun.

The bovine policewoman who interrogated me so unimaginatively during my initial detainment period bore an extraordinary resemblance to Shirley Abicair, the Australian zither player who performed superbly as Norman's love interest in Rank's 1954 hit comedy *One Good Turn*, although the *Evening News* critic found their sentimental scenes together an embarrassment.

I think I am going to enjoy my new role here. Newspapers are fighting for my story. They're already comparing me to Nilsen and Sutcliffe, although I would rather be compared to Christie or Crippen. Funny how everyone remembers the name of a murderer, but no one remembers the victim.

If they want to know, I will tell them everything. Just as long as I can tell them about my other pet interests.

My past is safe.

My future is known.

My present belongs to Norman.

# KIM NEWMAN

# Red Reign

KIM NEWMAN'S critically-acclaimed novel *Anno Dracula* was described by *Locus* as "the most comprehensive, brilliant, dazzlingly audacious vampire novel to date." "Red Reign" was the novella which inspired that work, and the version which appears here has been revised from that originally published in *The Mammoth Book of Vampires*.

The author's other novels include the equally audacious *The Night Mayor*, *Bad Dreams*, *Jago* and *The Quoram*. Under his not-so-secret "Jack Yeovil" pseudonym, Boxtree has finally published the author's *Warhammer* volume *Genevieve Undead*, a trilogy of vampire novellas and a follow-up to his previous books in the series, *Drachenfels* and *Beasts in Velvet*.

With Paul J. McAuley, he co-edited one of the best original anthologies of 1992, *In Dreams*; his tale "The Man Who Collected Barker" was recently adapted into a stage play in Los Angeles, and his fiction has appeared in *Dark Voices 5: The Pan Book of Horror*, *The Mammoth Book of Zombies*, *The Dedalus Book of Femmes Fatales* and *Narrow Houses*. A short story collection is forthcoming.

If you're a fan of vampire movies or fiction, get set to enter a bizarre alternate Victorian society, where the King of the Undead holds sway over many familiar characters . . .

# I

**Dr Seward's Diary**
**(Kept in phonograph)**

8 September, 1888. *Tonight's was easier than last week's. Perhaps, with practice, everything becomes easier. If never easy. Never . . . easy.*

*I'm sorry.*

*It is hard to keep one's thoughts in order, and this apparatus is unforgiving of digressions. I cannot ink over hasty words, terminate unthought-out thoughts, tear out a spoiled page. I must be concise. After all, I have had medical training. This record may be of importance to posterity.*

*Very well.*

*Subject: female, apparently in her twenties. Recently dead, I would say. Profession: obvious. Location: Hanbury Street, Whitechapel. Near the Salvation Army mission. Time: shortly before five in the morning. The fog was thick as mud, which is the best for my nightwork. In this year, fog is welcome. The less one can see of what London has become, the better.*

*She gave her name as Lulu. She was not English. From her accent, I would judge her German or Austrian by birth. A pretty thing, distinctive. Shiny black hair cut short and lacquered, in an almost Chinese style. In the fog and with the poor light of the street, her red lips seemed quite black. Like all of them, she smiled too easily, disclosing sharp little pearl-chip teeth. A cloud of cheap perfume, sickly sweet scent to cover the reek of decay.*

*The streets are filthy in Whitechapel, open sewers of vice and foulness. The dead are everywhere.*

*She laughed musically, the sound like something wrung from a mechanism, and beckoned me over, loosening the ragged feathers around her throat. Lulu's laugh reminded me of Lucy. Lucy when she was alive, not the leech-thing we finished in Kingstead Cemetery.*

*Three years ago, when only Van Helsing believed . . . The world has changed since then. Thanks to the Prince Consort.*

*Van Helsing would have understood my nightwork. When he was alive. And the others. A family, we were. My friend Arthur Holmwood, the Texan Morris, the clerk Harker, his wife. And the Dutch doctor, mangling the language and tutting over his impedimenta. Only I am left of the family. Alive. I must continue to fight . . .*

*I learned from last week's in Buck's Row—Polly Nicholls, the newspapers say her name was. Polly or Mary Ann—to do it quickly and precisely. Throat. Heart. Tripes. Then get the head off. That finishes the things. Clean silver, and a clean conscience. Van Helsing, blinkered by folklore and symbolism, spoke always of the heart, but any of the major organs will do. The kidneys are easiest to get to.*

*I had made my preparations carefully. For half an hour, I sat in my office, allowing myself to become aware of the pain in my right hand. The madman is dead—truly dead—but Renfield left his jaw-marks, semi-circles of deep indentations, scabbed over many times but never right again. With Nicholls, my mind was still dull from the laudanum I take for the pain, and I was not as precise as I might have been. Learning to be left-handed hasn't helped either. I missed the major artery, and the thing had time to screech before I could saw through the neck. I am afraid I lost control, and became a butcher when I should be a surgeon, a deliverer.*

*Lulu went better. She clung as tenaciously to life, but I think there was an acceptance of my gift. She was relieved, at the last, to have her soul cleansed by silver. It is hard to come by. Now, the coinage is all gold or copper. I kept back a store of sovereigns while the money was changing, and found a tradesman who would execute my commission. I've had the surgical instruments since my days at the Purfleet asylum. Now the blades are plated, a core of steel strength inside killing silver. Before venturing out into the fog, I unlocked my private cabinet and spent some time looking at the shine of the silver. This time, I selected the post-mortem scalpel. It is fitting, I think, to employ a tool intended for rooting around in the bodies of the dead.*

*Lulu invited me into a doorway to do her business, and wriggled her skirts up over slim white legs. I took the time to open her blouse, to get her collar and feathers away from her unmarked throat. She asked about my lumpily-gloved hand, and I told her it was an old wound. She smiled and I drew my silver edge across her neck, pressing firmly with my thumb, cutting deep into pristine deadflesh.*

*I held her up with my body, shielding my work from any passersby, and slipped the scalpel through her ribs into her heart. I felt her whole body shudder, and then fall lifeless. But I know how resilient the dead can be, and took care to finish the job, exposing as well as puncturing the heart, cutting a few of the tubes in the belly, taking out the kidneys and part of the uterus, then enlarging the throat wound until the head came loose. Having exposed the vertebrae, I worried the head back and forth until the neckbones parted.*

*There was little blood in her. She must not have fed tonight.*

## II

She rested in her tiny office at Toynbee Hall. It was as safe a place as any to pass the few days each month when lassitude came over her and she shared the sleep of the dead. Up high in the building, the room had only a tiny skylight and the door could be secured from the inside. It served its purpose, just as coffins and crypts served for those of the Prince Consort's bloodline.

She heard hammering. Insistent, repeated blows. Noise reached into her dark fog. Meat and bone pounding against wood.

In her dreams, Genevieve had been back in her warm girlhood. When she had been her father's daughter, not Chandagnac's get. Before she had been turned, before the Dark Kiss had made her what she had become.

Her tongue felt sleep-filmed teeth. Her eyes opened, and she tried to focus on the dingy glass of the skylight. The sun was not yet down.

In her dreams, the hammering had been a mallet striking the end of a snapped-in-half quarterstaff. The English captain had finished her father-in-darkness like a butterfly, pinning Chandagnac to the bloodied earth. Those had been barbarous times.

In an instant, dreams were washed away and she was awake, as if a gallon of icy water had been dashed into her face.

"Mademoiselle Dieudonné," a voice sounded, "Open up."

She sat up, the sheet falling away from her body. She slept on the floor, on a blanket laid over the rough planks.

"There's been another murder."

Genevieve took a Chinese silk robe from a hook by the door, and drew it around herself. It was not what etiquette recommended she wear while entertaining a gentleman caller, but it would have to do. Etiquette, so important a few short years ago, meant less and less. They were sleeping in coffins lined with earth in Mayfair, and drinking from their servants' necks, and so the correct form of address for a Bishop was hardly a major consideration this year.

She slid back the bolts, and the hammering stopped. She had traces of fog still in her head. Outside, the afternoon was dying. She would not be at her best until night was around her again. She pulled open her door, and saw a small new-born, with a long coat around him like a cloak and a bowler hat in his hand, standing in the corridor outside.

"Inspector Lestrade," she said, allowing the detective in. His jagged, irregular teeth stuck awkwardly out of his mouth, unconcealed by the scraggly moustache he had been cultivating. The sparse whiskers only made him look more like a rat than he had done when he was alive. He wore smoked glasses, but crimson points behind the lenses suggested active eyes.

The Scotland Yard man took off his hat, and set it down upon her desk.

"Last night," he began, hurriedly, "in Hanbury Street. It was butchery, plain and simple."

"Last night?"

"I'm sorry," he drew breath, making an allowance for her recent sleep. "It's the eighth now. Of September."

"I've been asleep three days."

"I thought it best to rouse you. Feelings are running high. The warm are getting restless, and the new-borns."

"You were quite right," she said. She rubbed sleep-gum from her eyes, and tried to clear her head. Even the last shards of sunlight, filtered through the grimy square of glass above, were icicles jammed into her forehead.

"When the sun is set," Lestrade was saying, "there'll be pandemonium on the streets. It could be another Bloody Sunday. Some say Van Helsing has come back."

"The Prince Consort would love that."

Lestrade shook his head. "It's just a rumour. Van Helsing is dead. His head is still on a spike outside the Palace."

"You've checked?"

"The Palace is always under guard. The Prince Consort has his Carpathians about him. Our kind cannot be too careful. We have many enemies."

"Our kind?"

"The Un-Dead."

Genevieve almost laughed. "I'm not your kind, Inspector. You are of the bloodline of Vlad Tepes, I am of the bloodline of Chandagnac. We are at best cousins."

The detective shrugged and snorted at the same time. Bloodline meant nothing to the vampires of London, Genevieve knew. Even at a third, a tenth or a twentieth remove, they all had the Prince Consort as father-in-darkness.

"Has the news travelled?"

"Fast," the detective told her. "The evening editions all carry the story. It'll be all over London by now. There are those among the warm who do not love us, Mademoiselle Dieudonné. They are rejoicing. And when the new-borns come out, there could be a panic. I've requested troops, but Commissioner Warren is leery of sending in the army. After that business last year . . ."

A group of warm insurrectionists, preaching sedition against the Crown, had rioted in Trafalgar Square. Someone declared a Republic, and tried to rally the anti-monarchist forces. Sir Charles Warren, the Commissioner of Scotland Yard, had called in the army, and a new-born lieutenant had ordered his men, a mixture of vampires and the living, to fire upon the demonstrators. The Revolution had nearly started then. If it had not been for the intervention of the Queen herself, the Empire could have exploded like a barrel of gunpowder.

"And what, pray, can I do," Genevieve asked, "to serve the purpose of the Prince Consort?"

Lestrade chewed his moustache, teeth glistening, flecks of froth on his lips.

"You may be needed, Mademoiselle. The hall is being overrun. Some don't want to be out on the streets with this murderer about. Some are spreading panic and sedition, firing up vigilante mobs. You have some influence . . ."

"I do, don't I?"

"I wish . . . I would humbly request . . . you would use your influence to calm the situation. Before any disaster occurs. Before any more are unnecessarily killed."

Genevieve was not above enjoying the taste of power. She slipped off her robe, shocking the detective with her nakedness. Death and rebirth had not shaken the prejudices of his time out of him. While Lestrade tried to shrink behind his smoked glasses, she swiftly dressed, fastening the seeming hundreds of small catches and buttons with neat movements of sharp-tipped fingers. After all these years, it was as if the costume of her warm days, as intricate and cumbersome as a full suit of armour, had returned to plague her again. As a new-born, she had, with relief, worn the simple tunics and trews made acceptable if not fashionable by the Maid of Orleans, vowing never again to let herself be sewed into breath-stopping formal dress.

The Inspector was too pale to blush properly, but penny-sized red patches appeared on his cheeks and he huffed involuntarily. Lestrade, like many new-borns, treated her as if she were the age of her face. She had been sixteen in 1432 when Chandagnac gave her the Dark Kiss. She was older, by a decade or more, than the Prince Consort. While he was a new-born, nailing Turks' turbans to their skulls and lowering his countrymen onto sharpened posts, she had been a full vampire, continuing the bloodline of her father-in-darkness, learning the skills that now made her among the longest-lived of her kind. With four and a half centuries behind her, it was hard not to be irritated when the fresh-risen dead, still barely cooled, patronised her.

"This murderer must be found, and stopped," Lestrade said, "before he kills again."

"Indubitably," Genevieve agreed, "it sounds like a problem for your old associate, the consulting detective."

She could sense, with the sharpened perceptions that told her night was falling, the chilling of the Inspector's heart.

"Mr Holmes is not available, Mademoiselle. He has his differences with the current government."

"You mean he has been removed—like so many of our finest minds—to those pens on the Sussex Downs. What are the newspapers calling them, concentration camps?"

"I regret his lack of vision . . ."

"Where is he? Devil's Dyke?"

Lestrade nodded, almost ashamed. There was a lot of the man left inside. Many new-borns clung to their warm lives as if nothing had changed, Genevieve wondered how long they would last before they grew like the bitch vampires the Prince Consort brought from the land beyond the mountains, an appetite on legs, mindlessly preying.

Genevieve finished with her cuffs, and turned to Lestrade, arms slightly out. That was a habit born of four hundred and fifty years without mirrors, always seeking an opinion on how she looked. The detective nodded grudging approval, and she was ready to face the world. She pulled a hooded cloak around her shoulders.

In the corridor outside her room, gaslamps were already lit. Beyond the row of windows, the hanging fog was purging itself of the last blood of the dying sun.

One window was open, letting in cold night air. Genevieve could taste life in it. She would have to feed soon, within two or three days. It was always that way after her sleep.

"I have to be at the inquest," Lestrade said. "It might be best if you came."

"Very well, but I must talk with the director first. Someone will have to take care of my duties."

They were on the stairs. Already, the building was coming to life. No matter how London had changed with the coming of the Prince Consort, Toynbee Hall was still required. The poor and destitute needed shelter, food, medical attention, education. The new-borns, potentially immortal destitutes, were hardly better off than their warm brothers and sisters. Sometimes, Genevieve felt like Sisyphus, forever rolling a rock uphill, always losing a yard for every foot gained.

On the first-floor landing, Lilly sat, rag-doll in her lap. One of her arms was withered, leathery membrane bunched in folds beneath it, the drab dress cut away to allow freedom of movement. The little girl smiled at Genevieve, teeth sharp but uneven, patches of dark fur on her neck and forehead. New-borns could not change their shape properly. But that didn't prevent them from trying, and mostly ending up in as bad a shape as Lilly, or worse . . .

The door of the director's office stood open. Genevieve stroked Lilly's hair, and went in, rapping a knuckle on the plaque as she passed. The director looked up from his desk, shutting a ledger he had been studying. He was a young man, still warm, but his face was deeply lined, and his hair was streaked grey. Many who had lived through the last few years looked like him, older than their years. He nodded, acknowledging the policeman.

"Jack," she said, "Inspector Lestrade wants me to attend an inquest. Can you spare me?"

"There's been another," the director said, making a statement not asking a question.

"A new-born," said Lestrade. "In Hanbury Street."

"Very well, Genevieve. Druitt can take your rounds if he's back from his regular jaunt. We weren't, ah, expecting you for a night or two yet anyway."

"Thank you."

"That's quite all right. Come and see me when you get back. Inspector Lestrade, good evening."

"Dr Seward," Lestrade said, putting on his hat, "good night."

## III

"What's to be done?" shouted a new-born in a peaked cap. "What's to stop this fiend murdering more of our women?"

Wynne Baxter, an old man of Gladstonian appearance, was angrily trying to keep control of the inquest. Unlike a high court judge, he had no gavel and so was forced to slap his wooden desk with an open fist.

"Any further interruptions," Baxter began, glaring, "and I shall be forced to clear the public from this court."

The new-born, a surly rough who must have looked hungry even when warm, slumped back into his chair. He was surrounded by a similar crew. They had long scarves, ragged coats, pockets distended by books, heavy boots and thin beards. Genevieve knew the type. Whitechapel had all manner of Republican, anarchist, socialist and insurrectionist factions.

"Thank you," said the coroner, rearranging his notes. New-borns did not like positions where someone warm had the authority. But a lifetime of cringing when official old men frowned on them left habits. Baxter was a familiar type too, resisting the Dark Kiss, wearing his wrinkles and bald pate as badges of humanity.

Dr Llewellyn, the local practitioner—well known at Toynbee Hall—who had done the preliminary examination of the body, had already given his testimony. It boiled down to the simple facts that Lulu Schön—a German girl, recently arrived in London and even more recently turned—had been heart-stabbed, disembowelled and decapitated. It had taken much desk-banging to quieten the outrage that followed the revelation of the method of murder.

Now, Baxter was hearing evidence from Dr Henry Jekyll, a scientific researcher. "Whenever a vampire's killed," Lestrade explained, "Jekyll comes creeping round. Something rum about him, if you get my drift . . ."

Genevieve thought the man, who was giving a detailed and anatomically precise description of the atrocities, a little stuffy, but listened with interest—more interest than expressed by the yawning newspaper reporters in the front row—to what he was saying.

". . . we have not learned enough about the precise changes in the human body that accompany the so-called transformation from normal life to the state of vampirism," Jekyll said. "Precise information is hard to come by, and superstition hangs like a London fog over the whole subject. My studies have been checked by official indifference, even hostility. We could all benefit from more research work. Perhaps the divisions which lead to tragic incidents like the death of this girl could then be erased from our society."

The anarchists were grumbling again. Without divisions, their cause would have no purpose.

"Too much of what we believe about vampirism is rooted in folklore," Jekyll continued. "The stake through the heart, the silver scythe to remove the head. The vampire *corpus* is remarkably resilient, but any major breach of the vital organs seems to produce true death, as here."

"Would you venture to suggest that the murderer was familiar with the workings of the human body, whether of a vampire or not?"

"Yes, your honour. The extent of the injuries betokens a certain frenzy of enthusiasm, but the actual wounds—one might almost say incisions—have been wrought with some skill."

"He's a bleedin' doctor." shouted the chief anarchist.

The court exploded into an uproar, again. The anarchists, who were about half-and-half warm and new-borns, stamped their feet and yelled, while others—a gaggle of haggard mainly un-dead women in colourful dresses who were presumably associates of the deceased, a scattering of well-dressed medical men, some of Lestrade's uniformed juniors, a sprinkling of sensation-seekers, press-men, clergymen and social reformers—just talked loudly among themselves. Baxter hurt his hand hitting his desk.

Genevieve noticed a man standing at the back of the courtroom, observing the clamour with cool interest. Well-dressed, with a cloak and top hat, he might have been a sensation-seeker but for a certain air of purpose. He was not a vampire, but—unlike the coroner, or even Dr Jekyll—he showed no signs of being disturbed to be among so many of the un-dead. He leant on a black cane.

"Who is that?" she asked Lestrade.

"Charles Beauregard," the new-born detective said, curling a lip. "Have you heard of the Diogenes Club?"

She shook her head.

"When they say 'high places', that's where they mean. Important people are taking an interest in this case. And Beauregard is their catspaw."

The coroner had order again. A clerk had nipped out of the room and returned with six more constables, all new-borns, and they were lining the walls like a guard. The anarchists were brooding again, their purpose obviously to cause just enough trouble to be an irritant but not enough to get their names noted.

"If I might be permitted to address the implied question raised by the gentleman in the second row," Jekyll asked, eliciting a nod from the coroner, "a knowledge of the position of the major organs does not necessarily betoken medical education. If you are not interested in preserving life, a butcher can have out a pair of kidneys as neatly as a surgeon. You need only a steady hand and a sharp knife, and there are plenty of those in Whitechapel."

"Do you have an opinion as to the instrument used by the murderer?"

"A blade of some sort, obviously. Silvered."

The word brought a collective gasp.

"Steel or iron would not have done such damage," Jekyll continued. "Vampire physiology is such that any wounds inflicted with ordinary weapons heal almost immediately. Tissue and bone regenerate, just as a lizard may grow a new tail. Silver has a counteractive effect on this process. Only a silver knife could do such permanent, fatal harm to a vampire."

Beauregard nodded. "You are familiar with the case of Mary Ann Nicholls?"

Jekyll nodded.

"Have you drawn any conclusions from a comparison of these two incidents?"

"Indeed. These two killings were undoubtably the work of the same individual. A left-handed man of above average height, with more than normal physical strength . . ."

"Mr Holmes would've been able to tell his mother's maiden name from a fleck of cigar ash," Lestrade muttered to Genevieve.

". . . I would add that, considering the case from an alienist's point of view, it is my belief that the murderer is not himself a vampire."

The anarchist was on his feet, but the coroner's extra constables were around him before he could even shout.

Smiling to himself at his subjugation of the court, Baxter made a note of the last point and thanked Dr Jekyll.

The man Beauregard, Genevieve noticed, was gone. The coroner began his elaborate summing-up of the situation, before delivering the verdict of "murder by person or persons unknown", adding that the murderer of Lulu Schön was judged to be the same man who had murdered, one week earlier, Mary Ann Nicholls.

Reporters began asking questions, all at once.

## IV

Beauregard strolled in the fog, trying to digest the information he had gleaned from the inquest. He would have to make a full report later, and so he wanted the facts ordered in his mind.

Somewhere nearby, a street organ ground into the night. The air was "Take a Pair of Crimson Eyes", from Gilbert and Sullivan's *The Vampyres of Venice: or: A Maid, a Shade and a Blade*. That seemed apt. The maid—so to speak—and the blade were obviously part of the case, and the shade was the murderer, obscured by fog and blood.

Despite Dr Jekyll's testimony, Beauregard had been toying with the notion that the crimes to date were the work of different men, ritual killings like *thuggee* stranglings, acts of revolt against the new masters. Such incidents were not uncommon. But these murders were different, the work of a madman not an insurrectionist. Of course, that would not prevent street-corner ranters like those who had interrupted the inquest from claiming these pathetic eviscerations as victories.

A vampire whore in Flower and Dean Street offered to make him immortal for an ounce or two of his blood. He flipped her a copper coin, and went on his way. He wondered how long he would have the strength to resist. At thirty-five, he was already aware that he was slowing. At fifty, at sixty, would his resolve to stay warm seem ridiculous, perverse? Sinful, even? Was refusing vampirism the moral equivalent of suicide? His father had been fifty-eight when he died.

Vampires needed the warm, to feed and succour them, to keep the country running through the days. There were already vampires—here in the East End, if not in the salons of Mayfair—starving as the poor always had done. How long before the "desperate measures" Lord Henry Wotton was always advocating in parliament—the penning-up of still more warm, not just criminals but any simply healthy specimens, to serve as cattle for the vampires of breeding who were essential to the governance of the country—were seriously considered. Stories crept back from Devil's Dyke that made Beauregard's heart turn to ice. Already the definition of "criminal" had extended to include too many good men and women who were simply unable to come to an accommodation with the new regime.

It took him a while to find a cab. After dark, Whitechapel was coming to life. Public houses and music halls were lit up, people crammed inside, laughing and shouting. And the streets were busy. Traders were selling sheet music, phials of "human" blood, scissors, Royal souvenirs. Chestnuts roasted in a barrel-fire on Half Moon Street were sold to new-born and warm alike. Vampires did not need to eat, but apparently the habit was hard to lose. Crowds took note of his clothes and mainly kept out of his way. Beauregard was conscious of the watch in his waistcoat and the wallet in his inside breast pocket. There were nimble fingers all around, and sharp nailed claws. Blood was not all the new-borns wanted. He swung his cane purposefully, warding off evil.

At length, he found a hansom and offered the cabbie three shillings to take him to Cheyne Walk, Chelsea. The man touched his whip to the brim of his bowler, and Beauregard slipped inside. The interior was upholstered in red, like the plush coffins displayed in the shops along Oxford Street. It seemed altogether too luxurious a conveyance for this quarter of the city, and Beauregard wondered whether it had brought a distinguished visitor or two from the West End, in search of amorous adventures. There were houses all over the district, catering to every taste. Women and boys, warm and vampire, were freely available for a few shillings. Drabs like Polly Nicholls and Lulu Schön could be had for coppers or a squirt of blood. It was possible that the murderer was not from Whitechapel, that he was just another toff pursuing his peculiar pleasures. In Whitechapel, they said, you could get anything, either by paying for it or taking it.

His duties, in what they called the Great Game, had taken him to worse places. He had spent weeks as a one-eyed beggar in Afghanistan, dogging the movements of a Russian envoy suspected of stirring up the hill-tribes.

During the Boer Rebellion, he had endeavoured to negotiate a treaty with the Amahagger, whose idea of an evening's entertainment was baking the heads of captives in pots. And, for a month, he had been entertained in the perfumed dungeons of an imaginative Chinese mandarin. However, it had been something of a surprise to return, after years abroad in the discreet service of Her Majesty, to find London itself transformed into a city more strange, dangerous and bizarre than any in his experience. It was no longer the heart of

Empire, just a sponge absorbing the blood of the Queen's domain until it burst.

The cab's wheels rattled against the cobbles, lulling him like the soft crash of waves under a ship.

While Beauregard had been away, the Prince Consort had taken London. He had wooed and won the Queen, persuading her to abandon her widow's black, then he had introduced vampirism to the British Isles, and reshaped the greatest Empire on the globe to suit his own desires. Charles Beauregard still served his Queen. He had promised death would not interfere with his loyalty to her person, but when he had made that vow he had thought he meant his own death.

The Prince Consort, who had taken for himself the additional title of Lord Protector, ruled Great Britain now, his get executing his wishes and whims. A vampire, Lord Ruthven, was Prime Minister, and another, Sir Francis Varney, Viceroy of India. An elite Carpathian guard, guised up in comic opera uniforms, patrolled the grounds of Buckingham Palace, and caroused throughout the West End like sacred terrors. The army, the navy, the diplomatic corps, the police and the Church of England all were in the Prince Consort's thrall, new-borns promoted over the warm at every opportunity.

While the business of the kingdom continued much as it always had done, there were other changes: people vanished from public and private life, camps such as Devil's Dyke springing up in remote areas of the country, and the apparatus of a government—secret police, sudden arrests, casual executions—he associated not with the Queen but with the Tsars and Taiping. There were Republican bands playing Robin Hood in the wilds of Scotland and Ireland, and cross-waving curates were always trying to brand new-born provincial mayors with the mark of Cain.

Something irritated him. He had grown used to trusting his occasional feelings of irritation. On several occasions, they had been the saving of his life.

The cab was in the Commercial Road, heading East, not West. He could smell the docks. Beauregard resolved to see this out. It was an interesting development, and he had hopes that the cabbie did not merely intend to murder and rob him.

He eased aside the catch in the head of his cane, and slid a few inches of shining steel out of the body of the stick. The sword would draw freely if he needed it. Still, it was only steel. He wondered whether silver might not have been wiser.

## V

At the Whitechapel Police Station, Lestrade introduced her to Inspector Abberline, who was in charge of the continuing murder investigation. Having handled the Nicholls case, without any notable results, he was now saddled with Lulu Schön, and any more yet to come. Jekyll's testimony confirmed what Genevieve had already intuited. These horrors would not stop of their own accord. The man with the silver knife would keep at his work until he was caught or killed.

Lestrade and Abberline went off together, to have a huddle. Abberline was warm, and elaborately—without realising it?—came up with other things to do with his hands whenever the possibility of pressing flesh with a vampire was raised. He lit his pipe and listened as Lestrade ticked off points on his fingers. Genevieve looked around the reception room, which was already busy.

Outside the station, there were several groups of interested parties. A Christian Crusade band, flying the cross of St George, were supporting a preacher, who was calling down God's Justice on vampirekind, upholding the Whitechapel Murderer as a true instrument of the Will of Christ. They were being heckled by a few professional insurrectionists, some of the crew she had seen at the inquest, and ridiculed by a knot of painted new-born women, who offered expensive kisses and changed lives. Genevieve understood that many new-borns paid to become some street tart's get, seeking vampirism as a way out of their warmth.

A sergeant was turning out some of the station's regulars. Genevieve recognised most of them. There were plenty—warm and vampire—who spent their lives shuffling between the holding cells and Toynbee Hall, in the constant search for a bed and a free meal.

"Miss Dee," said a woman, recognising her, "Miss Dee . . ."

"Cathy," she said, acknowledging the new-born, "are you being well treated?"

"Loverly, miss, loverly," she said, simpering at the sergeant, "it's an 'ome from 'ome."

Cathy Eddowes looked hardly better as a vampire than she must have done when warm. Gin and too many nights outdoors had raddled her, and the red shine in her eyes and on her hair didn't outweigh the mottled skin under her heavy rouge. Like many in Whitechapel, Cathy still exchanged her body for drink. Her customers' blood was probably as high in its alcohol content as the gin to which she used to be devoted.

The new-born primped her hair, arranging a red ribbon that kept her tight curls away from her wide face. There was a running sore on the back of her hand.

"Let me look at that, Cathy."

Genevieve had seen marks like these. New-borns had to be careful. They were stronger, more lasting than the warm. But too much of their diet was tainted. And disease was still a danger. The Dark Kiss did something strange—something Dr Jekyll would probably find of great interest—to any diseases a person happened to carry over from warm life to their undead state.

"Do you have many of these sores?"

Cathy shook her head, but Genevieve knew she meant yes.

A clear fluid was weeping from the red patch on the back of the new-born's hand, and there were damp marks on Cathy's tight bodice, suggesting more patches. She wore her scarf in an unnatural fashion, covering her neck and upper breasts. Genevieve peeled the wool away, and smelled the pungent discharge that glistened on Cathy's skin.

Genevieve looked into the woman's eyes, and saw fear. Cathy Eddowes knew something was wrong, but was superstitiously afraid of finding out what it was.

"Cathy, you must call in at the Hall tonight. See Mr Druitt, or, better yet, Dr Seward. Something can be done for your condition. I promise you."

"I'll be all right, love."

"Not unless you get some treatment, Cathy."

Cathy tried to laugh, and tottered out onto the streets. One of her boot heels was gone, so she had a music hall limp. She held up her head, wrapping her scarf around her like a duchess's fur stole, and wiggled provocatively past the Christian Crusade speaker, slipping into the fog.

"Dead in a year," said the sergeant, a red-eyed new-born with a snoutlike protrusion in the centre of his face.

"Not if I can help it."

## VI

The cab took him to Limehouse, somewhere near the Basin. It was not a part of the city he knew well, although he had been here in Her Majesty's Service several times. The door was opened for him, and a pair of red eyes glittered in the dark beyond.

"Sorry for the inconvenience, Beauregard," purred a silky voice, male but not entirely masculine, "but I hope you'll understand. It's a sticky wicket . . ."

Beauregard stepped down, and found himself in a yard off one of the warren of streets near the docks. There were people all around. The one who had spoken was an Englishman, a vampire with a good coat and soft hat, face in darkness. His posture was studied in its langour, he was an athlete at rest and Beauregard would not have liked to go four rounds with him. The others were Chinese, pig-tailed and bowed, hands in their sleeves. Most were warm, but the massive fellow by the cab-door was a new-born, naked to the waist to show off his dragon tattoos and his vampire indifference to the autumn chill.

The Englishman stepped forward, and moonlight caught his youthful face. He had pretty eyelashes, like a woman's, and Beauregard recognised him.

"I saw you get six sixes from six balls in '85," he said. "Gentlemen and Players, the MCC."

The sportsman shrugged modestly. "You play what's chucked at you. I always say."

Beauregard had heard the new-born's name in the Diogenes Club, tentatively linked with a series of daring jewel robberies. He supposed the sportsman's involvement in this evident kidnapping confirmed that he was indeed the author of those criminal feats.

"This way," said the amateur cracksman, indicating a wet stretch of stone wall. The new-born Chinese pressed a brick, and a section of the wall tilted upwards, forming a hatch-like door. "Duck down or you'll bash your bean. Deuced small, these chinks."

Beauregard followed the new-born, who could see in the dark better than he, and was in turn followed by some of the Chinese. They went down a passageway that sloped sharply, and he realised they must be below street level. Everything was damp and glistening, suggesting these underground chambers must be close to the river.

Doors were opened, and Beauregard was ushered into a dimly-lit drawing room, richly furnished. He noticed there were no windows, just *chinoiserie* screens. The centrepiece was a large desk, behind which sat an ancient Chinaman, his long, hard fingernails like knifepoints on his blotter. There were others in the room, in comfortable armchairs arranged in a half-circle about the desk.

One man turned his head, red cigar-end making a Devil's mask of his face. He was a vampire, but the Chinaman was not.

"Mr Beauregard," began the Celestial, "so kind of you to join our wretched and unworthy selves."

"So kind of you to invite me."

The Chinaman clapped his hands, and nodded to a dead-faced servant, a Burmese.

"Take our visitor's hat, cloak and *cane*."

Beauregard was relieved of his burdens. When the Burmese was close enough, Beauregard observed the singular earring, and the ritual tattooing about his neck.

"A Dacoit?" he inquired.

"Very observant."

"I have some experience of the world of secret societies."

"Indeed you have, Mr Beauregard. Our paths have crossed three times; in Egypt, in the Kashmir, and in Shansi Province. You caused me some little inconvenience."

Beauregard realised to whom he was talking. "My apologies, doctor."

The Chinaman leaned forward, his face emerging into the light, his fingernails clacking as he brushed away Beauregard's apologies. "Think nothing of it. Those were trivial matters, of no import beyond the ordinary."

They called this man the "Devil Doctor" or "the Lord of Strange Deaths", and he was reputed to be one of the Council of Seven, the ruling body of the Si-Fan, a *tong* whose influence extended from China to all the quarters of the Earth.

The amateur cracksman turned up the gaslight, and faces became clear, dark corners of the room were dispelled.

"Business," snorted a military-looking vampire, "time is money, remember . . ."

"A thousand pardons, Colonel Moran. In the East, things are different. Here, we must bow to your Western ways, hurry and bustle, haste and industry."

The cigar-smoker stood up, unbending a lanky figure from which hung a frock coat marked around the pockets with chalk. The Colonel deferred to him, and stepped back, eyes falling. The smoker's head oscillated from side to side like a lizard's, eyeteeth protruding over his lower lip.

"My associate is a businessman," he explained between puffs, "our cricketing friend is a dilettante. Sikes is continuing his family business. I am a mathematician, but you, my dear doctor, are an artist."

"The Professor flatters me."

Beauregard had heard of the Professor too. "With two of the three most dangerous men in the world in one room, I have to ask myself where the third might be?"

"I see our names and positions are not unknown to you, Mr Beauregard," said the Chinaman. "Dr Nikola is unavailable for our little gathering. I believe he may be found investigating some sunken ships off the coast of Tasmania. He no longer concerns us. He has his own interests."

Beauregard looked at the others in the meeting, those still unaccounted for. Sikes was a pig-faced man, warm, short, barrel-chested and brutal. With a loud check jacket and cheap oil on his hair, he looked out of place in such a distinguished gathering. Alone in the company, he was the image of a criminal.

"Professor, if you would care to explain . . ."

"Thank you, doctor," replied the man they called "The Napoleon of Crime". "Mr Beauregard, as you are aware, none of us in this room—and I include you among our number—has what we might call common cause. We pursue our own furrows, and if they happen to intersect . . . well, that is often unfortunate. Lately, the world has changed, but whatever personal metamorphoses we might have welcomed, our calling has remained essentially the same. We are a shadow community, and we always have been. To a great extent, we have come to an accommodation. We pit our wits against each other, but when the sun comes up, we draw a line, we let well enough alone. It grieves me greatly to have to say this, but that line seems not to be holding . . ."

"There was police raids all over the East End," Sikes interrupted. "Years of bloody work overturned in a single day. 'Ouses smashed. Gambling, opium, girls: nuffin' sacred. Our business 'as been bought and paid for, and the filthy peelers done us dirty when they went back on the deal."

"I have nothing to do with the police," Beauregard said.

"Do not think us naive," said the Professor. "Like all the members of the Diogenes Club, you have no official position at all. But what is official and what is effective are separate things."

"This persecution of our interests will continue," the Celestial said, "so long as the Whitechapel Murderer is at liberty."

Beauregard nodded. "I suppose so. There's always a chance the killer will be turned up by the raids."

"He's not one of us," snorted Colonel Moran.

"'E's a ravin' nutter, that's what 'e is. Listen, none of us is 'zactly squeamish—know what I mean?—but this bloke is takin' it too far. If an 'ore makes trouble, you takes a razor to 'er face not 'er bleedin' froat."

"There's never been any suggestion, so far as I know, that any of you were involved in the murders."

"That's not the point, Mr Beauregard," the Professor continued. "Our shadow empire is like a spiderweb. It extends throughout the world, but it is concentrated here, in this city. It is thick and complicated and surprisingly delicate. If enough threads are severed, it will fall. And threads are being severed left and right. We have all suffered since Mary Ann Nicholls was killed, and the inconvenience was redoubled tonight. Each time this murderer strikes at the public, he stabs at us also."

"My 'ores don't wanna go on the streets wiv 'im out there. It's 'urtin' me pockets."

"I'm sure the police will catch the man. There's a reward of fifty pounds for information."

"And we have posted a reward of a thousand guineas, but nothing has come of it."

"Mr Beauregard," said the Chinaman. "We should like to add our humble efforts to those of the most excellent police. We pledge that any knowledge which comes into our possession—as knowledge on so many matters so often does—shall be passed directly to you. In return, we ask that the personal interest in this matter, which we know the Diogenes Club has required you take, be persecuted with the utmost vigour."

Beauregard tried not to show it, but he was deeply shocked that the innermost workings of the Diogenes Club were somehow known to the Lord of Strange Deaths. And yet the insidious Chinaman evidently knew in detail of the briefing he had been given only hours earlier.

"This bounder is letting the side down," the amateur cracksman said, "and it would be best if he stripped his whites and went back to the bally pavilion."

"We've put up a thousand guineas for information," the Colonel said, "and two thousand for his rotten head."

"Do we have an understanding, Mr Beauregard?"

"Yes, Professor."

The new-born smiled a thin smile, fangs scraping his thin underlip. One murder meant very little to these men, but a loose cannon of crime was an inconvenience they would not brook.

"A cab will take you to Cheyne Walk," the Celestial explained, smile crinkling his eyes and lifting his thin moustaches. "This meeting is at an end. Serve our purpose, and you will be rewarded. Fail us, and the consequences will be . . . not so pleasant."

With a wave, Beauregard was dismissed.

As the amateur cracksman took him back through the passage, Beauregard wondered just how many Devils he would have to ally himself with in order to discharge his duty to the Crown.

His hat, cloak and cane were waiting for him inside the cab.

"Toodle-oo," said the cricketer, red eyes shining, "see you at Lords."

## VII

When the sun came up, the new-borns scurried to their coffins and corners, Genevieve trailed alone through the streets, never thinking to be afraid of the shrinking shadows, wandering back to Toynbee Hall. Like the Prince Consort, she was old enough not to shrivel in the sun as the more sensitive new-borns did, but she felt the energy that had come with the blood of the warm girl seep away as the first light of dawn filtered orange through the swirling fog. She passed a warm policeman on the Commercial Road, and nodded a greeting to him. He turned away, and kept on his beat. There were more policemen in Whitechapel even at this hour than there would be in six weeks' time at the Lord Mayor's Parade.

In the last week and a half, she had spent more time on the Ripper than on her work. Druitt was pulling double shifts, juggling the limited number of places at the Hall to deal with the most needy first. She had been seconded to a Vigilance Committee, and had been to so many meetings that even now words still rung in her ears as music rings in the ears of those who sit too near the orchestra. The socialists George Bernard Shaw and Beatrix Potter had been making speeches all over the city, using the murders to bring attention to the conditions of the East End. Toynbee Hall was momentarily the recipient of enough charitable donations to make Druitt propose that it would be a good idea to sponsor the Ripper's activities as a means of raising funds, a suggestion that did not amuse the serious-minded Jack Seward. Neither Shaw nor Potter were vampires themselves, and Shaw at least had been linked, Genevieve understood, with one of the Republican factions.

A poster up on the wall of an ostler's yard promised the latest reward for information leading to the capture of Jack the Ripper. It bore a photographic representation of the letter the Central News Agency had received, covered in a spidery red scrawl. Nobody had recognised the handwriting yet, and Genevieve guessed that tracing the prankster with the red ink would get the police no nearer the Whitechapel Murderer than they already were. Which was to say, not very near at all.

Rival groups of warm and new-born vigilantes had roamed the streets with billy-clubs and razors, scrapping with each other and setting upon dubiously innocent passersby. Since the last killing, the street girls had started complaining less about the danger of the murderer and more about the lack of custom noticeable since the vigilantes started harassing anyone who came to Whitechapel looking for a woman. Genevieve heard that the whores of Soho and Covent Garden were doing record business, and record gloating.

A lunatic—almost certainly not the killer—had written to the Central News Agency, wittering on in scarlet. "I am down on whores and leeches and shan't quit ripping them till I get buckled

... I saved some of the proper red stuff in a ginger beer bottle to write with but it went thick like glue and I can't use it. Red ink is fit enough I hope, ha ha ... My knife is silver and sharp and I want to get to work straight away if I can." The anonymous crank's letter had been signed "yours truly, Jack the Ripper", and the name had stuck.

Genevieve had heard Jack was a leather-aproned shoemaker, a Polish Jew carrying out ritual killings, a foreign sailor, a degenerate from the West End, the ghost of Abraham Van Helsing or Charley Peace. He was a policeman, a doctor, a midwife, a priest. With each rumour, more innocent people were thrown to the mob. A shoemaker named Pizer had been locked up in the police cells for his own protection when someone took it into their heads to write "Jack's Shack" on his shopfront. After a Christian Crusade speaker argued that the killer could walk unhindered about the area killing at will because he was a policeman, a vampire constable was dragged into a yard off Coke Street and impaled on a length of picket fence.

Genevieve passed the doorway where Lilly slept. The new-born child, who might grow old but never become an adult, was curling up for the day with some scraps of blanket that had been given to her at the Hall. Genevieve noticed the girl's half-shapeshifted arm was worse, useless wing sprouting from hip to armpit. Changing was a trick the Prince Consort kept to himself, and there were too many imperfect freaks about. Lilly had a cat nestled against her face, its neck in her mouth. The animal was still barely alive.

Abberline and Lestrade had questioned dozens, but made no arrests. There were always rival groups of protesters outside the police station. Genevieve heard rumours that psychic mediums like Lees and Carnacki had been called for. Sir Charles Warren had been forced to explain himself in private to the Prime Minister, and Ruthven would have the Commissioner's resignation if there was no action soon. Any number of consulting detectives—Sexton Blake, Max Carados, August Van Dusen—had prowled Whitechapel, hoping to turn something up. Even the venerable Hawkshaw had come out of retirement. But with their acknowledged master in Devil's Dyke, the enthusiasm of the detective community had ebbed considerably, and no solutions were forthcoming. The Queen, young again and plump, had expressed concern about "these ghastly murders", but nothing had been heard from the Prince Consort, to whom Genevieve assumed the lives of a few streetwalkers, vampire or not, were of as much importance as those of beetles.

Gradually, as she came to realise just how powerless she was to affect the behaviour of this unknown maniac, she also sensed just how important this case was becoming. Everyone involved seemed to begin their arguments by declaring that it was about more than just two dead vampire whores. It was about D'Israeli's "two nations", it was about the regrettable spread of vampirism among the lower orders, it was about the fragile equilibrium of the transformed kingdom. The murders were mere sparks, but the British Empire was a tinderbox.

She spent a lot of time with whores—she had been an outcast long enough to feel a certain identification with them—and shared their fears. Tonight, nearing dawn, she had found a warm girl in Mrs Warren's house off Raven Row and bled her, out of need not pleasure. After so many years, she should be used to her predator's life, but the Prince Consort had turned everything topsy-turvy and she was ashamed again, not of what she must do to prolong her existence, but of the things vampirekind, those of the bloodline of Vlad Tepes, did around her. The warm girl had been bitten several times, and was pale and fragile. Eventually, she would turn. Nobody's get, she would have to find her own way in the darkness, and doubtless end up as raddled as Cathy Eddowes or as truly dead as Polly Nicholls.

Her head was fuzzy from the gin her warm girl had drunk. The whole city seemed sick. Dawn shot the fog full of blood.

## VIII

**Dr Seward's Diary**

September 28, 1888. *Today, I went to Kingstead to lay the annual wreath. It is three years, to the day, since Lucy's death. Her destruction, rather. The tomb bears the date of her first death, and only I—or so I thought—remember the date of Van Helsing's expedition. The Prince Consort and Lord Protector, after all, is hardly likely to make it a national holiday. Then, we trailed along with the old Dutchman, not really believing what he had told us of Lucy. My load of grief at her death had been more than enough to bear, without being told that she had risen from her coffin and was the dark woman who had taken to biting children on Hampstead Heath.*

*I still dream of Lucy, too much. Once, I had hoped to take her for my wife. But Arthur's charms—not to mention his title and his wealth—prevailed. Her lips, her pale skin, her hair, her eyes. Many times have my dreams of Lucy been responsible for my nocturnal emissions. Wet kisses and wet dreams . . .*

*Lucy was the first in England of the Prince Consort's get, and the first to be destroyed. I only regret now that it was Arthur Holmwood—Lord Godalming—who did the honours, driving the wooden stake into her heart, setting her free of her unwelcome condition. I helped decapitate the hissing corpse, and filled her mouth with garlic. If only Van Helsing had been as quick to lead us to the second new-born, the third, the tenth, the hundredth. There was a point, I suppose, when Dracula could have been driven from these shores, could have been hounded back to his Transylvanian fastness, could have been properly dispatched with wood and silver and steel. But I don't know when that could have been.*

*I have chosen to work in Whitechapel because it is the ugliest part of the Prince Consort's realm. Here, the superficialities which some say make his rule tolerable are at their thinnest. With vampire sluts on every corner, baying for blood, and befuddled or dead men littering the cramped streets, it is possible to see the true, worm-eaten face of what has been wrought. It is hard to keep my control among so many of the leeches, but my vocation is strong. Once, I was a doctor, a specialist in mental disorders. Now, I am a vampire killer. My duty is to cut out the corrupt heart of the city.*

*The fog that shrouds London in autumn has got thicker since Dracula came. I understand all manner of vermin—rats, wild dogs, cats—have thrived, and some quarters of the city have even seen a resurgence of the medieval disease they carry. It is as if the Prince Consort were a bubbling sinkhole, disgorging filth from where he sits, grinning his wolf's grin as it seeps throughout his kingdom. The fog means there is less and less distinction between day and night. In Whitechapel, many days, the sun truly does not shine. That excites the new-borns. We've been seeing more and more go half-mad in the daytime, muddy light burning out their brains.*

*The rest of the city is more sedate, but no better. On the way to Kingstead, I stopped off at an inn in Hampstead for a pork pie and a pint of beer. In the gloom of the afternoon, gentlefolk paraded themselves on the Heath, skins pale, eyes shining red. It is quite the thing, I understand, to follow fashions set by the Queen, and vampirism—although resisted for several years—has now become more than acceptable. Prim, pretty girls in bonnets, ivory-dagger teeth artfully concealed by Japanese fans, flock to the Heath on sunless afternoons, thick black parasols held high. There is no difference, really, between them and the blood-sucking whores of the Ten Bells and the Vlad IV in Whitechapel.*

*The gates of Kingstead hung open, unattended. Since dying became unfashionable, churchyards have fallen into disuse. Most churches are empty too, although the court has its tame archbishops, trying desperately to reconcile Anglicanism with vampirism. When he was truly alive, the Prince Consort slaughtered thousands in the defence of the faith, and he still fancies himself a Christian. Entering the graveyard, I could not help but remember . . . Lucy's "sickness", her funeral. Van Helsing's diagnosis, the cure. We destroyed a thing, not the girl I had loved. Cutting through her neck, I found a calling.*

*My hand hurt damnably, a throbbing lump of tissue. I know I should seek treatment, but I think I need my pain. It gives me resolve.*

*At the start of it, some new-borns had taken to opening the tombs of their dead relatives, hoping by some strange osmosis to return them to vampire life. I had to watch my step to avoid the chasm-like holes left in the ground by these fruitless endeavours. The fog was thin up here, a muslin curtain.*

*It was something of a shock to see a figure outside the Westenra tomb. A young woman, slim and dark, in a velvet-collared coat, a straw hat with a dead bird on it perched on her tightly-bound hair.*

*Hearing my approach, she turned and I caught the glint of red eyes.*

*With the light behind her, it could have been Lucy.*

*"Sir?" she said, startled by my interruption. "Who might that be?"*

*The voice was Irish, uneducated, light. It was not Lucy.*

*I left my hat on, but nodded. There was something familiar about the new-born.*

*"Why," she said, "'tis Dr Seward, from the Toynbee."*

*A shaft of late sun speared through the fog, and the vampire flinched. I saw her face.*

*"Kelly, isn't it?"*

*"Marie, sir," she said, recovering her composure, remembering to simper, to smile, to ingratiate. "Come to pay your respects?"*

*I nodded, and laid my wreath. She had put her own at the door of the tomb, a penny posy now dwarfed by my shilling tribute.*

*"Did you know the young miss?"*

*"I did."*

*Arthur had beat me out with Lucy, as he beat me out with his hammer and stake. Lord Godalming was a vampire himself now, a sharp-faced blade and the ornament of any society gathering. Eventually, I must take my silver to his treacherous dead heart.*

*"She was a beauty," Kelly said. "Beautiful."*

*I could not conceive of any connection in life between my Lucy and this broad-boned drab. Mary Kelly—our records say Mary Jane, but she sometimes styles herself Marie Jeanette—is fresher than most, but she's just another whore, really. Like Nicholls, and Schön . . .*

*"She turned me," Kelly explained. "Found me on the Heath one night when I was walking home from the house of a gentleman, an' delivered me into my new life."*

*I looked more closely at Kelly. If she was Lucy's get, she bore out the theory I have heard that a vampire's progeny come to resemble their parent-in-darkness. There was definitely something of Lucy's delicacy about her red little mouth and her white little teeth.*

*"I'm her get, as she was the Prince Consort's. That makes me almost royalty. The Queen is my aunt-in-darkness."*

*Kelly giggled, fangs shining.*

*My hand was dipped in fire in my pocket, a tight fist at the centre of a ball of pain.*

*Kelly came close to me, so close I could whiff the rot on her breath under her perfume, and stroked the collar of my coat.*

*"That's good material, sir."*

*She kissed my neck, quick as a snake, and my heart spasmed. Even now, I cannot explain or excuse the feelings that came over me.*

*"I could turn you, warm sir, make royalty of you . . ."*

*My body was rigid as she moved against me, pressing forward with her hips, her hands slipping around my shoulders, my back.*

*I shook my head.*

*"'Tis your loss, sir."*

*She stood away. Blood pounded in my temples, my heart raced like a Wessex Cup winner. I was nauseated by the thing's presence. Had my scalpel been in my pocket, I would have ripped—hideous word, courtesy of the unknown jester who gave me my "trade name"—her heart out. But there were other emotions. She looked so like Lucy, so like the Lucy who bothers my dreams.*

*I tried to speak, but just croaked. Kelly understood. She must be experienced.*

*The leech turned and smiled, slipping near me again.*

*"Somethin' else, sir."*

*I nodded, and, slowly, she began to loosen my clothes. She took my hand out of my pocket, and cooed over the wound, licking the bled-through bandage with shudders of pleasure. I looked about.*

*"We won't be disturbed here, doctor, sir . . ."*

*"Jack," I muttered.*

*"Jack," she said, pleased with the sound.*

*(Who is the letter-writer? Jack or John is a common name. He can't know. If he knew, I would not still be alive.)*

*In the lea of Lucy's tomb, I rutted with the foul creature, tears on my face, a dreadful burning inside me. Her flesh was cool and white. Afterwards, she took me into her mouth and—with exquisite, torturous care—bled me slightly. I offered her coin, but my blood was enough for her. She looked at me with tenderness, almost with pity, before she left. If only I had had my scalpel.*

*Now, I am jittery, nervous. It has been too long since I last struck. Whitechapel has become dangerous. There have been people snooping around all the time, seeing the Ripper in every shadow.*

*My scalpel is on my desk, shining silver. Sharp as a whisper.*

*They say that I am mad. They do not understand my purpose.*

*Returning from Kingstead, I admitted something to myself. When I dream of Lucy, I do not dream of her as she was when she was alive, when I loved her. I dream of Lucy as a vampire.*

*It is nearly midnight. I must go out.*

## IX

The city was on fire!

As Genevieve understood it, the Ripper had struck twice last night. In Duffield Yard, off Berner Street, the murderer had cut a new-born whore's throat, but been disturbed by a passerby named Diemschutz and fled before he could finish his job. Within the hour, he had cornered Catherine Eddowes—Cathy!—in Mitre Square, and done a thorough dissection, going so far as to clip the ears and carry off some of the internal organs.

A double event!

She had spent the evening at the Hall. The director had put her in charge of the shift, since Druitt was off on some business of his own. Lilly was dying, and Genevieve had been with her. The girl's human body was immortal, but the animal she had tried to become was taking over, and that animal was dead. As Lilly's tissue transformed into leathery dead flesh, the girl was dying by inches. Genevieve wished for a silver knife like the Ripper's, to make the merciful cut. One of the warm nurses had given Lilly a little blood, but it was no use. Genevieve talked to the girl, sang the songs of her own long-ago childhood, but she did not know if Lilly could even hear.

An hour before dawn, the news had come. One of the pimps, arm laid open to the bone by someone's razor, was brought in, and the crowd with him had five different versions of the story. Jack the Ripper was caught, and was being held at the police station, his identity concealed because he was one of the Royal Family. Jack had gutted a dozen in full view, and eluded pursuers by leaping over a twenty-foot wall, escaping thanks to springs on his boots. Jack's face was a silver skull, his arms bloodied scythes, his breath purging fire.

Jack had killed. Again. Twice.

A police constable told her the bare facts. She had been shocked to hear about Cathy. The other woman she didn't think she had met.

"He's takin' them two at a time," the constable had said, "you almost have to admire him, the Devil."

Now, with the sun up, Genevieve was nearly dozing. She was tired of keeping things together, with Druitt and Seward away. A crowd of whores had been around, mainly in hysterical tears, begging for money to escape from the death-trap of Whitechapel. Actually, the district had been a death-trap long before the Ripper silvered his knives.

Noisily, Lilly died.

Genevieve wrapped the tiny corpse in a sheet. It was already starting to rot, and would have to be removed before the stink became too bad to bear. Whenever anyone she knew died, another grain of ice clung to her heart. She could see how easy it was to become a monster of callousness. A few more centuries, and she could be a match for Vlad Tepes, caring for nothing but power and hot blood in her throat.

There was a commotion—*another* commotion—downstairs in the receiving rooms. Genevieve had been expecting more injuries to come in during the day. After the murders, there would be street brawls, vigilante victims, maybe even a lynching in the American style . . .

Four uniformed policemen were in the hallway, something heavy slung in an oilcloth between them. Lestrade was pacing nervously, clothes in disarray. The coppers had had to fight their way through hostile crowds. "It's as if he's laughin' at us," the constable had said, "stirrin' them all up against us."

"Mademoiselle Dieudonné, clear a private room."

"Inspector . . . "

"Don't argue, just do it. One of them's still alive."

She understood at once, and checked her charts. Immediately, she realised she knew there was an empty room.

They followed her upstairs, grunting under their awkward burden, and she let them into Lilly's room. She shifted the tiny bundle from the bed, and the policemen manoeuvred the woman onto it, pulling away the oilcloth.

"Mademoiselle Dieudonné, meet Long Liz Stride."

The new-born was tall and thin, rouge smeared on her sunken cheeks, her hair a tatty grey. She wore a cotton shift, dyed red from neckline to waist. Her throat was opened to the bone, cut from ear to ear like a clown's smile.

She was gurgling, her cut pipes trying to mesh.

"Jackie Boy didn't have enough time for his usual," Lestrade explained. "Saved it up for Cathy Eddowes. Warm bastard"

Liz Stride tried to yell, but couldn't call up air from her lungs into her throat. A draught whispered through her wound. Her teeth were gone, but for four sharp incisors. Her limbs convulsed like galvanised frogs' legs. Two of the coppers had to hold her down. Her hands shook like trees in a storm.

"She won't last," Genevieve told him. "She's too far gone."

Another vampire might have survived such a wound—she had herself lived through worse—but Liz Stride was a new-born, and had been turned too late in life. She had been dying for years, poisoning herself with rough gin, taking too many hard knocks.

"She doesn't have to last, she just has to give a statement."

Genevieve was not sure that was a realistic hope.

"Inspector, I don't know if she *can* talk. I think her vocal cords have been severed."

Lestrade chewed his moustache. Liz Stride was his first chance at the Ripper, and he didn't want to let it go.

The door was pushed in, and people crowded through. Lestrade turned to shout "out" at them, but swallowed his command.

"Mr Beauregard, sir," he said.

The tall, well-dressed man Genevieve had seen at Lulu Schön's inquest came into the room, with Dr Seward in his wake. There were more people—nurses, attendants—in the corridor.

"Inspector," the tall man said. "May I . . ."

"Always a pleasure to help the Diogenes Club, Mr Beauregard," Lestrade said, in a tone which suggested it was rather more of a pleasure to pour caustic soda into one's own eyes.

Beauregard slid through the constables with an elegant movement, polite but forceful. He flicked his cloak over his shoulders, to give his arms freedom of movement.

"Good God," he said. "Can nothing be done for this poor wretch?"

Genevieve was strangely impressed. Beauregard was the first person who had said anything to suggest he thought Liz Stride was worth doing anything for, rather than someone whom something ought to be done about.

"It's too late," Genevieve explained. "She's trying to renew herself, but her injuries are too great, her reserves of strength too meagre . . ."

The torn flesh around Liz Stride's open throat swarmed, but failed to knit. Her convulsions were more regular now.

"Dr Seward?" Beauregard said, asking for a second opinion.

The director approached the bucking, thrashing woman. Genevieve saw again that he had a distaste—almost always held tightly in check—for vampires.

"Mademoiselle Dieudonné is right, I'm afraid. Poor creature, I have some silver salts upstairs. We could ease her passing. It would be the kindest course."

"Not until she gives us answers," Lestrade interrupted.

"For heaven's sake, man," Beauregard countered. "She's a human being, not a clue."

Seward touched Liz Stride's forehead, and looked into her eyes, which were red marbles. He shook his head.

Suddenly, the wounded new-born was possessed with a surge of strength. She threw off the constable who was holding down her shoulders, and lunged for the director, her jaws opening as wide as a cobra's.

Genevieve pushed Seward out of the way, and ducked to avoid Liz Stride's slashing talons.

"She's changing," someone shouted.

It was true. Liz Stride reared up, her backbone curving, her limbs drawing in. A wolfish snout grew out of her face, and swathes of hair ran over her exposed skin.

Seward crab-walked backwards to the wall. Lestrade called his men out of danger. Beauregard was reaching under his cloak for something.

Liz Stride was trying to become a wolf or a dog. But that was a hard trick—like her father-in-darkness before her, Genevieve could not shapeshift—and it took immense concentration and a strong sense of one's own self. Not the resources available to a gin-soaked mind, or to a new-born in mortal pain.

"Hell Fire," someone said.

Liz Stride's lower jaw stuck out like an alligator's, growing too large to fix properly to her skull. Her right leg and arm shrivelled, while her left side bloated, slabs of muscle forming around the bone. Her bloody clothes tore.

The wound in her throat mended over, and reformed, new yellow teeth shining at the edges of the cut. A taloned foot lashed out, and tore into a warm constable's uniformed chest. Blood gushed.

The half-creature was yelping screeches out of its neck-hole. She leaped, pushing through policemen, and landed in a clump, scrabbling across the floor, a powerfully-razored hand reaching for Seward.

"Aside," Beauregard ordered.

The man from the Diogenes Club held a revolver. He thumb-cocked the gun, and took a careful aim.

Liz Stride turned, and looked up at the barrel.

"That's useless," Genevieve protested.

Liz Stride sprung into the air.

Beauregard pulled the trigger. His shot took Liz Stride in the heart, and slammed her back against the wall. She fell, lifeless, onto Seward, body turning back into what it had been, and then into rotten meat.

Genevieve looked a question at Beauregard.

"Silver bullet," he explained, without pride.

Seward stood up, wiping the blood from his face. He was shaking, barely repressing his disgust.

"Well, you've finished the Ripper's business, and that's a fact," Lestrade muttered.

"I'm not complainin'," said Watkins, the gash-chested warm constable.

Genevieve bent over the corpse, and confirmed Liz Stride's death. Suddenly, with a last convulsion, her arm—still wolfish—leaped out, and her claws fastened in Seward's trousers-cuff.

# X

"I think she was trying to tell us something," he said.

"What," the vampire replied, "the murderer's name is . . . Sydney Trousers."

Beauregard laughed. What Genevieve had said was not especially funny, but humour from a vampire was unexpected. Not many of the un-dead bothered with jokes.

"Unlikely," he replied. "Mr Boot, perhaps."

"Or a boot-maker. Like Leather Apron."

"Pizer had an alibi for Polly Nicholls. And he left Whitechapel a week ago."

Lestrade was carting Liz Stride off to the mortuary. Beauregard was walking the distance between Berner Street and Mitre Square, and the vampire from Toynbee Hall was tagging along.

Genevieve Dieudonné dressed like a New Woman, tight jacket and simple dress, sensible flat-heeled boots, beret-like cap and waist-length cape. If Great Britain still had an elected parliament, she would have wanted the vote. And, he suspected, she would not have voted for Ruthven.

They arrived at the site of Catherine Eddowes' murder. The bloody patch was guarded by a warm policeman, and the crowds were staying away.

"The Ripper must be a sprinter," she said.

Beauregard checked his watch.

"We beat his time by five minutes, but we knew where we were going. He was presumably just looking for a girl."

"And a private place."

"It's not very private here."

There were faces behind the windows in the court, looking down.

"In Whitechapel, people are practised at not seeing things."

Genevieve was prowling the tiny walled-in court, as if trying to get the feel of the place.

"You're not like other vampires," he observed.

"No," she agreed.

"How . . ."

"Four hundred and fifty six."

Beauregard was puzzled.

"That's right," she said, "I am not of the Prince Consort's bloodline. My father-in-darkness was Chandagnac, and his mother-in-darkness was Lady Melissa d'Acques, and . . ."

"So all this – " he waved his hand "– is nothing to do with you?"

"Everything is to do with everyone, Mr Beauregard, Vlad Tepes is a sick monster, and his get spread their sickness. That woman this morning is what you can expect of his bloodline . . ."

"You work as a physician?"

She shrugged, "I've picked up a lot of skills over the years, I've been a whore, a soldier, a singer, a geographer, a criminal. Whatever has seemed right. Now, being a doctor is the best I can see."

Beauregard found himself liking this ancient girl. She wasn't like any of the women—warm or un-dead—he knew. Women, whether by choice or from necessity, seemed to stand to one side, watching, passing comments, never acting. Genevieve Dieudonné was not a spectator.

"Is this political?"

Beauregard thought carefully.

"I've asked about the Diogenes Club," she explained, "You're some sort of government office, aren't you?"

"I serve the Crown, yes."

"Well, why your interest in this matter?"

Genevieve stood over the bloody splash that was left of Catherine Eddowes.

"The Queen herself has expressed her concern. If she decrees we try to catch a murderer, then . . ."

"The Ripper might be an anarchist of some stripe," she mused. "Or a die-hard vampire hater."

A little way away from the square, a group of policemen were clustered, Lestrade and Abberline among them, a thin man with a sad moustache and a silk hat at their head. It was Sir Charles Warren, dragged down to a despised quarter of his parish by the killings.

Beauregard sauntered over, the vampire girl with him.

A new-born constable was shifting a square of packing-case away from the wall against which it had been resting. A fat rat, body as big and bloated as a rugby ball, shot out, and darted between the Commissioner's polished shoes, squeaking like rusty nails on a slate.

Lestrade moved aside to let them into the group.

The constable had disclosed a scrawl.

THE VAMPYRES
ARE NOT THE MEN THAT WILL BE
BLAMED FOR NOTHING

"So, obviously the vampires are to be blamed for something," deduced the Commissioner, astutely.

"Could the Ripper be one of us?" asked a distinguished-looking new-born civilian who had come with Sir Charles.

"One of you," Beauregard muttered.

"The man's obviously trying to throw us off," put in Abberline, who was still warm. "That's an educated man trying to make us think he's an illiterate. Only one misspelling, and a double negative not even the thickest coster-monger would actually use."

"Like the letters?" asked Genevieve.

Abberline thought, "Personally, I think the letters were some smart circulation drummer at the *Whitechapel Star* playing silly buggers to drive up sales. This is a different hand, and this was the Ripper. It's too close to be a coincidence."

"The graffito was not here yesterday?" Beauregard asked.

"The beat man swears not."

The constable agreed with the inspector.

"Wipe it off," Sir Charles said.

Nobody did anything.

"There'll be mob rule. We're still few, and the warm are many."

The Commissioner took his own handkerchief to the chalk, and rubbed it away. Nobody protested at the destruction of the evidence.

"There," Sir Charles said, job done. "Sometimes I think I have to do everything myself."

Beauregard saw a narrow-minded impulsiveness that might have passed for stouthearted valour at Rorke's Drift or Lucknow, and understood just how Sir Charles could make a decision that ended in a massacre.

The dignitaries drifted away, back to their cabs and clubs and comfort. And the East End coppers stayed behind to clean up.

"Right," said Lestrade, "I want the cells full by sundown. Haul in every tart, every pimp, every bruiser, every pickpocket. Threaten 'em with whatever you want. Someone knows something, and sooner or later, someone'll talk."

That would please the circle in Limehouse not a bit, Beauregard reflected. Furthermore, Lestrade was wrong. Beauregard had a high enough estimation of the Professor and his colleagues to believe that if any criminal in London knew so much as a hint as to the identity of the Ripper, it would have been passed directly to him. In the week and a half since he had been taken to meet with them, he had heard nothing.

He found himself alone with Genevieve as sun set. She took off her cap.

"There," she said, shaking her hair out, "that's better."

# XI

**Dr Seward's Diary**

October 22, 1888. *I am keeping Mary Kelly. She is so like Lucy, so like what Lucy became. I have paid her rent up to the end of the month. I visit her when I can, when my work at the Hall permits, and we indulge in our peculiar exchange of fluids.*

*The "double event"—hideous expression—has unnerved me, and I think I shall halt my nightwork. It is still necessary, but it is becoming too dangerous. The police are against me, and there are vampires everywhere. Besides, I am learning from Kelly, learning about myself.*

*She tells me, as we lie on the bed in her lodgings in Miller's Court. that she has gone off the game, that she is not seeing other men. I know she is lying, but do not make an issue of it. I open her pink flesh up and vent myself inside her, and she gently taps my blood, her teeth sliding into me. I have scars on my body, scars that itch like the wound Renfield gave me in Purfleet. I am determined not to turn, not to grow weak.*

*Money is not important. Kelly can have whatever I have left from my income. Since I came to Toynbee Hall. I've been drawing no salary and heavily subsidising the purchase of medical supplies and other necessaries. There has always been money in my family. No title, but always money.*

*Stride knew me when the police brought her to the Hall, and she would have identified me if Beauregard had not finished her. Others must have seen me about my nightwork—between Stride and Eddowes. I ran through the streets in a panic, bloodied and with a scalpel in my fist—and there is a not-bad description in the* Police Gazette—*There are so many fabulations about the Ripper—fuelled by still more silly notes to the press and police—that I can hide unnoticed among them, even if the occasional rumour strikes uncomfortably close.*

*A patient of mine, an uneducated immigrant named Kosminsky, confessed to me that he was Jack the Ripper, and I duly turned him over to Lestrade for examination. He showed me the file of similar confessions. And somewhere out there is the letter-writer, chortling over his silly red ink and arch jokes. George Lusk, chairman of the Vigilance Committee, was sent half a calf's kidney with a note headed "From Hell", claiming that the enclosure was from one of the dead women. "Tother piece I fried and ate, it was very nise."*

*I worry about Genevieve. Other vampires have a kind of red fog in their brains, but she is different. I read a piece by Henry Jekyll in* The Lancet—*speculating on the business of the vampire bloodline, as delicately as possible suggesting that there might be something impure about the royal strain the Prince Consort has imported. So many of Dracula's get are twisted, self-destructing creatures, torn apart by their changing bodies and uncontrollable desires. Royal blood, of course, is notoriously thin. And Jekyll has "disappeared". Lestrade denies that he has been carted off to Devil's Dyke, but many who dare venture an opinion against the Prince Consort seem to get lost in the fog.*

*I know what I do is right. I was right to save Lucy by cutting off her head, and I have been right to save the others. Nicholls, Schön, Stride, Eddowes. I am right.*

*But I shall stop.*

*I am an alienist, and Kelly has made me turn my look back upon myself. Is my behaviour so different from poor Renfield's, amassing his tiny deaths like a miser hoards pennies? Dracula made a freak of him, as he has made a monster of me.*

*And I am a monster. Jack the Ripper. I shall be classed with Sweeney Todd, Sawney Beane, Jonathan Wild, Billy Bonney and endlessly served up in the* Police Gazette *and* Famous Crimes: Past and Present—*Already, there are penny dreadfuls about Saucy Jack, Red Jack, Spring-Heel'd Jack, Bloody Jack. Soon, there will be music hall turns, sensational melodramas, a wax figure in Madame Tussaud's Chamber of Horrors.*

*I meant to destroy a monster, not to become one.*

*I have made Kelly tell me about Lucy. The story, I am no longer ashamed to realise, excites me. I cannot care for Kelly as herself, so I must care for her for Lucy's sake.*

*The Lucy I remember is smug and prim and properly flirtatious, delicately encouraging my attentions but then clumsily turning me away when Arthur dangled his title under her nose. Somewhere between that befuddling but enchanting girl and the screaming leech whose head I sawed free of its shoulders was the new-born who turned Kelly. Dracula's get. With each retelling of the nocturnal encounter on the Heath, Kelly adds new details. She either remembers more, or invents them for my sake.*

*I am not sure I care which.*

*Sometimes, Lucy's advances to Kelly are tender, seductive, mysterious, with heated caresses before the Dark Kiss. At other times, they are a brutal rape, with needle-teeth shredding flesh and muscle, pain mixed in with the pleasure.*

*We illustrate with our bodies Kelly's stories.*

*I can no longer remember the faces of the dead women. There is only Kelly's face. And that becomes more like Lucy with each passing night.*

*I have bought Kelly clothes similar to those Lucy wore. The nightgown she wears before we couple is very like the shroud in which Lucy was buried. Kelly styles her hair like Lucy's now. Her speech is improving, the Irish accent fading.*

*Soon, I hesitate to hope, Kelly will* be *Lucy.*

## XII

"It's been nearly a month, Charles," the vampire girl ventured, "perhaps it's over?"

Beauregard shook his head.

"No, Genevieve," he said, "Good things come to an end, bad things have to be stopped."

"You're right, of course."

It was well after dark, and they were in the Ten Bells. Beauregard was becoming as familiar with Whitechapel as he had with the other strange territories to which the Diogenes Club had despatched him. He spent his days asleep in Chelsea, and his nights in the East End, with Genevieve, hunting the Ripper. And not catching him.

Everyone was starting to relax. The vigilante groups who had roamed the streets two weeks ago, making mischief and abusing innocents, were still wearing their sashes and carrying coshes, but they spent more time in pubs than the fog. After a month of double- and triple-shifts, policemen were gradually being redistributed back to their regular duties. It was not as if the Ripper did anything to reduce crime elsewhere in the city.

A conspiracy against the Prince Consort had been exposed last week, and, outside Buckingham Palace, Van Helsing's head had company. Shaw, the socialist, was there, and an adventurous young man named Rassendyll. Among the conspirators had been a new-born or two, which added a new colour to the political spectrum. The police were required to exact reprisals upon the conspirators and their families. Devil's Dyke was overcrowded with agitators and insurrectionists. W. T. Stead, an editor who had spoken against the Prince Consort, had been dragged out of his offices by wolfish Carpathians, and torn apart for amusement.

Now, neither Genevieve nor Beauregard drank. They just watched the others. Beside the drunken vigilantes, the pub was full of women, either genuine prostitutes or police agents in disguise. That was one of the several daft schemes that had gone from being laughed at in Scotland Yard to being implemented.

In the Diogenes Club, there was talk of outright rebellion in India and the Far East. A reporter for the *Civil and Military Gazette* had tried to assassinate Varney during an official visit to Lahore, and he—at least—was still at liberty and plotting. Many in her dominions were ceasing to recognise the Queen as their rightful ruler, if only because they sensed that since her resurrection she had not truly worn the crown. Each week, more ambassadors were withdrawn from the Court of St James. The Turks, whose memories were longer than Beauregard had expected, were clamouring for reparations from the Prince Consort, with regard to crimes of war committed against them in the fifteenth century.

Beauregard tried to look at Genevieve without her noticing, without her penetrating his thoughts. In the light, she looked absurdly young. He had to be guarded with her. It was hard to keep his thoughts in rein, and impossible fully to trust any vampire.

"You're right," she said. "He's still out there. He hasn't given up."

"Perhaps the Ripper's taken a holiday?"

"Or been distracted."

"Some say he's a sea captain. He could be on a voyage."

Genevieve thought hard, then shook her head. "No. He's still here. I can sense it."

"You sound like Lees, the psychical fellow."

"It's part of what I am," she explained. "The Prince Consort shapeshifts, but I can sense things. It's to do with our bloodlines. There's a fog around everything, but I can feel the Ripper out there somewhere. He's not finished yet."

"This place is annoying me," he said. "Let's get out, and see if we can do some good."

They had been patrolling like policemen. When not following one of the innumerable false leads that cropped up daily in this case, they just wandered, hoping to come up against a man with a big bag of knives and darkness in his heart. It was absurd, when you thought about it.

"I'd like to call in on the Hall. Jack Seward has a new ladylove, and has been neglecting his duties."

They stood up, and he helped her arrange her cloak on her shoulders.

"Careless fellow," he observed.

"Not at all. He's just driven, obsessive. I'm glad he's found a distraction. He's been heading for a nervous collapse for years. He had a bad time of it when Vlad Tepes first came, I believe, although it's not something he cares to talk about much."

They pushed through the ornately-glassed doors and into the streets. Beauregard shivered in the cold, but Genevieve just breezed through the icy fog as if it were light spring sunshine. He had constantly to remind himself this sharp girl was not human.

Down the street stood a cab, the horse funnelling steam from its nostrils. Beauregard recognised the cabbie.

"What is it?" Genevieve asked, noticing his sudden tension.

"Recent acquaintances," he said.

The door drifted open, creating a swirl in the fog. Beauregard knew they were surrounded. The tramp huddled in the alleyway across the road, the idler hugging himself against the cold, the one he couldn't see in the shadows under the tobacconist's shop. He thumbed the catch of his cane, but did not think he could take them all and look after Genevieve.

Someone leaned out of the cab, and beckoned them. Beauregard, with casual care, walked over.

## XIII

"Genevieve Dieudonné," Beauregard introduced her, "Colonel Sebastian Moran, formerly of the First Bangalore Pioneers, author of *Heavy Game of the Western Himalayas*, and one of the greatest scoundrels unhanged . . ."

The new-born in the coach was an angry-looking brute, uncomfortable in evening dress, moustache bristling fiercely. When alive, he must have had the ruddy tan of an "Injah hand", but now he looked like a viper, poison sacs bulging under his chin.

Moran grunted something that might count as an acknowledgement, and ordered them to get into the coach.

Beauregard hesitated, then stepped back to allow her to go first. He was being clever, she realised. If the Colonel meant harm, he would keep an eye on the man he considered a threat. The new-born would not believe her four and a half centuries stronger than he. If it came to it, she could take him apart.

Genevieve sat opposite Moran, and Beauregard took the seat next to her. Moran tapped the roof, and the cab trundled off.

With the motion, the black-hooded bundle next to the Colonel nodded forwards, and had to be straightened up and leaned back.

"A friend?" Beauregard asked.

Moran snorted. Inside the bundle was a man, either dead or insensible.

"What would you say if I told you this was Jack the Ripper?"

"I suppose I'd have to take you seriously. I understand you only hunt the most dangerous game."

Moran grinned like a devil, tiger-fangs under his whiskers.

"Huntin' hunters," he said. "It's the only sport worth talkin' about."

"They say Quatermain and Roxton are better than you with a rifle, and that Russian general who uses the Tartar warbow is the best of all."

The Colonel brushed away the comparisons.

"They're all still warm."

Moran had a stiff arm out, holding back the clumsy bundle.

"We're on our own in this huntin' trip," he said. "The rest of them aren't in it."

Beauregard considered.

"It's been nearly a month since the last matter," the Colonel said, "Jack's finished. But that's not enough for us, is it? If business is to get back to the usual, Jack has to be seen to be finished."

They were near the river. The Thames was a sharp, foul undertaste in the air. All the filth of the city wound up in the river, and was disseminated into the seven seas. Garbage from Rotherhithe and Stepney drifted to Shanghai and Madagascar.

Moran got a grip on the black winding sheet, and wrenched it away from a pale, bloodied face. Genevieve recognised the man.

"Druitt," she said.

"Montague John Druitt, I believe," the Colonel said. "A colleague of yours, with very peculiar nocturnal habits."

This was not right.

Druitt's left eye opened in a rind of blood. He had been badly beaten, but was still alive.

"The police considered him early in the investigation," Beauregard said—a surprise to Genevieve—"but he was ruled out."

"He had easy access," Moran said, "Toynbee Hall is almost dead centre of the pattern made by the murder sites. He fits the popular picture, a crackpot toff with bizarre delusions. Nobody—begging your pardon, ma'am—really believes an educated man works among tarts and beggars out of Christian kindness. And nobody is goin' to object to Druitt hangin' for the slaughter of a handful of whores. He's not exactly royalty, is he? He don't even have an alibi for any of the killings."

"You evidently have close friends at the Yard?"

Moran flashed his feral grin again.

"So, do I extend my congratulations to you and your ladyfriend," the Colonel asked, "have you caught Jack the Ripper?"

Beauregard took a long pause and thought. Genevieve was confused, realising how much had been kept from her. Druitt was trying to say something, but his broken mouth couldn't frame words. The coach was thick with the smell of slick blood, and her own mouth was dry. She had not fed in too long.

"No," Beauregard said, "Druitt will not fit. He plays cricket."

"So does another blackguard I could name. That don't prevent him from bein' a filthy murderer."

"In this case, it does. On the mornings after the second and third and fourth murders, Druitt was on the field. After the double event, he made a half-century and took two wickets. I hardly think he could have managed that if he'd been up all night chasing and killing women."

Moran was not impressed.

"You're beginnin' to sound like that rotten detective. All clues and evidence and deductions. Druitt here is committin' suicide tonight, fillin' his pockets with stones and takin' a swim in the Thames. I dare say the body'll have been bashed about a bit before he's found. But before he does the deed, he'll leave behind a confession. And his handwritin' is goin' to look deuced like that on those bloody crank letters."

Moran made Druitt's head nod.

"It won't wash, Colonel. What if the real Ripper starts killing again?"

"Whores die, Beauregard. It happens often. We found one Ripper, we can always find another."

"Let me guess. Pedachenko, the Russian agent? The police considered him for a moment or two. Sir William Gull, the Queen's physician? The theosophist, Dr Donstan? The solicitor, Soames Forsyte? The cretin, Aron Kosminsky? Poor old Leather Apron

Pizer? Dr Jekyll? Prince Eddy? Walter Sickert? Dr Cream? It's a simple matter to put a scalpel into someone's hand and make him up for the part. But that won't stop the killing . . ."

"I didn't take you for such a fastidious sort, Beauregard. You don't mind servin' vampires, or – " a sharp nod at Genevieve "– consortin' with them. You may be warm, but you're chillin' by the hour. Your conscience lets you serve the Prince Consort . . ."

"I serve the Queen, Moran."

The Colonel started to laugh, but—after a flash of razor lightning in the dark of the cab—found Beauregard's sword-cane at his throat.

"I know a silversmith, too," Beauregard said. "Just like Jack."

Druitt tumbled off his seat, and Genevieve caught him. He was broken inside.

Moran's eyes glowed red in the gloom. The silvered length of steel held fast, its point dimpling the Colonel's adam's apple.

"I'm going to turn him," Genevieve said. "He's too badly hurt to be saved any other way."

Beauregard nodded to her, his hand steady.

With a nip, she bit into her wrist, and waited for the blood to well up. If Druitt could drink enough of her blood as she drained him, the transformation would begin.

It was a long time—centuries—since she had had any get. The years had made her cautious, or responsible.

"Another new-born," Moran snorted. "We should've been more selective when it all started."

"Drink," she cooed.

What did she really know about Montague John Druitt? Like her, he was a lay practitioner, not a doctor but with some medical knowledge. She did not even know why a man with some small income and position should want to work in Toynbee Hall. He was not an obsessive philanthropist, like Seward. He was not a religious man, like Booth. Genevieve had taken him for granted as a useful pair of hands. Now, she was going to have to take responsibility for him, possibly for ever.

If he became a monster, like Vlad Tepes or even like Colonel Sebastian Moran, then it would be her fault. She would be killing all the people Druitt killed.

And he had been a suspect. Even if innocent, there was something about Druitt that had made him seem a likely Ripper.

"Drink," she said, forcing the word from her mouth. Her wrist was dripping red.

She held her hand to Druitt's mouth. Her incisors slid from their gumsheaths, and she dipped her head. The scent of Druitt's blood was stinging in her nostrils.

Druitt had a convulsion, and she realised his need was urgent. If he did not drink her blood now, he would die.

She touched her wrist to his mashed lips. He flinched away, trembling.

"No," he gargled, refusing her gift, "no . . ."

A shudder of disgust ran through him, and he died.

"Not everybody wants to live forever at any price," Moran observed. "What a waste."

Genevieve reached across the space between them, and backhanded the Colonel across the face, knocking away Beauregard's cane.

Moran's red eyes shrank, and she could tell he was afraid of her. She was still hungry, having allowed the red thirst to rise in her. She could not drink Druitt's spoiled dead blood. She could not even drink Moran's second- or third-hand blood. But she could relieve her frustration by ripping meat off his face.

"Call her off," Moran spluttered.

One of her hands was at his throat, the other was drawn back, the fingers gathered into a point, sharp talons bunched like an arrowhead. It would be so easy to put a hole in Moran's face.

"It's not worth it," Beauregard said. Somehow, his words cut through her crimson rage, and she held back. "He may be a worm, but he has friends, Genevieve. Friends you wouldn't want to make enemies of."

Her teeth slipped back into her gums, and her sharpened fingernails settled. She was still itchy for blood, but she was in control again.

Beauregard nodded, and Moran had the coach stop.

The Colonel, his new-born's confidence in shreds, was shaking as they stepped down. A trickle of blood leaked from one eye. Beauregard sheathed his cane, and Moran wrapped a scarf around his pricked neck.

"Quatermain wouldn't have flinched, Colonel," Beauregard said. "Good night, and give my regards to the Professor."

Moran turned his face away into the darkness, and the cab wheeled away from the pavement, rushing into the fog.

Genevieve's head was spinning.

They were back where they had started. Near the Ten Bells. The pub was no quieter now than when they left. Women loitered by the doors, strutting for passersby.

Her mouth hurt, and her heart was hammering. She made fists, and tried to shut her eyes.

Beauregard held his wrist to her mouth.

"Here," he said, "take what you need."

A rush of gratitude made her ankles weak. She almost swooned, but at once dispelled the fog in her mind, concentrating on her need.

She bit him gently, and took as little as possible to slake the red thirst. His blood trickled down her throat, calming her, giving her strength. When it was over, she asked him if it were his first time, and he nodded.

"It's not unpleasant," he commented, neutrally.

"It can be less formal," she said. "Eventually."

"Good night, Genevieve," he said, turning away. He walked into the fog, and left her, his blood still on her lips.

She realised she knew as little about Charles Beauregard as she had about Druitt. He had never really told her why he was interested in the Ripper. Or why he continued to serve his vampire queen.

For a moment, she was frightened. Everyone around her wore a mask, and behind that mask might be . . .

Anything.

## XIV

She was who-the-bloody-ever she wanted to be, whoever *men* wanted her to be. Mary Jane, Marie Jeanette. Or Lucy. She would be Ellen Terry if she had to. Or Queen Victoria.

He sat by her bedside now.

She was telling him again how she had been turned. How his Lucy had come out of the night for her on the Heath, and given her the Dark Kiss. Only now, she was telling him as if she were Lucy, and Mary Jane some other person, some worthless whore . . .

"I was so cold, John, so hungry, so *new* . . ."

It was easy to know how Lucy had felt. She had felt the same when she woke from her deep sleep. Only Lucy had woke in a crypt, respectfully laid out. Mary Jane had been on a cart, minutes away from a lime pit. One of the unclaimed dead.

"She was warm, plump, alive, blood pounding in her sweet neck."

He was listening now, nodding his head. She supposed he was mad. But he was a gentleman. And he was good to her, good for her.

"The children hadn't been enough."

Mary Jane had been confused by the new desires. It had taken her weeks to adjust. She had ripped open dogs for their juice. She had not known enough to stay out of the sun, and her skin had turned to painful crackling.

But that was like a dream now. She was beginning to lose Mary Jane's memories. She was Lucy.

"I needed her, John. I needed her blood."

He sat by her bed, reserved and doctorly. Later, she would pleasure him. And she would drink from him.

Each time she drank, she became less Mary Jane and more Lucy. It must be something in his blood.

Since her rebirth, the mirror in her room was useless to her. No one had ever bothered to sketch her picture, so she could easily forget her own face. He had pictures of Lucy, looking like a little girl dressed up in her mother's clothes, and it was Lucy's face she imagined her eyes looked out of.

"I beckoned her from the path," she said, leaning over from the pile of pillows on the bed, her face close to his. "I sang under my breath, and I waved to her. I *wished* her to me, and she came . . ."

She stroked his cheek, and laid her head against his chest.

He was holding his breath, sweating a little, his posture awkward. She could soon make him unbend.

"There were red eyes in front of me, and a voice calling me. I left the path, and she was waiting. It was a cold night, but she wore only a white shift. Her skin was white in the moonlight. Her . . ."

She caught herself.

Mary Jane, she said inside, be careful . . .

He stood up, gently pushing her away, and walked across the room. Taking a grip of her washstand, he looked at himself in the mirror, trying to find something in his reflection.

She was confused. All her life, she had been giving men what they wanted. Now she was dead, and things were the same.

She went to him, and hugged him from behind. He jumped at her touch, surprised.

Of course, he had not seen her coming.

"John," she cooed at him, "come to bed, John. Make me warm."

He pushed her away again, roughly this time. She was not used to her vampire's strength. Imagining herself still a feeble girl, she was one, a reed easy to break.

"Lucy," he said, emptily, not to her . . .

Anger sparked in her mind.

"I'm not your bloody Lucy Westenra," she shouted. "I'm Mary Jane Kelly, and I don't care who knows it."

"No," he said, reaching into his jacket for something, gripping it hard, "you're not Lucy . . ."

## XV

Her touch had changed him. Beauregard had been troubled by

dreams since that night. Dreams in which Genevieve Dieudonné, sometimes herself and sometimes a needle-fanged cat, lapped at his blood.

He supposed it had always been in the cards. With the way things were, he would have been tapped by a vampire sooner or later. He was luckier than most, to have given his blood freely rather than have it taken by force.

The fog was thick tonight. And the November cold was like the caress of a razor. Or a scalpel.

Genevieve had taken from him, but given something in return. Something of herself.

He stood outside Toynbee Hall, on the point of entering. He had been here for half an hour. Nothing was that urgent.

She was inside. He *knew*.

He was afraid he wanted her to drink from him again. Not the simple thirst-slaking of an opened wrist, but the full embrace of the Dark Kiss. Genevieve Dieudonné was an extraordinary woman by the standards of any age. Together, they could live through the centuries.

It was a temptation.

A gaudily-painted child, unable to close her mouth over her new teeth, sauntered up to him, and lifted her skirts. He brushed her aside and, sulking, she retreated.

He remembered his duty.

For nearly a fortnight, duty had made him stay away from Toynbee Hall. Now, duty brought him back here.

At the Diogenes Club, he had received a brief note of apology from the Professor, informing him that Colonel Moran had been rebuked for his ill-advised actions. That could hardly be a comfort to Montague Druitt, who had washed ashore at Deptford days ago, face eaten away by fish.

Yet Moran had said something which still ticked away in the back of Beauregard's mind.

Genevieve's lips had been cool, her touch gentle, her tongue roughly pleasant as a cat's. The draining of his blood, so slow and so tender, had been an exquisite sensation, instantly addictive . . .

Toynbee Hall was named for its philanthropic founder. It was a mission to Whitechapel, Arnold Toynbee had said the Britishers of the East End were far more in need of Christian attention than the heathen Africans with whom Dr Livingstone had been so concerned.

The Hall was in the centre of the pattern of the Ripper murders.

Finally, Beauregard overcame his languid confusion, and spurred himself to action. He walked across the narrow street, and slipped into the Hall.

A warm matron sat at a reception desk, devouring the latest Marie Corelli, *Thelma*. Beauregard understood that since she became a new-born, the celebrated authoress's prose style had deteriorated still further. Genevieve had remarked once that vampires were never very creative, all their energies being diverted into the simple prolonging of life.

"Where is Mademoiselle Dieudonné?"

"She is filling in for the director, sir. She should be in Dr Seward's office."

"Thank you."

"Shall you be wanting to be announced?"

"No need to bother, thank you."

The matron frowned, and mentally added another complaint to a list she was keeping of Things Wrong With That Vampire Girl. Beauregard was briefly surprised to be party to her clear and vinegary thoughts, but swept that distraction aside as he made his way to the director's first floor office.

Genevieve was surprised to see him.

"Charles," she said.

She sat at Seward's desk, papers strewn about her. He fancied she was startled, as if found prying where she was not wanted.

"Where have you been?"

He had no answer.

Looking around the room, his eyes were drawn to a device in a glass dust-case. It was an affair of brass boxes, with a large trumpet-like attachment.

"This is an Edison-Bell phonograph, is it not?"

"Jack uses it for medical notes. He has a passion for tricks and toys."

He turned.

"Genevieve . . ."

She was near, now. He had not heard her come out from behind the desk.

"It's all right, Charles. I didn't mean to bewitch you. The symptoms will recede in a week or two. Believe me, I have experience with your condition."

"It's not that . . ."

He could not think along a straight line of reasoning. Butterfly insights fluttered in the back of his mind, never quite caught.

By an effort of will, he concentrated on the pressing matter of the Ripper.

"Why Whitechapel?" he asked. "Why not Soho, or Hyde Park, or anywhere? Vampirism is not limited to this district, nor prostitution. The Ripper hunts here because it is most convenient, because he *is* here. Somewhere, near . . ."

"I've been looking over our records," she said, tapping the pile on the desk. "The victims were all brought in at one time or another."

"It all comes back to Toynbee Hall by so many routes. Druitt and you work here, Stride was brought here, the killings are in a ring about the address, all the dead women were here . . ."

"Could Moran have been right? Could it have been Druitt? There have been no more murders."

Beauregard shook his head. "It's not over yet."

"If only Jack were here."

He made a fist. "We'd have the murderer then."

"No. I mean Jack Seward. He treated all the women. He might know if they had something in common."

Genevieve's words sank into his brain, and lightning swarmed behind his eyes. Suddenly, he *knew* . . .

"They had Dr Seward in common."

"But . . ."

"Dr *Jack* Seward."

She shook her head, but he could tell she was seeing what he saw, coming quickly to a realisation.

They both remembered Elizabeth Stride grasping Dr Seward's ankle. She had been trying to tell them something.

"Are there diaries around here?" Beauregard asked. "Private records, notes, anything? These maniacs are often compelled to keep souvenirs, keepsakes, memorabilia . . ."

"I've been through all his files tonight. They contain only the usual material."

"Locked drawers?"

"No, Only the phonograph cabinet. The wax cylinders are delicate and have to be protected from dust."

Beauregard wrenched the cover off the contraption, and pulled open the drawer of the stand. Its fragile lock splintered.

The cylinders were ranked in tubes, with neatly-inked labels.

"*Nicholls*," he read aloud, "*Schön Stride/Eddowes, Kelly, Kelly, Kelly, Lucy* . . ."

Genevieve was by him, delving deeper into the drawer.

"And these . . . *Lucy, Van Helsing, Renfield, Lucy's Tomb*."

Everyone remembered Van Helsing, and Beauregard even knew Renfield was the Prince Consort's martyred disciple in London. But . . .

"Kelly and Lucy. Who are they? Unknown victims?"

Genevieve was going again through the papers on the desk. She talked as she sorted.

"Lucy, at a guess, was Lucy Westenra, Vlad Tepes' first English conquest, the first of his bloodline here. Dr Van Helsing destroyed her, and Jack Seward, I'll wager, was in with Van Helsing's crowd. As for Kelly . . . well, we have lots of Kellys on our books. But only one who fits our Jack's requirements. Here."

She handed him a sheet of paper, with the details of a patient's treatment.

Kelly, Mary Jane. 13, Miller's Court.

# XVI

"Fucking Hell," said Beauregard.

Genevieve had to agree with him.

The stench of dead blood hit her in the stomach like a fist, and she had to hold the doorframe to keep from fainting. She had seen the leavings of murderers before, and blood-muddied battlefields, and plague holes, and torture chambers, and execution sites.

But 13, Miller's Court, was the worst of all.

Dr Seward knelt in the middle of the red ruin barely recognisable as a human being. He was still working, his apron and shirtsleeves dyed red, his silver scalpel flickering in the firelight as he made further pointless incisions.

Mary Kelly's room was a typical cramped lodging. A bed, a chair and a fireplace, with barely enough floor to walk around the bed. Seward's operations had spread the girl across the bed and the floor, and around the walls up to the height of three feet. The cheap muslin curtains were speckled with halfpenny-size dots.

In the grate, a bundle still burned, casting a red light that seared into Genevieve's night-sensitive eyes.

Seward did not seem overly concerned with their intrusion.

"Nearly done," he said, lifting out an eyeball from a pie-shaped expanse that had once been a face, and snipping deftly through the optic nerves. "I have to be sure Lucy is dead. Van Helsing says her soul will not rest until she is truly dead."

He was calm, not ranting.

Beauregard had his pistol out and aimed.

"Put down the knife, and step away from her," he said.

Seward placed the knife on the bedspread, and stood up, wiping his hands on an already-bloody patch of apron.

Mary Kelly was truly dead. Genevieve had no doubt about that.

"It's over," Seward said. "We've beaten him. We've beaten Dracula. The foul contagion cannot spread further."

Genevieve had nothing to say. Her stomach was still a tight fist.

Seward seemed to see Genevieve for the first time.

"Lucy," he said, seeing someone else, somewhere else. "Lucy, it was all for you . . ."

He bent to pick up his scalpel, and Beauregard shot him. In the shoulder.

Seward spun around, his fingers grasping air, and slammed against the wall. He pressed his gloved hand to the wall, and sank downwards, his knees protruding as he tried to make his body shrink. In the wall, a scrap of silver shone where Beauregard's bullet had lodged.

Genevieve had snatched the weapon away from the bed. Its silver blade itched, but she held it by the enamelled grip. It was such a small thing to have done so much damage.

"The shot will have alerted people," Beauregard said. "We have to get him out of here. A mob would tear him apart."

Genevieve hauled Seward upright, and between them they got him into the street. His clothes were sticky and tacky from the drying, foul-smelling gore.

It was nearing morning, and Genevieve was suddenly tired. The cold air did not dispel the throbbing in her head. The image of 13, Miller's Court was imprinted in her mind like a photograph upon paper. She would never, she thought, lose it.

Seward was easy to manipulate. He would walk with them to a police station, or to Hell.

From Hell, that's where the letters had come.

## XVII

As soon as they were out of the charnel house, Beauregard made his decision. The women were dead, and Seward was mad. No justice could be served by turning him over to Lestrade.

"Hold him up, Genevieve," he said. "Against the wall."

She knew what he was about, and gave her consent. Seward was propped against the wall of the alley. His face was wearily free of expression. Blood dribbled from his wound.

Beauregard drew his swordcane. The rasp cut through the tiny nightsounds.

"He bit me," the Ripper said, remembering some trivial incident, "the madman bit me."

Seward held out his gloved, swollen hand.

Genevieve nodded, and Beauregard slipped his blade through Seward's heart. The point scraped brickwork. Beauregard withdrew the sword, and sheathed it.

Seward, cleanly dead, crumpled.

"The Prince Consort would have made him immortal, just so he could torture him forever," he said.

Genevieve agreed with him.

"He was mad and not responsible."

"Then who," he asked, "was responsible?"

"The thing who drove him mad."

Beauregard looked up. A cloud had passed from the face of the moon, and it shone down through the thinning fog.

He fancied he had seen a bat, large and black, flitting up in the stratosphere.

His duty was not yet discharged.

## XVIII

The Queen's carriage had called for her at Toynbee Hall, and a fidgety coachman named Netley was delicately negotiating the way through the cramped streets of Whitechapel. Netley had already picked up Beauregard, from the Diogenes Club. The huge black horse and its discreetly imposing burden would feel less confined once they were on the wider thoroughfares of the city. Now, the carriage was like a panther in Hampton Court Maze, prowling rather than moving as elegantly and speedily as it was meant to. In the night, hostile eyes were aimed at the black coach, and at the coat of arms it bore.

Genevieve noticed Beauregard was somewhat subdued. She had seen him several times since the night of November 9th. Since 13, Miller's Court. She had even been admitted into the hallowed chambers of the Diogenes Club, to give evidence to a private hearing at which Beauregard was called upon to give an account of the death of Dr Seward. She understood the secret ways of government, and realised this tribunal had as much to do with deciding which truths should be concealed as which should be presented to the public at large. The chairman, a venerable and warm diplomat who had weathered many changes of government, took everything in, but gave out no verdict, simply absorbing the information, as each grain of truth shaped the policies of a club that was often more than a club. There were few vampires in the Diogenes Club, and Genevieve wondered whether it might not be a hiding place for the pillars of the *ancien régime* or a nest of insurrectionists.

An engraved invitation to the Palace had been delivered personally into her hand. As acting director of the Hall, she was busier than ever. A new strain of plague was running through the new-borns of Whitechapel, triggering off their undisciplined shapeshifting powers, creating a horde of short-lived, agonised freaks. But a summons from the Queen and the Prince Consort was not to be ignored.

Presumably, they were to be honoured for their part in ending the career of Jack the Ripper. A private honour, perhaps, but an honour nevertheless.

Genevieve wondered if Beauregard would be proud to meet his sovereign, or if her current state would sadden him. She had heard stories of the situation inside the Palace. And she knew more of Vlad Tepes than most. Among vampires, he had always been the Man Who Would Be King.

The carriage passed through Fleet Street—past the boarded-up and burned-out offices of the nation's great newspapers—and the Strand. There was no fog tonight, just an icy wind.

It had been generally decided, in the ruling cabal of the Diogenes Club, that the identity of the murderer should be witheld, although it was common knowledge that his crimes had come to an end. Arrangements had been made at Scotland Yard, the Commissioner's resignation exchanged for an overseas posting, and Lestrade and Abberline were on fresh cases. Nothing much had changed, Whitechapel was hunting a new madman now, a murderer of brutish disposition and appearance named Edward Hyde who had trampled a small child and then raised his ambitions by shoving a broken walking-stick through the heart of a new-born Member of Parliament. Once he was stopped, another murderer would come along, and another, and another . . .

In Trafalgar Square, there were bonfires. The red light filled the carriage as they passed Nelson's Column. The police kept dousing the fires, but insurrectionists started them up again. Scraps of wood were smuggled in. Items of clothing even were used to fuel the fires. Newborns were superstitiously afraid of fire, and did not like to get too close.

Beauregard looked out with interest at the blazes, heaped around the stone lions. Originally a memorial to the victims of Bloody Sunday, they had a new meaning now. News had come through from India, where there had been another mutiny, with many warm British troops and officials throwing in their lot with the natives. Sir Francis Varney, the unpopular vampire Viceroy, had been dragged from his hiding place at the Red Fort in Delhi by a mob and cast into just such a fire, burned down to ash and bones. The colony was in open revolt. And there were stirrings in Africa and Points East.

Crowds were scuffling by the fires, one of the Prince Consort's Carpathian Guard tossing warm young men about while the Fire Brigade perhaps half-heartedly, tried to train their horses. Placards were waved and slogans shouted.

JACK STILL RIPS, a graffito read.

The letters were still coming, the red-inked scrawls signed "Jack the Ripper". Now, they called for the warm to rally against their vampire masters. Whenever a new-born was killed, "Jack the Ripper" took the credit. Beauregard had said nothing, but Genevieve suspected that the letters were issued from the Diogenes Club. She saw that a dangerous game was being played in the halls of secret government, factions conspiring against each other, with the ruination of the Prince Consort as an end. Dr Seward might have been mad, but his work had not been entirely wasteful. Even if a monster became a hero, a new Guy Fawkes, a purpose was being served.

She was a vampire, but she was not of the bloodline of Vlad Tepes. That left her, as ever, on the sidelines of history. She had no real interest either way. It had been refreshing for a while not to have to pretend to be warm, but the Prince Consort's regime made things uncomfortable for most of the un-dead. For every noble vampire in his town house, with a harem of willing blood-slaves, there were twenty of Mary Kelly, Lilly, or Cathy Eddowes, as miserable as they had ever been, their vampire attributes addictions and handicaps rather than powers and potentials.

The carriage, able to breathe at last, rolled down the Mall towards Buckingham Palace. Insurrectionist leaders hung in chains from cruciform cages lining the road, some still barely alive. Within the last three nights, an open battle had raged in St James's Park, between the warm and the dead.

"Look," Beauregard said, sadly, "there's Van Helsing's head."

Genevieve craned her neck and saw the pathetic lump on the end of its raised pike. The story was that Abraham Van Helsing was still alive, in the Prince Consort's thrall, raised high so that his eyes might see the reign of Dracula over London. The story was a lie. What was left was a fly-blown skull, hung with ragged strips.

They were at the Palace. Two Carpathians, in midnight black uniforms slashed with crimson, hauled the huge ironwork frames aside as if they were silk curtains.

The exterior of the Palace was illuminated. The Union Jack flew, and the Crest of Dracula.

Beauregard's face was a blank.

The carriage pulled up at the entrance, and a footman opened the door, Genevieve stepped down first, and Beauregard followed.

She had selected a simple dress, having nothing better and knowing finery had never suited her. He wore his usual evening dress, and handed his cape and cane to the servant who took her cloak. A Carpathian, his face a mask of stiff hair, stood by to watch him hand over his cane. He turned over his revolver too. Silver bullets were frowned on at the Court. Smithing with silver was punishable by death.

The Palace's doors were hauled open in lurches, and a strange creature—a tailored parti-coloured suit emphasising the extensive and grotesque malformations of his body, growths the size of loaves sprouting from his torso, his huge head a knotted turnip in which human features were barely discernible—admitted them. Genevieve was overwhelmed with pity for the man, perceiving at once that this was a warm human being not the fruit of some catastrophically failed attempt at shapeshifting.

Beauregard nodded to the servant, and said "Good evening. Merrick, is it not?"

A smile formed somewhere in the doughy expanses of Merrick's face, and he returned the greeting, his words slurred by excess slews of flesh around his mouth.

"And how is the Queen this evening?"

Merrick did not reply, but Genevieve imagined she saw an expression in the unreadable map of his features. There was a sadness in his single exposed eye, and a grim set to his lips.

Beauregard gave Merrick a card, and said "Compliments of the Diogenes Club." Something conspiratorial passed between the perfectly-groomed gentleman-adventurer and the hideously deformed servant.

Merrick lead them down the hallway, hunched over like a gorilla, using one long arm to propel his body. He had one normal arm, which stuck uselessly from his body, penned in by lumpy swellings.

Obviously, it amused Vlad Tepes to keep this poor creature as a pet. He had always had a fondness for freaks and sports.

Merrick knocked on a door.

"Genevieve," Beauregard said, voice just above a whisper, "if what I do brings harm to you, I am sincerely sorry."

She did not understand him. As her mind raced to catch up with him, he leaned over and kissed her, on the mouth, the warm way. She tasted him, and was reminded. The sharing of blood had established a link between them.

The kiss broke, and he stood back, leaving her baffled. Then a door was opened, and they were admitted into the Royal Presences.

Nothing had prepared her for the sty the throne-room had become. Dilapidated beyond belief, its once-fine walls and paintings torn and stained, with the stench of dried blood and human ordure thick in the air, the room was ill-lit by battered chandeliers, and full of people and animals. Laughter and whimpering competed, and the marble floors were thick with filthy discharges. An armadillo rolled by, its rear-parts clogged with its own dirt.

Merrick announced them, his palate suffering as he got their names out. Someone made a crude remark, and gales of laughter cut through the din, then were cut off at a wave of the Prince Consort's ham-sized hand.

Vlad Tepes sat upon the throne, massive as a commemorative statue, his face enormously bloated, rich red under withered grey. Stinking moustaches hung to his chest, stiff with recent blood, and his black-stubbled chin was dotted with the gravy-stains of his last feeding. An ermine-collared cloak clung to his shoulders like the wings of a giant bat; otherwise, he was naked, his body thickly-coated with matted hair, blood and filth clotting on his chest and limbs. His white manhood, tipped scarlet as an adder's tongue, lay coiled like a snake in his lap. His body was swollen like a leech's, his rope-thick veins visibly pulsing.

Beauregard shook in the presence, the smell smiting him like blows. Genevieve held him up, and looked around the room.

"I never dreamed . . ." he muttered, "never . . ."

A warm girl ran across the room, pursued by one of the Carpathians, his uniform in tatters. He brought her down with a swipe of a bear-paw, and began to tear at her back and sides with triple-jointed jaws, taking meat as well as drink.

The Prince Consort smiled.

The Queen was kneeling by the throne, a silver spiked collar around her neck, a massive chain leading from it to a loose bracelet upon Dracula's wrist. She was in her shift and stockings, brown hair loose, blood on her face. It was impossible to see the round old woman she had been in this abused girl. Genevieve hoped she was mad, but feared she was only too well aware of what was going on about her. She turned away, not looking at the Carpathian's meal.

"Majesties," Beauregard said, bowing his head.

Vlad Tepes laughed, an enormous farting sound exploding from his jaggedly-fanged maw. The stench of his breath filled the room. It was everything dead and rotten.

A fastidiously-dressed vampire youth, an explosion of lace escaping at his collar from the tight black shine of his velvet suit, explained to the Prince Consort who these guests were. Genevieve recognised the Prime Minister, Lord Ruthven.

"These are the heroes of Whitechapel," the English vampire said, a fluttering handkerchief before his mouth and nose.

The Prince Consort grinned ferociously, eyes burning like crimson furnaces, moustaches creaking like leather straps.

"The lady and I are acquainted," he said, in surprisingly perfect and courteous English. "We met at the home of the Countess Dolingen of Graz, some hundred years ago."

Genevieve remembered well. The Countess, a snob beyond the grave, had summoned what she referred to as the un-dead aristocracy. The Karnsteins of Styria had been there, pale and uninteresting, and several of Vlad Tepes's Transylvanian associates, Princess Vajda, Countess Bathory, Count Iorga, Count Von Krolock. Also Saint-Germain from France, Villanueva from Spain, Duval from Mexico. At that gathering, Vlad Tepes had seemed an ill-mannered upstart, and his proposition of a vampire crusade, to subjugate petty humanity under his standard, had been ignored. Since then, Genevieve had done her best to avoid other vampires.

"You have served us well, Englishman," the Prince Consort said, praise sounding like a threat.

Beauregard stepped forward.

"I have a gift, majesties," he said, "a souvenir of our exploit in the East End."

Vlad Tepes's eyes gleamed with lust. At heart, he had the philistine avarice of a true barbarian. Despite his lofty titles, he was barely a generation away from the mountain bully-boys his ancestors had been. He liked nothing more than pretty things. Bright, shining toys.

Beauregard took something from his inside pocket, and unwrapped a cloth from it.

Silver shone.

Everyone in the throne room was quieted. Vampires had been feeding in the shadows, noisily suckling the flesh of youths and girls. Carpathians had been grunting their simple language at each other. All went silent.

Fury twisted the Prince Consort's brow, but then contempt and mirth turned his face into a wide-mouthed mask of obscene enjoyment.

Beauregard held Dr Seward's silver scalpel. He had taken it from Genevieve that night. As evidence, she thought.

"You think you can defy me with that tiny needle, Englishman?"

"It is a gift," Beauregard replied. "But not for you."

Genevieve was edging away, uncertain. The Carpathians had detached themselves from their amusements, and were forming a half circle around Beauregard. There was no one between Beauregard and the throne, but, if he made a move towards the Prince Consort, a wall of solid vampireflesh and bone would form.

"For my Queen," Beauregard said, tossing the knife.

Genevieve saw the silver reflect in Vlad Tepes's eyes, as anger exploded dark in the pupils. Then Victoria snatched the tumbling scalpel from the air . . .

It had all been for this moment, all to get Beauregard into the Royal Presence, all to serve this one duty. Genevieve, the taste of him in her mouth, understood.

Victoria slipped the blade under her breast, stapling her shift to her ribs, puncturing her heart. For her, it was over quickly.

With a look of triumph and joy, she fell from her dais, blood gouting from her fatal wound, and rolled down the steps, chain clanking with her.

Vlad Tepes—Prince Consort no more—was on his feet, cloak rippling around him like a thundercloud. Tusklike teeth exploded from his face, and his hands became spear-tipped clusters. Beauregard, Genevieve realised, was dead. But the monster's power was dealt a blow from which it could never recover. The Empire Vlad Tepes had usurped would rise against him. He had grown too arrogant.

The Carpathians were on Beauregard already, talons and mouths red and digging.

Genevieve thought she was to die too. Beauregard had tried to keep her from harm by not involving her in his designs. But she had been too stubborn, had insisted on being here, on seeing Vlad Tepes in the lair he had made for himself.

He came down from his throne for her, foul steam pouring from his mouth and nostrils.

But she was older than him. Less blinded by the ignorance of his selfish fantasies. For centuries, he had thought himself special, as a higher being apart from humanity, while she knew she was just a tick in the hide of the warm.

She ducked under his hands, and was not there when he overbalanced, falling to the floor like a felled tree, marble cracking under his face. He was slow in his age, in his bloated state. Too much indulgence. Too much isolation. Veins in his neck burst, spurting blood, and knitted together again.

While Vlad Tepes was scrambling to right himself, the rest of his court were in confusion. Some returned to their bloody pleasure, some fell insensate.

She could do nothing for Beauregard.

Ruthven was uncertain. With the Queen truly dead, things were going to change. He could have barred her way from the palace, but he hesitated—ever the politician—then stood aside.

Merrick had the doors open for her, and she escaped from the infernal heat and stench of the throne-room. He then slammed the doors shut, and put his back to them. He had been part of Beauregard's conspiracy, also willing to give his life for his sovereign. He nodded to the main doors, and made a long howl that might have meant "go."

She saluted the man, and ran from the Palace. Outside, in the night, fires were burning high. The news would soon be spreading.

A spark had touched the gunpowder keg.

# PETER ATKINS

## Aviatrix

PETER ATKINS was born in Liverpool in 1955—a year of birth he is proud to share with Disneyland, rock 'n' roll, and the movies *This Island Earth* and *Kiss Me Deadly*. For six years he acted with Clive Barker's experimental theatre group, The Dog Company, and then trod the boards for another half-decade, this time as composer, musician and singer with a band called The Chase. For twenty years he has been convinced that Buster Keaton is God.

Atkins is best known to horror fans for his movie scripts for *Hellbound: Hellraiser II* (1988) and *Hellraiser III: Hell on Earth* (1992), both based on concepts created by his old school-chum Barker.

However, he is also the author of *Morningstar*, an assured first novel which combines vampires and serial killers; his short fiction has been published in *Fear* and *Demons and Deviants*; he has contributed scripts to Epic's *Hellraiser* comic books and graphic novels, and has written two teleplays for Propaganda Films' *Inside-Out* TV series. His work has also appeared in the non-fiction volumes *Clive Barker's Shadows In Eden*, *Cut! Horror Writers on Horror Film*, *Pandemonium* and *The Hellraiser Chronicles*. Current projects include writing *Hellraiser IV* as well as an epic Egyptian fantasy/adventure co-scripted with director Anthony Hickox, and a new novel.

All you need to know about "Aviatrix" is explained by the author in his *Afterword* . . .

## I

WAY HE FIGURED IT WAS THIS. You go up in one of those things, it's going to crash. It crashes, you're going to die. You're going to die, what the hell's stopping you from going to Stan's Corner Donuts in Westwood Village three hours before check-in at LAX and eating your way through five Maple Bars? Shit, you'd be cinders and memory long before that superlative sweetness transformed itself into inches and artery-closure so who cared?

## II

He actually settled for three. He wasn't hedging his bets on survival or anything, it was just that three really were enough. Finishing the third, filling his mouth with the last two inches of maple-flavored frosting and soft warm dough, was the optimum point of pleasure. Starting another would undercut the sensual perfection. Better to stop. But God, they were good. Sugar and fat. It didn't get any better. The Western World had reached apotheosis at the moment that combinations of those two foodstuffs became readily available to anyone with half an income. Keep your Beethoven. Fuck your Goya. Sugar and Fat. That was culture.

"You wanna refill on the coffee, Steve?"

Dyson looked over his shoulder to the counter. His name wasn't Steve but he was the only customer in there so he figured it was him who was being asked.

"No. No thanks. I'm fine."

The guy behind the counter—young, long-haired, *loud* shirt—grinned.

"Can't be fine, Steve. Three donuts. Gotta be some kind of oral compensation going on."

Dyson (still not Steve, still Jonathan) hesitated. He'd always hated people guessing things about him, hated more the readiness of some strangers to break the social contract of silence with which we surround such guesses. Nevertheless, he answered. Probably because he also hated appearing to care.

"Flying," he said, "Hate it. Every time I *know* I'm going to die."

"And every time you haven't."

"God's oversight. Or his little joke."

"False sense of security thing?"

"Something like that."

"Get you to where you think maybe, just maybe, this is gonna be alright then—*bam*! Gotcha! Yeah?"

"Something like that."

"Don't wanna burst your bubble, Steve . . . but you're probably not that important. Know what I mean?"

"Oh, I don't feel special or anything. I . . ."

"You figure the joke's on all of us. 'As flies to wanton boys are we to the gods. They kill us for their sport.' Macbeth."

"Lear."

"What?"

"It's Lear. King Lear. Not Macbeth."

"Oh. Whatever. It's still bullshit. They've got better things to do."

"Yeah?"

"Yeah. Like watching us learn to fly. And being proud of us."

Dyson paused before replying, filling the silence by draining his cup of what little coffee remained. He looked over the styrofoam lip at the counterman, at his flawless young face, at his open smile. He didn't need this. He came to Stan's for donuts not facile New Age optimism. Worse; he'd conversed. Next time he came in and this guy was working there was a ready-made opening for more conversation. He hated that. Donuts were private. Stan's was ruined for him.

He put the cup down beside the wax-paper and crumpled napkins, mumbled a mock high-spirited hope-you're-right-see-ya, hefted up his on-flight bag, and left. It was only when he reached the taxi-rank at the corner of Westwood and Lindbrook that he realised he'd assumed there would be a Next Time at Stan's. The sudden anger he felt at the counterman for tricking him into such an expectation was subsumed in the nauseating warmth of the anxiety rush that flooded his system as punishment for hope. His legs were weak as he grinned inanely at the driver of the first cab in line and let himself into the back seat.

"Hi. Howya doin'?" he said, in response to the driver's enquiring eyes in the rear-view mirror. "LAX please."

## III

Dyson was always very strict with himself about when he could take the valium. Before check-in was no good—you might find out there that the flight was delayed and thus have wasted one of the precious little pills (increasingly harder to get because stupid doctors thought beta-blockers were healthier. Healthier! *Who fucking cares*?!)—but, equally, you didn't want to wait too long after getting your boarding pass—take-off was the worst part and God forbid you should be hurtled down that runway still waiting for the drug to kick in, embarrassing yourself and disturbing other passengers with your moans and copious sweating. No, there was a five or ten minute window immediately after check-in during which a bar could be found, a large scotch on the rocks ordered, a ten-milligram placed on the tongue, and the liquor swallowed in a single gulp, carrying the pill with it.

Dyson had done all that and was now strapped in his window seat pretending to read the airline's magazine. He glanced at his watch. Takeoff was in fifteen minutes. But he wasn't waiting for takeoff. He was waiting for that first evidence of the drug's efficacy, the half-sleep he always fell into immediately before the plane taxied. Mustn't prompt it, he thought, and looked back down at the article on French street-markets.

Apparently you could buy groceries there. And occasionally clothes. Sometimes prints. How fucking riveting. The disembodied voice of a cabin crew member began advising passengers about the safety features to be found on this 767. Several of the bookstalls by the Seine sold English paperbacks. In the unlikely event of an emergency wine was much cheaper than in the cafés. There were several exits near the market and clothes could be found under the banks of the river in front of you. The child by the bookstall was clearly indicated and even though oxygen was flowing would not inflate. Beside the river, far from the boy, was a woman who was speaking. People were walking by, not even noticing her strange manner of dress. She was clad in a bulky fur-lined leather jacket and had a tight-fitting leather helmet on her head, its unfastened straps hanging on either side of her face.

Dyson wanted to hear what she was saying and walked nearer to her. She smiled at his approach and continued her explanation even as she motioned for him to climb in the open seat behind the one in which she sat.

"Static is occasionally encountered on the radios of Heaven."

Her voice was confident and benign. Dyson fastened the belt around his waist and adjusted his goggles. He looked beyond the jarring geometries of the struts between the upper and lower sets of wood-and-canvas wings to the undisturbed green fields on either side of the sandy runway. The fields, perfectly flat, stretched to every horizon. He, the woman, and the biplane itself were the only foreign objects. It was important that they left.

The woman turned round in her seat to smile at him again.

"We must discover the horizontal movement of elevators," she said, and, turning away from him once more, started up the plane's small engine, sending the single front-mounted propeller spinning furiously. Transmuted by the propeller's frenzy, the formerly still air whipped back across Dyson's face as an intimate and exhilarating wind. He opened his mouth to it, excited, and placed his hands on either side of the narrow open cockpit as the plane began to rush forward across the sand. The runway was uneven and bumpy but Dyson felt no fear as the fragile biplane hurtled faster and faster along it. The machine and the moment were implicit with flight, pregnant with escape. The trajectory held no potential other than a leap into the sky and the freedom of the winds.

Dyson wondered how he could hear the pilot's voice against the combined roaring of engine and air but hear it he did.

"You need to put your seat in the upright position," she seemed to be saying, though he could see only her back and the waves of corn-blonde hair that hung below the back of her helmet. He looked down at himself. The seat was welded in position tight against the cockpit. How could he move it? He closed his eyes to think about this further.

"Sir? Your seat has to be upright for takeoff."

Dyson opened his eyes. A dark-haired Flight Attendant was smiling apologetically at him as she stood in the aisle beside the seat of the passenger next to him.

"I'm *sorry*," she stressed, stretching the word out to demonstrate further her distress at disturbing him. "But the Captain's about to take off and I need your seat to be upright."

Dyson nodded vigorously and blinked himself more thoroughly awake.

"Of course, of course," he said and pressed the button in the arm-rest beside him, leaning from the waist as he did so to allow the seat-back to inch forward into its takeoff position.

"*Thank* you," the Stewardess said, rewarding him with another smile before moving on to check the seat-positions of other passengers.

Dyson hadn't lowered his seat consciously. He'd never do that. He always fastened his seat-belt immediately he sat down, too. He hated having to be asked or reminded about either of those things. One of the masks he wore to hide his terror was the seasoned, bored-with-the-rituals, flier and he hated to be caught out. His thigh must have pressed against the button as he dozed and lowered his seat-back in his sleep. He looked out of his window. The plane had left the gate and was swinging round onto the designated runway to begin its launch. A wave of anxiety went through him, small (the valium was doing its job) but unpleasant enough. He was furious with his thigh. He'd really been asleep, so asleep that maybe for the first time he could have gotten through takeoff unconscious and woken only when the plane had already reached cruising altitude. That would have been great. But no, here he was as usual—convinced of death and powerless to do anything about it as the huge machine (*Too big. Too heavy. How could these things fly? How* could *they?*) thundered its way toward immolation. He sat bolt upright, tense in every muscle, conscious of every breath, and waited for the inevitable catastrophe.

## IV

Dyson finished his cognac and settled back a little in his seat. He felt a lot better now. The plane had been at a steady 31,000 feet for over an hour and all the banking and turning that made the first twenty minutes of any flight the worst were long over. Dyson had had two scotches before dinner, a red wine to accompany the filet mignon, and a cognac to accompany the coffee. And the Byrds were on one of the in-flight audio channels, the falling bass-line and soaring harmonies of *Turn, Turn, Turn* entering each of Dyson's ears and meeting somewhere in the middle of his head.

He often experienced these twenty or thirty-minute stretches of euphoria during a flight, times where he could gaze out of his window at the distant landscapes below him and feel genuinely good about being up in a plane. But it took a lot of alcohol to get him in such states and it took very little to get him out of them; ten seconds of turbulence was enough, or the sight of another plane through his window (distance and direction didn't matter—if there were two planes in the same cubic mile of air, he assumed they would find each other). But the Byrds and the booze and the unshaky sky had given him this period of peace and he luxuriated in it.

Over on the video monitor a couple of rows in front of him he could see actors mouthing words and buildings exploding silently. He wondered about tuning his headset to the movie soundtrack but decided against it. He closed his eyes instead, turned the music down slightly, and stretched his legs out as much as he could beneath the seat in front of him.

The sea below them was a pale purple. They'd left the glass mountains and their strange shifting subterranean contents long behind them, though the aviatrix had dipped the biplane sufficiently at the time for Dyson to catch a glimpse of one huge clouded eye the size of a shopping-mall parking-lot, which had blinked beneath the crystal as they'd buzzed past. Dyson was more impressed with the waves though; with no shore to break against save gravity, they rose in the middle of their ocean, losing their colour as they did so, to climb vertically in towering translucency and foam themselves into a fury of deep-white dissolution at their skyscraper-high peaks.

Occasionally, his pilot would turn half-round in her front seat to smile at him and to gesture with a directional hand at some other point of interest. They'd been flying for hours, it seemed, and Dyson felt he could fly forever. His pilot was beautiful and the sights they shared were wonderful. He was reaching forward to tap her shoulder and tell her this when a sharp pinging noise somewhere above his head distracted him and made him look up.

He found that he was looking at an illuminated sign telling him to fasten his seat-belt. For a moment he was terribly confused and then a quick glance around him reminded him of where he was. *His* seat-belt of course was still fastened but the heavy-set man beside him needed to fish the two halves of his belt out from beneath his expansive backside and clip them together. The senior Flight Attendant's voice emerged from the overhead speakers in the cabin to reinforce the instruction.

"Ladies and gentlemen, the Captain has found it necessary to illuminate the seat-belt signs while we go through this turbulence. If you are standing anywhere in the cabin, please return to your seats. Thank you."

Dyson's heart beat a little faster. The plane was bumping and rocking like an express train on a bad stretch of track. He dropped that simile bloody quickly; derailment here didn't mean ploughing up some farmer's field, it meant a drop. A big drop. Thirty. One. Thousand. Feet. *Stop it, stop it*, he told himself. Turbulence, that's all. Very normal. Very ordinary. He looked at his watch. Good. The flight was well past the halfway point—which probably meant nothing aeronautically but was always a good psychological signpost for him. He tried to summon up the feeling he had had in his dream in which flight was not only a miracle but an ecstasy. He failed of course but at least it gave him something to think about as the plane rode out the wind.

The dream from which he'd just awoken was plainly a continuation of the one he'd had immediately before takeoff. That was very strange. He'd never re-entered a dream before. The nearest he'd had to even a recurring dream was on those few occasions that he woke feeling that he'd visited places in the night which were geographically close to places he'd dreamed in before—as if somehow his night-time self might sometime meet a dream cartographer who would lay out for him route-marked maps demonstrating that this dream of a Tuesday in March, ten years ago, took place about four blocks from this one of a recent July, and that both were only a short cab-ride from the nightmare of December last.

This dream, though, felt like it had continued while he was busy being awake and that he had rejoined it after an elapsed time equivalent to the time he had spent away. Very strange—it gave the dream state an equal standing with the waking one that he had never before granted to it. It was as if he was waking from each into the other, moving between equally valid territories rather than simply being entertained by his unconscious.

He thought of the woman in his dream and her romantically anachronistic dress. He recognised the provenance of the imagery of course—those 1930s women fliers whose likenesses he had seen in magazine photos and documentary footage—but the aviatrix of his unconscious was something more than them. She was the paradigm of them all, the missing original from which they had been cast. It was as if he had dreamed of Amelia Earhart and dreamed not of the living woman who had disappeared during her last flight but of her spirit, of her principle, of the *idea* of which she had been simply the symbol.

His dreaming self had fashioned her into an Amelia Earhart who was never lost, but *translated*—an Amelia Earhart who had flown herself through the clouds of unknowing into a yonder never so blue nor so wild. Not lost, but escaped; flying forever across imagination's skies; borne on the secret winds that blow above the dream country.

Another *ping* from above his head stopped his analysis. He looked up. The seat-belt light had gone out. Dyson felt a rush of pleasure. She was still piloting him, it seemed; his thoughts of her had taken him through the turbulence into calmer skies without his usual neurotic attention to every second and every shudder.

He smiled. He missed her, he realised. He wondered where they were and over what wonders she was flying him while he was away. Would it be possible to go back? Could he *will* himself into that territory into which he had previously merely stumbled? Excited, he fished through the seat-pocket for the in-flight courtesy bag and pulled out the complimentary eye-mask. On his rare forays up and down the aisles of aircraft on which he'd flown he'd always thought the passengers wearing those things looked inordinately fucking stupid, but now he didn't give a shit what he looked like and he slipped the elasticated strap over his head and leaned back in his seat.

"*Aviatrix*," he said silently, relishing the word like a mantra or a spell of summoning, "*aviatrix*".

## VI

The desert was sentient.

It lay beneath them, an expanse of subtly shifting sands, and

Dyson, looking behind him, could see no beginning to its hugeness and, looking ahead, could see no end. What he could see, however, was that the desert observed their flight just as much as they observed it. For the most part its observation was implicit—a sensed thing rather than a seen—but occasionally, in a spirit of inquiry, it would reform part of itself, sending up into the air vast sheets of sand that would rise with breathtaking speed on either side of the biplane, so that where a moment before they had been high above a plain they were suddenly flying low between the towering walls of a valley, walls that shimmered with the constant movement of their countless grains.

Once, it even completed the canopy, curving the tops of its walls toward each other until they met so that Dyson and the aviatrix were flying within a tunnel, a tunnel that should have been lightless but was somehow not—as if the desert had widened the spaces between every tiny grain of itself to allow its visitors the luxury of sight.

They followed the tunnel for several minutes before the desert fell back around them to its passive state below. The woman turned in her cockpit to look at Dyson. Her hands were off the controls but he had realised some time back that she didn't really need physical contact with the machinery. She and the plane were essentially one. They drove themselves through these dream skies by desire, not science.

"Thunder has three sides, Steve," she said, "But no dalmatians."

Dyson nodded. He was beginning to understand her. And was already terribly in love. She nodded downwards and he looked to see.

They were flying over a hole in the world. Bounded like a midwest lake by long shore-roads, what Dyson saw was no body of water but a jet-black expanse of deep space, studded with distant stars and cloudy filaments of gases.

The roar of an explosion suddenly deafened him. He couldn't understand for a moment. He could see nothing that had happened that would explain the sound. Then he heard a voice to his side screaming in terminal panic.

"*Jesus fucking Christ! The wing's gone!*"

## VII

Dyson, already screaming himself, tore the eye-mask from his face with fingers tingling with prescient terror.

The fat man in the seat beside him was twitching like a speared beast, arms flapping uselessly in the air, the stink of his voided bowels invading Dyson's senses almost before anything else.

Dyson, unaware of the whimpers and screams coming from his own mouth, swept the cabin with his eyes. People were ripping themselves free of their restraining belts and clambering pointlessly into the aisles. There was nothing they could do for themselves, but they were listening to a primal voice within that decreed movement even when movement couldn't save them.

One Flight Attendant was paying lip service to procedure and shouting out for the passengers to remain calm while her colleagues, knowing it was over, joined in the atavistic dance of the civilians, running, scrambling, stumbling, screaming. The howls of the doomed filled the cabin of the aircraft and for one precious fleeting second Dyson had an absurd sense of satisfaction. He'd always known this terror—at least in embryo—and now that, fully born, it was running rampant through the souls of the previously complacent he felt the poisoned vindication of the doomsayer.

It was all of three seconds since the exploding engine had torn the wing from the 767 and, incredibly, apart from the shuddering lurch to the side that accompanied the sundering, the crippled plane had stayed more or less steady.

That stopped being true.

Nose first, it dropped like a stone.

Dyson's belt was still fastened around him. It hurt like fuck as all his weight pressed against it. The passengers who had found the time to snap their belts, though, fell screaming down the vertical chute that the cabin of the plane had become and smashed into the first solid objects that barred their way. Eight people died before the plane hit the ground. Twenty-three people wished they had. One hundred and fifty more were beyond thought, pushed howling into a primal state of animal terror.

Dyson was one of them. He was squealing like a three-day torture victim. There was nothing in his mind except dread and denial and nothing in his body save ice and emptiness. Nothing could save him and nothing did.

The plane arrowed itself into the unyielding rock of a mountain range and, fuel-tanks still one third full, exploded instantly into all-consuming fire, killing everyone on board.

## VIII

Dyson had been screaming the second before he died and was surprised to find he was still screaming the second after. He was still falling at a nauseating speed, as if the mountain and the explosion had not interrupted him at all. He was no longer in his seat, however, and no longer in the plane. It was just him, falling through complete blackness and screaming.

By the time a minute had passed, though, continuing to scream seemed a little stupid. And so he stopped. The blackness was still all around him and there seemed to be little he could do about that except continue to fall through it. Unless of course he opened his eyes. And so he did.

The sky was jade-green and tasted moist and slightly acidic. Far below, the ground was writhing. It was a mass of intertwined worm-like creatures, each the length of Europe and all of them the colours of bruising. Immediately in front of him, and falling just as fast, was the aviatrix.

Dyson tried to reach out to her but found it difficult to move his limbs against the rush of air. It was unnecessary. She turned toward him, riding the air like a sky-diver, and took hold of his hand. Instantly, their fall stopped. Dyson gasped. They were hovering in mid-air. Her eyes locked on his and he found himself unable to look away as her change began.

## IX

Above the unending territories of the dream country the great white bird flew as she had always flown, her vast shadow bringing night in her wake.

Invisible from the ground, in the warmth of that huge snowy breast, nestled Dyson, fingers clinging happily to the feathers of the white goddess as her great wings beat tireless against the skies and flew into forever.

## AFTERWORD

*Dave Rae, a friend of mine, works for Liverpool City Council. A year or so ago, a memo from the Council came down to all employees. Dave showed it to me. It was essentially a list of words which were deemed to be no longer acceptable. These words were Politically Incorrect. It was a very long list. Among it were the obvious words—chairman, postman, etc.—and many many more. One of them was aviatrix.*

*Now, the first thing to occur to us was how ludicrously unlikely it was that any city employee would ever have need to make use of such a glorious anachronism as "aviatrix" and Dave and I had many a drunken laugh trying to work the word into hypothetical Council communications. Secondly, we bemoaned the waste of time, energy and tax-payer's money that went into the production of such a thorough list when a general instruction to avoid words or phrasing that were redolent of racism or sexism would have done the job.*

*Thirdly—and this is what's scary—aviatrix is a beautiful word and these dickheads wanted to ban it. They wanted to remove it from the language because it had a feminine ending. It presupposed that there was a difference between a male flier and a female one and this was deemed unacceptable. Does the phrase "thought-police" occur to anyone? One of the primary functions of language is to provide us with a set of symbols by which we understand the world; to allow us to illuminate the tiniest shades of the meaning of things and of the differences between things. When any Authority attempts to control language, they are really trying to take away your ability to understand, to perceive subtle differences, to think.*

*A woman dressed in a flying uniform is different than a man dressed in a flying uniform. She's not inferior. She's not superior. But she's different. And a language that denies itself a word to illustrate that difference is a crippled language.*

*Further—don't these people have ears? Are they deaf to the music of language? Do they not hear that it's about sound as much as it's about sense? Aviatrix is a gorgeous set of sounds even if you don't know what it means. So these arbiters of ideological soundness not only want to rob us of subtle shades of meaning, they want to rob us of melody, too. Fuck 'em. Fuck 'em all. May they burn in a non-creed-specific Hell.*

*I wrote "Aviatrix" for several reasons, but one of them is to ensure that there are now in the world more pieces of paper bearing this beautiful banned word than there used to be. The story is dedicated to Dave Rae.*

*Peter Atkins*
*Los Angeles*
*September 1992*

# IAN R. MACLEOD

## Snodgrass

MUCH AS IAN MACLEOD would "sometimes like to say that I work part-time as a wall-of-death-rider or have just come back from a couple of months investigating the life cycle of the Tibetan swamp moth, I remain a writer and a house-husband, and reasonably content with my lot."

He actually lives in Britain's Sutton Coldfield with his wife Gillian and daughter Emily. After working for ten years in the Civil Service, he quit his job to become a full-time writer.

The first story he sold, "1/72nd Scale" (reprinted in *Best New Horror* 2), was nominated for a Nebula Award in 1990 by the Science Fiction Writers of America. He has made three successive appearances in Gardner Dozois' *The Year's Best Science Fiction/Best New SF* anthologies, and stories have been published in *Interzone*, *The Magazine of Fantasy & Science Fiction*, *Asimov's Science Fiction*, *Amazing Stories*, *Weird Tales*, *Pulphouse* and *In Dreams*. A hardback collection is possibly forthcoming in America, and he is currently re-writing the "first" novel following "various rejections, buggerings-about and near-misses with publishers."

About "Snodgrass", MacLeod confesses to "being no great Beatles or Lennon fan. I started wondering about the chances that brought the Beatles together, and the flukes of talent and history that made them what they were.

"I think that the driving engine of the story as far as I was concerned was actually a kind of fear—which perhaps helps to explain its inclusion in a horror collection. The fear in question is the fear of artistic failure, which, in the minds of most artists (i.e., me) is closely linked with failing in life as a whole. You want to shout things from the golden rooftops, but instead you end up mumbling in the gutter . . ."

## SNODGRASS

I'VE GOT ME WHOLE LIFE WORKED OUT. Today, give up smoking. Tomorrow, quit drinking. The day after, give up smoking again.

It's morning. Light me cig. Pick the fluff off me feet. Drag the curtain back, and the night's left everything in the same mess outside. Bin sacks by the kitchen door that Cal never gets around to taking out front. The garden jungleland gone brown with autumn. Houses this way and that, terraces queuing for something that'll never happen.

It's early. Daren't look at the clock. The stair carpet works greasegrit between me toes. Downstairs in the freezing kitchen, pull the cupboard where the handle's dropped off.

"Hey, Mother Hubbard," I shout up the stairs to Cal. "Why no fucking cornflakes?"

The lav flushes. Cal lumbers down in a grey nightie. "What's all this about cornflakes? Since when do you have breakfast, John?"

"Since John got a job."

"You? A job?"

"I wouldn't piss yer around about this, Cal."

"You owe me four weeks' rent," she says. "Plus I don't know how much for bog roll and soap. Then there's the TV licence."

"Don't tell me yer buy a TV licence."

"I don't, but I'm the householder. It's me who'd get sent to gaol."

"Every Wednesday, I'll visit yer," I say, rummaging in the bread bin.

"What's this job anyway?"

"I told yer on Saturday when you and Kevin came back from the Chinese. Must have been too pissed to notice." I hold up a stiff green slice of Mighty White. "Think this is edible?"

"Eat it and find out. And stop calling Steve Kevin. He's upstairs asleep right at this moment."

"Well there's a surprise. Rip Van and his tiny Winkle."

"I wish you wouldn't say things like that. You know what Steve's like if you give him an excuse."

"Yeah, but at least I don't have to sleep with him."

Cal sits down to watch me struggle through breakfast. Before Kevin, it was another Kevin, and a million other Kevins before that, all with grazed knuckles from the way they walk. Cal says she needs the protection even if it means the odd bruise.

I paste freckled marge over ye Mighty White. It tastes just like the doormat, and I should know.

"Why don't yer tell our Kev to stuff it?" I say.

She smiles and leans forward.

"Snuggle up to Dr Winston here," I wheedle.

"You'd be too old to look after me with the clients, John," she says, as though I'm being serious. Which I am.

"For what I'd charge to let them prod yer, Cal, yer wouldn't have any clients. Onassis couldn't afford yer."

"Onassis is dead, unless you mean the woman." She stands up, turning away, shaking the knots from her hair. She stares out of the window over the mess in the sink. Cal hates to talk about her work. "It's past eight, John," she says without looking at any clock. It's a knack she has. "Hadn't you better get ready for this job?"

Yeah, ye job. The people at the Jobbie are always on the look-out for something fresh for Dr Winston. They think of him as a challenge. Miss Nikki was behind ye spit-splattered perspex last week. She's an old hand—been there for at least three months.

"Name's Dr Winston O'Boogie," I drooled, doing me hunchback when I reached the front of ye queue.

"We've got something for you, Mr Lennon," she says. They always call yer Mister or Sir here, just like the fucking police. "How would you like to work in a Government Department?"

"Well, wow," I say, letting the hunchback slip. "You mean like a spy?"

That makes her smile. I hate it when they don't smile.

She passes me ye chit. Name, age, address. Skills, qualifications—none. That bit always kills me. Stapled to it we have details of something clerical.

"It's a new scheme, Mr Lennon," Nikki says. "The Government is committed to helping the long-term unemployed. You can start Monday."

So here's Dr Winston O'Boogie at the bus stop in the weird morning light. I've got on me best jacket, socks that match, even remembered me glasses so I can see what's happening. Cars are crawling. Men in suits are tapping fingers on the steering wheel as they groove to Katie Boyle. None of them live around here—they're all from Solihull—and this is just a place to complain about the traffic. And Monday's a drag cos daughter Celia has to back the Mini off the drive and be a darling and shift Mummy's Citroën too so yer poor hard-working Dad can get to the Sierra.

The bus into town lumbers up. The driver looks at me like I'm a freak when I don't know ye exact fare. Up on the top deck where there's No standing, No spitting, No ball games, I get me a window seat and light me a ciggy. I love it up here, looking down on the world, into people's bedroom windows. Always have. Me and me mate Pete used to drive the bus from the top front seat all the way from Menlove Avenue to Quarry Bank School. I remember the rows of semis, trees that used to brush like sea on shingle over the roof of the bus. Everything in Speke was Snodgrass of course, what with valve radios on the sideboard and the *Daily Excess*, but Snodgrass was different in them days. It was like watching a play, waiting for someone to forget their lines. Mimi used to tell me that anyone who said they were middle class probably wasn't. You knew just by checking whether they had one of them blocks that look like Kendal Mint Cake hooked around the rim of the loo. It was all tea and biscuits then, and Mind, dear, your slip's showing. You knew where you were, what you were fighting.

The bus crawls. We're up in the clouds here, the fumes on the pavement like dry ice at a big concert. Oh, yeah. I mean, Dr Winston may be nifty fifty with his whole death to look forward to but he knows what he's saying. Cal sometimes works at the NEC when she gets too proud to do the real business. Hands out leaflets and wiggles her ass. She got me a ticket last year to see Simply Red and we went together and she put on her best dress that looked just great and didn't show too much and I was proud to be with her, even if I did feel like her dad. Of course, the music was warmed-over shit. It always is. I hate the way that red-haired guy sings. She tried to get me to see Cliff too, but Dr Winston has his pride.

Everywhere is empty round here, knocked down and boarded up, postered over. There's a group called SideKick playing at Digbeth. And waddayouknow, the Beatles are playing this very evening at the NEC. The Greatest Hits Tour, it says here on ye corrugated fence. I mean, Fab Gear Man. Give It Bloody Foive. Macca and Stu and George and Ringo, and obviously the solo careers are up the kazoo again. Like, wow.

The bus dumps me in the middle of Brum. The office is just off Cherry Street. I stagger meself by finding it right away, me letter from the Jobbie in me hot little hand. I show it to a geezer in uniform, and he sends me up to the fifth floor. The whole place is new. It smells of formaldehyde—that stuff we used to pickle the spiders in at school. Me share the lift with ye office bimbo. Oh, after *you*.

Dr Winston does his iceberg cruise through the openplan. So this is what Monday morning really looks like.

Into an office at the far end. Smells of coffee. Snodgrass has got a filter machine bubbling away. A teapot ready for the afternoon.

"Mr Lennon."

We shake hands across the desk. "Mr Snodgrass."

Snodgrass cracks a smile. "There must have been some mistake down in General Admin. My name's Fenn. But everyone calls me Allen."

"Oh yeah. And why's that?" A voice inside that sounds like Mimi says *Stop this behaviour, John*. She's right, of course. Dr Winston needs the job, the money. Snodgrass tells me to sit down. I fumble for a ciggy and try to loosen up.

"No smoking please, Mr . . . er, *John*."

Oh, great.

"You're a lot, um, older than most of the casual workers we get."

"Well this is what being on the Giro does for yer. I'm nineteen really."

Snodgrass looks down at his file. "Born 1940." He looks up again. "And is that a Liverpool accent I detect?"

I look around me. "Where?"

Snodgrass has got a crazy grin on his face. I think the bastard likes me. "So you're John Lennon, from Liverpool. I thought the name rang a faint bell." He leans forward. "I am right, aren't I?"

Oh fucking Jesus. A faint bell. This happens about once every six months. Why *now*? "Oh yeah," I say. "I used to play the squeezebox for Gerry and the Pacemakers. Just session work. And it was a big thrill to work with Shirley Bassey, I can tell yer. She's the King as far as I'm concerned. Got bigger balls than Elvis."

"You were the guy who left the Beatles."

"That was Pete Best, Mr Snodgrass."

"You *and* Pete Best. Pete Best was the one who was dumped for Ringo. You walked out on Paul McCartney and Stuart Sutcliffe. I collect records, you see. I've read all the books about Merseybeat. And my elder sister was a big fan of those old bands. The Fourmost, Billy J. Kramer, Cilla, the Beatles. Of course, it was all before my time."

"Dinosaurs ruled the earth."

"You must have some stories to tell."

"Oh, yeah." I lean forward across the desk. "Did yer know that Paul McCartney was really a woman?"

"Well, John, I – "

"It figures if yer think about it, Mr Snodgrass. I mean, have *you* ever seen his dick?"

"Just call me Allen, please, will you? Now, I'll show you your desk."

Snodgrass takes me out into the openplan. Introduces me to a pile of envelopes, a pile of letters. Well, Hi. Seems like Dr Winston is supposed to put one into the other.

"What do I do when I've finished?" I ask.

"We'll find you some more."

All the faces in the openplan are staring. A phone's ringing, but no one bothers to answer. "Yeah," I say, "I can see there's a big rush on."

On his way back to his office, Snodgrass takes a detour to have a word with a fat Doris in a floral print sitting over by the filing cabinets. He says something to her that includes the word Beatle. Soon, the whole office knows.

"I bet you could write a book," fat Doris says, standing over me, smelling of pot noodles. "Everyone's interested in those days now. Of course, the Who and the Stones were the ones for me. Brian Jones. Keith Moon, for some reason. All the ones who died. I was a real rebel. I went to Heathrow airport once, chewed my handbag to shreds."

"Did yer piss yourself too, Doris? That's what usually happened."

Fat Doris twitches a smile. "Never quite made it to the very top, the Beatles, did they? Still, that Paul McCartney wrote some lovely songs. "Yesterday", you still hear that one in lifts don't you? And Stu was *so* good-looking then. Must be a real tragedy in your life that you didn't stay. How does it feel, carrying that around with you, licking envelopes for a living?"

"Yer know what your trouble is don't yer, Doris?"

Seems she don't, so I tell her.

Winston's got no money for the bus home. His old joints ache—never realised it was this bloody far to walk. The kids are playing in our road like it's a holiday, which it always is for most of them. A tennis ball hits me hard on the noddle. I pretend it don't hurt, then I growl at them to fuck off as they follow me down the street. Kevin's van's disappeared from outside the house. Musta gone out. Pity, shame.

Cal's wrapped up in a rug on the sofa, smoking a joint and watching *Home and Away*. She jumps up when she sees me in the hall like she thought I was dead already.

"Look, Cal," I say. "I really wanted this job, but yer wouldn't get Adolf Hitler to do what they asked, God rest his soul. There were all these little puppies in cages and I was supposed to push knitting needles down into their eyes. Jesus, it was – "

"Just shaddup for one minute will you, John!"

"I'll get the rent somehow, Cal, I – "

"– Paul McCartney was here!"

"Who the hell's Paul McCartney?"

"Be serious for a minute, John. He was *here*. There was a car the size of a tank parked outside the house. You should have seen the curtains twitch."

Cal hands me the joint. I take a pull, but I really need something stronger. And I still don't believe what she's saying. "And why the fuck should Macca come here?"

"To see *you*, John. He said he'd used a private detective to trace you here. Somehow got the address through your wife Cynthia. I didn't even know you were *married*, John. And a kid named Julian who's nearly thirty. He's married too, he's – "

"– What else did that bastard tell yer?"

"Look, we just talked. He was very charming."

Charming. That figures. *Now* I'm beginning to believe.

"I thought you told me you used to be best mates."

"Too bloody right. Then he nicked me band. It was John Lennon and the Quarrymen. I should never have let the bastard join. Then Johnny and the Moondogs. Then Long John and the Silver Beatles. It was *my* name, *my* idea to shorten it to just the Beatles. They all said it was daft, but they went along with it because it was *my* fucking band."

"Look, nobody doubts that, John. But what's the point in being bitter? Paul just wanted to know how you were."

"Oh, it's *Paul* now is it? Did yer let him shag yer, did yer put out for free, ask him to autograph yer fanny?"

"Come on, John. Climb down off the bloody wall. It didn't happen, you're not rich and famous. It's like not winning the pools, happens to everyone you meet. After all, the Beatles were just another rock band. It's not like they were the Stones."

"Oh, no. The Stones weren't crap for a start. Bang bang Maxwell's Silver bloody Hammer. Give me Cliff any day."

"You never want to talk about it, do you? You just let it stay inside you, boiling up. Look, why will you never believe that people care? *I* care. Will you accept that for a start? Do you think I put up with you here for the sodding rent which incidentally I never get anyway? You're old enough to be my bloody father, John. So stop acting like a kid." Her face starts to go wet. I hate these kind of scenes. "You *could* be my father, John. Seeing as I didn't have one, you'd do fine. Just believe in yourself for a change."

"At least yer had a bloody *mother*," I growl. But I can't keep the nasty up. Open me arms and she's trembling like a rabbit, smelling of salt and grass. All these years, all these *bloody* years. Why is it you can never leave anything behind?

Cal sniffs and steps back and pulls these bits of paper from her pocket. "He gave me these. Two tickets for tonight's show, and a pass for the do afterwards."

I look around at chez nous. The air smells of old stew that I can never remember eating. I mean, who the hell cooks *stew*? And Macca was here. Did them feet in ancient whathaveyou.

Cal plonks the tickets on the telly and brews some tea. She's humming in the kitchen, it's her big day, a famous rock star has come on down. I wonder if I should tear ye tickets up now, but decide to leave it for later. Something to look forward to for a change. All these years, all these *bloody* years. There was a journalist caught up with Dr Winston a while back. Oh Mr Lennon, I'm doing background. We'll pay yer of course, and perhaps we could have lunch? Which we did, and I can reveal exclusively for the first time that the Doctor got well and truly rat-arsed. And then the cheque came and the Doctor saw it all in black and white, serialised in the *Sunday* bloody *Excess*. A sad and bitter man, it said. So it's in the papers and I know it's true.

Cal clears a space for the mugs on the carpet and plonks them down. "I know you don't mean to go tonight," she says. "I'm not going to argue about it now."

She sits down on the sofa and lets me put an arm around her waist. We get warm and cosy. It's nice sometimes with Cal. You don't have to argue or explain.

"You know, John," she murmurs. "The secret of happiness is not trying."

"And you're the world expert? Happiness sure ain't living on the Giro in bloody Birmingham."

"Birmingham isn't the end of the world."

"No, but yer can see it from here."

Cal smiles. I love it when she smiles. She leans over and lights more blow from somewhere. She puts it to my lips. I breathe it in. The smoke. Tastes like harvest bonfires. We're snug as two bunnies. "Think of when you were happy," she whispers. "There must have been a time."

Oh, yeah: 1966, after I'd recorded the five singles that made up the entire creative output of the Nowhere Men and some git at the record company was given the job of saying, Well, John, we don't feel we can give yer act the attention it deserves. And let's be honest the Beatles link isn't really bankable any more is it? Walking out into the London traffic, it was just a huge load off me back. John, yer don't have to be a rock star after all. No more backs of vans. No more Watford Gap Sizzlers for breakfast. No more chord changes. No more launches and re-launches. No more telling the bloody bass player how to use his instrument. Of course, there was Cyn and little Julian back in Liverpool, but let's face it I was always a bastard when it came to family. I kidded meself they were better off without me.

But 1966. There *was* something then, the light had a sharp edge. Not just acid and grass although that was part of it. A girl with ribbons came up to me along Tottenham Court Road. Gave me a dogeared postcard of a white foreign beach, a blue sea. Told me she'd been there that very morning, just held it to her eyes in the dark. She kissed me cheek and she said she wanted to pass the blessing on. Well, the Doctor has never been much of a dreamer, but he could feel the surf of that beach through his toes as he dodged the traffic. He knew there were easier ways of getting there than closing yer eyes. So I took all me money and I bought me a ticket and I took a plane to Spain, la, la. Seemed like everyone was heading that way then, drifting in some warm current from the sun.

Lived on Formentera for sunbaked years I couldn't count. It was a sweet way of life, bumming this, bumming that, me and the Walrus walking hand in hand, counting the sand. Sheltering under a fig tree in the rain, I met this Welsh girl who called herself Morwenna. We all had strange names then. She took me to a house made of driftwood and canvas washed up on the shore. She had bells between her breasts and they tinkled as we made love. When the clouds had cleared we bought fish fresh from the nets in the white-washed harbour. Then we talked in firelight and the dolphins sang to the lobsters as the waves advanced. She told me under the stars that she knew other places, other worlds. There's another John at your shoulder, she said. He's so like you I can't understand what's different.

But Formentera was a long way from anything. It was so timeless we knew it couldn't last. The tourists, the government, the locals, the police—every Snodgrass in the universe—moved in. Turned out Morwenna's parents had money so it was all just fine and dandy for the cunt, leaving me one morning before the sun was up, taking a little boat to the airport on Ibiza, then all the way back to bloody Cardiff. The clouds greyed over the Med and the Doctor stayed on too long. Shot the wrong shit, scored the wrong deals. Somehow, I ended up in Paris, sleeping in a box and not speaking a bloody word of the lingo. Then somewhere else. The whole thing is a haze. Another time, I was sobbing on Mimi's doorstep in pebbledash Menlove Avenue and the dog next door was barking and Mendips looked just the same. The porch where I used to play me guitar. Wallpaper and cooking smells inside. She gave me egg and chips and tea in thick white china, just like the old days when she used to go on about me drainpipes.

So I stayed on a while in Liverpool, slept in me old bed with me feet sticking out the bottom. Mimi had taken down all me Brigitte Bardot posters but nothing else had changed. I could almost believe that me mate Paul was gonna come around on the wag from the Inny and we'd spend the afternoon with our guitars and pickle sandwiches, rewriting Buddy Holly and dreaming of the days to come. The songs never came out the way we meant and the gigs at the Casbah were a mess. But things were *possible*, then, yer know?

I roused meself from bed after a few weeks and Mimi nagged me down the Jobbie. Then I had to give up kidding meself that time had stood still. Did yer know all the docks have gone? I've never seen anything so empty. God knows what the people do with themselves when they're not getting pissed. I couldn't even find the fucking Cavern, or Eppy's old record shop where he used to sell that Sibelius crap until he chanced upon us rough lads.

When I got back to Mendips I suddenly saw how old Mimi had got. Mimi, I said, yer're a senior citizen. *I* should be looking after *you*. She just laughed that off, of course; Mimi was sweet and sour as ever. Wagged her finger at me and put something tasty on the stove. When Mimi's around, I'm still just a kid, can't help it. And she couldn't resist saying, I told you all this guitar stuff would get you nowhere, John. But at least she said it with a smile and hug. I guess I could have stayed there forever, but that's not the Doctor's way. Like Mimi says, he's got ants in his pants. Just like his poor dead mum. So I started to worry that things were getting too cosy, that maybe it was time to dump everything and start again, again.

What finally happened was that I met this bloke one day on me way back from the Jobbie. The original Snodgrass, no less—the one I used to sneer at during calligraphy in Art School. In them days I was James Dean and Elvis combined with me drainpipes and me duck's arse quiff. A one man revolution—Cynthia, the rest of the class were so hip they were trying to look like Kenny Ball and his Sodding Jazzmen. This kid Snodgrass couldn't even manage that, probably dug Frank Ifield. He had spots on his neck, a green sports jacket that looked like his mum had knitted it. Christ knows what his real name was. Of course, Dr Winston used to take the piss something rancid, specially when he'd sunk a few pints of black velvet down at Ye Cracke. Anyway, twenty years on and the Doctor was watching ye seagulls on Paradise Street and waiting for the lights to change, when this sports car shaped like a dildo slides up and a window purrs down.

"Hi, John! Bet you don't remember me."

All I can smell is leather and aftershave. I squint and lean forward to see. The guy's got red-rimmed glasses on. A grin like a slab of marble.

"Yeah," I say, although I really don't know how I know. "You're the prat from college. The one with the spotty neck."

"I got into advertising," he said. "My own company now. You were in that band, weren't you, John? Left just before they made it. You always did talk big."

"Fuck off, Snodgrass," I tell him, and head across the road. Nearly walk straight into a bus.

Somehow, it's the last straw. I saunter down to Lime Street, get me a platform ticket and take the first Intercity that comes in, la, la. They throw me off at Brum, which I swear to Jesus God is the only reason why I'm here. Oh, yeah. I let Mimi know what had happened after a few weeks when me conscience got too heavy. She must have told Cyn. Maybe they send each other Crimble cards.

Damn.

Cal's gone.

Cold. The sofa. How can anyone *sleep* on this thing? Hurts me old bones just to sit on it. The sun is fading at the window. Must be late afternoon. No sign of Cal. Probably has to do the biz with some Arab our Kev's found for her. Now seems as good a time as any to sort out Macca's tickets, but when I look on top ye telly they've done a runner. The cunt's gone and hidden them, la, la.

Kevin's back. I can hear him farting and snoring upstairs in Cal's room. I shift the dead begonia off ye sideboard and rummage in the cigar box behind. Juicy stuff, near on sixty quid. Cal hides her money somewhere different about once a fortnight, and she don't think the Doctor has worked out where she's put it this time. Me, I've known for ages, was just saving for ye rainy day. Which is now.

So yer thought yer could get Dr Winston O'Boogie to go and see Stu and Paulie just by hiding the tickets did yer? The fucking NEC! Ah-ha. The Doctor's got other ideas. He pulls on ye jacket, his best and only shoes. Checks himself in the hall mirror. Puts on glasses. Looks like Age Concern. Takes them off again. Heads out. Pulls the door quiet in case Kev should stir. The air outside is grainy, smells of diesel. The sky is pink and all the street lights that work are coming on. The kids are still playing, busy breaking the aerial off a car. They're too absorbed to look up at ye passing Doctor, which is somehow worse than being taunted. I recognise the cracks in ye pavement. This one looks like a moon buggy. This one looks like me mum's face after the car hit her outside Mendips. Not that I saw, but still, yer dream, don't yer? You still dream. And maybe things were getting a bit too cosy here with Cal anyway, starting to feel sorry for her instead of myself. Too cosy. And the Doctor's not sure if he's ever coming back.

I walk ye streets. Sixty quid, so which pub's it gonna be? But it turns out the boozers are still all shut anyway. It don't feel early, but it is—children's hour on the telly, just the time of year for smoke and darkness.

End up on the hill on top of the High Street. See the rooftops from here, cars crawling, all them paper warriors on the way home, Tracy doing lipstick on the bus, dreaming of her boyfriend's busy hands and the night to come. Whole of Birmingham's pouring with light. A few more right turns in the Sierra to where the avenues drip sweet evening and Snodgrass says I'm home darling. Deep in the sea arms of love and bolognese for tea. Streets of Solihull and Sutton Coldfield where the kids know how to work a computer instead of just nick one, wear ye uniform at school, places where the grass is velvet and there are magic fountains amid the fairy trees.

The buses drift by on sails of exhaust and the sky is the colour of Ribena. Soon the stars will come. I can feel the whole night pouring in, humming words I can never quite find. Jesus, does *everyone* feel this way? Does Snodgrass carry this around when he's watching Tracy's legs, on holy Sunday before the Big Match polishing the GL badge on his fucking Sierra? Does he dream of the dark tide, seaweed combers of the ocean parting like the lips he never touched?

Me, I'm Snodgrass, Kevin, Tracy, fat Doris in her print dress. I'm every bit part player in the whole bloody horror-show. Everyone except John Lennon. Oh Jesus Mary Joseph and Winston, I dreamed I could circle the world with me arms, take the crowd with me guitar, stomp the beat on dirty floors so it would never end, whisper the dream for every kid under the starch sheets of radio nights. Show them how to shine.

Christ, I need a drink. Find me way easily, growl at dogs and passers-by, but Dave the barman's a mate. Everything's deep red in here and tastes of old booze and cigs and the dodgy Gents, just like swimming through me own blood. Dave is wiping the counter with a filthy rag and it's Getting pissed tonight are we, John? Yet bet, wac. Notice two rastas in the corner. Give em the old comic Livipud accent. Ken Dodd and his Diddymen. Makes em smile. I hate it when they don't smile. Ansells and a chaser. Even got change for the juke-box. Not a Beatles song in sight. No "Yesterday", no "C Moon", no "Mull of Kinbloodytyre". Hey, me shout at ye rastas, Now Bob Marley, he was the biz, reet? At least he had the sense to die. Like Jimi, Jim, Janis, all the good ones who kept the anger and the dream. The rastas say something unintelligible back. Rock and roll, lets. The rastas and Winston, we're on the same wavelength. Buy em a drink. Clap their backs. They're exchanging grins like they think I don't notice. Man, will you look at this sad old git? But he's buying. Yeah I'm buying thanks to Cal. By the way lads, these Rothmans taste like shit, now surely you guys must have something a little stronger?

The evening starts to fill out. I can see everything happening even before it does. Maybe the Doctor will have a little puke round about eight to make room for a greasy chippy. Oh, yeah, and plenty of time for more booze and then maybe a bit of bother later. Rock and roll. The rastas have got their mates with them now and they're saying Hey man, how much money you got there? I wave it in their faces. Wipe yer arse on this, Sambo. Hey, Dave, yer serving or what? Drinky here, drinky there. The good Doctor give drinky everywhere.

Juke-box is pounding. Arms in arms, I'm singing words I don't know. Dave he tell me, Take it easy now, John. And I tell him exactly what to stuff, and precisely where. Oh, yeah. Need to sit down. There's an arm on me shoulder. I push it off. The arm comes again. The Doctor's ready to lash out, so maybe the bother is coming earlier than expected. Well, that's just fine and me turn to face ye foe.

It's Cal.

"John, you just can't hold your booze any longer."

She's leading me out ye door. I wave me rastas an ocean wave. The bar waves back.

The night air hits me like a truncheon. "How the fuck did yer find me?"

"Not very difficult. How many pubs are there around here?"

"I've never counted." No, seriously. "Just dump me here, Cal. Don't give me another chance to piss yer around. Look." I fumble me pockets. Twenty pee. Turns out I'm skint again. "I nicked all yer money. Behind the begonia."

"On the sideboard? That's not mine, it's Kevin's. After last time do you think I'm stupid enough to leave money around where you could find it?"

"Ah-ha!" I point at her in triumph. "You called him Kevin."

"Just get in the bloody car."

I get in the bloody car. Some geezer in the front says Okay guv, and off we zoom. It's a big car. Smells like a new camera. I do me royal wave past Kwiksave. I tell the driver, Hey me man, just step on it and follow that car.

"Plenty of time, sir," he tells me. He looks like a chauffeur. He's wearing a bloody cap.

Time for what?

And Jesus, we're heading to Solihull. I've got me glasses on somehow. Trees and a big dual carriageway, the sort you never see from a bus.

The Doctor does the interior a favour. Says, Stop the car. Do a spastic sprint across ye lay-by and yawn me guts out over the verge. The stars stop spinning. I wipe me face. The Sierras are swishing by.

There's a road sign the size of the Liverpool Empire over me head. Says NEC, two miles. So *that's* it.

Rock and roll. NEC. I've been here and seen Simply Red on Cal's free tickets, all them pretty tunes with their balls lopped off at birth. Knew what to expect. The place is all car park, like a bloody airport but less fun. Cal says Hi to the staff at the big doors, twilight workers in Butlin's blazers. Got any jobs on here, Cal? asks the pretty girl with the pretty programmes. It's Max Bygraves next week. Cal just smiles. The Doctor toys with a witty riposte about how she gets more dough lying with her legs open but decides not to. But Jesus, this is Snodgrass city. I've never seen so many casual suits.

I nick a programme from the pile when no one's looking. Got so much gloss on it, feels like a sheet of glass. The Greatest Hits Tour. Two photos of the Fab Foursome, then and now. George still looks like his mum, and Ringo's Ringo. Stu is wasted, but he always was. And Macca is Cliff on steroids.

"Stop muttering, John," Cal says, and takes me arm.

We go into this aircraft hangar. Half an hour later, we've got to our seat. It's right at the bloody front of what I presume must be the stage. Looks more like Apollo Nine. Another small step backwards for mankind. Oh, yeah. I *know* what a stage should look like. Like the bloody Indra in Hamburg where we took turns between the striptease. A stage is a place where yer stand and fight against the booze and the boredom and the sodding silence. A place where yer make people listen. Like the Cavern too before all the Tracys got their lunchtime jollies by screaming over the music. Magic days where I could feel the power through me Rickenbacker. And that guitar cost me a fortune and where the bloody hell did it get to? Vanished with every other dream.

Lights go down. A smoothie in a pink suit runs up to a mike and says ladeeez and gennnlemen, Paul McCartney, Stuart Sutcliffe, George Harrison, Ringo Starr—the Beatles! Hey, rock and roll. Everyone cheers as they run on stage. Seems like there's about ten of them nowadays, not counting the background chicks. They're all tiny up on that launch pad, but I manage to recognise Paul from the photies. He says Hello (pause) Birrrmingham just like he's Mick Hucknall and shakes his mop top that's still kinda cut the way Astrid did all them years back in Hamburg. Ringo's about half a mile back hidden behind the drums but that's okay cos there's some session guy up there too. George is looking down at his guitar like he's Bert Weedon. And there's Stu almost as far back as Ringo, still having difficulty playing the bass after all these bloody years. Should have stuck with the painting, me lad, something yer were good at. And

Jesus, I don't believe it, Paul shoots Stu an exasperated glance as they kick into the riff for "Long Tall Sally" and he comes in two bars late. Jesus, has *anything* changed.

Yeah, John Lennon's not up there. Would never have lasted this long with the Doctor anyway. I mean, thirty *years*. That's as bad as Status Quo, and at least they know how to rock, even if they've only learnt the one tune.

Days in me life. Number one in a series of one. Collect the fucking set. It's 1962. Eppy's sent us rough lads a telegram from down the Smoke. Great news, boys. A contract. This is just when we're all starting to wonder, and Stu in particular is pining for Astrid back in Hamburg. But we're all giving it a go and the Doctor's even agreed to that stupid haircut that never quite caught on and to sacking Pete Best and getting Ringo in and the bloody suit with the bloody collar and the bloody fucking tie. So down to London it is. And then ta ran ta rah! A real single, a real recording studio! We meet this producer dude in a suit called Martin. He and Eppy get on like old buddies, upper crust and all that and me wonders out loud if he's a queer Jew too, but Paul says Can it John we can't afford to blow this.

So we gets in ye studio which is like a rabbit hutch. Do a roll Ringo, Martin says through the mike. So Ringo gets down on the mat and turns over. We all piss ourselves over that and all the time there's Mr Producer looking schoolmasterish. Me, I say, Hey, did yer really produce the Goons, Meester Martin. I got the "Ying Tong Song" note perfect. They all think I'm kidding. Let's get on with it, John, Eppy says, and oils a grin through the glass, giving me the doe eyes. And don't yer believe it, John knows exactly what he wants. Oh, yeah. Like, did Colonel Parker fancy Elvis? Wow. So this is rock and roll.

Me and Paul, we got it all worked out. Hit the charts with "Love Me Do", by Lennon and McCartney, the credits on the record label just the way we agreed years back in the front parlour of his Dad's house even though we've always done our own stuff separately. It's Macca's song, but we're democratic, right? And what really makes it is me harmonica riff. So that's what we play and we're all nervous as shit but even Stu manages to get the bass part right just the way Paul's shown him.

Silence. The amps are humming. Okay, says Mr Martin, putting on a voice, That was just great, lads. An interesting song. *Interesting*? Never one to beat about the proverbial, I say, yer mean it was shit, right? Just cos we wrote it ourselves and don't live down Tin Pan bloody Alley. But he says, I think we're looking at a B side for that one lads. Now, listen to this.

Oh, yeah. We listen. Martin plays us this tape of a demo of some ditty called "How Do You Do It". Definite Top Ten material for somebody, he says significantly. Gerry and the Pacemakers are already interested but I'll give you first refusal. And Eppy nods beside him through the glass. It's like watching Sooty and bloody Sweep in there. So Ringo smashes a cymbal and Stu tries to tune his bass and George goes over to help and I look at Paul and Paul looks at me.

"It's a decent tune, John," Paul says.

"You're kidding. It's a heap of shit."

Eppy tuts through the glass. Now *John*.

And so it goes. Me, I grab me Rickenbacker and walk out the fucking studio. There's a boozer round the corner. London prices are a joke but I sink one pint and then another, waiting for someone to come and say, You're so right, John. But Paul don't come. Eppy don't come either even though I thought it was me of all the lads that he was after. After the third pint, I'm fucking glad. The haircuts, the suits, and now playing tunes that belong in the bloody adverts. It's all gone too far.

And there it was. John Quits The Beatles in some local snotrag called *Merseybeat* the week after before I've had a chance to change me mind. And after that I've got me pride. When I saw Paul down Victoria Street a couple a months later yer could tell the single was doing well just by his bloody walk. Said Hi John, yer know it's not too late and God knows how *Merseybeat* got hold of the story. He said it as though he and Eppy hadn't jumped at the chance to dump me and make sure everybody knew. There was Macca putting on the charm the way he always did when he was in a tight situation. I told him to stuff it where the fucking sun don't shine. And that was that. I stomped off down ye street, had a cup of tea in Littlewoods. Walked out on Cynthia and the kid. Formed me own band. Did a few gigs. Bolloxed up me life good and proper.

And here we have the Beatles, still gigging, nearly a full house here at the NEC, almost as big as Phil Collins or the Bee Gees. Paul does his old thumbs-up routine between songs. Awwrright. He's a real rock and roll dude, him and George play their own solos just like Dire Straights. The music drifts from the poppy older stuff to the druggy middle stuff back to the poppy later stuff. "Things We Said Today". "Good Day Sun Shine". "Dizzy Miss Lizzy". "Jet". They even do "How Do You Do It". No sign of "Love Me Do", of course. That never got recorded, although I'll bet they could do me harmonica riff on ye synthesiser as easy as shit. It all sounds smooth and tight and sweetly nostalgic, just the way it would on the Sony music centre back at home after Snodgrass has loosened his tie from a hard day watching Tracy wriggle her ass over the fax machine in Accounts. The pretty lights flash, the dry ice fumes, but the spaceship never quite takes off. Me, I shout for "Maxwell's Silver Hammer", and in a sudden wave of silence, it seems like Paul actually hears. He squints down at the front row and grins for a moment like he understands the joke. Then the lights dim to purple and Paul sits down at ye piano, gives the seat a little tug just the way he used to when he was practising on his Dad's old upright in the parlour at home. Plays the opening chords of "Let It Be". I look around me and several thousand flames are held up. It's a forest of candles, and Jesus it's a beautiful song. There's a lump in me throat, God help me. For a moment, it feels like everyone here is close to touching the dream.

The moment lasts longer than it decently should. Right through "No More Lonely Nights" until "Hey Judi" peters out like something half-finished and the band kick into "Lady Madonna", which has a thundering bass riff even though Stu is still picking up his Fender. And the fucking stage starts to revolve. Me, I've had enough.

Cal looks at me as I stand up. She's bopping along like a Tracy. I mouth the word Bog and point to me crotch. She nods. Either she's given up worrying about the Doctor doing a runner or she don't care. Fact is, the booze has wrung me dry and I've got me a headache coming. I stumble me way up the aisles. The music pushes me along. He really *is* gonna do "C Moon". Makes yer want to piss just hearing it.

The lav is deliciously quiet. White tiles and some poor geezer in grey mopping up the piss. The Doctor straddles the porcelain. It takes about a minute's concentration to get a decent flow. Maybe this is what getting old is all about. I wonder if superstars like Macca have the same problem, but I doubt it. Probably pay some geezer to go for them, and oh, Kevin, can yer manage a good dump for me while yer're there?

Once it starts, the flow keeps up for a long time. Gets boring. I flush down ye stray hair, dismantle ye cigarette butt, looking at the grouting on the tiles, stare around. The guy with the mop is leaning on it, watching me.

"Must be a real groove in here," I say.

"Oh, no," he laughs. "Don't get the wrong idea."

I give percy a shake and zip up. The last spurt still runs down me bloody leg. Bet that don't happen to Paul either.

*The wrong idea*? The guy's got the plump face of a thirty-year-old choirboy. Pity poor Eppy ain't still alive, he'd be in his fucking element.

"I think all queers should be shot," fat choirboy assures me.

"Well, seeing it from your perspective . . ." The Doctor starts to back away. This guy's out-weirding me without even trying.

"What's the concert like?"

The music comes around the corner as a grey echo, drowned in the smell of piss and disinfectant. "It's mostly shit, what do yer expect?"

"Yeah," he nods. His accent is funny. I think it's some bastard kind of Brummy until I suddenly realise he's American. "They sold out, didn't they?"

"The Beatles never sold in."

"Bloody hypocrites. All that money going to waste."

Some other guy comes in, stares at us as he wees. Gives his leg a shake, walks out again. Choirboy and I stand in stupid silence. It's one of them situations yer find yerself in. But anyone who thinks that the Beatles are crap can't be all bad.

"You used to be in the Beatles, didn't you?"

I stare at him. No one's recognised me just from me face in years. I've got me glasses on, me specially grey and wrinkled disguise.

"Oh, I've read all about the Beatles," he assures me, giving his mop a twirl.

I've half a mind to say, If yer're that interested give me the fucking mop and yer can have me seat, but there's something about him that I wouldn't trust next to Cal.

"Hey," he smiles. "Listen in there. Sounds like they're doing the encore."

Which of course is "Yesterday", like Oh deary me, we left it out by accident from the main show and thought we would just pop it in here. Not a dry seat in the bloody house.

Choirboy's still grinning at me. I see he's got a paperback in the pocket of his overall. *Catcher in the Rye*. "They'll be a big rush in a minute," he says. "More mess for me to clean up. Even Jesus wouldn't like this job."

"Then why do yer do it? The pay can't be spectacular."

"Well, this is just casual work. I'll probably quit after tonight."

"Yeah, pal. I know all about casual work."

"But this is interesting, gets you into places. I like to be near to the stars. I need to see how bad they are." He cracks that grin a little wider. "Tell me," he says, "what's Paul really like?"

"How the fuck should I know? I haven't seen the guy in nearly thirty years. But, there's . . . there's some do on afterwards . . . he's asked me and me bird to come along. Yer know, for old times I guess." *Jesus, John, who are yer trying to impress*?

"Oh," he says, "and where's that taking place? I sometimes look in, you know. The security round here's a joke. Last week, I was *that* close to Madonna." He demonstrates the distance with his broom.

Cal's got the invites in her handybag, but I can picture them clear enough. I've got a great memory for crap. They're all scrolled like it's a wedding and there's a signed pass tacked on the back just to make it official. Admit two, The Excelsior, Meriden. Boogie on down, and I bet the Lord Mayor's coming. And tomorrow it's Reading. I mean, do these guys paarrty every night?

Choirboy grins. "It's here at the Metropole, right?"

"Oh, yeah, the Metropole." I saw the neon on the way in. "That's the place just outside? Saves the bastards having to walk too far." I scratch me head. "Well maybe I'll see yer there. And just let me know if yer have any trouble at all getting in, right?"

"Right on." He holds out his hand. I don't bother to shake it—and it's not simply because this guy cleans bogs. I don't want him near me, and somehow I don't want him near Paul or the others either. He's a fruitcase, and I feel briefly and absurdly pleased with meself that I've sent him off to ye wrong hotel.

I give him a wave and head on out ye bog. In the aircraft hangar, music's still playing. Let's all get up and dance to a song de da de da de dum de dum. Snodgrass and Tracy are trying to be enthusiastic so they can tell everyone how great it was in the office tomorrow. I wander down the aisles, wondering if it might be easier not to meet up with Cal. On reflection, this seems as good a place as any to duck out of her life. Do the cunt a favour. After all, she deserves it. And to be honest, I really don't fancy explaining to Kevin where all his money went. He's a big lad, is our Kev. Useful, like.

The music stops. The crowd claps like they're really not sure whether they want any more and Paul raises an unnecessary arm to still them.

"Hey, one more song then we'll let yer go," he says with probably unintentional irony. I doubt if they know what the fuck is going on up there in Mission Control.

He puts down his Gibson and a roadie hands him something silver. Stu's grinning like a skull. He even wanders within spitting distance of the front of the stage. A match-stick figure, I can see he looks the way Keith Richards would have done if he *really* hadn't taken care of himself. He nods to George. George picks up a twelve string.

"This one's for an old friend," Paul says.

The session musicians are looking at each other like What the fuck's going on? Could this really be an unrehearsed moment? Seems unlikely, but then Paul muffs the count in on a swift four/four beat. There's nervous laughter amongst the Fab Fearsome, silence in the auditorium. Then again. One. Two. Three. And.

Macca puts the harmonica to his lips. Plays me *riff*. "Love Me Do". Oh, yeah. I really can't believe it. The audience are looking a bit bemused, but probably reckon it's just something from the new LP that's stacked by the yard out in the foyer and no one's bothered to buy. The song's over quickly. Them kind of songs always were. Me, I'm crying.

The End. Finis, like they say in cartoon. Ye Beatles give a wave and duck off stage. I get swept back in the rush to get to ye doors. I hear snatches of, Doesn't he look *old*, They *never* knew how to rock, Absolutely *brilliant*, and *How* much did you pay the babysitter? I wipe the snot off on me sleeve and look around. Cal catches hold of me by the largely unpatronised T-shirt stall before I have a chance to see her coming.

"What did you think?"

"A load of shit," I say, hoping she won't notice I've been crying.

She smiles. "Is that all you can manage, John? That must mean you liked it."

Touché, Monsieur Pussycat. "Truth is, I could need a drink."

"Well, let's get down the Excelsior. You can meet your old mates and get as pissed as you like."

She glides me out towards the door. Me feet feel like they're on rollers. And there's me chauffeur pal with the boy scout uniform. People stare at us as he opens the door like we're George Michael. Pity he don't salute, but still, I'd look a right pillock trying to squirm me way away from a pretty woman and the back seat of a Jag.

The car pulls slowly through the crowds. I do me wave like I'm the Queen Mum although the old bint's probably too hip to be seen at a Beatles concert. Turns out there's a special exit for us VIPs. I mean, rock and roll. It's just a few minutes' drive, me mate up front tells us.

Cal settles back. "This is the life."

"Call this life?"

"Might as well make the most of it, John."

"Oh, yeah. I bet you get taken in this kind of limo all the time. Blowjobs in the back seat. It's what pays, right?" I bite me lip and look out the window. Jesus, I'm starting to cry again.

"Why do you say things like that, John?"

"Because I'm a bastard. I mean, you of all people must know about bastards having to put up with Steve."

Cal laughed. "You called him Steve!"

I really must be going ta bits. "Yeah, well I must have puked up me wits over that lay-by."

"Anyway," she touches me arm. "Call him whatever you like. I took your advice this evening. Told him where to stuff it."

I look carefully at her face. She obviously ain't kidding, but I can't see any bruises. "And what about the money I nicked?"

"Well, that's not a problem for me, is it? I simply told him the truth, that it was you." She smiled. "Come on, John. I'd almost believe you were frightened of him. He's just some bloke. He's got another girl he's after anyway, the other side of town and good luck to her."

"So it's just you and me is it, Cal. Cosy, like. Don't expect me to sort out yer customers for yer."

"I'm getting too old for that, John. It costs you more than they pay. Maybe I'll do more work at the NEC. Of course, you'll have to start paying your sodding rent."

I hear meself say, "I think there's a vacancy coming up in the NEC Gents. How about that for a funky job for Dr Winston? At least you get to sweep the shit up there rather than having to stuff it into envelopes."

"What are you talking about, John?"

"Forget it. Maybe I'll explain in the morning. You've got influence there, haven't you?"

"I'll help you get a job, if that's what you're trying to say."

I lookouta ye window. The houses streaming past, yellow windows, where ye Snodgrasses who weren't at the concert are chomping pipe and slippers while the wife makes spaniel eyes. The kids tucked upstairs in pink and blue rooms that smell of Persil and Playdough. Me, I'm just the guy who used to be in a halfway-famous band before they were anybody. I got me no book club subscription, I got me no life so clean yer could eat yer bloody dinner off it. Of course, I still got me rebellion, oh yeah, I got me that, and all it amounts to is cadging cigs off Cal and lifting packets of Cheesy Wotsits from the bargain bin in Kwiksave when Doris and Tracy ain't looking. Oh, yeah, rebellion. The milkman shouts at me when I go near his float in case the Mad Old Git nicks another bottle.

I can remember when we used to stand up and face the crowd, do all them songs I've forgotten how to play. When Paul still knew how to rock. When Stu was half an artist, dreamy and scary at the same time. When George was just a neat kid behind a huge guitar, lying about his age. When Ringo was funny and the beat went on forever. Down the smoggily lit stairways and greasy tunnels, along burrows and byways where the cheesy reek of the bogs hit yer like a wall. Then the booze was free afterwards and the girls would gather round, press softly against yer arm as they smiled. Their boyfriends would mutter at the bar but you knew they were afraid of yer.

Knew they could sense the power of the music that carried off the stage. Jesus, the girls were as sweet as the rain in those grey cities, the shining streets, the forest wharves, the dark doorways where there was laughter in the dripping brick-paved night. And sleeping afterwards, yer head spinning from the booze and the wakeups and the downers, taking turns on that stained mattress with the cinema below booming in yer head and the music still pouring through. Diving down into carousel dreams.

Oh, the beat went on all right. Used to think it would carry up into daylight and the real air, touch the eyes and ears of the pretty dreamers, even make Snodgrass stir a little in his slumbers, take the shine off the Sierra, make him look up at the angels in the sky once in a while, or even just down at the shit on the pavement.

"Well, here we are," Cal says.

Oh, yeah. Some hotel. Out in the pretty pretty. Trees and lights across a fucking lake. The boy scout opens the door for me and Cal. Unsteady on me pins, I take a breath, then have me a good retching cough. The air out here reeks of roses or something, like one of them expensive bog fresheners that Cal sprays around when our Kev's had a dump.

"Hey." Cal holds out the crook of her arm. "Aren't you going to escort me in?"

"Let's wait here."

There are other cars pulling up, some old git dressed like he's the Duke of Wellington standing at the doors. Straight ahead to the Clarendon Suite, sir, he smooths greyly to the passing suits. I suppose these must be record industry types. And then there's this bigger car than the rest starts to pull up. It just goes on and on, like one of them gags in *Tom and Jerry*. Everyone steps back like it's the Pope. Instead, turns out it's just the Beatles. They blink around in the darkness like mad owls, dressed in them ridiculous loose cotton suits that Clapton always looks such a prat in. Lawyers tremble around them like little fish. Paul pauses to give a motorcycle policeman his autograph, flashes the famous Macca grin. Some guy in a suit who looks like the hotel manager shakes hands with Stu. Rock and roll. I mean, this is what we were always fighting for. The Beatles don't register the good Doctor before they head inside, but maybe that's because he's taken three steps back into the toilet freshener darkness.

"What are we waiting for?" Cal asks as the rest of the rubbernecks drift in.

"This isn't easy, Cal."

"Who said anything about *easy*?"

I give the Duke of Wellington a salute as he holds ye door open.

"Straight ahead to the Clarendon Suite, sir."

"Hey," I tell him, "I used to be Beatle John."

"Stop mucking about, John." Cal does her Kenneth Williams impression, then gets all serious. "This is important. Just forget about the past and let's concentrate on the rest of your life. All you have to say to Paul is Hello. He's a decent guy. And I'm sure that the rest of them haven't changed as much as you imagine."

Cal wheels me in. The hotel lobby looks like a hotel lobby. The Tracy at reception gives me a cutglass smile. Catch a glimpse of meself in the mirror and unbelievably I really don't look too bad. Must be slipping.

"Jesus, Cal. I need a smoke."

"Here." She rumbles in me pocket, produces Kevin's Rothmans. "I suppose you want a bloody light."

All the expensive fish are drifting by. Some bint in an evening dress so low at the back that you can see the crack of her arse puts her arm on this Snodgrass and gives him a peck on the cheek. That was *delightful*, darrling, she purrs. She really does.

"I mean a *real* smoke, Cal. Haven't you got some blow?" I make a lunge for her handbag.

"Bloody hell, John," she whispers, looking close to losing her cool. She pushes something into my hand. "Have it outside, if you must. Share it with the bloody doorman."

"Thanks Cal." I give her a peck on the cheek and she looks at me oddly. "I'll never forget."

"Forget what?" she asks as I back towards the door. Then she begins to understand. But the Duke holds the door open for me and already I'm out in the forest night air.

The door swings back, then open again. The hotel lights fan out across the grass. I look back. There's some figure.

"Hey, *John*!"

It's a guy's voice, not Cal's after all. Sounds almost Liverpool.

"Hey, wait a minute! Can't we just talk?"

The voice rings in silence.

"John! It's me!"

Paul's walking into the darkness towards me. He's holding out his hand. I stumble against chrome. The big cars are all around. Then I'm kicking white stripes down the road. Turns to gravel underfoot and I can see blue sea, a white beach steaming after the warm rain, a place where a woman is waiting and the bells jingle between her breasts. Just close your eyes and you're there.

Me throat me legs me head hurts. But there's a gated side road here that leads off through trees and scuffing the dirt at the end of a field to some big houses that nod and sway with the sleepy night.

I risk a look behind. Everything is peaceful. There's no one around. Snodgrass is dreaming. Stars upon the rooftops, and the Sierra's in the drive. Trees and privet, lawns neat as velvet. Just some suburban road at the back of the hotel. People living their lives.

I catch me breath, and start to run again.

# KATE WILHELM

# The Day of the Sharks

KATE WILHELM was born in Louisville, Kentucky, and lives in Eugene, Oregon with her husband, noted writer and critic Damon Knight. *Locus* has described her novels as being "among the most immediate, trenchant commentaries on our world and our lives available today."

She received her first Nebula Award in 1968 for her story "The Planners", and her latest Nebula in 1988 for "Forever Yours, Anna". She has also been honoured with a Hugo Award (for her novel *Where Late the Sweet Birds Sang*), a Prix Apollo Award and a Jupiter Award.

Her recent books include a fantasy novel, *Cambio Bay*, and a mystery entitled *Justice for Some*. "The Day of the Sharks" originally appeared in her landmark collection *And the Angels Sing*. Set during a seemingly idyllic Florida vacation, a faltering marriage takes a disturbingly nightmarish turn in the powerful narrative which follows . . .

HER TRANQUILIZER IS WEARING OFF, Gary thinks, when Veronica begins to tell him about it again. He stops listening almost immediately, and watches the road.

"... that thin voice coming in my ears, hour after hour. You know, he doesn't dictate it like that. He pauses and goes out, has coffee, sees other patients, but day after day, having that box talk to me ..."

The road is a glare, the sun straight ahead, centered in the dazzling whiteness of the concrete; the bay they are skirting is without a ripple, an endless mirror of eye-hurting brilliance. It will be beautiful when the sun is actually setting, he thinks, but now his eyes burn, and the damn air-conditioning in the rented car is malfunctioning, alternately shocking them with random cold blasts, or leaving them sweltering in the airless machine that smells of deodorizers and cleaning fluids.

"... and they weren't people. Not after a while. They were gall bladders and thyroids and kidney stones. I began to wonder if there were any people even connected to them. You know? Free-floating kidney stones."

A flight of birds catches his attention; they just clear the water, almost touching the surface with their broad wings that look tattered, old, as if they have been at war, are flak-torn.

"... system's supposed to help with the filing, for the computers, or something. Everything by number, not even parts of the anatomy any longer. Just numbers and prices. Case histories of numbers."

Her voice is getting high, tight, the way it does these days. Her posture has become rigid, her gaze fixed on a point straight ahead; she can stay this way for hours, unmoving, seeing what? He can't imagine what she sees. He grasps the steering wheel harder, wishes she would take another damn tranquilizer and be done with it. She will eventually. But she is afraid of them throughout the day until after dinner when it doesn't matter if she falls asleep. She took two at breakfast and dozed on the flight from Chicago to Tampa; it was a peaceful flight.

Ahead, a squat, ugly complex comes into view, black against the glaring sky, his next landmark. He slows to make the turn off the highway over a bridge onto a narrower road. Now, with the sun to his right, he can drive faster. The islands have nothing on them, a few palm trees, some dunes, scrub that looks like felled palm trees, more birds. Sea gulls, he thinks, with near triumph. At least he knows sea gulls. Six miles farther.

His thoughts turn to Bill Hendrix and his wife Shar. And then he is thinking only of Shar. For the first time after she and Bill moved down here she pleaded with him to come visit. He could fake a business trip. He could meet her in Tallahassee, or Miami, or somewhere. Then no more begging, no more anything, until the call from Bill. "If you're going to the Bahamas, hell, man, you've got to come for the weekend, at least. You can fly on from Tampa on Monday."

"We should have gone straight on to Grand Bahama," Veronica mumbles, facing the arrowlike road that seems to plunge into the blue water in the distance. A low dense clump of green rises on the left. The greenery expands, becomes pine trees, motionless in the still, late afternoon. "Turn again just after the pines," Bill's instructions went on. There is only one way to turn, left. They enter the subdivision under construction.

Unfinished houses are ugly, Gary thinks, obscenely ugly, naked, no illusions about them, the land around the buildings cluttered with junk that will be hidden away by the bulldozers, but there, always there. The landfill is dazzling white: sand, shells, the detritus dredged from the bay to create land, brought up long enough ago to have bleached to snow white.

"We should have gone straight on to Grand Bahama," Veronica says again, louder, still not looking at him.

"I told you, I have this business with Bill. We'll leave first thing Monday morning."

They wind through the subdivision, following instructions. A short causeway, to the end of the street, on to the point. There is Bill's house, with a yard fully landscaped, green and flowering. Gary's eyes narrow as he looks at it. The house is almost hidden from the street, but what shows is expensive, and the landscaping cost a fortune.

Bill said only three houses were finished, and that one is still vacant. The buyers will move in on the first of the month. They have not passed the other completed houses.

"I hardly even know them," Veronica says, not quite whining although a petulant tone has entered her voice. Gary doesn't know what that is supposed to mean. They were friends for more than five years. Gary wonders if she ever suspected Shar, if Bill ever did. He is almost certain no one did, but still, there is the possibility. Veronica knows there was someone. She always knows.

He parks in the driveway, but before they can get out of the car, they are suddenly chilled by a last effort of the air conditioner. He feels goose bumps rise; Veronica's skin takes on a bluish cast. Bill and Shar are coming out to meet them.

She has a beautiful tan, the same dark gold all over her legs, her arms, her face. Her hair is blonder than it was before; she might have been a little thinner before, but otherwise she looks exactly the same. There is a sheen on her skin, as if she has been polished. She is tall and strong, a Viking type, she calls herself. Nothing willowy about her, nothing fat or slack. She has long, smooth muscles in her legs; her stomach is as firm and flat as a boy's. She wears white briefs and a halter, and rubber thongs on her feet. Bill is a bit shorter than she is, thickly built, very powerful, with thick wrists and a thick neck. Size seventeen. They are both so tanned that Gary feels he and Veronica must both look like invalids.

"My God! Ghosts!" Shar cries, as Gary and Veronica get out of the car. She embraces them with too much enthusiasm and warmth, and Gary can sense Veronica's withdrawal. Next to Shar, Veronica appears used up, old. She is only thirty-one, but she looks ill, as she is, and she looks frightened and suspicious, and very tired. There are circles under her eyes; he feels guilty that he has not seen them before, that only now, contrasting her with Shar does he recognize the signs of illness, remember that this isn't simply a vacation.

"Hey, it's good to see you," Bill says, putting his arm across Gary's back. "Come on in. A drink is what you people need. And tomorrow we'll get out in the sun and put some color in your cheeks."

It should be warm and friendly, but it isn't. It is like walking into a scenario where every line has been rehearsed, the stage sets done by art majors; even the sky has been given an extra touch of the brush. It is gaudy now with sunset, the ambient light peach colored, and out back, visible through a wall of sliding glass doors, the bay is brilliant, touched with gold.

"Two hundred sixty-five thou," Bill says, waving his hand as they enter the house where the furniture is either white or sleek, shiny black. He goes to a bar and pours martinis already made up, and they sit down where they can watch the lights on the bay. Between them and the golden water are red and yellow flowering bushes, an Olympic-size swimming pool, a terrace with enough seating and tables to serve as a cafe. "Too much, isn't it?" Bill says, grinning. "Just too goddam much."

"Are you hungry?" Shar asks. "Dinner won't be until pretty late. We're having a little party, buffet about ten. How about a sandwich, something to tide you over?"

"Oh, Gary," Veronica says, stricken.

"No sweat," Bill says. "It's a business party. You know, people I owe. Just happened to coincide. Don't feel you're interrupting anything."

Still, Veronica looks at Gary as if pleading with him; he shrugs. "It'll be all right," he says, trying to make his impatience sound like patience. "She hasn't been feeling very well," he adds, glancing at Shar.

"It won't be too much of a drag, I hope," Shar says lightly. "Wind us up and watch us entertain. Isn't that right, Bill?"

He laughs and pours more drinks. "You'll fit right in, Gary. Just watch how their eyes gleam when I tell them you're an investment counselor." He laughs again.

The party is little more than an excuse to get loud and drunk, Gary admits to himself later, wandering on the terrace with a drink in his hand, tired from the over-long day, bored with people he doesn't know, doesn't want to know. He knows their types, he thinks, watching a heavy-set man in a flowered shirt mock-push a nearly bare-breasted woman into the pool, laughing, leering, lusting. Shar touches his arm.

"Dance?"

They dance, his hand warmed by her golden back that is almost too smooth to be human. "Can I see you alone later?"

She smiles and doesn't answer.

He dances her to the end of the terrace, more discreetly lighted than the other areas, and kisses her. "Later?"

"Don't be an idiot. With your wife and my husband on the scene?"

"Veronica will be knocked out with tranquilizers, and Bill's on his way to passing out."

"What's wrong with Veronica?"

"Nerves, I guess. She flipped out at work. Tried to burn down the office or something."

"Good God! Did she really?"

"She says she was only burning the files, but the whole place would have gone up if it hadn't been caught when it was."

"What did they do to her?"

He is tired of talking about Veronica, tired of thinking about her. "Hospital. Two weeks. Now a vacation, and then into analysis, I guess. She's under a shrink's care."

"Poor Gary," Shar says, her voice amused.

He can't see her features, but can feel the warmth of her skin, smell the elusive scent that she wears, that she always wore. When he starts to kiss her again, she moves away and walks back toward the house. "Later," he says, this time not asking.

She smiles over her shoulder and stops to chat with a group of men standing at the sliding door to the Florida room.

Finally, Gary spots Veronica at a table by a man, clutching her glass tightly, her eyes glazed in the way they do when she drinks more than a glass of wine. He curses silently and turns to see Bill approaching with another man in tow. Bill is red faced, perspiring heavily, and the grace that he displays when sober is gone. He lumbers, stumbles into things, loses coordination in a way that seems to suggest that his limbs have different reaction times. He wards off a table before he is within reach, then hits it with his thigh, and belatedly clutches a chair to steady himself. Gary moves closer to Veronica and the unknown man; he doesn't want to talk to a drunken Bill.

". . . density ratio so fouled up that no one knows what the hell they're going to do. Six hundred units per acre. Now I ask you, does that sound too terrible to you, a city girl? You know Chicago can handle that many people, what's the difference?"

Veronica shakes her head helplessly. "Units?"

"Yep. They're saying no more than two fifty per acre. Two hundred fifty! What kind of condo can you put up with only two fifty?"

Veronica looks almost desperate; relief relaxes her face when Gary draws near. "Have you eaten yet?" he asks.

She stands up, nods to the man, and takes Gary's arm. Her fingers dig in convulsively. "How long will this go on?" she whispers, as they walk toward the buffet.

She looks and sounds terrible; she should go to bed. Her tension is almost a palpable thing, electric. He feels that he could touch it, be burned by it.

Bill blocks their way, still with the tall man. "Gary, want you to meet Dwight Scanlon, president of the development company I was telling you about. My good friend, Gary Ingalls, and Veronica."

"Hear you're on your way to Grand Bahama," Dwight Scanlon says, taking Gary's hand. "Lovely place. We've got a hotel over there, in fact. You have your rooms reserved? Look, cancel them, why don't you? I've got this suite, nobody in it, nobody scheduled for it until June. Yours for the taking."

Before Gary can refuse, Scanlon has turned to Veronica. "Have you seen the moon coming up over that bay yet? What a sight!" He offers his arm; she puts her hand on it tentatively, and they walk out together.

Bill downs his drink and runs his hand over his face. "Gotta turn on that air conditioner pretty soon."

The air conditioner is on, but the house is jammed with guests, and waiters and caterers. The sliding doors to the terrace have been open all evening. Gary wanders back outside where he sits down at a wrought-iron table. His head is buzzing, not unpleasantly, and there is a lightness in his legs and arms, also not unpleasant. He watches a sinuous woman work her way through a cluster of people to approach his table with evident purpose.

"I'm Audrey Scanlon," she says, and sits down after pulling a tiny chair very close to his. "You're Gary, aren't you?"

He nods.

"Perhaps you'd like to help us launch our boat Sunday," she says. She does not touch him, but he has the feeling that she is all over him.

"No way," Shar says coolly, suddenly at Gary's side. "He's ours until Monday morning; aren't you, Gary, darling?"

Audrey stands up. "Maybe we'll see you in Grand Bahama," she whispers and now she does touch him. Her hand lingers a moment on his arm, and when she moves away, she doesn't lift it, but lets her fingers trail over his skin very lightly.

"Bitch," Shar says, when she is gone.

"No doubt, they just happen to have this little company that they would love to have recommended to prospective buyers." He sounds bitter even to his ears. Shar pats his arm. Someone calls her and she leaves him.

Soon Veronica returns from the dock; her eyes are shining. "I've been propositioned, I think."

"Scanlon?"

She nods. She looks very happy.

"His wife just did the same with me. They must be fresh in from the swamps."

"Don't make it sound like that," Veronica cries. "Maybe he just found me attractive! Wouldn't it occur to you that someone else might still find me attractive?"

"He wants me to list his company," Gary says. "And he has as much finesse about it as a hippo humping a hippo."

"I wouldn't have done it." Her face twitches and settles into the newly familiar rigid lines. "I wouldn't have done anything," she says woodenly. "Why couldn't you let me have my little fantasy?"

"You should go to bed. You're so tired, you're ready to keel over."

She walks away unsteadily.

Someone falls into the pool; within minutes there are a number of rescuers in the water. After that it seems almost spontaneous, although it never really is, he knows, for others to begin shedding their clothes to jump in. Gary swims naked, as do Shar and Audrey, and a dozen others. All laughing and playing and then huddling in towels and drinking again.

Guests are leaving now, and presently there are only three or four remaining, drinking with Bill, nostalgic about old times, before the islands were bought. Veronica has vanished, possibly to go to bed. Gary takes Shar's hand and leads her to the terrace, beyond it to the velvet lawn where he spreads his towel and hers to make a bed. He lowers her to the ground; she doesn't resist.

Immediately afterward she draws away. "I have to go in," she murmurs. "I can't stay out here." She stands over him; he sits up and puts his arms around her hips, pulls her to him, presses his face into her pubic hair and bites softly. She moans and sways, but then pushes him away. "No more. Not now."

She runs, naked, gleaming in the patio lights briefly, then vanishes into one of the rooms that open to the terrace.

Gary swims again, but he knows he is too drunk to be in the water alone; he climbs out shivering, with exhaustion as much as from the cold. The guest room has an outside door, he remembers; he finds it and goes in to shower and dry himself and dress again. Veronica is not in the room. When he returns to the living room, all the guests are gone. Bill has brought out champagne that he, Veronica, and Shar are drinking.

They drink until dawn flames the sky and then they go to bed. It is eleven when Gary awakens with a pounding headache; Veronica is already up and out.

"Take this," Bill says when he enters the dining room. "Don't ask questions, just drink it." It is a juice drink, heavily spiked with bourbon. For a moment Gary feels his stomach churn, then it settles down again. The drink is very good.

Veronica looks awful; her eyes are red rimmed and blood-shot, sunken in her face. "Why don't you try to sleep some more?" he says, too miserable to care one way or the other.

From the kitchen come sounds of things being banged about. Bill winces. "Caterers' clean-up crew," he says. "Let's go out to the dock until they finish."

"I'll bring the cart," Shar says. "God knows we all need something to eat, and coffee, lots of coffee."

The sun is hot, but the breeze is refreshing. The bay is about a mile wide; there are no signs of civilization, as long as they face away from this subdivision. Now and again a jumping fish makes ripples that undulate in the water as the tide flows in like a river.

"Twelve feet deep here," Bill says. "It's shallow up in the fingers. Point's the place to be." His boat is thirty-five feet, two-forty horsepower Westinghouse . . .

Gary gazes at the gently moving water and doesn't listen to Bill cataloguing his treasures. Objects and wielders, he thinks. They all were objects and wielders of objects last night. Changing roles as easily as they changed their clothes. Even his too-brief contact with Shar was object and wielder, and he does not know who played which part.

Suddenly he recalls the scene when he first visited Veronica in the hospital. She was stupefied from Thorazine, or something they gave her. Her voice was singsong. "I don't think there are any people, Gary. Nowhere. They're all gone, and I don't know where they went. I'm so afraid." She did not sound afraid, only dull and drug-stupid.

Later, Bill will make his pitch, Gary knows. *Hit a little snag, old buddy. You know how it goes.* He knows. He drinks the strong black coffee, thinking how distant his head has become, throbbing like drums not quite heard, but felt as pressure. Across the bay the land has not been developed yet and shows a low green, irregular skyline, a fitting place for the drums to originate from. He watches a boat sail up the channel, nearly all the way across the bay.

"We'll just rest up this afternoon," Bill says. "Take life easy, that's the motto down here. Not like your big city, eh?"

No one replies. Veronica is nibbling on a piece of toast; some color has come back to her face, but it is probably only the beginning of a sunburn. Shar's gaze meets Gary's and she lets her eyes close slightly, a very faint smile on her mouth.

"And tomorrow, bright and early, we'll take the boat out," Bill says. "Do a little fishing out in the gulf." He pours more coffee and lights a cigarette.

"What's that?" Veronica says suddenly, sitting upright. She points. "A shark, or something."

They all look as a dark form breaks the smooth surface of the water, arches up, and vanishes again. It is on their side of the channel, several hundred yards out.

"I'll be damned," Bill says. "One of those whales. I thought they all died." He watches and when it breaks the water again, he nods in satisfaction. "It's a false killer whale."

"Killer whale? Here?" Gary asks.

"*False* killer whale. Harmless, just looks like the real thing. Listen, let me tell you what I saw a few weeks ago. Damnedest thing I ever saw in my life. Over near Fort Myers. I was driving along, heard this report on the car radio about whales beaching themselves. So I thought, what the hell, I'd go have a look. Beach was crowded with people by the time I got there, but nothing was happening. I keep binoculars in the car, you know? So I got them out, and watched. There was a line of those animals out there in the water, quarter of a mile offshore, just laying there in the water. Not moving a muscle. No surf, no wind, as calm as that bay is right now. I kept watching, beginning to get bored with the whole thing, you know? They weren't doing a damn thing. Just laying there. Then, by God, they started to move in. All at once, all together, like a goddam chorus line. And they kept coming, and kept coming until they were in water too shallow to swim in and they began to roll. People were jumping in from everywhere, yanking on them, trying to get them turned around, headed back out. Some people had rowboats, a couple of motorboats, people in the water up to their necks, just trying to get those things back out to sea. And while they're working with this bunch, another bunch was starting in, the females and young. They'd been waiting half a mile offshore for some kind of a damn signal, or something, and now they were coming in. People kept getting the first ones turned around, and those whales would just sort of swerve a couple of feet to one side or the other and back they'd come in to shore. It went on for hours. Some of the boats towed a couple of the big males out to sea again, I guess hoping that the others would follow them. They didn't."

His voice is low, awed, his gaze following the movements of the whale in the bay. "They got a lot of them out to sea again, but a dozen of them made it in. They died on the beach. Mass suicide. The damnedest thing I ever saw."

No one speaks for several moments, then Veronica says, "Why?" Her voice is tight and high. "Were they sick?"

"Marine biologists couldn't find anything wrong. No sharks in the water. No storms to mix them up, and it was too deliberate to think they just made a mistake, misjudged the depth of the water. No one knows why."

"That's crazy!" Veronica cries, jumping up. "There has to be a reason. There's always a reason!" The shrillness of her voice is startling. She clamps her lips and runs up the dock, back inside the house.

"God, I'm sorry," Bill says, his big face contrite. "I shouldn't have told that story. It . . . it haunts me."

"Forget it," Gary says. "What happened to the rest of the whales? You thought they all died?"

"That's the worst part," Bill says soberly. "The next day they found them down in the Keys. Beached on one of the islands down there."

Shar stands up. "I'll go do something about lunch. The caterers must be gone by now."

The whale continues to swim in great circles out in the bay, close in, then farther out again. Bill begins to tell Gary about the financial problems his company has encountered, through no fault of their own. Gary promises nothing. He will study the financial statements, the local restrictions, and so on. Bill understands. He lays his hand on Gary's arm and assures him that he understands.

Veronica doesn't come out for lunch, and after the others eat, Shar and Bill withdraw to nap. Gary puts on his trunks and swims in the pool, then stretches out under a cluster of palm trees, something *Reclinatus*, Bill said. You can transplant full-grown palm trees, instant garden, Gary thinks, listening to the wind in the fronds, a soothing rainlike sound. You dredge up the bay bottom, smooth it out, cover it with a carpet of sod, plant trees, flowers, shrubs, plant a house, plant people. Instant paradise. And there are no insects in the ground. Barren, pseudodirt. Not real.

Veronica said, after her hospitalization, "Sometimes I wonder, if I reach out to touch you when you're not looking, not thinking about me, not concentrating on being you, will my hand go through you?"

"Meaning?"

"I don't know. Nothing you do is real. You work with money—bits of paper that have no meaning. You don't even see the money. It isn't real, just figures on paper, symbols in the computer. You don't make anything, or fix anything. After you finish for the day, does the office lose its shape, melt down to nothing until you get back and give it a pseudoreality again?"

"Veronica! For heaven's sake!" He reached for her and she drew away sharply, in recoil almost.

"No! That isn't real either. A touch, a kiss, a fuck. Pseudoreal."

"I don't know what the hell you're talking about."

"You can tell if it's real. You can tell. If it's there years later. If you can go to it and find it years later." Her voice became a whisper, her gaze on something he could not see. "Money becomes figures on paper. Patients become organs that become numbers in the computer. Pseudoreal."

After she is well again, they will separate. He has already decided. She is young, pretty until she became ill. She will marry again, maybe even have children. She wants children; he said later, after we're established, a little money saved. Later. And he will find someone new, someone with gaiety in her laugh, who isn't sick. Someone who will bring fun into his life again.

He dozes in the shade and awakens to find that the sun is burning his legs. The distant throbbing has entered his head; it is his head, but there is another noise, screeching and screaming.

"Hey, old buddy, you want a gin and tonic?" Bill calls from the doorway.

"I sure as hell want something," Gary says. He feels worse than he did that morning.

Bill steps out to the terrace, shielding his eyes with his hand, looking at gulls screaming, diving, shrieking, just off the end of the dock. "Must be a school running," he says, and starts to walk toward the commotion.

Gary follows him slowly. They stop halfway up the dock. The whale is alongside the structure, the entire animal clearly visible in the quiet water. Blood is flowing from under it. The gulls wheel and scream overhead; now and then one of them dips to the surface of the water, darts up again.

"I will be God damned!" Bill says in wonder. "She's going to give birth. For Christ's sake!"

The whale pays no attention to the men on the dock. Now and then a long shudder passes through her, rippling from her great black head down to her tail. She is gleaming black, nine feet long, sleek; her blowhole opens and closes convulsively. She shudders; her body twists. She sinks, surfaces again.

"She's in trouble," Gary says.

Bill looks at him blankly.

"It shouldn't take more than a minute or so. I read that somewhere. And she's bleeding too much."

The stain rises in the water, spreads like a cloud. It seems to rise like smoke signals.

"There must be someone who knows what to do," Gary says, staring at the helpless animal. "The university?"

"It's after five, Saturday," Bill says. "The Coast Guard. I'll call them. Someone there will know."

Gary stands on the dock, his hands clenched, watching the animal and the distress signals dispersing through the water. He doesn't hear the others until Shar says, "Oh, my God!" He turns to see her and Veronica staring at the whale.

"They'll find someone to send," Bill says, hurrying across the yard. "It might take a while, though."

The animal doesn't have a while, Gary knows. He doesn't say it. They continue to watch in horrified fascination as the ripples that are pain reactions spread throughout the animal regularly.

Suddenly Shar draws her breath in. "Oh, no!" she cries. She is staring out at the bay. "Sharks!"

Gary sees them, two fins moving through the water almost leisurely, as if they know there is no need to hurry. Bill turns and runs to the house. He comes back moments later with a rifle. He puts a handful of shells on the dock and loads a clip.

"Where are they?" His voice is hoarse, the words slurred. Shar points. He doesn't raise the rifle. "Too far," he says in his strange voice.

It is excitement, Gary realizes; his own mouth is dry and he feels prickly with sweat and goose bumps, as if something loathsome has touched him.

"It won't do any good," Veronica says, and her voice is different, too, high and clear, but steady. "As soon as the baby is born, she'll want to go out to sea, won't she? They'll be waiting for her."

She is looking out at the channel. There are more fins. A pack then. They must have followed the trail of blood from out in the gulf. Veronica appears transfixed, as if in a trance.

"You'd better go inside," he says. She does not give any sign that she heard him. He touches her arm and she twitches with a convulsive shudder, like the whale's. She does not look at him. "Get inside, damn it!" His hand falls from her arm and he turns away. She wants to see the blood fest, he realizes, sickened. The near rapture on her face makes her look like a transcendent Joan at the moment when the torch touches the faggots. He takes a few long steps away from her, but then comes back; he can't leave, neither can he stand still and watch. He hunches his shoulders and paces back and forth, back and forth.

Suddenly the rifle goes off and the sound is a shock that hurts. It rolls over the water, echoing.

"You can't kill them from here!" Shar cries.

"Only wanted to nick one," Bill says, aiming again. "They'll turn on one that's wounded, maybe leave her alone." The sharks move in a great semicircle, not coming directly toward the dock. They are swimming faster. He fires again.

"The bastards! The bastards!" Bill says over and over, nearly sobbing. "The bastards!"

Without warning the false killer whale moves away from the dock. She swims for about ten feet and rolls to her side. A cloud of blood spreads over the water. The gulls screech in a frenzy. They swoop down on the water, hiding the whale from view. She jerks and makes a great splash; they rise, screaming.

The baby is being expelled. Gary can see the body, the curled tail already straightening, and now the head is free. With what must have been an agony of effort the mother whale rolls suddenly, away from the infant, making a complete turn in the water in one swift, sharp movement. She has broken the cord. As she finishes the turn she comes up under the infant and nudges it to the surface. It rolls to one side and does not move. It is white underneath, three feet long, and it is dead. It starts to sink and again the mother whale nudges it to the surface of the water. And again. And again. Gary turns away.

He hears Shar being sick over the rail of the dock.

"They're coming!" Veronica screams.

Gary swings around in time to see Veronica snatch the rifle from Bill's limp hands; Bill is staring at the whale as if in a daze. Veronica points the rifle and begins to fire very fast, not at the sharks, but downward. The sleek black whale thrashes in the water, she tries to jump, but doesn't clear the surface, and then a paroxysm of jerks overtake her; finally she rolls over. The sharks begin to hit her.

Veronica turns toward the house; the rifle in her hands is pointed directly at Gary. He does not move. Her face is closed and hard, a stranger's face. She opens her hands and the rifle falls, clatters on the shells still on the dock. She walks past him without another glance at the sharks, at him, at anyone.

The water churns and froths; it is all red. Shar staggers away from the rail. She reaches for Gary's arm to steady herself and he jerks away involuntarily. Her hand would go through him, he thinks; she begins to run toward the house.

"She's afraid your wife will burn it down," Bill says in a thick, dull voice. For a moment his face is naked; he knows. "I might burn it down myself one day. Just might do that." He walks away, his shoulders bowed, his head lowered.

The frenzied gulls, the boiling water, the heat of the sun, all that's real, Gary thinks. Veronica firing the rifle, that was real. He remains on the dock until the Coast Guard cutter comes into sight, speeding toward the dock. The water is calm again; there is nothing for them to see, nothing for them to do. He doesn't even bother to wave to them. One of the men is standing in the boat scanning the water, and suddenly he points. The sharks are still in the channel. The boat veers, makes waves as it swings around and heads out away from the dock.

They didn't even see him, Gary knows. He is not surprised. Slowly he lifts his hands and looks at them, and then lets them drop to his sides. In his mind is an image of a raging inferno.

# M. JOHN HARRISON

## Anima

M. JOHN HARRISON says that he's "working too hard to have a biography at the moment." After being closely identified with Michael Moorcock's *New Worlds* magazine in the late 1960s, his debut novel, *The Committed Men*, set in a post-holocaust Britain, was published in 1971.

Since then, Harrison has written in a variety of genres, including horror, science fiction, sword & sorcery, graphic novels and rock climbing. In the UK, Flamingo has recently published his novel *The Course of the Heart* as a lead title, along with reissues of *Climbers* (winner of The Boardman Tasker Award) and his disturbing collection, *The Ice Monkey and Other Stories*. He also reviews for the *Times Literary Supplement*.

"I'm working on a novel, *Signs of Life*," reveals the author, "and a semi-autobiographical non-fiction centred on 'high access' engineering, *The Drop*, some of the research for which gave rise to the character Choe Ashton in 'Anima'."

For his second contribution to this volume of *Best New Horror*, Harrison takes us on a quest into one man's secret past . . .

A WEEK AGO LAST TUESDAY I dreamed all night of trying to find out what had happened to the woman I loved. She was a pianist and a writer. We had met in New York when she played a concert of American and British music. She had reminded me how I had once been able to dance. Now, some time later, she had come to Britain to find me. But she could no longer speak, only weep. How had she travelled here? Where did she live? What was she trying to say? It was a dream heavy with sadness and urgency. All avenues of inquiry were blocked. There were people who might know about her, but always some reason why they could not be asked, or would not tell. I walked up and down the streets, examining the goods on the market stalls, my only clue the re-issue date of a once-banned medicine.

I never dreamed anything like this until I met Choe Ashton –

Ten past ten on a Saturday night in December, the weekend Bush talked to Gorbachev on the *Maxim Gorki* in half a gale in Valetta Harbour. In the east, governments were going over like tired middleweights—saggy, puzzled, almost apologetic. I sat in the upper rooms of a media drinking club in central London. The occasion was the birthday of a corporate executive called Dawes who sometimes commissioned work from me. Shortly they would be giving him a cake-shaped like half a football on which had been iced the words: OVER THE MOON BUT NOT OVER THE HILL!

Meanwhile they were eating pasta.

"Now that's two thousand calories. How much more do you want?"

"So far I've had cheese but not much else, which is interesting – "

"Are we going to get that fettucini we've paid for?"

The women were in TV: the last of the power dressers. The men were in advertising, balding to a pony tail. Men or women, they all had a Range Rover in the car park at Poland Street. They were already thinking of exchanging it for one of the new Mazdas. I moved away from them and went to stare out of the window. The sky over towards Trafalgar Square looked like a thundery summer afternoon. The buildings, side-lit by street lamps, stood out against it, and against one another, like buildings cut from cardboard. I followed an obscure line of neon. A string of fairy lights slanting away along the edge of a roof. Then cars going to and fro down at the junction by St Martin-in-the-Fields, appearing very much smaller than they were. I had been there about a minute when someone came up behind me and said:

"Guess what? I was just in the bog. I switched the hand-drier on and it talked to me. No, come on, it's true! I put my hands under it and it said, 'Choe, I really like drying your hands.'"

I knew his name, and I had seen him around: no more. He was in his forties, short and wiry, full of energy, with the flat-top haircut and earring of a much younger man. His 501s were ripped at the knees. With them he wore a softly-tailored French Connection blouson which made his face, reddened as if by some kind of outdoor work, look incongruous and hard.

"Has anything like that ever happened to you? I'm not kidding you, you know. It talked to me!"

I shrugged.

"OK. Give us a fag then, if you don't believe me. Eh?"

He was delighted by my embarrassment.

"I don't smoke," I said.

"Come on," he wheedled. "Every fucker smokes. Dawsie only knows people who smoke. Give us a fag."

I had spent all day feeling as if my eyes were focusing at different lengths. Every so often, things—especially print—swam in a way which suggested that though for one eye the ideal distance was eighteen inches, the other felt happier at twelve. Choe Ashton turned out to be the perfect object for this augmented kind of vision, slipping naturally in and out of view, one part of his personality clear and sharp, the rest vague and impressionistic. What did he do? Whose friend was he? Any attempt to bring the whole of him into view produced a constant sense of strain, as your brain fought to equalize the different focal lengths.

"I'm sick of this," he said. "Let's fuck off to Lisle Street and have a Chinese. Eh?"

He gave me a sly, beautiful smile. An ageing boy in a French Connection jacket.

"Come on, you know you want to."

I did. I was bored. As we were leaving, they brought the birthday cake in. People always seem very human on occasions like this. Dawes made several efforts to blow the candles out, to diminishing applause; and ended up pouring wine over them. Then an odd thing happened. The candles, which—blackened, but fizzing and bubbling grossly, dripping thick coloured wax down the sides of the football—had seemed to be completely extinguished, began to burn again. Blinking happily around, Dawes had taken the incident as a powerful metaphor for his own vitality, and was already pouring more wine on them.

"Did you see that?" I asked Choe Ashton.

But he was halfway out of the door.

At first we walked rapidly, not talking. Head down, hands rammed into the pockets of his coat, Ashton paused only to glance at the enormous neon currency symbols above the Bureau de Change on Charing Cross Road. "Ah, money!" But as soon as he recognized Ed's Easy Diner, he seemed content to slow down and take his time. It was a warm night for December. Soho was full of the most carefully dressed people. Ashton pulled me towards a group standing outside the Groucho, so that he could admire their louche haircuts and beautifully crumpled chinos. "Can't you feel the light coming off them?" he asked me in a voice loud enough for them to hear. "I just want to bask in it."

For a moment after he had said this, there did seem to be a light round them—like the soft light in a 70s movie, or the kind of watery nimbus you sometimes see when you are peering through a window in the rain. I pulled him away, but he kept yearning back along the pavement towards them, laughing. "I love you!" he called to them despairingly. "I love you!" They moved uncomfortably under his approval, like cattle the other side of a fence.

"The middle classes are always on watch," he complained.

We dodged briefly into a pick-up bar and tried to talk. The only free table was on a kind of mezzanine floor on the way to the ladies' lavatory. Up there you were on a level with the sound system. Drunken girls pushed past, or fell heavily into the table.

"I love them all!" shouted Ashton.

"Pardon?"

"I love them!"

"What, these too?"

"Everything they do is wonderful!"

Actually they just sat under the ads for Jello-shots, Schlitz and Molson's Canadian and drank Lowenbrau: boys in soft three-button shirts and Timberline boots, girls with tailored jackets over white silk trousers. I couldn't see how they had arrived there from Manor House or Finsbury Park, all those dull, broken, littered places on the Piccadilly line; or why. Eventually we got sick of bawling at one another over the music and let it drive us back out into Cambridge Circus.

"I was here this afternoon," he said. "I thought I heard my name called out."

"Someone you knew."

"I couldn't see anyone."

We ended up in one of those Lisle Street restaurants which specialize in degree-zero décor, cheap crockery and grudging service. There were seven tables crammed into an area smaller than a newsagent's shop. The lavatory—with its broken door handle and empty paper roll—was downstairs in the kitchens. Outside it on a hard chair sat a waitress, who stared angrily at you as you went past. They had a payphone: but if you wanted to use it, or even collect your coat from the coat rack, you had to lean over someone else's dinner. Choe Ashton, delighted, went straight to the crepe paper shrine mounted in the alcove to show me a vase of plastic flowers, a red-and-gold tin censer from which the stubs of old incense sticks protruded like burnt-out fireworks, two boxes of safety matches.

"See this? Make a wish!"

With considerable gentleness he put fresh incense in the censer and struck a match.

"I love these places –" he said.

He sat down and rubbed his hands.

"– but I'm bored with Hot and Sour."

He stared away from the menu and up at the industrial ceiling, which had been lowered with yellow-painted slats. Through them you could still see wires, bitumen, ventilator boxes. A few faded strings ejected from some exhausted Christmas party-popper still hung up there, as if someone had flung noodles about in a claustrophobic fit or paddy.

"Let's have some Bitter and Unfulfilled here!" he called to the waitress. "No. Wait a minute. I want Imitation Pine Board Soup, with a Loon Fung calendar.

"But it has to have copulating pandas on it."

After that we began to drink Tsing Tao beer. Its packaging, he said, the pale grey ground and green, red and gold label, reminded him of something. He arranged several empty cans across the table between us and stared at them thoughtfully for some time, but nothing came of it. I don't remember eating, though we ordered a lot of food. Later he transferred his obsession from the Tsing Tao label to the reflections of the street neon in the mirror behind the bar. SOHO. PEEP SHOW. They were red, greenish-yellow, a cold blue. A strobe flickered inside the door of the peep show. Six people had been in there in two minutes. Two of them had come out again almost immediately. "Fucking hell, sex, eh? Why do we bother?" Ashton looked at me. "I fucking hate it," he said. Suddenly he stood up and addressed the people at the nearer tables. "Anyone who hates sex, stand up!" he tried to persuade them. "Fucking sex." He laughed. "Fucking fucking," he said. "Get it?" The waitresses began to move towards us.

But they had only come to bring the bill and offer him another beer. He smiled at them, moved his hands apart, palms forward, fingers spread.

"No thanks," he said shyly.

"The bill's in Chinese!" he shouted. He brandished it delightedly at the rest of the diners. "Hey!"

I agreed to drive him home. For the first few minutes he showed some interest in my car. At that time I had an Escort RS Turbo. But I didn't drive it fast enough for him, and he was silent again until we were passing The Flying Dutchman in Camberwell. There, he asked in an irritable voice: "Another thing. Why is this pub always in the same place?" He lived on the other side of Peckham, where it nudges up against Dulwich. It took him some time to find the right street. "I've only just moved in." I got him upstairs then consulted my watch. "I think I'd better sleep on your floor," I said. But he had passed out. It seemed like a nice flat, although he hadn't bought much furniture.

I woke late the next morning. Ten o'clock. Sleet was falling. A minicab driver had parked his Renault under the front window, switched its engine off, and turned up Capital Radio so that I could hear clearly a preview of a new track by the Psychedelic Furs. Every thirty seconds he leaned on his horn. At that, the woman who had called him leant out of a fourth floor window in one of the point blocks on the other side of the road and shrieked:

"Cammin dahn!"

Beep.

"Cammin dahn!"

Beep.

"Cammin dahn!"

Beep. Beep. Beep.

"Cammin dahn! Cammin dahn!"

At the back the flat overlooked a row of gardens. They were long and narrow and generally untended; so choked, some of them, with bramble, elder and buddleia stalks, that they reminded you of overgrown lanes between walls of sagging, sugary old brick. In the bleaker ones, you knew, a dog would trot restlessly all day between piles of household or builders' rubbish, under a complex array of washing lines. Choe Ashton's garden had once been kept in better order. There was a patio of black and white flagstones like a chess board, a few roses pruned savagely back to bare earth. The little pond was full of leaves. Suddenly I saw that there was a fox sniffing round the board fence at the bottom of the garden.

At first I thought it was some breed of cat I had never seen before: long-backed, reddish, brindling towards its hindquarters and long tail. It was moving a bit like a cat, sinuously and close to the ground. After a minute or two it found the pond and drank at length, looking up every so often, but too wet and tired, perhaps too ill to be wary or nervous.

I watched with my heart in my mouth, afraid to move even behind the window in case it saw me and ran off. Choe Ashton came into the room.

"Fucking hell," he said. "Are you still here?"

"Sssh. There's a fox in your garden."

He stood beside me. As he watched, the fox moved into the middle of the overgrown lawn, pawing and sniffing at the earth. It yawned. I couldn't see anything there it might eat. I wondered if it might have smelt another fox. It sat down suddenly and stared vaguely into the sleet.

"I can't see anything."

I stared at him.

"Choe, you must be blind – "

He gripped my arm very hard, just above the elbow.

"That hurts," I said.

"I can't fucking see any fucking fox," he said quietly.

We stood like that for thirty or forty seconds. In that time the fox went all round the lawn, not moving very fast, then crossed the low brick wall into the next garden, where it vanished among some elders, leafless laburnum bushes and apple trees.

"OK, Choe."

People like Choe are like moths in a restaurant on a summer evening just as it gets dark. They bang from lamp to lamp then streak across the room in long flat wounded trajectories. We make a lot of their confusion but less of their rage. They dash themselves to pieces out of sheer need to be more than they are. It would have been better to leave him alone to do it, but I was already fascinated.

I phoned everyone who had been at the Dawes party. No one knew the whole story. But they all agreed he was older than he appeared and, careerwise at least, a bit of a wimp. He was from the north of England. He had taken one of the first really good media degrees—from East Sussex—but never followed it up. He did the odd design job for one of the smaller agencies that operate out of top rooms above Wardour Street. In addition, he had some film work, some advertising work. But who didn't? The interesting thing was how he had filled his time until he appeared in Soho. After East Sussex he had moved back north and taken a job as a scaffolder, then joined a Manchester steeplejacking firm. He had worked in the massive stone quarries around Buxton, and out in the North Sea on the rigs. Returning to London obsessed with motorcycles, he had opened one of the first courier operations of the Thatcher boom.

He never kept any job for long. Boredom came too easily to him. Anything hard and dangerous attracted him, and the stories I heard about him, true or not, would have filled a book. He told me some of them himself, later:

Stripping old render near the top of a thirty storey council high-rise in Glasgow, he found himself working from scaffolding fifty feet above a brick-net. These devices—essentially a few square feet of strong plastic netting stretched on a metal frame—are designed to catch dropped tools or bits of falling masonry. With a brick-net, you don't need safety bunting or a spotter on the ground to protect unwary pedestrians. Ashton quickly became obsessed. He thought about the bricknet in his digs at night. (Everyone else was watching *Prisoner in Cell Block H*.) During the day everything that fell seemed to go down into it in slow motion. Things were slow in his life too. One cold windy Monday ten minutes before lunch, he took a sly look sideways at the other jacks working on the scaffolding. Then he screamed and jumped off, turning over twice in the air and landing flat on his back. The breath went out of him—boof! Everything in the net flew up into the air and fell down again on top of him—old mastic tubes, bits of window frame, half bricks.

"I'd forgotten that stuff," he said with a grin.

"Were you injured?"

"I walked a bit stiff that week."

"Was it worth it?"

"It was a fucking trip."

Later, induced by money to take a long-running steelworks job, he decided to commute to Rotherham from London on a Kawasaki 750 racer. Each working week began in the early hours of Monday morning, when, still wobbly from the excesses of the weekend, he pushed this overpowered bright green monster up the motorway at a hundred and fifty miles an hour in the dark. He was never caught, but quite soon he grew bored. So he taught himself to lie along the Kawa with his feet on the back pegs, wedge the throttle open with a broken matchstick so that he could take both hands off the handlebars and roll a joint in the tiny pocket of still air behind the fairing. At the right speed, he claimed, Kawasaki engineering was good enough to hold the machine on track.

"The idea," he said, "is not to slow down."

I wasn't sure boredom was entirely the issue. Some form of exploration was taking place, as if Choe Ashton wanted to know the real limits of the world, not in the abstract but by experience. I grew used to identifying the common ground of these stories—the point at which they intersected—because there, I believed, I had found Choe's myth of himself, and it was this myth that energized him. I was quite wrong. He was not going to let himself be seen so easily. But that didn't become plain until later. Meanwhile, when I heard him say, "We're sitting on the roof one dinner time, and suddenly I've poured lighter fuel on my overalls and set myself on fire," I would nod sagely and think of Aleister Crowley's friend Russell, discharged from the US Navy after he had shot up forty grains of medical-grade cocaine and tried to set fire to a piece of glass by willpower alone.

"I just did it to see what people would do," Choe said. "They had to beat me out with their hands."

In a broad fake Northern accent he added:

"I'm scared of nowt, me." Then in a more normal voice: "Do you believe that?"

"I think I do," I said, watching with some interest the moth on its flat, savage, wounded trajectory.

He gave me a look of contempt.

This didn't prevent him from flirting all winter, slipping away—but never too far—between the sets of a comically complex personality: always waiting for me to catch up, or catch my breath.

Drunk in bars, he would suggest going to the first night of a photographic exhibition, a new production of Ionesco, ballet at the Royal Opera House: arrive on the night in some immaculate designer two-piece with baggy trousers and immense shoulder pads: and then say –

"I've got the Kawa parked round the corner."

"I'm sure you have, Choe."

"You don't believe I came on it, do you?" And again, appealing to a foyer full of people who had arrived in BMWs:

"This fucker doesn't believe I came on me bike!"

To see how far he would go, I took him to a dance version of *Beauty and the Beast*. He sat there quietly, entranced by the colour and movement, quite unconcerned by the awful costumes and Persil white sentimentality, until the interval. Then he said loudly: "It's like the fucking fish tank at the dentist's in here. Look at them!" He meant the audience, which, gorgeously dressed and vaguely smiling, had begun to come and go in the depopulated front stalls like moonlight gourami or neon tetras nosing among the silver bubbles of the oxygenator. Quiet, aimless, decorative, they had come, just like the dancers, to be seen.

"They're a bit more self-conscious than fish, Choe."

"Are they?"

He stood up.

"Let's go and get some fucking beer. I'm bored with this."

Two or three weeks later, having heard I liked Turgenev, he sent me an expensive old edition of *Sketches from a Hunter's Notebook*, on the front endpapers of which he had written in his careful designer hand:

"Turgenev records how women posted flowers—pressed marguerites and immortelles—to the childmurderer Tropmann in the days before his execution. It was as if Tropmann were going to be 'sent on before.' Each small bouquet or floret was a confused memory of the pre-Christian plea 'Intercede for us' which accompanied the sacrifice of the king or his substitute. But more, it was a special plea: 'Intercede for me.' These notes, with their careful, complex folds, arrived from the suicide provinces—bare, empty coastal towns, agricultural plains, the suburbs of industrial cities. They had been loaded carefully into their envelopes by white hands whose patience was running out between their own fingers like water."

I phoned him up.

"Choe, what a weird quote. Where did you find it?"

"I'm not stupid, you know," he said, and put the phone down. He had written it himself. For two weeks he refused to speak to me, and in the end I won him round only by promising him I would go to the Tate and spend a whole afternoon with the Turners. He shivered his way down to the Embankment from Pimlico tube station to meet me. The sleeves of the French Connection jacket were pushed up to his elbows, to show off slim but powerful forearms tattooed with brilliantly coloured peacock feathers which fanned down the muscle to gently clasp his thin wrists.

"Like them? They're new."

"Like what, Choe?"

He laughed. I was learning. Inside the gallery, the Turners deliquesced into light: *Procession of Boats with Distant Smoke*, circa 1845; *The Sun of Venice Going Down to Sea*, 1843. He stood reverentially in front of them for a moment or two. Then the tattooed arms flashed, and he dragged me over to *Pilate Washing his Hands*.

"This fucker though! It can't have been painted by the same man!"

He looked at me almost plaintively.

"Can it?"

Formless, decaying faces. Light somehow dripping itself apart to reveal its own opposite.

"It looks like an Ensor."

"It looks like a fucking Emil Nolde. Let's go to the zoo."

"What?"

He consulted his watch. "There's still plenty of daylight left," he said. "Let's go to the zoo." On the way out he pulled me over to

John Singer Sargent's *Carnation, Lily, Lily, Rose*. "Isn't that fucking brilliant?" And, as I turned my head up to the painting, "No, not that, you fucking dickhead, the title. Isn't that the most brilliant title in the world? I always come here to read it."

Regents Park. Winter. Trees like fan coral. Squirrel monkeys with fur a distinct shade of green scatter and run for their houses, squeaking with one high pitched voice. A strange, far-off, ululating call—lyrical but animalistic—goes out from the zoo as if something is signalling. Choe took me straight to its source: lar gibbons. "My favourite fucking animal." These sad, creamy-coloured little things, with their dark eyes and curved arthritic hands, live in a long tall cage shaped like a sailing vessel. Inside, concrete blocks and hutches give the effect of deck and bridge fittings. The tallest of these is at the prow, where you can often see one gibbon on its own, crouched staring into the distance past the rhino house.

"Just look at them!" Choe said.

He showed me how they fold up when not in use, the curve of their hands and arms fitting exactly into the curve of their thigh. Knees under their chins they sit hunched in the last bit of winter sun, picking over a pile of lettuce leaves; or swing through the rigging of their vessel with a kind of absent-minded agility. They send out their call, aching and musical. It is raw speech, the speech of desires that can never be fulfilled, only suffered.

"Aren't they perfect?"

We watched them companionably for a few minutes.

"See the way they move?" Choe said suddenly. Then:

"When someone loves you, you feel this whole marvellous confidence in yourself. In your body, I mean."

I said nothing. I couldn't think how the two ideas were linked. He had turned his back on the cage and was staring angrily away into the park, where in the distance some children were running and shouting happily. He was inviting me to laugh at him. When I didn't, he relaxed.

"You feel good in it," he said. "For once it isn't just some bag of shit that carries you around. I – "

"Is that why you're trying to kill yourself, Choe?"

He stared at me.

"For fuck's sake," he said wearily.

Behind us the lar gibbons steered their long strange ship into the wind with an enormous effort of will. A small plaque mounted on the wire netting of the cage explained: "the very loud call is used to tell other gibbons the limit of its territory, especially in the mornings." I thought that was a pity.

* * *

In the spring he gave up his job with the agency and went offshore.

"I need some money," he said. "The rigs are the place for that. Besides, I like the helicopter ditching course."

He wanted to take the Kawa round Europe that summer.

"You need dosh to pay the speeding tickets." He thought for a moment. "I like Europe."

And then, as if trying to sum up an entire continent:

"I once jumped over a dog in Switzerland. It was just lying in the middle of the road asleep. I was doing a hundred and ten. Bloke behind me saw it too late and ran it over."

He was away for two or three months, but he hadn't forgotten anything. Whatever it was he wanted me for remained as important to him as it had been when he singled me out at the Dawes party. He came back at the height of summer and knocked at my door in Camden, wearing Levi 620s, brand new 16-hole DMs, a black sleeveless T shirt which had faded to a perfect fusty green, and a single gold earring. We walked up between the market stalls to Camden Lock, where he sat in the sunshine blinking at the old curved bridge which lifts the towpath over the canal. His arms had been baked brown in Provence and Chamonix, but the peacock feathers still rioted down them, purple, green and electric blue, a surf of eyes; and on his upper left arm one tiny perfect rose had appeared, flushed and pink.

"How was Europe?" I asked him.

"Fucking brilliant," he said absently. "It was great."

"Get many tickets?"

"Too fucking right."

"I like the new tattoo."

"It's good."

We were silent for a bit. Then he said:

"I want to show you something."

"What?"

"It would mean driving up north."

Determined not to make a mistake this time, I said:

"Would two days' time do?"

"Are you sure you want to know this?"

I wasn't sure. But I said yes anyway. In fact it was four or five days before he was free to leave. He wheedled me into letting him drive. A blip in the weather brought strong south-west winds which butted and banged at the RS as he stroked it up the motorway at a steady hundred and twenty. Plumes of spray drifted across the carriageways, so that even the heaviest vehicle, glimpsed briefly through a streaming windscreen, seemed to be moving sideways as well as forwards, caught in some long dreamlike fatal skid. Beyond Nottingham, though, where the road petered out into roadworks, blocked exits and confusing temporary signboards, the cloud thinned suddenly.

"Blue sky!" said Choe, braking heavily to avoid the back of a fleet Cavalier, then dipping briefly into the middle lane to overtake it. Hunched forward over the steering wheel until his face was pressed against the windscreen, he squinted upwards.

"I can see sunshine!"

"Will you watch where you're fucking going?"

He abandoned the motorway and urged the RS into the curving back roads of the White Peak, redlining the rev counter between gear changes, braking only when the bend filled the windscreen with black and white chevrons, pirouetting out along some undrawn line between will and physics. I should have been frightened, but it was full summer, and the rain had brought the flowers out, and all I could see were horses up to their knees in moon-daisies. The verges were fat with clover and cow parsley. The foxgloves were like girls. Thick clusters of creamy flowers weighed down the elders, and wherever I looked there were wild roses the most tremulous pink and white. Every field's edge was banked with red poppies. That would have been enough—fields of red poppies!—but among them, perhaps one to five hundred, one to a thousand, there were sports or hybrids of a completely different colour, a dull waxy purple, rather sombre but fine.

"How odd! Did you see that, Choe?"

"Don't talk."

After about twenty minutes he stopped the car and switched the engine off.

"This is near enough for now."

We were in a long bleak lay-by somewhere on the A6. The road fell away from us in a gentle curve until it reached the flatter country west and north. Down there I could see a town—houses for quarry workers, a junction with traffic lights, a tall steel chimney designed to pump hot gases up through the chronic inversion layers of Spring and Autumn.

"When I was a kid," Choe said, "I lived a few miles outside that place. "He undid his seatbelt and turned to face me. "What you've got to understand is that it's a fucking dump. It's got that fucking big chimney, and a Sainsburys and a Woolworths, and a fucking bus station." He adjusted the driving mirror so that he could see his own face in it. "I hated that fucking bus station. You know why? Because it was the only way in and out. I went in and out on one of those fucking buses every day for ten years, to take exams, look for jobs, go round the record shop on a wet Saturday afternoon." He pushed the mirror back into its proper place. "Ever spend any time in bus stations?"

"Never."

"I didn't think you had. Let me tell you they're death on a stick. Only people who are socially dead use a bus station."

Everything warm, he said, went on at a distance from people like that. Their lives were at an ebb. At a loss. They had to watch the clean, the happy, the successfully employed, stepping out of new cars and into the lobbies of warm hotels. If the dead had ever been able to do that, they would never be able to do it again. They would never be able to dress out of choice or eat what they would like.

"They're old, or they're bankrupt, or they've just come out of a long-stay mental ward. They're fucked."

All over the north of England they stood around at ten in the evening waiting for the last bus to places called Chinley Cross, or Farfield or Penistone. By day it was worse.

"Because you can see every fucking back-end village you're going through. The bus is fucked, and it never gets up any speed." He appealed to me: "It stinks of diesel and old woollen coats. *And the fuckers who get on are carrying sandwich boxes*."

I laughed.

"There's nothing intrinsically wrong with a sandwich box," I said.

"Do you want to hear this or not?"

"Sorry, Choe."

"I hated those fucking buses except for one thing – "

He was seventeen or eighteen years old. It was his last summer in the town. By September he would be at East Sussex. He would be free. This only seemed to make him more impatient. Women were everywhere, walking ahead of him on every pavement, packed into the vegetarian coffee-shop at lunchtime, laughing all afternoon on the benches in the new shopping plaza. Plump brown arms, the napes of necks: he could feel their limbs moving beneath the white summer dresses. He didn't want them. At night he fell out with his parents and then went upstairs to masturbate savagely over images of red-haired preRaphaelite women he had cut from a book of prints. He hardly understood himself. One afternoon a girl of his own age got on the bus at Stand 18. She was perfectly plain—a bit short and fat, wearing a cardigan of a colour he described as "a sort of Huddersfield pink"—until she turned round and he saw that she had the most extraordinary green eyes. "Every different green was in them." They were the green of grass, of laurel leaves, the pale green of a bird's egg. They were the deep blue-green of every sea-cliché he had ever read. "And all at the same time. Not in different lights or on different days. All at the same time." Eyes intelligent, reflective of the light, not human: the eyes of a bird or an animal. They seemed independent of her, as if they saw things on behalf of someone else: as if whatever intelligence inhabited them was quite different to her own. They examined him briefly. In that glance, he believed, "she'd seen everything about me. There was nothing left to know." He was transfixed. If you had ridden that bus as an adult, he said, and seen those eyes, you might have thought that angels travel route X39 to Sheffield in disguise.

"But they don't. They fucking don't."

After that first afternoon she often travelled from Stand 18. He was so astonished by her that when she got off the bus one day at a place called Jumble Wood, he got off too and followed her. A nice middle-class road wound up between bungalows in the sunshine. Above them, on the lip of a short steep gritstone scarp, hung the trees: green and tangled, rather impenetrable. She walked past the houses and he lost sight of her: so he went up to the wood itself. Inside, it was smaller than he had expected, full of a kind of hot stillness. He sat down for a minute or two, tranquilized by the greenish gold light filtering down into the gloom between the oaks; then walked on, to find himself suddenly on the edge of a dry limestone valley. There was a white cliff, fringed with yew and whitebeam. There were grassy banks scattered with ferns and sycamore saplings. At his feet purple vetches twined their tendrils like nylon monofilament round the stems of the moon daisies. He was astonished by the wood avens, pure art nouveau with their complaisantly bowed yellow-brown flowerheads and strange spiky seed cases. He had never seen them before: or the heath spotted orchids, tiny delicate patterns like intaglio on each pale violet petal.

When he looked up again, sunshine was pouring into the narrow valley from its southwestern end, spilling through the translucent leaves of young ash trees, transfiguring the stones and illuminating the grassy slopes as *if from inside*—as if the whole landscape might suddenly split open and pour its own mysterious devouring light back into the world.

"So what did happen, Choe?"

Instead of answering he stared away from me through the windscreen, started the car up, and let it roll gently down the hill, until, on the right, I saw the turning and the sign:

JUMBLE WOOD.

"You decide," he said. "We'll walk up."

I don't know what he wanted me to see, except what he had seen all those years ago. All I found is what he had already described—the wood, smaller than you would expect, full of dust motes suspended in sunshine—and beyond that, on the knife-edge of the geological interface, the curious little limestone valley with its presiding crag like a white church.

"You're going to have to give me a bit more help," I said.

He knelt down.

"See this? Wood avens. I had to look it up in a book."

He picked one and offered it to me.

"It's pretty. Choe, what happened here?"

"Would you believe me if I told you the world really did split open?"

He gazed miserably away from me.

"What?" I said.

"Somehow the light peeled itself open and showed me what was inside. It was her. She walked out of it, with those eyes every green in the world." He laughed. "Would you believe me if I said she was naked, and she stank of sex, and she let me push her down there and then and fuck her in the sunshine? And then somehow she went back into the world and it sealed itself up behind her and I never saw her again?"

"Choe – "

"I was eighteen years old," he said. "It was my first fuck."

He turned away suddenly.

"It was my only fuck," he said. "I've never done it since. Whatever lives here loves us. I know it does. But it only loves us once."

He drove back to London in silence, parked the Escort in Camden and walked off to the tube. I telephoned him daily for two weeks, and then weekly for two months. All I got was his answering machine. In the end I gave up. Someone told me he had moved to Chiswick; someone else that he had left Britain altogether. Then one day in December I got a call from him. He was living in Gravesend.

"All that Jumble Wood stuff," he said. "I made it up. I only told you that to get you going, you know."

I said I would still like to talk.

"Can you get down here?"

I said I could, and we arranged a meeting. He rang to cancel three or four times. Each time it was back on within an hour or two. First I was to meet him at the bar of a pub called the Harbour Lights. Then, if I was bringing a car, at his flat. Finally he agreed to be in the main car park at one o'clock.

I drove down there along the coast road, past the rows of empty caravans, exhausted amusement parks and chemical factories which occupied the low ground between the road and the sea. Wet sleet had fallen on them all that month without once turning into snow. You could hear the women in the supermarkets congratulating themselves on being born on a warm coast, though in fact it was quite raw in the town that afternoon. I found Choe sitting on the wall of the car-park, kicking his feet, his jeans rolled up to show off a pair of paint-splattered workboots. He had shaved his hair off, then let it grow out two or three millimetres so that the bony plates of his skull showed through, aggressive and vulnerable at the same time. He seemed bored and lonely, as if he had been sitting there all morning, his nose running, his face and arms reddening in the wind from the sea.

He jumped off the wall.

"You'll love the Harbour Lights!" he promised, and we began to walk down through the town towards the sea. Quite soon, everything was exciting him again: a girl getting out of a new car; brilliantly-coloured skateboard components displayed in the window of the Surf Shack; an advertisement for a film he hadn't seen. "See that? Wow!" He waved his arm. "And look at those fucking gannets up there!" Thinking perhaps that he had thrown them something, the circling birds—they were actually herring gulls—dipped and veered abruptly in their flight.

"They could wait forever!"

"They're big strong birds," I agreed.

He stared at me.

"I'm fucking scared of them," he said.

"I thought you were scared of nowt."

He laughed.

We had come out on to the sea-front, and there was the Harbour Lights, facing out across the bay where a handful of wind-surfers bobbed around on a low swell, their bright sails signalling in acid greens and pinks from a lost summer. "You should see the pies in here," Choe said delightedly. "There's a kind of black residue in them. It's the meat."

We went in and sat down.

"Tell me about what you do," he said.

I opened my mouth but he interrupted immediately.

"Look at this place!"

It seemed no different to any other pub on a flat coast, but perhaps that was what he meant. The brewery had put in an imitation ship's bell; a jukebox played 60s surfer classics. At one end of the long cavernous bar were a few empty seafood trays under chipped glass, while at the other the barman was saying to a woman in a torn fur coat, "You've picked a bad day." He hurried off down to the other end, where he seemed to fall into a dream. She smiled vaguely after him, then took off one shoe to examine the heel. A small tan and white dog, driven to hysteria by this act, rushed barking at her bare foot. The locals laughed and winked at one another.

Choe stared at them with dislike.

"You went along with all this so you'd have something to write," he accused me.

I got my notebook out and put it on the table between us.

"It's a living, Choe."

I went to the bar to get the drinks. "Write something about me then," he said when I came back. He grinned. "Go on! Now! I bet you can!"

"I don't do portraits, Choe."

The lies liberated from this statement skittered off into infinity like images between two mirrors. He must have sensed them go, because instead of answering he stood up and turned his back on me and pretended to look out of the window at the aimless evolutions of the windsurfers –

They would tack hesitantly towards one another until they had gathered in a slow drift like a lot of ducks on a pond: then one of them, his sail like neon in the sleety afternoon light, would shoot out of the mass and fly for quarter of a mile across the bay in a fast, delirious curve, spray shuddering up around him as he leapt from wave to wave. During this drive he seemed to have broken free not just from the other surfers but from Gravesend, winter, everything. Every line of his body tautened against the pull of the sail—braced feet, bent legs, yellow flotation jacket—was like an advert for another climate.

Sooner or later, though, the board would swerve, slow down suddenly, subside. Abandoned by the wind the bright sail, after hunting about for a second or two in surprise, sagged and fell into the water like a butterfly into a bath, clinging to a moment of self-awareness too confused to be of any use. This made Choe Ashton shiver and stare round the bar.

"These fuckers have all committed suicide," he said. His face was so pale I thought he was going to be sick.

"Be fair, Choe," I said cruelly. "You like the pies."

"I won't let you write anything about me."

"How can you stop that, Choe?"

He shrugged.

"I could beat the fuck out of you," he said.

Outside, the tide was coming in resolutely; the light was fading. I went out to the lavatory. Among the stickers on the bar door was one saying, "Prevent Hangovers—Stay Drunk." When I got back the woman at the bar was doing up her coat. "I'd put far too much cayenne in," she told the barman, "but we had to eat it anyway!" The tan and white dog was begging from table to table, and Choe Ashton had gone. I found him outside. Twenty or thirty herring gulls had gathered shrieking above him in the darkening air, and he was throwing stones at them with single-minded ferocity. It was some time before he noticed me. He was panting.

"These fuckers," he said. "They can wait forever." He rubbed the inside of his elbow. "I've hurt my arm."

"They only live a year or two, Choe."

He picked up another stone. The gulls shrieked.

"I only told you that stuff to get you going," he said. "None of it was true. I never even lived there."

I have no idea what happened to Choe Ashton in Jumble Wood. Whatever he says now though, I believe he returns there year after year, probably on the day he took me, the anniversary of his first and perhaps single sexual experience. It is as much an attempt to reassure himself of his own existence as that of the girl he believes came out of the inside of the world. I imagine he stands there all afternoon watching the golden light angle moment to moment across the valley. Seen in the promise of this light, the shadows of the sycamore saplings are full of significance; the little crag resembles a white church. Behind him, on the gritstone side of the geological divide, the wood is hot and tranquil and full of insects. His hand resting on the rough bark of an oak he appeals time and again to whatever lives in that place—"Bring her back. Bring her back to me."—only to be hurt time and again by its lack of response.

I understand that. I understand why he might want to obscure it. From me. From himself. What I don't understand is my own dream.

I've lost no one. My life is perfectly whole. I never dreamed anything like this until I met Choe Ashton. It's since then that I can no longer accept a universe empty of meaning, even if I must put it there myself.

# DOUGLAS E. WINTER

## Bright Lights, Big Zombie

DOUGLAS WINTER is an honour graduate of Harvard Law School and a Washington D.C. attorney. However, we suppose we shouldn't hold that against him, as he also happens to be the horror genre's premier critic, regularly reviewing for magazines and newspapers. His non-fiction books include *Shadowings: The Reader's Guide to Horror Fiction 1981–82*, *Faces of Fear* and *Stephen King: The Art of Darkness*.

He has edited the anthologies *Black Wine*, *Night Visions 5* and the worldwide bestseller, *Prime Evil*. He is currently working on a follow-up to that volume, and is writing a biography of Clive Barker. For relaxation, he watches countless obscure horror videos, admitting to a special fondness for such Italian *auteurs* as Dario Argento and Lucio Fulci.

In recent years, Winter has also turned his considerable talents to writing fiction, with great success, as the following story (which draws extensively upon his knowledge of European zombie movies) proves . . .

*DOUGLAS E. WINTER*

*When I started using dynamite, I believed in many things . . . Finally, I believe only in dynamite.*

*Sergio Leone*, Giu la testa

## IT'S SIX A.M. DO YOU KNOW WHERE YOUR BRAINS ARE?

YOU ARE NOT THE KIND OF ZOMBIE who would be at a place like this at this time of the morning. You are not a zombie at all; not yet. But here you are, and you cannot say that the videotape is entirely unfamiliar, although it is a copy of a copy and the details are fuzzy. You are at an after hours club near SoHo watching a frantic young gentleman named Bob as the grooved and swiftly spinning point of a power drill chews its way through the left side of his skull. The film is known alternatively as *City of the Living Dead* and *The Gates of Hell*, and you're not certain whether this version is missing anything or not. All might come clear if you could actually hear the soundtrack. Then again, it might not. The one the other night was in Swedish or Danish or Dutch, and a small voice inside you insists that this epidemic lack of clarity is a result of too much of this stuff already. The night has turned on that imperceptible pivot where two A.M. changes to six A.M. Somewhere back there you could have cut your losses, but you rode past that moment on a comet trail of bulletblown heads and gobbled intestines and now you are trying to hang onto the rush. Your brain at this moment is somewhere else, spread in grey-smeared stains on the pavement or coughed up in bright patterns against a concrete wall. There is a hole at the top of your skull wider than the path that could be corkscrewed by a power drill, and it hungers to be filled. It needs to be fed. It needs more blood.

## THE DEPARTMENT OF VICTUAL FALSIFICATION

Morning arrives on schedule. You sleepwalk through the subway stations from Canal Street to Union Square, then switch to the Number 6 Local on the Lexington Avenue Line. You come up from the Thirty-third Street exit blinking. Waiting for a light at Thirty-second, you scope the headline of the *Daily News*: STILL DEAD. There is a blurred photograph of something that looks vaguely like a hospital room. You think about those four unmoving bodies, locked somewhere inside the Center for Disease Control in

Atlanta. You think about your mother. You think about Miranda. But the light has changed. You're late for work again and you've worn out the line about the delays at the checkpoints. There is no time for new lies.

Your boss, Tony Kettle, runs the Department of Victual Falsification like a pocket calculator, and lately your twos and twos have not added up to fours. If Kettledrum had his way, you would have been subtracted from the staff long ago, but the magazine has been shorthanded since Black Wednesday and sooner or later you manage to get your work done. And let's face it, you know splatter films better than almost anyone left alive.

The offices of the magazine cover a single floor. Once there were several journals published here, from sci-fi to soft porn to professional wrestling. Now there is only the magazine, a subtenant called Engel Enterprises, and quiet desperation. You navigate the water-stained carpet to the Department of Victual Falsification. Directly across the hall is Tony's office, and you stagger past with the hope that he's not there.

"Good morning, gorehounds," you say as you enter the department. There are six desks, but only three of them are occupied. Brooks is reading the back of his cigarette package: Camel Lights. Elaine shakes her head and puts her blue pencil through line after line of typescript. Stan, who has been bowdlerizing an old Jess Franco retrospective for weeks, shuffles a stack of stills and whistles an Oingo Boingo tune. J. Peter and Olivia are dead.

What once was your desk is now a prop stand for a mad maze of paper. An autographed photo of David Warbeck is pinned to the wall, and looks out over old issues of *Film Comment, Video Watchdog, Ecco, Eyeball*, the *Daily News*. Here are the curled and coffee-stained manuscripts, and there the rows of reference volumes, from *Gray's Anatomy* to Hardy's *Encyclopedia of Horror Film*. Somewhere in the shuffle are two lonely pages of printout, the copy you managed to eke out yesterday from the press kit for John Woo's latest bullet ballet, smuggled through Customs between the pages of a Bible.

Atop it all is a pink message slip with today's date: Ruggero Deodato called. Don't forget about tonight. "And hey," Brooks says, finally lighting up a cigarette. "We had another visit from the Brain Police." You are given a look that is meant to be serious and significant.

You have spent the last five years of your life presenting images of horror, full color and in closeup, to a readership—perhaps you should say viewership—of what you suspected were mostly lonely, adolescent and alienated males who loved these kinds of films. The bloodier the better. Special effects—the tearing of latex flesh, the splash of stage crimson, the eating of rubber entrails—were the magazine's focus, and in better days, after a particularly vivid drunk that followed a screening of the latest *Night of the Living Dead* ripoff, you and J. Peter and Tony came to call yourself the Department of Victual Falsification.

That was then, and this is now. The dead came back, not for a night, but for forever. Your mother. Black Wednesday. Miranda. Cannibals in the streets. The bonfires in Union Square. Law and order. Congressional hearings. Peace, complete with special ID cards and checkpoints and military censors.

You remember, just before the Gulf War, reading newspaper articles about high school students who paged through magazines that were to be sent to the troops in Saudi Arabia, coloring over bras and bare chests, skirts that were too short, cigarettes caught up in dangling hands. You thought that this was supremely funny. Now each month you do something much the same. The magazine publishes the latest additions to the lists, recounts the seizures from the shelves of the warehouses and rental stores. At first the banished titles were the inevitable ones, the old Xs and the newer NC-17s and, of course, anything to do with the living dead. In recent months the lists have expanded into the Rs and a few of the PG-13s.

You are detectives of the dying commodity called horror, and there are fewer places where the magazine is sold, and fewer things that you can say, and fewer photos for you to run and, of course, there are fewer people left alive, fewer still who care.

## THE FUTILITY OF FICTION

You see yourself as the kind of zombie who would appreciate a quiet night at home with a good book. You watch tv instead. Tonight there is the Local News, followed by the National News, and then, of course, the game shows begin and will continue on until the Local News, followed by the National News, and then, of course, the game shows again. There are 106 other channels on your television set, but all of them are awash in a sea of speckled grey and have been for nearly a year.

The path that awaits you is clear. You reach into the back of your bookcase, behind the wall of unread Literary Guild Alternate Selections, to slip out tonight's first videotape, a pristine copy, recorded on TDK Pro High Grade at SP, of the Japanese LaserDisc of Ruggero Deodato's *Cannibal Holocaust*. You waited months for your dealer to get this one, and now you wait patiently for the first real moment of truth, that glimpse of the tribesmen as they tear off and eat the flesh of their prey. Although you tell yourself that this is what you want, that this is really what you want, this is not what you get. There is a cornfield on your forty-inch television monitor. It is late summer, nearly the harvest, and there in the tall stalks is Miranda, walking with racehorse grace in her bleached jeans and turtleneck sweater, hair in golden braids and face shining with the sun.

You turn your back on the monitor and you listen. For some time after Miranda died, you knocked on the door of the apartment before you entered. You would turn the key slowly in the lock and then pause here in the living room in the hope that you would hear her in the bedroom, that she had returned, that she was waiting for you, that none of this had happened, that none of this was real.

The video plays on. "How could you explain what a movie is?" A voice calls to you from the screen: "They're all dead, aren't they?" You look back and the cannibals at last are feasting. You watch, and you wish. Nothing seems to be what you want to do until you consider horror. A random sampling of the titles hidden at the back of the bookcase induces a delicious expectancy: *Anthropophagus. Eaten Alive. Trap Them and Kill Them.* Little wonder that the Gore Commission should have found so many of these films so wanting. The covers of the video boxes are themselves a kind of foreplay, wet and bright with colors, most of them red. *Make Them Die Slowly.* Here the label reads: "Banned in 31 countries." Make that 32. You know so much about these motion pictures, about the stories that they have to tell. You feel that if only they had given you the camera back then in the eighties, back when such things could be, you could have given shape to this uncertain passion that nightly inhabits your gut.

You have always wanted to make films. Getting the job at the magazine was only the first step toward cinematic celebrity. You never stopped thinking of yourself as a writer and director of horror films, biding his time in the Department of Victual Falsification. But between the job and the life there wasn't much time for the screenplays or even the short experimental films. That first, and only, Christmas, Miranda had given you the videocamera. For a few weeks afterward, you would shoot Miranda as she walked around the apartment, Miranda with shampoo in her hair, Miranda and the new kitten, Miranda at the stove, Miranda at the fireplace, Miranda and Miranda and Miranda. Then, what with the zombies and everything, life started getting more interesting and complicated. You worked for the magazine and you had once met George A. Romero and you had your collection of videos, so chic now that the lists were out and the tapes were gone from the rental shelves. People were happy to meet you and to invite you to their parties. Then things got worse, and then came Black Wednesday and the bodies in the streets and the soldiers and the fires in Union Square.

You pull your videocamera from its hiding place beneath the floorboards of the closet and set it up on its tripod. You have no blank videotape, of course. You take the cassette from the VCR and push it into the camera. You decide to start immediately with the film you have in mind. You aim the camera at the far wall of the apartment, bare and white. The autofocus blurs, then holds. Through the viewfinder you see exactly what you want. You press the start button. You tape nothing.

## A TOMB WITH A VIEW

You dream about the Still Dead. You sneak down the corridors of the Center for Disease Control. Nobody can see you. A door with a plaque reading *C'est La Mort* opens into the Department of Victual Falsification. Miranda is spreadeagled across the top of your desk, her wrists and ankles bound with strips of celluloid, the censored seconds from the first reel of Deodato's *Inferno in diretta*. Around her in white hospital beds, like the four points on a compass, are the Still Dead. You approach and discover that she isn't moving. You touch her. She is cold. Quiet. One of them. Still dead. But then she opens her eyes and looks at you. You make a sound like a scream but it is the telephone ringing. The receiver is hot and wet in your hand.

"I'm sick." You expect the caller to be Elaine or, worse yet, the Kettledrum himself. *Ta-dum, ta-dee, ta . . .*

"I knew that from the day I met you." The voice is unmistakable. In his prime he made the covers of *New York* and *Interview* and *Spy*. Now no one cares; but you never know, perhaps they will again. Sunlight is in your eyes. The clock says ten. You listen to Jay's latest proposition. A duplication center somewhere in the Bronx. Edit onto one-inch tape, copies to VHS. Sales in back rooms, some bars, the private clubs, on the street. Money to be made. Fame. And most important, screen credits. "Your name in lights."

In this new world there is no longer a place for dreams. Yet you have no doubt that he can do these things. It is the catch that troubles you, but only for a moment. You know you can be had. Jay says *ciao* and he's gone.

You're not dressed and out of the apartment until eleven. The uptown train pulls away just as you make the platform. Clutched beneath your elbow, the *Daily News* is screaming: BRIDGE BLOWN.

This time it was the George Washington. You wonder whether the dead are being kept out, or the living kept in. Now if you want to get to New Jersey, you swim. The Still Dead are buried on page five. No new developments: "Still Dead." The CDC will issue another statement on Sunday. Billy Graham will lead a candlelight prayer vigil. The President has expressed cautious optimism.

It's eleven-thirty when you reach Park Avenue South, eleven-forty by the time you get a cup of coffee and an elevator. Kettledrum is waiting, and he holds his glasses in his hand. A bad sign. You consider saying something. An excuse, an apology. Just offering a smile. It is all a joke. The glasses start to twirl. You know you are in trouble.

Tony does not waste words. The magazine has had visitors again. The military censor took a hard look at the new issue and found not one, but two, discussions of the contents of listed videos in your article on Umberto Lenzi.

"What about the First Amendment?" Tony looks at you. You look at Tony. Tony is the first to laugh. You decide to nod your head and join in when you see the photo in Tony's hands. Black and white and red all over. It's Miranda. Her legs are spread wide, left hand fondling the rope of raw intestine that dangles provocatively between them, dripping wet blots of blood onto the headless body on the floor. You look again and it is not Miranda. Of course not. It is some actress from a splatter film, and this is a publicity photo. A still. Still life.

## LES YEUX SANS VISAGE

You met her in one of those midwestern towns where the sunsets were gold and not impaled by tall buildings. You had gone from NYU Film School to waiting for jobs to waiting tables at the Salvador Deli, and when the magazine asked, you answered. Soon after you had written the expected fanboy froth about Troma and Incarnate and the rest of the local scene, you were sent into the heartland to write the set report on the latest annual installment in the film life of a hockey-masked hooligan. At night you would stand around for hours while thirty-year-olds trying to act like teenagers were taped up with rubber tubes that would, for the few seconds of a take, spout out a mixture of Karo Syrup and melted chocolate that looked something like blood. In the mornings you would sleep and then, in the afternoons, write a few pandering paragraphs of the usual nonsense before taking a walk around the town, the reporter from the big city, and stop by the Rexall and the Kroger and the Payless Shoe Store and on the third day, after boredom had set in soundly, you found her in a place called Kenny's. You remember that she was drinking a Nehi, leaning easily against a wall, one bluejeaned leg crossed over the other. She was wearing black Keds. Her eyes were closed and she was listening to a song on the jukebox, something by Public Image Limited, the two of them so out of place there in Hicksville that you thought you had walked into a dream. You wanted to shoot her, just to shoot her right then and there, and you wished that you had a camera. You told her she should be in movies, and of course this is what she wanted to hear.

Within the week she had moved in with you. She talked about the day your movie would go into production. All your plans were aimed at Hollywood. She wanted to live in the Malibu and you wished to join the film life of El Lay. You watched videocassettes of Lang and Franju, Bava and Pasolini, and bullshitted her with beginning film theory until you both had enough to drink and then you went to bed. It wasn't long before you decided you would marry her.

You returned to New York with the question of what Miranda was going to do. She had talked about college, talked about modeling, talked about children. She wasn't sure what she wanted to do. People were always telling Miranda that she should be in movies. At dinners you would talk about directors and their actress wives: Bardot and Vadim, Russell and Roeg, Rossellini and Lynch. About how only you could direct her. About how only you could show the world Miranda. And then, of course, she died.

## STILL DEAD

No one is kind. Their jobs are on the line. You have been inclined of late to underestimate the value of the dollar. Now you wonder what you would do if the magazine were gone.

You wander down the hall to the archives and browse through back issues. That first appearance of the magazine, way back in 1979, wore Godzilla on the cover and promised a photo preview of *Alien*. It seems like a century ago. No one in this country had heard of Deodato or Lenzi or Fulci; certainly no one cared. You flip through the years, and the bright-blooded covers, and you wonder at everything that has changed.

Later you find an empty office and make the call. You take a deep breath and dial the number of Jay's loft. You don't recognize the voice at the other end. "Tell him I'll do it." The voice asks you to identify yourself. "Tell him that Dario Argento called, and that he'll do it." The voice says that she has no idea what you are talking about, but that if you would leave your number, Jay would call right back. You hang up the phone and wonder whether it could have been traced. In your mind are images of men in blue suits with badges.

You escape the building without incident. It is a cold, snowy morning. Fall or winter. Miranda died in October. They called it Black Wednesday, but the day was bright and clear. There were leaves on the ground the morning she died, a blanket of green and gold that turned wet and red by noon and then grey with ash by night. It was midafternoon before the National Guardsmen had secured the apartment building. It was two weeks until the barricades were complete and the city was safe again. Each morning you would awaken to the smell of Miranda on your pillow, and then the other smell, the smell of the corpses burning in the midnight heaps at Union Square.

You slip into a bar near Penn Station. On the large-screen TV is a repeat of the Morning News. The daily CDC press conference is uninformative. As is that from Central Command. Protests continue outside the White House. The bartender rolls his eyes and says, "Fucking hippies." No one trusts a man who will not wear a flag on his lapel or tie a yellow ribbon to the antenna of his car. You nod and drink your beer.

It's late when you leave the bar, your footsteps uncertain, the sidewalk slick with ice. You haven't seen a taxi in months. Ahead is a checkpoint and you brush your pockets, trying to remember if you're holding. You imagine a patdown, the sound of a gloved hand on a plastic case. A copy of Fulci's *Zombie* in your coat could get you six months, maybe a year with the right judge; don't even think about the contents of your apartment. You're next at the gate. The soldier shines a flashlight into your eyes and you say, "Jack Valenti." No smile. "Forty-fifth President of the United States." He doesn't appreciate the joke, just waves you through, and you can't help but feel that you have escaped something.

At your apartment you discover an envelope with the logo of Jay's former employer, a comic book company, stuck beneath the door. Inside there is a note: *Soon.*

## CANNIBALS, QUESTI, AND GUINEA PIGS

Your interest in film doesn't normally take you beyond the racks marked Horror and Suspense, but at the moment there seems to be a shortage of inventory in both departments. This morning you are standing on the second floor of RKO Video on Broadway, where a patron is complaining to the cashier about the quality of her copy of

*Pretty Woman*. You are looking for something, anything, with the word "dead" in its title. Nothing is to be found. You start looking instead for the word "living."

He walks past you, blood-brown Armani coat flapping like wounded wings. "Mister . . ."

"Fulci," you say, slipping a copy of *Heaven Can Wait* from the shelf in front of you.

He nods and smiles and follows you back to the checkout counter. The woman there looks like she would rather be at the dentist's. It could be a mistake to rent this tape and leave some sort of record of where you were and when. You excuse your way to the front of the line and announce in a loud but tempered voice that you would like to special order *Faces of Death*, all three installments, and by the time that the kid has hold of you, pulling you back, people are talking and the woman at the counter has a telephone in her hand.

You run for the doorway and the lights suddenly are bright. A security guard looms in front of you; he doesn't like what he sees. You toss him the video and his hands react. A perfect catch. You feel the kid pushing and you look back over your shoulder as you reach the exit. You are laughing a little too hard.

Outside you take opposite sides of Broadway, and when you watch the kid wander into an alley off Fifty-seventh, you step in after him and try on a smile.

"Got it, dude." Now he is smiling, too. "All yours. Uncut *Django Kill*. From Argentina. *Se habla? No más, mi muchacho. Inglés*, my man, with subtitles."

"How much?"

"Hundred dollar."

"Get lost."

"Pure stuff. Uncut. Got the scalping scene."

"Right. Twenty-five."

"I ain't giving the stuff away."

"I can't do more than fifty."

"It's a steal. Fifty. You're robbing me."

You can't believe you're doing this. Finally you follow the kid farther down the alley. "I want a look."

"Shit," he says. "Who do you think you are, Siskel and Ebert? This is a steal, man. I'm telling you it's good."

You give him the fifty and then there is nothing to do but hustle it back to your apartment and give it a try. The tape is unmarked but for a torn handwritten label that reads GIULIO QUESTI. You want to believe that this means something. Images of dust and blood and molten gold are burning in your mind. You watch a few seconds of noise, and then a faded color spectrum appears. Finally you see a picture, so grainy that you need to squint. It's not *Django Kill*, oh no, not at all. You *think* you can see something happening, something with a Japanese girl tied to a dingy bed, and there is a man in a samurai helmet standing over her, the lights turned blue and a longhandled knife that dips down into her torso and comes up wet. He cuts away her right hand, throws blood onto the walls. You seem to think that this video is called *Guinea Pig*. There is no story to it, just the girl kidnapped, bound, and slowly cut into pieces. Finally the psycho eats her eyeballs. You want to feel something, do something, say something, but it's only eleven-thirty in the morning and everyone else in the world is dead or has a job.

## NO CULTURE

Over coffee and toast you read the *Daily News*. Miami is gone, carpet-bombed back into swampland. The President is regretful but unshaken in his resolve. Food riots in Boston and Providence. A news team in Palm Springs got footage of what looks like a zombied Tom Cruise, his buttocks chewed away but otherwise intact. And there is another entry in the Still Dead. This makes five of them. Five who have died only once. Five who have not returned. They wait in that white room at the CDC, and the whole world waits for them.

At dawn you woke like a man accustomed to the hour, your vision clear and in focus. You are committed to the task that awaits you. You wanted to call Jay again, maybe tell him you see the storyboards, you see frame by frame, you see and see and see.

It is Saturday and your apartment is a dungeon from which you must escape. You decide to go to the movies. The only remaining theatres are in Times Square, but the Times Square you remember is gone. A Holiday Inn has supplanted the Pussycat empire on Broadway. What was the Peppermint Lounge is now Tower 45. You pass the Marriott Marquis and walk onto Forty-second Street. The UDC has done its work so very well. Ghosts of grindhouses past fade in and out like distant television signals. The Adonis, the XXXtasy Video Center, Peepland: all gone. Even the Funny Store has vanished beneath the weight of another office tower. Progress is our most important product, and progress has taken them, one by one.

The new theatres on Forty-second Street are sedate and shadowless waiting rooms, places of pleasant dreams, not nightmares. The first is showing Disney cartoons, the next *Jesus of Nazareth*. You wonder what they will do about Lazarus. There is no choice but the third one, which does not admit children. You are hopeful, but there is no doubting the fear.

With two cans of beer hidden in your coat, you move away from the ticket booth and find a seat in the middle of the theater. The lights dim. An animated usherette tells you not to smoke and to use the trash receptacles as you exit. The following preview has been approved for all audiences by the Motion Picture Association of America. *The Absent-Minded Professor*. Your knees are shaky. You sip at the first beer. You stand and walk back up the aisle. This will not work.

Finally the previews are at an end. You sneak another drink of beer and take a seat on the aisle, just in case. The following motion picture has been rated PG-13 by the Motion Picture Association of America. This is a London Film Production. There is a clock tower, Big Ben; the time is eleven. The music is so very strange, plucking strings, a zither. The film is called *The Third Man*. Written by Graham Greene. Directed by Carol Reed. It is set in Vienna, after the Second World War. Some man named Holly Martins, a writer, comes to visit his friend Harry Lime, but Harry Lime is dead. There is no color. The faces look out at you in black-and-white. Nothing is happening. The actors are just talking and talking, walking and walking.

You clutch at the armrests and wait for the next surge to hit you. It comes just as you begin to understand. Harry Lime is back from the dead. He was never dead, not really. It was a joke of some kind. "We should have dug deeper than a grave." As the audience murmurs, you stand up, knowing that Harry Lime is alive, yes alive, even to the very end, when the bullets find him. You think about the squibs that could explode from beneath his clothing, sending clots of blood across the grey walls of the sewers, and you hear yourself groan with the knowledge of what is missing, what is gone, what was never there.

People are turning in their seats to look at you. They are saying *Sit down*! and *What does he want*? An usher in a suit is hurrying down the aisle. At least he is in color. Another usher is coming from the other side. You move along the row of seats, bumping knees and outstretched hands. The beer falls onto the carpet, another unseen stain. You do not resist as one of the ushers takes your arm.

In the lobby you see nothing but the poster for the film, and then the night waiting outside. There, in black-and-white, is the knowledge of the way that we have chosen to be entertained, like a book read once too often, leaving a trail of images and emotions so familiar that there is nothing left to see or feel. You know the future, and it is now; it always will be now.

## BLOOD AND SYMPATHY

Later you return to the scene of your crimes. You wonder at the silence, whether it is absolute or only the hour. There are no signs that the magazine has been closed down. Still you feel strange stepping out of the elevator and into an unlit corridor. That the hour is past midnight doesn't help.

Tony's door is closed and dark. There's a light on in the Department of Victual Falsification. Elaine is at her desk. She looks up when you come in, but she does not seem surprised. You tell her that you've come to get your things. "Don't bother," she tells you. Then: "I've been waiting here all day for you." Waiting for what? "You could have called." That is when you notice that your desk is clear. The photo on the wall looks down on nothing. You don't need to look to know that the drawers are empty.

"We had more trouble here this morning," Elaine says. "A search warrant." Now you realize that she is holding a pistol in her left hand. "Tony says it's over. Done. Finished." The pistol looks like it might be loaded. "What do you think?"

You want to tell her the truth. Instead you say: "I think it's only just begun."

She's smiling. The pistol is back in her purse. "I thought you might want these." Four plastic cases. "My secret stash."

You hold up the first of the videos, factory fresh and labeled: *Revenge of the Dead*. It is Pupi Avati's *Zeder*. You deep-breathe and feel your nostrils go like ice.

"Elaine." She raises her eyebrows. Now you are committed. In the elevator, you ask her where she wants to go.

"How about your place?"

You walk and walk and at Fifth Avenue, just past the Flatiron Building, Elaine takes your hand and leads you into a Chinese carryout, where she orders dim sum for you both. From the restaurant you walk toward Union Square. Each step takes you closer to your apartment, to the place where Miranda lived. Where Miranda died. This was your neighborhood. That boarded-up storefront was your grocer, the next your video store. Now the vista has gone upside down, and nothing will ever be the same.

"Best bonfire in the city," Elaine says, pointing to Union Square. A trio of National Guardsmen in urban camouflage huddle with their cigarettes. They watch over a graveyard of concrete and ash, circled with rolls of barbed wire. The fragrance reminds you of the mornings after Black Wednesday, when you woke to the smell of the corpses burning, the perfumed ghost of Miranda sleeping beside you. It seems a lifetime ago, but still you can see her sleeping, the flicker of flames across the face that wasn't there.

Soon Elaine is lying next to you in that same room, her dark hair a shadow on the pillow. The only light is from the small bedside television. After *Zeder* you watch the uncut *Apocalypse Domani*, and after that she opens your shirt, her hand against your chest. You watch the tv screen go blank, then grey, and in the moments before you try, but fail, to make love, she says: "When there are no more films, we'll have to make our own."

## SOMETIMES A VOGUE NATION

You wake up with a severed head on your chest. Its lips are moving but you can't hear the words. After a few seconds you realize that the head isn't talking, it is chewing. A hand rises into view, clutching a fistful of entrails. The clock on the VCR blinks a continuous 12:00. That would be noon, judging by the sunlight that zigzags through the blinds. The last thing you remember was that Elaine was sleeping while you watched the final moments of Deodato's *L'ultima cannibali*. The tribesmen had split Mei Mei Lay open from groin to breastbone, dug out her organs, and sewn her back up for cooking. You have the feeling that you may have missed something good.

You remove the little television from your chest just as Doctor Butcher begins to rev up his band saw. The shot is static, almost matter-of-fact. The stage blood, when it comes, is orangish, surreal. You would have given the scene depth, momentum; not simply shock, but true anguish. There is a note on the nightstand, a few lines in black ink; you read it and smile a thank-you to Elaine. You are on your second cup of coffee and the final moments of *Doctor Butcher, M.D.* when the telephone rings. It's Joe D'Amato. He wants to take you sightseeing, probably tonight or tomorrow, sometime after ten. He'll call again. You tell him you'll be waiting.

Then you hit the streets, in search of a sandwich and today's *Daily News*. You wonder what Jay will do for lighting and whether you will need your tripod. At your favorite Greek diner you order chicken salad and more coffee. When you spread the newspaper across the counter, you learn that the first of the Still Dead, a thirty-three-year-old black male from suburban Chicago, otherwise unidentified, came back last night and was trepanned with a surgical power saw. Life is still imitating art. Doctor Butcher would have been proud.

Across a few more streets and down an alley is the backdoor to Forbidden Planet. You keep your head down, feel like you look guilty, and shove your hands deep into your pockets. Money talks and bullshit walks. You need an extra battery for your camera, and maybe somebody at the Planet will be selling.

"Got what you want," someone says, though it's hard to hear over the noise of a boom box, an incessant orgy of doom thrash metal. The kids lean into the walls and don't look at you. They wear their biker jackets, black t-shirts and jeans like uniforms.

"Say man." A skinheaded nymphet in torn fishnets twists down the volume, raises her pastewhite face to you. "You know where we could get some stuff?"

"Stuff?" You want to keep walking, get this over with as quickly as you can. Who knows who might be watching?

"You know." Her eyes, black circles scored at their far corners with silver, dart around, mock fugitive. She sucks at her cigarette, blows back smoke and the word of the hour. "Some good G-O-R-E?"

"No can do." Your hands seem caught in your pockets. These are your readers. Your public. They sent you letters, sometimes. But you never thought of them when you wrote not really. You thought about something else, something –

"Like *New York Ripper*?"

"No." But you can't walk away. You are –

"*Eaten Alive*, maybe? *Man from Deep River*? Some cannibal – "

"Listen, I – "

"I do," she says, and for the first time she is alive truly alive. She bites at her purple lips, finally works up a smile. "Like we know where we can score something but we don't got the dollars. You wanna go in with us, maybe?"

You look at them, and they look back at you, expectant; line of lost moviegoers, waiting for what you can show them. You tell yourself that you are not this desperate. You are looking for a battery. That's all. At last you shrug and start to walk away. She turns the music back up, and now that rotten Johnny Lydon is ranting away:

*This is what you want*
*This is what you get*
*This is what you want*
*This is what you get. . . .*

You feel them pulling at you, pulling you back. But it's not them, not really. You want so desperately to see. You came here in search of something, something you thought you wanted, but now you aren't sure. You wonder if you ever were sure. You want to give in to it, let it take you away again to that place where you never need to be sure.

Whether you want to or not, you think about Miranda. You try to remember the way she was before Black Wednesday, before the night she died, before the dead came back and the apartment walls went red with blood. And before everything was whitewashed back into this thing they call reality.

## THE NIGHT SHIFTS

You are hungry and you are thirsty; you need to see something, but you're not sure what. Nothing hidden on your bookshelf is enough anymore.

You walk down into SoHo, past all the empty restaurants and art galleries, a showplace of spraypaint and shattered glass. When you cross Prince Street, a walkie-talkie crackles at you from the darkness. A cough and clipped voices. Soldiers are on the street corners. All of the city seems armed and ready. Like the morning after Black Wednesday.

At first you could not believe that Miranda was dead. Now you find it hard to believe that she was ever really alive. That you were married. Shared wine and loud music and laughter. That there ever was anything but this.

You decided long ago not to think about that day. It was months after the first reports came in from the Pennsylvania countryside. About the dead that came back to life.

The dead that walked. The dead that ate the living. You had your doubts about the stories, even when it was Dan Rather who told them. After all, this was the stuff of horror movies.

Before it happened you had never thought about Miranda's death. You were too young, too happy, to think about it. You spent no time in anticipation of it because death was something that would not happen, could not happen, at least until you yourself were old and tired and ready.

Helicopters flutter overhead. Their searchlights bite holes in the darkness. At Houston you find a market that is still open, buy a carton of beer, and head back to the apartment.

"Do you love her?" your mother had asked that first, and last, time the two of you visited. You didn't know what to say. Of course you loved her. You had married her hadn't you?

You thought you would faint when you came home that night, in those long lost moments of shadow and flame. Miranda had been beautiful. That was the way you wanted to remember her. Like in the photographs her parents had sent, now on the mantle of the apartment, taken when she was younger than you had ever known her.

You could have given her life eternal through the lens of your camera. Video. Film. Pictures. You could have loved her forever.

How could you explain the feeling of being misplaced, of always standing to one side of the world, of watching the world as if it existed only when recorded and replayed on tape, and wondering if this was how everyone felt. You always believed that other people could see more directly, could actually see and understand the world through their own eyes, and didn't worry quite so much about why. You could see it only through a lens, through what you could record and edit and assemble into a tangible, meaningful whole, locked safely and securely within the four walls of a picture. Then, and only then, could you see and understand . . . and yes, love.

You drink more than one beer on your trek back to the apartment, and once there you drink more than one more. You slip another video into the deck. Deodato again. *Camping del terrore*, although for once you prefer the English title: *Body Count*. More beer and another video, and then another and another, and after a time the images blur and bleed into a single color.

Sooner or later the telephone rings. It is time.

## GONE

The barricades are back up at the major intersections, and the city has become very small. Your head is hollow, cracked and scooped out like an oyster on the half shell. You followed the flicker of red video across the television screen in pursuit of some kind of answer. Then the tapes ran out; as you watched the last line of credits, superimposed on a staggering horde of zombies as they crossed the Brooklyn Bridge, you suddenly saw yourself in hideous closeup, gapemouthed in worship before a forty-inch altar of flickering light.

You caught the telephone on the second ring. Through the noise and a distant sound that sooner or later you realized was gunfire, you heard that it was Jay, that he wanted you to meet him at Patchin Place. This is not a test. Your presence, and your videocamera, are required. You told him you'd be there in minutes, and now you're there, camera in hand, and you can feel it about to happen.

The alleyway is awash in the yellow spray of flares and flashlights. Elaine stands in the shadows, her pistol pointed into the night sky; at her side is some black guy with a shotgun. Jay is watchful; waiting, waiting. Finally he looks at you.

"Do it," he says, and then gestures grandly to the others. "Lights." Shadows twist over a gas generator; a ratcheting, a cough, and a spray of white cuts the alley into an urban dreamscape, the stuff of Lang and Reed.

"Something's happening, uptown and down . . ." He wears a

joker's grin, a shotgun in his black-gloved hand. "Could be Black Wednesday all over again." You hear a shout, footsteps racing on wet concrete. He shrugs and nods into the darkness. "Someone has to shoot the picture." His hand busses your shoulder. "So do it," he says again. "Sound," he announces; and, as he walks away, "Speed." Then you're alone, with your finger on the trigger.

Through the viewfinder you see the world, your world, the world made flesh on the grey-silver screen. Mad shadows chase one of Jay's nerdy protégés into view, and he dances before you, arms in flight, and mugs breathlessly for the camera. Finally he leans in at you and cries: "They're heeeeer!"

Then he is gone, and your world is the world of the dead. The first one is an oldtimer, workshirt and spotted trousers, shuffling around the corner in vague pursuit. The left side of his face is gone; eaten. You can see the teeth marks as you smashzoom in on him. From somewhere to your left comes the bullroar of the black guy's shotgun. The top of the oldtimer's head lifts away. You watch him fall and see your take replayed endlessly on the monitors of an editing bay. Perfect. Picture perfect. He collapses to the sidewalk in an unceremonious and uncinematic heap.

You slide the camera over the corpse and up the wall, where the shadow of the next one spiderwebs nicely into p.o.v. "Got him," you hear Elaine call. This one is a kid, your random Puerto Rican street punk, and he looks fairly fresh. You hit him with a medium closeup just in time to catch the jagged line of bulletholes that Elaine punches into his chest. Craters erupt—grey skin, blood and squirming maggots—and you zoom into one then out just in time to catch the headshot as the black guy steps in stage right, swings his shotgun up and lets both barrels go. The body cartwheels back, out of the light, and you've lost it to the black beyond.

"Take . . . it . . . easy." Jay sounds anxious and upset. "Not . . . so . . . fast." But there are sirens in the distance and the sound, you think, of radios and marching feet. White noise and distant voices. Order is about to be restored. You don't have much time.

You peek over the viewfinder and there is another shadow climbing the wall. Elaine is twisting a speedloader from her belt. Shell casings ping-pong down the alley. You look in again and see shadow turn to skin. It's a woman. Tall. Long blond hair. Pale skin. As you squint and let the focus go, ready for a soft fade-in, you hear her footsteps stumble forward. Your finger finds the autofocus as you let the lens sweep the pavement slowly to her feet. Black Keds. Then up. Bleached jeans. Slowly. White blouse, half-unbuttoned, a tiny pearl necklace at her throat, and pale, pale skin. Slowly up to her face. Her beautiful face. A small clicking sound is coming from your throat.

The picture shivers once, twice, then dims. Finally you hear your voice: "Mir-an-da!"

You pull the shot away from her and left. Elaine kneels, stiffarms the handgun. You hear sounds like belches and swing your eyes, the camera, back. Miranda's left forearm angles impossibly, then breaks, strands of flesh stretching, then snapping, hand clutching at empty air as it spins and floats away. You see the shot in slow motion, a mad Peckinpah pirouette, suddenly shattered in midturn as the force of a shotgun blast kicks out her legs. You fall to your knees with her, losing your balance, nearly dropping the camera; still you hold onto the shot. You have her now. She can't escape you. You feel the urge for a closeup, but you cannot risk moving from the medium shot as Miranda rears back into frame. Another roar, and the top of her right shoulder explodes. A great brown geyser of blood erupts, grey flesh and bone graffiti the alley wall.

Somehow she stands, keeps walking. Her head jerks to the right as the black guy chunks in another round; the shotgun kicks again, a miss that showers a grey snow of brick and dust. You swing the camera down then up from her bulletblown knees in time to catch Elaine's next volley, three shots that spit through Miranda's chest and neck and crease her cheek. Her mouth opens wide in response. You don't know if it is a laugh or a scream.

Still she is coming, past the black guy, past Elaine, who looks at you with angry fear. They can't fire now, not back at you and Jay and the rest of the crew. Your shot is steady, sure, a reverse zoom that frames her just so, the alley seeming to widen behind her as she approaches. Now your back is against the wall and the lens is open wide; she walks on and gives you your closeup. She is yours, all yours.

A flash of movement cuts the picture; the camera is nearly lost from your arms as she skitters backward. Then you see the muzzle and hardwood butt of the shotgun, and Jay's gloved right hand as he hits her again, and you hold the shot as she falls and you're down on the ground with her, the camera looking up across her body into a night sky punctured by distant stars. You can see her tongue through the open left side of her face. One of her eyes is blinking out of control; the other one is gone. You know she has never been more beautiful than now. She is yours, and will be yours forever.

You watch as Jay joins you at her side. He lowers the shotgun; the barrel slides along her stomach, her chest, her neck, to the tip of her chin. Finally its hot and smoking mouth kisses hers. And as you hold her in lingering close-up, he shoves the barrel down. You hear the crack of teeth and bone and then the shotgun kicks and there is a shriek and you are caught in a warm wet rain that washes over the lens until you can see nothing, nothing, nothing at all but red.

You hear laughter and you know that it is your own. You can no longer see, but you can run, and you drop the camera, hear the shatter of glass and plastic, the whir of the eject as you grab at the tape and you run, you run and run into the darkness, into the night until at last you can see a distant light, and you run in its direction. You hold on to your tape and run.

Finally you see the sanitation trucks lined before you on this side of Union Square. You watch as body bags are carried out by men in gasmasks and white camouflaged parkas, and dumped onto the fire, sending smoke, and the smell, over you. No matter how far you run, the smell will follow you. It recalls you to another morning. You arrived home from the magazine after drinking most of the night; Miranda had called just before midnight, wondering where you were. When you arrived, the apartment was steeped in this same aroma. The soldiers stood warming themselves around the flames. Miranda was gone. You could count the bullet holes across the lobby, the stairway, and the walls of the apartment itself; you could count the bodies sprawled in the streets, fuel for the flames. You had seen it all before; you had seen it all, but you had never believed in it. It wasn't real; it could never be real. But it was. The films, the videos, were just the coming attractions, a sneak preview of the epic now playing around the clock in the world outside.

You approach the last of the trucks. A sanitation worker hefts another body bag from its wide belly, drops the heavy plastic cocoon unceremoniously to the pavement.

"Dead." This is what you say to him, although you meant to say something more.

"What was your first clue?" He turns and walks toward the Square. The fire rages high, a false dawn. The workers, and the soldiers who guard them, look at the flames, and not at you.

You get down on your knees and tear open the body bag. The smell of the corpse envelops you. When you touch it your hands find something soft and wet. The first bite sticks in your throat and when you try to swallow, you almost gag.

You will have to go very slowly.

You will have to forget most everything you have ever learned.

for *Steve Bissette*

# PETER STRAUB

## The Ghost Village

PETER STRAUB is one of America's most respected authors. He was born in Milwaukee, Wisconsin, and was a teacher before his first novel, *Marriages*, was published in 1973.

Since then he has published a number of acclaimed books, including *Under Venus*, *Julia* (filmed as *Full Circle/The Haunting of Julia*), *If You Could See Me Now*, *Ghost Story* (filmed with an all-star cast), *Shadowland*, *Floating Dragon* (currently being developed for TV), *The Talisman* (a collaboration with Stephen King), *Koko*, *Mystery*, *Mrs God* and *The Throat*.

A winner of both the British Fantasy Award and the World Fantasy Award, Straub has published two books of poetry, *Open Air* and *Leeson Park & Belsize Square*, and some of his best short fiction is collected in *Houses Without Doors*.

"'The Ghost Village' is an early version of a section of *The Throat*," explains the author, "and a condensed and altered form of the story still exists in that novel."

We are proud to present a powerful novella of ancient myth and modern hauntings by one of the genre's finest craftsmen . . .

IN VIETNAM I KNEW A MAN who went quietly and purposefully crazy because his wife wrote him that his son had been sexually abused—"messed with"—by the leader of their church choir. This man was a black six-foot-six grunt named Leonard Hamnet, from a small town in Tennessee named Archibald. Before writing, his wife had waited until she had endured the entire business of going to the police, talking to other parents, returning to the police with another accusation, and finally succeeding in having the man charged. He was up for trial in two months. Leonard Hamnet was no happier about that than he was about the original injury.

"I got to murder him, you know, but I'm seriously thinking on murdering her too," he said. He still held the letter in his hands, and he was speaking to Spanky Burrage, Michael Poole, Conor Linklater, SP4 Cotton, Calvin Hill, Tina Pumo, the magnificent M. O. Dengler, and myself. "All this is going on, my boy needs help, this here Mr Brewster needs to be dismantled, needs to be *racked* and *stacked*, and she don't tell me! Makes me want to put her *down*, man. Take her damn head off and put it up on a stake in the yard, man. With a sign saying: *Here is one stupid woman.*"

We were in the unofficial part of Camp Crandall known as No Man's Land, located between the wire perimeter and a shack, also unofficial, where a cunning little weasel named Wilson Manly sold contraband beer and liquor. No Man's Land, so called because the C.O. pretended it did not exist, contained a mound of old tires, a pisstube, and a lot of dusty red ground. Leonard Hamnet gave the letter in his hand a dispirited look, folded it into the pocket of his fatigues, and began to roam around the heap of tires, aiming kicks at the ones that stuck out furthest. "One stupid woman," he repeated. Dust exploded up from a burst, worn-down wheel of rubber.

I wanted to make sure Hamnet knew he was angry with Mr Brewster, not his wife, and said, "She was trying – "

Hamnet's great glistening bull's head turned toward me.

"Look at what the woman did. She nailed that bastard. She got other people to admit that he messed with their kids too. That must be almost impossible. And she had the guy arrested. He's going to be put away for a long time."

"I'll put that bitch away, too," Hamnet said, and kicked an old grey tire hard enough to push it nearly a foot back into the heap. All the other tires shuddered and moved. For a second it seemed that the entire mound might collapse.

"This is my *boy* I'm talking about here," Hamnet said. "This shit has gone far enough."

"The important thing," Dengler said, "is to take care of your boy. You have to see he gets help."

"How'm I gonna do that from here?" Hamnet shouted.

"Write him a letter," Dengler said. "Tell him you love him. Tell him he did right to go to his mother. Tell him you think about him all the time."

Hamnet took the letter from his pocket and stared at it. It was already stained and wrinkled. I did not think it could survive many more of Hamnet's readings. His face seemed to get heavier, no easy trick with a face like Hamnet's. "I got to get home," he said. "I got to get back home and take *care* of these people."

Hamnet began putting in requests for compassionate leave relentlessly—one request a day. When we were out on patrol, sometimes I saw him unfold the tattered sheet of notepaper from his shirt pocket and read it two or three times, concentrating intensely. When the letter began to shred along the folds, Hamnet taped it together.

We were going out on four- and five-day patrols during that period, taking a lot of casualties. Hamnet performed well in the field, but he had retreated so far within himself that he spoke in monosyllables. He wore a dull, glazed look, and moved like a man who had just eaten a heavy dinner. I thought he looked like he had given up, and when people gave up they did not last long—they were already very close to death, and other people avoided them.

We were camped in a stand of trees at the edge of a paddy. That day we had lost two men so new that I had already forgotten their names. We had to eat cold C rations because heating them with C-4 it would have been like putting up billboards and arc lights. We couldn't smoke, and we were not supposed to talk. Hamnet's C rations consisted of an old can of Spam that dated from an earlier war and a can of peaches. He saw Spanky staring at the peaches and tossed him the can. Then he dropped the Spam between his legs. Death was almost visible around him. He fingered the note out of his pocket and tried to read it in the damp grey twilight.

At that moment someone started shooting at us, and the Lieutenant yelled "*Shit!*", and we dropped our food and returned fire at the invisible people trying to kill us. When they kept shooting back, we had to go through the paddy.

The warm water came up to our chests. At the dikes, we scrambled over and splashed down into the muck on the other side. A boy from Santa Cruz, California, named Thomas Blevins got a round in the back of his neck and dropped dead into the water just short of the first dike, and another boy named Tyrell Budd coughed and dropped down right beside him. The F.O. called in an artillery strike. We leaned against the backs of the last two dikes when the big shells came thudding in. The ground shook and the water rippled, and the edge of the forest went up in a series of fireballs. We could hear the monkeys screaming.

One by one we crawled over the last dike onto the damp but solid ground on the other side of the paddy. Here the trees were much sparser, and a little group of thatched huts was visible through them.

Then two things I did not understand happened, one after the other. Someone off in the forest fired a mortar round at us—just one. One mortar, one round. That was the first thing. I fell down and shoved my face in the muck, and everybody around me did the same. I considered that this might be my last second on earth, and greedily inhaled whatever life might be left to me. Whoever fired the mortar should have had an excellent idea of our location, and I experienced that endless moment of pure, terrifying helplessness—a moment in which the soul simultaneously clings to the body and readies itself to let go of it—until the shell landed on top of the last dike and blew it to bits. Dirt, mud, and water slopped down around us, and shell fragments whizzed through the air. One of the fragments sailed over us, sliced a hamburger-sized wad of bark and wood from a tree, and clanged into Spanky Burrage's helmet with a sound like a brick hitting a garbage can. The fragment fell to the ground, and a little smoke drifted up from it.

We picked ourselves up. Spanky looked dead, except that he was breathing. Hamnet shouldered his pack and picked up Spanky and slung him over his shoulder. He saw me looking at him.

"I gotta take *care* of these people," he said.

The other thing I did not understand—apart from why there had been only one mortar round—came when we entered the village.

Lieutenant Harry Beevers had yet to join us, and we were nearly a year away from the events at Ia Thuc, when everything, the world and ourselves within the world, went crazy. I have to explain what happened. Lieutenant Harry Beevers killed thirty children in a cave at Ia Thuc and their bodies disappeared, but Michael Poole and I went into that cave and knew that something obscene had happened in there. We smelled evil, we touched its wings with our hands. A pitiful character named Victor Spitalny ran into the cave when he heard gunfire, and came pinwheeling out right away, screaming, covered with welts or hives that vanished almost as soon as he came out into the air. Poor Spitalny had touched it too. Because I was twenty and already writing books in my head, I thought that the cave was the place where the other *Tom Sawyer* ended, where Injun Joe raped Becky Thatcher and slit Tom's throat.

When we walked into the little village in the woods on the other side of the rice paddy, I experienced a kind of foretaste of Ia Thuc.

If I can say this without setting off all the Gothic bells, the place seemed intrinsically, inherently wrong—it was too quiet, too still, completely without noise or movement. There were no chickens, dogs, or pigs; no old women came out to look us over, no old men offered conciliatory smiles. The little huts, still inhabitable, were empty—something I had never seen before in Vietnam, and never saw again. It was a ghost village, in a country where people thought the earth was sanctified by their ancestor's bodies.

Poole's map said that the place was named Bong To.

Hamnet lowered Spanky into the long grass as soon as we reached the center of the empty village. I bawled out a few words in my poor Vietnamese.

Spanky groaned. He gently touched the sides of his helmet. "I caught a head wound," he said.

"You wouldn't have a head at all, you was only wearing your liner," Hamnet said.

Spanky bit his lips and pushed the helmet up off his head. He groaned. A finger of blood ran down beside his ear. Finally the helmet passed over a lump the size of an apple that rose up from under his hair. Wincing, Spanky fingered this enormous knot. "I see double," he said. "I'll never get that helmet back on."

The medic said, "Take it easy, we'll get you out of here."

"Out of *here*?" Spanky brightened up.

"Back to Crandall," the medic said.

Spitalny sidled up, and Spanky frowned at him. "There ain't nobody here," Spitalny said. "What the fuck is going on?" He took the emptiness of the village as a personal affront.

Leonard Hamnet turned his back and spat.

"Spitalny, Tiano," the Lieutenant said. "Go into the paddy and get Tyrell and Blevins. Now."

Tattoo Tiano, who was due to die six and a half months later and was Spitalny's only friend, said, "You do it this time, Lieutenant."

Hamnet turned around and began moving toward Tiano and Spitalny. He looked as if he had grown two sizes larger, as if his hands could pick up boulders. I had forgotten how big he was. His head was lowered, and a rim of clear white showed above the irises. I wouldn't have been surprised if he had blown smoke from his nostrils.

"Hey, I'm gone, I'm already there," Tiano said. He and Spitalny began moving quickly through the sparse trees. Whoever had fired the mortar had packed up and gone. By now it was nearly dark, and the mosquitos had found us.

"So?" Poole said.

Hamnet sat down heavily enough for me to feel the shock in my boots. He said, "I have to go home, Lieutenant. I don't mean no disrespect, but I cannot take this shit much longer."

The Lieutenant said he was working on it.

Poole, Hamnet, and I looked around at the village.

Spanky Burrage said, "Good quiet place for Ham to catch up on his reading."

"Maybe I better take a look," the Lieutenant said. He flicked the lighter a couple of times and walked off toward the nearest hut. The rest of us stood around like fools, listening to the mosquitos and the sounds of Tiano and Spitalny pulling the dead men up over the dikes. Every now and then Spanky groaned and shook his head. Too much time passed.

The Lieutenant said something almost inaudible from inside the hut. He came back outside in a hurry, looking disturbed and puzzled even in the darkness.

"Underhill, Poole," he said, "I want you to see this."

Poole and I glanced at each other. I wondered if I looked as bad as he did. Poole seemed to be a couple of psychic inches from either taking a poke at the Lieutenant or exploding altogether. In his muddy face his eyes were the size of hen's eggs. He was wound up like a cheap watch. I thought that I probably looked pretty much the same.

"What is it, Lieutenant?" he asked.

The Lieutenant gestured for us to come to the hut, then turned around and went back inside. There was no reason for us not to follow him. The Lieutenant was a jerk, but Harry Beevers, our next Lieutenant, was a baron, an earl among jerks, and we nearly always did whatever dumb thing he told us to do. Poole was so ragged and edgy that he looked as if he felt like shooting the Lieutenant in the back. *I* felt like shooting the Lieutenant in the back, I realized a second later. I didn't have an idea in the world what was going on in Poole's mind. I grumbled something and moved toward the hut. Poole followed.

The Lieutenant was standing in the doorway, looking over his shoulder and fingering his sidearm. He frowned at us to let us know we had been slow to obey him, then flicked on the lighter. The sudden hollows and shadows in his face made him resemble one of the corpses I had opened up when I was in graves registration at Camp White Star.

"You want to know what it is, Poole? Okay, you tell me what it is."

He held the lighter before him like a torch and marched into the hut. I imagined the entire dry, flimsy structure bursting into heat and flame. This Lieutenant was not destined to get home walking and breathing, and I pitied and hated him about equally, but I did not want to turn into toast because he had found an American body inside a hut and didn't know what to do about it. I'd heard of platoons finding the mutilated corpses of American prisoners, and hoped that this was not our turn.

And then, in the instant before I smelled blood and saw the Lieutenant stoop to lift a panel on the floor, I thought that what had spooked him was not the body of an American POW but of a child who had been murdered and left behind in this empty place. The Lieutenant had probably not seen any dead children yet. Some part of the Lieutenant was still worrying about what a girl named Becky Roddenburger was getting up to back at Idaho State, and a dead child would be too much reality for him.

He pulled up the wooden panel in the floor, and I caught the smell of blood. The Zippo died, and darkness closed down on us. The Lieutenant yanked the panel back on its hinges. The smell of blood floated up from whatever was beneath the floor. The Lieutenant flicked the Zippo, and his face jumped out of the darkness. "Now. Tell me what this is."

"It's where they hide the kids when people like us show up," I said. "Smells like something went wrong. Did you take a look?"

I saw in his tight cheeks and almost lipless mouth that he had not. He wasn't about to go down there and get killed by the Minotaur while his platoon stood around outside.

"Taking a look is your job, Underhill," he said.

For a second we both looked at the ladder, made of peeled branches lashed together with rags, that led down into the pit.

"Give me the lighter," Poole said, and grabbed it away from the Lieutenant. He sat on the edge of the hole and leaned over, bringing the flame beneath the level of the floor. He grunted at whatever he saw, and surprised both the Lieutenant and myself by pushing himself off the ledge into the opening. The light went out. The Lieutenant and I looked down into the dark open rectangle in the floor.

The lighter flared again. I could see Poole's extended arm, the jittering little fire, a packed-earth floor. The top of the concealed room was less than an inch above the top of Poole's head. He moved away from the opening.

"What is it? Are there any –" The Lieutenant's voice made a creaky sound. "Any bodies?"

"Come down here, Tim," Poole called up.

I sat on the floor and swung my legs into the pit. Then I jumped down.

Beneath the floor, the smell of blood was almost sickeningly strong.

"What do you see?" the Lieutenant shouted. He was trying to sound like a leader, and his voice squeaked on the last word.

I saw an empty room shaped like a giant grave. The walls were covered by some kind of thick paper held in place by wooden struts sunk into the earth. Both the thick brown paper and two of the struts showed old bloodstains.

"Hot," Poole said, and closed the lighter.

"Come *on*, damn it," came the Lieutenant's voice. "Get out of there."

"Yes, sir," Poole said. He flicked the lighter back on. Many layers of thick paper formed an absorbent pad between the earth and the room, and the topmost, thinnest layer had been covered with vertical lines of Vietnamese writing. The writing looked like poetry, like the left-hand pages of Kenneth Rexroth's translations of Tu Fu and Li Po.

"Well, well," Poole said, and I turned to see him pointing at what first looked like intricately woven strands of rope fixed to the bloodstained wooden uprights. Poole stepped forward and the weave jumped into sharp relief. About four feet off the ground, iron chains had been screwed to the uprights. The thick pad between the two lengths of chain had been soaked with blood. The three feet of ground between the posts looked rusty. Poole moved the lighter closer to the chains, and we saw dried blood on the metal links.

"I want you guys out of there, and I mean *now*," whined the Lieutenant.

Poole snapped the lighter shut.

"I just changed my mind," I said softly. "I'm putting twenty bucks into the Elijah fund. For two weeks from today. That's what, June twentieth?"

"Tell it to Spanky," he said. Spanky Burrage had invented the pool we called the Elijah fund, and he held the money. Michael had not put any money into the pool. He thought that a new Lieutenant might be even worse than the one we had. Of course he was right. Harry Beevers was our next Lieutenant. Elijah Joys, Lieutenant Elijah Joys of New Utrecht, Idaho, a graduate of the University of Idaho and basic training at Fort Benning, Georgia, was an inept, weak Lieutenant, not a disastrous one. If Spanky could have seen what was coming, he would have given back the money and prayed for the safety of Lieutenant Joys.

Poole and I moved back toward the opening. I felt as if I had seen a shrine to an obscene deity. The Lieutenant leaned over and stuck out his hand—uselessly, because he did not bend down far enough for us to reach him. We levered ourselves up out of the hole stiff-armed, as if we were leaving a swimming pool. The Lieutenant stepped back. He had a thin face and thick, fleshy nose, and his Adam's apple danced around in his neck like a jumping bean. He might not have been Harry Beevers, but he was no prize. "Well, how many?"

"How many what?" I asked.

"How many are there?" He wanted to go back to Camp Crandall with a good body count.

"There weren't exactly any bodies, Lieutenant," said Poole, trying to let him down easily. He described what we had seen.

"Well, what's that good for?" He meant, *How is that going to help me*?

"Interrogations, probably," Poole said. "If you questioned someone down there, no one outside the hut would hear anything. At night, you could just drag the body into the woods."

Lieutenant Joys nodded. "Field Interrogation Post," he said, trying out the phrase. "Torture, Use of, Highly Indicated." He nodded again. "Right?"

"Highly," Poole said.

"Shows you what kind of enemy we're dealing with in this conflict."

I could no longer stand being in the same three square feet of space with Elijah Joys, and I took a step toward the door of the hut. I did not know what Poole and I had seen, but I knew it was not a Field Interrogation Post, Torture, Use of, Highly Indicated, unless the Vietnamese had begun to interrogate monkeys. It occurred to me that the writing on the wall might have been names instead of poetry—I thought that we had stumbled into a mystery that had nothing to do with the war, a Vietnamese mystery.

For a second, music from my old life, music too beautiful to be endurable, started playing in my head. Finally I recognized it: "The Walk to the Paradise Gardens," from *A Village Romeo and Juliet* by Frederick Delius. Back in Berkeley, I had listened to it hundreds of times.

If nothing else had happened, I think I could have replayed the whole piece in my head. Tears filled my eyes, and I stepped toward the door of the hut. Then I froze. A ragged Vietnamese boy of seven or eight was regarding me with great seriousness from the far corner of the hut. I knew he was not there—I knew he was a spirit. I had no belief in spirits, but that's what he was. Some part of my mind as detached as a crime reporter reminded me that "The Walk to the Paradise Gardens" was about two children who were about to die, and that in a sense the music *was* their death. I wiped my eyes with my hand, and when I lowered my arm, the boy was still there. He was beautiful, beautiful in the ordinary way, as Vietnamese children nearly always seemed beautiful to me. Then he vanished all at once, like the flickering light of the Zippo. I nearly groaned aloud. That child had been murdered in the hut: he had not just died, he had been murdered.

I said something to the other two men and went through the door into the growing darkness. I was very dimly aware of the Lieutenant asking Poole to repeat his description of the uprights and the bloody chain. Hamnet and Burrage and Calvin Hill were sitting down and leaning against a tree. Victor Spitalny was wiping his hands on his filthy shirt. White smoke curled up from Hill's cigarette, and Tina Pumo exhaled a long white stream of vapor. The unhinged thought came to me with an absolute conviction that *this* was the Paradise Gardens. The men lounging in the darkness; the pattern of the cigarette smoke, and the patterns they made, sitting or standing; the in-drawing darkness, as physical as a blanket; the frame of the trees and the flat gray-green background of the paddy.

My soul had come back to life.

Then I became aware that there was something wrong about the men arranged before me, and again it took a moment for my intelligence to catch up to my intuition. Every member of a combat unit makes unconscious adjustments as members of the unit go down in the field; survival sometimes depends on the number of people you know are with you, and you keep count without being quite aware of doing it. I had registered that two men too many were in front of me. Instead of seven, there were nine, and the two men that made up the nine of us left were still behind me in the hut. M. O. Dengler was looking at me with growing curiosity, and I thought he knew exactly what I was thinking. A sick chill went through me. I saw Tom Blevins and Tyrell Budd standing together at the far right of the platoon, a little muddier than the others but otherwise different from the rest only in that, like Dengler, they were looking directly at me.

Hill tossed his cigarette away in an arc of light. Poole and Lieutenant Joys came out of the hut behind me. Leonard Hamnet patted his pocket to reassure himself that he still had his letter. I looked back at the right of the group, and the two dead men were gone.

"Let's saddle up," the Lieutenant said. "We aren't doing any good around here."

"Tim?" Dengler asked. He had not taken his eyes off me since I had come out of the hut. I shook my head.

"Well, what was it?" asked Tina Pumo. "Was it juicy?"

Spanky and Calvin Hill laughed and slapped hands.

"Aren't we gonna torch this place?" asked Spitalny.

The Lieutenant ignored him. "Juicy enough, Pumo. Interrogation Post. Field Interrogation Post."

"No shit," said Pumo.

"These people are into torture, Pumo. It's just another indication."

"Gotcha." Pumo glanced at me and his eyes grew curious. Dengler moved closer.

"I was just remembering something," I said. "Something from the world."

"You better forget about the world while you're over here, Underhill," the Lieutenant told me. "I'm trying to keep you alive, in case you hadn't noticed, but you have to cooperate with me." His Adam's apple jumped like a begging puppy.

As soon as he went ahead to lead us out of the village, I gave twenty dollars to Spanky and said, "Two weeks from today."

"My man," Spanky said.

The rest of the patrol was uneventful.

The next night we had showers, real food, alcohol, cots to sleep in. Sheets and pillows. Two new guys replaced Tyrell Budd and Thomas Blevins, whose names were never mentioned again, at least by me, until long after the war was over and Poole, Linklater, Pumo, and I looked them up, along with the rest of our dead, on the Wall in Washington. I wanted to forget the patrol, especially what I had seen and experienced inside the hut. I wanted the oblivion which came in powdered form.

I remember that it was raining. I remember the steam lifting off the ground, and the condensation dripping down the metal poles in the tents. Moisture shone on the faces around me. I was sitting in the brothers' tent, listening to the music Spanky Burrage played on the big reel-to-reel recorder he had bought on R&R in Taipei. Spanky Burrage never played Delius, but what he played was paradisal: great jazz from Armstrong to Coltrane, on reels recorded for him by his friends back in Little Rock and which he knew so well he could find individual tracks and performances without bothering to look at the counter. Spanky liked to play disc jockey during these long sessions, changing reels and speeding past thousands of feet of tape to play the same songs by different musicians, even the same song hiding under different names—"Cherokee" and "KoKo," "Indiana" and "Donna Lee"—or long series of songs connected by titles that used the same words—"I Thought About You" (Art Tatum), "You and the Night and the Music" (Sonny Rollins), "I Love You" (Bill Evans), "If I Could Be with You" (Ike Quebec), "You Leave Me Breathless," (Milt Jackson), even, for the sake of the joke, "Thou Swell," by Glenroy Breakstone. In his single-artist mode on this day, Spanky was ranging through the work of a great trumpet player named Clifford Brown.

On this sweltering, rainy day, Clifford Brown's music sounded regal and unearthly. Clifford Brown was walking to the Paradise Gardens. Listening to him was like watching a smiling man shouldering open an enormous door to let in great dazzling rays of light. We were out of the war. The world we were in transcended pain and loss, and imagination had banished fear. Even SP4 Cotton and Calvin Hill, who preferred James Brown to Clifford Brown, lay on their bunks listening as Spanky followed his instincts from one track to another.

After he had played disc jockey for something like two hours, Spanky rewound the long tape and said, "Enough." The end of the tape slapped against the reel. I looked at Dengler, who seemed dazed, as if awakening from a long sleep. The memory of the music was still all around us: light still poured in through the crack in the great door.

"I'm gonna have a smoke *and* a drink," Cotton announced, and pushed himself up off his cot. He walked to the door of the tent and pulled the flap aside to expose the green wet drizzle. That dazzling light, the light from another world, began to fade. Cotton sighed, plopped a wide-brimmed hat on his head, and slipped outside. Before the stiff flap fell shut, I saw him jumping through the puddles on the way to Wilson Manly's shack. I felt as though I had returned from a long journey.

Spanky finished putting the Clifford Brown reel back into its cardboard box. Someone in the rear of the tent switched on Armed Forces Radio. Spanky looked at me and shrugged. Leonard Hamnet took his letter out of his pocket, unfolded it, and read it through very slowly.

"Leonard," I said, and he swung his big buffalo's head toward me. "You still putting in for compassionate leave?"

He nodded. "You know what I gotta do."

"Yes," Dengler said, in a slow quiet voice.

"They gonna let me take care of my people. They gonna send me back."

He spoke with a complete absence of nuance, like a man who had learned to get what he wanted by parroting words without knowing what they meant.

Dengler looked at me and smiled. For a second he seemed as alien as Hamnet. "What do you think is going to happen? To us, I mean. Do you think it'll just go on like this day after day until some of us get killed and the rest of us go home, or do you think it's going to get stranger and stranger?" He did not wait for me to answer. "I think it'll always sort of look the same, but it won't be—I think the edges are starting to melt. I think that's what happens when you're out here long enough. The edges melt."

"Your edges melted a long time ago, Dengler," Spanky said, and applauded his own joke.

Dengler was still staring at me. He always resembled a serious, dark-haired child, and never looked as though he belonged in uniform. "Here's what I mean, kind of," he said. "When we were listening to that trumpet player – "

"*Brownie*, Clifford *Brown*," Spanky whispered.

"– I could see the notes in the air. Like they were written out on a long scroll. And after he played them, they stayed in the air for a long time."

"Sweetie-*pie*," Spanky said softly. "You pretty hip, for a little ofay square."

"When we were back in that village, last week," Dengler said. "Tell me about that."

I said that he had been there too.

"But something happened to you. Something special."

"I put twenty bucks in the Elijah fund," I said.

"Only twenty?" Cotton asked.

"What was in that hut?" Dengler asked.

I shook my head.

"All right," Dengler said. "But it's happening, isn't it? Things are changing."

I could not speak. I could not tell Dengler in front of Cotton and Spanky Burrage that I had imagined seeing the ghosts of Blevins, Budd, and a murdered child. I smiled and shook my head.

"Fine," Dengler said.

"What the fuck you sayin' is *fine*?" Cotton said. "I don't mind listening to that music, but I do draw the line at this bullshit." He flipped himself off his bunk and pointed a finger at me. "What date you give Spanky?"

"Fifteenth."

"He last longer than that." Cotton tilted his head as the song on the radio ended. Armed Forces Radio began playing a song by Moby Grape. Disgusted, he turned back to me. "Check it out. End of August. He be so tired, he be *sleepwalkin'*. Be halfway through his tour. The fool will go to pieces, and that's when he'll get it."

Cotton had put thirty dollars on August thirty-first, exactly the midpoint of Lieutenant Joys' tour of duty. He had a long time to adjust to the loss of the money, because he himself stayed alive until a sniper killed him at the beginning of February. Then he became a member of the ghost platoon that followed us wherever we went. I think this ghost platoon, filled with men I had loved and detested, whose names I could or could not remember, disbanded only when I went to the Wall in Washington, D.C., and by then I felt that I was a member of it myself.

## II

I left the tent with a vague notion of getting outside and enjoying the slight coolness that followed the rain. The packet of Si Van Vo's white powder rested at the bottom of my right front pocket, which was so deep that my fingers just brushed its top. I decided that what I needed was a beer.

Wilson Manly's shack was all the way on the other side of camp. I never liked going to the enlisted men's club, where they were rumored to serve cheap Vietnamese beer in American bottles. Certainly the bottles had often been stripped of their labels, and to a suspicious eye the caps looked dented; also, the beer there never quite tasted like the stuff Manly sold.

One other place remained, farther away than the enlisted men's club but closer than Manly's shack and somewhere between them in official status. About twenty minutes' walk from where I stood, just at the curve in the steeply descending road to the airfield and the motor pool, stood an isolated wooden structure called Billy's. Billy himself, supposedly a Green Beret Captain who had installed a handful of bar girls in an old French command post, had gone home long ago, but his club had endured. There were no more girls, if there ever had been, and the brand-name liquor was about as reliable as the enlisted men's club's beer. When it was open, a succession of slender Montagnard boys who slept in the nearly empty upstairs rooms served drinks. I visited these rooms two or three times, but I never learned where the boys went when Billy's was closed. They spoke almost no English. Billy's did not look anything like a French command post, even one that had been transformed into a bordello: it looked like a roadhouse.

A long time ago, the building had been painted brown. The wood was soft with rot. Someone had once boarded up the two front windows on the lower floor, and someone else had torn off a narrow band of boards across each of the windows, so that light entered in two flat white bands that traveled across the floor during the day. Around six thirty the light bounced off the long foxed mirror that stood behind the row of bottles. After five minutes of blinding light, the sun disappeared beneath the pine boards, and for ten or fifteen minutes a shadowy pink glow filled the barroom. There was no electricity and no ice. Fingerprints covered the glasses. When you needed a toilet, you went to a cubicle with inverted metal boot-prints on either side of a hole in the floor.

The building stood in a little grove of trees in the curve of the descending road, and as I walked toward it in the diffuse reddish light of the sunset, a mud-spattered jeep painted in the colors of camouflage gradually came into view to the right of the bar, emerging from invisibility like an optical illusion. The jeep seemed to have floated out of the trees behind it, to be a part of them.

I heard low male voices, which stopped when I stepped onto the soft boards of the front porch. I glanced at the jeep, looking for insignia or identification, but the mud covered the door panels. Something white gleamed dully from the back seat. When I looked more closely, I saw in a coil of rope an oval of bone that it took me a moment to recognize as the top of a painstakingly cleaned and bleached human skull.

Before I could reach the handle, the door opened. A boy named Mike stood before me, in loose khaki shorts and a dirty white shirt much too large for him. Then he saw who I was. "Oh," he said. "Yes. Tim. Okay. You can come in." His real name was not Mike, but Mike was what it sounded like. He carried himself with an odd defensive alertness, and he shot me a tight, uncomfortable smile. "Far table, right side."

"It's okay?" I asked, because everything about him told me that it wasn't.

"*Yesss.*" He stepped back to let me in.

I smelled cordite before I saw the other men. The bar looked empty, and the band of light coming in through the opening over the windows had already reached the long mirror, creating a bright dazzle, a white fire. I took a couple of steps inside, and Mike moved around me to return to his post.

"Oh, hell," someone said from off to my left. "We have to put up with *this*?"

I turned my head to look into the murk of that side of the bar, and saw three men sitting against the wall at a round table. None of the kerosene lamps had been lighted yet, and the dazzle from the mirror made the far reaches of the bar even less distinct.

"Is okay, is okay," said Mike. "Old customer. Old friend."

"I bet he is," the voice said. "Just don't let any women in here."

"No women," Mike said. "No problem."

I went through the tables to the furthest one on the right.

"You want whiskey, Tim?" Mike asked.

"Tim?" the man said. "*Tim*?"

"Beer," I said, and sat down.

A nearly empty bottle of Johnnie Walker Black, three glasses, and about a dozen cans of beer covered the table before them. The soldier with his back against the wall shoved aside some of the beer cans so that I could see the .45 next to the Johnnie Walker bottle. He leaned forward with a drunk's guarded coordination. The sleeves had been ripped off his shirt, and dirt darkened his skin as if he had not bathed in years. His hair had been cut with a knife, and had once been blond.

"I just want to make sure about this," he said. "You're not a woman, right? You swear to that?"

"Anything you say," I said.

"No woman walks into this place." He put his hand on the gun. "No nurse. No wife. No *anything*. You got that?"

"Got it," I said. Mike hurried around the bar with my beer.

"Tim. Funny name. Tom, now—that's a name. Tim sounds like a little guy—like him." He pointed at Mike with his left hand, the whole hand and not merely the index finger, while his right still rested on the .45. "Little fucker ought to be wearing a dress. Hell, he practically *is* wearing a dress."

"Don't you like women?" I asked. Mike put a can of Budweiser on my table and shook his head rapidly, twice. He had wanted me in the club because he was afraid the drunken soldier was going to shoot him, and now I was just making things worse.

I looked at the two men with the drunken officer. They were dirty and exhausted—whatever had happened to the drunk had also happened to them. The difference was that they were not drunk yet.

"That is a complicated question," the drunk said. "There are questions of responsibility. You can be responsible for yourself. You can be responsible for your children and your tribe. You are responsible for anyone you want to protect. But can you be responsible for women? If so, how responsible?"

Mike quietly moved behind the bar and sat on a stool with his arms out of sight. I knew he had a shotgun under there.

"You don't have any idea what I'm talking about, do you, Tim, you rear-echelon dipshit?"

"You're afraid you'll shoot any women who come in here, so you told the bartender to keep them out."

"This wise-ass sergeant is personally interfering with my state of mind," the drunk said to the burly man on his right. "Tell him to get out of here, or a certain degree of unpleasantness will ensue."

"Leave him alone," the other man said. Stripes of dried mud lay across his lean, haggard face.

The drunken officer Beret startled me by leaning toward the other man and speaking in a clear, carrying Vietnamese. It was an old-fashioned, almost literary Vietnamese, and he must have thought and dreamed in it to speak it so well. He assumed that neither I nor the Montagnard boy would understand him.

*This is serious*, he said, *and I am serious. If you wish to see how serious, just sit in your chair and do nothing. Do you know of what I am capable by now? Have you learned nothing? You know what I know. I know what you know. A great heaviness is between us. Of all the people in the world at this moment, the only ones I do not despise are already dead, or should be. At this moment, murder is weightless.*

There was more, and I cannot swear that this was exactly what he said, but it's pretty close. He may have said that murder was *empty*.

Then he said, in that same flowing Vietnamese that even to my ears sounded as stilted as the language of a third-rate Victorian novel: *Recall what is in our vehicle (carriage); you should remember what we have brought with us, because I shall never forget it. Is it so easy for you to forget?*

It takes a long time and a lot of patience to clean and bleach bone. A skull would be more difficult than most of a skeleton.

*Your leader requires more of this nectar*, he said, and rolled back in his chair, looking at me with his hand on his gun.

"Whiskey," said the burly soldier. Mike was already pulling the bottle off the shelf. He understood that the officer was trying to knock himself out before he would find it necessary to shoot someone.

For a moment I thought that the burly soldier to his right looked familiar. His head had been shaved so close he looked bald, and his eyes were enormous above the streaks of dirt. A stainless-steel watch hung from a slot in his collar. He extended a muscular arm for the bottle Mike passed him while keeping as far from the table as he could. The soldier twisted off the cap and poured into all three glasses. The man in the center immediately drank all the whiskey in his glass and banged the glass down on the table for a refill.

The haggard soldier who had been silent until now said, "Something is gonna happen here." He looked straight at me. "Pal?"

"That man is nobody's pal," the drunk said. Before anyone could stop him, he snatched up the gun, pointed it across the room, and fired. There was a flash of fire, a huge explosion, and the reek of cordite. The bullet went straight through the soft wooden wall, about eight feet to my left. A stray bit of light slanted through the hole it made.

For a moment I was deaf. I swallowed the last of my beer and stood up. My head was ringing.

"Is it clear that I hate the necessity for this kind of shit?" said the drunk. "Is that much understood?"

The soldier who had called me pal laughed, and the burly soldier poured more whiskey into the drunk's glass. Then he stood up and started coming toward me. Beneath the exhaustion and the stripes of dirt, his face was taut with anxiety. He put himself between me and the man with the gun.

"I am not a rear-echelon dipshit," I said. "I don't want any trouble, but people like him do not own this war."

"Will you maybe let me save your ass, Sergeant?" he whispered. "Major Bachelor hasn't been anywhere near white men in three years, and he's having a little trouble readjusting. Compared to him, we're all rear-echelon dipshits."

I looked at his tattered shirt. "Are you his babysitter, Captain?"

He gave me an exasperated look, and glanced over his shoulder at the Major. "Major, put down your damn weapon. The sergeant is a combat soldier. He is on his way back to camp."

*I don't care what he is*, the Major said in Vietnamese.

The Captain began pulling me toward the door, keeping his body between me and the other table. I motioned for Mike to come out with me.

"Don't worry, the Major won't shoot him, Major Bachelor loves the Yards," the Captain said. He gave me an impatient glance because I had refused to move at his pace. Then I saw him notice my pupils. "God damn," he said, and then he stopped moving altogether and said "God damn" again, but in a different tone of voice.

I started laughing.

"Oh, this is –" He shook his head. "This is really – "

"Where have you *been?*" I asked him.

John Ransom turned to the table. "Hey, I know this guy. He's an old football friend of mine."

Major Bachelor shrugged and put the .45 back on the table. His eyelids had nearly closed. "I don't care about football," he said, but he kept his hand off the weapon.

"Buy the sergeant a drink," said the haggard officer.

"Buy the fucking sergeant a drink," the Major chimed in.

John Ransom quickly moved to the bar and reached for a glass, which the confused Mike put into his hand. Ransom went through the tables, filled his glass and mine, and carried both back to join me.

We watched the Major's head slip down by notches toward his chest. When his chin finally reached the unbuttoned top of his ruined shirt, Ransom said, "All right, Bob," and the other man slid the .45 out from under the Major's hand. He pushed it beneath his belt.

"The man is out," Bob said.

Ransom turned back to me. "He was up three days straight with us, God knows how long before that." Ransom did not have to specify who *he* was. "Bob and I got some sleep, trading off, but he just kept on talking." He fell into one of the chairs at my table and tilted his glass to his mouth. I sat down beside him.

For a moment no one in the bar spoke. The line of light from the open space across the windows had already left the mirror, and was now approaching the place on the wall that meant it would soon disappear. Mike lifted the cover from one of the lamps and began trimming the wick.

"How come you're always fucked up when I see you?"

"You have to ask?"

He smiled. He looked very different from when I had seen him preparing to give a sales pitch to Senator Burrman at Camp White Star. His body had thickened and hardened, and his eyes had retreated far back into his head. He seemed to me to have moved a long step nearer the goal I had always seen in him than when he had given me the zealot's word about stopping the spread of Communism. This man had taken in more of the war, and that much more of the war was inside him now.

"I got you off graves registration at White Star, didn't I?"

I agreed that he had.

"What did you call it, the body squad? It wasn't even a real graves registration unit, was it?" He smiled and shook his head. "I took care of your Captain McCue, too—he was using it as a kind of dumping ground. I don't know how he got away with it as long as he did. The only one with any training was that sergeant, what's his name. Italian."

"DeMaestro."

Ransom nodded. "The whole operation was going off the rails." Mike lit a big kitchen match and touched it to the wick of the kerosene lamp. "I heard some things –" He slumped against the wall and swallowed whiskey. I wondered if he had heard about Captain Havens. He closed his eyes. "Some crazy stuff went on back there."

I asked if he was still stationed in the highlands up around the Laotian border. He almost sighed when he shook his head.

"You're not with the tribesmen anymore? What were they, Khatu?"

He opened his eyes. "You have a good memory. No, I'm not there anymore." He considered saying more, but decided not to.

He had failed himself. "I'm kind of on hold until they send me up around Khe Sahn. It'll be better up there—the Bru are tremendous. But right now, all I want to do is take a bath and get into bed. Any bed. Actually, I'd settle for a dry level place on the ground."

"Where did you come from now?"

"Incountry." His face creased and he showed his teeth. The effect was so unsettling that I did not immediately realize that he was smiling. "Way incountry. We had to get the Major out."

"Looks more like you had to pull him out, like a tooth."

My ignorance made him sit up straight. "You mean you never heard of him? Franklin Bachelor?"

And then I thought I had, that someone had mentioned him to me a long time ago.

"In the bush for years. Bachelor did stuff that ordinary people don't even *dream* of—he's a legend."

A legend, I thought. Like the Green Berets Ransom had mentioned a lifetime ago at White Star.

"Ran what amounted to a private army, did a lot of good work in Darlac Province. He was out there on his own. The man was a hero. That's straight. Bachelor got to places we couldn't even get close to—he got *inside* an NVA encampment, you hear me, *inside* the encampment and *silently* killed about an entire division."

Of all the people in the world at this minute, I remembered, the only ones he did not detest were already dead. I thought I must have heard it wrong.

"He was absorbed right into Rhade life," Ransom said. I could hear the awe in his voice. "The man even got married. Rhade ceremony. His wife went with him on missions. I hear she was beautiful."

Then I knew where I had heard of Franklin Bachelor before. He had been a captain when Ratman and his platoon had run into him after a private named Bobby Swett had been blown to pieces on a trail in Darlac Province. Ratman had thought his wife was a black-haired angel.

And then I knew whose skull lay wound in rope in the back seat of the jeep.

"I did hear of him," I said. "I knew someone who met him. The Rhade woman, too."

"His *wife*," Ransom said.

I asked him where they were taking Bachelor.

"We're stopping overnight at Crandall for some rest. Then we hop to Tan Son Nhut and bring him back to the States—Langley. I thought we might have to strap him down, but I guess we'll just keep pouring whiskey into him."

"He's going to want his gun back."

"Maybe I'll give it to him." His look told me what he thought Major Bachelor would do with his .45, if he was left alone with it long enough. "He's in for a rough time at Langley. There'll be some heat."

"Why Langley?"

"Don't ask. But don't be naïve, either. Don't you think they're . . ." He would not finish that sentence. "Why do you think we had to bring him out in the first place?"

"Because something went wrong."

"Oh, everything went wrong. Bachelor went totally out of control. He had his own war. Ran a lot of sidelines, some of which were supposed to be under shall we say tighter controls?"

He had lost me.

"Ventures into Laos. Business trips to Cambodia. Sometimes he wound up in control of airfields Air America was using, and that meant he was in control of the cargo."

When I shook my head, he said, "Don't you have a little something in your pocket? A little package?"

A secret world—inside this world, another, secret world.

"You understand, I don't care what he did any more than I care about what *you* do. I think Langley can go fuck itself. Bachelor wrote the book. In spite of his sidelines. In spite of whatever *trouble* he got into. The man was effective. He stepped over a boundary, maybe a lot of boundaries—but tell me that you can do what we're supposed to do without stepping over boundaries."

I wondered why he seemed to be defending himself, and asked if he would have to testify at Langley.

"It's not a trial."

"A debriefing."

"Sure, a debriefing. They can ask me anything they want. All I can tell them is what I saw. That's *my* evidence, right? What I saw? They don't have any evidence, except maybe this, uh, these human remains the Major insisted on bringing out."

For a second, I wished that I could see the sober shadowy gentlemen of Langley, Virginia, the gentlemen with slicked-back hair and pinstriped suits, question Major Bachelor. They thought *they* were serious men.

"It was like Bong To, in a funny way." Ransom waited for me to ask. When I did not, he said, "A ghost town, I mean. I don't suppose you've ever heard of Bong To."

"My unit was just there." His head jerked up. "A mortar round scared us into the village."

"You saw the place?"

I nodded.

"Funny story." Now he was sorry he had ever mentioned it. "Well, think about Bachelor, now. I think he must have been in Cambodia or someplace, doing what he does, when his village was overrun. He comes back and finds everybody dead, his wife included. I mean, I don't think *Bachelor* killed those people—they weren't just dead, they'd been made to beg for it. So Bachelor wasn't there, and his assistant, a Captain Bennington, must have just run off—we never did find him. Officially, Bennington's MIA. It's simple. You can't find the main guy, so you make sure he can see how mad you are when he gets back. You do a little grievous bodily harm on his people. They were not nice to his wife, Tim, to her they were especially not nice. What does he do? He buries all the bodies in the village graveyard, because that's a sacred responsibility. Don't ask me what else he does, because you don't have to know this, okay? But the bodies are buried. Generally speaking. Captain Bennington never does show up. We arrive and take Bachelor away. But sooner or later, some of the people who escaped are going to come back to that village. They're going to go on living there. The worst thing in the world happened to them in that place, but they won't leave. Eventually, other people in their family will join them, if they're still alive, and the terrible thing will be a part of their lives. Because it is not thinkable to leave your dead."

"But they did in Bong To," I said.

"In Bong To, they did."

I saw the look of regret on his face again, and said that I wasn't asking him to tell me any secrets.

"It's not a secret. It's not even military."

"It's just a ghost town."

Ransom was still uncomfortable. He turned his glass around and around in his hands before he drank. "I have to get the Major into camp."

"It's a real ghost town," I said. "Complete with ghosts."

"I honestly wouldn't be surprised." He drank what was left in his glass and stood up. He had decided not to say any more about it. "Let's take care of Major Bachelor, Bob," he said.

"Right."

Ransom carried our bottle to the bar and paid Mike. I stepped toward him to do the same, and Ransom said, "Taken care of."

There was that phrase again—it seemed I had been hearing it all day, and that its meaning would not stay still.

Ransom and Bob picked up the Major between them. They were strong enough to lift him easily. Bachelor's greasy head rolled forward. Bob put the .45 into his pocket, and Ransom put the bottle into his own pocket. Together they carried the Major to the door.

I followed them outside. Artillery pounded hills a long way off. It was dark now, and light from the lanterns spilled out through the gaps in the windows.

All of us went down the rotting steps, the Major bobbing between the other two.

Ransom opened the jeep, and they took a while to maneuver the Major into the back seat. Bob squeezed in beside him and pulled him upright.

John Ransom got in behind the wheel and sighed. He had no taste for the next part of his job.

"I'll give you a ride back to camp," he said. "We don't want an MP to get a close look at you."

I took the seat beside him. Ransom started the engine and turned on the lights. He jerked the gearshift into reverse and rolled backwards. "You know why that mortar round came in, don't you?" he asked me. He grinned at me, and we bounced onto the road back to the main part of camp. "He was trying to chase you away from Bong To, and your fool of a Lieutenant went straight for the place instead." He was still grinning. "It must have steamed him, seeing a bunch of round-eyes going in there."

"He didn't send in any more fire."

"No. He didn't want to damage the place. It's supposed to stay the way it is. I don't think they'd use the word, but that village is supposed to be like a kind of monument." He glanced at me again. "To shame."

For some reason, all I could think of was the drunken Major in the seat behind me, who had said that you were responsible for the people you wanted to protect. Ransom said, "Did you go into any of the huts? Did you see anything unusual there?"

"I went into a hut. I saw something unusual."

"A list of names?"

"I thought that's what they were."

"Okay," Ransom said. "You know a little Vietnamese?"

"A little."

"You notice anything about those names?"

I could not remember. My Vietnamese had been picked up in bars and markets, and was almost completely oral.

"Four of them were from a family named Trang. Trang was the village chief, like his father before him, and his grandfather before him. Trang had four daughters. As each one got to the age of six or seven, he took them down into that underground room and chained them to the posts and raped them. A lot of those huts have hidden storage areas, but Trang must have modified his after his first daughter was born. The funny thing is, I think everybody in the village knew what he was doing. I'm not saying they thought it was okay, but they let it happen. They could pretend they didn't know: the girls never complained, and nobody ever heard any screams. I guess Trang was a good-enough chief. When the daughters got to sixteen, they left for the cities. Sent back money, too. So maybe they thought it was okay, but I don't think they did, myself, do you?"

"How would I know? But there's a man in my platoon, a guy from – "

"I think there's a difference between private and public shame. Between what's acknowledged and what is not acknowledged. That's what Bachelor has to cope with, when he gets to Langley. Some things are acceptable, as long as you don't talk about them." He looked sideways at me as we began to approach the northern end of the camp proper. He wiped his face, and flakes of dried mud fell off his cheek. The exposed skin looked red, and so did his eyes. "Because the way I see it, this is a whole general issue. The issue is: what is *expressible*? This goes way beyond the tendency of people to tolerate thoughts, actions, or behavior they would otherwise find unacceptable."

I had never heard a soldier speak this way before. It was a little bit like being back in Berkeley.

"I'm talking about the difference between what is expressed and what is described," Ransom said. "A lot of experience is unacknowledged. Religion lets us handle some of the unacknowledged stuff in an acceptable way. But suppose—just suppose—that you were forced to confront extreme experience directly, without any mediation?"

"I have," I said. "You have, too."

"More extreme than combat, more extreme than terror. Something like that happened to the Major: he *encountered* God. Demands were made upon him. He had to move out of the ordinary, even as *he* defined it."

Ransom was telling me how Major Bachelor had wound up being brought to Camp Crandall with his wife's skull, but none of it was clear to me.

"I've been learning things," Ransom told me. He was almost whispering. "Think about what would make all the people of a village pick up and leave, when sacred obligation ties them to that village."

"I don't know the answer," I said.

"An even more sacred obligation, created by a really spectacular sense of shame. When a crime is too great to live with, the memory of it becomes sacred. Becomes the crime itself – "

I remembered thinking that the arrangement in the hut's basement had been a shrine to an obscene deity.

"Here we have this village and its chief. The village knows but does not know what the chief has been doing. They are used to consulting and obeying him. Then—one day, a little boy disappears."

My heart gave a thud.

"A little boy. Say: three. Old enough to talk and get into trouble, but too young to take care of himself. He's just gone—*poof*. Well, this is Vietnam, right? You turn your back, your kid wanders away, some animal gets him. He could get lost in the jungle and wander into a claymore. Someone like you might even shoot him. He could fall into a boobytrap and never be seen again. It could happen.

"A couple of months later, it happens again. Mom turns her back, where the hell did Junior go? This time they really look, not just Mom and Grandma, all their friends. They scour the village. The *villagers* scour the village, every square foot of that place, and then they do the same to the rice paddy, and then they look through the forest.

"And guess what happens next. This is the interesting part. An old woman goes out one morning to fetch water from the well, and she sees a ghost. This old lady is part of the extended family of the first lost kid, but the ghost she sees isn't the kid's—it's the ghost of a disreputable old man from another village, a drunkard, in fact. A local no-good, in fact. He's just standing near the well with his hands together, he's hungry—that's what these people know about ghosts. The skinny old bastard wants *more*. He wants to be *fed*. The old lady gives a squawk and passes out. When she comes to again, the ghost is gone.

"Well, the old lady tells everybody what she saw, and the whole village gets in a panic. Evil forces have been set loose. Next thing you know, two thirteen-year-old girls are working in the paddy, they look up and see an old woman who died when they were ten—she's about six feet away from them. Her hair is stringy and grey and her fingernails are about a foot long. She used to be a friendly old lady, but she doesn't look too friendly now. She's hungry too, like all ghosts. They start screaming and crying, but no one else can see her, and she comes closer and closer, and they try to get away but one of them falls down, and the old woman is on her like a cat. And do you know what she does? She rubs her filthy hands over the screaming girl's face, and licks the tears and slobber off her fingers.

"The next night, another little boy disappears. Two men go looking around the village latrine behind the houses, and they see two ghosts down in the pit, shoving excrement into their mouths. They rush back into the village, and then they both see half a dozen ghosts around the chief's hut. Among them are a sister who died during the war with the

French and a twenty-year-old first wife who died of dengue fever. They want to eat. One of the men screeches, because not only did he see his dead wife, who looks something like what we could call a vampire, he saw her pass into the chief's hut without the benefit of the door.

"These people believe in ghosts, Underhill, they know ghosts exist, but it is extremely rare for them to see these ghosts. And these people are like psychoanalysts, because they do not believe in accidents. Every event contains meaning.

"The dead twenty-year-old wife comes back out through the wall of the chief's hut. Her hands are empty but dripping with red, and she is licking them like a starving cat.

"The former husband stands there pointing and jabbering, and the mothers and grandmothers of the missing boys come out of their huts. They are as afraid of what they're thinking as they are of all the ghosts moving around them. The ghosts are part of what they know they know, even though most of them have never seen one until now. What is going through their minds is something new: new because it was hidden.

"The mothers and grandmothers go to the chief's door and begin howling like dogs. When the chief comes out, they push past him and they take the hut apart. And you know what they find. They found the end of Bong To."

Ransom had parked the jeep near my battalion headquarters five minutes before, and now he smiled as if he had explained everything.

"But what *happened*?" I asked. "How did you hear about it?"

He shrugged. "We learned all this in interrogation. When the women found the underground room, they knew the chief had forced the boys into sex, and then killed them. They didn't know what he had done with the bodies, but they knew he had killed the boys. The next time the VC paid one of their courtesy calls, they told the cadre leader what they knew. The VC did the rest. They were disgusted—Trang had betrayed *them*, too—betrayed everything he was supposed to represent. One of the VC we captured took the chief downstairs into his underground room and chained the man to the posts, wrote the names of the dead boys and Trang's daughters on the padding that covered the walls, and then . . . then they did what they did to him. They probably carried out the pieces and threw them into the excrement-pit. And over months, bit by bit, not all at once but slowly, everybody in the village moved out. By that time, they were seeing ghosts all the time. They had crossed a kind of border."

"Do you think they really saw ghosts?" I asked him. "I mean, do you think they were real ghosts?"

"If you want an expert opinion, you'd have to ask Major Bachelor. He has a lot to say about ghosts." He hesitated for a moment, and then leaned over to open my door. "But if you ask me, sure they did."

I got out of the jeep and closed the door.

Ransom peered at me through the jeep's window. "Take better care of yourself."

"Good luck with your Bru."

"The Bru are fantastic." He slammed the jeep into gear and shot away, cranking the wheel to turn the jeep around in a giant circle in front of the battalion headquarters before he jammed it into second and took off to wherever he was going.

Two weeks later Leonard Hamnet managed to get the Lutheran chaplain at Crandall to write a letter to the Tin Man for him, and two days after that he was in a clean uniform, packing up his kit for an overnight flight to an Air Force base in California. From there he was connecting to a Memphis flight, and from there the Army had booked him onto a six-passenger puddlejumper to Look-out Mountain.

When I came into Hamnet's tent he was zipping his bag shut in a zone of quiet afforded him by the other men. He did not want to talk about where he was going or the reason he was going there, and instead of answering my questions about his flights, he unzipped a pocket on the side of his bag and handed me a thick folder of airline tickets.

I looked through them and gave them back. "Hard travel," I said.

"From now on, everything is easy," Hamnet said. He seemed rigid and constrained as he zipped the precious tickets back into the bag. By this time his wife's letter was a rag held together with scotch tape. I could picture him reading and rereading it, for the thousandth or two thousandth time, on the long flight over the Pacific.

"They need your help," I said. "I'm glad they're going to get it."

"That's right." Hamnet waited for me to leave him alone.

Because his bag seemed heavy, I asked about the length of his leave. He wanted to get the tickets back out of the bag rather than answer me directly, but he forced himself to speak. "They gave me seven days. Plus travel time."

"Good," I said, meaninglessly, and then there was nothing left to say, and we both knew it. Hamnet hoisted his bag off his bunk and turned to the door without any of the usual farewells and embraces. Some of the other men called to him, but he seemed to hear nothing but his own thoughts. I followed him outside and stood beside him in the heat. Hamnet was wearing a tie and his boots had a high polish. He was already sweating through his stiff khaki shirt. He would not meet my eyes. In a minute a jeep pulled up before us. The Lutheran chaplain had surpassed himself.

"Goodbye, Leonard," I said, and Hamnet tossed his bag in back and got into the jeep. He sat up straight as a statue. The private driving the jeep said something to him as they drove off, but Hamnet did not reply. I bet he did not say a word to the stewardesses, either, or to the cab drivers or baggage handlers or anyone else who witnessed his long journey home.

## III

On the day after Leonard Hamnet was scheduled to return, Lieutenant Joys called Michael Poole and myself into his quarters to tell us what had happened back in Tennessee. He held a sheaf of papers in his hand, and he seemed both angry and embarrassed. Hamnet would not be returning to the platoon. It was a little funny. Well, of course it wasn't funny at all. The whole thing was terrible—that was what it was. Someone was to blame, too. Irresponsible decisions had been made, and we'd all be lucky if there wasn't an investigation. We were closest to the man, hadn't we seen what was likely to happen? If not, what the hell was our excuse?

Didn't we have any inkling of what the man was planning to do?

Well, yes, at the beginning, Poole and I said. But he seemed to have adjusted.

We have stupidity and incompetence all the way down the line here, said Lieutenant Elijah Joys. Here is a man who manages to carry a semi-automatic weapon through security at three different airports, bring it into a court-house, and carry out threats he made months before, without anybody stopping him.

I remembered the bag Hamnet had tossed into the back of the jeep; I remembered the reluctance with which he had zipped it open to show me his tickets. Hamnet had not carried his weapon through airport security. He had just shipped it home in his bag and walked straight through customs in his clean uniform and shiny boots.

As soon as the foreman had announced the guilty verdict, Leonard Hamnet had gotten to his feet, pulled the semiautomatic pistol from inside his jacket, and executed Mr Brewster where he was sitting at the defense table. While people shouted and screamed and dove for cover, while the courthouse officer tried to unsnap his gun, Hamnet killed his wife and his son. By the time he raised the pistol to his own head, the security officer had shot him twice in the chest. He died on the operating table at Lookout Mountain Lutheran Hospital, and his mother had requested that his remains receive burial at Arlington National Cemetery.

His mother. Arlington. I ask you.

That was what the Lieutenant said. *His mother. Arlington. I ask you.*

A private from Indianapolis named E. W. Burroughs won the six hundred and twenty dollars in the Elijah Fund when Lieutenant Joys was killed by a fragmentation bomb thirty-two days before the end of his tour. After that we were delivered unsuspecting into the hands of Harry Beevers, the Lost Boss, the worst lieutenant in the world. Private Burroughs died a week later, down in Dragon Valley along with Tiano and Calvin Hill and lots of others, when Lieutenant Beevers walked us into a mined field where we spent forty-eight hours under fire between two companies of NVA. I suppose Burroughs' mother back in Indianapolis got the six hundred and twenty dollars.

# STEPHEN JONES & KIM NEWMAN

# Necrology: 1992

AS WE MOVE FURTHER INTO THE 1990s, it is inevitable that we will continue to lose many of those who have significantly shaped the horror, science fiction and fantasy genres in fiction and film. 1992 was another bad year, when death once more claimed the writers, artists, performers and technicians who are remembered here . . .

## AUTHORS/ARTISTS

Italian-born artist **Joseph Mugnaini**, best known for his illustrations for Ray Bradbury books such as *Fahrenheit 451*, *The Martian Chronicles*, *The October Country* and *The Halloween Tree*, amongst many others, died on January 23 after suffering an aneurism. He was 79. His short film, *Icarus*, based on a Bradbury story, was nominated for an Academy Award.

Award-winning British author **Angela Carter** (aka Angela Olive Stalker) died of lung cancer on February 16, aged 51. Her acclaimed novels and collections include *The Magic Toyshop* (which she later adapted for TV), *Heroes and Villains*, *The Infernal Desire Machines of Dr Hoffman*, *The Passion of New Eve*, *The Bloody Chamber and Other Stories*, *Nights at the Circus*, *Black Venus* and *Wise Children*. She also co-scripted the 1984 movie *The Company of Wolves*, based on her published radio play.

Pulp author **Dwight V.** (Vreeland) **Swain** died of a self-inflicted gunshot on February 24, aged 76. A regular contributor to *Amazing*,

*Imagination* and *Imaginative Tales*, he also published novels under the pseudonyms "Nick Carter" and "John Cleve".

Probably the most famous and prolific science fiction author ever, Russian-born **Isaac Asimov** (aka Isaak Ludich Azimov), died on April 6 from heart and kidney failure, aged 72. His first SF story appeared in a 1939 issue of *Amazing Stories*, and he subsequently published almost 500 books in all genres and was the winner of numerous awards.

Controversial artist **Francis Bacon**, noted for his bizarre and distorted imagery, died of a heart attack on April 28, aged 82.

**Michael Talbot**, author of such horror novels as *The Delicate Dependency*, *The Bog* and *Night Things*, died of leukaemia on May 27. He was 38.

**William M. Gaines**, the founder and publisher of EC comics, died on June 3, aged 70. He was a pioneer of superior horror, science fiction, crime and war comics, publishing such titles as *Tales from the Crypt*, *The Vault of Horror*, *The Haunt of Fear*, *Weird Science*, *Weird Fantasy* and *Incredible Science Fiction*, until they were closed down by the Comics Code Authority in the mid-1950s. In 1952 he launched *Mad* as a comic book (created by Harvey Kurtzman) and three years later turned it into a satirical magazine which is still published. Numerous stories from the comics have been adapted into movies and form the basis for the HBO TV series *Tales from the Crypt*.

**Martin Goodman**, who in 1939 founded the company that would become Marvel Comics, died on June 6, aged 84. He sold the company in 1968 and retired.

Screenwriter and Blacklist survivor **Frederic I.** (aka Fred) **Rinaldo** died on June 22, aged 78, from complications following surgery for a broken hip. His credits include *The Invisible Woman*, *The Black Cat* (1941), *Robot Monster*, and the Abbott and Costello comedies, *Hold That Ghost*, *Meet Frankenstein* and . . . *Meet the Invisible Man*.

Russian-born science fiction author **Reginald Bretnor**, aged 80, died on July 15. He is best remembered for his series of stories featuring the characters Papa Schimmelhorn and Ferdinand Feghoot.

Author and physician **Alan E. Nourse** died on July 19 from congestive heart failure. He was 64. He wrote a number of medical science fiction books for adults and younger readers.

Historical novelist **Rosemary Sutcliff**, whose books include the classic Arthurian novel *Sword at Sunset*, died from a progressive wasting disease on July 23, aged 71.

Fan artist **Joe Shuster** died on July 30 of congestive heart failure. He was 78. In 1934, he co-created Superman with Jerry Siegal, and four years later they sold all rights in the character to Detective

Comics for $130. After working on the comic book for several years, they were fired when they asked for a share of the profits. Decades later, due to public pressure, the destitute pair were granted a yearly pension of $30,000 by DC Comics.

Award-winning movie poster artist **Robert Peak** died from a brain hemorrhage on August 7, aged 64. He created the distinctive images for *West Side Story*, *My Fair Lady*, *Camelot*, *Apocalypse Now*, *Rollerball*, *Superman*, *Excalibur* and the first five *Star Trek* films.

Children's author **Mary Norton** died after suffering a stroke on August 29, aged 88. Her novel *The Magic Bed-Knob* was filmed by Disney in 1971 as *Bedknobs and Broomsticks*, while her five books about the six-inch tall Borrowers have been adapted for television.

One of the greatest writers of the modern horror story, **Fritz Leiber**, died on September 5 from a series of small strokes after complications following a convention in Ontario, Canada. He was 81. Fritz Reuter Leiber Jr was the son of the noted Shakespearean/Hollywood actor. The winner of multiple awards (including the Lifetime Achievement from both the World Fantasy Convention and the Horror Writers of America), Leiber's first published story featured his enduring heroic fantasy duo Fafhrd and the Gray Mouser (co-created with Harry Fischer): 'Two Sought Adventure' appeared in *Unknown* in 1939. Many memorable novels and short stories followed, spanning the genres. His best horror fiction can be found in the collections *Night's Black Agents* and *Shadows With Eyes*, and the novels *Conjure Wife* (filmed several times) and *Our Lady of Darkness*. He also novelised the 1965 movie *Tarzan and the Valley of Gold*.

Belgian cartoonist **Pierre Culliford**, creator of the Smurfs (originally the Schtroumpfs), died on December 24, aged 64. The characters have been adapted into films and television, with the books translated into more than twenty languages.

## ACTORS/ACTRESSES

Australian stage and screen actress **Dame Judith Anderson** died from a brain tumour and pneumonia on January 3, aged 94. Her film roles include the sinister housekeeper in Hitchcock's *Rebecca* and a Vulcan High Priestess in *Star Trek III The Search for Spock*. She also appeared in *Laura* and *And Then There Were None*.

B-movie tough guy **Steve Brodie** died of cancer on January 9. He was 72, and his many credits include Ray Harryhausen's *The Beast from 20,000 Fathoms, Donovan's Brain, The Wild World of Batwoman, The Giant Spider Invasion* and *Frankenstein Island*.

Veteran character actor **Ian Wolfe** died from natural causes on January 23, aged 95. In a career spanning seven decades, he appeared in more than 200 films. His numerous genre credits include *The Raven* (1935, with Karloff and Lugosi), *Mad Love* (with Peter Lorre), plus *On Borrowed Time, Sherlock Holmes Faces Death, Flesh and Fantasy, Murder in the Blue Room, The Pearl of Death, The Scarlet Claw, The Invisible Man's Revenge, Zombies on Broadway, Bedlam* (with Karloff), *Dressed to Kill* (1946), *The Lost World* (1960), *Diary of a Madman* (with Vincent Price), *Games, THX 1138, The Terminal Man* and the recent *Dick Tracy* (1990).

The same day saw the death for former child star **Freddie Bartholomew**, at the age of 61. Born in Ireland, he played well-bred English boys in such Hollywood productions as *David Copperfield* (with Basil Rathbone), *Little Lord Fauntleroy* (1936), *Captains Courageous* and *Kidnapped* (the latter two with John Carradine).

Puerto Rican-born Hollywood star/director **Jose Ferrer** (aka Jose Vincente Ferrer y Centron) died on January 26, after a short illness. He was aged 80. His varied career included the Academy Award-winning title role of *Cyrano de Bergerac* (1950), plus *The Sentinel, Crash, Dracula's Dog, The Swarm, Blood Tide, Dune* and the title role in TV's *The Return of Captain Nemo*.

Veteran stage actress **Dame Gwen Ffrangcon-Davies** died from natural causes on January 27, aged 101. The last link with the Victorian theatre, she made her stage debut as a fairy in *A Midsummer Night's Dream* in 1911. Her few film credits include Hammer's *The Devil Rides Out* and the recent Sherlock Holmes TV movie *The Master Blackmailer.*

Dependable character actor **John Dehner** died on February 4, of emphysema and diabetes, aged 76. He began his career as an animator for Walt Disney (*Fantasia, Bambi* etc) and later became a regular guest star on TV. His film roles include *The Catman of Paris, The Bowery Boys Meet the Monsters, Carousel, The Day of the Dolphin, The Boys from Brazil, Jagged Edge* and *Creator.*

American leading man **Ray Danton** died on February 11, from kidney disease. He was 60. Besides his acting roles, he also directed *Psychic Killer, The Deathmaster* and *Crypt of the Living Dead.*

Best remembered for her appearance in the original *Star Trek* TV episode "The Gamesters of Triskelion" and as a regular on *Get Smart*, American actress **Angelique Pettyjohn** died from cancer on February 14, at the age 48. Her film appearances include *The Lost Empire, Repo Man, Biohazard, The Mad Doctor of Blood Island, The Wizard of Speed and Time* and several porno roles under the names Angelique and Heaven St John.

**Dick York,** best known as the original Darren (1964–9, before health problems forced him to leave) in the TV series *Bewitched*, died on February 20, from emphysema and a degenerative spinal condition. He was 63.

American actress **Sandy Dennis** died of cancer on March 2. She was 54. She won the Academy Award for Best Supporting Actress for *Who's Afraid of Virginia Woolf?*, and her other credits include *Parents, 976-Evil* and the TV movies *The Man Who Wanted to Live Forever* and Steven Spielberg's *Something Evil*.

Canadian actor **Robert Beatty** died of pneumonia on March 3, aged 82. His many films include *2001: A Space Odyssey*.

**Gracie Lantz** (aka Grace Stafford), the creator and voice of cartoon character Woody Woodpecker for forty years, died from spinal cancer on March 17, aged 88.

Italian-born actor **Cesare Danova** died from a heart attack on March 19, during a meeting of the Foreign Film Committee. He was 66. As a leading man, his film credits include *Tarzan the Ape Man* (1959), *Valley of the Dragons, The Invisible Strangler, Chamber of Horrors* and *Tentacles*.

Canadian-born **John Ireland** died of leukaemia on March 21, aged 78. As a Hollywood leading man, he appeared in many westerns before ending up in *I Saw What You Did, The House of Seven Corpses, Welcome to Arrow Beach*, TV's *The Phantom of Hollywood, Satan's Cheerleaders, The Shape of Things to Come, Guyana: Cult of the Damned, Miami Golem, Incubus, Sundown The Vampire in Retreat* and *Waxwork II: Lost in Time*.

Best remembered as Mildred the housekeeper on TV's *McMillan and Wife* series and the classic Jewish mother in *Rhoda*, American comedienne **Nancy Walker** (aka Ann Swoyer Barto) died from lung cancer on March 25, aged 69. Her film appearances include *Murder By Death, The World's Greatest Athlete* and *Human Feelings* (as God). She was also the unlikely director of the disco disaster *Can't Stop the Music*.

Austrian-born Hollywood leading man **Paul Henried** (aka Paul von Hernreid) died from pneumonia on March 29, aged 84. His films include *Now Voyager, Casablanca, Between Two Worlds, Thief of Damascus*, Hammer's *Stolen Face, Siren of Baghdad* and *Exorcist II The Heretic*. In 1964 he directed the psychological thriller *Dead Ringer*.

Actress **Alix Talton**, who starred in *The Deadly Mantis* and also appeared in Hitchcock's 1956 remake of his own *The Man Who Knew Too Much*, died of lung cancer on April 7. She was 72.

Screen tough guy **Neville Brand** died of emphysema on April 16, aged 71. He entered the film industry in 1948 after ten years in the US Army where he was the fourth most decorated soldier in

World War Two. His movie credits include TV's *Killdozer*, *Eaten Alive*, *Psychic Killer*, *The Ninth Configuration*, *Without Warning* and *Evils of the Night*. He was a semi-regular as Al Capone on TV's *The Untouchables* (1959–62).

Saucy British TV comedian **Benny** (aka Alfred) **Hill** died on April 18, aged 67. His film appearances include *Who Done It?* (1956), *Those Magnificent Men in Their Flying Machines* and *Chitty Chitty Bang Bang*.

Another famous British comedian, **Frankie Howerd**, died of a heart attack the following day, aged 70. Although better known for his TV work, his movie credits include a couple of *Carry On* films, *Mouse on the Moon*, the underrated *The House in Nightmare Park* and the dire *Sgt Pepper's Lonely Hearts Club Band*.

The original bride of Frankenstein, American actress **Mae Clarke**, died of cancer on April 29. She was 81. Besides being a victim of Karloff's monster in *Frankenstein* (1931), she also had a grapefruit smashed in her face by James Cagney in *Public Enemy*, starred in the serial *King of the Rocket Men* and appeared in the 1960s *Batman* TV series.

**Lon Ralph Chaney**, great-grandson of the silent film star, was killed in a car crash on May 5.

German singer-actress and screen legend **Marlene Dietrich** (aka Maria Magdalena von Losch) died on May 6, aged 90. Her numerous films include *The Blue Angel*, *The Scarlet Empress*, *The Garden of Allah*, *Destry Rides Again*, Hitchcock's *Stage Fright*, *Around the World in Eighty Days* and Orson Welles' *Touch of Evil*.

American actor **Richard Derr**, who portrayed pulp hero The Shadow in *Invisible Avenger* (1958), died on May 8, aged 74. His other movie credits include *Castle in the Desert*, *When Worlds Collide* and *Terror is a Man*.

TV actor **Robert Reed** (*The Brady Bunch* etc.) died of bowel cancer on May 12, aged 59. Among his film appearances are *The Maltese Bippy*, and the TV movies *Haunts of the Very Rich* and *Mandrake*.

Italian actress **Marisa Mell**, who co-starred with John Phillip Law in Mario Bava's *Danger: Diabolik*, died of cancer on May 16. She was 53.

B-movie hero **Marshall Thompson** died of heart failure on May 18, aged 66. Best known to TV audiences for the series *World of the Giants* (1959), *Men Into Space* (1959–60) and *Daktari* (1966–8), his many film roles include *Cult of the Cobra*, *It! The Terror Beyond Space*, *Fiend Without a Face*, *First Man Into Space*, *Bog* and the TV movie *Cruise Into Terror*.

British actress **Pippa Steel**(e), who appeared in Hammer's *The*

*Vampire Lovers* and *Lust for a Vampire*, died from cancer on May 29. She was 44.

Portly British character actor and playwright **Robert Morley** died on June 3 from a stroke. He was 84. Amongst his many films are *The Ghosts of Berkeley Square*, *Beat the Devil*, *Around the World in Eighty Days*, *A Study in Terror* (as Mycroft Holmes), *Way Way Out*, *Some Girls Do*, *Theatre of Blood* (with Vincent Price), *The Blue Bird* (1976) and *The Wind*.

Veteran British character actor **Laurence Naismith** died on June 5, after a short illness. He was 83. His numerous movies include Ray Harryhausen's *Jason and the Argonauts* and *The Valley of Gwangi*, *Village of the Damned*, *Eye of the Cat*, *Scrooge* (1970), *Quest for Love* and *The Amazing Mr Blunden*.

Singer/actress **Georgia Brown** died on June 6, aged 58. She appeared in the movies *A Study in Terror*, *Tales That Witness Madness*, *Nothing But the Night* (with Lee and Cushing) and *The Seven-Per-Cent Solution*, and played Klingon Worf's human stepmother on TV's *Star Trek: The Next Generation*.

British stage actress **Maxine Audley**, who appeared in *Peeping Tom* and Hammer's *Frankenstein Must Be Destroyed*, died of a heart attack on June 23. She was 69.

Leading 1940s American actress **Brenda Marshall** (aka Ardis Ankerson Gaines) died on July 30, aged 76. Her credits include *The Sea Hawk*, *The Smiling Ghost* and *Strange Impersonation*. She married William Holden and retired in the 1950s.

American TV actor **John Anderson** died on August 7 from a heart attack, aged 69. He appeared in such films as *Psycho* and *The Satan Bug*.

Welsh-born character actor **Mervyn Johns** died on September 6, aged 93. The father of actress Glynis, he appeared in Hitchcock's *Jamaica Inn*, *The Halfway House*, *Scrooge* (1951), *The Day of the Triffids*, Hammer's remake of *The Old Dark House* (1962) and was the star of the classic 1945 *Dead of Night*.

One of the screen's best purveyors of crazies, **Anthony Perkins**, died of an AIDS-related illness on September 12. He was 60. Perkins portrayed Norman Bates in Hitchcock's classic *Psycho* and three sequels (directing *Psycho III* in 1986). He also appeared in *On the Beach*, *The Trial*, *The Black Hole*, *Crimes of Passion*, *Edge of Sanity* and the TV movies *How Awful About Allan*, *The Sins of Dorian Gray*, *Daughter of Darkness* and *I'm Dangerous Tonight*. He starred in the 1990 syndicated TV series *Ghost Writer* and directed the cannibalism comedy *Lucky Stiff*.

Respected British stage and screen actor **Denholm Elliott** died of AIDS on October 6, aged 70. His numerous movie credits include

*The House That Dripped Blood* (with Lee and Cushing), *Quest for Love*, *Madame Sin*, Hammer's *To the Devil a Daughter* (with Christopher Lee), *Vault of Horror*, *The Boys from Brazil*, *Hound of the Baskervilles* (1977 and 1983 versions), *Brimstone and Treacle*, *Underworld* (scripted by Clive Barker) and as Indiana Jones' friend Marcus Brody in *Raiders of the Lost Ark* and *Indiana Jones and the Last Crusade*. On TV he appeared in the 1968 version of *The Strange Case of Dr Jekyll and Mr. Hyde* and portrayed the title role in the 1969 adaptation of *Dracula*.

Comedy actor **Cleavon Little**, best known for his starring role in Mel Brooks' *Blazing Saddles*, died of colon cancer on October 22, aged 53. He also appeared in the vampire comedy *Once Bitten*.

Singer **Roger Miller**, whose hits include "King of the Road" and "England Swings", died on October 25 from cancer, aged 56. He voiced Allan-a-Dale in Disney's animated *Robin Hood*.

Actress **Regina Carrol**, wife of director Al Adamson, died on November 4 of cancer. She was 49 and appeared in such grade-Z horrors (often directed by her husband) as *Blood of Ghastly Horror*, *The Female Bunch*, *Brain of Blood*, *Dracula vs. Frankenstein*, *Satan's Sadists*, *Doctor Dracula* and *Carnival Magic*.

Character actor **Sterling Holloway** died from cardiac arrest on November 22, aged 87. He appeared in such films as *Professor Beware*, *International House* (with W. C. Fields and Bela Lugosi), *Alice in Wonderland* (1933) and *The Blue Bird* (1940), before lending his vocal talents to Disney's *Dumbo*, *Bambi*, *Alice in Wonderland* (1952), *The Jungle Book*, *The Aristocats*, and the *Winnie the Pooh* series.

Anglo-Swiss born **Paula** (aka Rita) **Corday** died during gall bladder surgery on November 23. She was 68, and appeared in *The Body Snatcher* (with Karloff and Lugosi), *Dick Tracy vs. Cueball* and *The Black Castle* (also with Karloff).

Veteran genre actor **Robert Shayne** died from lung cancer, aged 92, on November 29. A regular on the TV series *Superman* (as Inspector Henderson) and *The Flash*, his numerous film credits include *The Face of Marble* (with John Carradine), *The Neanderthal Man*, *Invaders from Mars*, *The Indestructible Man* (with Lon Chaney, Jr.), *Tobor the Great*, *War of the Satellites*, *Kronos*, *The Giant Claw*, *Spook Chasers*, *Teenage Caveman*, *How to Make a Monster* and *Son of Flubber*.

**Robert F. Simon**, who portrayed J. J. Jameson in the *Spider-man* TV series, died from a heart attack on November 29, aged 83. His film credits include *Face of Fire*, *The Wizard of Baghdad* and *The Reluctant Astronaut*.

**Harry Ellerbe**, who appeared in *The Magnetic Monster* and with

Vincent Price in *The Fall of the House of Usher* (1960) and *The Haunted Palace*, died on December 3. He was 91.

Veteran character actor **Hank Worden**, who found cult fame late in his career on TV's *Twin Peaks*, died from natural causes on December 6, aged 91. His movie credits include *The Searchers* (as Mose Harper), *The Secret Life of Walter Mitty* (with Karloff) and *The Ice Pirates*.

British character actor **Percy Herbert** died the same day from a heart attack. He was aged 72. His many films include Hammer's *One Million Years BC* and *Quatermass 2*, *Night of the Demon*, *Night of the Big Heat* (with Cushing and Lee), Ray Harryhausen's *The Mysterious Island*, *Casino Royale* and *Doomwatch*. He also appeared in the "Killer With a Knife" episode of TV's *Cimarron Strip*, a feature-length Jack the Ripper western scripted by Harlan Ellison.

**Vincent Gardenia** (aka Scognamiglio), who played Mushnik in the musical remake of *Little Shop of Horrors* (1986), died on December 9 from a heart attack. He was 71 and also appeared in the remake of *Heaven Can Wait* (1978) and the TV movie *The Screaming Skull* (1973).

American leading man **Dana Andrews** (aka Carver Daniel Andrews) died of pneumonia on December 17, aged 83. Best remembered as the hero of *Laura* and *Night of the Demon*, his other movie credits include *Crack in the World*, *The Satan Bug*, *Brainstorm* (1965), *The Loved One*, *Spy in Your Eye*, *The Frozen Dead* and *Airport 1975*.

## FILM/TV TECHNICIANS

Hungarian-born **Andrew Marton**, aged 87, died on January 7. As second unit director he filmed the classic chariot race in *Ben Hur* (1959), co-directed *King Solomon's Mines* (1950), and directed the science fiction adventures *Crack in the World* and *Around the World Under the Sea*.

Veteran Walt Disney animator **Jack Kinney** died on February 9, aged 82. His many films include *Pinocchio*, *Dumbo*, and such classic shorts as *Der Fuehrer's Face* (which he directed), *The Reluctant Dragon* and *The Three Caballeros*.

Screenwriter/director **Richard Brooks** died on March 11, aged 79. Best known for his film *The Blackboard Jungle* and his Oscar-winning screenplay for *Elmer Gantry* (which he directed), Brooks also scripted *Cobra Woman* and produced and directed *In Cold Blood*.

Hungarian-born director **Laslo Benedek** died the same day, aged

65. His credits include *The Wild One* and the 1971 chiller *The Night Visitor*.

Genre director **Jack Arnold** died of arteriosclerosis on March 17, aged 75. His classics of the genre include *The Creature from the Black Lagoon, Revenge of the Creature, It Came from Outer Space, Tarantula, The Incredible Shrinking Man, The Space Children* and *Monster on the Campus*.

Indian director **Satyajit Ray** died April 23, aged 70, less than a month after receiving an honorary Academy Award. His 1968 movie *The Adventures of Goopy and Bagha* contained many fantasy sequences, *The Music Room* benefited from its Gothic atmosphere, and one of the trio of episodes in *Three Daughters* was an old-fashioned ghost story.

Action director **John Sturges** died on August 8 from a heart attack, aged 82. His films include *Bad Day at Black Rock*, *The Satan Bug* and *Marooned*.

Cameraman and special effects pioneer **Hans F. Koenkamp** died on September 12, at the age of 100. His many credits include the 1925 *Wizard of Oz*, *Noah's Ark*, *Moby Dick* (1930), *Svengali* (1931), *A Midsummer Night's Dream* (1935) and *The Beast With Five Fingers*.

Pioneer Hollywood producer **Hal Roach** died on November 2 from pneumonia. He was 100 years old. After teaming up with Harold Lloyd in 1916, he made comedies with Our Gang, Will Rogers and Laurel and Hardy. His later sound films include *Topper*, *Topper Returns*, *Topper Takes a Trip*, *Turnabout* and *One Million BC*.